Sophie's Daughters Trilogy

Sophie's Daughters Trilogy

Mary Connealy

BARBOUR
PUBLISHING

Doctor *in* Petticoats

Dedication

I like to include tough women in my books, in case you haven't noticed. I like to think I've raised four tough women. Not so tough in the ways of gun slinging and buck skinning but tough in ways that really count: good hearts, intelligence, and faith. This book is dedicated to them—my daughters Joslyn, Wendy, Shelly, and Katy.

One

Mosqueros, Texas, 1879

Beth McClellen would die before she missed Mandy's wedding.

That wasn't some cute expression. It was a plain, bald fact.

She would probably be pounded to death any minute now.

The stagecoach, in its four-day-long quest to hit every bump and rock in northwest Texas, lurched into the air then slammed back onto its wheels. She'd planned to take the train all the way to Mosqueros, but a cyclone had ripped out a bridge somewhere and the trains weren't running. So Beth had no choice but to take the much slower stagecoach.

She'd still hoped to make the wedding. But it was cutting things really close. Even with the irritating delay, the stage had appealed to her. Horses, fresh air, Texas scenery—after four years in the teeming city of Boston, she thought the stage was brilliant.

She was an idiot.

The coach tilted up sharply as the trail rose. Beth fell against the seat back. "How can this thing stay in one piece?"

She didn't expect an answer from the drunk across from her

and she didn't get one.

He did slide farther down on the seat, slumping sideways, growling in his—well, Beth wasn't about to call it sleep. Stupor was more like it. She braced herself to shove him to the floor if he fell forward onto her. She'd use him as a footrest, and for the first time in days the man would serve some use on this earth.

Give me strength to keep from knocking him to the floor on purpose, Lord.

They reached the hilltop and the ascent switched to descent. The stage picked up speed and the hooves of the horses rose from plodding walks to fast clips.

Beth knew it by sound and feel, not sight. She'd closed the curtains to block out the sun, hoping to also block some of the billowing dust that seeped through the windows. And if it lessened the stifling heat of an August Texas a few degrees, it might also lessen the stench of her fellow rider.

Darkness might keep him asleep, too. She could only pray to the good Lord it would. The few times he'd been semi-lucid, he tended to break into rants about the dreadful state of the world. He'd start with generalities then launch into particulars, muttering to himself as if she wasn't there and he was a lunatic.

Well, if he thought he was alone, then he was wrong, wrong, wrong. But he was right on one count—he was definitely a lunatic.

More than once in the last four days, she'd been tempted to shut him up with the butt end of the pistol she had strapped to her ankle.

The driver shouted over the thundering hooves of his four horses. He'd been shouting at the poor horses for days.

Beth was tempted to swing out the door, clamber onto the top of the stage, and beat the man to within an inch of his life for the way he pushed his horses. And it didn't pass unnoticed that Beth was contemplating violence against every man within her reach.

It had been a long trip home.

The driver wasn't completely heartless. They'd stopped several times and gotten a new team, but the relentless pace, the shouting of the driver—they wore the poor horses down long before they finished their run.

Another shout had Beth sitting straighter. It was a new shout, laced with fear—nothing she'd heard from the driver before. She pushed aside the curtain on the window and saw the same desolate, broken range she'd been seeing all day. West Texas, a brutal, barren place.

Her family had found a fertile valley in this desolation, but almost the only one. A rugged, man-eating, soul-crushing country that either hardened people into gleaming white diamonds or pulverized them into useless coal dust.

Beth liked to think she was a diamond. And she'd crushed her share of men into dust right along with Texas.

The trail was narrow. They were rolling quickly down one of the thousand dips in the mountainous area.

The driver shouted again. "Whoa."

That *really* caught her attention. The man never said whoa. Not outside of town. He stopped for *nothing*.

She leaned forward, holding her breath because she was a little too close to the snoring, reeking passenger. She'd been on this stage for four days in the sweltering heat and roiling dust and she was no fresh posy herself, but this guy was ridiculous.

The stagecoach slowed, slid sideways, and picked up speed. The driver shouted and cursed and Beth could see, if she angled her head, the man battling with the brake.

Had the brake given out? Was the stagecoach a runaway? No, not a runaway. She could feel the brakes dragging on the wheels, hear the scrape of the brake as it tried to slow the heavy stage.

"Keep your head. Keep your head." Muttering, Beth knew the side she'd just looked out of rode too close to a rock face that rose high on her left. She slid to the other side of the coach. Before, she'd been too close to the man's feet. Now she could smell his breath.

Inhaling the dusty air and stench through her mouth to make it bearable, she pushed back the curtain on this side and her stomach twisted.

The whole world fell away from this side of the coach.

She stood, holding on to the rocking, jouncing stagecoach. Letting go with one hand, she shoved the door open. Poking her head out she saw. . .disaster. Dead ahead.

Emphasis on dead.

No way was she getting home for that wedding.

A stagecoach lay on its side not a hundred yards down the trail. Bodies everywhere. A quick glance told Beth that five people were unconscious or dead on the ground. If they hit that wreckage, they'd kill any passengers left alive then plunge over the side of the mountain.

Beth saw a horse racing away far down the trail, dragging harness leather behind him. No sign of the three other horses that had pulled the ruined stage. A sudden twist in the trail concealed the accident, but it was still coming.

Beth started praying with every breath. And she asked for the thing this country demanded most.

Lord, give me strength.

The driver shouted again, throwing his whole body on the brake while he sawed on the reins. His horses leaned back until they were nearly sitting on their haunches, fighting the forward motion of the heavy stagecoach. He didn't have the strength to hold the brake *and* the horses on this steep incline.

Beth's ma hadn't raised her to spend a lot of time fretting and wringing her hands. If there was a bronc to bust, Beth busted it. If there was a wagon to pull, Beth hopped out and started pulling before anyone had to ask.

That was the McClellen way.

So helping was a given, and it didn't take but a second to know she wasn't going out on the side that might crush her between the mountain and a racing stage. So the cliff side was her only choice.

One horse whinnied, a terrible, frightened sound. Beth could have wept for the scared animal if she was inclined toward tears—which she wasn't.

The shout and the frightened horse jerked the nasty scourge of a man who was Beth's traveling companion upright in the seat, as if he'd been poked by a pin. "Wha'waz'at?"

Ignoring the idiot, Beth swung herself onto the roof, grateful she'd changed into her riding skirt for the journey home. Just as she heaved herself upward, the stage rounded a bend in this poisonous sidewinder of a trail.

Beth's feet had just hooked over the top of the stage and they slipped. For a terrible second, Beth was thrown out. Her legs dangled over nothingness. Her fingers clawed at the railing atop the stage. Her wrists creaked as the weight of her body fought her slender hands. One hand lost its grip. She clawed frantically for a hold. Her fingers ached; the palms of her hands were scraped raw.

Give me strength.

After heart-pounding seconds of doubt that she had the strength, she regained her hold.

Then the trail straightened and Beth's legs swung back with nearly as much force as they'd flown out. Her boots, with their pointed leather toes, smacked into her fellow passenger.

"Hey!"

It felt like she hit him in the head. That cheered her somewhat and helped her ignore her now-bleeding hands.

Give me strength, Lord. Give me strength.

Scowling at the mess ahead of them on the trail, Beth assumed—if they figured out a way not to die in the next five minutes—they'd be held up for a good long time. She was definitely going to miss the wedding, and that made her mad clean through.

Rage gave her the burst of energy she needed to drag herself onto the roof. She landed on her side on top of her wretched home for the last few days with an *oomph* of pain. She didn't know if God gave strength in the form of rage, but she took it as a gift anyway.

Rolling to her hands and knees, she scooted forward. "Get over!"

The stage driver shouted in surprise and practically jumped off the seat. A stage driver ought to have steadier nerves.

"I can drive a team. Get over and hand me the reins. You concentrate on the brakes."

The man didn't move, staring at her like he was a half-wit.

Beth dropped down beside him and wrenched the reins out of his hands.

"You can't drive this thing." But before he was done yelling, the lout must have noted her experienced grip on the handful of reins. He left her to the horses, turned to the brake, and threw every ounce of his considerable weight against it.

The wheels scratched on the rocky trail, skidding, slowing, shoving the horses along in front of it.

"Whoa!" Beth shouted, rising to her feet, hauling with all her strength—and some strength besides that must have been supplied by the Almighty because the horses responded.

With the stage slowing from the brake, the horses weren't being pushed as hard. They slowed.

It was taking too long.

They came around the next curve. Death and destruction loomed only yards ahead.

Beth leaned harder, bracing her feet, calling to the team in a voice she'd learned years ago got an uncommon response from animals. Her family being the exception, she'd rather be with animals than most people she'd met.

Give me strength. Give me strength. Give me strength.

Suddenly, a weight hit her from behind and almost tossed her headfirst onto the horses' hooves. A viselike arm snaked around her waist to stop her fall. Then, the second she was steady, two hands gripped the reins. And she had the strength of ten.

And the stench told her who was helping her.

High time the drunk got involved in saving his own worthless hide.

The stage driver shouted with exertion. The stage slowed. The wheels locked, sliding now, scratching on the coarse, rocky trail.

They skidded straight for the wreckage. The trail narrowed. No getting around it.

Just ahead the stage lay on its side. It looked like it had rolled at least once, judging by the damage. Doors were broken off, wheels shattered.

Only a miracle had kept the coach from plunging off the edge.

One woman lay closest to Beth's stage. Her four horses would trample the injured woman. Then the stage would roll over what was left of her.

She shouted to the team, but the horses were nearly sitting on their haunches now. The lead horse on the left, a dark red chestnut with black mane and tail, screamed in terror at what lay straight in their path.

Give me strength. Give me strength. Give me strength.

The man's arms flexed. Muscle like corded steel flexed as he pulled and added his voice to the shouts of "Whoa!"

The woman on the ground lying facedown stirred. She raised her chest up with her arms and turned to the noise. Blood soaked her hair and face. Her blue gingham dress had one arm ripped off and the woman's bare shoulder looked raw. Her eyes widened at the oncoming stage. Her mouth gaped in horror as the stage skidded nearer, nearer, nearer.

Twenty feet, then ten, then five.

Give me strength, Lord.

The man behind found more strength and pulled until his muscles bulged.

The stage passed over the woman.

The skidding stopped.

Too late.

15

Two

Dust swallowed the stage. Beth was blinded.

The horses had trampled the poor woman.

Give me strength. Give me strength. Give me strength.

Practically throwing herself to the ground in the choking dirt, one battered, bleeding hand slipped on the stage seat and Beth nearly fell. Ignoring her own pain, she hung on grimly, scrambled to the ground, and rushed to the horses' heads.

The woman had rolled off to the side or they'd have crushed her to death. She'd saved herself.

Beth wanted to shout in triumph and give the woman a big hug. Instead, Beth dropped to the rocky, dusty trail beside the bleeding woman. "Lie still. Please." She guided the woman to her back. "Let me make sure you don't have any broken bones."

Beth had trained four years for this. But this was her first real chance to use her medical skills—more doctor than nurse thanks to the generosity of the doctor she'd apprenticed with.

Out of the corner of her eye, Beth saw the stage driver lead the horses to the side, tie them to a scrub pine on the uphill slope, and then rush to the closest victim.

The woman stared sightlessly upward as if the horror had taken a firm hold of her mind and wouldn't release her.

"Don't be afraid." Beth used her horse-soothing voice. People responded well to it, too. Finally she slipped past the lady's terror.

"My husband. Is my husband all right?" The injured lady's face was coated in drying blood. She grabbed the front of Beth's dress with one hand. Her other, more battered arm moved weakly, nearly useless. Beth let the woman drag her forward until their noses almost touched.

Smoothing back the woman's hair, Beth tried to soothe her. "I'll go check your husband."

Beth didn't waste time prying the overwrought woman's hands loose. Instead, she murmured comfort and, even with her head held tight, managed to check the woman's arms and legs, her ribs and head, searching for injuries.

There was obvious swelling along her ribs and the woman winced with pain when Beth pressed, but the bones held. Cracked, not broken—Beth hoped. The bleeding arm was cut to shreds, but the bone was intact. The woman gritted her teeth and dragged in a painful breath when Beth touched too close to the shoulder.

Beth noted the bleeding head wound was more dried than wet. That told its own story of how long these folks had been here—hours most likely, but not days. There was a chance the wounded could still be helped. "Please, let me go so I can check on your husband."

No response.

Give me strength. Give me strength.

This time Beth's strength might be required to tear loose from the death grip.

Suddenly the woman released Beth's collar. "Go." The woman's pain-filled eyes seemed rational. "I—I can tell my arms and legs work. I'll be fine. Go check the others."

Beth gasped for breath then nodded, satisfied the woman

didn't need anything right now. God willing, this one would survive. Beth patted the woman's hand. "I'll see to your husband."

Beth stood and raced toward the next victim. She noticed the drunk climbing down from the stage at last, unsteady, more of a danger to the injured than a help. He might trip over them, and if that didn't kill them, his breath would finish them off.

Beth scolded herself. They'd have never gotten the stage stopped without his help.

Fine, she'd stop thinking of him as a waste of human flesh. Now if only the bum would stay downwind.

The stage driver rushed to another victim.

Beth headed for a man pinned under the wrecked coach. His body was crushed. The man was beyond help, and Beth prayed for his soul and any loved ones he'd left behind as she raced on. Another man lay dead beneath the wheels of the stage, his neck bent at a horrible angle, his eyes gaping and empty.

There were six in all. Four alive. Only the woman was conscious.

The woman finally got to her feet and assisted. She found her husband, unconscious but among the living, and turned her attention to him.

The stage driver got a canteen of water and the three of them washed wounds.

Two more of the victims began rousing. One had a badly broken leg.

The woman's husband had a dislocated shoulder. As he awakened, he was maddened with pain. Still only partly conscious, he couldn't lie still, yet every move caused cries of anguish, awful to hear from anyone but somehow worse from a man.

Beth had read of dislocated joints in her studies, but she'd never had the opportunity to try and repair one.

His wife struggled to calm him. Every time he lashed out he'd bump her somehow and she'd gasp with pain.

"What's your name?" Beth asked, trying to get the situation

under control. Maybe if they all just took a minute to calm down. . .

"It's Camilla. Camilla Armitage. My husband's name is Leo."

"Mrs. Armitage, you've got to stay away from him," Beth urged the woman. "Leo doesn't know you're here so you're not helping. Your arm has started bleeding again. We don't want that to get worse. And I'm sure you have cracked ribs. A blow landed just right could break them. Your husband will be sick to think he did such a thing to you. Please just move back."

"He needs me. I'll be fine." The woman's chin firmed stubbornly and Beth didn't waste more time trying to get her to move away.

Beth couldn't restrain the poor man. With one furious glance at the drunk who sat, staring away from the carnage, turning his back to the whole mess, Beth said to the driver, "We've got to pop his shoulder back into its socket. It takes a lot of strength. And someone needs to hold him down bodily. That will anchor him and give me something to pull against."

The driver gave her a long, quiet look. "I should be the one pulling. I've never done it before, but I can try."

"You should, but I don't have the weight to anchor him." She reached for Leo's arm. "It has to be held out straight, jerked hard—"

Before Beth could do more than lift the arm, the man screamed in pain and struck out. He caught her in the face and knocked her flat on her backside.

Beth felt her temper rise.

The woman must have noticed and been afraid of what Beth might do. "Please, my Leo is a good man. A gentle man. He'd never do such a thing if he was awake."

It was the absolute truth that the man was beyond rational thought.

The stage driver knelt beside the flailing man. These struggles deepened Leo's agony.

Beth knew it would take three people. One to hold his shoulders down—the man's wife was already trying to do that, through her tears, and failing. One to restrain his feet so he was motionless. One to jerk on the arm and hopefully to reset the joint.

Shuddering to think of the pain they'd soon cause the man, Beth was suddenly furious at the bum who sat there, not helping. True, he'd come through and helped pull the stage to a stop, but that was to save his own pathetic, drunken life. Wasn't it? When it came to helping others, he was worthless.

She hadn't actually seen him take a single drink on the whole trip. She suspected he'd drained his flask quite a while ago. In fact, she'd never seen the flask, assuming he was sneaking nips on the sly at the beginning of the trip then sleeping it off the rest of the way.

Beth surged to her feet. "We need help over here!"

The man didn't even look up. He stared as if asleep with his eyes open.

Well, Beth wasn't one to let a good temper tantrum go to waste, and seriously, this afternoon had worn her out right to her last bit of restraint. . .and beyond. Who better to punish?

She looked down at the stage driver and the woman, struggling to hold the man in place. "I'm going to get us some help."

The stage driver looked with distaste at the other passenger. "Good luck."

Beth whirled and used the hundred-foot downhill march to get her knees to stop shaking. Not because she was afraid of this man—she still had her gun butt—but because the afternoon had just been more than too much.

She stomped to the man's side, and carefully considering her approach—or maybe not so carefully—she grabbed the man's filthy, flattened, black Stetson off his head and swatted him with it.

"Hey!" He turned as if surprised to see her.

"I didn't exactly sneak up on you, now did I?" She whaled on him again.

He shielded his face. His once-white shirt tore up one side at his sudden movement. "Will you stop that?"

The sound of the ripping fabric—good grief, it looked like silk—gave Beth a sense of doing the Lord's work. She wondered how long he'd been wearing it. The cloth must be rotten to tear so easily.

"Do I have your attention, you miserable worm?" Beth threw the hat at his head.

He held his arms over his face, the bedraggled white sleeves rolled up nearly to his elbows, and glared through his wrists at her. His eyes narrowed.

It occurred to Beth that the man might be dangerous. Well, she could be dangerous, too. If he was, she'd make him sorry he showed that side of himself.

Doing her very best to set his skin on fire with her eyes, she leaned down, hoping to find a balance where she could rage at him without Mrs. Armitage hearing her. The poor woman had been through enough. "You get up off the ground and help us, you worthless skunk!"

And wasn't *skunk* just exactly the right word for the filthy pig?

"Get away from me." The wormy, skunky pig's eyes flashed like he had rabies.

Gritting her teeth so she could look fierce and still breathe through her mouth, she leaned closer. "You stand up right now." She hissed at him like a rattlesnake, so she had a few animal attributes of her own. "I need *help*. I don't care how drunk you are, how lazy you are, or how *stupid* you are. Right now I need some muscle, and I know you've got it. Get on your feet and get over there and help us, or so help me I will rip your arm off and beat you to *death* with the bloody stump."

The man's eyes seemed to clear. Maybe she'd pierced the alcoholic fog. "I'm not drunk."

Interesting that he hadn't protested being called stupid or worthless or a skunk. . .what else had she called him? She'd lost track of her insults somewhere along the line.

"Oh, *puh-leeze*, you expect me to believe you're this worthless without the help of whiskey?" Beth jammed her fists on her hips and straightened away from him. She had to get some air. "If that's true then I might as well shoot you here and now. Do the whole world a favor."

The drunk's eyes slid from her to the writhing man.

Beth had always been sensitive to others. Her ma had told her many times that was her finest gift. Right now it felt like a curse.

Beth saw something so vulnerable and fragile in the man's eyes that she almost regretted asking for help. It wasn't fear or laziness or stupidity or drunkenness. It was as if Leo's suffering ate into this man's soul.

"What's your name?" Beth asked quietly, very much afraid the man was on the verge of running.

"Alexander." He rubbed one hand over his grizzled, unshaven cheeks, his eyes imprisoned by the sight of the man's agony. "Alex Buchanan."

What horror had Alex seen to put such a look in his eyes? Beth couldn't give him the break he so desperately needed. "I can't do it without help. Please, Alex. Please. We can end Leo's suffering."

"He'll still hurt. Dislocated shoulders take a long time to heal."

Beth realized what the man had just admitted. He knew something about healing.

"Yes, it'll take time to heal, but the second that joint is back in place the pain will lessen. Please." She stiffened her compassionate spine. "You've got one more chance to say yes then I'm taking your hat to you again."

Alex didn't look at her. Instead, riveted on Leo, he pushed himself to his feet. His eyes filled with tears. His lips moved silently.

She wondered if it was a prayer. He didn't strike her as the praying kind.

He swiped his sleeve across his forehead, in a way meant to

disguise wiping his eyes. "I. . .I can't. I can't help him." He wheeled away from the blood and pain.

Beth caught his forearm with a hard slap of flesh on flesh. "You don't have a choice."

"I do."

Beth was afraid she might have to tackle him. "I'm not giving you one."

Alex turned, stared at her. Their eyes locked.

Seconds stretched to a minute, maybe longer. Growing slowly, a sensation Beth had never felt before almost made her let go, back away. Those eyes, it was as if he was looking all the way into her soul. She felt strength drain from her as if he was drawing on reserves within her, soaking up courage like desert ground in a rainstorm.

Her hand was on his wrist, and out of habit, she slid her fingers a bit to feel his pulse slamming at double the rate it should have. To Beth's sensitive touch it was as if his very blood cried out to be delivered from what he had to do.

God, give me strength. Strength enough for us both.

Still Alex watched her, drew from her. Leo fell silent, or maybe Beth was drawn so deeply into Alex's eyes that she couldn't connect with the world anymore.

Finally, Alex's eyes fell shut. Beth saw tears again, along the rims of his lashes, thick dark lashes to match hair, hanging long, nearly in ringlets around his neck.

His lips kept moving. She held on to his wrist, to lend support now rather than to restrain him. Then he started nodding. He physically changed—he seemed to grow taller, his shoulders squared, his chin came up. When he opened his eyes, a new man was there. Or maybe an old man, the man Alex Buchanan used to be before he crawled inside a bottle.

Beth could see what this was costing him. As if he paid for this courage by stripping off his skin with a razor.

He'd awakened something in her while their eyes were locked, something brand new.

"Let's do it," he said.

She'd never been so proud of anyone in her life.

Three

Alex had never been so ashamed.

He turned away from the little spitfire who had more guts in one arched, white-blond eyebrow than he had in his whole body.

The blood. No, never again. . .Shut up. Do it and forget it.

Alex had played this game the whole time he'd been in the army. Talking to himself, beating himself up, goading himself until he could do what needed to be done. He'd gotten out, and after four years he was still haunted by the things he'd seen.

Ignoring what it did to him. Ignoring the agony in his soul. Turning away from *this* feeling and *that* feeling, until he'd turned away from so much of himself he was barely human.

By the time he'd stopped, it had been far too late to regain his humanity.

He stumbled. The pretty blond steadied him.

A weakling, held up by a slender girl.

Why did he let this tear him apart?

He moved closer to the man.

Do it. Forget it. Don't feel it. . . . The blood. The pain.

25

Alex was going to make it so much worse.

But then he'll get better. Hurt him to heal him.

Alex knew all the reasons behind inflicting agony on patients. He detached himself from his feelings to the extent possible.

She thought he was a drunk. If only it were that simple. If only drink helped. He lived like a drunk—slept most of the time, was haunted the rest. Always moving, worthless, broke—or as good as because the money he had was like poison to him, dollars earned in blood and pain.

Digging deep into his scarred soul, Alex crouched by the man's side. He began speaking. He had a knack, he knew it. But there was a terrible cost to remaining calm in the midst of mayhem.

The spitfire had said his name. Alex wished he didn't remember. "Leo?"

The man wasn't lucid. His eyes opened, maybe in response to his name but more likely just in response to a voice. His pupils were dilated. There was no focus, no reason.

Alex ran his hands over the man's skull while he studied the wife. "What's your name, ma'am?"

He wasn't used to women. There'd been a few he'd had to work with but not many. Women were the worst. This one was so battered, covered in her own blood; Alex wondered if he might start crying like a girl child. The final shame—or no, who was he kidding? There was no end to the shame.

"Camilla Armitage."

"I had a creek that ran by my home in upstate New York when I was a child. We call it Camy Creek. I wonder if it was named after a woman named Camilla. You've had a terrible day, haven't you, Camilla?"

She nodded. "My Leo calls me Camy sometimes." Her hand moved on her husband's arm, caressing, comforting, strong enough to stick even when it was so hard. Stronger than Alex.

"Your husband is going to be fine. He's in terrible pain and this is going to hurt for a while. He's got torn tendons and muscle damage but it will all heal. He'll favor the arm for a few weeks, maybe a month, but even at that, with a sling, he'll be able to be up and walking. He'll be fine."

Some of the fear eased from Mrs. Armitage's eyes. Alex thought the man calmed a bit, too, still not clearheaded, but Alex's voice was reaching past the confusion. There was a terrible goose egg on the crown of the man's head that explained his incoherence.

Alex continued speaking softly, practically singing as he moved from Leo's head, down his unaffected arm, trying to get the man to just be calm, relax, trust.

My touch doesn't hurt you. My hands are healing hands.

Duping him to relax so Alex could turn to the ugly dislocated shoulder and betray his patient, inflict horrible pain on him. "No injury to this arm. No fractures anywhere. No stitches needed. Your shoulder will be tender for a few days, but the humerus isn't compromised. The clavicle and scapula are intact."

He heard the little spitfire who'd slapped him around gasp. That might well mean she knew some of these words. Well, she thought she knew everything, so why not this?

She knelt beside him, by Leo's knees, across from the driver. Poor Leo was surrounded.

Alex reminded himself that there were other wounded and he'd soon be called upon to help them. Controlling a deep inner shaking, he kept talking. "The deltoideus muscle is the one on top of the shoulder." Information meant little to the suffering couple, but any words were comforting. "And pectoralis muscles are on the chest. They're bruised and they'll be sore like any strained muscle, but they'll heal."

Leo had a wild look—the whites showing around his pupils like a terrified horse. But that eased. He still wasn't fully conscious, and he'd probably be addled for the next twenty-four hours and, in the end, not remember a thing Alex did to him.

But in the next few seconds, the man was going to hate Alex enough to kill.

The stage driver was holding the man's feet so securely that Leo had quit trying to fight the driver's firm grip.

As Alex slid one hand over Leo's chest, testing for cracked ribs, he reached sideways for the spitfire's hand and guided her to touch Leo's chest, flattening her hands. He flicked a glance at her, telling her with his eyes that it was time—never letting that warning sound in his voice as he soothed Leo.

She nodded. She knew what lay ahead. Good.

"Now." In one smooth motion, Alex grabbed Leo's wrist and upper arm, straightened it, and jerked.

An audible pop sounded a split second before the man's scream. His shoulder snapped back into its socket.

Leo's wife held his other hand, but she didn't have a good enough grip. The man flailed, shouted with agony, wrenched his hand free, and slugged Alex in the face so hard he fell over backward.

Alex kept going, scrambling backward like a frightened bug.

After the first eruption, Leo subsided. All his screaming cut off. The pain was manageable now. The madness was over.

And Alex felt the blood pouring from his nose and turned. Crawling on his hands and knees like a baby, he made it to the cliff alongside the trail, hung his head over the edge, and vomited.

The spitfire came up beside him and steadied him with a hand on his shoulders. Whispering gracious words, thanks, encouragement, Alex thought she'd have done the world a favor if she just shoved him over the edge.

Then, maybe, his nightmares would finally stop. The accumulated screams of agony would be quieted in his brain, the flashes of blood and gore, severed limbs, the dead and dying.

When it was over, he sank to his belly on the ground, his head still extended in midair as all the memories flooded back.

A cloth wiped his face. Damp. The spitfire had found water. Well, of course there'd have been a canteen or two on the stage.

He lay there, looking down, down, down.

The spitfire had her own soothing voice. He recognized it.

Then his eyes sharpened on the broken crags beneath him, and he saw that they hadn't counted all the dead. A young woman lay down there, way off to his right. Her eyes, wide, locked right on him, looked into him as if she hated him for not saving her.

He had to get down there, help her somehow. Alex launched himself to his feet. His legs went out from under him.

The spitfire knocked him away from the ledge, flipped him on his back, and wrapped his hands in something that immobilized them. "Give me strength," the woman muttered under her breath.

Why would she want even more strength than she already had? Near as Alex could make out, the woman could have subdued the entire unsettled West with one hand tied behind her back.

"What are you doing?" He found himself hog-tied as tightly as a calf set for branding.

She knelt beside him and glared down into his eyes. But her voice was sweet as sugar. "I still need you, so you're not going down there."

"I've got to save her."

"She's dead," the spitfire hissed as if someone had splattered water on her red-hot temper. She took a quick look behind her, and Alex realized Mrs. Armitage, now cradling her husband's head in her lap and cooing to him, was listening to every word they said.

Was that young woman at the bottom of the cliff the Armitages' daughter? He couldn't know, but a shouting match over the poor thing wouldn't help anyone.

He quit struggling. "Untie me."

"No."

"No?" He wanted to launch his body at her, tackle her, but he didn't.

"That's right. No. You understand short words. That's a good sign, but even half-wits understand that, so I'm still leaving you tied up."

"You can't just say no."

"Can and did. You're staying right here until I believe you've got yourself under control."

Alex saw the stage driver kneeling beside someone else. Another victim. Alex hadn't even gone to take a look at this one.

Yet.

He looked back at Miss Spitfire. He was on real thin ice...as if there'd ever be anything so cool as ice in this brutal, arid stretch of Texas. He decided to try and act sane...for a change.

"I—I know she's—" He couldn't say it.

"Dead." The fire faded from her eyes, replaced by worry. "I'm sorry but the word you're looking for is—*dead*."

Alex flinched. "I'm not looking for that word."

"You say you need to go down and help her, but it seemed to me like you were getting ready to throw yourself off a cliff. Considering the semi-lunatic behavior you've exhibited up until now, I suppose it's possible you thought you could help her. But since there's no path, nothing but a sheer drop, it amounted to killing yourself. I decided to act first and ask questions later. Not much good asking questions once you'd pitched yourself over the edge, now was there?"

He tasted the panic over seeing that girl down there, obviously another victim of this stagecoach accident. It was a terrible fall. Of course she was beyond help. He *was* looking for the word dead.

"You're right. I wasn't thinking clearly. All I could hear was her—" No sense removing all doubt from her mind that she was dealing with a crazy man. Alex had gotten lost in the gaping eyes and the woman's hate for him because he failed her.

"She seemed to be begging for help. I heard it, too."

He snapped back into the present and looked into the spitfire's eyes. Blue eyes. Blue. So blue. His were as dark as his broken soul. Her voice, too. She had the gift of soothing with her voice. A caretaker's voice. He shared that with her. Except he hadn't shared his soothing voice with anyone for a long time.

And he hoped to never share it again.

Now she was soothing him. He wanted so desperately to believe that was possible, to calm the madness of his memories.

She'd called it right. He *was* a crazy man.

"I'd like for you to untie me. I need to check the other victims and make a sling for Leo's arm."

She studied him, weighing his demeanor, thinking, he knew, about that moment when he'd almost gone over that ledge. Then she produced a knife that gleamed in the late afternoon sun and slashed the leather straps on his arms. "I can use the help. We're going to have to get that other stagecoach out of the way so we can drive on. It's going to take all the strength we have. And then some."

Alex sat up. The spitfire stood and extended her hand. He took it but did his best to stand on his own and not tax her strength, though she had so much.

When he was upright, he found himself far too close to those blue eyes and a craving was in him to hear her voice again, soothing him. "Thank you."

"You're a doctor." She wound the strips of leather around her waist. She'd tied him up with her belt?

He hadn't noticed it there before, but he didn't notice much anymore. "No, I'm not."

"Yes, you are. I don't know anyone else who would use the terms you did. *Humerus, clavicle, deltoideus*—those are words only doctors and nurses know. And you handled that dislocated shoulder with too much skill to have picked up some tricks on the trail. You've had training. You're a doctor."

"If you can call four years sucked into the carnage of war training. If hacking off limbs with little more than a butcher knife, digging bullets out of the arms and legs of screaming men, and using a branding iron to cauterize a wound is training, then yes, I guess I'm a doctor."

"It counted today. You helped that man." Such kindness,

such a beautiful tone.

He felt like he dared to admit some of what boiled inside. "I had to hurt him to help him."

The spitfire used her eyes on him, as if she was hunting around inside his head, looking for—what? Some sign of intelligence probably.

"It figures you'd look at the help you gave that man and find a reason to hate yourself for healing him. It just figures."

Alex knew he shouldn't ask. He'd lived too long to ask. But she was so lovely, and her eyes were so blue, and she was talking and he wanted her to keep on. "Why does it figure?"

"Because, Alexander Buchanan"—

He saw it in her eyes and he'd asked, so he had it coming.

—"you are measuring up to be a complete idiot."

And that was nothing less than the truth, his high grades in medical school notwithstanding.

"Now don't make me tie you up again, because the next time, I swear, when I'm done with you, you'll be taking a nap all the way to the next town."

Alex turned to Leo, hoping for a bit more kindness from the man he'd put through torture a few minutes ago.

Four

Beth thought it was fair to say she had a God-given gift for compassion mixed with toughness.

But it'd been a long day.

Right now, she was within a hair's breadth of showing her toughness with the back of her hand on her brand-new friend, Alex "The Skunk" Buchanan—guaranteed mental patient. She was slap out of compassion.

This wasn't the first time Beth had noticed that in Texas they let mental patients roam free. Texans figured living in Texas cleared their heads or killed them, either one solving the problem.

Beth fetched her doctor's bag out of the stagecoach and set to work on the wounded. The rest of the troop of injured were finally seen to. Alex seemed capable enough, but there was a mild thread of panic running under every word he spoke and every move he made. Alex expertly splinted one older man's leg. Beth put Leo's arm in a sling and bandaged Mrs. Armitage's head. Camilla was working as hard as Beth and the stage driver.

The third victim, a youngish man dressed like he lived in the city, came around and, though battered, seemed to have no major injuries. He was addled enough to be no help though. And Beth could have used more help.

"What about the young woman?" Beth asked Mrs. Armitage after a final adjustment to the older man's broken leg.

Mrs. Armitage's jaw clenched and her eyes went to the ledge as if she felt guilty for not looking. "The one who fell to her death?"

Beth caught her arm. "You don't need to see her. Did you know her name?"

"It was Celeste. Celeste Gray."

Gray. Beth recognized the name of the man Mandy had just married. Not a common name but not that rare either. Was this young woman on her way to Mandy's wedding? She could very well be. The cyclone that had torn out the bridge had come through several days ago.

Suddenly it was far more personal. That young woman down there might well be Mandy's sister-in-law or perhaps a cousin. That made her Beth's family, too. Beth had no idea what to do about it. No one could go down there to get her, but leaving her in the open was obscene. They'd dragged the bodies of the two dead men off to the side of the trail with plans to come back later for them. There'd be no burial on this stony ground. Maybe whoever came back could bring enough rope to go down for poor Celeste.

With a sharp shake of her head, Beth turned back to Mrs. Armitage. "We've got everyone as patched as we're going to get them. We need to move."

The stage driver, who called himself Whip, heard Beth and turned to study the wreckage and his own restless team.

"Can we get turned around and go back?" Beth asked.

"Nope, too narrow."

"Then we either walk out of here or shove the wrecked coach off the ledge. It's beyond repair, so setting it on its wheels would do no good." Beth studied the terrain, her available help, and the weight of that broken-down stage.

"There's a nice length of rope on the back of your stage, Whip. Go fetch it and unharness your team." Beth went to the damaged stage and took every inch of rope and leather off it she could find.

"What'a'ya got in mind?" the driver asked.

"We'll rig a pulley to that overhanging tree up there"—Beth pointed—"and use the horses' strength to knock that stage the rest of the way off the trail."

"No, wait!" Mrs. Armitage cried out.

Beth turned. The distraught woman was still bloody. They didn't have enough water to spare to wash her clean. Under the blood her skin had gone deathly pale.

"What is it?"

"My husband's satchel—it has money in it. I don't know what we'll do if we lose it. I have to get it out."

"No." Alex had moved away from the group once the doctoring was done and had been studiously looking down the trail with longing eyes as if tempted nearly beyond control to desert them all. "That stage is too close to the edge. No one's going in there to get anything."

"It's wedged tight, Alex." Beth regretted overruling him the first time he'd shown any spunk, but there was no reason they couldn't give poor Camilla this bit of comfort. "I'll get it."

"No!" Alex strode toward Beth. "You won't! No amount of money is worth your life." He came close enough that his voice, dropping to a barely audible whisper, only reached her. "You only get one life, you understand? Don't kid yourself that you'll get lucky or be fast enough or smart enough to get in and out. It's too big a risk."

Beth tried to help him. She understood, at least somewhat, that he was traumatized, and she felt sympathy for him. But the stage wasn't going to slide anywhere. "It's going to take every ounce of strength every one of us *and* the horses have to pull it off those rocks and get it off the trail." She rested her hand on his forearm and tried to soothe him. "I know life is precious,

Alex. I would never put myself in danger for money. But there's no danger. You're overreacting."

"I'm not." His arm jerked away from her touch and he grabbed her wrist. "And you're not doing it."

Beth—short on compassion—was tempted to hog-tie him again. In fact, she was looking forward to it. In fact, she found herself looking forward to it so much she decided she couldn't trust herself and held up. Rather than jerk away from him—and honesty forced her to admit she wasn't all that sure she could break his iron hold—she leaned closer. "Get your hands off of me. I don't know if you're sane enough to know you're about half-crazy, but your judgment is pathetic. I can't trust a single thing you say. There is no risk, and if getting that woman's things will put her mind at ease then I'm doing it. Now let go of me *right now* or I will make you regret you were ever born."

Alex's fingers tightened. Their eyes held. It wasn't like before when Beth felt him sucking the energy from her. He was trying to dominate her with his will, his fierceness, his grip.

She almost smiled. It was kind of sweet, his trying that when he had to know he didn't stand a chance. Crazy or not, he did have her best interests at heart. Still, she knew she'd slug him if he didn't let go and do it fast. "I'm gonna count to three."

Alex's hand almost had a spasm, but at last he let go. "Fine!" He practically threw her arm away from him. "Risk your life, maybe die for a few dollars. That's what most people would do. I expected better of you though. You seem like a woman with a shred or two of sense."

Well, that hurt.

She glared at him then turned to the stage. "It's wedged in that narrow part of the trail like a rock. It couldn't begin to fall."

Alex's response was a noise so rude Beth barely kept her back to him. Averting her eyes from the two men pinned and dead beneath the coach, she called out, "I'm going to throw everything out. Gather what needs to be taken."

Beth tried her very best to give Alex credit for worrying about her. But she'd already learned the poor guy worried about everything, so this was no great surprise.

Grimly, she climbed up the stage, which lay on its side. It was a shame it wasn't teetering on the cliff's edge. Then one good shove might have solved their problems. Instead it had slammed into a rocky outcropping on the downhill side and was wedged tight.

Gaining the top, which was in fact the side, she found the door ripped off and gone. Inside, a few satchels and bags were jumbled around. Any larger parcels and crates would have been strapped on the roof, and she'd noticed a few scattered here and there.

She lightly swung her body down into the tipped-over box. It was disorienting to be in the stage while it was on its side. She didn't like the feeling of the whole world being tipped on its axis, so she quickly began tossing things out the door, making sure they went onto the trail rather than over the cliff.

Wedged under the seat lay a heavy reticule of black velvet. Maybe Mrs. Armitage's purse?

Beth grabbed it just as an awful crack sounded from outside the stage. A crash of tumbling stones scared her as if she'd heard a gunshot.

The stage rolled toward the cliff.

Five

Sophie, I'm worried about Beth." Clay McClellen clamped his hat on his head and stared down the trail out of town to the east.

"She's late. And she's going to want to see you, Mandy." Sophie didn't grab Mandy's arm, but Mandy could tell her ma wanted to, badly. And it was all Mandy could do to not grab right back.

"Ma, we've gotta go." Mandy hated it, but Sidney was right, they needed to hit the trail. They were already getting a late start. Yes, it was still blazing hot. But winter came early in the mountains. Pa knew it and admitted that every day lessened their chances of settling in well before winter came to the Colorado Rockies.

Mandy adjusted her Winchester 73 on her shoulder, so the rifle hung at an angle on her back, the muzzle pointing down by her right hip, the butt end of the gun pointing up by her left shoulder. She was barely aware of touching the rifle, and yet she never forgot it was there. She felt vulnerable without it and had rearmed herself immediately following her wedding ceremony.

Sidney didn't like her rifle much. But apparently he liked her enough to put up with the ever-present firearm.

The Wild West was a lot tamer when a body had a steady hand and was a dead eye with a Winchester. And Mandy had both and she liked tame, even if she had to do the taming herself.

And now it looked like she was going somewhere even wilder than West Texas, if there was such a thing.

"Beth was hoping to be here on the afternoon stage. She'll want to see you. Surely you can wait until tomorrow morning."

Mandy threw her arms around her mother's neck, mostly so Ma couldn't see her face and know how scared she was of setting off across half the country in search of a new, better home. The home she had right now was as nice as any Mandy had ever dreamed of, so the idea didn't hold much appeal. When she'd accepted Sidney's proposal, she'd never reckoned on moving halfway across the country.

Sidney came close and slid his arm around Mandy's waist and pulled her close. "We've got to go, Mrs. Gray." He was on her left. Sidney had learned fast she didn't like her shooting arm impeded. It gave her an itch between her shoulder blades.

Letting loose of her ma almost felt like tearing her own skin, but Mandy needed to leave her mother and her home and cleave unto her husband. The Bible was clear.

Settling against his side, Mandy's heart raced. This happened every time Sidney got close. Love had hit her so hard it left her breathless, and when Sidney had proposed after they'd only known each other a month, she'd felt such joy she could have sprouted wings and flown straight to heaven.

"I'm sorry," he whispered in her ear and made her shiver. "If we don't catch this stage, we'll miss the train. It'll be another week before there's a stage heading north out of Mosqueros. I really am sorry." His hand caressed her side, up and down. His voice settled somewhere deep in Mandy's heart.

She couldn't believe her good luck in snaring such a fine man. Handsome and strong and sweet. Rich, too, and he looked so nice in his store-bought suit. He had studied the possibilities of opening a law office in Mosqueros. But he decided a week before their wedding—after a month and three weeks of almost no lawyer business—that he had to go elsewhere. He had a line on a law office that needed a partner near bustling Denver, Colorado.

The jingle of iron in the traces made Mandy glance over her shoulder. The stage driver was almost finished getting his fresh team harnessed.

Not seeing Beth was unthinkable. Her little sister hadn't been home for four long years. But Sidney was her husband now. He was head of the house. Mandy had promised to obey and she intended to keep that promise.

She looked at the trail, praying for Beth's stage to round the corner of Mosqueros's rutted Main Street, bringing her little sister home. Just a hug, just ten seconds to tell Beth how much she'd missed her.

Mandy knew how far away this journey would take her. It was very possible—probable in fact—that she would never see her family again. She fought the tears by thinking of sweet Sidney. Mandy couldn't let Ma sway her into cajoling Sidney to wait yet again. "Ma, she was supposed to be here three days ago on the train. We held the wedding off until this morning for her because her telegram said she'd be coming on the stage yesterday."

Sidney had been irritated. He'd made no secret of not wanting to spend his wedding night sitting up on a bouncing stage. He'd complied with her wishes finally, but it had been their first fight, the first time she'd really gotten a glimpse of Sidney's hot temper, and it was all Mandy's fault. She was going to do her best to be a perfect wife and never make him unhappy again. She didn't dare ask him to delay their departure.

"You know they've broken down or something, Ma. She's not going to get here."

"I'm going to ride out and meet the stage." Pa glared at the street as if he blamed the very ground for preventing Beth's homecoming. "If there's trouble, I'll help 'em clear it up. I'm taking an extra horse, and even if they're broke down, Beth could ride hard for home and get here by morning."

Leaving Pa was almost harder than leaving Ma, but Mandy had found a man just as brave and true. That made it bearable.

"I don't think you gave the law office in Mosqueros a fair try, Sid. Taking off for the mountains this time of year, with winter only a couple of months away, is reckless. Winter comes early in the Rockies. I know. I grew up there."

A quick, almost painful spasm of Sidney's fingers on her side reminded her how annoyed he got when someone called him Sid. "We'll be fine if we go now, sir." His fingers relaxed and he caressed her side again.

Mandy loved the respectful way Sidney talked to her pa. Even if he was irritated, he remained a real gentleman.

Pa didn't approve of this marriage, just because it had happened so fast. Mandy got half a dozen stern lectures since she'd announced her engagement, but she knew her heart and she wanted Sidney.

She was too old to still be single, an old maid of twenty-two. And the truth was, she'd run off her share of men waiting for a prince. He'd finally come. Just an hour ago they'd said their vows and she was now Mrs. Sidney Gray.

And anyway, Mandy'd never had a boyfriend that Clay McClellen thought was good enough, so Pa's disapproval didn't mean a whole lot.

"Denver is a fast-growing town." Sidney's hand moved steadily on her side, so comforting. "I've got work lined up."

"I thought you just had a line on a job." Pa adjusted his hat, pulling the front brim low. "It didn't sound like a sure thing to me."

"We'll be fine, sir. We'll be settled and safe before the first snow flies."

"You should spend the winter here. There's room in our house if you don't find the right place in Mosqueros. Then you could start out in the spring if the lawyer business hasn't picked up here." Pa held Sidney's eyes for too long.

Mandy looked at her ma and glared, hoping for once Sophie could control her husband.

With a little shrug, Ma just stayed out of it. Ma never stayed out of anything unless she wanted to, which meant she wanted Mandy to stay, too. It was understandable. Her parents loved her and she loved them. But it was time to grow up.

"Load up!" the stage driver hollered. There were two other people waiting on the wooden sidewalk by the stage station.

Mandy threw her arms around first Ma, then Pa. Then she went down the line, hugging her two little sisters.

Sally, a reckless tomboy of seventeen, was dressed—under protest—in a riding skirt. She wore buckskin pants on the range. Ma had given up trying to make her behave like a proper lady, except in town, and Sally almost never came to town except for church, so the girl nearly lived in disgraceful men's pants. But despite her boyish behavior, Sally hugged her fiercely with all the love in her unconventional little heart.

Eleven-year-old Laurie was next. She was overly proper, as if her whole life was a reaction against Sally's refusal to be ladylike. Laurie's eyes filled with tears as she hugged Mandy tight. "I don't want you to go." Laurie's voice broke and Mandy remembered the hand she'd had in raising her littlest sister.

Four little brothers needed a hug, then Adam, a longtime friend of the McClellen family who owned a ranch near them, and his wife, Tillie, a former slave who'd been kept in chains long after the War Between the States had ended. Mandy considered them and their brood family. She didn't bother trying to hug Buff—she knew it'd embarrass him to death—but she said good-bye. "Where's Luther?" How could he have missed seeing her off?

Buff stood, clutching his coonskin cap in both hands, dressed in heavy leather that had to be smothering in the heat. He turned his head toward the end of the street and nodded.

Mandy turned and saw Luther coming, riding his horse and pulling a second horse behind him.

"I had Luther pack some things for you to set up housekeeping," Ma said.

"We're burnin' daylight!" the stage driver shouted and gave Mandy and Sidney a surly look. The other passengers were aboard.

Mandy glanced frantically at Luther. She had to tell him good-bye. She had to.

Luther helped load a big box on the stage, giving Mandy a chance to hug everyone one more time. When she threw her arms around Luther, his cheeks turned pink under his full beard. He and Buff had been like kindly uncles to the McClellen brood for years.

With a smile that she kept locked on her face to keep the tears at bay, Mandy let Sidney pull her toward the stage. Amid waves and shouts of good-bye, she climbed aboard the crowded stage, heartbroken to leave her family, devastated to miss Beth, and thrilled to be with the man she adored.

She slid the strap of her Winchester off over her head and settled her rifle between her and the stagecoach wall, the trigger close to her right hand. She rubbed on the little callus that had formed on her trigger finger and fought down the flicker of fury toward her new husband who couldn't wait another week to take her halfway across the country. When she had her anger under control, she looked out the window to wave one last time. They all waved back almost frantically. Then Pa tipped his hat to the family, swung up onto his horse, and rode off in the direction of Beth.

Sidney's arm slipped around her waist.

She smiled at him but tried, with her eyes, to warn him to behave with the two men sitting across from them.

Sidney leaned down and kissed her on the neck.

Mandy was embarrassed to death and slid as far from him as

possible in the cramped space.

Sidney just followed. "We'll be in town late tonight." When he had her cornered, he dropped his voice to a whisper. "We'll have ourselves a wedding night, Mandy."

She shivered, but it wasn't with pleasure. The two passengers were watching every move. One had his eyes fixed on them. The other was pretending not to stare, but Mandy caught him peeking.

"We should have been married days ago. . .weeks ago. We would have if we hadn't put the wedding off for so long for your sister."

Mandy pushed on Sidney's chest forcefully and spoke sharply. "Now behave." She smiled at him when she realized how harsh she'd sounded.

He frowned. She'd seen him frown before, but never quite like this and never at her. She'd annoyed him. Her heart trembled to know she'd made him unhappy. How could she fix it? Certainly not by letting him kiss her in front of others.

"Tell me when the train we're meeting is coming in." Distract him. That might do it.

"Early tomorrow morning."

With a sigh, Mandy said, "We had to take this stage, I know, to get there, but I would have loved to see Beth." Tears burned at her eyes.

"I'm your family now, Mandy." He straightened away from her. The annoyance in his eyes flashed to true anger. "Your loyalty is supposed to be to me."

Mandy noticed both men straighten subtly as if. . . But no, they couldn't think she would need protection from her husband. Rushing to calm Sidney down, she smiled. "It is to you. I just love my sister and miss her, but I'm here with you now, aren't I? I love you, and I'm excited about our new life in Colorado."

She was stunned by her new life in Colorado. She'd had no notion that Sidney wasn't settled in Mosqueros when she'd accepted his proposal. But she loved him and would follow him anywhere.

His mouth was a tense line and he watched her, as if judging her words. Finally, he turned and put the length of the seat between them and pushed the curtain aside to look out the window.

Mandy felt awful. Married two hours and she'd already done something wrong. She had no way to fix it now though, not with an audience, so she settled into the corner of the stage and did her best to rest her head, wishing sleep would come and this uncomfortable part of their journey was over so they could settle in and be happy.

Six

It's rolling!" Alex's shout only told her what she already knew.

Beth took one look up at the tilting doorway that was right about head high. It was going the wrong way for her to climb up there to get out. Both doors had been torn off and Beth now stood on the ground, but the stage wouldn't clear her head when it went over.

She dropped. Shouts grew louder. The stage tipped. When the opening on which she now stood rose, she looked under it and saw dangling feet—

The stage stopped.

—Alex's battered cowboy boots. He must have his hands on the top of the stage, using his weight to stop it from rolling.

Then, instead of rolling, the stage slid.

If it rolled, she had a chance of getting out. If it slid, it'd scrape her right off the cliff with it.

"Let go!" She snaked her hands out the door opening and caught his feet and yanked. "Let go and get down here."

The lunatic either didn't hear her or didn't think she was

46

making sense because he hung on and the stage slid again. Alex's feet rose higher, risking his fool neck.

Another few inches and Beth could slide out of the stage on her belly. "Alex, let go and get down here." Then she thought of what the crazy man might respond to. "I need help. Catch my hand. Please."

Alex dropped to the ground, all the way down to look at her. The stage, without his weight, began rolling again. Alex thrust his hand forward.

Beth grabbed him. She needed another five inches, a space wider than she was, and she could get her body through. It rose three, then four.

The stage slid suddenly, instead of rolling.

"No!" Alex's free hand grabbed the door frame and lifted. Beth's grabbed right beside his hand. While keeping a firm grip on each other, they lifted with such strength a groan ripped out of Beth's throat. The stage canted just enough. Beth dropped flat on her belly in the dirt.

The stage slid again with her between the ground and the heavy vehicle. Alex pulled until she thought her own shoulder might be dislocated. Her head was under the stage now. If it dropped she'd be crushed.

Another pair of hands appeared, lifting on the stage door frame, rugged hands—the stage driver. A third single, feminine hand caught hold—Camilla Armitage. Then another pair of man's hands, smooth—the young man in the dark suit, fit for city life.

The stage lifted, lifted. Alex pulled and Beth shoved off whatever purchase she could find inside the stage and propelled herself forward. Alex dragged her.

With a roar of tumbling stone and scraping wood on rock and dirt, the stage was gone, rolling down the cliff, cracking and slamming into granite and stunted brush that clung to the rugged cliffs.

Beth's feet dangled over the ledge for only a split second. Alex used that amazing strength of his to pull her all the way to safety. She flew forward and knocked her rescuer over backward. With a grunt of pain, she sprawled full length on top of him.

Their eyes met.

"Thank you." She only had a moment to say it because the others were easing her onto her back, talking. Mrs. Armitage was crying. Beth saw that they'd all come rushing to help her—Whip, the stage driver; Mrs. Armitage; and the young man. Only Leo and the man with the broken leg hadn't rushed to help. Beth suspected Leo was still somewhat addle-headed or he'd have chipped in, too.

It was all Beth could do to keep tears from coming to her eyes. But tears were nonsense for the most part, a waste of salt and water, Pa liked to say. So she didn't take the time to break down and cry. Instead, she stood, noticed she still had Camilla's reticule looped over her wrist, and offered it to her.

Camilla shook her head. "That's not mine. You threw out the satchel we needed almost first thing."

"I noticed the young woman carrying it," Whip said. "I wonder if she had family we should notify?"

"Well, we got the stage off the trail then. Let's be on our way." Beth smiled at the driver and hung on to the reticule with no idea what to do with it.

The driver didn't react. He seemed dazed, as if the scare had gone to his head as much as the blow had to Leo's.

Beth could sympathize. It'd been a long day. She decided to give him just a few more minutes to settle down.

She looked at Alex, still lying on his back. Reaching down, she offered him a hand.

"Thanks, Alex." Beth didn't think he heard her. And he'd really been through a lot, considering whatever trauma still pounded inside the man's head. "You were right about the stage being dangerous. Thank you for saving me."

His eyes flashed. He reached up and caught hold of Beth's

hand with a slap of flesh on flesh and a death grip.

Beth felt a little thrill of fear race up her spine—well, more thrill than fear, honestly. She knew the feeling of fear well. No one grew up in West Texas without learning to have a healthy fear of the rugged land. Thrill though, oh yes.

"Let's get loaded." The driver seemed to come out of his daze, and the group straggled toward the waiting stage.

Beth tugged on Alex. He came to his feet in a move so graceful he could have been a mountain lion. . .a pouncing mountain lion. . .a pouncing mountain lion who smelled really bad.

"I told you not to go in there." He didn't yell. Beth wished he would because the stage driver might come and save her. Alex looked for all the world like, after all the trouble he'd gone to saving her, he was now considering tossing her over the cliff.

But since when had Beth ever needed someone else to save her? She'd save herself, thanks very much. "I had no idea those rocks might crumble. They looked as solid as. . .well, as solid as a rock."

"I told you it was dangerous." He ignored her explanation and, his hand like a vise on her wrist, took a step toward her, using his height to loom over her.

Give me strength. Strength not to clobber Alex.

Beth wanted to sympathize with the poor, half-crazy man, but honestly, she'd had a hard day, too. "You were right." If she couldn't say that with complete humility, she blamed it on stress.

"I told you the stage might roll."

"I was wrong." The words were good, but Beth knew the tone didn't sound a bit contrite. In fact, it sounded like a child's chant, something a body might hear on a schoolyard at recess. "Neener, neener, neener."

She jerked but he didn't let go. Chanting again, she said, "You were right. I was wrong. You're smart. I'm stupid. Is that what you need to hear?"

His eyes narrowed at her mocking tone. His grip tightened. "I tried to make you use your head."

Well fine. He wanted her close, she'd get close. She took a step forward. "Can we go now?"

"No amount of money is worth dying for. Not even *risking* death." He shook her arm hard.

Oh, dear God, give me strength not to pound this guy. And if I do pound him, give me plenty of strength for that.

"But you wouldn't listen." His fingers were starting to hurt. He was insane, so she decided to give him one more chance.

"You don't know me well." There, that sounded rational and calm and adult. No schoolyard taunt.

"You almost killed yourself for a *purse.*" He was so mad his hair might have been standing up a bit straighter, not that easy with his battered hat.

"So you couldn't possibly know how much I hate, 'I told you so.'" It was only fair to warn him. . .before.

"I almost *died* saving you." He dragged her forward until her forearm was pressed against his chest.

She tried to sound reasonable. "So you couldn't know that you are within about ten words—"

"We *all* almost died saving you." His nose almost touched hers.

The man seriously, profoundly reeked. "Of losing your ability to—"

"Life is *precious.*" His eyes shot out blue flames until she thought they singed her lashes.

"Stand upright if you don't—" Beth wasn't counting, but she figured he had about one word to go.

"You risked your life for *nothing!*" His burning eyes connected and Beth felt that tug again, like they saw inside her, in her mind, in her heart, drawing from her. Compassion, understanding, hope, strength.

Terror—it made her feel terror. Because she didn't want to feel any of that for a crazy man. Which made her react in the way any good McClellen girl would. "Get your hand off of me. Last chance."

He didn't.

She quit relying on words.

He dropped over backward with a cry of pain.

She hated to hurt him. Not because she hated his *being* hurt—shameful to admit, but she kind of liked that. But it was going to make more work for her, and she was worn clean out.

The man stank. He was heavy. Now someone had to toss him into the stage—which picked that moment to roll up beside her.

Everyone loaded.

It had to be her to load him. No one else but the driver was up to it. And he'd be slow climbing down from his perch.

She reached down and, hurt though he was, Alex seemed to learn it was best to work with her and not against her. She hoisted him in.

There was really no room for him. Three people on one side— the Armitages and the young man. On the other side, the man with the broken leg took up the whole seat. His leg was neatly bound.

Beth was relieved. She'd have had to tend him once they got to town if he'd needed more help. Beth shoved Alex inside onto the floor, still curled up with pain. She stuffed his legs in and slammed the door and swung up beside Whip on the high seat.

There was barely room. Whip had stowed everything saved from the wrecked stage up here, including on the seat beside him.

She lifted a box onto her lap and smiled at the crusty old driver. "Let's head for Mosqueros."

He slapped the reins so quickly and obediently, she suspected he'd witnessed her encounter with Alex.

The stage pulled to a stop about the same time Alex's blood started circulating again.

He had recovered enough that he'd grown sick of the floor and decided he'd use this opportunity to sit on the roof for the rest of the ride.

Even if it did mean being within striking distance of the spitfire. Beth, she'd said her name was Beth. It was a peaceful, gentle name.

Inaccurate as all get-out.

He swung the door open, still on the floor, and scooted out. A tall stranger riding a gray mare and pulling two black mustangs behind him rode to a stop, smiling up at the driver. "Beth, honey, we've been wondering what kept you."

He wasn't looking at the driver at all. He was obviously riding out to meet the spitfire. The cowboy looked to be around forty. He rode with a steady hand. His eyes wrinkled in the corners as if he'd seen a lot of Texas summers. He had a cool, competent gaze, a revolver on his hip and a rifle in a boot on his saddle. A man who'd seen his share of trouble in his life and expected more.

"Is Mandy gone, Pa?" The spitfire could handle herself, but now, just in case she needed more firepower, she had a well-armed, cool-eyed Pa on the scene.

Alex did his best not to groan out load. The cowboy didn't look as Alex stood and swung the stage door shut, but Alex had a good suspicion that the man didn't miss much.

"She had to go, honey." The cowboy swung down from his horse just as the spitfire hopped off the driver's seat. "It's so good to see you again," the man murmured as he drew her into a bear hug. There was more warmth and love in that one hug than Alex had seen since his own pa died.

"I wanted to see her so bad, Pa." The spitfire started crying.

"Now, Beth, don't start that." The cowboy set her away from him, his eyes wide as if she scared him.

Alex sensed that the man could handle most anything. But apparently not tears.

Alex could relate.

The spitfire shook her head and dashed the back of her hand across her eyes. "Sorry, Pa. I just wanted to see her so bad. I wanted to meet her husband."

The cowboy grunted as if the spitfire hadn't missed much.

"We've gotta get on to Mosqueros, folks."

"I'll ride in with you, Pa."

The driver nodded and lifted the reins.

"Hey, wait a minute!"

The spitfire, her pa, and the driver all looked at Alex. He regretted earning their attention, but the driver was going to drive off without him. "I'll ride up top with you. It's too crowded in there."

"Pa, this is Alex Buchanan. Alex, my pa, Clay McClellen." She said it as if she wanted her pa to know exactly who he was going to shoot.

Alex felt a little shiver of fear. He then thought of her strong, slender arm in his grip and how he'd dragged her against him. And he remembered how intelligent and compassionate and strong she was, and what had passed between them when their eyes had locked.

He might deserve to be shot. Although the spitfire had punished him pretty well on her own, Alex would just as soon that didn't come up.

"Can you give him a lift, McClellen?" the stage driver asked. "There wasn't really room for your girl up here, and the stage is full. We picked up passengers and stowed some luggage from a wreck we found back up the trail."

Clay McClellen's eyes were assessing, cool. Alex wondered what the man saw. Filth, tattered cloths, a bad attitude. Whatever he saw must not have worried him much. "Sure, grab a horse." Most likely because McClellen figured it'd be no problem to shoot him down like a mangy coyote, should the necessity arise.

"Make sure the injured are helped to a good room in town. Tell them I'll check on them tomorrow after Sunday services."

The spitfire gave orders in a polite tone, but Alex never doubted she was in charge.

"Sure enough, Miss McClellen. I'll see to 'em."

Riding along with these two was way down on the list of things Alex wanted to do right now. But even lower was crouching on the floor of that stage for the rest of the trip or sitting squashed up against the driver. "Obliged for the use of the horse, McClellen," Alex said.

The spitfire took a few minutes to check on everyone in the stage while McClellen got the particulars on the accident from the stage driver.

Alex moved toward his horse, not wanting to get pulled into the doctor exams but listening to the spitfire's quiet questions and her patients' answers. He heard her promise to check on them all again.

Then she swung up onto horseback. "We left three dead behind, Pa."

Alex noticed the way she moved, as if she was part of the horse, completely at home.

Reins slapped into Alex's hands and caught him lightly across the face. Alex looked up and saw McClellen watching him, scowling. Alex wondered just exactly what expression had been on his face as he watched the heavily armed man's daughter.

From now on, keep your eyes strictly on the horse, idiot.

"Pa, I'll just ride on for home. I don't want to go all the way into Mosqueros now."

"No, I'm not letting you ride the range alone. You know better'n that."

"Mosqueros is an hour out of our way. If you want to ride in with Alex—"

"I'll stay with the stage." Alex cut her off and handed the reins back to McClellen.

"You got a destination in mind, Buchanan? A job or family in town waiting, or are you just passing through?"

"I thought to stay in Mosqueros a while. Maybe for the winter." Alex had no idea how he'd live through the winter, but he couldn't stand the thought of going back East to his father's home, even if it was well heated and there was plenty of money for food and comfort. That inheritance was never going to be his. If his father would've lived, he'd've disinherited Alex for the things he'd done—so Alex disinherited himself.

"You huntin' work?"

Alex shrugged.

"Ride with us to the ranch. You can sleep in the bunkhouse, eat with the men, clean up."

Alex looked closer at McClellen when he said "clean up" to see if the man was sneering, but the man's expression was contained, unreadable.

"We always go to town for Sunday services. You can ride along then to Mosqueros, and we'll be handy to lead the horse home."

From the cool look in McClellen's eyes, Alex suspected this was a test. He just wasn't sure what to say to pass or fail. Was it about attending church? Coming to McClellen's ranch? Accepting a handout? Probably not knowing was the *real* test and just hesitating proved he was flunking. Well, that was something McClellen had probably figured out just by looking, so what difference did it make?

Since Alex couldn't figure right and wrong out, he decided to just do as he wished, and the meal and a bed were too tempting to pass up. "Thanks. I'll accept." Maybe he ought to ask for a job while he was at the ranch. He'd done a bit of cattle wrangling in the last four years as he'd drifted. He'd done just enough to know he was pathetic at it. He'd be found out as incompetent and fired within days. But in the meantime, he'd eat. Eating was good.

Not wanting to ask for work in front of the spitfire, he decided to wait until later.

"Pa, we've got to send someone back to bring in the dead from that stage wreck."

"I'll handle it." McClellen kicked his horse to pick up the pace.

The three of them set off at about five times the speed of the stage, which creaked along in their wake and was soon left far behind.

"Pa, Alex is a doctor." She smiled as if she'd done him a favor with her announcement.

"He is?" The look the rancher gave him was as close to shocked as someone so contained could muster.

"No, I'm not!"

"You're not?" McClellen asked as he and the spitfire turned off the trail and struck out to the south while the well-traveled trail headed on west. Alex had to hustle to keep up. It was all he could do to ignore the lingering ache left behind by Beth's. . . annoyance.

"Yes, he is."

McClellen looked between them. "Well, which is it?"

"I'm not."

"He's a doctor, but he's not doctoring these days."

"Mosqueros could use a doctor."

"Pa"—she gave him a disgruntled look—"Alex can't be the *Mosqueros* doctor. *I'm* going to—"

"You can't be a doctor!" Alex cut her off.

"Do it." She glared at him.

"No, you're not." McClellen talked over her this time. "Doctoring's not a proper job for a female."

Alex looked at the spitfire's father and found a kindred spirit.

The spitfire, however, wasn't having it. "I spent the last four year training to be a doctor."

"A nurse, you mean," her pa said.

"No, a doctor. It's true I went to nursing school."

"Then you're a nurse." Alex flinched a bit when she turned her fiery eyes on him.

"But I apprenticed with a doctor. He knew I'd be the only

person in the area with doctoring skills. He taught me everything. He let me do surgery."

"With a knife?" Alex gasped.

"No, I cut my patients open with a carrot, idiot," Beth snapped. "Of course with a knife."

"That's awful. That guy oughta be reported." McClellen's jaw stiffened with anger.

He ought to be arrested and shot and maybe hanged, too, Alex thought. "What all'd he let you do? A woman can't be examining a man."

"None of your business, Alex."

"You're not gonna be a doctor and that's that." Her pa rode right up close so he could tower over her whilst he laid down the law. "You can do some midwifin' if your ma says it's okay and she goes along, and maybe a few other little things with women and young children, but you'll be living at the ranch, and you aren't going off alone in the night to care for sick people. That's just asking for trouble."

"Amen!" Alex slapped his pommel and McClellen looked at him. They jerked their chins in agreement.

"He can be the doctor." McClellen jabbed his thumb at Alex.

Beth glared at Alex. "He's not a doctor."

"I'm not a doctor." Alex and the spitfire had spoken at the same time.

"You just said he was a doctor." McClellen looked between the two of them.

"I'm not." Alex knew that even if the spitfire didn't.

"He's not." Now she was just being stubborn because she wanted the job herself.

McClellen shook his head in disgust and kicked his horse into a faster gait, which took him out from between them.

They glared at each other for too long.

Then Alex got his own horse moving faster. He liked it better when he couldn't see her pretty blue eyes anyway.

Seven

A loud whistle jerked Mandy awake. Her hand slapped down and found her rifle and she felt better. Sleep had been a wish, but she'd never expected to really get any.

It was pitch-dark.

Truly, it made sense that even in the rattling stagecoach she'd nodded off. It had been a stressful week. She hadn't slept much since Sidney had announced they were moving to Colorado and Mandy realized she would have to leave her family.

The stage pulled to a stop. Mandy heard the nervous snorting of the horses, most likely unhappy with the roaring train.

"What's that?" Sidney asked.

"A train." One of their fellow passengers said in a voice that seemed to call Sidney stupid.

Her door swung open and the stage driver stuck his head in. "We don't have much time to move your bags from the stage to the train. Let's get moving."

"We aren't going yet?" Sidney sounded outraged. "Our train leaves in the morning."

Mandy knew he was overly anxious for the wedding night. He'd made it abundantly clear. Mandy admitted to relief on several occasions that her pa and ma had been fierce about chaperoning them because Mandy had been nearly alarmed with Sidney's forward behavior when the two of them were alone. He'd acted like delaying the wedding in hopes Beth would arrive was done strictly to thwart him.

The driver shook his head. "Someone was waiting with the news when I pulled up. This is tomorrow's train. It's early. This is the one you folks have to take if you're goin' north. Let's get you loaded."

The stage driver vanished from the door, and Mandy felt the coach sway as he climbed to the top. A valise flew off the top, followed by a trunk.

The two men in the stage hesitated. Mandy assumed it was to let her and Sidney go first. She moved toward the door away from the flying luggage.

Sidney caught Mandy's arm and looked at the men. "Go ahead."

They exchanged glances then left.

Sidney turned her around to face him. "Now we're getting on a train? Our tickets go straight through to Colorado. We won't be alone together for days." He whispered, but it sounded like anger rather than discretion. "Let's wait and take a later train."

"We've got our whole lives, Sidney. You're the one who said we don't dare miss the train."

"Yeah, but that was mainly to get away from your family. Colorado will still be there in a week."

With a pang of sorrow, Mandy asked, "You mean we could have waited longer for Beth?"

"I wanted to get you alone."

"But I might never see my sister again, Sidney. It breaks my heart to think of it. If we can wait a week, let's go back to Mosqueros and—"

"You need to grow up, little girl."

Devastated to think Sidney would make such a choice for so frivolous a reason, Mandy ignored his insulting tone, turned, and moved to leave the stage.

Sidney caught her upper arm and jerked her back. "You're my wife now." He leaned over her. Sidney wasn't very tall—an inch or so taller than Mandy's own five foot five. And he was going soft like so many city men, so his strength surprised her. "You're not Clay McClellen's daughter anymore."

Even in the dim starlight, Mandy saw Sidney's face redden with anger, and she felt that cold, that strange cold that came over her when there was trouble. Her thumb slid over that callus on her index finger once before she could stop herself.

Protect me, Lord.

What she felt wasn't new bride nerves. It was real, solid fear that she might be in danger. Fear was something Mandy had experienced many times in her life. And she knew to face it head-on, usually with a rifle. Her hand slid to her trusty Winchester as she glared at Sidney. "I'm *both*. I'll *always* be both. And more importantly, I'm *Sophie McClellen's* daughter."

"What's that supposed to mean?" The grip on her forearm began to hurt until she knew she'd have a bruise tomorrow.

Her parents could fight like a house afire. Mandy had seen them squabble many times, though not so much after the first year or so. But her pa had never put his hands on her ma, and Ma had never, ever backed down. Well, maybe she did just for peace and quiet, but *never* out of fear.

Fearing a man she loved was ridiculous, and Mandy refused to do it. "It means that if you know what's good for you, you'll get your hand off of me right this minute."

"I'll let you go when—"

A grunt drew Mandy's head around. The stage coach driver stood there, his eyes narrow. They went from Mandy to her arm to Sidney's florid face.

60

Sidney released her arm so quickly there was no doubt he'd gotten the driver's message.

She had a message or two of her own. But now wasn't the time. "Let's get loaded onto the train." She grabbed her rifle, swung out of the stage, and dropped to the ground, not caring if Sidney came along or not. As she settled the gun into place and gathered up her things, she wondered just how much trouble marriage was going to be.

A vague, troubling memory flirted around inside her head. Her pa—but not Clay McClellen, her first pa. Mandy had only shadowy memories of him, and those were muddled because, of course, being twin brothers, her first pa, Cliff, looked exactly like her second pa, Clay. It was hard to separate memories.

But she had one that was crystal clear. The day her first pa died.

Pa had only been back from the war for a little while. He was a quiet man. Her second pa was quiet, too, but a pleasant, good-natured kind of quiet. Her first pa was sullen quiet. Moody. Mandy remembered how they all tried hard to placate the man. . . . The dinner table. On the day he died.

Ma told Pa there was a baby on the way. Mandy had started laughing, and she and her sisters, Beth and Sally, had giggled and talked about the new baby.

"It better be a boy. I'm sick of nothing but girl children." Pa slapped his hand on the table and made the plates and silverware jump and clatter. Then he jabbed a finger at Ma. "Try not to kill my son this time."

All of them fell silent.

Mandy had no idea what he meant, though later she'd learned Ma had lost a baby boy between Beth and Sally. She'd been thrown from a horse, doing man's work Pa wouldn't do.

Tears brimmed in Sally's eyes, and for one second Mandy hated her pa. Mandy was eight, a big girl, and she'd gotten used to him. He didn't hurt her feelings hardly at all anymore. Beth was pretty good at ignoring him, too. They'd learned to protect their hearts. But Sally was only three and she adored him. She took all his hard little digs and stuck by him, defended him, loved him. She tried so hard to be good enough to earn Pa's love. But no one could be good enough to earn something that didn't exist.

Ma had looked around the table on that long-ago day, with her eyes wide, sad, full of love—apologizing wordlessly for Pa's cruelty. Mandy knew her ma was glad she'd given birth to girl children.

Ma's gaze settled on Sally's hurt little face for a second then Ma's eyes lit with fire. Absolute rage ignited.

Mandy felt a chill of fear.

"These *girls* are the best children any man could have." Ma spent her life trying to keep the ornery man she'd married happy. She almost never lost her temper—a fearsome thing when she did. "The *only* one in this family who doesn't measure up is *you*." Ma glared from her end of the table.

Pa glared back.

They looked as if they hated each other.

Mandy could remember the slashing pain of the first moment in her life when she'd realized finally, fully, that her pa didn't love her, never would. That heartbreaking truth hurt nearly as much as if she'd been stabbed. But even then she knew it wasn't her. There was something broken in her pa. He didn't know how to love.

Even at eight years old, Mandy wanted to beg Ma not to fight. Ma was decent and strong. Pa was selfish and weak. The decent, strong person had to do decent, strong things like love unlovable people and keep peace even when it wasn't easy.

Pa had shoved his chair back hard enough that it tipped over with a loud crash. Without another word—silence was so often his way—he left, slamming the cabin door behind him.

Ma stormed after him.

As she swung the door open, a crowd of men rode into the

yard, yelling, guns drawn, surrounding Pa.

Someone shouted, "Horse thief."

Shouting threats and accusations, the crowd grabbed Pa and rode off.

Ma screamed and ran out of the house. But they left her behind in a cloud of cruel laughter and dust. Within the hour, Pa was dead and Ma was digging him a hole in the ground.

I've married a man just like my pa. Oh, God, protect me. Protect me. Protect me.

There would be children of course, and Mandy would spend her life praying this prayer for herself and her young'uns.

Mandy felt sick. Then she remembered that Sidney had a charming side, too. He wasn't all sullen and angry like Pa. There would be good times, plenty of them if Mandy could just be good enough, cheerful enough, obedient enough to keep him happy.

And on the days she couldn't do enough, she'd find a more painful way—painful for Sidney—to calm him down. No man was *ever* going to put his hands on her in anger. And she'd shoot any man who did such a thing to her children. Being her husband wouldn't save him. She'd make sure Sidney knew that for a fact.

She lifted all the luggage she could carry, squared her gun-toting shoulders, and headed for the *chuffing* train now pulling to a stop in the darkened town. She suspected this load of work was her lot from now on.

The driver came alongside her, carrying the heavy box Pa had sent along, leaving behind the single large trunk for Sidney. "You don't have to go with him if you don't want." The driver spoke quietly to her so his voice didn't carry past the screeching brakes and steaming locomotive engine.

Mandy exchanged a look with the man. She didn't know him, but she knew his kind. Gruff, taciturn Western men didn't talk much. They minded their own business except when it came to protecting women. The grizzled driver would take care of Mandy if she asked him to.

But he was wrong. Mandy had said her vows before man and God. She had to go.

Oh, Lord, protect me.

"Thank you, but he's my husband. I do have to go."

With a shrug, the man fell silent as he helped her load her things onto the train. Then he left to tend his own horses.

She still hadn't spoken to Sidney when the train pulled out on a journey that left her precious family behind forever.

"I've brought in three more. They all resisted. They're dead."

The colonel's blue eyes narrowed.

"I'm here to collect my reward." Cletus Slaughter knew what the man was thinking. He'd have let all these cowards roam free if it was up to him.

They'd had this fight before. But the colonel always paid.

"What poor men did you catch this time, Slaughter?" Lifting the papers up, the colonel read the three names, his fussy, trimmed white beard quivering a bit with anger.

Cletus enjoyed watching the man hate him while having to fork over the money because it was the law. "They're deserters and cowards. I hate a coward."

"So you shoot them in the back?" The colonel slammed a fist on his heavy desk. "I'd say a back shooter is the worst kind of coward."

Everything about this office was polished, uppity. But no amount of fancy furniture and slick uniform could make Cletus answer to anyone. He'd had his time in the cavalry. Now he savored shoving the rules and regulations down this pompous officer's throat.

"They're wanted men. I'm claimin' the reward." Cletus crossed his arms, enjoying the feel of his new shirt. He'd been livin' high since he'd found out the army paid for the return of deserters. Most of them begged and crawled, and a few of them tried to run.

Yes, he'd put a few bullets in a coward's back. Glad to do it.

"This is the end, Slaughter. I've sent a wire back East asking the War Department to drop this business of hunting down deserters. This dead-or-alive rule for deserters is left from the War Between the States. They don't intend to enforce it now. Most of the time, if deserters are caught the only punishment is asking the men to serve out their times. Sometimes pay is even negotiated for them."

"Long as it's the law, I'm gonna keep huntin'. Now where's my money?"

"The purser has it." The colonel grudgingly wrote up the order to pay the bounty. "What poor fool are you going after this time?"

Cletus didn't trust the colonel not to interfere if he knew. "None'a your business, Colonel. You'll find out when I bring him in." Cletus snatched the note and smirked at the colonel, using the writ to give him a sloppy salute. Officers hated that.

He collected his bounty and rode out. When he was settled into a ground-eating walk on his thoroughbred—a grand horse, paid for on the backs of cowards—he pulled out his list and saw that it wasn't that far of a ride to a place one of the cowards had been sighted. Cletus had informers everywhere.

A deserter on a stagecoach riding along, enjoying the fat of the land—a land he'd betrayed. A doctor. Most likely left men to die. Now somewhere putting his filthy hands on unsuspecting citizens and living rich.

Cletus couldn't hold back a smile as he imagined this one making a run for it. He caressed his brand new Colt single-action army revolver. Best gun made. Cletus had the best of everything now. And he would for as long as the cowards remained.

Spinning the gun's cylinder to check that it was fully loaded, Cletus thought about the cowardly doctor. He hoped Alex Buchanan would run.

Eight

Alex finally felt good enough to concentrate on hating himself.

He preferred to starve wallowing in filth. It kept his mind occupied. But tonight he ate well, then bathed and went to bed. He could concentrate on self-loathing.

Clay McClellen had tossed him a change of clothes, even a worn but decent pair of boots and a battered hat, shoved a bar of soap in his hands, and directed him to a farm pond to bathe. There'd be no supper until Alex got back.

Alex had refused the clothes, but McClellen got gruff and said they had a mountain of old clothes left behind by former hands. Alex wondered about that. He was about McClellen's height. The clothes were probably his. But Alex was so hungry his belly button was rubbing against his backbone, so he took the clothes and scrubbed himself clean. It took a while because the filth was worked deep into his skin.

The beef stew in the bunkhouse was so delicious Alex almost made himself sick gobbling it down. The rest of the hands went for the chow with just as much enthusiasm, so Alex wasn't even embarrassed to be seen eating with the manners of a wolf.

Then Alex rolled into a hard bunk that felt like he'd floated into heaven compared to a lot of the places he'd slept. And the nightmares came.

Alex jerked awake to find a grizzled cowhand named Whitey shaking his shoulder. Alex looked around in the dim light of dawn to see every man in the building awake and staring at him.

As soon as he'd come fully awake, Whitey slapped him on the arm. "Been to war myself, son. A lot of the hands have. And had my share of bad dreams. We have a light day on Sunday. See if you can get another hour of sleep."

Whitey handled the cooking in the bunkhouse, and he'd done a fine job last night. He was gray-haired and had knowing eyes. He walked away with a slight limp. The men flopped back on their beds, minding their own business the way only cowpokes could. Alex was too afraid to let himself sleep again.

His dreams were so real he seemed to be reliving the horror. The blood.

Alex closed his eyes, as if that could stop it, but it only made it worse. His dreams felt like his leg was being amputated. They tore a hole in Alex's soul as surely as a hacksaw tore through muscle and bone. Something he'd done and done and done. Now he was left with that hole, big enough to let the devil in. Because Alex felt the devil inside him, felt the rage and hate and evil.

He was lost.

God, I'm so lost.

He threw the blanket off and stood, grabbed his boots, and slipped out, even though he knew every man there heard him. They were a salty lot, plenty of soldiers in the bunch. McClellen knew how to hire hands. . . . That meant he'd know enough not to hire Alex.

Outside, in the dim light of early morning, Alex pulled on his boots and strode toward the pond where he'd bathed yesterday.

Maybe if he soaked his head in cold water the nightmares would fade.

He neared the crest of a low hill, covered with scrub pines that blocked his view of the pond. Clay McClellen stood from an old tree stump and started toward him, carrying his rifle.

That's when Alex heard the distant sound of laughter, women's laughter.

He stopped and let McClellen come the rest of the way. The man was guarding his women. So many women. Alex had heard all about the beautiful McClellen women from the cowhands last night.

Clay had daughters, one married and gone to a man who wasn't good enough for her, although it sounded like no man could ever be good enough for her. Beth, the spitfire—they'd asked about her as if their own long lost daughter had returned. Some grumbling had erupted about her going off to school when she'd been way too young. But she'd been headstrong and gotten her way. Harum-scarum Sally, she sounded like their favorite. And Laurie, still young but so obviously adored. Which left Sophie, the prettiest and toughest wife any man ever had. Plus McClellen had himself a passel of sons.

The cowhands talked in absolutely respectful terms. In fact their tone was more in the way of a warning of stark and horrible pain should Alex ever dare to say a wrong word or give a wrong look to one of the McClellen women. They'd put it nicely— for brusque, Western men. He'd gotten the message.

And now here he was, most likely intruding on the women bathing.

Alex noticed that McClellen had stationed himself so he couldn't see the pond either, mindful of his daughters' modesty. Alex envied the man until he could hardly breathe.

"Sorry, McClellen. I didn't know there'd be anyone out here." Alex said it quick before McClellen could start shooting.

"Call me Clay. Don't worry about it. That's why I came out,

so as to warn men away. The girls come out lotsa mornings for a little while, but only if I've got time to guard 'em."

"So, Clay, you looking for any more cowhands?"

McClellen's eyes narrowed, not with anger but with thinking, considering. "You're a doctor. Why do you want to be a cowhand?"

"I don't want to be a doctor anymore."

Clay shook his head. "Try to make some sense."

Alex almost smiled. Almost. He didn't do much smiling. He didn't exactly keep his past a secret. He just didn't talk to anyone about anything.

"I doctored on the frontier for the cavalry." Alex couldn't hold Clay's eyes anymore so he looked at the ground and saw his nightmares again. "It was bad is all. I got a belly full of sick and hurting people. I can't do it anymore."

"Beth told us last night you really helped that man on the stage. She said you were pretty good."

"She said that?" Alex looked up, startled. He'd just flunked another test judging from the scowl on Clay's face.

"You stay away from my girls." Clay took a step forward and Alex backed up quick. "No cowhand on this ranch gets two chances, you understand. And my girls' word is *law*. If one of 'em doesn't like you for any reason at *all*, you're gone. I don't listen to two sides of a story when one of my girls is telling one side of it. Understand?"

"Sure. That's the way it oughta be."

"There's a man in the federal penitentiary right now who was schoolmaster here and made the mistake of slapping Sally's hand with a ruler."

"They put him in prison for that?" Alex knew women were treated with respect in the West. But that seemed a little extreme.

"He did a couple of other things, too. But none of it mattered a lick to me 'cept what he did to my girl. She was five years old and her teacher convinced her I'd be on *his* side. So she didn't tell me he was thrashing her. Now they know I'll take their side. Always."

"Good. That's the way it ought to be." Alex had half a notion to ride to the federal penitentiary himself and take a piece of the man's hide. "Before you say I'm hired, I might as well tell you I'm not a hand on the range. I'll work hard for you but I'm. . .I haven't been at it very long."

"So go back to doctorin'."

Alex ignored the advice. "I just don't want you hiring me based on lies. I admit I've got a lot to learn."

Clay shook his head as if he were already tired and it was just past sunup. "Fine. I'll expect you to be worthless for a while. But Alex?" The tone of Clay's voice was frightening.

"What?"

"If one of my cowhands breaks an arm or needs a cut sewn up, you'll help us out." It wasn't a request. It was an order.

"I'm not a doctor anymore. I told you."

"And I don't expect you to be one. You'll be busting broncos and branding cattle with everyone else. But I'm trying to keep Beth under control, and I don't want her doctoring a bunch of beat-up cowpokes. It ain't proper. She's been a hand at healing all her life. I swear they used to *pretend* to be hurt so she'd come and make a fuss over them. That was part of the reason I finally gave in and let her go back East to study."

"Part of the reason? What's the other part?"

"She cried."

Alex flinched. He'd have let her go, too.

"I. . .I've seen some things. . .ugly things." Alex held Clay's eyes for too long. He didn't want to make that promise about doctoring. He didn't know if he *could* make that promise. And Clay McClellen didn't look like the kind of man who had much patience for weaklings. "It's a hard promise you're asking me to make. And I don't make promises I can't keep. All I can say is. . . I. . .I'll try. I'll do my best."

Clay stared as if a hard enough look could go all the way into Alex's brain. Finally Clay relaxed.

Alex didn't know if that meant Clay had managed to read his mind or he'd realized Alex had no mind to read so he'd given up.

"That's all any man can do, I reckon."

Alex nodded and turned back to the bunkhouse.

"Oh, Alex?"

"Yeah?" Alex wondered what other promises McClellen was going to wring out of him.

"The ranch hands all ride along with us to church."

His shoulders slumped. "I'm not a churchgoing man, not anymore."

"The only other job I've got this morning is to send some hands out to fetch back the dead bodies from the stage wreck. You're welcome to ride along with them."

Alex would rather go to church. He'd also rather take a beating. That must have shown on his face.

"Ride in with us then. I don't make attending church a requirement of the job. That's between you and God, but I like a big enough group that no one will consider messing with my girls. It's still a dangerous country. So you'll be expected to come."

"I'll be ready." One set of clothes. A borrowed horse. Alex was ready now.

Nine

I missed Texas something fierce." Beth turned to Sally, marveling at how her little sister had grown up. "You're as tall as me. And Laurie! I can't believe how she's changed. She's almost my height. And the twins are nine now."

"It's been so long, Beth. It figured we'd do some growing." Sally had her hair tied back and her Sunday best dress and bonnet on. But no female finery could mask the fire in her eyes and the restlessness that marked every move and word from Beth's hoyden sister.

Sally liked to ride the range. Pa encouraged it and Ma had given up fighting it. Sally worked as hard as any cowhand on the place.

The twins, Cliff and Jarrod, nine, did their best to keep up with her. Seven-year-old Edward was dying to be allowed to ride herd and he did go out, but only with Pa or Sally riding beside him. Little Jeffrey, five, whom they all called Buck, could throw a screaming tantrum, but even so, he wasn't allowed to help yet. He could throw a loop over a standing calf and ride horseback, but he wasn't allowed to herd cattle. Pa didn't give him that much freedom.

Sally had already done cowhand work at age five, but that was out of necessity. Now when Beth thought back on it, she couldn't believe the things Ma had let them do at so young an age.

Looking at her family crowded beside her in the back of the buckboard, Beth was struck by how much they'd changed. Buck had been tiny when she'd gone to Boston to study. She'd missed so much. She was never going to be so far away from them again.

Which reminded her of Mandy—which made her want to cry. So she looked away from all the blond-headed little brothers and sisters and noticed Alex riding along to church.

He cleaned up well. And he noticed her noticing him. Their eyes connected in that same weird way, and Beth looked quickly away before she could get drawn in.

When they got to Mosqueros, she saw Alex head for a nearby stand of trees instead of coming inside to services. As he leaned against a shady oak, Beth ached for him and all his emotional scars. Finding a faith in God would be the best first step in healing those scars, but Alex would never know if he kept leaning. She was tempted to go have a talk with him, but there was no time.

Parson Radcliff, who'd just taken over for Parson Roscoe, called them inside. Beth thought the skinny, energetic young man and his pretty wife, who expected a baby—their second—any time, were going to be a letdown after Parson Roscoe's years of support and kindness.

Beth noticed the Reeveses sitting in the back on the right as they'd always done. Except now they took up two pews. The older twins were missing—grown and gone just like Mandy most likely. But the triplets remained. At fifteen, Mark, Luke, and John were tall as adult men but gangly still. Then there was a second row of squirming, whispering blond boys. Beth counted five, but they were stair steps, thank heavens. No more Reeves babies born in bunches.

Beth sat in the front pew beside her family through the service, and it pulled on her just like her family and Texas and being a caretaker. This church was part of her, part of home. Beth noticed her little brothers were more wiggly than usual. Although what did she know about usual anymore?

Ma whispered to Sally and she took fidgety Buck's hand and led her youngest brother outside as the congregation rose to sing a closing hymn.

They were just finishing "Shall We Gather at the River" when Sally screamed in what sounded like agony. "Buck, run!" Sally screamed again. Beth had never heard her tough little sister make such a horrible sound.

Pa was down the aisle and out the door like a shot, Ma half a step behind.

Laura yelled at Beth, "I'll take care of the young'uns."

Beth raced after her parents. When she stepped outside, she saw Sally screaming at Buck to run faster.

Buck cried out in pain.

"Go, Buck. Run to Pa!" Sally was behind Buck. She looked up and her eyes locked on Pa, then she veered off, waving her arms wildly.

Buck slammed into Pa's legs. Beth took one look at the welts on Buck's face and knew they'd wrangled with a beehive.

Sally raced, doing more shouting than screaming, her arms flailing. She headed straight toward a water trough standing on Mosqueros' Main Street.

Beth knew, whatever stings Buck had gotten, Sally's had to be worse. She'd shoved her little brother out of the way and led the bees after her. Beth raced toward Sally.

Sally hurled herself into the water. A swarm of bees lifted into the air above the trough and buzzed away in a dark cloud, back toward open country.

Beth reached Sally and caught her arm. Ma was a step behind her on the other side of the trough. Together they lifted Sally until her head was above water.

"Buck! Where's Buck?" Sally's face and neck were already lumpy and swollen from the stings. She had on long sleeves, but Beth saw that her hands were swelling. Bees floated to the surface, drowned, but too late to stop many of them from stinging.

More churchgoers crowded out, everyone rushing toward Sally, talking wildly.

"Buck's okay, Sally. You saved him. He's crying, stung a little, but he's fine." Beth slid her arm behind Sally's shoulders and, with Ma's help, lifted her from the water trough.

Pa came up beside them and took Sally into his arms. Buck clung to Pa's leg sobbing.

Beth took a second to inspect her little brother. He was stung, too, but nothing like Sally. She'd pushed him away and taken the brunt of the enraged bees on herself.

"Laurie!" Beth made eye contact with Laurie, who had the other little brothers with her. "Take care of him!"

"Got him, Beth." Laurie scooped Buck into her arms and began soothing him. She took him to the trough and bathed his welts with the tepid water.

Beth scanned the area. The bees, wherever they'd come from, were long gone.

"Pa, I hurt!" Sally began crying.

Beth nearly froze from the shock. Sally knew hard work. She knew broken fingers and bitter heat and bruised muscles. She knew how to keep going and she never complained—except when Ma insisted she wear a dress to town. And they all knew how much Pa hated tears. All of them tried to avoid crying for their pa's sake, and all of them failed on occasion.

Except Sally. Sally never, ever cried.

Pa took Sally to a grassy spot, one of the few in this rugged land around Mosqueros. He lowered Sally to the ground. Beth saw more and more little white welts rising on her sister's face and hands. The rest of her body was protected by her clothes, unless they'd gotten under her skirts, but she had hundreds of stings on her exposed skin.

Sally's uncharacteristic tears scared Beth right to her gut.

Pa knelt on one side of Sally, talking quietly, for once in his life not letting tears send him running.

Beth eased Sally's skirts up a bit and found drowned bees and ugly welts all over her legs. She also found a knife stuck into Sally's boot and wasn't a bit surprised. The McClellens, whether girl or boy, were a tough bunch. Pa and Ma had taught them well. And Sally was the toughest of them all.

Ice. Cold compresses, that's what helped bee stings. And ice in Texas in midsummer was not even possible. She thought of the tepid water in the trough and doubted it would do any good.

"We need water! The cooler the better," Beth shouted.

"I'll get it from the town well." Vivian Radcliff, young and dark haired with kind eyes, looked to be ten months along toward birthing a baby, but the parson's wife could move.

Beth knelt opposite of Pa and studied Sally's condition. Her face continued to swell. One eye was nearly closed. She'd be in terrible pain for days.

A sudden high-pitched wheeze came from Sally's puffy lips. Her eyes went wide to the extent possible. She lurched into a sitting position, her mouth open. The noise came again, as sharp as the cawing of a crow. Sally's throat was swelling shut.

Beth had heard of this when so much poison entered someone's system she couldn't help but react. She even knew of a tiny surgery that could help, but she'd never done it. To cut at Sally's throat, if her incision was misplaced, would kill instantly. Her hands shook as she prayed Sally's throat didn't swell completely shut.

A high whistling gasp for breath came again. Then it stopped. Sally's nearly closed eyes gaped open. Her mouth moved silently. She reached for her neck as if to pull someone's strangling hands away.

At that second Beth's eyes landed on Alex, hanging to the back of the gathering crowd. Terror had bled the color from Alex's face. His eyes riveted on Sally.

Beth knew. Without asking, she knew that Alex could help. "Get over here!"

Alex's eyes went from Sally to Beth. He took a step backward, shaking his head.

She erupted from the ground and ran around her dying sister. Shoving her way through the crowd, she caught Alex's arm in a vise. "You have to help me, Alex."

Their eyes locked again. She remembered well the way he'd drawn strength from her before. She didn't have time for him to work up his nerve. This wasn't a dislocated shoulder. Her sister would be dead in minutes without Alex's immediate assistance. Even now, this second, her body was being starved of oxygen and she might have brain damage.

She gave him ten seconds then she sank her fingers into his arms, digging in with her nails. "Now! Right now!"

Her orders had a visible effect on Alex. His eyes focused. He nodded and charged to Sally's side and shouted, "Clay, let me in. Now!"

Pa jerked his head up then moved quickly aside.

Alex fell to his knees.

Beth rounded Sally's body, knelt across from Alex, and prayed.

Give him strength, Lord God. Give him courage. Give him speed and a steady hand.

"Who has a knife?" she shouted.

Pa drew a knife out of his boot. Beth knew Pa kept his knife razor sharp. It would work, but she shuddered to think of how dirty the blade might be. She thought of the knife in Sally's boot, but it wouldn't be even close to clean either.

At the same instant Laurie, breathing hard from a fast run, shoved Beth's beloved doctor bag into her hands. "I got it from the wagon. I thought you might need it."

With a shout of relief, Beth tore open the black leather satchel and dug inside, extracting her scalpel. Her mentor in Boston had given her this bag and the supplies in it after she'd been working with him a year. She kept it with her at all times, even on a buckboard ride to church.

"Hang on to this, Laurie." She gave her precious bag into her sister's keeping and extended the scalpel to Alex.

Beth saw the moment the doctor in Alex took over. Color returned to his face. Alex took the knife with confident fingers.

Beth caught hold of Sally, holding her still as she jerked and battled for any tiny breath of air. "We can sterilize the knife." Beth grabbed her bag back from Laurie and pulled the top wide open.

"Have you got carbolic acid?" Alex glanced at Beth's precious supplies.

"Yes, a good supply." She looked at Laurie, standing close, desperate to help. "Can you get the bottle of carbolic acid out of my bag?" Beth quickly described it.

Laurie produced a small container.

"No, not that. Dover's Powder is an emetic."

"What's that?"

"Well, it is a painkiller but Sally doesn't need that now. And if you give an overly strong dose, it'll make you sick to your stomach." Beth thought of what an understatement that was. She took the bag from Laurie and pulled out the bottle of carbolic acid, carefully wrapped to prevent breakage.

"Pour some over the knife and my hands then swab some on her neck."

Beth removed the stopper from the glass bottle and the sharp odor of carbolic acid raised her hopes that Sally wouldn't end up with an infection. She obeyed Alex quickly. Beth bent down and looked straight into Sally's eyes.

Terrified. She'd seen the knife. She couldn't breathe.

"Sally, hang on," Beth whispered, trying to get through Sally's pain and fear. Her hand slid to Sally's wrist.

The pulse was strong; her sister was strong.

"We'll save you. I'll save you." Beth had never spoken words that she meant so passionately. And she needed Alex-the-Madman to make them come true.

Alex pressed the razor-sharp scalpel to Sally's throat.

Ten

Pa grabbed Alex's arm. "What are you doing?"

Alex pulled the sharp blade back away from Sally's delicate throat.

Beth realized she was witnessing a first. Alex was right and her pa was wrong. Her pa knew everything.

"Let him go, Pa. Alex has to cut into Sally's airway. He has to do it *right now.*"

"You can't cut someone's throat. She'll bleed to death."

"Clay, I know right where to cut. I won't get near the carotid artery. That's the artery that would make her hemorrhage." Alex's voice was deeper than usual, or maybe stronger, more confident. He was no longer the addled man in need of food and clothes.

Beth knew the medical words would help Pa and everyone else trust Alex's abilities. She knew it helped her. Alex had chosen his words deliberately for that purpose.

Pa exchanged a look with Beth.

She nodded her head. "Let him go, Pa. He knows what he's doing."

Sally's body suddenly went into a spasm.

Pa let Alex go.

"Hold her very still." The command in Alex's voice was the same one she'd heard during her apprenticeship from the doctor who trained her. Alex was very much in charge.

Beth gripped Sally's shoulders. Ma was at Sally's head, holding her still so a stranger could slit her throat. Then Pa and Laurie had Sally's legs. Adam, the McClellen's oldest family friend, appeared at Sally's feet and he knelt and held. They all trusted Alex on Beth's say-so.

"Beth, have you got any small tube?" Alex looked up, his gaze hard, almost cruel.

Beth nodded.

"Get it as soon as I've made the incision."

Beth knew all of the people around Sally prayed as hard as they held on. The congregation of Mosqueros's only church stood in a circle around them, praying, too.

Alex made the tiniest possible incision. Blood ran free and nearly everyone in the crowd gasped.

Beth quickly released Sally.

Laurie grabbed Sally's now-free arm, which started reaching for her neck.

Beth found a tiny syringe, part of the standard equipment. Every doctor had a bag and cherished the instruments it contained. What had happened to Alex's?

Alex ripped the syringe apart until all he had left was a slender tube and slid it into Sally's bleeding incision. Then Alex bent over the tube and blew. Sally's chest rose. Alex pulled back and Sally's chest fell, slowly, naturally. The air expelling from the exposed end of the tube ruffled Alex's hair.

After Alex blew life into Sally's lungs a few more breaths, Sally's spasms stopped. Beth felt Sally's terrible tension ease. She no longer needed to be restrained once air flowed in and out of her body. The whole crowd sighed as if they'd been holding their breath, too.

Alex repeated the movements, blowing, pulling away to allow an exhale, blowing. Sally's chest moved naturally as if she were breathing, but it was through the tube, not her mouth. Alex finally stopped, and Beth realized Sally was doing the tube breathing herself.

Beth looked over at Alex. He wiped the sweat off his forehead and smeared blood across his face. Her heart turned over at the unsteady movement. Those calm, knowledgeable hands were now trembling like an oak tree in a windstorm.

He said, in that authoritative voice, "Cloth."

Beth handed him a square of clean white cotton, remembering well how she'd assisted in operations. Alex stemmed the blood that flowed around the tube as Sally breathed.

Speaking to Beth's parents, Alex said, "Sally will be able to breathe through this tube until the swelling goes down in her throat. That could take a while, maybe an hour or so. She'll regain consciousness any time now and we'll have our hands full keeping her still. When her throat clears, I'll suture this incision and she'll be fine. There's the risk of an infection of course, although Beth's carbolic acid will help fight that. Still, it's always a danger."

Alex went on, talking about caring for the wound. Beth knew he was talking more to ease Pa's and Ma's minds than because what he said was important. She knew well the strong effect of a calm presence in times of trouble.

When Alex's instructions were done, he said, "Where can we take her? I don't want her in a buckboard. It's too rough a ride out to the ranch, so she needs a place in town."

"Bring her to my house," Parson Radcliff said.

"No," the banker, Royce Badje, spoke up. "There's an empty building next to the bank. I own it and I'd be glad to see it used for a doctor's office."

"I don't need an office." Alex looked up, his eyes suddenly

losing all the confidence and strength that had carried him through until now.

Before he could humiliate himself, which Beth felt sure was inevitable, she reached her hand across Sally's body. "Hush." Anyone within ten feet heard her. But Alex obeyed, and Beth's saying, "Hush," didn't give away much.

"That will be fine, Mr. Badje. Is it empty? We could use a bedroll on the floor for Sally to lie on."

"It's furnished upstairs, so you can live there, Doc. And there are shelves and counters downstairs. It used to be a dry goods store. No hospital beds though. But the town can help get it set up for a doctor."

"I'll run and dust the counters and put down sheets." Royce Badje's wife hurried away, and several women followed her, eager to help.

Alex reacted to the sudden action as if someone had fired the starting pistol of a race. He rose to his feet as if to run.

Beth jumped up and grabbed his wrist across Sally's body. "Not now, Alex. Please. We need you. Sally needs you."

A murmur went through the crowd and Beth knew everyone was wondering what she meant. Ignoring her old friends, she did her best not to shame Alex, but if she had to, she'd hog-tie him before she let him leave. Clutching his wrist with such force it drew him out of whatever nightmare he'd descended into, Beth whispered, "If you hadn't been here, my sister would have died."

Alex came to her again, locking their eyes, that look, the fear, that drawing force, using her strength and courage because he had none. With the same intuition that guided her in caring for patients, Beth knew Alex hated himself for needing her. Judged himself to be a coward and a failure, contemptible. Or at least he held himself in contempt even as he was surrounded by a town full of people praising God for his presence. "I. . .I'm not a—"

"Let's get Sally inside." Beth's voice cut through what was

most likely going to be a further denial of what Alex was. Not what he *did* but what he *was*. The man was a born healer, a caretaker all the way to his bludgeoned soul.

As surely as she knew he needed her by his side for strength, she knew there was no way out for Alex. To walk away from this God-given gift was to walk away from his soul. And that is exactly what Alex had done.

And now it was given to Beth as a charge from the Almighty, to help him regain that part of himself. Only then could Alex be healthy and whole again. Beth assured the Lord she would gladly take on that role for the man who had saved her sister.

Pa lifted Sally, with Ma carefully steadying her head. Sally's soaking wet hair streamed down. Blood coated Sally's neck. Her eyes remained swollen and closed. Her face was so covered with welts that her pretty face, so like Beth's, was disfigured. Ma and Pa kept their eyes locked on the cut and the little tube in her neck. They headed—two people who'd learned to work well together as a unit—toward the empty dry goods store.

Beth was able to get Alex moving without his saying anything more. When at last they reached the store, Beth noticed that many folks had trailed along behind. "Please wait outside," she asked politely. "And, Laurie, can you get the rest of the family—"

"I'll take care of them, Beth," Adam cut in. His ebony black skin wrinkled in concern, but his eyes, as always, were calm and competent. "You just see to Sally."

"Thank you." Beth had no idea what she'd been going to say, really. Should the family go home? Should they find a place to stay in town? Whatever were they to do with Ma and Pa and Beth and Sally all unable to take care of them? Laurie could handle it, but she was so young and upset about Sally, too. Adam's taking over was perfect.

Tillie was at his side. She rested one of her gentle, competent hands on Beth's wrist. "For now we'll take them to Parson Radcliff's. They've invited us. We'll be praying for Sally, honey."

Adam, Tillie, and their three little ones were close friends to the McClellens.

"Thanks, Tillie." Sighing with relief, Beth kept her tight grip on Alex and dragged him into the store after Ma and Pa. The door swung shut as Pa lay Sally on a counter that looked perfect to hold a cash box and piles of fabric and notions...not an injured young woman, but it worked fine. It was about waist high, the perfect height for them to tend Sally. And there was a soft blanket spread on top.

Mrs. Badje fussed, swiping dust away from every surface in the room, to make a cleaner spot for the wounded girl. Several other church ladies bustled about tidying the store up.

"I'll need boiling hot water," Beth said to the kindly Mrs. Badje.

She nodded then vanished out the back as if her only goal in life was to help and be a bother to no one.

Beth turned to her captive—Alex—who, despite his nearly miraculous gift for doctoring, seemed bent on bothering everyone.

He sure as certain bothered Beth something fierce.

Eleven

"Let go." Alex jerked his arm away from the claws Beth had sunk into him. "We're alone. You don't have to cover for me anymore."

"We're not alone." Beth jerked her head toward her worried parents who so far only had eyes for Sally. The church ladies had finished their quick cleanup and left, following Mrs. Badje.

"I already told your pa I'm not interested in doctoring and some of the whys." Alex stalked past her to Sally's side, clinging to his anger because it was a strong emotion. He could force the weak cowardice away as long as he was furious. "She's breathing well." Alex ran one finger over Sally's swollen, lumpy face. "Terrible stings. Poor girl." He saw his hand shaking and pulled back. "Beth, bring your kit around here. Do you have tweezers? Let's get these stingers out of her."

Beth extended the tweezers to him.

"You do it." He barked, just like the yellow dog he was.

The kindness and understanding in her eyes near to killed him. She didn't argue; she just did it. Alex became the nurse handing her anything she asked for out of her well-equipped doctor's bag.

Alex had thrown his away somewhere in western New Mexico. He'd run from the army's demands. That bag, so much a part of him for so long, seemed to burn his hand every time he touched it. . .the guilt, the failure at deserting.

But the nightmares! He couldn't face another day of adding to them. One more Indian campaign, always one more. Why couldn't people live side-by-side without taking up arms? What was the matter with the world? Where was God?

Where are You, God?

Alex knew God hadn't moved. It was Alex who had gone to a place beyond salvation. He even believed God would forgive him. He was just too ashamed to ask. He too richly deserved any punishment God chose to give.

The quiet lady who'd brought the blankets returned with rags and water, cool in a basin, blazing hot in a bucket. She slipped out again.

Alex took a second to envy the woman her escape, then dipped a cloth into the cool water and began bathing the pretty young woman's face and hands, hoping the chill would reduce the swelling. "She looks like you," he whispered to Beth.

Beth looked up from where she worked with her tweezers on the dozens of stingers visible on the girl's face.

"My little sister Sally. She's the toughest of the bunch. She drew those bees toward herself to save Buck." Beth looked at him then shifted her eyes to her hovering parents.

They nodded. "Sally'd do that," Pa said.

"The swelling isn't getting worse anymore," Alex reassured Beth's family. All he could see was that welling blood where he'd cut a young woman's throat.

"How long will she need that thing to breathe?" Clay asked.

"A few hours is probably all." Beth was answering the questions.

Good, Alex was afraid of what might come out of his mouth if he started talking.

"She'll be able to breathe on her own real soon." Beth's hands were steady as iron. Alex heard prayers escape her lips as she tended her sister.

Without making a conscious choice, Alex added his own. As he prayed, the thought invaded that he should go back, face his fate for being a deserter, even if it was a firing squad. The frontier fighting with the Indians had finally stopped, except for isolated incidents. He wouldn't have to doctor on a battlefield again.

The fact that he never had turned himself in only deepened his self-contempt. But even if he was beyond God's grace, that didn't mean God wouldn't hear a prayer from Alex for someone else, did it?

They worked for an hour or more. Beth with her tweezers, then bathing the throat wound with blazing hot water. Alex with his cold cloths. Mrs. Badje came in repeatedly keeping the water hot and cold.

As Sally continued breathing steadily, Alex noticed Sophie leave quietly then return much later with the parson at her side. "The children needed to know Sally was doing well." Sophie took up her place at Beth's side. Clay stayed at Alex's left.

The parson shared a quiet prayer with Sophie and Clay. Then the three talked quietly, standing near, ready to help.

Alex heard all of this, but his focus was on the patient and Beth's steadiness. How could a woman be so calm in the eye of a cyclone? And with her own sister riding that cyclone.

Alex wondered how anyone had the nerve to bring children into this dangerous world. Alex's prayers for this girl's healing went up steadily to God.

Beth glanced at him once, which made him aware that he'd been praying audibly. " 'The Lord is my shepherd,' " she began quietly reciting the Twenty-third Psalm.

He knew it well and prayed along. " 'Yea, though I walk through the valley of the shadow of death. . .' " He'd been too long in the valley of the shadow of death.

" 'Thou anointest my head with oil. . .' " Their words became unison as Sophie, Clay, and the parson joined in. "'And I will dwell in the house of the Lord forever.'"

Just as they finished, Sally's eyes flickered open. It wasn't much because they were so swollen, but Alex felt the young woman's muscles go taut. Leaning close, Alex saw awareness in those barely open eyes.

Alex leaned down and felt a faintest of breaths come easing out from Sally's lips. "She's breathing." Alex looked up at Beth. She smiled and Alex felt as if the sun had come out after a month-long rain. "The swelling has gone down in her throat."

"Can we close the incision then?" She had strength Alex couldn't fathom. And somehow he'd found himself able to use it himself. Borrow it, absorb it. Surely that wasn't possible, but it was the only way Alex could explain what he was capable of, as long as he could look into Beth McClellen's eyes.

Alex nodded. "I made the incision tiny so hopefully one or two stitches, taken from the outside, will close her trachea. Before I take any stitches, we'll make sure Sally is breathing well."

"Good idea." She smiled then turned to brush Sally's hair back off her forehead. "You're all right, Sally. You're going to be fine. Lie very still."

"Beth?"

"Yes, honey."

"I hurt." Sally's words were more a movement of her lips than audible, but she did manage to breathe out a whisper of sound, which meant air was now passing through her throat.

Beth looked at her parents. "Come over and talk to her and keep her still."

They rushed to stand close to Sally's head and bent so she could make eye contact as Alex removed the tube.

"She'll be vulnerable to infection and hard to keep still." Alex couldn't seem to stop himself from acting like a doctor. Giving instructions and dark warnings. His was the last voice so many had heard, the voice of doom.

"You don't know the half of keeping her still." Beth nodded down at her sister, who managed a twisted smile.

"How's Buck?" The voice, weak and shaky, was further proof Sally was pushing air through her throat.

"Buck's fine, only a few stings. You saved him, little sister." Beth smiled and Sally visibly relaxed.

Alex looked at Sally's concerned but very able parents. Speaking in a calm, matter-of-fact voice, Alex said, "Sophie, Clay, can you help us hold her?"

Sophie braced Sally's head, but at the same time began talking, distracting her, urging her to be very still. Clay steadied the girl's shoulders. The parson stood by her feet, ready if needed. Everyone in this room, including the patient, was stronger than Alex.

Alex knew that for the next twenty-four to forty-eight hours someone would need to be with Sally every minute. Moving her was out of the question so, for as long as Sally needed help, Alex was the doctor.

Not that Alex hadn't turned his back on a patient in need before. God forgive him, he'd done it in cold blood.

But not this time. With Beth's help, Alex could stay—especially if he didn't sleep. And then once the incision was healing well, without infection—*God, please don't let there be an infection*—Alex would go back to his plans to work for Clay. The man would definitely give him a good chance as a cowhand now. Saving a man's child ought to earn a man some security on his new job.

Just as Alex laid it all out in his mind, the door flew open. Laurie, wild-eyed, burst into the room. "Parson, your wife fell. She's hurt. She says to bring the doctor. The baby's coming."

Alex's gaze latched onto Beth's.

"Go." She gave him a nod of complete confidence. "I can take care of Sally."

"No. Not without you."

The parson grabbed Alex's arm. He hadn't registered Alex's

words to Beth. "This way, Doc." He was a slight man, and a man of worship and love, but he had a grip like a mule skinner.

"I—I—Beth, please," Alex implored her.

Beth's lips thinned with temper and Alex well remembered how she'd knocked him to his knees just yesterday. Then she swiftly looked at her mother. "Can you keep her still, Ma? This might take both of us."

"Yes, go if you need to."

"We'll be fine," Pa added.

"Maybe we can bring Mrs. Radcliff back here." Beth grabbed her doctor's bag, rushed around the counter serving as Sally's hospital bed, and was at Alex's side as they ran out.

Parson Radcliff let go of Alex's arm and sprinted toward his house. Alex did his best to keep up. A few heads poked out of upper windows along the street, Mosqueros residents who had heard Laurie hollering as she ran to get help.

Alex couldn't believe it. His second patient in one day. Bitterly, he wondered how he was ever going to convince these people that he wasn't a doctor.

Twelve

As she ran, Beth thanked God Alex was a doctor.

Standing helplessly beside Sally had brought it home clearly to Beth that she wasn't one. She had the potential and she would be able to help a lot of hurting people, but she didn't really have the training she needed. And Alex did. And he had years of experience after schooling. He'd hated it, but he'd learned what he needed to know.

He had the skill; she had the nerve. Together, they made a great team.

They raced down the Mosqueros street toward their next patient. Beth felt Alex slowing, and, worried that he might duck down an alley and run the wrong way, she caught his hand and hoped he thought she was trying to impart courage when in fact she was taking him prisoner.

Parson Radcliff whipped around a corner. Beth remembered the tidy house the Roscoes had lived in. As they turned the corner, Beth saw Adam outside surrounded by crying children. Tillie must have stayed in with Mrs. Radcliff, leaving Adam to care for the three McClellen boys, Radcliff's toddler, as well as Adam's own three children, two older boys and a little girl nearly school-aged.

Adam looked overwhelmed. Well, he wasn't the only one.

Parson Radcliff slammed through the door and they heard his frantic voice.

Beth followed, still hanging on tight to Alex who, in fairness, had made no escape attempt. Exchanging one worried look with Adam, Beth left him to his fate, kept hold of Alex, and ran inside.

"It happened so fast. Little Andrew knocked his milk over." Tillie referred to the Radcliff's toddler.

Beth was relieved one of her rambunctious little brothers hadn't taken the poor woman out.

"Then Mrs. Radcliff slipped and fell so hard." Tillie shook her head.

That was all the time Beth gave her. The sobbing coming from the back room had her towing Alex along.

Laurie darted up and whispered as if she didn't want to say the words out loud. "I think she broke her leg, the poor woman."

Beth nodded. "Adam looks overwhelmed. Go see if you need to save him."

Laurie rushed out as Beth hurried after Alex to find him hanging back as he listened to the poor woman.

Tillie followed them into the room, and when Beth glanced at Tillie, the older woman's eyes narrowed as she stared at Alex and Beth.

Beth wondered what she saw. Probably the truth. Alex—for all his skill at doctoring—appeared to be the slightest bit insane. Beth caught the sleeve of his blue shirt, thinking she recognized a stain on the back of the shoulder. This was Pa's shirt.

Once she was there, lending support, or rather pushing Alex around, he gathered his nerve and switched from lunatic to doctor. Beth would be able to write a medical textbook based on her dealings with poor, wounded mental patient, Dr. Buchanan.

She set her bag on a table beside the bed. "Tillie, will you get some bandages out of that bag and. . ." Beth listed the things she thought necessary.

Tillie opened the bag. She set a small container beside the table. "Is this what you needed?"

Beth saw the Dover's Powder and flinched. "No. Good heavens, no, Tillie."

"Then why do you have it in your bag?"

"It's got many uses. It's a good painkiller. But you have to give it very carefully. Even a small overdose will make you cast up everything in your belly and it can last for day and days. Put it away."

A furrow cut through Tillie's brow and she turned back to the bag.

Alex finally entered the fray. He gently but firmly shouldered the parson aside from his place, opposite the bed from Beth. "Mrs.—" Alex gave Beth a wild look.

"Radcliff," Beth supplied.

Alex nodded. "Mrs. Radcliff, please calm down and let's see what's happened."

That voice. It was like a musical instrument. Beth felt her own calm deepening and spreading. Her impatience with Dr. Crazy eased.

Alex asked questions as he ran his hands down the poor woman's leg. He reached her ankle, and Mrs. Radcliff's indrawn breath was nearly a scream. His shoulders sagging, Alex kept examining the area until finally he said, "I hope it's just a bad sprain."

Beth saw the badly swollen ankle. She knew a bad sprain and a break had to be treated very much the same. But a sprain was much less upsetting, and keeping Mrs. Radcliff calm right now was—

The woman lurched up in bed, sitting erect. She clutched her stomach. "The baby. Christopher, the baby is coming. Oh,

Christopher, my water broke shortly after I fell. The pains are coming."

—was out of the question, obviously.

The afternoon turned into the longest day of Beth's life.

With no plaster to make a cast, Alex did his best to splint and bind the ankle into immobility. When he had Mrs. Radcliff settled as well as could be expected, he grabbed Beth and rushed back to check on Sally.

Beth insisted he go and leave her to tend Mrs. Radcliff. She was still insisting when he dragged her into the building where Sally lay being coddled and fussed over by Ma and Pa.

Showing no signs of their mad dash except for breathing hard, Alex checked Sally quickly but thoroughly, his words reassuring as he explained the reason for their absence.

Ma gave Beth a significant look, shifting her eyes to Alex, very obviously asking what in the world was going on with the man. Beth shrugged, and Ma shook her head and went back to watching Sally.

When Alex finished his exam, he said, "Things look as if they're going well here. We need to get back to Mrs. Radcliff."

"One of us will come down if she shows any sign of trouble," Pa said. "You stay and tend to the parson's wife now."

"Alex, I could stay and watch—" Beth didn't get to finish. He had her in hand again.

As they hustled down the sidewalk, Alex gave her a frantic look. "Quit trying to get rid of me. I'll never survive this afternoon without you."

"That's a ridiculous thing to say."

"I know. That doesn't mean it's not true."

And since the crazy man was absolutely serious, Beth kept up as they raced back to Mrs. Radcliff's side. Whatever he did— and he did a lot that afternoon—he was professional, skilled, and kind. And through every second of it, he clung to Beth like she was some kind of talisman who was the source of his power.

He wouldn't let her step away for even an instant.

Four long years of hard work, long nights, intense training, and massive textbooks, and Beth had been reduced to a lucky charm.

Thirteen

Ⅱis name's Buchanan." Cletus knew he'd put the question wrong. He'd not get a single word out of this bunch. Still, he couldn't stop himself from goading them. "Man claims he's a doctor but he's got blood on his hands, and I'm here to see that he's brought to justice before he kills again."

Stony silence greeted him. These shiftless skunks didn't know Cletus was a lawman. He'd been a no-account himself at one time but no more. He had money and a fine horse and a sharp outfit of clothes and the best gun money could buy. This scum needed to learn how to treat their betters, and Cletus burned with the need to teach them at the end of a shooting iron. But the four men sitting at the table dealing into a card game had watchful eyes and they kept their gun hands loose and ready.

Cletus should've come in and asked if he could join the game. He knew how to play cards and men with equal skill. But he'd been edgy and anxious to track down the doc and he'd gone straight to questioning them. Knowing he'd lost out, Cletus tried to act as if he didn't care. With a shrug, he said, "I heard tell of a man by that name down this'a way matched his description."

"We mind our own business, mister," the closest poker player said, drawing long on his cigar. "Healthy man might wanta do the same."

A little chill climbed Cletus's spine at the measured drawl, clearly a threat. Cletus nodded. There were others in town. He'd handle them better than he had this trash. Probably a bunch of outlaws themselves. Cletus decided then and there he'd start bounty hunting as soon as the last of the deserting cowards were rounded up.

Cletus sidled away from the men, not wanting to turn his back. He stepped out on the wooden sidewalk in the little cow town and stalked away, his feet thudding hard on the boards, grumbling. Seeing a diner ahead, he headed for it.

Gathering the frayed edges of his temper, he walked inside and noticed three long tables, two of them empty. Normal for mid-morning. The third had four men sitting at it. A hefty, grizzled man with a cigar dangling from his lips came through swinging doors carrying a coffeepot.

"Want a cup?"

"Yep. Obliged." Cletus sat at the table with the others.

One looked like he lived in town. Dark pants and a vest over a white shirt. Two others were dusty and sweat soaked, with a Stetson lying on the table beside each. Most likely cowpokes. The third wore a black leather vest, and when he shifted, Cletus noticed a star on his chest. A lawman. Cletus never went directly to the law in any town. Too much chance of the lawman going after the deserter and claiming the reward for himself.

The coffee slapped onto the table in front of him and Cletus was good and trapped. He couldn't ask any questions and he couldn't leave without drawing notice. For now he was thwarted, but not for long. Instead of asking questions, Cletus listened. Sometimes he learned more keeping his mouth shut anyway.

Alex had no idea why he hadn't kept his mouth shut.

Not today. It'd already been too late today.

But yesterday, on the stage. *Deltoideus.* He could have helped Beth like an untrained cowboy. But oh no, he had to say the word *deltoideus.* He had to spout off medical words. Now here he was, as good as branded with the name of doctor.

He almost ran screaming when he saw the Armitages. Mrs. Armitage supported her husband. Leo's arm was in a sling, and his face was pasty white. No doubt from exhaustion and pain, but what if he'd reinjured himself?

"Doctor." Mrs. Armitage waved as if he might have missed them coming straight at him on the one and only sidewalk.

He'd just checked Sally for the fourth time and he needed to get back to Vivian Radcliff. Her time was coming close. Beth had promised to look in on Leo and Camilla today. Fine, these were her patients. Except he hadn't let Beth out of his sight.

Beth must have sensed his desire to cut and run because she grabbed his hand in a vise.

"This way, folks. Come on in to Dr. Buchanan's office." Beth waved her arm toward the building Sally was lying in.

Dr. Buchanan's office? Where had that come from? "I am *not* a doctor," Alex growled under his breath.

"Shut up and get in there. I'm going to go get help to move Mrs. Radcliff down here so you can tend everyone at once without running back and forth."

Alex dug his fingers into hers. He could out-vise her any day of the week. "If you leave, I swear I'll make a break for it and you'll never see me again."

The Armitages narrowed the gap between them.

"I should anyway. You can handle this." Alex's gaze met hers. "I'll go. You take over. You needed me for your sister but not for the rest of this."

"Give me strength."

Alex was pretty sure she was praying. Good, let God give her all the strength she needed, and while she was at it, she oughta ask for some strength for him, too. Alex didn't think he had much coming from God. Or more honestly, Alex admitted he was too ashamed to ask.

"I'll get Pa to help the parson move his wife."

"She'll be loud and out of control birthing a baby. We can't have that while we're trying to keep Sally quiet."

"My sister's tougher than you think. I'd wager Mrs. *Radcliff* is tougher than you think. And no matter *how* wimpy they are, it's a sure bet that they're all tougher than *you*."

"Hey, Doc." Leo Armitage was looking straight at Alex. Beth had done more for him yesterday than Alex had. The guy was a jerk to pretend Alex was the doctor.

Alex looked at her, expecting resentment.

She smiled, the picture of competence and calm. . .and strength. "Step right in here to the doctor's office. Dr. Buchanan will have a look at your arm. We've had a busy day already today. Is it all right if we go check on the parson's wife while you wait? She's in labor."

"Of course. We don't mind waiting." Mrs. Armitage acted like she was a bit early for her appointment.

"There aren't any chairs. Won't you get tired standing so long?" Alex focused on the sick one of the group. Let Mr. Armitage decide his own fate.

"I'll be fine. I might settle on the floor though. We'll find a place to get comfortable. I appreciate the help you gave me yesterday, Dr. Buchanan." He let his wife get the door then thanked her so kindly, Alex was humbled. Sure, he'd punched Alex in the nose, but other than that, the guy was a true gentleman.

The couple went in.

Beth went back to dragging Alex.

"I am *not* a doctor," Alex said.

"Give me strength." Beth looked up toward heaven.

The parson's wife, brave pioneer woman that she was, agreed

to move to the doctor's office on her injured ankle. Adam and Laurie had vanished with all the children. Tillie was put in charge of moving bedding to the office. As soon as Tillie headed out, and the poor laboring woman was between pains, Alex and the parson carried Mrs. Radcliff down the street with Beth holding the doors.

Alex's doctor's office now had a delivery room, a post-surgical recovery room, and a waiting room. All in the *same* room, granted, but still, it was almost a city hospital.

Tillie left. She said she was determined to find Adam and save all those children. Alex snorted. Adam was probably in more danger than the kids. Pa rode with Tillie, promising to return as soon as Tillie was safe at home.

Leo Armitage was checked over thoroughly and sent on his way.

Mrs. Radcliff was delivered of a squalling son.

Sally went to sleep.

Beth settled in to sit with Sally and her mother for the night.

Parson Radcliff was busy helping his wife get comfortable on a bedroll on the floor, propping her up so she could cradle her baby.

The door swung open and Alex jumped, afraid of what else might happen.

Clay McClellen's spurs clinked as he stepped inside, dragging his Stetson off his head. "I left your son with Adam for the night, Parson. I didn't see any sense bringing him back here. I can ride out and fetch him home in the morning."

"Thanks, Clay. Obliged to you and Adam and Tillie for caring for him. I haven't been a very good father to Andy today."

Clay gave him a good-natured slap on the back. "You're doing fine. That's what a church family is for."

"Clay, why don't you ride on home with Beth now," Ma said.

"She's not going anywhere." Alex found his doctor voice somewhere.

"I'm staying, Ma. Alex has to keep watch over Mrs. Radcliff for a while longer then help Parson carry her home. I'll be needed here with Sally. You go on home and get some rest. Alex and I'll watch Sally. In the morning, ride in with Pa when he picks up Andrew and you can spell me."

"No, you're not staying in here tonight." All Clay's good humor vanished. "It ain't proper."

Alex tensed at the narrow-eyed look on Clay's face.

"Nothing improper will go on here, Clay." Alex wasn't letting Beth go. If she went, he went.

"It's out of the question," Sophie stood next to Beth like a guardian angel in a petticoat.

"No, Alex, she can't spend the night here with you." Clay spoke on top of his wife.

If she left he couldn't do it. He'd look at the poor girl with her throat slit and think of that woman dead over the cliff yesterday. Without Beth he'd start seeing the dead and dying in war. He might fall asleep. He might dream.

"I'll stay," Sophie said. Alex looked at the dark circles of fatigue under Sophie's eyes. The woman needed rest.

"You'll have your hands full with Sally tomorrow, Sophie." Clay clutched his hat brim in both hands, clearly worried. "She'll be feeling better, and you'll be the only one who can keep her quiet. You know I don't have the knack. But I can stay tonight when she's probably going to mostly sleep."

"Isn't that shipment of horses being driven in tomorrow?" Sophie asked. "You have to be home."

Clay paused, his eyes narrow. "I'll manage. Or Eustace can see to caring for the new stock."

Beth snorted as if she was fed up. "If you don't sleep tonight you'll have to sleep tomorrow, Ma. I might as well do my turn now."

"You're just as tired as I am." Sophie didn't budge.

"I worked long shifts at the hospital. I'm used to it. And I can't sleep now anyway. I need to wait until Mrs. Radcliff's ready to go home and Sally is settled for the night. Until then I can't leave anyway. You and Pa go."

"No." Clay stood firm.

"I'm fine." Beth crossed her arms.

"You can't stay here alone with Dr. Buchanan," Parson Radcliff chimed in. "Sally isn't a sufficient chaperone. I assume you've been raised to know what's good and proper." The parson gave Alex a fire-and-brimstone look if ever there was one.

Alex wondered if maybe *his* throat was swelling shut. Beth could *not* leave him. He looked at the traitor pastor. "You've been falling all over yourself thanking me for helping your wife. And now you accuse me of treating Beth with anything but the utmost respect."

"That's not the point." The parson sounded downright starchy.

"Beth leaves or you leave." Clay jabbed his finger at Alex. "Or someone else stays." Clay said it like he was reading it straight off a stone tablet carved by the finger of God.

Alex felt all the old fear, the nightmarish torment, welling up inside him. He took a half step backward. "She can't leave. Don't you want to stay with me, Beth?"

"I do." Beth was at his side in an instant, holding his hand firmly, sounding as if she'd just taken a vow. And Alex supposed she had. She was still trying to protect him. Stop him from making a fool of himself.

"That's the perfect answer." The parson slapped his forehead with the heel of his hands. "I mean it's as if God Himself is shaking us, trying to see what's right before our eyes."

"What?" Alex felt hope.

"Right before our eyes where?" Sophie looked up from watching every breath Sally took.

"Give me strength," Beth whispered her standard prayer.

"Absolutely not." Clay slapped his thigh with his hat.

That must mean Clay at least knew what the crazy parson was

talking about. He had a hunch Beth did, too. What else did she need strength for right now?

"I thought of it when Beth said, 'I do.' They can get married." The parson smiled as pleased as if he'd just given birth himself. He had—to a harebrained idea.

"What?" Alex looked down at their joined hands. It made no more sense now that it'd been said out loud.

"That idea isn't before *my* eyes." Sophie's blond brows lowered to a straight, angry line. "They only met yesterday."

"Absolutely not." Clay *had* known what the parson meant.

"And how long did you and Clay know each other before you got hitched?" the parson asked.

"I'm not sure even God can give me that much strength," Beth muttered.

Strength enough to run away from Alex? Or to marry him? Because suddenly, to Alex, it made perfect sense. For some reason the world made sense with Beth at his side. Having, holding, from this day forward. Yes! He found stores of strength and courage inside himself. God himself was shaking Alex for sure. He might even be able to go back to doctoring. . .not that he was a doctor.

"Beth, will you marry me?"

Fourteen

Beth's eyes locked on Alex's and she couldn't get free. That same weird, deep contact that seemed to tap energy from her bones and heart and soul.

She considered herself a levelheaded person. Good in a crisis. Thinking things through, but at the same time acting fast.

Right this minute, her brain seemed to be stuffed with gauze padding. Gauze padding soaked in laudanum. Stupid and numb, pinned by Alex's gaze.

"Uhhh. . ." Beth drew that sound out awhile.

"No. That isn't a possibility." Ma was talking but she wasn't making sense, not through the laudanum and gauze.

"Let's get home, Beth." Pa crossed his arms with that "I've got a revolver and I'm not afraid to use it" look he sometimes got; but that didn't break the connection with Alex.

"One day," Parson Radcliff said so loudly Beth almost understood what that meant. "Parson Roscoe told me the whole story. Clay, you knew Sophie one day and not a full day at that when you married her. And you spent most of that day unconscious."

"That was different." Pa's voice came from far away and nearby at the same time. He'd come to stand next to Beth, Alex clinging to her hand.

Ma had rounded that counter that before had been between her and the rest of the room. She still kept one hand resting on Sally to make sure she didn't move, but she'd narrowed the gap between herself and Beth.

The parson came close and kept telling the story of Ma and Pa's wedding day, a story Beth had heard many times. Which is why it seemed so easy to ignore the telling now.

"He was family." Sophie kept her hand on Sally.

Beth glanced down at Sally, sleeping. Alive because Alex had known what to do. And Alex would never have come through if Beth hadn't been handy to browbeat him. Not exactly a good basis for a marriage...marriage...marriage. Marriage? Beth's head went numb again. She'd almost pulled out of it there for a minute.

Parson Radcliff's son started crying, underscoring to Beth why she needed to stay. The baby was fine. Mrs. Radcliff's ankle would heal. Mr. Armitage's arm was going to be fine. Beth could have maybe done all of that, though not as well as Dr. Loco here who now spoke.

"We'll be fine. We've made a connection today that will get us through." Alex's gaze took on a desperate edge. His hand tightened on hers until the pain almost seeped through the numbness in her head. The man was afraid she'd leave him.

And she was afraid he'd abandon her little sister. Not because Alex was weak. His behavior was too completely out of control for such a normal word. The man was a lunatic who somehow could tap into sanity when he looked her in the eye. What did that make her? A human straitjacket?

"What do you say, Beth? Will you marry me?"

"Uh. . ." So far that was the only sound Beth was capable of.

"I told you no." They'd formed a tight circle, but Pa pushed in farther so he stood between Beth and Alex, not squarely between, though. Alex still held her gaze, drawing strength, sanity. "I'm Beth's pa and I make a decision like this."

"I saved your daughter's life today, Clay." Alex looked away from Beth and it was like having skin ripped from her body. She almost cried out in pain. Then she watched her crazy would-be fiancé square off against Pa. The madman didn't do half bad standing up to him. That was something that could be said of very few men. Of course Alex was insane. "Why would you deny me Beth's hand in marriage?"

"Don't you put my Sally's life up as if we owe you and Beth is the payment." Sophie left Sally's side.

"Ma, she'll fall off that counter!" With the eye contact broken, Beth found words beyond "uh." Though her head still had that numb, stupid feel. And Ma obeyed quickly, which just showed how upset Ma was by all this. She'd have never left Sally's side otherwise.

The baby started crying louder. "Doctor, are you sure my son is all right?" Mrs. Radcliff sounded fretful, not an uncommon occurrence after a child was born. The woman needed quiet and peace and sleep. Instead she had ringside seats at a circus.

"Dr. Buchanan, you and Beth can't leave my wife so soon after our baby is born, and with a sprained ankle besides." The parson looked scared, and Beth got the impression he thought Alex and Beth getting married boiled down to life and death.

Sally groaned and reached unsteady hands toward her neck, which no doubt hurt terribly. After all, she'd had her throat cut just that morning.

"Settle down, Sally." Sophie abandoned the battlefield.

The parson turned to his wife, went to her side, and knelt by her, where she lay on a pallet on the floor. He reached for his tiny son. "Let me take him, Viv."

Pa turned and looked down at Beth, blocking the whole room from her vision. "Let's go now, Beth. If you have a serious interest in marriage, it'll keep until you know him better."

"Uh. . ." Beth felt some reason returning. She could make sense any minute now.

"Clay, help me." Sophie had Sally's hands, but suddenly Sally was thrashing her head and moaning.

Pa left, and in the midst of the Radcliffs calming the baby and the McClellens calming Sally, Beth and Alex were alone in a little cocoon surrounded by chaos.

And the connection returned. Alex stepped closer. Beth noted that the man was ignoring his patients in order to talk with her. Not admirable behavior. Of course she was ignoring them, too.

"You know how desperately I need you." Alex whispered, stepping even closer so the words were only between them. If there'd been romance between them, those would have been beautiful, loving words.

"I know." It was the simple truth. For whatever reason, Alex needed her nearly as much as he needed air. Oh, he didn't need her if he remained a useless lump sleeping in a stagecoach. But for doctoring, it wasn't about want. It was about need. Maybe after a time he'd be able to function as a doctor on his own, but for now, Beth didn't think he had a chance.

"And you need me, too." Alex's eyes changed, became warm, burning, glittering. . .maybe with madness.

Beth felt her heartbeat speed up, but it wasn't out of fear. "Why do I need you?" The gauze and laudanum must be thinning because she was sure she didn't need Alex for anything.

"Because they won't let you be a doctor here without me." He leaned closer, almost as if he wanted to kiss her. The words held that kind of intimacy. "But with me, you can doctor this whole town. They'll call you my nurse or a midwife, but the label isn't important. Not even the respect. You have a passion to heal."

"How do you know that?" Beth's breathing sped up.

Alex's voice rose from a whisper to something dark and husky and alive. "I know it because I recognize the same thing in you

108

that I have in myself. If you were smart, you'd run. The kind of calling, obsession even, to help people hurts."

"No, it doesn't. It's never hurt me."

"That's because you've never failed."

"I've failed. I've had patients die. I know my place in their lives is to help, but survival, life and death, is up to God."

"You haven't failed like I've failed. You haven't seen butchery. You haven't been surrounded by death and dying, blood and screams, women and children, young men with their whole lives in front of them. . ."

"War. You're talking about a war. What war?" The Civil War was long over. Alex was too young to have been through it.

"The frontier. I was a doctor for the cavalry. I saw the troops, but also the Indian villages. I saw—I saw. . ." Alex's voice faded away. The look of horror in his eyes shook Beth and she wished so terribly she could take that vision from him, that memory.

Alex's hand trembled as it reached to rest against her face. "It's not about love, Beth. It's about something bigger, more important."

Beth wanted to tell Alex there was nothing more important than love. Nothing. "It's about helping these people, using the gift God put in you. A gift that glows and burns like red hot coals and makes you feel like the suffering of others is your own."

Alex nodded his head slowly. His hand settled more firmly against her face and lifted and lowered, gently guiding her to nod along with him.

Somehow that motion of agreement transferred itself inside her, and she knew Alex was right. She did need to heal. And it hurt. And it burned inside her, a flame that never went out.

"You need me as much as I need you." He leaned closer still, his voice only for her. "With me beside you, the work of a doctor is possible for you."

"I'll do it." Beth reached up to rest her hand on his, where it cradled her face. Nodding under her own power now. "I'll marry you."

Alex lowered his head and she thought he'd kiss her. She realized she was intensely curious about how the connection between them would feel if it was expressed in a kiss.

Instead he closed his eyes and rested his forehead on hers. "I'm sorry. I should just go."

"Beth, lend us a hand."

Beth turned at her mother's urgent voice. Sally was half-asleep and only reacting to the pain now, thrashing. Her little sister was going to be fine, but right now she couldn't stand to lie still another second. Sally needed Beth's calming voice.

She felt like she had to tear at something that bound her to Alex, but her mother's need for help wasn't something she could ignore. She rushed to Sally's side and began crooning.

Behind her, she heard Alex go to the Radcliffs and talk with that same soothing tone as she had. A quick glance and she saw he held the fretful baby in his arms.

A miraculous voice. He'd just used it on her to persuade her to commit an act of madness. She was as crazy as Alex. But she was going to do it.

"Sally, honey, listen to me. It's Beth." Her sister's thrashing slowed. Her growing hysteria eased and her eyes focused. She let Beth soothe her. The struggles gradually ceased. While she crooned, Beth considered the madness of what she'd agreed to. But was it madness? Or genius?

As a single woman, she'd never be allowed to use her God-given gift for doctoring. And "God-given" was the key part of that thought. This gift was hers from her earliest memory. The compassion, the gentling voice, the healing touch, the gift for reaching all living creatures.

And now here stood Alex, who had connected to her in a way beyond her understanding. His proposal gave her the chance to fulfill God's call. To Beth it seemed that his very proposal was guided by God.

She needed Alex even more than he needed her.

Yes, she'd marry him.

Fifteen

I know what you're thinking, Beth."

Beth didn't doubt it. Her ma had always been one step ahead of everyone.

As Sally finally subsided into sleep, Beth smiled at her mother, so tough, so smart, the best woman Beth had ever known. "I told Alex yes. I'm going to marry him, Ma."

"It's true I got married fast, Beth, honey. But my situation was completely different from yours. I had no other prospects, and Clay was your pa's brother. Even though I hadn't known him long—"

"About twenty hours as I recall, and he spent sixteen of those hours either unconscious or in town or riding ahead of you on his horse when we went back to the ranch. I think you probably actually talked to the man for about a half an hour." Beth grinned.

Ma's eyes narrowed. She didn't like not getting her way.

"Alex doesn't seem all that—" Ma's eyes slid to Alex, who was on his knees beside the parson's wife, talking quietly to her. He held the Radcliffs' new son in his arms.

Alex seemed pretty wonderful to Beth right at that second. Sure, she'd thought he was a lunatic at first. But he was coming around. Showing flashes of occasional sanity. At least as long as she was at his side. "There's something between us, Ma. I feel it. It's meant to be."

"You can't have fallen in love with the man this fast."

"I didn't say love. You're right that it's too soon. But I can—I can *see* into him. He's no good at covering his feelings. I can see he's got a gift for healing like I do. I can see he's wounded from giving too much. And I can see—" Beth looked up at her ma, a woman she respected more than anyone else on earth. "I can see that I will be able to heal him by supporting him and encouraging him." And maybe, occasionally, beating on him with his hat. Beth didn't rule it out.

Ma frowned and shook her head doubtfully. "Beth, honey—"

"He needs me, Ma," Beth cut her off. "And I need him."

"You don't need anyone, Beth."

Pa was there, too. He wasn't ever going to agree to this. Beth knew for a fact that her pa didn't think there was a man alive good enough for any of his daughters. So she wasn't too worried about convincing him. He wouldn't kidnap her to stop the wedding and he wouldn't shoot Alex, unless Alex really provoked him. So Pa wasn't the one who needed convincing—since it was hopeless. But she'd really like her mother's blessing.

"This town—the whole West—will never let me tend to the sick. I thought they would. I did a lot of doctoring when I was back East. But now I know it was because I was at a doctor's side. Alone, I won't be able to do anything."

Alex came up to her side. They exchanged a glance, and Beth knew he'd heard everything. He didn't interfere though. Instead he stood beside Pa, across from Beth, and bent down to examine Sally's throat. "We can't let Sally eat for twenty-four hours. We need to get the trachea incision to close. I don't want to suture the outer layer of skin because we'll need to take the inner stitches out.

She can have a bit of water in about twelve hours. She'll be hungry so it won't be easy to hold her back. She needs careful watching. It's best if she stays here rather than goes home. Jouncing her around could slow down the healing."

Alex looked away from the incision, right at Beth. Then his eyes cut to Ma. Beth was afraid of what he'd say. Things were balanced on the very edge of disaster. If he said the wrong thing, it could tip the wrong way.

"Sophie"—he looked sideways at Pa—"Clay, I want permission to marry your daughter. I know we haven't known each other long enough. I know that. But we are suited to each other." Alex looked at Beth now.

She nodded. "We are."

"She fills an empty place inside of me. And I think—I hope—I will be a good mate for her, too." Alex looked back at her parents. "We'd like your blessing. We've already decided that we will get married. And we're doing it right now tonight. But to have your support and blessing would mean a lot to Beth, and because her feelings are important to me, they'd mean a lot to me, too." He looked directly at Pa then. "I will treat her with kindness and respect, Clay. I already respect her more than any woman I've ever met."

The two men stared at each other.

Pa had his usual grim, narrow-eyed look, the one he always got when there was a male paying attention to his girls. He looked away first to Ma. "What do you think, Sophie?"

Ma rolled her eyes. "He can't be much worse than your brother, I suppose. And we'll be here to take care of her if he turns out to be worthless, as I firmly believe he will."

A disgusted huff of breath escaped Pa's lips. He looked at Beth. "Marry him then. You can always come on back home."

Beth almost laughed at the depth of her parents' low expectations. She did smile at Alex, who looked offended and hurt and a bit angry. "That's as close to a blessing as you're likely to get from my folks. Maybe if you shape up to be a decent husband they'll give it after a few years. Five or ten."

"Can't say as I blame them." Alex sighed then called over his shoulder, "Can you spare a minute, Parson Radcliff? Beth and I'd like to get married."

"Sure, won't take but a second."

Beth remembered that the parson had been all for this. He was a man of God. Surely that meant something. What though, she couldn't exactly say.

The parson came to stand by Sally's head carrying his fussing son. Beth and Alex stood facing each other over Sally. Her parents stood in such a way they'd almost work as a best man and matron of honor. Except for her little sister stretched out on a counter, it was a little like a wedding. Not a lot, but a little.

The vows were short and to the point because Parson Radcliff's baby started crying. Beth never knew if Alex would have kissed her because the parson didn't take the time to order it and the counter and wounded young woman between them didn't make it convenient.

"You can go home now, Ma and Pa. We're married now and that makes it proper and legal and safe for you to leave us alone."

"Legal, definitely," Ma said. "Proper—I suppose. But safe?"

Pa shook his head. "No, she's safe. Beth knows how to take care of herself. Alex here looks none too tough. You can handle him if he gets to being trouble. You have your knife, right? Where's your rifle?"

"I don't usually bring it to church." Beth didn't look at Alex for fear of what she'd see while they talked rifles and knifes.

"I'll bring it in tomorrow." Pa patted Sally on the ankle.

"I can turn him into one of my patients in a flicker of an eyelash. Don't worry. I've already proved that one."

"Oh, brother." Alex turned and went to check on Mrs. Radcliff and urged the parson to go home. Alex kept the baby.

Satisfied that her new husband had been reminded of exactly whom he was dealing with, Beth kissed her folks good-bye and went back to tending her now-sleeping little sister.

Sixteen

The hospital was settled quickly. The parson and the McClellens left. The baby and Mrs. Radcliff slept quietly on the pallet on the floor.

Alex made up another pallet on the floor and gently moved Sally to a spot where she wasn't at risk of falling. "Strange," Alex whispered to himself.

"What's strange?"

Alex jumped. He'd been so focused on Sally he hadn't heard Beth come up behind him. He glanced down, afraid he'd jostled the girl and awakened her, but Sally slept on. Alex rose to his feet and faced Beth. Almost alone with his wife. "I just realized I've got a little sister." Alex smiled. "I kinda like the idea."

Beth's expression lightened. He saw exhaustion on her face, but the serenity and compassion were still there. And the strength, under it all, more strength than he'd ever had.

"Well, once you get to know her, I'm sure you'll find out she and my other brothers and sisters will drive you crazy." Beth grinned. "They're a wild bunch, all right."

"And a wife." Alex almost regretted saying the words, because Beth's smile shrank like wool underwear in boiling water. But there wasn't much point in denying it.

"You've got yourself a wife." Beth nodded but commented no further.

"And you've got a new name. Beth Buchanan. Pretty."

"The name?" Beth's forehead furrowed.

"The name is pretty. . .too." Alex leaned forward and kissed her. He was there and away so fast she didn't have time to use her strength to beat on him. He even took a few steps back.

"Now, Alex." Pink rose in Beth's cheeks. "This marriage isn't going to be—be—about—about k–kissing."

Suddenly Alex was absolutely determined to prove her wrong.

"It's going to be about caring for sick people in Mosqueros," she added.

He'd seen her mad and compassionate. He'd seen her smiling and courageous and tough. He'd seen her thrilled to see her pa and loving with her little sisters and brothers. But he'd never seen her blush. It made his brand spankin' new wife prettier than ever.

"Agreed." Alex didn't agree. He'd break that news to her later. He was watching her so intently he noticed the tiny flinch of hurt when he agreed so quickly. The madness, the haunting seemed a bit further away with every moment he spent in her company. He knew it was just another kind of weakness to think a woman could heal a tormented soul. Alex had to figure out a way to save himself.

And then he thought of Someone else who could save him. God.

He'd believed that fiercely when he was young. But for so long, Alex had believed that his actions put him beyond the pale. Maybe not. Maybe he had reason to hope.

Smiling at his blushing wife, he said, "Our marriage is going to be about caring for sick people."

She squared her shoulders and nodded, as if there'd been no

flinch, no hurt. "Good, I'm glad we see it the same way."

"Me, too. We need to get some rest." Alex leaned in and kissed her again.

Mandy was awakened with a kiss.

She made a poor princess because she'd have rather stayed asleep. The jerking, huffing train had beaten on her until it felt as if she'd walked into the middle of a fistfight. She'd finally fallen asleep, after trying futilely to sleep sitting up in the uncomfortable seats most of the night.

And now Sidney smiled into her barely open eyes as if waking up a woman half-dead from exhaustion was a romantic idea.

And her Winchester was close enough to grab.

Shocked at that unworthy thought, Mandy forced herself to smile. She also quit breathing because Sidney's breath was foul enough to raise blisters on her skin and his odor was the worse for having ridden all day yesterday in the sweltering heat.

It was still almost completely dark. There was a bit of a cast of gray to the train car so she could see Sidney. . .and smell him.

"Good morning." Her voice sounded as rough and rocky as ten miles of mountain trail.

Sidney pulled her into another kiss. Mandy did her best to hold her breath and kiss at the same time, hoping the kiss ended before her lungs exploded.

"Honey, I found a luggage car near the end of the train." Sidney's eyes were warm, coaxing. His voice was sultry and suggestive. A voice Mandy loved in the normal course of things. "Why don't we go back there and spend some time alone?"

Uh-oh. *Alone* had gotten to be one of Mandy's least favorite words. The man had suggested it many times since they'd met. Propriety had always been a sufficient excuse.

She wanted to be Sidney's wife in all regards. And she would be. As soon as they found some quiet, comfortable, clean spot. With a bathtub.

No luggage car. And she knew all too well that Sidney didn't like the word *no*. She braced herself for the pouting to begin.

"Good morning." An elderly woman moved up beside them. "I've been waiting for you to wake up. Nothing more tedious than a long train ride." She lowered herself onto the bench seat facing Mandy and Sidney as if her joints ached.

Thank You, dear Lord.

Mandy had a moment of pause at that thought. She wasn't sure escaping a time alone with her grimy husband should be such a relief. Certainly she smelled rather—travel worn—herself. But then if she did, why was Sidney so eager to be alone with her?

"We'd be pleased for the company, ma'am." And when Mandy said "we" she meant "I" because Sidney did *not* look pleased. "Have you done a lot of train travel?" Mandy nodded at the seat that faced her.

Sidney was on her left, crowding her up against the window, but he eased away as the woman settled in. A lucky break for Mandy and her assaulted sense of smell.

"Oh my, yes. I'm an old hand. I've got children spread here and there along the rail lines. And I'm always on my way to see one or the other of them."

"Are you riding all the way to Denver?"

"Why yes, dear, I am."

Mandy smiled. "Where are you from?"

The elderly lady, grimy from travel, smiled with the kind eyes of an angel as she began knitting and chattering away.

The woman really had been everywhere and her stories were so interesting Mandy barely minded her sullen, moping husband.

Beth had gotten precious little sleep. She was exhausted and groggy. Which is why she remained calm when she noticed a hand on her stomach.

A man's hand.

Not calm after all.

Beth launched herself to sit up straight. The hand remained resting on her belly.

It all came flooding back. . .the hand belonged to her husband. She'd gotten married last night.

Her eyes warily turned to follow that hand up to Alex's eyes, wide open. She caught his hand and returned it to him.

Alex smiled.

Finding a smile curling her own lips, Beth was shocked at the impulse. She'd been out of her mind. What other possible reason could there be for marrying a lunatic? She must be one, too. But at around midnight last night—Beth shifted around in her head and couldn't remember exactly what time it had been—marrying Alex had seemed like a really good idea.

To her surprise she still liked it. She was truly delighted to find herself married to the lunatic. Terrified, too, and the two—delight and terror—were an uncomfortable combination. But still she smiled. She had definitely lost her mind.

"Good morning, Mrs. Buchanan." Alex's voice was gravelly with sleep. His eyes were heavy-lidded. He had a bristly morning set of whiskers.

"Good morning, Alex."

Having him take a bath, shave, and get into clean clothes had made a world of difference in how she reacted to Alex. She hadn't wanted to slug him for hours. Well, there'd been a few mild moments of temptation. Bathing seemed like a really shallow reason to marry a man, but honestly, he'd cleaned up very nicely. Now he had morning whiskers.

An odd thing to be waking up for the first time with a husband.

Alex sat up. He was close enough that it brought up memories of last night's kiss. And then he reminded her of it in an unmistakable way. He kissed her again.

Beth wondered at her willingness to let this near stranger kiss her. It couldn't be a sign of good character on her part. But she let him anyway.

His arms came around her waist and she found her own entwining his neck.

"I'm well, Beth. Let's go home." Sally was awake.

Alex pulled back, grinned down at her, and then turned to her sister.

Beth moved out of Alex's way and went to Sally's other side.

"You had a hard day yesterday, Sally." Alex took Sally's hand. "I think you're going to be fine, and your ma and pa will be in to see you soon, but for now. . ." He took her hand and guided her fingers to the tiny cut in her neck. Alex was careful not to let Sally touch the actual wound, but he let her touch close enough that it helped her understand the source of her main discomfort. "I had to perform a very small operation. You got stung by bees. Do you remember that?"

Sally's fingers were slow-moving and careful, two words Beth had never used to describe her active little sister. A sure sign she was still feeling poorly. The bee stings had mostly gone down, but there were still tiny traces of each and every one of them.

"Now let me explain exactly what I did. Because I need you to understand why you have to lie very still for the rest of today. And not talk unless you absolutely must. I'm not going to let you eat either. A few sips of water is all. I know that will be hard, but Beth, and soon your parents, and I are here if you need any help. Okay?"

Sally nodded cautiously. "Okay."

As well as possible, Beth concealed a sigh of relief to hear Sally speak clearly.

"Your voice sounds good. You can talk if it feels okay, but no yelling, okay? We're trying to be very gentle with your throat today."

Sally smiled and nodded.

"Good. Now, you had a bad reaction to so many bee stings."

Alex went on to explain with his soothing voice in very simple terms what he'd done. It was so clear that Beth suspected that, if it was ever asked of her, she could now perform this procedure herself.

The baby started to cry, and Alex glanced over his shoulder at his other patient. Then with one last pat of Sally's hand, he got up quickly and rushed to the infant.

Beth knew without being told that he was trying to let Mrs. Radcliff sleep awhile longer.

"It's a very good sign that you're wanting to go home, Sally." Beth took up the task of distracting Sally from her natural inclination, which was to run wild.

As she soothed, Beth took occasional glances at her husband, handling a baby so comfortably, so calmly. She'd helped him find this part of himself. And he still needed her, even more than she needed him.

How strange to be married to a man she'd just met and actually feel good about that. She didn't love him—that would be a bit much—but she felt connected in a way that reminded her of God's words, *"The twain shall be one."* Then she flinched as she thought the verse all the way to the end. *"The twain shall be one flesh."*

Beth had an inkling of what that meant. Well, that wasn't for her. She and Alex were partners, business partners.

Except for that kiss. That had felt like more than partners. And she couldn't say Alex had stolen that kiss, either. He'd given her plenty of time to duck. But there she'd stood, like a brainless sheep, and let him kiss her. In honesty, she had to admit she'd kissed him back and enjoyed every moment.

Not as much as she'd enjoyed whacking him with his hat after the stage wreck, but almost. Very close to as much.

"Doc, come quick!" Mrs. Farley, who'd run the general store by her husband's side for as long as Beth could remember, slammed through the door yelling, "My husband fell. Bart knocked himself insensible. And his head is bleedin' something fierce."

The loud entrance woke up Mrs. Radcliff. She rose to her feet, a pioneer woman after all. Having a baby, even with a sprained ankle, didn't keep her down long. "Give me the boy and go, Dr. Buchanan. Go along with him Beth. I can mind Sally."

"No, your ankle—"

Alex grabbed a chair and sat it with a loud clatter next to Sally. He then swept Mrs. Radcliff into his arms, baby and all. The surprise of it shook a giggle out of the woman. Alex sat his passenger down at Sally's side.

"Thank you, ma'am." Alex grabbed Beth's hand while he rushed for the door. "Appreciate it. Sophie and probably the parson will be along anytime. I can really use Beth's help. Sally, you lie still." They hurried on Mrs. Farley's heels toward the store. The woman was round and her dark hair shot through with gray, but she set a fast pace.

"Alex, I should stay and—"

"There's your ma." Alex jerked his head toward the hitching post outside the doctor's office as they swept past.

"Ma, help keep Sally still," Beth yelled over her shoulder. "Mr. Farley's hurt. We'll be back as soon as possible."

Beth caught a glimpse of Ma's startled face as they rushed across the street, but she left it to Mrs. Radcliff to explain. The town was small and the general store was across the street and only a few doors down from the newly created doctor's office. Alex dragged her inside before she could tell her ma anymore.

Bart Farley was on his hands and knees, groaning. A good sign that the blow hadn't knocked him cold for any longer. A ladder lay toppled over next to the gray-haired man.

Alex was at the man's side instantly, dropping to his knees. "Lie back, sir. Just let me look at you."

Bart resisted Alex's touch, his eyes glazed and unfocused.

His wife knelt beside Alex. "You heard him, Bart. Now you mind the doctor."

124

"Don't need no doctor, Gina. No sense fussin'." He sounded groggy, his voice faint and unsteady.

Alex got him onto his back despite the resistance and started talking. "You've gone and split your head clean open, Bart. Just stay still. It'll take me but a minute to check you over."

Beth saw at a glance that the man needed stitches. "I'm going for my bag." She whirled for the door.

"Beth, wait!"

Freezing, she looked at Alex and saw his panic. She said, "You go for the bag then."

Alex's throat worked as if he were trying desperately to swallow. His eyes went from Bart, still struggling to sit up, to Beth. "N–no, no, that's fine. You go."

"I'll hurry." Beth wanted to shake the man. But being needed like this had an amazing effect on her heart. She ran.

Panic seemed to blow straight out of the top of Alex's head.

Beth was gone. All he saw was blood.

He reached for the man's shoulders and tried to get him to lie back. The blood had flowed down the side of Bart's face. It coated his neck and shoulder, and now Alex's right hand. It was a titanic battle to keep from jumping away.

Light wavered. Bart faded, replaced by another man in another time and place. The man under Alex's hands moaned in agony. An explosion blasted dirt into Alex's back. He reeled forward. Maybe shrapnel instead of dirt. He couldn't feel any pain. The impact blasted him like bullets. The force of the explosion knocked him onto his hands and knees, so he sheltered the man beneath him, covering the horrible wounds from flying debris.

The scene before him widened from the bleeding man. He was outside. Blazing hot, arid, deafening noise, inhospitable sand stretching in all directions. Men, dead men, dying men lay bleeding, limbs severed.

Alex needed to get up, go to them. He looked back at the man he shielded with his body and scrambled back onto his knees. A shredded, blood-soaked United States Cavalry uniform. The soldier's disemboweled stomach gaped open. The man cried out, as if Alex had slit him open with a knife instead of the Comanche Indian who lay dead only feet away, a half dozen bullet holes ripped through the Indian warrior's chest. Blood seeped into the thirsty sand. The earth drinking up life. Feeding on men too foolish to avoid war. The man bleeding and moaning by Alex was dead. He just didn't know it yet. Alex had to fight back vomit as he watched the man try to stuff his guts back into his own belly. Death was imminent, but the man was beyond pain, acting on instinct, mindless.

Like war.

More explosions, bullets whizzed in all directions. Alex's back burned with pain. He'd been hit.

"Stay down!"

Alex hunched low over the man. Ignoring the dead. Protecting himself like a coward while life spilled, crimson and hot, out of Comanche and cavalry alike. Alex couldn't help. He was too terrified, too selfish, too stupid and cowardly. The smell of blood was like a drug, leaving him unable to think of anything but surviving this madness. Weak beyond salvation for letting everyone bleed and scream and die while he cowered and did nothing.

Alex groped for his doctor bag. Lifted it. Gore dripped from it, and entrails and stinking foul blood. He threw the ugly thing aside with a cry of horror. Threw it hard and far as if he could throw away failure and death. But no one could throw that hard. Failure and death were like a stench soaked into his soul. They never left.

"Alex!" The voice cut through the smoke.

The explosions stopped sharply, as if Alex had gone deaf. He looked up into blue eyes. Pretty, living, wise, compassionate eyes. Annoyed eyes.

The room came back into focus. The battlefield left behind.
Beth.

The general store. Bart. Another patient he failed.

Alex's eyes fell shut. He dropped his head in shame as Beth
ministered to this man. Not badly hurt at all.

How long had he been gone? How long had it taken Beth
to restore him to fragile sanity? To pull him back to the present?
How much of a madman had he appeared to be in front of
Bart's wife?

Tears burned in Alex's eyes. He hadn't cried in a long time.
He'd learned how to cry in war and spent a lot of time fighting
that show of weakness. Then finally the tears had dried up and
turned to stone in his heart.

Alex's prayers had gone, too. That ugly battle, toward the end
of what they called the Red River War, was when Alex knew
he couldn't do it anymore. That blood-soaked bag represented
everything he'd failed at. It represented the day he'd walked away
from his duties as an American, betrayed his country, his fellow
soldiers, his wounded patients. He'd walked away to let them
all die.

Only days later did he even notice the shrapnel in his back
and arms. He was soaked with blood from his neck to his knees.
A shocked man in a town with no name cared for Alex. The
wounds didn't kill him. But he was dead just the same. Just like
that eviscerated soldier, Alex was dead but still moving, too stupid
to lie down.

He started to rise to his feet and get away from this single
bleeding man. No decent person would want him if he knew the
whole ugly truth.

Beth grabbed his hand. "Can we be alone for a few minutes,
Mrs. Farley?"

"Well, I suppose. You're sure you don't need me?"

"We will need you in a bit, but for right now, we need things
absolutely quiet. Just step outside. I'll call you back in."

"Is. . .is the doctor all right?" Mrs. Farley asked unsteadily. "Is Bart hurt seriously?"

Alex wondered what in heaven's name he'd done. He opened his mouth to ask, but before he could speak, Beth did the talking for them.

"Yes, the doctor's fine. Bart's going to be fine, too. We just need a minute alone." Beth's voice soothed Mrs. Farley and Alex, too.

His senses seemed to heal. He finally had the presence of mind to look at her again.

That's where my strength lies. I have none of my own. I can't find my way back to You, God. Only with Beth can I be a doctor.

A prayer.

Alex had prayed more in the days since he'd met Beth than he had in the years he'd spent wandering the West since he'd run, a broken, cowardly traitor, from that brutal, ugly, senseless war.

The United States Government had allowed the decimation of the Indians' food source, turned a blind eye to the ruthless near-extermination of the buffalo. Then they'd made promises, food in exchange for the native people going to a reservation. The promises were largely broken and the Indians faced starvation if they stayed within their treaty borders, so they returned to their hunting grounds, more out of desperation than defiance.

Cattlemen came along with their herds of longhorns, and the Indians, hunters for countless generations, considered the cattle fair game. Clashes came, as was bound to happen.

The United States Army had turned its attention to the Civil War, and for a while the native people had been allowed to live their lives, which had included harassment of white settlers. Finally, with peace restored in the East, the government turned to settle the West. The time for treaties and talks was over and the cavalry was given the assignment of ridding the West of Indians. They went to the reservations and died or they left the reservations and died. The devil's own bargain.

Alex had been there to watch them die. His commander had insisted Alex focus on wounded soldiers first, and heaven knew there were plenty of them. Alex stood by during the deaths of so many.

They'd fought Comanche, Arapahoe, Cheyenne, and Kiowa. Alex had come to recognize their arrows and clothing and temperament. And fear them all. That part didn't make him a coward. Only a fool didn't fear a Comanche warrior.

But there were plenty of ways to show a yellow belly. And Alex had found them all. Alex wasn't fit to be near decent folks. He'd lived the last years denying his God-given gift for healing and remaining with those who were as indecent as he could find.

But Beth wouldn't let him go back where he belonged. She'd hate him if she knew all he'd done. Instead she'd married him.

He should never have allowed it. She'd be stained with his filth and failure. He'd kill again with his tenuous hold on reason. At least as a derelict who ran with drinkers and gamblers, though he didn't drink or gamble himself, he hadn't tainted anyone else.

God, forgive me. Protect Beth. Maybe I'll die and set her free.

But Alex had discovered, despite his best efforts, that he didn't die easily.

His nerves calmed. Beth's soothing voice rained her gentle ministrations down on Bart and healed Alex, too. He was able to turn to the wounded man and help. He could survive as long as she was within his grasp.

And from the assurance that he should shove her away to protect her came a soul-deep desire to hold her close forever. He'd married his very own personal savior. He knew that belonged to Jesus Christ, and that was where he should turn for strength. But for now, he needed Beth. Maybe when she'd healed him enough, strengthened him enough, he could turn back to God.

Seventeen

She'd married a lunatic and that was that.

Beth did her best not to care that she was married to a lunatic, but honestly, it was perturbing. A nice swat to Alex's head with a Stetson would have suited her right now, but there wasn't one handy. She held the idea in reserve for later.

"Here is the thread and needle, Alex." She talked to him in short words, enunciated clearly, to penetrate the fog he seemed to have sunk into. "You sew him up while I get the bandages out." *Ban-da-ges*, three syllable word. She hoped her lunatic husband could handle it.

Reaching for the thread with trembling hands, Beth thought how ridiculous it was that *he* was the doctor. *He* was the one everyone turned to. Worse yet, they might be right to do it. It galled her to admit it, but Alex was a better hand than she with the sutures. At least he was when his hands weren't shaking.

She did a nice job, but she didn't have his skill. She knew the work Alex did would heal faster and leave less of a scar.

The big, dumb jerk.

Beth didn't wander off in case her beloved husband drifted off into whatever asylum he lived in when she stepped away from his side.

Being married was going to be a pure nuisance. She did fetch a washbasin, found fortunately right in the same room. Alex would probably sew his own brains away from his backbone if she left his sight. Blessed, or possibly cursed, with incredible empathy, Beth couldn't help wondering what Alex had gone through to have scarred him so deeply.

The poor, big, dumb jerk.

They soon had Bart Farley sewn up, washed up, and tucked into bed with the help of Mrs. Farley. Bart was already grousing about going to bed when there was work to be done, which Beth took as a good sign. They left him to Mrs. Farley's capable care.

Heading back to the hospital, Beth saw that her ma's and pa's horses were tied up in front of the building where Sally rested. Her folks would have things in hand. Now was as good a time as any. She grabbed Alex's wrist and dragged him into an alley. She needed to figure out the source of his madness before she could fix him. Now was the time to dig into his head. And she intended to do that digging even if she needed to use a pickax. She opened her mouth to start yelling.

"Thank you." Alex pulled her so close she couldn't breathe and kissed every angry thought right out of her head.

"I heard you're looking for a man?" A ferretlike man scuttled out of an alley.

Cletus looked the man over. He knew better than to trust this one, but most of his information came from sources like this. Purchased for the price of a pint of whiskey usually. It was Cletus's job to sort the truth from the lies, but he was good at it. "I am."

"C–can we have this—this meeting over there?" The man's hands trembled as he pointed toward a saloon. His lips quivered.

He had a thirsty look, a desperate thirsty look.

"Let's go." Cletus led the way.

A half hour later, and a few bits poorer, Cletus smiled down at the notes he'd taken. This was it. The most promising description yet. He stepped out of the bar, missing the smoke and stench of liquor and men enjoying themselves.

A woman gasped and crossed in the middle of the dirt street to get away from him.

Maybe his smile was a little mean. Grunting in satisfaction, he tucked the paper in his pocket. Cletus swung up on his horse and turned it toward the trail. If it was true, Buchanan had been brought low. He'd be easy to catch. Cletus liked things easy.

Of course, in a dead-or-alive situation, Cletus preferred dead. Easier to transport a dead body than a live one. No escape attempts. But if Buchanan was as low-down as it sounded, turning his back on dying men, running like a yellow coward to save himself, it might not be that easy to find an excuse to shoot the man.

Chuckling, Cletus decided not to spend time pondering it. He'd find a way. Or wait until he was alone and make up something.

When it came to dead or alive, Cletus liked to keep things simple.

Alex wrapped her up tight and made her part of him. He was a married man. Right in front of God, he'd said his vows to the prettiest woman he'd ever seen, with strength enough for both of them.

"I can be a doctor if you're with me." He eased himself back and saw Beth, her eyes focused on his lips. She wanted this closeness as badly as he did. Well, it was more than Alex had ever hoped for. And he saw no reason not to send all his mending patients home—right now—and close up the doctor's office for the day and just practice being married as the good Lord intended. He lowered his head toward those pretty pink lips.

"Buchanan, get out here."

Alex's eyes dropped shut. His father-in-law. Wonderful, just whom he hoped to see right now.

Alex let loose of Beth with considerable reluctance, slid one arm around her waist to remind Clay the woman belonged to him. He had a moment of such power and pleasure that he was tempted to call Clay "Pa" just to see what would happen. Surely Beth wouldn't let her pa kill him.

Fighting the smile that wanted to spread across his face, Alex said, "What's the problem?" He tried to sound interested, since Clay's daughter was one of the patients back at the doctor's office.

"Luther took some of the men out to bury the bodies in from the stage wreck, and we've got a big problem."

Alex felt his throat begin to swell shut from panic. He glanced at Beth. "How close did you watch yesterday when I did that throat surgery on Sally?"

"Real close." Beth blinked her eyes like a sleepy owl being forced awake in the daylight. "Why?"

"No reason. Just good to know you could perform the surgery should it be called for." Alex turned back to Clay, who'd narrowed his eyes. That look probably came from finding his daughter being kissed in an alley. Wife or not, it was a disrespectful location for such a thing, no denying it. He hoped to find a spare moment, before Clay killed him, to point out that Beth had dragged Alex in there, not the other way around.

"Come on out here. I need to talk to you about the folks who died in that stagecoach wreck." Clay worded it like a request, but Alex saw no choice but to obey, even knowing what his brand-new Pa wanted. Alex was going to be asked to deal with the dead bodies.

Alex walked toward Clay, compelled to move by a will one thousand times stronger than his own—his wife dragged him. "I'm not a mortician, McClellen. I don't get bodies ready for burial."

"You come, too, Beth. I need to ask you some questions. I've sent for the Armitages, too."

Suddenly Alex wasn't quite so scared. This wasn't about laying out a line of corpses. This was about what had happened out on that trail. Alex could handle that. Probably.

Beth came alongside Alex and he slid his arm back around her, this time to hold himself steady.

Coward. Weakling. Failure. Traitor.

The words described him perfectly. He should let go of her, send her back to her pa. Go crawl out in the desert to die. Instead he clung tightly to his wife.

The alley was shaded, and when Beth and Alex stepped out into the sunlight, Alex blinked before he focused on the men standing across the street. No bodies.

Two fully bearded old men and a black man, younger but still with shots of gray through his hair. Alex had seen the old men at McClellen's ranch. Luther and Buff, they'd been called. Adam had been at church yesterday and, with his wife, took the McClellens' children after the accident. He remembered Tillie had been there at the parson's house. Lots of yesterday was a blur.

"They already buried the bodies, Alex." Clay leaned down, nearly whispering into Beth's ear. Alex could hear but no one else was close enough. "But this morning the sheriff rode out to the ranch real early. He went through the papers that didn't belong to any survivors. Figured to find heirs and send word back, along with any money, to whomever would miss those folks. The driver and the man riding with him are known men around here, but the sheriff found papers that had to belong to the woman who died."

Alex remembered that poor woman, lying dead, her eyes begging him to help her. He'd have killed himself trying if Beth hadn't stopped him.

Through the window to Alex's doctor's office, Sophie was visible at Sally's side. Parson Radcliff came pacing down the street, most likely to visit his wife.

The sheriff was talking with Luther, Buff, and Adam, glancing over at Clay every few seconds.

"This young woman has the same name as Mandy's husband. You told me that the other night, Beth."

"Yes, I remember." Beth sounded as if she grieved for a woman she'd never known. She sounded wounded. Alex hated to think of all the wounds that were in store for her as a doctor. "She's the right age. I wondered if she could be Mandy's sister-in-law. Celeste Gray could have been our family."

Clay made a sound so rude it shocked Alex. Why disparage the poor dead woman? "We found her satchel. The paperwork in it is almighty troubling. The only reason I'm telling you two is because you know her name and I don't want you saying anything about her being family to that low-down, yellow coyote of a husband of Mandy's."

Alex, leaning in to listen, jerked his head up at the venom in Clay's voice.

Beth jumped, too, so Alex wasn't wrong in thinking this was a level of anger Beth wasn't used to. "What's wrong, Pa?"

"The sheriff, Buff, Luther, and Adam are the only ones but me who've seen those papers. If we're readin' 'em right, that young woman was *married* to Sidney Gray. The man your sister married just two days ago."

Beth gasped. "What?"

Alex's eyes felt as if they bulged out of his head. A married man, courting Clay McClellen's daughter, and marrying her to boot. The man was a fool.

He glanced at Beth and saw the outrage on her face. She might be a kindly, compassionate woman, but she was a Texas cowgirl at heart. She looked ready to saddle a horse and set out after her sister.

Alex hoped Mandy was as tough, because a man who would tell such lies couldn't be trusted in anything. And right now he had Mandy at his mercy. He'd never even *met* Mandy and Alex was ready to hunt Sidney Gray down.

"I've already wired the town up the trail, hoping to catch Mandy before she gets on the train. I told her it was urgent she come home."

The four men—the sheriff, Buff, Luther, and Adam—approached Alex's little circle as Clay went on. "But I didn't put the truth of what we found in a telegram for the whole world to see, so she might not mind me. I ought to hear right away if she's headed back. If she's not, I know they're heading for Denver. I'll ride out to fetch her home."

"The wire already came, Clay," Luther said. "The telegraph office said the train for Denver went through last night late, and Mandy was on it for sure. She's gone."

Clay's teeth ground together. With a short, hard jerk of his chin, he turned toward his horse. "I'll be going then."

Luther's hand landed hard on Clay's arm. "Nope, you can't ride off to save your daughter and abandon the rest of your family, Clay. You'll be gone for weeks getting to Denver. And it's a big city. Finding her will be hard work."

"Oh—yes—I—can—go get my daughter." Clay's tone made Alex's stomach twist. The man was furious at this dishonor of Mandy.

"Clay, think for a second," Luther said. "You know we'd watch the ranch and your family while you were gone. But you could be all winter hunting Mandy up."

Alex saw Clay's eyes go to the window framing Sophie.

"Your young'uns and Sophie need you. Buff and I have already decided. We're riding out for Mandy as soon as we get the packhorses loaded. We'll bring her back."

Clay's deadly eyes went from Luther to Buff to Sophie. "It don't sit right to let anyone else take care of this business. This is a father's duty."

Those words cut at Alex's heart. A father's duty. His father had used that word many times. *Duty*. But he'd always talked about Alex's duty to the family business. But Alex had no interest in running an industry. He'd wanted to heal. He'd been called to it. A father had a duty, too.

His father hadn't seen that side of things. Clay McClellen did.

Beth spoke up. "You know, Pa, Mandy is legally married to Sidney. That woman was dead for hours before the time you told me Mandy said her wedding vows."

"Sidney didn't know that. He went right ahead and married her. Then he took off with her, probably knew he had a wife out there looking for him."

"That don't make the wedding less legal." Beth looked at Alex, and Alex saw fear in Beth's eyes. "He's got rights over Mandy now."

Which meant Alex had rights over Beth. He felt a little dizzy just thinking about it.

Clay looked at Beth as if she were a puzzle he'd been trying to solve for years. "You think Mandy'll see it that way?"

"It's the truth. Why would she see it any other way?"

"Then she'll have to divorce him."

Beth shuddered. "That would be a scandal for sure."

Even Alex nodded. He'd barely heard of a divorce. It was a word spoken rarely and then in hushed, horrified tones. To get a divorce was a slap in God's face. A blatant breaking of a vow made straight to heaven. Alex had never known anyone to do such a thing.

"I can solve that problem right quick, Clay. Reckon Sidney'll make it easy for me, too." Luther turned and headed for his horse.

Buff followed silently.

Clay nodded as he watched the old men.

As Luther swung up on his horse, Alex couldn't quite keep his mouth shut. "How can he solve a problem like that?"

Clay turned back to Alex and gave him a look that turned him ice cold in the burning Texas heat. "He can unmarry 'em with his Winchester."

Eighteen

Mandy had taken a beating.

After days on the rough-riding train, which stopped in every little town along the way, zigzagged east, then back west on its way north, even Sidney had lapsed into a sullen stupor. No more nonsense about sneaking off to luggage cars.

They were rushing to beat winter, but Mandy knew there was more involved than just getting there. They needed to get settled.

Nights were cooler as they headed north, but the late August weather was hot and sunny, turning the train car into an oven. Mandy felt about half-baked.

The train stopped now and again, and Mandy and Sidney got off to eat on Sidney's dwindling money. They'd stretch their legs, but the train paused only long enough to take on water and coal, then they went straight back to chugging along.

With every chuff of smoke, every clack of the wheels, Mandy felt herself moving farther and farther from her beloved family. Although she wept in the dark of night, when Sidney slept, she refused to let the tears fall during the day.

138

Sidney hated tears even more than Pa. Although Pa was more afraid of tears—the only thing Mandy knew of that her father feared—they made Sidney angry. Sidney said her loyalty belonged to him. And he was right. So the tears hardened in her throat until they felt like stones she carried inside her chest.

Mandy couldn't see why Sidney thought she couldn't love him and her family. Her heart had room for both. Some days those unshed tears seemed to lodge in her heart and focus on Sidney.

Please, God, don't let me be unloving to my husband. Protect me from that. Forgive me for that. Protect me from the heartache I've felt ever since I left my family behind. Protect me.

One morning, after another brutally uncomfortable night of trying to sleep sitting up, Mandy looked out the window in the first light of dawn. She gasped at the view.

Mountains. Majestic, beautiful mountains. They were finally getting to their destination if the mountains were near.

It took the whole day, but they finally saw signs of a big town ahead. Denver. They'd made it.

Mandy watched out the window as the outskirts of town slipped by the ever-slowing train. She reached out and grabbed Sidney's hand. "It's so big!"

Sidney laughed. "This is nothin'. I grew up in Boston. Now *that's* a big town."

A magnificent building loomed ahead of them and above them as they drew nearer. It was built as if it wanted to rival the mountains for grandeur. Mandy saw a crowd gathered near the front of the massive, intimidating building. No doubt the spot the train would stop.

Mandy's heart began pounding.

Oh, Lord, protect me.

She'd never left Mosqueros before. She'd never seen a town like this. She'd read Beth's letters and thought she knew what a city was like, but nothing had prepared her for this reality. She didn't know how a person lived in a town. How did a person hunt for food? Grow a garden? Find lumber to build a log cabin?

A man stood on a box or something to boost him higher than the surrounding mob. He was yelling.

Mandy could hear the anger in his voice but not the actual words over the locomotive's blasting whistle and screeching brakes. The roiling crowd shoved and grumbled. She saw someone draw a gun and aim it straight up. The sharp crack split the air.

Mandy's hand went to her Winchester, leaning on the seat at her side. Her blood cooled as it did in times of danger. Her senses sharpened until she could swear she smelled that crowd of men and the burn of gunpowder. She rubbed on the callus on her trigger finger while sleet shot through her veins and she waited to fight, protect, defend. It was what she was best at.

As they drew closer, Mandy realized that the only place to leave the train was going to be right into that crowd. Cool, she turned to her new husband, the man who had vowed to love and cherish her. And protect her. Though she probably would be the one doing the protecting.

"I've never been in a city this big before." She kept her eyes flat. Even watching Sidney she was aware of all that went on around her. The growing noise, the anger in the crowd. "If we get separated we might never find each other. I don't think we should step out into that crowd."

Protect me, Lord. Protect us both.

"Don't be childish. You'll be fine." Sidney scowled.

Then the gun fired again and again. A woman screamed.

Sidney flinched. "Maybe you're right. Just looking at that building makes me wonder. Denver isn't the way I heard it was. They might not be so interested in a man with a few lawyer skills." Sidney gave her a weak, nervous smile, then cleared his throat. "I don't know what's going on, but we can't go out into that mess."

Mandy would have gone. She had her hand tight on her rifle and she'd have done it if Sidney insisted, but she was delighted not to step out into that mob scene. "You can be a lawyer anywhere, can't you? Let's find a smaller town. A place where we can homestead. We'll check the land offices in the towns up the trail. I'll help get a place set up for us. I know the land. We'll live close enough to town for you to go in and earn money while I get us settled. I've even helped build a cabin before. Ma and Pa saw to it that all of us learned survival skills. I know how that works in the country but not in the city. I couldn't hunt a deer or find firewood in a city."

Sidney looked between the shoving crowd and Mandy. He finally turned to her and said, "I think you're right. It's. . .it's different from how I thought it'd be. I was going to find us a hotel. Someone gave me the name of a lawyer he heard wanted help."

Sidney's eyes shifted as he said that, and Mandy wondered if Sidney was so sure about that job. "But I'd have to find work fast. We don't have a lot of money to live on until some starts coming in."

"Surely you have enough to pay for another day's fare." Mandy had some, but her ma had recommended not mentioning that, saving it for emergencies. Mandy wondered if that was dishonest, but Ma had talked about hard times and the years they spent living a meager life before Pa—Mandy's second pa, Clay—had come and taken them out of their awful little shack hidden in a thicket.

"Hard times can come on a family." Ma had pressed the paper bills into Mandy's hand during a private moment before the wedding. "My pa sent me off with some money, and now I'll do the same for you. But it's just between you and me, Mandy. It's best to always lay a bit of money up and try your best to live without it. And it might—might hurt Sidney's pride to think I helped you. Best not to tell him, not unless it's absolutely necessary."

Now that rather large roll of bills lay tucked in the bottom of Mandy's shoe. An uncomfortable lump that suddenly seemed to offer security in a world gone mad.

Mandy hadn't counted it and she didn't intend to for a while. Not if she could convince Sidney to leave this awful, dirty, sprawling city. If she could just find a patch of land to homestead, with good hunting nearby. Mandy had heard Pa, Luther, and Buff talk about the mountains. She thought she'd picked up enough details to know what to look for, come hunting time. And maybe she could even do some trapping, have fur pelts to sell. She had her rifle and a Colt revolver in her trunk. Pa had packed in a hunting knife, a whetstone, and a few basic tools, plus enough ammunition to start a war. Mandy and Sidney could live without the money for now.

Sidney turned and looked at her. "You want to homestead? I've heard it's a hard life."

"I'm used to hard work. It doesn't scare me. Maybe we can ride until we find some flat land tucked right up against the mountains. I could grow a garden. The mountains are covered with trees to build a house. And the Rockies are rich hunting land." Mandy felt devious, but she decided to add, "Maybe we could even find a bit of gold if we're lucky. My pa's father found gold and left it to Pa when he died. It helped us buy our ranch back after some bad men took it from us. You're always hearing about gold strikes in the Rockies."

Sidney's eyes took on a strange gleam. She'd finally said the magic word to persuade him to continue on.

The train conductor walked through the half-filled train car. "We can't pull in here, folks. The engineer has decided not to face that mob at the station. Those of you who wanted to get off here, we'll let you off farther down the rails a bit and we'll find wagons to transport you, or if you can, just ride on to the next stop."

All of the passengers stared at the ruckus then stayed firmly in their seats. Because of the irregularity of the train avoiding the mob, the conductor didn't ask for tickets after they'd let the passengers off who were staying in Denver.

Mandy was content to leave the city far behind. She and

Sidney went to the land office in each little town. They'd ask questions about homesteading and come away disappointed each time at the distance they'd have to live from town. Mandy wasn't worried about living far out of town. She liked the idea. But Sidney wouldn't hear of it.

Nothing was just right, even as they passed Laramie and headed into Montana. The days began to fade together as Mandy waited for Sidney to find a place to suit him. There was no money to leave the train, even for a day or two, so the wedding night Sidney had so longed for seemed to be long forgotten.

He did finally decide to leave the train though. Not because it suited him but because the rails ended in Butte, Montana. With a sigh of relief, Mandy saw the beautiful landscape and thought they'd be able to find a nice place near Butte.

And then the land office manager said the exact wrong thing to Sidney about little Helena, Montana, the territorial capital. "Gold."

Sidney decided their journey wasn't yet over. Helena was yet another day's ride by stagecoach. There, Mandy hoped and prayed they'd stop.

Mandy needed to write her family and tell them where she was, except first she needed to know where this journey would finally end.

Nineteen

Doctor, where are you?" The voice from downstairs almost sounded like the woman was singing.

Alex cringed. Beth rolled her eyes. They were finishing a quick noon meal in their rooms above the doctor's office.

"That woman is *not* sick." Alex gave Beth a look so comically painful, it was all she could do not to start laughing.

"She just needs the attention." Beth, thanks to Ma and Pa's help, now felt nearly at home. Her family had brought in some furniture and her clothing. Ma had even scrounged up some clothes for Alex and stocked the cupboards. Beth and Alex had been too busy to give it a thought.

Now Beth sat in a white shirtwaist and dark gray riding skirt. Alex had a change of pants and shirt. All of it had been provided by someone else. Not out of financial need, but because in the week they'd been married, the rush hadn't stopped, day or night.

"Well, you go down and pay attention to her," he hissed. They had to whisper because Mrs. Gallup was already coming upstairs. There was no hiding from Nora Gallup. Fastest

Whimper in the West.

"Me?" Beth rested her fingertips on her chest with playful grace. "Why, I'd love to, you generous man. But of course—"

"There you are, Dr. Buchanan." Nora barged right into their living quarters.

Beth smirked at Alex. No one would do for Mrs. Gallup but the doctor. The *real* doctor. Beth had never been so happy to be a woman. She let it irritate her a tiny bit that the woman invaded their living space, then shrugged. If they wanted to stop the woman, they were going to have to buy a lock and that was that. Beth looked at the determined woman. Nearly five foot nine, over two hundred pounds, fast moving, and as healthy as a horse.

It would have to be a sturdy lock.

"I'm frantic, Dr. Buchanan. I've had a terrible stabbing pain in my chest all morning. I'm afraid it's my heart again."

Beth doubted it. "Go on down, Doctor. I'll clean up here then join you."

Alex's hand landed on Beth's wrist in its usual vise-like way. But in this case, Beth didn't think Alex was actually turning to her for strength and courage. Well, courage maybe, but only because Nora was seriously scary. By the end of this woman's complaint-filled visit, Beth would be ready to cry for her mama.

"I can use the assistance, Mrs. Buchanan." Alex smiled but his eyes were pathetic. Begging. He did *not* want to be alone with Mrs. Gallup.

Beth knew why, too. The woman seemed bent on being examined from head to foot. Closely examined—*everywhere.*

It wasn't as if the middle-aged woman had designs on Alex. Beth knew that. The woman was just determined to discover an illness. She brought a well-worn medical book along to the exams and gave Alex suggestions.

She didn't insist on the extremely close examination if Beth was around, but Beth had stepped out back to the privy one time and Mrs. Gallup had come in during Beth's absence. Alex had barely lived to tell the tale. Beth came along quietly, to spare all three of them the embarrassment of watching Alex beg.

Mrs. Gallup was cosseted and encouraged and given treatment for stress. Alex suggested soothing baths, chamomile tea, long walks, and he'd even lent her Beth's beloved copy of Jane Austen's *Sense and Sensibility*. For a while, Beth clung to the book desperately. But, being the next thing to a doctor's assigned treatment, Mrs. Gallup was desperate to read it and promised to care for it and bring it back soon. Beth finally acquiesced, quietly gloating because Alex had just ensured yet another visit, which was inevitable in any case. *Sense and Sensibility* was no medical textbook, but Beth didn't underestimate Mrs. Gallup's ability to find something within those pages that she could mangle until it alerted her to a new illness. All told, it took Alex and Beth an hour to convince the woman she wasn't dying.

"You know, Doctor," Beth said sardonically as the woman closed the door behind her, "one of these days that woman really is going to be sick, and you'll miss it because you're so used to ignoring and patronizing her."

Alex groaned out loud and rubbed his face. "You're probably right."

Beth snickered and poked Alex in the ribs.

He grabbed her hand to stop her. "She'll come in with a broken arm and I'll pat her on the head and send her on her way."

"I'm picturing how it will be at her funeral." Beth swept the hand Alex wasn't restraining grandly in front of them.

"In the unlikely event that woman doesn't outlive us both." Alex tugged Beth toward him.

She was spun to face him and gasped in surprise at how close they were and how comfortable being close felt. "The parson will stand there and talk about that poor, poor woman and how nobody listened to her."

Alex clamped his arms around Beth's waist. "Then he'll

spend an hour yelling at me for prescribing hot tea for a woman whose heart was failing."

Beth settled her hands on his chest, fighting a smile. "They'll forbid you to ever practice medicine again."

"No chance." Alex shook his head with a mock scowl. "I would never be that lucky."

Beth laughed and a smile bloomed on Alex's lips. He didn't smile much and when he flashed his shining white teeth and lifted the dour expression he so often wore, Beth felt like it was a personal victory. She enjoyed coaxing an upturn out of his lips.

Then those smiling lips leaned close and kissed her. Freezing like a startled animal, Beth drew in her breath until Alex's lips sealed her away from air.

They'd been so busy. Running day and night since they'd gotten married days ago, but Beth had wondered when this might happen. She was her mother's daughter after all. Ma had told her what marriage meant. And how it could be.

Then Alex deepened the kiss and pulled her closer. Beth quit thinking and wound her arms around her husband's neck with a small sound of pleasure. Moments passed and Beth enjoyed the touch of her husband.

"Beth," Alex whispered against her lips, "I feel like I'm alive again."

Beth ran one hand into his dark, closely shorn hair. "You've always been alive, Alex."

Nodding, Alex said, "I just haven't been living. I look back on my life and see that I've wasted so much time. I just couldn't handle all the bad things I'd seen." His eyes darkened.

Beth spoke quickly to keep her husband from sinking into the morose thoughts that plagued him. "I've been praying so hard that you'd find peace."

"Peace. Yeah, maybe that's what this is. I haven't had a nightmare in days."

Beth knew he'd been pulled into some kind of waking

nightmare when he'd doctored Mr. Farley. But she slept beside him every night and his sleep hadn't been disturbed. "Peace with your memories and, I hope, peace with God." Beth waited, hoping her husband would really talk to her for once. If he could talk about the emotional scars he carried, maybe they'd lose the power to haunt him.

"God." Alex ran one finger down Beth's cheek while his arm stayed wrapped tight around her waist. "Yes, I started praying again the day I met you. I believe I've found Him again. I started believing that maybe, just maybe, I deserved God's forgiveness for all that I've done."

"None of us deserves forgiveness. None of us is guiltless. 'For all have sinned and come short of the glory of God.'"

"But there's sin and there's sin. Mine were very close to unforgivable. But I've always believed in God's ability to forgive. It's just these last days that I've felt like I even had a right to ask."

"So you've asked at last? You've come back to your faith?" Beth had a hard time imagining softhearted Alex doing something truly awful.

"No, but I've been praying for my patients and for you."

"For me, really?"

"Yes, all prayers of thanksgiving." Alex's eyes caressed her face as gently as that one finger. "If you're willing, maybe you could pray with me now, while I finally dare to ask Him."

"I would love to pray with you, Alex." Beth leaned close and kissed him gently.

They held each other while Alex turned and faced God, for himself and his own sins. Beth felt him stand straight, as if a weight lifted off his shoulders. He didn't speak aloud exactly what burden he carried, and Beth hoped it wasn't because he was still harboring guilt.

When Alex's prayer ended, Beth asked, "Do you want to tell me what you've been through? Would it help?"

"Maybe someday." Alex pulled her closer and lowered his lips to hers, returning the kiss she'd given him. He raised his head. "But right now, I feel like being close to my sweet, new wife. Would you like that, Beth? Do you want a real marriage to me?"

She smiled and curled her arms around his neck.

He surprised her when he swept her up into his arms. She broke the kiss and their eyes met. Their bond was as strong as ever, but it had changed. For the first time what passed between them was laced with something other than Alex's need for her strength. He gave instead of took. He leaned closer, lowering his lips to hers.

The office door slammed open.

Alex as good as dropped her as he turned to face the Armitages. Fortunately, Beth was clinging to his neck and only her feet swung to the floor.

Mr. Armitage. Due to have his arm checked.

Beth gave Alex a quick pat on the back. She said, "Have a seat, Mr. Armitage." His wife came in right behind him.

Beth walked away from Alex quickly to keep herself from grabbing him and abandoning the Armitages to doctor themselves.

As she began removing Mr. Armitage's sling from his perfectly healing arm, the door slammed open again. They were lucky not to have lost a window.

"Doctor, my boy's got a fever and a rash." A young woman rushed in, nearly staggering under the weight of a young child.

Beth saw Alex's shoulder slump, then he got hold of himself and hurried to the woman, relieving her of the burden of her little boy. "Looks like measles."

Highly contagious. They'd soon be overrun.

Beth gave up on stealing away with her husband and rolled up the sleeves of her white shirtwaist to get back to doctoring. With a quiet sigh, Beth reminded herself sternly that this was what she'd always wanted.

Mandy stepped off the stagecoach and her legs buckled.

Sidney caught her, but he stumbled back and let the stage catch him.

Mandy looked behind her. "Thank you."

Sidney set her on her feet with a wan smile. "We made it."

She nodded. They hadn't quite made it really, but it was finally close. Sidney had found the place he wanted to be.

Thank You, Jesus.

Mandy squared her shoulders, hooked her Winchester over her shoulder where it belonged, and oversaw the unloading of the things her parents had sent along. Not a lot, but Mandy knew her folks. Even while they were trying to convince Mandy to stay, they'd been planning for if she went. Ma and Pa would have seen to the right supplies.

The town of Helena was much bigger than Mandy had expected, but still only a fraction of the size of Denver. The land office was right next door to the stage station and still open for the day, although the sun was low in the sky. After a quick talk with the station manager, they left their box, trunk, and satchels behind under his watchful eyes and hurried to the land office.

Homesteading wasn't difficult—at least the part where they claimed the land. The closest they could get to town was over twenty miles, but there was water on the claim, or so the land agent said, and trees to build a cabin. More woodland than pasture land, they were told.

Mandy looked at Sidney. "We can't live there. You won't be able to get into town to work." If they pushed hard they could hopefully make it in two days with all their things to carry.

She thought of her few precious dollars from her ma and knew they wouldn't last long if they had to rent a room in Helena.

"This is fine. I can take a twenty-mile ride twice a day on a good horse." Sidney signed the homesteading agreement with a flourish.

Mandy didn't contradict him in front of the agent, thinking

to his manly feelings. But once they'd taken the careful directions and stepped outside, Mandy whispered, "Sidney, we don't have a horse."

Sidney smiled at her, that cheerful, confident smile that had first drawn her to him. "We'll get one before long."

"How?" Mandy thought of her money.

"I'm planning to find gold." Sidney smiled then marched to the stage station. He stumbled to a stop when he reached the heavy box and trunk they needed to cart twenty miles. "Why did your parents send all this junk along? Let's just leave it here."

"I can rent a handcart for two bits." Mandy pointed to a sign.

Sidney frowned as if it was just occurring to him how far twenty miles was.

Mandy arranged for the cart and they loaded their belongings into it and headed southwest. Each of them grabbed a handle on the cart, and Mandy enjoyed the sense of their working together. Life could be good if they built a tight cabin and the hunting was easy.

"We'll get out of town and find a sheltered spot to camp for the night," Mandy said as they left Helena behind. "Then we'll get an early start tomorrow."

Sidney turned to her with a light in his eyes. "So we'll finally have us a wedding night."

Trust her husband to focus on the frivolous. Mandy wondered how long it would take Sidney to realize they didn't have any food for supper. It had been a long day on the trail. Her muscles were cramped and battered. Sidney hadn't shaved since they'd left Mosqueros, and neither of them smelled any too good. Mandy felt a headache coming on but didn't mention it.

As they began to put space behind them from bustling Helena, the light left the sky. It was then Mandy saw a fire flickering ahead. She heard the deep lowing of cattle from behind an outcropping of rock on the rugged land and knew what they'd come upon. Someone was holding a herd of cattle just outside of

151

town. No doubt to sell it. Mandy had eaten many a meal around a campfire in her life and her stomach growled at the thought of piping hot coffee and tough, savory beef.

"Hold up, Sidney." She set her side of the cart down. Sidney's forehead was soaked with sweat and he was breathing hard. Mandy was more used to the rugged life, but she was feeling overwhelmed at the thought of the long walk ahead and the brutally hard work they faced to be ready for winter.

Sidney gladly set his side of the cart down. "Time to stop for the night?"

Mandy pointed at the flickering fire. "It's a campsite. Let's go in and see if we can sleep near their fire."

"What about the two of us being alone?" Sidney's impatience was clear.

They heard a voice yell, "Come and get it!"

Sidney's impatience was overridden by hunger. "It's proper for a camp like that to welcome strangers, isn't it? I've heard that."

"I reckon they'll share a meal with us." Mandy smiled and Sidney smiled back. Good, the man had some common sense after all.

"Let's go say howdy." Sidney's smile widened, and Mandy remembered why she loved him.

Which wasn't to say she'd forgotten. She'd just been really tired ever since she'd said, "I do."

They headed for the fire towing their cart. When they were within hailing distance, she put out her hand to stop Sidney.

"What is it?" He sounded eager to be on his way to dinner.

"There's a proper way to approach a cow camp. This close to town I doubt they're apt to suspect us of mischief, but a cattle drive crew is always ready for trouble. We want to make sure they don't think we qualify." Mandy felt her nerves steady and her blood cool, but not overly.

Sidney swallowed and looked lost.

"Let me do it." Mandy waited until Sidney nodded. She

shouted, "Hello, the camp."

Her female voice was probably a good idea. A bunch of cowpokes weren't likely to start shooting at a woman. Not unless they were severely provoked. Mandy heard about ten guns being cocked. It didn't scare her. She could see the makings of a well-run cow camp, and she respected the tough life on a cattle drive. Having a fire iron drawn and cocked was just good sense.

"Come on in slow," another woman answered.

The female voice surprised Mandy. She was also surprised by her urge to cry. A woman, out here, with the cattle drive. All of the loneliness for her family hit her like a closed fist. Mandy had her hands full not just breaking straight into tears and howling her head off.

"Let's go." She didn't look at Sidney because she didn't want him to see the tears she felt brimming in her eyes. To stop the nonsense, she hollered as she walked forward, "We're homesteading about twenty miles from town. We're just looking for a place to sleep for the night. Then we'll be on our way." Mandy walked and talked, her cart between her and Sidney.

As she got close in the settling dusk, she saw several women. The one who'd called out stood to the front, her rifle out but pointed to the ground. Even in the dim light, Mandy noticed the woman's deep tan. She looked like she might be Indian. But as Mandy got closer, she saw the woman had hazel eyes and that didn't fit.

The woman wore a fringed buckskin jacket with some of the fringe missing. That meant she was a working cowpoke, because the point of having the fringe was to have a piggin' string handy. And just from the look of the setup, it appeared the woman was in charge.

Mandy's heart pounded harder as she recognized the strength, the command. It was a look Mandy had seen in her own mother's eyes many times.

The woman had on a split riding skirt made of softly tanned

doeskin, worn and dirty and obviously the clothes of a rancher.

Mandy was every bit as dirty, but it wasn't the honest dirt of hard work.

"You're welcome at our fire." The woman set her gun aside, but Mandy noticed none of the others did.

"I'm Mandy, and this is my husband, Sidney Gray. We're new to Montana."

"I'm Belle Harden and this is my family and my cowhands. C'mon in and rest yourselves."

Mandy looked around and saw more women. No, not women, girls. The oldest two might be a bit younger than Mandy, but full grown. The older ones had white-blond hair, one was a fiery redhead younger than Laurie, another just a toddler, so dark she really might be Indian.

"These are my girls, Lindsay and Emma." Belle pointed to the blonds. "Sarah's toting my son, Tanner." The redhead had a baby strapped on her back.

"And the little one running around is Betsy." Belle pointed fondly at the three-year-old who waved and yelled, "Hi."

"Betsy?" Mandy felt as if her throat was swelling shut. "As in Elizabeth?"

"Yep." Belle came up close to Mandy, taking note of her rifle.

"I've got a sister named Elizabeth. We call her Beth." Mandy shook her head to fight off a sudden urge to cry. She noticed lots of men. It was a strong crew driving a few hundred head of cattle. Mandy did a quick estimate with her experienced eye and guessed three or four hundred head. This reminded her so much of the times she and her sisters and Ma had horned in on a roundup, Mandy couldn't help herself.

Despite the years of her father's scolding and pleading, despite Sidney's moody way of punishing her, despite her own common sense. . .Mandy burst into tears.

The woman's forehead wrinkled briefly. Then she strode forward and pulled Mandy into her arms.

Twenty

It's a girl!" Beth lifted the messy, wriggling newborn up so her mother could see.

"My girl. I got my girl. Oh, I wanted her so badly." Mrs. Stoddard burst into tears of joy.

Beth spared the baby her first spanking when the tiny darling started squalling the cry of a healthy, lively infant. Beth couldn't quit smiling as she quickly washed up the baby. It was just the two of them. Oops. Beth grinned as she wrapped the little one in a soft blanket. Three not two.

Alex had gone out of the room to sit with the expectant father. The older children, three active, handsome sons, all school-aged, had long ago gone to bed.

Beth and Mrs. Stoddard had done this peacefully by themselves. Mrs. Stoddard had even protested that her husband had sent for the doctor. She'd given birth to all three of her older boys without help. But her husband went all nervous on her and snuck away for help. Mrs. Stoddard had been a good sport about it, on the condition that only Beth stay with her.

Alex had agreed with the woman's request for privacy. He had left, assuring Mr. Stoddard he'd stay close in the event of need, and he went to rock by the fire with the anxious father.

Beth crooned at the baby as she settled her into her mother's arms then went to invite Mr. Stoddard in to meet his daughter.

The man almost ran over Beth in his haste to reach his wife's side.

Beth could see that Alex's eyes were heavy with sleep. She couldn't keep the smile off her face when she scolded. "You've been napping while I've been hard at work."

Alex didn't deny it. He walked by her side to the buckboard and lent a hand to boost her up. They drove out of the Stoddards' yard on the long trail for Mosqueros.

Slipping his arm around Beth's waist, he said, "Lean on me. Try and sleep."

"I can't. I'm wide awake. I love delivering babies." Beth did lay her head on his strong shoulder. But her blood was coursing through her veins, as it always did after a birth.

"You get all the good jobs." Alex's supporting arm tightened and Beth enjoyed the feeling.

"Can you believe how hectic it's been since we opened the doctor's office?"

"It was bad enough without the measles outbreak." Alex shook his head.

Beth knew he was every bit as tired as she was.

They'd had a steady flow of folks asking for a doctor. They'd delivered three babies, including the parson's wife's that first night. And there'd been someone staying in their makeshift hospital almost every night, thanks to a couple of broken bones and a cowpoke who tangled with a cantankerous longhorn, besides the measles. Everyone recovered well, but Alex and Beth had been running ever since they'd started doctoring.

Until now. Unless some sick or injured person lay in wait for them back in town, their hospital was empty and their town was healthy.

"I guess they really needed us, didn't they?" Alex took his eyes off the trail, which was fine. The way was straight and the horses were placid and calm and interested in going home. "We've helped a lot of people."

Beth saw the hope in Alex's eyes. They prayed together every day, and Alex seemed to bloom during their times of closeness to God. He still insisted she be at his side while he doctored, but Beth hoped he was remembering why he'd loved healing. She prayed that he'd keep getting stronger, steadier, until the day she didn't have to be by his side every minute. Not that she minded being here.

"You're a really good doctor, Alex." Beth hesitated but she went ahead. "I think you're replacing all the bad memories with good ones. Most of doctoring is a blessing. Getting to help people mend, using our God-given talents matched with training to heal. Are you feeling better these days?"

"I still want you by my side."

Beth felt his fingers dig into her waist a bit too hard. She knew she'd trod on dangerous ground by bringing this up. "I plan to be."

The fingers relaxed before they caused pain. Which was lucky for Alex because Beth wouldn't have put up with that graciously.

"But yes, I am feeling better. I'm not ready to test doctoring on my own. And it works, the two of us together, doesn't it?" He turned to look in her eyes.

She felt that connection that they'd had from the very beginning. It was substantial, almost solid, like they were locked together somehow. A team hitched into the same yoke, pulling together. Stronger together than apart.

Alex was obsessed with needing her, but Beth knew that connection went two ways. She needed him, too.

"Yes, it works." There was no reason for her to whisper. There was certainly no one out and about this evening to be disturbed by their voices.

Alex leaned closer, watching her. Supporting her. His eyes flickered to her lips, which suddenly felt dry. She licked them and he noticed.

Then he kissed her and she sure as certain noticed that.

In the silent night, broken by the sound of the horses' hooves and a gentle gusting wind, Beth kissed him back.

He pulled away. Only inches. "We're married, Beth, honey. You know what that means?"

Beth did indeed. Her mother had not shirked.

Alex leaned in again, and this time not even the sound of the horses could find its way into the world where Alex swept her.

She was a married woman in every way now.

Beth woke in the first light of dawn feeling perfect peace. They had a home and a doctor's practice and now a true affection. She turned, wanting to study Alex sleeping beside her, holding her close.

He was awake. Watching.

Instantly she felt their connection. Only now it was more solid than ever. Truly there were ties binding them now. A union of the flesh, the possibility of a child.

Those were good things. And she was married to a good man. Beth smiled.

There were no patients knocking at their door, but it was very early. Some would most likely appear. But for now, it was only the two of them.

Alex drew her into his arms. They spent the early hours of the quiet morning deepening those ties.

Alex couldn't believe they'd been left alone so long. Late in the afternoon, he bandaged the nasty burn on the little boy's arm while Beth distracted the child with a licorice stick and her sweet voice. When that didn't work, she and the boy's mother held him still and dabbed at his tears.

It gave Alex chills to listen to the hurting child cry. But Beth was here, and he was able to go on.

Doctoring was better. Still awful, but so much better. He finished the bandage and sent mother and child on their way, then pulled Beth close. "Having you near has always been wonderful. But now, after last night, it's even better. Your eyes give me strength, but your arms help even more."

Beth stayed in his arms, holding him close, her head on his shoulder. So generous.

God had given him a miracle when He'd sent this little spitfire into his life.

Finally she pulled away only far enough to smile. "Let's go eat at the diner. The sun is setting, and I haven't had a chance to lay in supplies for the week. Our cupboards are about bare."

Alex shuddered. He'd eaten Esther's food before. "Please, not the diner."

Beth laughed. "I'll tell you a secret that will get you through."

"You know a secret that makes Esther's food better?"

Beth nodded. "No coffee. No dessert. In fact, I recommend just eating her bread. It's pretty good. Her meat is tough, but it doesn't taste that bad. It's not really dangerous."

"I thought I'd broken a tooth." Alex tugged at her waist so she stumbled a bit and he grinned, letting her know he did it deliberately to hold her close.

"I meant dangerous like poisonous." Beth snickered. "You made the mistake of having pie and coffee last time. I tried to warn you."

"Try harder next time."

Beth laughed, and they left the doctor's office arm-in-arm. They'd walked about ten steps down the sidewalk when they saw Esther pulling down the window shade on the diner. Beth turned, her brow furrowed. "How late is it?"

Alex looked at the lowering sun. "Later than I thought. I guess past Esther's closing time. Or she's got somewhere special to go."

Beth shrugged. "Well, we'll make do with yesterday's biscuits and honey, I suppose."

They turned to go home and Alex felt a spring in his step. Home. He had a home and a beautiful wife and he'd remembered how to be a doctor. . .not alone yet, but that didn't matter because he didn't have to do it alone. He had Beth. Life was good.

A tiny flicker of unease broke through his contented haze. He had trouble on his trail, he knew that, but he'd left it far behind.

In the encroaching dusk, a sudden movement to his right made him jump. A man rushing toward them, a dirty, skinny, stump of a man, but healthy looking. Not in need of a doctor.

"I need a doctor. My brother's hurt." The man grabbed Alex's arm and began dragging him.

Alex caught ahold of Beth and brought her.

The frantic man stopped when he saw Beth coming. "No, not her. My brother, he don't want no womenfolk tending to him. He—he won't accept help if she's along."

Alex's stomach plunged. "Then I can't go. I'm sorry, but we work together."

Alex wrenched his arm loose from the fingers that clung to him. He shuddered a bit when the man scowled, revealing broken teeth and an ugliness in his eyes that had nothing to do with physical appearances.

The man took all of five seconds to consider the situation. "She'll have to come then. My brother will put up with it or die. It's a long ride. I've got a horse but—"

Alex exchanged a look with Beth. It was wrong to bring her along, out at night with this unknown man. But—

"We'll hitch up our buckboard and be right behind you." Beth tugged Alex's arm toward the stable where their horses boarded.

Alex fell into step beside her.

"Wait!" Beth stopped so quickly Alex lost his grip on her.

Somehow that made the whole unsettling situation worse, no Beth.

Forgive me, Lord, for being so weak, so cowardly.

"What?" Alex turned and went after her as she rushed for their building.

"I...uh...we...uh...you need the doctor's bag." Beth glanced at Alex, silently apologizing for the slip. They both knew that for the public to trust them Alex had to be the doctor, not Beth.

"Hurry." The anxious, unpleasant man seemed to think they were making an escape. He followed right along with them. "I was over an hour on the trail and my brother doesn't have much time."

"Tell me what happened." Alex opened the door.

Beth darted inside and back out so fast Alex didn't even have a chance to join her. She had her doctor's bag in one hand and her rifle strapped on her back, the muzzle showing by her right hand, the butt above her left shoulder. She always wore it this way when they went doctoring out in the country. The two of them turned and rushed toward the stable.

Only as they entered the livery and began, as a team, buckling the traces on their gleaming brown thoroughbreds, the whole outfit given to them as a wedding gift by Beth's parents, did Alex realize the man hadn't answered his questions.

He'd vanished. Now he reappeared at the livery door on horseback.

The man's nervous rush had Alex pushing. "I didn't even hear what was wrong with the brother."

Beth looked across the horses' broad backs, her concerned eyes a match for his. "Okay, done. Let's go. He seems worried to death."

"Do you know him? Is he from around here?" Boosting Beth up onto the high seat of the buckboard, Alex vaulted up behind her as she scooted over.

"Nope. But I've been away a long time. Half the people in town are strangers."

Alex slapped the reins to his horses' backs and they rushed out the open door of the stable.

The man rode ahead, setting a pace to the south that would exhaust the horses before long.

"What's he going this way for?" Beth asked.

"Why not this way?"

"There's nothing out this way. This land is so rugged and rocky, anyone who's trying to carve a living out of this land is in for a bad time of it."

"I can barely keep up with this guy. Does this trail ever branch off?" Alex slapped the horses with the reins. The man rounded a twist in the trail that climbed steadily upward. The trail got steeper and fell away on the left into a deep canyon.

Beth caught at Alex's arm. "I don't know anyone who lives out this way."

Alex looked away from the increasingly narrow trail. "No one?" He carefully skirted a particularly slender section of the trail where the ground had caved away.

The road was shadowed from the setting sun and the notch in the trail seemed to open on an abyss. Who knew how far they'd drop if they went over. To Alex's overactive imagination, it seemed like they'd fall for eternity.

Beth clenched her jaw and remained silent until they passed that spot. Now the trail, still narrow, was less treacherous. "Well, of course someone could be out here I don't know, but look at how rugged it is. Look at the land. No cattle graze out here. This is wasteland. I've heard my folks talk about it plenty of times, that these highlands can't support a ranch. And these woods go on and on for miles. They lead into the desert to the south, and the west is not much better. So where exactly are we going?"

"What do you think?" Alex looked up the trail. The man had vanished. What was going on? Why would he leave them so far behind? What if the trail branched off and Alex chose the wrong branch?

Alex slowed the team. They were losing speed anyway on the steep trail so it was more a matter of not goading the team forward. There was only one way to get the answers they needed.

"Hey!" His voice echoed off the hills and valleys. There was no answer. "Hey, mister." Alex realized they didn't know the man's name. He'd told them nothing about himself.

"Stop the team!" Beth's voice acted like a jammed-on brake.

Alex drew the team to a halt just before a bend in the trail that wound around an outcropping of rock. Gnarled trees blocked their view of the trail ahead so Alex couldn't see the man.

The wind blew, whistling through the hills that rose around them. Alex strained to see the trail better as dusk grew heavier. One of the horses blew a whoosh of breath and shook his head, jingling the traces.

The darkness deepened.

"I don't like this, Alex." Beth surprised him by opening her doctor's bag and producing a Colt revolver. "Something's going on. Why did he lead us out here and abandon us?"

Alex looked from the gun to the bright gleam in Beth's eyes and knew she'd use that weapon to defend herself if she had to. She'd defend him, too. Which sent a wash of failure and shame through him. He was still a coward. He didn't even have the courage to prepare in the event of danger.

"Back the team up. Slowly," Beth ordered.

"There's a nasty cliff back a few yards. Help me watch for it."

Beth was studying the back trail, the rocks overhead. Near as Alex could tell the woman was considering every possible problem before it happened. "Once we're past that, there's a wide enough spot to turn around."

"I could go forward. I think the trail widens near that bend ahead."

"No!" Beth raised her rifle so it was pointing at the sky, her hand on the trigger. "Back up. If he's really in need of a doctor, he'll come back after us. If he's up to something, lying in wait right around that bend would be a real likely idea. Back the team up now!"

Alex obeyed her. Despite his years farther west with the cavalry and the training he'd had in survival, he'd never been in command. He'd taken orders, not given them, unless he was doctoring. Now wasn't the time to start being in charge.

Alex eased the team back, watching the wheels as they neared the sheared-off spot that looked like a mountain-sized cougar had slashed at the trail. The horses seemed more than willing to push downhill instead of pulling up.

Beth watched for about ten seconds then a breath of relief caught Alex's attention. "We're past it. Now let's go back another twenty feet."

"There's a spot where we can turn around." Despite being something of a weakling in his wife's eyes, Alex had driven his share of buckboards so he got the team backed properly and soon had them headed downhill back toward Mosqueros. They came past that treacherously narrow spot and Alex kept the team as close to the uphill side as possible.

"I wonder where he went." Beth twisted to look back.

A bullet whizzed past her face. Missed her only because she'd turned.

"Get down!" Alex threw himself at Beth and the two of them tumbled over the side of the buckboard. . .and right down that cutout in the trail, into the abyss.

★ Twenty-one ★

We'll ride out with you tomorrow and help you get settled." Silas Harden handed Mandy a plate of food.

Beans, beefsteak, biscuits, and blazing hot coffee. The Harden crew had already eaten but their pot wasn't empty, and they all settled in around the campfire, eager to listen to new voices. Mandy had told them their plans, and the Hardens had volunteered to help them get to the homestead. Mandy could barely conceal her almost desperate relief.

"Not necessary." Sidney spoke around a scoop full of beans. He'd been eager to take their food, but Mandy could see his pride was stung by her tears. Sidney wasn't going to accept anything else from the Hardens.

"I didn't ask if we could." Silas settled next to Belle without looking at Sidney. "I told you we were going to. You can ride with us, or trail after us if you prefer."

Belle's cool eyes went to Sidney with a very strange look Mandy couldn't quite understand. Almost like Sidney was everything Belle expected a man to be. As if his behavior was no surprise.

"We're coming." Belle gave Silas a look of such solid support, Mandy could have built a cabin on that foundation. "We've got a while. It's early enough we don't have to worry about beating the weather. Silas and a few hands can run the herd in tomorrow morning and get settled up while we head for your property and get a cabin put together. My Silas is a hand at building."

Silas smiled a private smile at his wife that made Mandy's heart beat harder. She'd seen that smile pass between her parents many times. It was love, a private kind of love.

She and Sidney had never exchanged such a look. Would they ever? It occurred to her that a smile like that might come with time. And with knowing a person inside and out. She didn't know much about Sidney, his childhood, his growing-up years. He'd come from Boston and he was a lawyer. There wasn't much else.

"You'll be glad for the help," Silas said. "Winter comes early up here."

"And stays late." One of the blond girls, Emma, stretched her legs out toward the fire. She had a riding skirt on like Belle, and the same calm, competent look in her eyes. But there the resemblance ended. Mandy knew all these girls plus the baby boy were Belle's children, but none of them looked a bit like their ma or pa except the little boy. Strange.

Mandy had a sudden flash of a wonderful idea. She clamped her mouth shut hard not to beg them to let her and Sidney go home with them. Why couldn't they ask if the Hardens needed help? No shame in working for a ranch. They had some time before they had to put up a cabin. She and Sidney could come back to their homestead in the spring, have the whole summer to get settled. Mandy knew without a doubt, just from the way Belle had hugged her while she cried, that they'd be welcome, whether the Hardens needed hands or not.

It wasn't a comfortable realization to Mandy that she wasn't looking forward to being utterly alone with a gold-mining husband through a long, cold Montana winter. She suddenly felt ridiculously young and wanted her mama.

In Ma's absence, Belle Harden would do.

They made quiet conversation around the fire. Mandy was surprised to learn that an old man among the hands, name of Shorty, recognized her pa's name. He'd known Jarrod McClellen from years back in Colorado. It gave Mandy a strange feeling to get this glimpse of a grandfather she'd never known.

They talked about the life of a fur trapper in the Rockies and Mandy told about her family back in Texas until it was time to sleep. The Hardens provided Sidney and Mandy with bedrolls, but it was immediately obvious that the women slept on one side of the camp and the men on the other, neither Belle nor her married daughter, Lindsay, shared blankets with their men. Proper for a cattle drive, Mandy knew. The best way to preserve a smidgen of propriety when men and women traveled together like this.

Sidney only growled a bit as he went to bed down with the men. Not even he had much energy for nonsense. After the long days being bounced along on the train, stealing sleep in snatches, and the long rough day on the stagecoach, Mandy was falling asleep on her feet. She didn't have a full minute to worry about how Sidney was handling another thwarted "wedding night." Mandy was asleep before her head finished settling on her blanket.

She jerked awake in the pitch-dark and was on her feet and moving, her rifle around her neck and over her shoulder, before she was conscious of what had awakened her. She listened as her hand slid down the muzzle of her Winchester. She could pull that muzzle forward in one jerk, have her right hand on the trigger and her left steadyin' the muzzle in half a heartbeat. She was the best shot in her family, better'n Pa or Ma, better even than Sally, and that was saying something.

It was coming from out in the pasture a ways, beyond the meager light cast by the red coals of the low-burning fire. Before she could step out into the dark, she heard movement and raised her gun, only to see Belle come up beside her, Silas right behind, and the whole camp stirring.

Mandy returned her Winchester to hang on her back and they all stood, frozen, listening.

"Horse." Mandy said. "Have you got one foaling?"

Belle shook her head then said, "Least ways we're not supposed to."

The faint, distressed sound came again, and Belle made a noise of disgust. "It's the blasted stallion of Tom Linscott's." Belle strode into the dark.

Mandy hurried to keep up. "A stallion is out there bothering the horses in your string?"

"Nope," Silas said with a smile in his voice that Mandy couldn't see in the dark, but she knew it was there all the same. "One of our mares ran off from town a few months back, and when we found her, she was running with Linscott's stallion. We're gonna have us a fine little foal. And that Linscott gets a stud fee for his horse. So we got us a bargain."

Mandy and Silas moved after Belle, but slowly. No sense startling a mare busy adding to the horse population. As Mandy's eyes adjusted to the dark away from the fire, she saw Belle kneeling beside a dark, wriggling lump on the ground. The mother licked and nudged at her baby.

"It's a little colt," Belle said, looking up from the baby. "I might just see if I can't earn a few dollars on stud fees, like Linscott does."

"We're not raising that thing up as a stallion, Belle. That horse of Linscott's is a brute. No one is safe within a country mile of the critter, and you know it." Silas crossed his arms. "We have to geld him."

Mandy noted that Silas's order wasn't given with an over supply of hope.

"We'll see, Silas. We don't have to decide tonight. I just

didn't think the horse'd been run off long enough to settle." Belle laughed. "I can't wait to tell Linscott. He's *loco* on the subject of that horse of his. He'll probably try and make me pay."

Belle and Silas both laughed at that, and Mandy almost felt sorry for Tom Linscott.

The next morning they were up, fed a hearty breakfast, and heading for the homestead just as the sun began to lighten the sky. One of the hands made a fast trip to town and came back with some building tools. So, they could commence putting up a cabin right away.

Silas stayed with the cattle but promised to catch up with them as soon as he'd dealt with the cattle buyers and laid in supplies.

"Look at the colt, Sidney." Mandy rode alongside her husband in the cool morning breeze.

The colt was pure black. Mandy recognized his regal lines, even in his skinny, uncoordinated movements. Mandy was tempted to agree with Belle that he ought to be held back for breeding.

Sidney glanced at the colt and shrugged. "A baby horse. So what?"

"He was born just last night." Mandy knew Sidney hadn't awakened. He was the only one in camp who hadn't, save Tanner. "He's a beauty."

Mandy rode slowly, making sure the foal stayed ahead of her as it gamboled along behind its mother. With some trepidation, she leaned closer to Sidney. "What would you think about asking the Hardens if we could hire on for the winter? We could work for them and come back to put up the cabin in the spring."

"No." Sidney scowled at her in an expression Mandy was already fully tired of. "I'm not a ranch hand. I'm a lawyer. And besides, I'm going to dig for gold."

"Being a miner isn't any easier than being a cowhand, and a cowhand usually makes more money." Mandy should have never brought the idea up.

Belle dropped back beside them just as Sidney mentioned gold. "Best to use the land for wild game and a garden and lumber. You can live rich on the plants and on the animals that roam wild here and raise a good herd of beef with the sweat of your brow. It's a rich land in ways other than gold. Gold is worth so much because it's mighty scarce. Hard to find, harder yet to hold on to if you do find it. Helena started as a mining town and it only turned civilized when the gold played out. Finding gold is a purely uncivilized business."

Sidney gave Belle the benefit of his scowl.

Belle held his gaze for far too long, as if she were studying him, looking inside his head, probably searching for a lick of sense.

Sidney turned away first and spurred his horse to ride with the men.

"I told Silas to send a telegram to your people in Texas, telling them you made it here safe and sound."

Mandy gasped. "I meant to write a letter. I was so tired last night it never crossed my mind."

"Well, just tell me what you'd like said. I don't have any paper with me, but I can contrive a letter and get it to your folks. Maybe I'll have Lindsay write it. She doesn't get snowed in so early."

Mandy reached out and caught Belle's hand. "Thank you. That would mean so much to me." For a second, Mandy was afraid she might cry again. "I never cry. What is wrong with me?"

Mandy looked away and her eyes settled on the foal. She tried to focus on the little guy to distract herself from the nonsense of tears. His mother, working today as a pack animal, was at the end of a string of horses. Because Mandy had dropped back to follow the colt, now she and Belle were bringing up the rear.

The shining black colt kicked up his heels and ran away from its mother. Mandy smiled to see his vigor.

Nodding, Belle said quietly, her eyes on Sidney, "Silas is my fourth husband and the first one who's amounted to much."

A squeak escaped from Mandy's lips. "Four husbands?" She'd never heard of such a thing.

"The Rockies are a brutally hard land, Mandy."

"So's West Texas."

Nodding, Belle added, "Weaklings and idlers don't last long out here. None of 'em." Belle's eyes never left Sidney. "So how much do you like that husband of yours?"

"L–like him? I *love* him."

Belle made a little sound deep in her throat. "Reckon that's usually the way, at least at first."

Looking away from Sidney, Belle said, "You ever need any help, you get yourself back to Helena and ask for Roy and Lindsay Adams. My place gets cut off in the winter, but my girl, Lindsay, lives not that far from Helena, south and west of town, up in the high-up hills. And they're known in town. Someone can ride out for them. She and Roy will come a'runnin' to help or take you in with them. I promise you."

"A–alright." The offer made Mandy jumpy. She didn't need to be taken in by anyone.

"Lindsay!" Belle called. "Girls! All of you come on back here."

As Belle's girls fell back beside them, Mandy tried to ignore the niggling of worry in her stomach. It was almost as if Belle *knew* there was going to be trouble. Not so much a warning as it was a *plan* for when the inevitable happened.

Just as the three older girls, with Betsy riding double with Emma and Tanner strapped on Lindsay's back, came into line with Mandy and Belle, a sharp snarl turned them toward where the foal had pranced.

Wolves sprang out of a copse of trees toward the wobbly baby.

Mandy jerked her rifle up and fired one-handed while she slung the strap off her shoulder with the other. She jacked the next bullet into the gun with a whirl of her hand and fired again, whirled and fired, whirled and fired. She had four wolves down, all within a foot or two of the colt before anyone else got off a shot. The foal stumbled back and tripped over the body of a still quivering wolf.

Cold, the way she always felt when she was shooting, iced over her nerves as she saw a shadowy movement in the woods. Her Winchester came around.

Belle fired before Mandy could, then Emma followed. Two more wolves fell forward and revealed themselves from where they'd crouched, lying in wait for an easy meal.

The foal's mother whinnied frantically, pulling against the lead string. Their whole party stopped in its tracks to stare at the dead wolves.

"Done?" Emma asked.

"One ran off before I could get him." Belle stuck her fire iron into its spot in the boot of her saddle.

Mandy slung her rifle back into place as she noticed Belle's gun. It was a Spencer like Ma preferred. It made Mandy homesick.

"I'll get the colt and calm the mare." Emma rode toward the foal and herded it back to its mother's side. The nervous mama licked her baby then nudged it toward her udder. The foal found comfort in warm milk.

Belle turned hazel eyes on Mandy, and those eyes glittered as gold as Sidney's dreams. "Where'd you learn to shoot like that?"

Mandy felt the ice recede from her veins and she looked down at the barely visible muzzle of her gun. She'd already returned the fire iron to its proper position angled across her back, butt high on the left, muzzle low on the right. She'd honed her skill, worked hard to give herself every edge. She'd tried a dozen different grips and made the strap herself to suit her. All to get it into action fast. It was the only way she'd found to best Sally and Ma, and then they'd copied her and taken to wearing their own strapped guns, so she'd practiced even more.

Though honesty forced her to admit she'd found a gift for shooting from an early age.

"My ma taught me, I reckon."

A smile quirked on Belle's face. "Your ma? Not your pa, Clay, the man Shorty said he knew as a boy?"

"Pa helped, too. All my sisters are hands around the ranch and shooting is part of it. You oughta see Sally. I can beat her for speed and accuracy, but when there's trouble, running, fighting, then it's a mighty close thing. I reckon I win out, but Sally's steady when there's trouble."

"Like wolves jumping out of the woods aren't trouble." Belle smiled.

"And my sister Beth, she's not so fast as any of the rest of us. Pretty fast, but we can beat her. But she's a hand at ghosting around in the woods. She's so quiet she can slip up on a deer in the woods and slap it on the rump before it sees her comin'." Mandy thought that might be a bit of an exaggeration, but Beth was a hand at sneakin' and no one could deny it.

Belle studied her. Then Mandy looked past Belle and saw all her girls staring straight at the strap she'd created just to suit her.

"Can I see it?" Belle asked. "Up close? I might rig something like that for my Spencer."

"Ma has always favored a Spencer. I prefer a Winchester like my pa." Mandy handed the gun over with a grin. "You and Emma are crack shots, too."

Belle was focused on the gun. "We've run afoul of our share of wolves in these mountains, I reckon."

Then Mandy looked past Belle and her girls and saw Sidney staring at her, clearly appalled. He knew she was a fast, accurate shot, because she'd told him and because she took her Winchester with her everywhere, wore it as faithfully as a bonnet. But she'd never really demonstrated it before. She'd thought he'd be impressed, respectful, proud. Instead he was disgusted.

Mandy's smile shrank like a Texas morning glory in the noonday sun. Belle looked up, saw the direction of Mandy's gaze, and followed it. Mandy immediately schooled her expression, sorry she'd let it show that Sidney had hurt her feelings. Judging by the frown on Belle's face, Mandy had gotten control of herself too late.

Poor Sidney, Belle was not impressed. Well, he wasn't at his best. Mandy made allowances for that, but Belle could only know what was in front of her eyes. Mandy knew she and Sidney would be fine. Whatever needed done, Mandy could do it herself, so having Sidney around to help, even if he was just digging for gold, would be better than being alone. They'd survive.

Having the girls studying her gun and talking with her made Mandy so homesick she could barely talk.

"We're going to have a time of it getting that foal home. It's a long walk. It'll be hard on the mare, too." Belle studied her mare with a furrowed brow. "She's older and she's one of our best. I'd have liked to get a few more years out of her, but that trail ride home might be too much for a new mother. I had no idea she was so close to foaling." Belle shook her head and kicked her horse back into motion. They all made their way toward Mandy's homestead, talking guns and wolves and foals.

Mandy worried about Sidney but couldn't help enjoying the female companionship. It made her think of her sisters. Especially Beth. What she'd give to have seen Beth again before she left. Sweet Beth with the healing touch. Beth had such dreams of helping others. Mandy knew her little sister would find a way to make those dreams come true.

By now Beth was settled into the ranch, surrounded by the family, doing what doctoring Pa would allow and wrangling with him to do more. Mandy smiled to think of her sweet sister living the safe, quiet, nurturing life of healing, just as she'd always dreamed.

Alex lost hold of Beth as they plunged over the cliff. He bounced off rock outcroppings, rolling along with stone and scraping mesquite. Alex's head cracked on something solid and he was only aware of sliding until he rammed to a stop. Alex heard the crack of a rifle and a rock spattered his face, slitting his skin.

He forced his dirt-gritted eyes open and saw Beth, her expression dazed, skidding to a stop beside him. He forced himself to move, urged on by another whining bullet even closer than the last. Grabbing Beth by the back of her collar, he took a fast look around and saw they'd landed on a ledge about twenty feet below the trail.

A bullet cut his arm and he had no choice—he pulled Beth with him over the edge. Again they fell. Then Alex hit something and rolled. His hand was ripped loose from Beth and he lost track of her until he landed hard again.

Bullets roared overhead, but from where they lay none came close.

Alex searched and found Beth flat on her back about ten feet down the still steep rock face. He slipped and slid down to her just as she tried to get to her knees. He dropped dizzily to the ground beside her. Blood soaked the hand he reached out to her.

"We're out of range." Alex's voice drew Beth's eyes around and he saw her face burned raw by the rocks. "Honey." He hated knowing she was hurt.

She shook her head hard. "We've got to move. He'll come down to check that we're dead."

"No one's crazy enough to follow us over that cliff."

Rock's rained down off to their side and they both looked up. They couldn't see to the top, but someone was definitely coming down.

Beth shoved herself to her feet. Alex noticed she had her doctor's bag hanging from her shoulder and the Winchester on her back.

"You held on to the gun?"

Beth gave him a wild look. "Of course I held on to the gun."

"You had time to think of grabbing the doctor's bag while we were diving away from gunfire and going over a cliff?"

Beth arched a blood-soaked brow. "Of course."

"In the half second before we jumped, I was praying, figuring we were going to die."

Beth shrugged and managed a grin. "In the half second before we jumped I jammed the handle of my doctor's bag hard onto my wrist and took a firm hold of the strap on the Winchester, figuring we were going to live." Then Beth's smile widened. "But I prayed while I did it."

"You are the perfect woman." Alex smiled back.

The rocks tumbled down from overhead again. Beth and Alex glanced up. Then their eyes locked. They staggered to their feet and ran.

A bullet tore through the air as Beth dragged Alex over yet another steep slope.

Beth did her best to keep them well ahead of the man pursuing them, but he kept coming. He was on high ground so he had a shot at them every so often and the bullets were so close it was terrifying. Their pursuer was a top hand with a gun. He'd been after them for over an hour. The night had settled into full dark, but bright stars overhead made too much visible. That was just a pure shame.

"You've never seen that man before?" Alex asked.

"Why, you think he's after me?" Beth skidded down the rocky incline, stones clattering away under her feet, her rugged riding skirt protecting her as much as possible.

"Well, I've never seen him before." Alex lost his footing and slid along on his belly for a while. Downward, always downward out of this high country.

Beth knew with a sickening certainty that they were being driven toward the desert. Their only possible path was directly away from her parents' ranch and Mosqueros, the places that offered safety. No one she knew of lived this way. Once they entered the driest part of this land, they'd be trapped, either dying of thirst or facing their assailant with his sharp eye and endless supply of bullets.

Thinking out loud, Beth said, "We could try and dig in, make a stand. Even hide and hope he goes past us in the dark. We're going to have to lose this guy or fight him. He's not giving up." Beth touched her rifle, slung down her back, to make sure it was in place while she tried to think of a way to do either.

"Can we get back up that cliff we came over?"

"I don't know. That man came down by choice. He didn't jump, so maybe, but I'd hate to go back and find out we were stuck."

"We'd be trapped back there, him in front of us, our backs to that rock wall."

She'd married a lunatic, but he was a smart, logical lunatic. "I've thought of another way, but it's a long, hard run and a long, long chance, and it will carry us even farther from safety."

"But we'll be alive, right?" Alex was breathing hard, but he was keeping up, even pulling her along.

"And Pa will come. It shouldn't take long for someone to miss us and Pa knows tracking."

"And we left the team and wagon behind. Hopefully they'll head for the livery. Your pa can back trail it."

"Yep, he can read sign like the written word. He'll come with the whole of his ranch hands backing him and save us."

"So we just need to stay alive until he gets here." Alex glanced at her. "You're sure we can't stand and fight on our own? We've got two guns and plenty of bullets."

Beth puffed as she ran. How long could they keep going? "He's a dead shot, Alex. He missed me by inches through pure luck and he was a long way up that trail. We're up against a tough man." Beth got to the bottom of this latest rugged gully and scrambled to her feet, pulling Alex up, grimacing at his bleeding arm with its slipshod bandage.

"Then I guess, at least for now, we'd better keep running."

Alex had never uttered a single note of protest or pain, she'd give him that. For a semi-crazy man who thought himself a coward, Alex was holding up really well.

"What do you think he wants? It's not to rob us, because we left the team behind and they're the most valuable thing we have."

"He may think we've got money."

"No low-down thief works this hard for money." Beth thought of what lay ahead of them if she followed the only plan she could think of—at least ten miles over country more apt to sit on end than lay flat.

There was a creek that wound this way, that had at one time run past a little shack she'd lived in, when her ma was between husbands. That creek was fast moving by the thicket where they'd used to live, but this far out it faded into an arroyo that only ran during the rainy season. It would be flat and smooth.

They'd make good time and hunt for the right place to leave the arroyo and circle around to head back north. They couldn't stay on it long though, because it ended in the Pecos and she wanted no part of that wild runaway river. Beth had heard the stories many times. The Pecos had killed nearly as many people as the desert.

It was late summer though. The arroyo would be easy to traverse and just as easy to abandon. They'd leave these treacherous hills behind and gain some space between them and their pursuer. . .if they couldn't shake him.

A sharp crack overhead had Beth looking back and expecting to see the gunman gaining. Instead she saw lightning. Rain. Coming from the north. Beth shuddered at the thought of floodwaters. "Alex, do you know how to swim?" Beth breathed hard as they ran hand-in-hand on the broken ground.

"That's a strange question to ask right now." Alex puffed the words out. He was right. They shouldn't be wasting a single breath. Only it wasn't wasted breath, Beth knew that.

"Just answer the question." A mesquite bush slapped her arm

and nearly snatched the rifle away. She didn't dare lose that.

"Can't say that I do. I've never tried it. Why would you ask that?"

Alex was right, it was a strange question. Even more, it wasn't a question that required an answer. Because whatever Alex said, they were going for a swim.

"Never mind." Beth groaned and tightened her grip even more securely on the rifle.

★ Twenty-two ★

For a girl who never cried, Mandy had been at. . .or over. . .the brink about ten times in the days since she'd gotten married. She hoped it wasn't some new affliction.

But watching Belle and her family and cowhands prepare to ride away brought tears to her eyes. Silas and his drovers had arrived a few hours after the rest of them had gotten there—land was already cleared for a cabin and a stack of trees had been felled, using the ax and other tools Silas and Belle had provided plus a few things in the crate Pa had packed for them.

Once he'd arrived, Silas took over. The man could build a house so well, Mandy nearly heard music playing while everybody followed his orders.

Pausing with one hand on the saddle horn, ready to mount up, Silas said, "You know we could take another day or two." He looked at a couple of his hands. "And some of these men are riding to Divide, not taking the high trail back to the Harden ranch. They could stay even longer. Help you split the kindling and mud the cabin."

Mandy looked at the solid cabin behind her. True, it needed the cracks chinked but Silas had told her and Sidney how. "Thanks, but we're fine."

Belle, already mounted, said, "We've left a lot of work for two people alone. There's no shame in accepting help from your neighbors."

The whole crew had been here for three long, hard days. Belle and Silas were leaving behind a good, tight log house, with a solidly built barn close to hand and a well-built corral. That was so much more than Mandy had ever dreamed of having done so quickly. Her hopes and prayers for protection had been to just survive the coming winter. She'd expected to spend it in a cabin the size of a line shack—if she was lucky.

But the Hardens had done even more. They'd also chopped wood for the winter, stocked the cupboards, and left behind two riding horses, leather for those horses, and a milk cow, a brood of chickens in a little henhouse, and a buckboard. They'd also built a few rustic pieces of furniture. And, the most wondrous thing of all, they'd left the little newborn foal and its mama.

Belle nodded then spotted the stupid, brimming tears, Mandy assumed, and rode up close. "I'm mighty grateful for you watchin' after my horse. We'd have lost the foal for sure if he'd taken that long trip home. It'd be mighty hard on the mare, too. She's an old one. I'll be back for the pair in the spring." Belle's warm, yellow-gold eyes said far more than her words.

Mandy knew Belle was worried about leaving. And she knew Belle and Silas would have gotten that foal and mare home somehow. But it would have been hard on the pair. That was the truth. So it was best to leave them behind for now. Of course Belle's daughter, Lindsay, lived a short day's ride in the direction of home, but even that was a long, steep trek.

The Hardens had come up with the only real thing Mandy could do for them and asked for it—and then acted as if the Hardens owed the Grays.

"I'm so glad there was something we could do to help." Mandy fought back the tears, not proud of this new inclination. "It doesn't begin to make up for all you've done for Sidney and me."

Sidney was hanging back by the steps. Every thank-you had been grudging. It was all Mandy could do not to rap him on the head with the butt of her Winchester.

Mandy neither yelled at her husband nor cried, knowing either would delay the Hardens, and they needed to get on the trail. Mandy had done everything she could to convince them she could finish their winter preparations on her own. And she could.

They could have survived with no help. But God had sent people in her path. Mandy prayed for protection steadily. It was the longing of her heart to feel close to God and protected from the often rugged life in the West. Both here and back in Texas.

God had certainly provided beyond any hope Mandy had dared. She and Sidney would live comfortably through the winter because of Belle and Silas Harden.

"I found the straightest trees I could"—Silas studied the cabin—"but there are plenty of gaps. You remember how to mix up the mud and daub it in, right?"

Silas had done one whole side already, most of the higher logs on the cabin, and he'd given the barn a first coating of mud, keeping his men working late into the night. But the plaster of mud needed to dry before more could be added, and where knots in the trees had forced them to leave good-sized gaps, the cabin was going to need several days worth of patching.

Now the Hardens were riding out, leaving behind supplies and the riding horses—which Mandy hadn't realized were a gift until a few minutes ago—and the foal, which meant the Hardens would return in the spring—and it was more than Mandy could stand without tears.

Sidney stood behind her glowering. Mandy expected taking the charity—Belle had called them housewarming gifts and payment for sheltering the mare and foal—had pinched him.

182

"They're rich people," Sidney grumbled as soon as the Harden company was out of earshot. "They don't know what it's like starting out. They could have given me better advice about where to hunt gold. All Harden would do was talk about caring for the horses and how to lay in wait for a deer. And how to mix the stupid mud up to patch holes in the cabin."

Mandy caught herself rubbing the little callus on her trigger finger and stopped that telling action. "We'll look around, Sidney. We'll find a place for you to dig your gold mine. But winter's coming down on us. We need to add a new layer of mud right away and jerk that venison."

Mandy looked out the door at the two big bucks hanging from a tree just outside the door. Emma had gone hunting and brought them in.

Mandy looked at Sidney and gave him an encouraging smile. "We're going to be happy here. If you don't find gold soon enough, you can ride to town and work until the winter settles in. We're going to make a good life."

She looked at the trees and scrub brush surrounding their home, cutting the wind. "It's a likely place we picked for a home." The Hardens had picked the exact site and done it well, but Sidney had picked Montana.

Sidney looked away from the hanging deer. "You really know how to butcher those deer?"

Mandy nodded, proud she'd be able to help make them comfortable.

He shared his most charming smile, and Mandy remembered fully why she'd agreed to marry him. "Will it hurt anything if you wait an hour or two to get started?"

"No, they can hang a while. But it's best to get a job tackled if it needs doing." Mandy took one step away from their little cabin.

Sidney slid an arm around Mandy's waist and pulled her back hard against him. Then he leaned in and kissed her. "I know something else that needs doing."

Mandy let the kiss drive every other thought straight out of her mind.

Sidney was right. The deer would still be there. It was far past time to give the man his wedding night.

They hadn't seen their pursuer in a while, but who needed a gunman when Beth was determined to kill them both?

Alex thought his legs were giving out. His arm burned like fire where it'd been creased by a bullet. They'd run all night through pouring, soaking rain. When he'd suggested they seek shelter, Beth had bullied him into moving on. The storm had cleared off about the time the sun came up.

The one good thing was they hadn't been fired on in hours. Maybe they'd lost that madman in the storm.

Alex had never been a lucky man so he wasn't optimistic. They ran on. Alex had long ago given up on doing anything but keeping pace with his wife.

"There it is!" Beth yelled.

"There what is?" Alex looked at the little slave driver he'd married.

"The arroyo I was looking for." She pointed and Alex caught a glimpse of shimmering water curving far below them. They'd been coming down out of high country all day, but from the look of the cut the arroyo ran through, they were still pretty high. She'd never said a word about an arroyo. Except, she had said—

"Wait a minute. About the time it started raining, you asked me if I could swim. I said I can't." They reached the edge of the cliff that fell thirty or more feet into what looked like raging floodwaters.

"I remember." Beth looked downstream. "Maybe we can run alongside it. We don't necessarily need to jump in."

A sharp report of a gun cut the air and a rock exploded. The ricochet slit Alex's face.

Beth gave Alex one wild look. "Sorry."

She grabbed his hand and, swim or not, he knew that while the fast moving water was only *apt* to kill them both, the bullets were for sure deadly. He clutched her hand and they jumped.

When Alex fought his way to the surface, his first thought was that he'd lost hold of Beth. As the water swept him along, he looked frantically for her. His eyes landed on that madman who'd lured them out into the mountains last night. The man was a long way away. Out of rifle range. At least Alex sure hoped so.

The man was so focused that Alex knew this hunter was staring straight at him, not Beth. The man yelled, and the canyons and water echoed the words until Alex couldn't possibly miss what he said, even over the roar of the rushing water. "Dead or alive, Buchanan! Dead or alive!"

And suddenly it all made sense. Alex knew exactly what this man was after. And he knew that unless they were very lucky— and Alex had never been lucky—Beth was going to die to pay for Alex's sins.

Alex caught sight of Beth being swept along by the current a few feet behind him. Their eyes locked. He knew she'd heard that awful shout. As they were rushed along by the raging floodwater, and since luck was unlikely, Alex started to pray.

Then the flood waters sucked him under.

"Dead or alive, Buchanan!" Cletus might as well have been howling at the moon. Buchanan and his woman couldn't hear him. Didn't matter. It suited Cletus to blow off some steam by yelling, so he did. No one around to care, so why not?

Cletus's druthers were to get a man before that man knew he was being hunted. Made life easier. Now Buchanan was warned. But Cletus had been hunting men for a long time and he knew the main trick was to just keep coming. Always coming. Like a hungry wolf on the trail of blood.

Cletus had left his horse behind. His gun wouldn't fire if he jumped in the water, and he wasn't going up against Buchanan without a gun. So he'd come along slow. No harm in slow as long as it was sure and steady. These waters flowed fast, and the walls of this washed-out arroyo were steep most of the way to the Pecos. There'd be little chance for Buchanan to climb out of that water for long, brutal miles.

Chances were Cletus would just scout downstream and pick up Buchanan's body. Smiling, he turned back. In the daylight he could cut his time in half and he could get his horse and ride around this mess of mountains instead of through them. If he didn't get there in time to cut Buchanan off, he'd get there later and track the man down. Buchanan was wanted. No law would protect him.

If the yellow-bellied doctor heard nothing else, Cletus hoped the deserter heard laughter echoing off the walls of the wild mountain canyon.

"Montana?" Sophie looked at the telegraph and was stunned. "What in the world is Mandy doing in Montana?" And who in the world was Silas Harden, the man who'd sent the wire?

She marched out of the telegraph office. Sophie had heard everything about that skunk Mandy had hitched herself to. She'd never liked the man. Too smooth to suit Sophie from the first day. Didn't have a callus on a single finger. Bad sign.

Clay would have to find Luther and Buff and send them in the right direction. Sophie had no doubt he'd do it. Her husband was a good man. A man to count on. Not like Sidney Gray.

But if Clay didn't fix this, Sophie vowed to the good Lord she'd saddle a horse and go herself. And yes, she'd take all the young'uns with her. That skunk who'd stolen her Mandy was not going to get away with marrying Mandy when he was already married. Yes, Sophie determined with grim resolve, she really did want to go herself.

"Clay!" Sophie saw Clay coming out of the doctor's office with Sally at his side. Sally, her girl. She'd almost died.

Sophie couldn't find it in herself to hate the strange Alex Buchanan even if it galled her that Beth had married the man. Even if the man stacked up to be some kind of lunatic. Still, she'd be grateful to him forever.

She had two daughters married. Both married to men Sophie thought were mighty strange picks.

"Sophie!" Clay marched toward her, Sally nearly running to keep up.

Sophie hurried just as fast toward him. They met in the middle of the mud-soaked main street in Mosqueros.

"Beth's gone!" Clay raged.

"Mandy's in Montana," Sophie said at the same moment.

"What?" they spoke the word in unison.

"Beth has disappeared." Clay talked faster and his words distracted Sophie from her disturbing news about Mandy. "Her horses came in last night, pulling the doctor's wagon. No one's see her all day."

Since it was nearly noon, something had definitely happened to Beth. All thoughts of Mandy and her plight were put aside. For now.

Sophie and Clay turned and walked side-by-side. Sally fell in line with them. All three of them jerked on their buckskin gloves as they headed for their horses, tied three in a row in front of the general store.

Sophie looked at Sally and could see the still-raw scar on her throat. A tiny scar that saved her life. "Is Alex gone, too?" She'd forgotten about her son-in-law.

"Yep." Clay jerked his reins loose from the hitching post and swung up onto his black gelding. "No one saw 'em leave town, but the wagon came in from the south. Rain washed out all the tracks from last night, but the wagon must have come down after the rain passed." Clay wheeled his horse to the south. "The horses stood, still in their traces, out front of the stable this morning. There's wagon tracks heading south."

He paused and turned back to Sophie. "Mandy's in Montana?" Clay's voice almost screeched. "What in the world is Mandy doing in Montana?"

"Who can say? Let's go save Beth. Then you'll need to wire Luther." Sophie spurred her horse south, Sally one step behind.

The tracks just kept on going south out of town, the one direction Beth would never go.

Sally was the first to notice a second set of tracks. "Someone rode out after them."

Clay swung down to study the sign. "The wagon came down the mountain empty. You can tell by the way the trail left by the buckboard wanders that there was no driver on the way back. That means—" Clay looked up.

Sophie read his fear as if he'd shouted it. Beth had been led up this lonely trail by someone and that someone had come back alone.

They were at a full gallop in seconds.

"Grab the log, Alex!" Beth saw their chance. Not to get out of here—there didn't seem to be a spot where the banks weren't straight up and high above their heads—but a log would help them stay afloat.

Alex heard her over the roar of the surging floodwaters. He must have because he obeyed. He grabbed for one of the dozens of branches of the stout trunk and, glory be to God, he held on.

Beth was behind him. For the first time, instead of fighting the current, she kicked hard to speed herself up. The Winchester was still wrapped around her head and one shoulder. The doctor's bag, with its medical supplies and the trusty Colt revolver, was slid hard up her arm until the handles were stuck tight. They'd been awkward to hang on to, but she'd done it, clung to them like they meant life or death.

They very well might.

She dragged herself forward, thinking of her sharpshooting sister, Mandy. It was Mandy who'd started using a strap so she could get her gun into play faster. Beth might well owe Mandy her life, if things came down to life and death, and the gun made the difference.

Fighting the water an inch at a time, she was battered and bruised and half-drowned from this wild ride. But at last she got to the tree and clung to the gnarled roots. The tree looked like it had been torn whole right out of the ground.

She was on the off side of the tree from Alex so she hoisted herself up to lie on her belly across the trunk. And there he was, doing the same thing with a frantic expression on his face—looking upstream.

When she appeared, he saw her and smiled. That frantic look had been his worrying about her. "Beth. Thank God you made it." He breathed hard twice, changing his grip so his body was more fully supported by the tree. "I'm so glad you're all right."

Beth squirmed around, too, trying to get a firmer grasp on the tree. She felt like she was using her last ounce of energy to pull herself up. She set her now soaked Winchester and her waterlogged doctor's bag on her lap. Maybe everything was ruined. Maybe the rifle and the Colt wouldn't fire. But she'd held on all this way down the flooded creek.

The branches spread out to the sides in a way that kept the tree from rolling. Alex and Beth raced along on their clumsy raft at a sickening speed, and every second swept them farther from the safety of Beth's family. But for this one second, they were alive. They were even sort of safe. At least safe from that back shooter. The river might still get them.

"We both made it." Alex panted as if he were storing up air for the future. As if he were planning to be underwater again soon.

The creek roared. No gunfire split the air. No human voices. A bird cawed in the early morning sun as the water splashed and rumbled along. Beth smiled. "Even you. Even I-can't-swim-Alex made it."

"I'm not sure what I did once I hit the water qualifies as swimming, but if it does, then, yes, I can swim." Alex sighed.

Beth leaned back and found the roots of the tree made a fair backrest. "We'll keep going downstream until we find a place with low banks where we can climb out. Then we'll circle around, give the arroyo a wide berth in case that man's coming downstream, and head back for Mosqueros."

"No!" Alex shook his head—dead serious. The day was breaking and Beth could see it clearly in his face that, for the first time, Alex wasn't going to obey her.

Well, that was annoying.

"We're not going back north to Mosqueros. We're going west to Fort Union."

Beth patted the flat of her hand on one ear, hoping to dislodge water so she could hear what the man was saying. Maybe the water in her ears had kept it from making sense.

"I've heard of Fort Union. It's in New Mexico. It's a long, hard ride over some mean country." Beth didn't bother to mention that they didn't have a horse. "Why would we go there for safety when we can just go back to Mosqueros?"

Alex sighed.

Beth saw something so kind and wise and gentle in his eyes that she wanted to crawl along this swirling, splashing log to his side and give him a hug.

"We're going there because we've been swept so far west that we may actually be closer to it than we are to Mosqueros."

Beth doubted it. They'd definitely come a long way in the right direction. But still—

"And we're also going there because I figured out who that man is."

"You know him?" Beth felt some meager satisfaction to know the man had been gunning for someone other than her. It was very meager.

"I don't know his name, but I know his type. He's a bounty hunter."

"And he's after you because—" Beth waited.

"Because I'm a wanted man, Beth. There's a price on my head. I should have told you. I should never have married you."

Beth gasped then sucked in some of the water still streaming off her face. She started choking. At last she managed to say, "Alex, what did you do?"

"I'm a deserter from the cavalry. As that man so cruelly reminded me, I'm wanted dead or alive. Only it's pretty clear to me that he's only interested in dead and he's going to make sure you're dead right along with me. I'm not going to stand for that. We'll make a run for Fort Union and I'll turn myself in."

"What do they do to deserters, Alex?"

Alex's eyes finally fell. He'd been pretty brave when he announced he was turning himself in to the cavalry. Now he wasn't quite so courageous.

"What, Alex? Tell me." Dread came in waves just from looking at Alex's expression.

"The punishment for desertion"—Alex swallowed hard but he raised his head to look her square in the eye—"is a firing squad."

★ Twenty-three ★

Mandy skinned the buck with a smile on her face. She was truly Sidney's wife now.

She wondered how long it would be until she had a little one to raise. She'd mothered her little brothers and sisters all her life, of course with her ma in charge, but Mandy knew the way of mothering, and all the fun and love and hard work. She couldn't wait.

God, protect me and Sidney and our children.

Her married life had finally, truly begun.

She made quick work of skinning the bucks then set the hides aside to tan, a process that would give them thick, comfortable blankets for the winter—or she could use them to make shoes or coats or gloves. She knew how to do all those things.

She hoped Sidney would show some interest in learning, because it was a big job. But she enjoyed the labor of her hands and took great satisfaction in knowing she could make a good life for herself with the strength of her back. Sidney liked to say he was working with his head not his back. But Mandy figured

God had given her a strong back for a reason so she didn't mind using it.

She cut the meat of both bucks into strips, setting aside a haunch to hang in a cool cave Silas Harden had scouted out. They'd eat venison steaks and roasts, and Mandy could contrive a good stew with the supplies the Hardens had brought for them. The rest of the meat would be smoked and stockpiled for the winter that she'd been grimly warned would come early and stay late.

"Mandy, I'm going to hike around, see if there are any likely spots for mining." Sidney came out of the house tugging his suspenders over his shoulders. Broad shoulders that had cradled Mandy last night.

She was truly in love with her husband. She knew he wasn't perfect. He was a city boy, not used to frontier living. But he'd learn, and if he took a notion to hunt for gold for a while, she'd let him. A man needed a dream.

Sidney had the shovel that Pa had packed with him. He slung it over his shoulder and whistled as he headed into the woods.

"Sidney, there's a cave just a bit up this trail that way." Mandy pointed to the west. "I don't know much about gold mining, but a cave might be a likely place to look." She'd heard of mines and she'd heard of panning for gold. They had no pan, so the cave sounded good.

Sidney turned away from his own direction and walked over to Mandy, who was covered neck to ankle in a huge apron, her hands bloody from butchering, her hair a bit flyaway, because when it had escaped in bits from its knot she'd been careful not to tuck it back in, considering the mess.

Sidney leaned down and kissed her gently, then pulled back to smile. "We're going to be happy here, Mandy. If I find a vein of gold, we'll be so rich we can buy and sell that Harden clan and we'll eat roast beef every day and not have to hunt."

Mandy knew she'd married a dreamer, but his dream seemed

to have shifted. What about being a lawyer? Well, he could always be one of those, too; and in the meantime, she'd keep venison on the table.

"Can you leave that and show me this cave?" Sidney looked uneasily at the deer, as if worried that he'd be remembering this mess when he was eating later.

Mandy fought a smile. "I'd love to walk over there with you." She set aside her heavy knife, then wiped her hands as best she could on the apron and took it off. She was still untidy and she suspected she smelled none too good, but she left the worst of the mess behind.

They strolled through the woods until Mandy came upon the cave mouth, nearly concealed by a clump of quaking aspen that was just showing the first signs of fall color. Mandy had listened closely while Belle and her whole family talked yesterday, educating her in the way of mountain living. What woods burned and carved well, which were best for building, what plants had medicinal uses. What wildlife was about, some dangerous, some not. Some tasty, some not.

Emma Harden had found a good spring, which is why they'd built where they had. A steady water source made a well unnecessary.

The whole group had talked and taught and been so kind. Mandy had sensed their quiet worry about leaving Mandy and Sidney here alone, but Mandy had convinced them she was a frontier woman, same as them. In the end they'd left her and Sidney to saddle their own broncos, which was the way of the West, be it in Texas or Montana.

Mandy slipped through the nearly solid wall of aspens. The Hardens had stacked rocks and rigged a gate in front of the cave entrance so it was a trick to get inside.

"Couldn't they find a cave around here that was easier to get in and out of?" Sidney asked. It was his first querulous comment of the day. Of course he'd only been out of bed about ten minutes.

"They picked this and blocked it off to keep out wild animals. I'm going to hang my jerked meat in here. We don't want to be feeding the local grizzly bears and mountain lions and wolves, now do we?" Mandy grinned at him as they entered the cave. It wasn't huge but once they'd passed the entrance, they could stand upright in it and it went back nearly twenty feet. The light was dim but Mandy saw that someone had rigged a sturdy branch in one corner to use as a hanger for meat. That was going to save her a lot of time.

She sure didn't see any gold, but that wasn't her project. "I've got a deer to cut up and a hide to tan. Then I'm going to chink the cabin and barn. Two people would make it go a lot faster." A hint she wished he'd take.

"Maybe later, honey." Sidney came near and tossed the shovel on the ground. He wrapped his arms around her waist and kissed her. When he finished he said, "I'm so proud of all you know how to do. You can really tan a deer hide?"

"Sure. It'll be great, strong leather when I'm done. I'll use the deer's brain to tan the hide then smoke it to keep it soft."

"The brain?" Sidney flinched.

Patting him on the chest, Mandy smiled at her city-boy husband. "We can use the hide all winter as a blanket. I even know how to make moccasins and pants for you. You might want them if you're doing hard work. They're a lot sturdier than broadcloth."

Sidney kissed her again. "I have married myself a fine woman."

The next kiss lasted longer.

"Now I want you to quit distracting me and let me get to work." His smile told her he was teasing.

She smiled back. "Good luck. I hope you find a wagonload of gold." She almost added, "But don't get your hopes up," but why discourage him? She'd leave that task to the Rocky Mountains.

"I'll be back here in a while to hang the haunch of venison so I'll see you soon."

"Bye." Sidney turned to the very barren walls of the cave with

195

a bit of a bewildered look on his face.

Mandy couldn't help him. She had no idea how to go about finding gold.

Slipping out the narrow opening of the cave, she started thinking of what they'd have for a noon meal. Something encouraging.

Mandy needed to keep her husband happy.

Beth needed to keep her husband alive.

"We are not going to some fort hundreds of miles over rugged desert and mountains to turn you over to a firing squad."

"It's the only way to keep you alive, Beth."

"No, it isn't." Their tree trunk rounded a curve in the flooded arroyo and Beth yelled, "Hang on."

She could have skipped yelling. Alex was watching the banks as carefully as she was. He'd already seen the curve ahead and gotten his arms wrapped tight around the branches he balanced between.

But she felt like yelling so it suited her to do it. They'd been floating along all morning, half the time squabbling, half the time sitting in grudge-soaked silence, all the time clinging to their tree. It had a tendency to slam into the bank like it was going to right now.

Beth sat leaning against the roots. Alex was on the other end of the tree. He'd slid closer to Beth slowly, inch by inch, until they were almost within arm's length of each other. But that last gap between them had no branches so there was nothing for him to hold on to. So they'd stayed apart, when Beth would have dearly loved him to hold her in his arms through this wretched ride.

They clung to their handholds as the tree jammed straight into the sheer wall that lined this arroyo. It hit so hard Beth lost her grip for a second, but she scrambled to regain it and stayed atop the God-supplied raft. The top ten feet of the tree snapped off with a sharp crack. Beth wondered how long before their boat was battered down to firewood. There were no low banks to climb out on.

The collision sent the tree spinning. Beth ended up downstream of Alex, but it wouldn't last. The tree would swivel again soon though. Many branches had been stripped away, leaving the top of the tree slender, but the roots were tough and still showed some green in places scraped raw. So the current tended to catch them and hold them back, letting the top of the tree get ahead again. They finally settled in again, with the rushing waters.

Beth's legs dangled into the flood. It helped her keep her balance to straddle the tree. She was exhausted, starved, and battered from the events of the last twenty-four hours. She wanted her ma so badly she felt like, inside, she'd reverted to a three-year-old. But outside, where it counted, she was a lawfully wedded woman trying to talk some sense into the half-wit she'd married. "It isn't the only way to keep me alive. We'll just make our way back to Mosqueros. I'll be safe there."

"But that man will keep coming. He'll be after me, and from the underhanded way he went about trying to take me in, I'd say he was definitely more interested in the 'dead' than the 'alive' on that wanted poster. And if he's gunning for me, you could get caught in the crossfire."

"I'll be careful. Pa was a major in the army during the Civil War. He might know someone who could give you advice."

Alex shook his head. "I'm going in, Beth. And you're coming with me. I'll face my punishment like a man and y–you'll be set free. I've been half out of my head for a long time. I should have gone back and faced this years ago. But I was too much of a coward."

"What happened, Alex? Why did you run? Is that why you were acting so crazy on the stagecoach? Is that why you can't do any doctoring unless you keep me at your side?"

Alex kept his eye on the bank.

Beth was always looking, too, hoping to find a lower spot where they had a chance of climbing out. But there'd been nothing.

"Ever hear of the Red River War?" Alex sounded so tense Beth almost stopped him. If he sank into that awful place he'd gone when she left him alone with Mr. Farley at the general store, Alex might not remember to hang on to the tree.

"That's not familiar. I've heard of a Red River in Texas." Beth adjusted her grip, wondering if she was going to have to shimmy along this tree at the risk of her own life to drag her husband out of his dark thoughts. "We don't have to talk about this now, Alex. It might be best to wait until we've reached the shore."

As if he hadn't heard her, Alex said, "I was in the cavalry when it broke out. I'd defied my father's wish to go into business with him. He was part owner of a railroad back East and very wealthy. But I was always drawn to doctoring." Alex raised his eyes to meet hers and she felt that deep connect. "You understand that, don't you?"

"Yes, I do." It was a tie almost as binding as their wedding vows and the ties of the flesh.

"I fought with my father for years, and when I went off to college, I was so rude, so defiant. When I was finally ready to practice medicine, I deliberately chose the West, the military because I felt led to the great need I believed was out here in the frontier. And I got here and the campaign started they called the Red River War."

Beth sat silently and prayed for strength for her and Alex. Her eyes still locked on Alex's, letting him draw strength.

"The Indians had a choice. Register and go peacefully to a reservation or be taken there by force. Only trouble was too many of the Indians were starving on the reservations. They'd go in, surrender, and then stay put until they realized none of the promised food was coming. Then they'd run away. Die on the reservation, die off the reservation. Some choice, huh?" Alex gave her a bitter smile.

"So, I was helping the cavalry round up the ones who'd refused to surrender." Alex shook his head. "It was so awful. It was nothing like I thought it would be when I set out to be a doctor. I had to go right onto the battlefield with the soldiers—guns firing, sometimes cannons. Knifes, bows and arrows. Hate, so much fighting and killing and hate. My job in that carnage was to save the wounded. It was so stupid. Why not just fight to begin with, instead of having the battles then trying to tend to those ugly wounds? Severed limbs, gut shots, men slashed by knives. And it wasn't just men. There were women and children in some of the Indian villages, and I had to tend to them, too. Little children savaged. Women dead or dying. Both soldiers and Indians lay side by side, bleeding. And I had to save the soldiers first. Even if one of the cavalry men was clearly beyond saving, I had to tend him while a less badly wounded warrior or even a woman or child lay close at hand. I could've saved them if I'd been allowed to give up on the soldiers."

"So you deserted when you couldn't take that anymore?" Beth wanted to hold him. She was afraid she'd send them all into the water if she scooted forward, but he needed her. Right now his pain was almost as bad as that of the bleeding, dying soldiers. She moved forward, carefully, an inch at a time, knowing she shouldn't—but her heart wouldn't allow her to stay away from someone who needed her so badly.

"I was kneeling beside a dying man who was soaked in blood. He'd been slashed across the belly and his insides were spilling out. He was—was—" Alex flinched, swallowed hard, and went on. "He was trying to put himself back together, out of his head, just driven by some freakish instinct. I picked up my doctor's bag and it was soaked in blood. My hands, my clothes, the ground, the whole world was soaked in blood."

Alex rubbed his head. "There were horses, too. Someone was shooting horses. I can't remember exactly what I saw, but I can hear those horses screaming. The gunfire. My bag swimming with blood."

Shaking his head, looking into the past, he said, "I just threw the bag and ran. A coward. I couldn't do it anymore. I betrayed my country when I ran, and the punishment for that is a firing squad. I've been so out of my head. I have dreams about that dying man, my doctor's bag, those dying horses. I haven't slept in years because of the nightmares. I tried drinking to shut down the madness, but the drinking made it worse. I had the dreams when I was wide awake then. I haven't done anything but move, as if I could run away from the horror when it's stuck inside my head."

Beth finally reached him and pulled him into her arms. He jumped a bit, as if he'd been so far gone inside his memories that he hadn't noticed she was close. Their eyes met. It was the same powerful connection they'd had from the very first.

"Until you, Beth. Until you dragged me out of the madness that's been plaguing me and forced me to help Mr. Armitage. And even as terrified as I was of doctoring again, the strength I stole from you gave me the first moments of peace I've had in years. I wanted it so badly that I just took it, took you, took everything you offered."

Alex slid his hands deep into her bedraggled hair. "And now I could get you killed. I won't do it." He shouted the words, his fists clutched her wind-dried tresses. His jaw set into a tight, hard line. "I'll die myself before I hurt you. I'll die gladly."

He pulled her tight and kissed her as if he was desperate for her touch. Desperate to feel her and hold her.

Beth fought back the tears until she heard the tight choking sound coming from Alex's throat. Then a sob broke free and Alex gave in to tears. Beth couldn't hold hers a moment longer, despite years of training to the contrary.

Together, they held each other and cried.

"They went over that cliff?" Sophie couldn't keep the horror out of her voice.

"Yep. I've looked hard. It's a long way down, but I see clear sign at the bottom that they got up and moved, so they survived the fall. And one rider led them up here then went back down the trail."

Sophie and Clay's eyes met as they stood silently adding things up.

"If they went down this cliff and he went back to town, then the way to find them is to find him." Clay arched his brows as if daring Sophie to deny the obvious.

"I'll go over the side here, Pa." Sally studied the steep slope and walked along the edge, looking for a better place to go down. "I'll trail Beth and see where she got to from this direction."

"Nope, you're not going down there alone."

"Where does this end up?" Sophie searched through her memory. This was a barren, forbidding stretch of land, and she was only slightly familiar with it.

Clay stared down the twisted and gullied terrain. Then his head lifted and he had a shine in his eyes that lifted Sophie's dread. "The arroyo. That's where Beth would go if she had to run this way. She'd head for that dried-up streambed."

"Except it's not dried up after last night's rain," Sophie reminded him.

"Which means they might be getting swept down, maybe all the way to the river," Clay added.

"If they don't drown first," Sally added somberly. "Remember those floodwaters that almost swept Pa away that first night he came to us?" Sally looked at Sophie.

Only years of practicing being brave kept Sophie from visibly shuddering. "I remember. A flood is a fearsome thing. Where do we go, Clay? Where do we ride to fetch Beth home? Alex and Beth." Sophie kept forgetting about him. But she glanced at Sally's scar and knew she'd never really forget. And she'd never be able to repay him. Yes, they'd definitely ride to save both Alex and Beth.

"If she makes it to the water and gets herself a ride on it, I know right where she'll be able to climb out. And that arroyo twists and turns so much we might even be able to get there ahead of her. If not, we'll be able to pick up sign."

"Or meet her heading for home," Sophie added hopefully as she swung up on her roan. "We can send word to the ranch and have Adam and Tillie look after the young'uns along with Laurie. And maybe Adam can send that wire to Luther, too."

"You know," Sally said as she spurred her horse after Clay and Sophie, bringing up the rear, "that man who came down this trail might well be riding to intercept her just like we are. And he's hours ahead of us."

No one said more. They were too busy riding for all they were worth without breaking their necks on the steep, muddy trail back to Mosqueros.

★ Twenty-four ★

Sidney came in from the woods, his shoulders slumped, the light waning. He'd been gone all day.

She'd even taken his dinner out to the cave because he didn't come in. Besides, she'd hauled the deer haunch to the cave. That had been the real point of the cave after all—cool storage for meat.

She'd finished the deer, started tanning the hide, put another layer of mud on the cabin, fed the animals, started dinner, and even found time to play with the little black colt. And still her husband didn't come. Now, just as she was starting to worry that the venison roast would dry out, here he came. With a sigh of relief, she stepped outside to wave hello.

When he caught sight of her, he straightened and began walking faster, a determined, if slightly forced smile on his dirty face.

Mandy didn't think she'd ever seen Sidney dirty before. Not from work at least. "Dinner is ready as soon as you wash up."

Nodding, Sidney came up onto the three steps that made a

stoop on the back of the house. "I had a good day. It takes some practice to get the shovel to work and I kept hitting stone. I might ride to Helena tomorrow and buy a pickax."

Mandy didn't mention that they had almost no money left. And she certainly didn't mention her ma's money. Sidney probably had enough for a pick. And though it came in very handy, she didn't really need money to survive.

A pickax—one tool her folks hadn't included in the supplies they'd sent, nor had the Hardens included one in their housewarming gifts, even though they knew Sidney wanted to dig for gold. Mandy was sorely afraid that omission showed their dim view of gold mining.

"Do you want me to ride along?" Mandy wasn't sure Sidney knew the way to Helena. It was a long and poorly marked trail through broken ground and heavy woods. She worried that he'd ride off and not find his way back to her.

"No need. You'll be alright here alone, won't you?" Sidney was suddenly very attentive, despite the lines of exhaustion on his face. "Are you afraid to stay here without me?"

"I'll be fine. I just thought the two of us together might scout the trail better. Are you considering asking around about a lawyerin' job?"

Shaking his head, Sidney said, "Of course not. Why work as a lawyer when there's gold to be carved out of these mountains?"

Mandy was careful not to let him see her sigh. Why work indeed—as if Sidney hadn't worked himself to the bone today. For no money.

Sidney ate heartily of the roast but didn't talk much. He kept yawning and rubbing his eyes.

Mandy noticed ugly blisters on his hands and knew the man would harden up if he kept mining. That might not be a bad thing.

He went directly to bed after he ate, and Mandy felt a twinge of hurt that he hadn't stayed to talk with her while she cleaned up after the meal or invited her to turn in along with him for the night. After all, there was no one else to talk to around here. If they didn't talk to each other, then they talked to no one at all. That would be a lonely life indeed.

Mandy had grown up surrounded by people. Lots of brothers and sisters on a thriving cattle ranch. There was always plenty of company. Now she washed the dishes alone, to the sound of her husband snoring in the little bedroom the Hardens had included on this tightly built cabin. The aloneness almost echoed in her ears.

She said a long, heartfelt prayer for her family, and things she needed protection from: homesickness, loneliness, resentment.

She missed her family terribly. It was all she could do to keep from crying when she thought that she might never see them again.

Afraid she could slip into a life seeded with envy, she turned her thoughts to praise, fighting off feelings of jealousy that Beth was now living at home, soaking in that peaceful, settled life.

Their log hurled toward the bank. The canyon narrowed.

"Brace yourself, Alex!" Beth swallowed a mouthful of dirty water, choking as she clung to the log.

She saw Alex jerk awake. He'd nodded off for a minute when the water had calmed briefly. He grabbed for the log and held on tight.

The current picked up. The water churned white and rough, a sudden dip of their tree splashed water high.

Beth was heartily sick of this ride. They'd been careening along for a good chunk of the day. The sheer canyon walls lining this arroyo had prevented them from climbing out.

Alex blinked his eyes and tightened his hold on the nearest branch. The tree was now about six feet long. The narrow end had been battered and snapped off repeatedly.

Then Beth saw what she'd been looking for all day. "There's a break in the canyon wall, Alex." She pointed to the arroyo wall, just past this narrow spot.

They had to survive the narrows first, but past the white, churning water breaking over protruding stones was their first chance to get out of here. They'd be very lucky to get through the rapids, but once through, they could finally get out of here and go. . .where?

Alex said Fort Union.

Beth said home.

He was too big to knock senseless and drag along back to her parents' ranch. If she'd had a horse she could manage it.

The log rammed into one of the bigger stones.

Beth flew forward, clinging to her handhold, the rifle and doctor's bag securely hitched to her body. She stayed with the bouncing, twisting log for a few seconds, remembering a particularly feisty bronco she'd busted when she'd been growing up. Then a second jolt tore her loose from the tree and sent her tumbling head over heels into the water.

She went under and resisted gasping for breath—barely. She rammed into a stone with her shoulder and flipped onto her stomach. Slashing at the water with her arms, she surfaced, dragged her lungs full of air, and then was plunged beneath the water again. Battling the rushing current, she emerged from the torrent once again and sighted that low spot in the arroyo bank. She struck out for the shore using strength born of desperation. She wanted out of this place, and who knew when she and Alex would get another chance.

The low spot was a tumbled-down pile of rocks, looking as if the bank had caved in. It wasn't a long stretch, and the water seemed to be taunting her by sweeping her away from that chance for escape.

Submerged again, she collided with something soft. Her head cleared the water and she was face-to-face with Alex. His eyes looked glazed and a rivulet of blood trickled down from his temple.

Beth slung one arm around him and continued kicking toward the shore. They looked to be going past when a sudden eddy swirled them around and kicked them out so hard they landed with a thud on the scattered rocks.

"Hang on, Alex. We made it, but you have to hang on." Beth's legs were still in the water, and it was as if there was a gripping hand on her feet, determined to drag her into the depths. But she was a tough Texas cowgirl and she hadn't gotten to her ripe old age of twenty without facing trouble head-on. Her grip on the rocks held as if God Himself gave her strength, which she suspected He did.

Alex's movements were clumsy, but he dragged himself forward, inch by inch. Slightly ahead of her, he turned back. Some of the daze was gone from his eyes and he caught hold of her wrist and tugged her up beside him.

The streaming water gave one last yank, like a spoiled child denied its toy, then she surged forward and landed like a beleaguered catfish, *splat*, beside Alex.

They were truly on dry land.

Beth used every ounce of strength she had to turn her head, now resting on the forbidding scratchy rocks, and open her eyes to see Alex.

He stared at her, bleeding but with a weary smile. "We made it, Beth. We're safe."

Beth closed her eyes and dragged in more precious air. "We are." Then her head cleared enough for her to add, "Except for that bounty hunter behind us and a firing squad ahead of us."

"Just give me this moment, okay?" Alex asked.

Beth lay there breathing until she had the energy to do more than breathe. With a groan, she pushed herself to her hands and knees and looked at the mess in front of her. Yes, they'd found a break in the arroyo wall, but they still had about a hundred yards of jagged rock to climb before they could really say they'd made it.

"Let's go, Alex." She looked at him, to goad him into moving. The whole left side of his face was soaked with blood. Beth reared up on her knees as Alex tried to rise. "Stop. Don't move." She wrenched her doctor's bag off her arm and saw that she'd left a deep welt from having the bag so tightly wedged. Opening the bag, water spilled out and Beth poured the soggy stream onto the rocks, careful to protect her precious, and possibly destroyed, contents.

"I'm fine, Beth. Let's get up this rubble of rock before we worry about a little scratch."

"Hush, you've lost a lot of blood. It will only take a minute for me to get the bleeding stopped."

Alex shook his head, but Beth suspected he felt terrible because instead of arguing more, he rested the unwounded side of his face on a warm, mostly flat stone and let her work on him.

She found a roll of cotton bandages and quickly formed a tidy, if soggy, pad to press on the small cut.

"Ouch!" Alex lifted his head. "Be careful. My head's taken all the abuse it can for one day."

With a gentle laugh, Beth started crooning to him. "I'm sorry you're hurt. Just be still. Let me help you. Let me—"

"Don't use that voice on me like I'm a scared little girl," Alex grumbled, but he lay his head back down and quit scolding.

Stifling another laugh, Beth kept up her soothing talk as she tended Alex, pressing on the wound until she was satisfied the bleeding had stopped. Then using another length of the bandage, she wrapped it tight around Alex's head. She bathed away the blood that made him look so terribly injured and decided he'd live after all.

By the time she was done, Alex had seemed to fully rouse from the daze left by the head bashing. "Thanks, honey. You're a good doctor."

"Only good?" Beth arched a brow.

"Great." Alex got to his knees, leaned forward, and kissed her. "The best." His eyes met hers and he kissed her again, slowly, deeply, beautifully.

Beth had never felt anything like that kiss. It was "thank you" and "I'm glad I'm alive," and, to her wary heart, it was "I love you."

She kissed him back just as fervently as he kissed her. When the kiss ended, their eyes met and Beth knew. He'd said it with a kiss. Now it was time for her to be just as brave with her words. "I love you."

Alex's eyes showed shock then deep abiding gratitude. "I love you, too." He pulled her hard against him and this time the kiss was pure passion.

And that's when reality finally, fully returned. Beth jerked away from him and grabbed his wrist. She felt his pulse beating strong and alive and vital. "I love you too much to stand by while you turn yourself over to a firing squad."

The pleasure in Alex's eyes faded, replaced by grim determination. "And I love you too much to stand by while a heartless man kills you because you happen to be sitting next to me on a wagon seat. I won't do it, Beth. I won't save my own life at the cost of yours."

"We can move." Beth grabbed his hand. "We can leave the area, go back East. That man wouldn't follow us to Boston. We could go where your father lives."

"Lived. My father's dead. He died ashamed of me because his son had turned deserter and run rather than face danger. I disgraced him and failed him in the lowest way possible, and I never had a chance to make it right. I'm not doing it again, disgracing you and myself the way I did him. I'm going to stand up to what I've done and take the punishment.

"I'd do it for you, to protect you, and no other reason. But there *is* another reason. A good one. It's the right thing to do. I turned my back on God and honor and country when I ran. And I won't live with that on my conscience anymore. I can't be a husband to you with that stain on my soul. I've made my peace with God. Now I'm going to face my punishment from my country and do it with honor. I can't call myself a man unless I do."

The fear of losing a man she now knew she loved was agonizing. Beth wanted to scream at him. She wanted to knock him over the head and drag him far from danger. But what she saw in his eyes stopped her. It was sanity. He was more fully lucid than he'd ever been. He wasn't drawing strength by being near her. He was finding strength of his own. She hated it. But she couldn't deny him.

God, give me the strength to do what's right.

Tears burned at her eyes and she had to force the words through her tightened throat. "All right, Alex. We'll go back, together. We'll make it right. And maybe the cavalry will punish you in some way less than a death penalty. Whatever they decide, I'm yours now. I love you and I'll stand beside you."

"I should go alone. I should have faced this first. I should never have married you and dragged you into my mess." Alex shook his head and those tears threatened again. "But I'm so glad I did." Alex's tears spilled over and he swiped quickly at his eyes with his wrist.

Beth had never seen a man cry before Alex. Her pa would die before he'd do such a thing, and she'd always considered that strength. But Alex's tears had their own kind of strength. He had the courage to let her see deep in his heart. To know his fear. To share his sense of honor. To respect his courage—more courage than she suspected she had—she'd have definitely run from this.

Or maybe not.

Alex pulled her into his arms and held her as if he were drowning again, with no floodwaters involved. Then at last he straightened. "Let's go. Let's find that fort."

They clambered up the treacherous rocks, and after some discussion and Beth's careful study of where the sun stood in the sky and Alex's vague memory of where Fort Union stood in the world, they set out, knowing Alex might never come home.

Sidney had set out for town midmorning. It wasn't that long of a ride but he didn't return all day. Mandy waited up long past bedtime and slept fitfully until first light.

Frantic, she saddled the remaining horse the Hardens had left her; strapped her rifle on her back with firm, determined movements; and headed to town at sunup to track him down. "He's lost or dead. I should have never let him go alone, Lord. Help me find him. Protect him."

Her prayers were continuous as she raced toward the city. She followed Sidney's tracks easily. She tried to be furious, thinking he'd been delayed in town and had just stayed over, unmindful of her worry. But she knew better. Deep in her heart, she knew Sidney would have come home.

But maybe he was just lost. That could have happened. She prayed that *had* happened. She should have started searching last night, but she hadn't truly begun to fear the worst until after sunset. By then, if his trail led in an unexpected direction, she might have missed it in the dark and wandered all night.

She prayed fervently as she rode.

Protect him, Lord. Protect him. Protect us both.

She found him facedown on the ground about halfway to Helena. His horse stood nearby. Its reins hung down, ground hitching the well-trained animal. Mandy noticed a pickax strapped to the saddle.

"Sidney!" Mandy threw herself off her horse's back and dropped to her knees. She gently tried to roll her husband over, and as she did, he groaned, deeply, quietly, but he was alive.

"Thank You, God," Mandy said through her tears as she leaned close to see where he'd been hurt. "Sidney, speak to me."

Her husband's eyes flickered open, heavy lidded. He grinned at her and hiccupped.

Mandy smelled liquor on his breath and sat back on her heels. All her terror twisted into fury. "You're drunk!"

Sidney's smile faded, and he rubbed his forehead then winced. Mandy saw a welt just below his hairline. He probably was injured, from falling off his horse on his ride home. Then either knocked senseless or too unsteady to get up, he'd slept here, flat out on this cold, stony trail all night. While she'd been beside herself with worry.

Sidney had never had a drink in his life. He'd told her that clearly when they'd talked of marriage and Mandy had expressed her dislike of hard spirits.

"Get up, Sidney Gray. Get on your horse and let's get home!" Mandy realized she was using the same voice on Sidney that her ma used on the little boys. Not a good sign.

Moaning, Sidney said, "Don't yell. It hurts my head."

Clenching her jaw tight, Mandy stood and stepped back as Sidney clumsily got to his feet. Without speaking another word to him, she swung up on her horse and headed home. She didn't even look back. He didn't want her to yell? Fine, she just might not ever speak to him again. Because honestly, she just didn't know what to say.

When she reached home, she hung her rifle on its pegs over the door, thinking it might be best to step far from her fire iron in her current mood. Not that she'd shoot her husband, but a rifle made a likely club and she wasn't sure of her self-control.

She set about making lunch. The time for breakfast had long passed.

Sidney didn't show up for over an hour, and when he came in, he was walking, leading his horse. Mandy wondered if he'd been unable to mount or if he had fallen off again. She was too angry to ask.

He put his horse away, came into the house, shoved his hands deep into his pockets, and spoke directly to his toes. "I'm sorry, Mandy. That never should have happened. I was tricked into it.

212

I told you I've never had a drink before, and it's true. But I wanted to ask some questions about gold mining and the only place I could find men gathered was in a saloon. I sat down with a group and they offered me some whiskey. I could barely keep it down, but I wanted them to think I was one of them." Sidney shrugged. His voice was heavy with regret. "It will never happen again. You've got my word."

"Do you know how worried I was when you didn't come home last night?" Mandy slammed a plate laden with venison stew on the table. "I almost set out for you then, but I kept waiting and hoping you'd come home. I should have gone hunting, but the night falls early. I'm still not really used to it. Then I was afraid I'd miss you. You riding home, me riding to Helena. I kept making excuses and waiting and waiting and waiting. I've spent the night believing you were dead, Sidney!" Mandy's voice rose to a screech and she turned away from him, shocked at the tears that tore loose. Marriage to Sidney was, she was sorely afraid, going to be a tearful business.

"I'm sorry. I promise you, before God, it will never happen again." Her wayward husband came up behind her and slipped his arms around her waist, pulling her snug into his arms. "I should have taken you with me. Then no man would have expected me to go in that filthy saloon. I will never put you through anything like that again. Please, Mandy. Please, can you forgive me for hurting you and failing myself?"

The words flowed from Sidney like poetry, soothing Mandy's anguish. She gradually, prayerfully released her anger and fear. He continued with promises and vows of love, interspersed with quiet kisses on her neck. Finally she leaned back against him, letting her head fall back onto his shoulder.

"Do you forgive me, Mandy love? Please tell me you still love me. If your heart hardened toward me I wouldn't want to live." He turned her slowly around. His words fell like sweet breaths on her face, and she realized he'd washed and cleaned his breath

213

before he came in. That was thoughtful of him.

She allowed his kisses, praying for God to release her from the anger she still harbored. At last she was able to return his affection fully. And when that moment came, Sidney pulled back, his eyes glittering with something that looked far too satisfied for Mandy's taste. But he poured out on her vows both lavish and contrite. His kisses were generous and passionate. The combination lulled her into trust.

At last she could not deny him the words he begged for. "I forgive you, Sidney. I love you. You know I do."

He swept her into his arms and carried her away to their bedroom to rebuild their bonds of love. If she, for one instant, considered denying him, she recognized it as an unworthy part of herself.

★ Twenty-five ★

Sophie nearly screamed with the tension of waiting. Clay was running as fast as he could. So was she. Sally was hard at work, too. They were all doing what had to be done before the two of them set out on a journey that could last days.

She and Sally took care of procuring spare horses and packing for a journey.

Sally squabbled with Sophie the entire time. "I can help, Ma. Let me come along." Sally tied the string of horses together. A spare for Clay and Sophie, so they could ride fast, switching saddles to let their animals rest. Plus a packhorse loaded with food and supplies, everything Beth and Alex might need if they were in dire straits.

Watching Sally's competent handling of the animals, Sophie knew that indeed her daughter could help. "You're not full strength yet. Alex told you to take it easy or you could end up with a relapse. Your throat could even possibly swell again. Taking a long, hard ride to save your sister doesn't qualify as easy."

"But Ma—"

"And the young'uns need you. It's going to be you and Laurie caring for them. We might be gone for days, even weeks." Sophie didn't have time but she couldn't stop herself from dragging Sally into her arms.

"Let me go instead of you." Sally's arms wrapped tight. "I can stick by Pa better'n you. And you know it."

"I do know it." Sophie pulled back and ran her hand through Sally's long white-blond hair, so like Sophie's. All her daughters took after her with their slenderness and strength and grit. "I'd let you go if you weren't still healing from those bee stings. You know you're not at full strength. Now don't get so set on going that you end up slowing us down and risking yourself and Beth with your stubbornness."

Sally's mouth formed a mutinous line, but she was an honest girl, and she couldn't deny that she still tired easily and that wound on her throat was still tender.

Sophie knew her daughter. And this wasn't something Sophie was doing on a whim. Sally had to stay. Sophie had to go.

Muttering dire-sounding but unintelligible words, Sally finished loading a packhorse just as Clay rushed out of the telegraph office. Clay mounted his horse, rapping orders and worries at Sally that ought to make the girl feel badly needed at the ranch. Sophie was glad her tomboy daughter was staying with the family. She was a young woman to count on in an emergency.

"I sent word to Adam so he and Tilly'll likely come over and check on you. Maybe even stay for the duration. Until he gets there, you'll have to care for the children and fill everybody in on what's happened with Beth. I wired Luther about Mandy being in Montana, and there might be an answer, so send someone in every day to check at the telegraph office."

Sally jerked her chin in agreement while shooting Sophie rebellious glances.

Clay grabbed the string of horses and turned for the trail. Sophie was after him instantly.

They set a blistering pace and didn't speak as they rode hard through the afternoon and evening.

It was long after the sun had set that they finally had to admit they couldn't go on in the dark. They made a cold camp and ate jerky and biscuits. As they collapsed on their bedrolls, Clay pulled Sophie close to him. She wanted to pour out her fear for Beth but she kept her lips tightly closed. Talk solved nothing and she'd learned Clay wasn't inclined toward unnecessary words.

But some were necessary. "Where are we headed?" Asking that earlier would have been a waste of time. Clay obviously had a direction in mind. Sophie was content to trust him and follow. But now there was time.

"There's a break in the arroyo wall. I've seen it once or twice. Beth will likely climb out there."

If she hasn't drowned in the floodwaters. If the fast-moving water doesn't sweep her on downstream. If whoever was after them hadn't found a perch and shot them dead as they floated past. Sophie didn't utter her black thoughts. They qualified as unnecessary words.

"It's on the western side of that canyon. The man trailing her went down the eastern side. He doesn't know the lay of the land. We'll beat him to Beth and Alex and be there to protect them if that coyote does turn up."

Sophie had ten more questions and she asked none of them. They had a long day tomorrow and they needed sleep to get through it. Sophie was a woman used to doing what needed doing. Right now, what she needed to do was sleep. She closed her eyes, but her unspoken fears proved stronger than all her years of self-control. She tucked up tight against Clay and held him. She noticed he held on right back.

That was enough communication from her husband to let her fall asleep.

The land was still mighty rugged, but Beth found a trail

straightaway that led in the direction her stubborn husband wanted to go. Since the only other choice was to head back to Mosqueros and maybe face down that dry-gulching bounty hunter, Beth chose to head on west.

They set a blistering pace for two people on foot, and walked far into the night. Their clothing dried on their backs and the squishing of their boots finally was silent.

Beth knew they'd intersect with people somewhere along this way. And she had enough money tucked in her shoe to buy a horse and some dry bullets. She might get some food, too, although if she could get the bullets, she could take care of the food on her own.

They finally had to give up for the night, and Beth searched for a likely place to sleep. They'd had nothing to eat all day, though they'd swallowed their share of water. She was too tired to think of food now, and it was too dark for her to even search for greens or berries.

She found a felled ponderosa pine that had fallen down a steep slope and brought an avalanche of rock with it, creating a decent cave. The tree looked as if it had been lying there for years, its needles shed until they made a fair bed. Beth decided to hope the tree would stay wedged over their heads for one more night.

With nothing to use as a cover, they snuggled together in the dark. Beth rested her head on Alex's strong shoulder, but her mind was in such a turmoil that sleep wouldn't come, despite her exhaustion. "Alex, is there nothing I can do to convince you to come back to Mosqueros with me? We can talk to someone. Get advice. Maybe there's a way you can—can serve out your time. Maybe we could talk with a lawyer, or maybe the sheriff would know the right way to turn yourself in."

Alex's lips stopped her talk. He didn't reply to her suggestions, which was a reply in itself. His kiss, first just one of comfort, became more. It was as if he was desperate to be close to her. But though they'd been together as man and wife fully, he didn't urge her to that closeness. Instead, he kissed her for long moments then finally pulled back.

"I love you, Beth. I want you to be safe. While we tried to find a trick to get me out of the punishment I deserve, you might be killed. If one man is after me, there may be ten."

"But I caused this, Alex." Beth reached up a hand to rest on Alex's mouth. She could barely see him in the shadow of their little cave. "He'd have never endangered you if I'd let you go on with the life you were living. You told no one your name. You stayed to yourself. He'd have searched in vain for years. It's my fault that you're being hunted."

"No, it's not." She felt more than saw him shake his head. "It's my own fault. This all happened because of my actions."

"You said you weren't a doctor, and this man was probably looking for a doctor."

She felt Alex kiss each of her fingertips. "I was a pathetic wretch of a man. You brought me back to life, and now I have to clean up the mess created by my cowardice."

"It sounds to me as if you were pushed beyond what any man could bear, Alex." Beth pulled away and tried to see his eyes in the night. "Surely the cavalry will have something short of execution for a man who served long and honorably until that one horrible day."

Silence stretched between them. Alex's hand stroked her hair. She could see the darkness of his tanned skin against her white hair.

"If they do, then I'll serve my time, be it in the cavalry or in prison. But I don't want you to wait for me, Beth. It could be years, and even if I serve my time, I'll be a marked man. A disgrace."

"Not a marked man, Alex. A fallen, broken man. Disgraced is the opposite of graced and God is gracious. He can wash it all away. I don't care what kind of past you have or what kind of punishment you have to face. I know you to be a decent, honorable man. I will wait for you forever."

"No!" Alex shook his head almost violently. "You can't waste your life on me."

"I can't do anything else, Alex. I love you." Beth kissed him and felt his kindness and his love and his regret. "Don't ask me to abandon you because I can't. I won't."

"I love you, too, Beth. It's another act of cowardice and selfishness to let you stay with me. I'm so sorry I'm not strong enough to turn you away." Alex pulled her close again. He whispered against her lips, "I have no right to be so blessed."

"You're going to town again?" Mandy felt a chill of pure fear.

"If you want to come along, you're welcome to." Sidney smiled that charming smile, and Mandy remembered his promises of just a few days ago. He'd never make such a mistake again as going into that saloon. "I should have bought a gold pan so I can work that spring."

"I've already got a rising of bread started."

Sidney had slept late and Mandy had let him. He'd worked hard with the pickax every day since his wretched visit to Helena.

"And I've got the willow lathes soaking to make the bedstead. I thought you'd help me with it." Mandy knew how to stretch those lathes to make a foundation for the straw tick mattress she planned to build. But once they started soaking, she couldn't take them out of the water unless she planned to use them. They'd harden. Worse yet, once they hardened they'd not soften and be pliable again. She spent hours yesterday hunting these tough, flexible branches. But if it meant not letting Sidney go to town alone again, maybe she should just abandon the work. There were more willows to be stripped.

"I forgot to buy what I need to pan for gold." Sidney was so earnest in his quest. "I'd never heard of that before. They said it's a lot easier than a pickax."

Mandy didn't know all that much about gold, there being a distinct lack of it in her part of Texas. But her pa had money from a gold strike her grandfather made in the Rockies, so it stood to reason that there was gold around here somewhere. All Mandy really knew about gold was one wild tale after another passed on from campfires. Most of it wasn't for the delicate ears of women, but Mandy knew how to listen when it was thought she was rolled up in a blanket asleep by a campfire.

"You know there'll be no more saloons for me, don't you, honey? I've given you my word and I intend to keep it. Come along if you're doubtful. I'd prefer to have you along with me." Sidney pulled her into his arms and proved himself to be very persuasive.

The air was colder today. Mandy was positive she smelled snow. She'd faced snow often enough in Texas to know the signs. A heavy snow might prevent her from searching out new willows. If she didn't get this bed made today, they'd spend the winter on the dirt floor. The Hardens had offered to stay longer and build more furniture and put down a wooden floor, but Mandy was capable of both.

Mandy knew she wasn't treating her husband like she trusted him, and that was a wifely sin to her way of thinking. "I'd best stay home. You go on in and buy your gold pan. I trust you, Sidney."

"Thank you." Sidney kissed her and distracted her from even her mildest worry. Then he saddled up and rode away while she went to work on their bedstead.

Mandy prayed steadily for her untrusting heart as she worked on weaving the lathe around a frame the Hardens had built for her. This would get them up off the floor. She had the bedstead done and just needed to wait for the lathe to dry so she could drag the mattress inside. She heard a horse trotting into the yard. It was long enough since Sidney left, if he pushed hard into Helena and back. She hurried outside, hoping to welcome her husband.

A strange man was dismounting from the most magnificent black stallion Mandy had ever seen. She ducked back inside, jerked her rifle off the pegs over her front door, and stood with the weapon cocked and pointed before the man had his stallion lashed to the hitching post.

"Move along, stranger." Mandy held the gun dead-level and didn't so much as blink. The man was less than ten feet away from her, but she felt her blood cool and her hands steady. She had the nerve to pull the trigger if he made any sudden moves. It worried her sometimes this chill that over came her when she needed to shoot. And she hated the thought of killing a man. But she knew she could do it.

"Howdy, ma'am." The man smiled but stayed at a respectful distance. He had golden yellow hair that dangled down to his shoulders. He was tall and broad, his shoulders wrapped in a coat tanned nearly white, with long fringe and slightly darker brown chaps. He looked to be young, under thirty, but he had eyes that understood the business end of a Winchester and enough sense to refrain from startling her.

Mandy didn't shift her focus, but only a blind woman could fail to notice the midnight black horse standing tied to her hitching post. The horse fairly vibrated with indignation at being restrained. It stood, its head high, its legs braced as if it was one wrong move from attack.

"Recognize the horse, Mrs. Gray?" The man's eyes were so blue Mandy felt as if she could see right through them to the sky behind. For a young man, he had a fair supply of wrinkles at the corners of his eyes, like many a man who'd spent long hours in the hot summer sun and bitter winter wind.

"No, I've never seen this horse before. I'd remember." She dared a glance at the horse.

The man made no move toward her or toward his gun. He seemed satisfied to stand, his hand raised just a bit, a look in his eyes that said he understood and even respected the gun aimed straight at his belly. "You've never seen him, but I was hoping you'd say you'd met his son."

The foal. Yes, the little black fireball could be a miniature of this fierce steed.

"You're Linscott." Mandy thought hard, searching for a first name. "Tom Linscott."

"That's right. The Tanners sent word that their mare had put a foal on the ground out of my black." Linscott reached a hand very cautiously out and patted his stallion on his massive, well-muscled shoulder.

"Tanners?" All Mandy's suspicions roared back to life and she raised the gun an inch, taking a bead.

Linscott recognized her doubts and smiled. "Oh yes, I mean Harden. They call it the Harden ranch now, I reckon. Hard to keep track, Belle and all her husbands."

Four, Mandy remembered that well enough.

"We've gotten so we don't pay no attention to the name of a new husband and just keep on calling it the Tanner ranch, although Silas is shaping up to be less worthless than the earlier men she married. They named their boy Tanner so that makes it even harder to forget the ranch's real name. . .or I guess I should say its former name."

Mandy didn't lower the fire iron. "I don't know you, Mr. Linscott. And the Hardens said they were running for home, expecting to be snowed into their high mountain valley for the winter, so they couldn't have told you about the foal."

"I didn't talk to the Hardens." Linscott's eyes narrowed as if he was growing tired of explaining himself.

Well, too bad for him.

"The cowhands I talked to said you were a pretty little thing and fast with your rifle. Said you shot four wolves in the time it takes most people to draw and aim. Said you even beat Belle to the draw, and that's sayin' somethin'. I'd have to admit they got it right."

Got what right? Her shooting or that she was pretty? Sidney always told her how pretty she was. She'd heard it from her pa, too, but Pa always said it was a nuisance being pretty in the West. Made more men for him to run off.

Linscott's eyes were warm as he studied her, paying particular attention to the long gun she had braced against her shoulder. She thought that's what he was looking at. She hoped it was.

"The Hardens get snowed in, but the hands that helped with the drive don't live at their ranch. Silas and Belle handle the ranch themselves except at branding and when they run cattle to market. A good share of the drovers who were with them spend the winter in Divide, and a few of them hired on to my outfit at the Double L. I was interested in the little guy. I always go visit foals of my black sires."

Linscott heard the soft whinny of a horse and turned to look over his stallion's tall shoulders toward the corral. "There he is." He spoke like a prayer. He had eyes for nothing but the baby frolicking at its mama's side. Then suddenly, as if he couldn't hold himself back, he strode toward the barn without another word.

Mandy felt like a fool standing there with her rifle aimed at nothing. "Mr. Linscott, I insist that you ride on. I don't want. . ."

The man wasn't even close enough to hear what she was saying anymore.

Mandy lowered the rifle. With a quick motion that she'd made a thousand times before, she slung it over her shoulder by its strap and hung it angled across her back, muzzle hanging down on her right, gun butt up on her left. Then she followed after her visitor, pausing to pat the cranky stallion on the nose as she passed him.

The horse tried to bite her hand off. She laughed and rounded him, giving his iron-shod heels their due respect.

As she tagged along after Mr. Linscott, it crossed her mind to threaten him with her husband. It might be wise to cloud the issue of how alone she was here. She could say her man would come a'runnin' if she gave a shout, but Tom Linscott had a solid look to him. Trail wise and straightforward, she doubted he'd bluff easy. And since Sidney was in town, all it'd be was a bluff. She kept herself away from Linscott but went up to the fence to watch the beautiful little colt.

Whistling softly, Mr. Linscott said, "He's perfect. A pure imitation of his papa." Linscott pulled off a worn glove, tucked it behind his belt buckle, and fished around in the pocket of his fringed, buckskin jacket. He crouched low and reached a hand through the split-rail fence. He opened his hand to reveal a chunk of carrot.

The colt noticed and froze, staring at that hand. The more civilized mare wandered slowly toward the offered treat.

"C'mon, good girl. You got yourself a prize of a baby, didn't you, lucky lady? Good girl. Good girl."

Mandy almost went for the carrot herself. She was amazed at Mr. Linscott's voice. It was familiar. She'd heard those soothing tones from cattlemen all her life as they gentled a nervous horse and fractious cattle that needed doctoring.

A lot of ranching was done with pure muscle and a sturdy rope, containing the animals for whatever purpose. But when a body needed to handle the critter, to break a horse or to doctor one, most good cowpokes could croon to them, ease their fears. No one was better at it than Beth. She had as much of a gift with animals as she did with people. This man wasn't in her league but he was good, very good.

The mare was obviously an old, well-trained cowpony. Belle had said she was too old to make the long trek home so soon after foaling. The mare didn't hesitate to approach a human hand attached to Linscott's gentle voice.

The foal danced and skittered, his wide black eyes showed white around his pupils as he watched his mother approach that dangerous hand. He pranced forward, then turned and ran a few paces away, then wheeled and rushed toward the security of his mama again. The baby pawed the dirt and shook its short mane.

Mandy crouched so she could look through the railing on eye level with the colt. She used her own animal soothing tones. "You are your father's son, sure enough."

The foal heard her voice and calmed and gamboled forward. She'd talked with him every day since his birth, while she'd tended his mother and the other two horses.

The mare nipped at the carrot, and Tom reached through and ruffled her ears. He looked sideways at Mandy. "The little guy knows you."

"I've been introducing myself to him every day when I feed the mare and brush her coat. He's a long way from tame, but he's not too afraid."

The foal came as far as his mother's hindquarters and ducked low to steal a comforting sip of milk.

Mr. Linscott's low chuckle deepened Mandy's enjoyment of the little colt. He slowly rose from where he crouched and the mare stayed close, letting him pet her, a reward for the carrot.

Mandy stood, too, realizing just how tall Mr. Linscott was— as oversized as his stallion.

Mr. Linscott turned to look at her while he caressed the mare.

Mandy recognized his type, right down to the ground. A cowboy. A man who fought nature every day and won, or at least survived to fight again the next day. A man like her pa.

Her eyes traveled from where he touched the mare up his long, strong arm to his square shoulders, and she looked straight into his eyes.

And he looked back.

Their gazes held for a second as she looked into those eyes. Blue eyes. As blue as hers. As blue as the heart of a flame.

Why had she thought she wanted a city man like Sidney? The moment that thought fully formed, she turned away and gripped the fence, riveting her gaze on the little colt.

Think of something to say. Think. Think.

Suddenly what had been pleasant and familiar was awkward and the silence, before companionable, was uncomfortable. "So, uh—B–Belle, um. . .said you'd try and get her to pay stud fees. Is that right?" There, a safe subject.

"Oh, I'll try." His voice called to her. She almost glanced over to see if he was offering her a carrot. "I got a reputation for guardin' that stallion like he was made of pure gold. But I know Belle Tanner, uh, Harden, I mean. Gotta learn that woman's new name, I reckon." Mr. Linscott chuckled again.

"I won't get anywhere with Belle. She's a tough one. And truth be told, my stallion probably lured this little lady into breakin' her reins and runnin' off with him. Belle don't owe me nothin'. But I won't admit that right up front. I'll be surprised if that confounded woman don't try and charge me money for the lost use of her mare over the winter." Mr. Linscott laughed harder. "But that woman sure got herself a rare little foal. My stallion breeds true, but I don't know as I've seen a prettier little baby born from him."

Mandy made a point not to turn and smile at the invitation Mr. Linscott gave her with his good-natured talk.

A touch on her shoulder brought her around and backed her about five feet down the corral fence. She fumbled again to speak. "Well, I—I need to get on with—with my—"

"Let me split that firewood there." Mr. Linscott still had his hand raised where he'd touched her, to draw her attention to where he was looking. He nodded toward the mountain of firewood the Harden clan had left behind. A little of it split but plenty left that wasn't.

Mandy glanced up and saw those eyes again. She looked quickly away. "There's no need of that. Thanks for offering. But no, I have a busy day laid out, so I'll say good-bye now and—"

"And I heard you needed to daub your house again. When I rode in, I saw a patch of clay soil, not far from here. That works faster and better than mud. I'll go dig up a supply and do some chinking. I need to thank you for takin' care of this little guy."

Mr. Linscott leaned his elbow on the fence. "Belle owes you, but my hands said they helped you. . .uh, you and—and your man get settled." Mr. Linscott straightened, and out of the corner of her eye, Mandy saw him adjust his hat. "They said your. . .uh. . . h–husband. . ." There was a few seconds of silence then Tom went on. "He isn't used to ranch life and maybe he'd be willing to accept some neighborly help. I like knowing my black's offspring are well cared for, and I can see that this one is. To my way of thinking, I owe you for that, and I pay what I owe."

Mr. Linscott turned away from her, and finally she felt free to turn and watch him. He headed straight for the woodpile. "Splittin' wood is heavy work for a woman. I can take some of that weight off your shoulders."

It was the honest truth that of all the chores that needed doing before winter landed hard on Mandy's head, splitting that mountain of cord wood was the most daunting. She could do it, but it would be long hours of hard labor just to keep even with what they needed to burn, and she needed to do more than keep even. She needed to get ahead and store up the wood before winter made that work impossible. And the chance of Sidney splitting all that wood was slim. "There's no need for that, Mr. Linscott."

"Call me Tom." He grabbed the ax, checked the edge with his thumb, then pulled the glove he'd shed back on. "And I'm doing it. Even a sharpshootin' cowgirl like you can't stop me."

He caught a length of wood, about three feet long, and up and settled it on the log used for a cutting block. He hefted the ax, testing the weight of it in his hands. Then taking a firm grip, he swung the ax with a single, smooth motion, and the log split in half. He set one of the three-foot-long halves back on the block and split it again.

Mandy watched his well-oiled movements, envying him his strength. She wasn't really thinking about much except the hard work Tom made look so easy, until he stopped in midswing and looked up at her, glaring. "Did you need something?"

Mandy realized she was staring. "No, no, I'm sorry. I—I have chores." She turned and almost ran to the cabin. Slipping inside, she hesitated to remove her gun from her back. Then knowing Linscott was no danger—not only was he no danger, he'd protect her—she hung her gun on its pegs and went back to building her bedstead. She was fully conscious of the steady music of the swinging ax and the presence of a man who was not her husband doing a husband's job.

She remembered the way Tom had assumed that the job was hers. It struck her like a blow that somehow he knew Sidney wasn't going to help. What had the cowpokes he'd talked to said that gave him that impression?

She didn't have to wonder though. She knew exactly what they'd said, nothing she didn't already know. Sidney was a city boy with no skills necessary to survive in the West.

Dismayed, Mandy forced herself to stay inside and work, alone, on the bed she shared with Sidney. It damaged something fragile, deep in her heart, to admit that she was ashamed of her husband.

Twenty-six

Beth was so proud of Alex she could hardly speak.

She also was sorely tempted to bash him over the head.

She suspected that made theirs a marriage like most.

They'd pushed hard all day up a trail and down. Beth kept a lookout for signs of a ranch or a larger trail—one that led them away from Fort Union.

Beth had found a skinny stream and they'd had plenty to drink. She'd gathered pinecones and carried them in her skirt. They could get nuts out of them if nothing easier and tastier showed itself. The nuts needed to be baked to crack out of their shells so that meant a fire and too much time. It had to wait until they camped for the night.

So they'd had no food all day and the front of Beth's stomach was rubbing against her backbone. They needed energy to keep up a good pace, so meager though the nuts were, they'd eat them.

Beth had done her best to dry out the firearms and she thought the bullets looked useable. They'd never really know until she fired the gun, but she wondered if they were being pursued, and gunshots sounded for miles. So she hoped for the best and decided to set a rabbit snare and hope they snagged something bigger for breakfast.

The sun was dropping in the sky and Beth had begun scouting for a place to sleep when she heard a twig snap. Beth grabbed Alex's arm, jerked him off the trail, and dove behind a bank of mesquite trees.

"What—"

"Shh!" Beth cut him off as she looked back and saw nothing. Someone was coming. She had no doubt. If it looked like the someone was friendly, she'd go out and ask for help. If it was the bounty hunter—

Beth lifted the Winchester off Alex's shoulder. He'd carried the heavy gun and her loaded doctor's bag all day. She quickly and as silently as possible loaded the rifle then did the same with the Colt. She'd left the chambers empty so they'd dry thoroughly. Hopefully one of them would fire. To be prepared in case one didn't, she eased her knife out of her boot and set it close to hand. She didn't offer one of the weapons to Alex, and he didn't ask.

Minutes ticked by and the rider or riders didn't come along. A thrill of fear climbed Beth's neck. Someone was riding carefully. Maybe even hunting.

Catching Alex's arm, she dropped back farther off the trail, not wanting to let anyone get behind them. The trail sloped upward into a wooded area and Beth saw some heavy boulders that would give them protection while affording her a good field of fire. She did her best to not make a sound, no twigs snapping for Beth. Alex was trying, too. And Beth appreciated it. She finally reached the rocks and ducked behind them.

"Beth, honey, it's Pa."

"Pa?" Beth shot to her feet. Pa and Ma came out from behind a bank of scrub pines. Both had their pistols drawn. Ma had her trusty Spencer repeating rifle hanging from her back. Pa toted his Winchester 73 the same way. They'd left their horses hidden somewhere.

"Ma!" Beth rushed around the boulders, barely aware of Alex rising to his feet as she dashed away. She flung herself into her mother's arms, and Ma holstered her gun and hugged her so tight it hurt. Beth had never felt anything better.

"Howdy, Clay. We're glad to see you two." Beth glanced sideways to see Alex shaking hands with her pa. Pa clapped her husband on the back and smiled.

"How'd you find us?" Beth liked thinking her pa had some affection for her husband.

"We've been following your trail all day. We knew you'd have to climb out of that arroyo to the west side. It's the only low spot. We crossed the arroyo north of where you jumped in and headed south to meet up with you heading home. But we went south a far piece before we crossed your trail. You're heading northwest instead of northeast toward Mosqueros."

Beth grinned at Ma, then turned and threw herself into her father's arms.

"I'm happy to see you're both alive and well." Ma gave Alex a quick hug. "Mostly well."

Alex pointed to the bedraggled bandage on his head. "I had a run-in with some rocks, but Beth took care of me. She's a fine doctor."

Beth heard Alex's generous words and turned to smile at him. She really did love this man.

"So'd you get lost? What are you headed this way for?" Pa lifted his hat and scratched his head.

All the excitement went out of the reunion.

Beth went into Alex's arms and wondered how hard it'd be to kidnap the stubborn man.

"Clay, Sophie, we were heading to—"

The sharp crack of rifle fire split the air.

Pa staggered forward. "Get down." Vivid red bloomed on his shirt. "Everyone! Get behind those rocks."

He fell against Beth, reaching out his arm to grab Ma, then

slammed into Alex as he fell, taking them all to the ground. As they landed, another shot ricocheted off the boulder nearest at hand. Pa was conscious and the four of them crawled and dragged themselves to shelter.

The rifle fired again. Bits of stone exploded into the air but the rocks were a solid shield.

"How many?" Pa gasped and pulled his Colt from his holster.

Beth knelt beside Pa, tearing his shirt open to see where he'd been hit. High on the shoulder. Maybe a broken collarbone.

Ma had her Spencer out, her head down but listening for movement. There were no more shots fired. "What's going on, Beth?"

"There's one man out there. A man came to us last night. No, two nights ago now, I guess."

"It was just last night." Ma said quietly, her attention riveted on any noise from beyond their shelter.

Beth shook her head and didn't bother trying to sort it out. The sickening wound pouring blood from her father's chest was too much to deal with and count back days, too. "He told us he had a sick brother. We followed him, then he started shooting and we've been on the run ever since."

"We saw signs of him. Only one man?" Ma asked.

"Yep."

"Why didn't you just shoot him like a hydrophobic skunk?"

Beth dragged her doctor's bag off her arm and jerked it open. *Please, God, give me enough of the healing gift to save Pa.*

"Thought of it, but he was a crack shot, and once he got above us on that cliff we had no place to lie in wait for him. We just headed out as fast as we could. Then we reached that arroyo and it was flooded. The shooter was still on our trail so we jumped in."

Ma glanced over. "Let Alex take care of your pa. You get over here and help me keep an eye out. If we pinpoint him, I can slip around and get a drop on him."

"Don't you dare, Sophie," Pa gasped as Alex pressed on the gushing wound.

"Lie still, Clay." Alex moved up to the side opposite Beth. "You're losing too much blood. You'll be passed out in a few minute if I don't get the bleeding stopped, and then you won't be able to give orders to anyone." Alex pushed hard, his arms straight, as much weight as he could muster on the wound. "Beth, stay right here. I need two hands."

"No, Alex. You'll have to do this one on your own." Beth leaned over and jerked Pa's Colt from its holster and scooted to the far end of the boulders. They were unprotected on both ends but had a rock wall behind them, which curved around and made it impossible for someone to sneak up or come at them from above.

Beth nearly fell backward when Alex grabbed her arm and pulled. "I'm not asking because I need you to encourage me. I'm asking because I need two hands to save your Pa's life. Get over here."

Beth exchanged a look with Ma.

"Help him, girl. I won't go slipping out. I'll just keep us covered."

With a jerk of her chin, Beth went back to Alex's side. Together they fought a short, brutal fight for her Pa's life.

"Forceps," Alex ordered. "Bullet's still in there."

"That's good, Pa." Beth slapped the instrument into Alex's hand.

"Beth, I've got to keep pressure on his back while I take the bullet out from the front. Get on this side with me. He's losing too much blood."

Beth nearly threw herself around to the other side of her poor pa.

Alex, his hand soaked in raging scarlet, took her hands and guided them beneath Pa's shoulder. "Press up hard. Plug that hole. As soon as the bullet's out, I can sew him up." Alex dug.

Pa lay still, silent, his face twisted in pain, his teeth gritted, his face sallow, letting Alex jab at his wound.

At last a dull scratch of metal on metal told Beth Alex had found the bullet. With a sickening scrape, he got hold of it and dragged the ugly bit of lead free.

Beth pressed on Pa's back, the entrance wound, with all of her might. She'd have lifted him if Pa hadn't worked with her to keep his shoulder firmly against her fingers. She nearly cried out in grief to think of how badly she was hurting him.

A sudden burst of rifle fire startled her. Then Ma returned fire—slow and steady she shredded an area directly in front of the boulder, without exposing herself. Ma lay down a field of fire, to the left and right of where the shots had come.

The bounty hunter's rifle fire ended.

"I've got to get over there," Pa spoke between his teeth, a deep groan escaping as he struggled to sit up. Beth noticed Pa pushed with his left hand but not his right. It wasn't working since he'd been hit.

"Sophie," Alex's voice was all doctor now. All authority.

Sophie quit shooting. "What?"

"Tell your husband to lie still if he wants to live."

"Clay!" Ma's voice must have penetrated Pa's fierce determination to protect his family. "I'm all right. I'll tell you if I need help. Now let Alex patch you up."

Pa's eyes met Ma's, and they communicated so much in that one look. Love and respect and fear and rage. All mixed up with deadly determination not to let this man do them any more harm.

Beth had never loved her parents more than she did at this very instant.

Pa subsided.

Alex worked so fast Beth could hardly follow his movements. He poured carbolic acid on Pa's wound and began sewing, cutting off the flow of blood. "I don't think he got a lung or an artery. It looks like his collarbone is broken."

Alex finished with motions so swift and sure that Beth could imagine him on a battlefield, racing from one wounded soldier to the next. Dispensing life in the midst of death.

"Clay, we need to roll you over and close the hole in your back." Alex spoke slowly, his voice low so as not to give information to their enemy, but clear to get past the agony.

"Beth, now, help me." Alex's voice was rock solid but his face was utterly colorless, and after he spoke, he clenched his jaw so tightly she was afraid he might break his teeth.

Beth hated every second of treating her pa. She thanked God fervently that Alex was here for this because causing Pa pain, even if she knew it was absolutely necessary, nearly sent her into fits.

They got Pa onto his belly and Alex dosed the wound with the sterilizing liquid then attacked it as if he had a hundred patients waiting, all screaming for help.

Beth had a clear view of how it was for Alex during war. The relentless pressure. The bleeding and dying. The cries of pain. The stench of death. All surrounded him as he fought for life in the midst of it.

She'd have run away, too. Now she knew she would never have stood it. She loved Alex more fiercely than ever and she vowed to God that she'd do everything in her power to protect him from whatever punishment the cavalry had in store, even if she had to write to the president of the United States.

The rifle fire began again, higher this time, so shattered fragments of rock blasted down on them. The gunman thought he'd found a way to force them out of their hiding place.

"Cover his wound, Beth. Don't let anything fall into it." Alex took the last few stitches, and quickly, as if he was working under threat of his own death, he pulled bandages from the doctor's bag.

Beth had hung them over her shoulders to dry during the day and she prayed now they hadn't become so dirty during the time they were in the air that they'd poison Pa's wound and bring on an infection.

Alex surprised her by soaking a pad of the bandage with the carbolic acid. Then he pressed it against Pa's injury and used more bandage, this time left dry, to fasten the bandage in place.

The rifle fire continued, deafening. The shards of rock rained down.

Ma returned fire with her Colt. The smoke and smell of the fired rounds made Beth wonder how much ammunition they had with them. She hoped it didn't come down to the stuff she'd hauled through floodwater today.

Splintering rock and shredded leaves, cut from overhead by their assailant's bullets, rained down on them.

"Get him on his back again. I didn't bandage the exit wound yet." He'd been in too big a hurry to close the back wound.

Beth helped, feeling her hands tremble as she shoved her father around like a. . .like a. . .a *patient*. She'd helped with Sally, but Alex hadn't needed her this desperately. He'd only needed her presence to give him strength. Now they had four medical hands working as hard and fast as they knew how, fighting for Pa's life.

The gunfire stopped. A heavy grunt sounded from beyond their fortressed position.

"I think I got him." Ma sounded grim and angry. There was no pleasure for her in shooting a person, no matter how evil that man.

Alex poured on more of the sterilizing carbolic acid.

Beth silently thanked God for Dr. Lister's brilliant invention. A wound could turn septic so easily. She asked for divine help in the healing of her beloved pa.

Alex quickly finished the bandaging then looked up at her, his stern doctor demeanor only for show. She saw beneath it to something so fragile that Beth was afraid he might splinter into pieces right in front of Beth's eyes. With a hard jerk of his chin that didn't reach his eyes, he said, "Okay, go help your ma. I just need to watch and make sure the bleeding has stopped."

Alex's hands were coated in blood. It had gotten on his disheveled white shirt, and his pants were sticky and crimson.

Beth saw those hands start to shake.

Alex wiped sweat off his forehead and smeared blood across his face without realizing it.

Beth was afraid if he knew he'd fall apart. She said, "Alex!"

He looked at her. She let her eyes connect with his. She saw the awareness in him that he hadn't clung to her, not for strength. They hadn't had that sharing Alex had relied on at first. He'd done this on his own. But now he drew from her. She felt him calm as their eyes held.

His voice sounded steady when he finally spoke. "We're done here. Your ma needs you more. Doesn't she, Clay?" Alex looked down at his patient.

"Yes." Clay's voice was barely a whisper. "Go, honey. Alex and I will be fine."

Beth's eyes went back to Alex's and he gave her an encouraging nod. "Go. I'm all right."

She felt as if her flesh tore when she turned away from Alex. It was possible she needed him as much as he needed her. She crawled to Ma's side.

Ma shoved Pa's rifle in Beth's hands. There was an ammunition belt on the ground in front of them. Ma looked at her and gave her a little smile. "We've fought bad men before together, Beth honey. Fought 'em and won."

Beth returned the smile, looked down at her father's blood all over her own hands and clothes, and felt her heart harden for the task ahead. "And we'll win again this time, won't we, Ma?"

There was a loud groan from about a hundred feet away.

One blond brow arched on her ma's confident face. "Maybe I've already finished the job."

Beth took a quick glance in the direction of that sound, then leaned close to her mother and whispered quiet, so no man would hear. "I'm glad you're my ma."

With a quick jerk of her chin, Ma whispered, "I'm glad you're my daughter, Beth. Now let's snake out of here. I'll go right, you go left."

"Pa ordered us to stay under cover." But that was before the dry-gulcher was down.

"Your pa always was one for giving orders." Ma smiled.

Beth smiled back.

"That coyote is hurt, but he's not dead," Ma added. "So we've got to go careful. You're the best there is at ghostin' around, girl."

Beth eased down on her belly. She took one quick look at Alex and Pa.

Alex had moved around so he had his back to them. Pa had let his eyes fall closed, which wasn't like him.

She braced herself to move out of the sheltering rock. Hoping she was up to the task ahead, she prayed, "Give me strength, Lord. Give me strength."

As she moved forward, she saw her ma vanish around the other side of the rock whispering, "Help me. Help me. Help me."

Beth scooted along quiet as a sliding snake. She rounded the sheltering boulders and headed in the direction of the shrubs where the man lay groaning in pain. She headed for the man's feet.

Her ma would be coming from where it sounded as if his head rested. They both slipped along, using every bit of cover in case the man was up to caring that they were coming for him.

Beth got to the edge of the bushes and saw the man's boots twitching. He was making plenty of noise now so he must be beyond caution. Beth got her gun leveled in front of her, mindful of where Ma would emerge from the bushes. She inched in until she could see the man's legs, then his belly. Her gun held steady and she saw up to the bounty hunter's arms, which were holding a gun aimed straight at Ma.

"Hey!" Beth shouted, drawing the man's attention.

His gun swung around. Ma slid out of the bushes and swung her gun hard at the man's head. It hit with a thud. The bounty hunter dropped back unconscious, but a spasm made his gun go off.

"Look out!" Ma yelled.

Beth heard a crack from overhead, where the bullet had hit. She threw herself sideways, hoping to pick right. She had no idea which way to dive. She rolled onto her back and saw a heavy branch plunging toward her like a spear.

The impact was the last thing she saw before the world went black.

★ Twenty-seven ★

"Alex, get over here!"

Alex heard the shot and was moving before Sophie shouted at him. And why was Sophie's the only voice he heard? He had time to die a thousand deaths in the seconds it took to reach Beth, who lay crushed under a huge, dead tree limb.

Sophie was already at Beth's side. "Grab the other end. This fell when the gun went off."

Alex lifted on his end and he and Sophie staggered under the weight, edging it away from Beth then throwing it to the side.

"What's going on!" Clay's voice was furious.

It sounded to Alex like he was getting up. "You've got to go to him." He used his doctor voice on Sophie and even she minded him. "Keep him still. If he starts bleeding again we could lose him."

"I'll be right back." Sophie rushed away.

Alex turned to Beth and saw blood. Crimson rushing blood. Then there were two of her, then one, then three. Alex sank to his knees beside her.

Stay here. Stay here. Keep me here, God.

Alex knew where else he was likely to go. Where he went every time he doctored, unless Beth was at his side. His mind went to war.

God, keep me here. Give me the strength to help her.

His vision faded and widened but Alex fought it. Brought himself back to Beth. He fumbled at her neck until he found a heartbeat. Strong, steady. Her neck was already soaked in blood but Alex found no injuries to her neck's arteries that would drain the life out of her in seconds, with nothing he could do to stop it.

Alex heard distant explosions. Cannon fire. Thundering horses' hooves on a battlefield. His hands were coated in blood, blood that had left the soldier's body, taking his life along with it.

Fighting the madness, he dragged himself back to Beth, ripped his shirt off and wadded it up and found the worst source of the bleeding. "Head wound." The sound of his own voice steadied him a bit. Maybe if he kept speaking aloud. "Head wounds bleed. That doesn't always mean they're serious."

Where was Beth's doctor's bag? The wounds needed to be sutured. If only all he needed to do was put in stitches, maybe he could stand it. But what else was hurt? Her spine? Her brain? Were there broken bones? Was she busted up inside? Alex tried to check while he staunched the blood.

He needed help. He needed his faithful nurse and assistant and fellow doctor. He needed his wife.

"Beth, honey, please stay with me." Alex pressed on two freely bleeding wounds, one on her jawline, one on her temple, and worried about an injury to her backbone. If she woke up, if she could talk to him while he cared for her. . .

Please, God, please. Let her be all right. Give me the strength to care for her. Give me strength. Give me strength.

For a moment he heard Beth's voice praying that prayer. Almost like God had sent her to be with him, even when she was asleep. The blood lived and grew. He put the pressure on the wounds again. Still the blood seemed to gush and grow and fight. It soaked into Alex's bunched-up shirt, then crawled up his arms and leapt at his body.

Shaking his head to keep it clear, Alex held fast on the mean gash on Beth's temple and the other on her chin. An awful, scarring cut on her beautiful face. Alex used both hands, trying to attend both wounds at once. He noticed blood trickle down from the corner of her mouth. From that cut on her chin? Or was she bleeding in her mouth or had she been crushed inside, her lungs or her heart? If that had happened she'd die. There was nothing he knew that would save her.

Seconds ticked past. Alex raised his crimson shirt away from the gash on her chin, hoping the bleeding had stopped. Blood trickled still.

His vision blurred and focused on a cavalryman. He reached for the wounded man. A horse screamed in pain. A cannon blasted. Dirt and shrapnel pummeled Alex's body, knocking him forward over the wounded, dying soldier's form as the man fumbled at the wound in his stomach, pushing to get his intestines back inside his belly. Alex reached for his doctor's bag and saw it covered in gore.

A sudden blow snapped Alex's head around and he stared into the furious face of his mother-in-law.

"Help her." Sophie nearly peeled his eardrums away with her harsh order. She raised her hand and slapped him hard across the face. "Get busy and help her."

Alex suddenly realized where his wife had learned her bed-side manner. Staring at Sophie, he braced himself to get slugged again and realized that the strength he'd drawn from Beth was in this woman, too. She seemed to know. Rather than draw back her hand she let him look, let him steady himself by using her courage when he had none of his own. It was enough for the world to come fully back.

"Y–yes, ma'am." Alex turned back to Beth. He'd stopped

243

working on her head wounds, let the shirt slip from his hands. She was coated in blood.

"Don't you have something else to do to my daughter besides try to stop a bleeding cut?"

Alex felt like a mother mountain lion had just roared in his face.

Sophie snatched the shirt from Alex and pressed on the wounds herself. "Is that all that's wrong with her?"

"I don't s–see any other injuries. Nothing external." Alex shook his head almost violently. "She needs stitches to stop this bleeding. M–my bag."

"Go get it yourself. I'll stay with her. And tell Clay to lay still or I'll hog-tie him."

Alex knew well that he faced a will far stronger than his own. If possible, a will even stronger than Beth's. He scrambled to his feet and stumbled forward, then lurched toward the boulder that hid his wounded father-in-law.

Cold blue eyes waited for him around that boulder. "How's Beth?"

"I need to put some stitches in. I think. . .I hope she's just knocked out from a tree branch falling on her." Alex remembered that trickle of blood coming from the corner of Beth's mouth. "Stay here. I can't doctor two people at once so don't do anything to tear those stitches. Your wife is helping me."

Clay seemed willing to drill holes in Alex's brain with his fiery blue gaze. That spurred Alex to hurry just so he could get back to yet another McClellen who was willing to do him damage if he didn't stay clearheaded. Alex decided being terrorized worked surprisingly well in this case to keep him focused.

Grabbing Beth's doctor's bag, which they'd been struggling to dry out all day, he rushed back to his wife, lying soaked in blood, her skin pure white against the sticky crimson flow.

Alex had a needle ready in seconds. Trying to detach from what lay ahead, piercing his wife's lovely skin to put in the barbaric sutures, he pushed, rushed along, letting his hands work and trying to keep his addled brain out of it. Going for the worse of her wounds first, Alex snapped, "Move the rag and hold the edges of this wound closed."

He barely heard the dictatorial tone of his voice but knew it for the take-charge doctor voice he was fully capable of using. Being knocked on his backside was one possible reaction to his dictatorial voice.

It didn't happen. Instead she obeyed all his instructions and proved to be an able assistant. She lacked Beth's finesse, but the woman had steady hands. Alex wasn't much surprised.

It took ten stitches to close up the gash on Beth's forehead. It ran along her hairline. There'd be a scar, but her hair would cover it.

Sophie had kept steady pressure on Beth's chin while she minded Alex's orders about the cut he was suturing.

Alex glanced up at Sophie. "We'll do her chin now."

"Ready." She nodded and smiled. That strength was still there; Alex didn't even have to look in Sophie's eyes to feel it steady him.

"You're a good doctor, Alex. I hope the day will come when you can trust yourself again."

"So do I." Alex turned back to his patient. When Beth's other cut was closed, Alex hoped that scar would fall just beneath the curve of her chin. Maybe that wouldn't harm her pretty face much either. But Alex knew without a doubt he wanted his wife alive and well, however scarred. And he knew Beth and her clear, level head well enough to know she'd agree. It occurred to Alex that Beth's scars would be visible while Alex's were invisible, but they were both scarred nonetheless.

"Look at this." Sophie ran her hand, smeared red with mostly dried blood, over Beth's head. "There's a big bump on this side, as well as the cut. Hopefully she just took a bad whack and got knocked cold. If we give her time, she'll come out of it."

A low groan turned Alex and Sophie toward the outlaw.

Though he didn't move, Sophie dived at the man and had him hog-tied and gagged so fast Alex could barely see Sophie's hands move. There was violence in Sophie's expression, but it didn't pass to the man overly much, though he was securely and tightly bound.

Turning her back on the bounty hunter, Sophie went back to caressing Beth's head. Part gentle mother, part grizzly—Sophie McClellen.

"I'm glad you're my wife's mother. I'm glad I got to know your whole brood."

Sophie looked away from Beth, her eyes narrow, her gaze sharp. "You say that like it's in the past. Like we're not going to be part of your life anymore."

Swallowing hard, Alex couldn't do other than tell the truth. "That man chasing us is after me to arrest me and turn me in to the cavalry at Fort Union. I'm a deserter. I told Beth we needed to get to the fort so I could turn myself in. That way she'd be safe. I'm wanted dead or alive, like all deserters, and this man is a bounty hunter. He didn't seem overly concerned about the 'alive' part of 'dead or alive,' and he didn't seem too worried about Beth getting caught in his crossfire."

Sophie held his gaze.

Alex waited, giving her plenty of time to realize that it was that act of cowardice, deserting from the cavalry, that had led to Beth's injuries. Clay's, too. This was all on Alex's head.

"You look at my daughter with eyes shining with love, Alex. Do you love her?"

Alex turned to stare at Beth, ashen white, completely un-moving. He felt as if his love had nearly killed her. "Yes." His words were barely audible. He said them to Beth rather than to Sophie. "Yes, I love her. And I almost got her killed." Alex felt tears burn at his eyes and felt them spill over.

Sophie gasped and Alex looked away from his silent, fragile wife. Sophie looked at what must be obvious signs of crying on

Alex's face as if he'd suddenly sprouted a second nose.

Dashing the tears away, Alex said, "Stay with Beth. I need to go check on Clay again."

One hard hand snaked out and grabbed Alex by the wrist. "No, don't let him see you"—Sophie's voice fell to a breath of a whisper—"crying. It'll kill him faster'n a bullet."

That made no sense. "Okay, you go. Tell him she's going to be fine."

"Is she going to be fine?"

"Yes, everyone's going to be fine." Alex felt confident of that. Everyone but him. He was facing a noose.

"I'll stay here with you until they're well enough to travel, then I'll go on to the fort alone. No sense taking Beth with me any farther."

"I've heard some of what they do to deserters. Lots of room for a decision to go hard against a man or go easy. I think it'd be best if your family rode along with you to that fort."

His family. Alex's eyes fell shut from the sweetness of those words. Sophie was counting him as family. It had been a long, long time since anyone had.

Sophie released Alex's arm and went to check on her husband.

Seconds after Alex heard Sophie speaking quietly to Clay, he saw Beth's eyes flutter open.

He bent down and angled himself so he was right in her line of vision, so she wouldn't move an inch. "Hey, you're awake."

There was a glazed look in Beth's eyes, but he saw her fighting it, trying to make sense of the world around her. At last her head cleared enough that she saw him. "What happened?"

"A tree fell on your head." Alex smiled, ignoring the terror he'd felt.

"That would explain the pain."

"I can get you some laudanum."

"Not right now. I've had it before. It makes me feel so stupid and groggy. Let's give the headache a chance to ease without it."

"Okay." He didn't mention the stitches. It was a lot more than just a headache.

A loud grunt from a few paces beyond Beth's wounded head drew Alex's attention and he saw Beth react. "Lie still. We're fine, honey. That's the polecat who was after us." Alex suddenly straightened. "You know, I think your ma shot him. I oughta go have a look, huh?"

Beth managed a smile. "It'd be the right thing to do."

"Even if I'm more inclined to shoot him again?"

"Even then."

"I'll do it then." Alex studied the man.

His piggish eyes blinked open and the man glared at Alex, but thanks to Sophie's skillful hands, the man would neither move nor speak a word.

"Okay, it looks like your ma's bullet creased his skull. Knocked him cold and cut him good, but nothing that won't heal, unless he gets infected." Alex turned back to Beth. "I'm done checking him."

Beth nodded. "Sounds good to me. Maybe a little later you could dose him with the carbolic acid."

"Why waste that on a man I want to see get a fever and die?"

Beth shrugged, then winced, but managed to pat Alex on his arm. "Well, it burns like the very dickens. So pouring it on his open wound would be worth something."

"True." Alex nodded as he imagined tossing a little salt in on top of the carbolic acid. He liked the image. "Okay, I'll do it. Later. When I'm done doctoring you."

Alarm flared in Beth's eyes. "You're not done yet?"

"I'm done, but I want to closely observe my patient for a while yet." Alex said, "Lie still now. I'm going to wash some of the blood away."

"Blood?" Beth started to sit up.

Alex restrained her. "Just be still. You've got a cut on your head and a few stitches where you bled. But you're fine. No sense joggling your head around and causing yourself pain just because you're so vain you want a mirror to pretty up in."

She narrowed her eyes and he'd have kissed her if she hadn't been such a gory, bloody mess.

He found a canteen among Sophie and Clay's supplies and had Beth looking much less horrifying very soon. Then he kissed her as a reward for her taking his ministrations so well, just as Sophie returned from fussing over Clay. "How's Clay?" he asked her.

"As growly as a grizzly bear because I told him he had to lie still. If it was up to him, he'd get up and ride right now. How's Beth?"

"She's awake."

Sophie's eyes went to Beth and a smile bloomed on her face. Alex noted the resemblance between his wife and Sophie and decided Beth would only get more beautiful.

"I think"—Alex looked up at Sophie and smiled—"both our patients are going to make it."

Then Alex thought of Fort Union and what he had coming there. Beth would get more beautiful, no doubt about it, but her beauty would be for her second husband...after the United States Cavalry disposed of her first one.

A hard knock at the door had Mandy scampering out of the bedroom to answer it. She didn't even want to meet Tom's eyes, but she had to thank him.

He was covered with wood chips and he'd taken off his coat and hung it over the hitching post. Mandy saw that his stallion was now in the corral with the mare and foal.

She frowned at Tom. "Is it safe to put your stallion in with the little colt? Sometimes a stallion can attack."

"The black's not like that. He's next thing to a killer in the normal course of things. No one rides him but me and he barely tolerates me. But he's gentle with his brood mares and the babies."

Mandy saw the regal horse sniff the baby, then lift his head and look around, as if scouting for danger.

"I put him in there a while ago. I hated to leave him hitched for hours. Hope that's okay. I had a bait of corn with me so he's not eating your feed."

"It's fine. I should have thought of it myself." She would have if she hadn't been strictly avoiding this man ever since she'd come inside.

"I'm just back with a load of clay." Tom nodded at a bucket full of red mud sitting on the ground beside him. "I didn't finish splitting the wood because I decided it'd be a better idea to work on the cabin a while. There's a patch of red ground about a hundred yards that way." Tom nodded toward the west. "I'm just letting you know that I'll be working close around the house for a while now. Thought you might hear me working and think I was prowling around." Tom reached down for the bucket.

Simple human decency for Mandy to speak. "I'll help. I want to see how the clay works patching the cabin. And I want to know where you found it."

Tom nodded and headed around the corner of the house.

"Wait!"

Pausing, Tom turned back, a brow arched.

"I'll make you something to eat. I've got biscuits and some roast venison. I could bring you out a sandwich."

Tom nodded. "I'm hungry enough to eat the deer with the fur still on, ma'am. I'd be obliged for a sandwich." He looked down at his hands, coated in red clay. "I'll wash a layer or two of this off first." He set the bucket down and went to the watering trough.

By the time he was done washing, Mandy was back with the food. She'd made two thick sandwiches with the salty meat and brought along a cup of steaming hot coffee for him and one for herself. "I'm sorry I didn't think of it earlier. All your hard work and I didn't even offer to feed you." She didn't feel quite right inviting him inside, so instead she came down the two little steps from her cabin and gestured to them. "Have a seat."

When Tom was settled, Mandy handed him the tin plate.

With a generous smile, Tom said, "I had jerky in my saddlebags if I'd have gotten too hungry. Never was one to eat by the clock. Not much use for a clock out here." He turned to the house. "I see Silas and his men mudded the north side, but it needs a second coat. The worst of the bitter wind comes howling down from the north."

Mandy followed his gaze.

He turned back to her and smiled. "But cold winds come from all directions out here, and sometimes all at once it seems, so we need to do the whole cabin."

Using the word *we* jolted Mandy into thoughts of Sidney. He should be here. He should put the cold winter winds ahead of his gold mining.

"So tell me about my colt and the wolves you saved him from?"

"*Your* colt?" Mandy laughed and Tom smiled and shrugged.

Then, sipping the savory coffee, talking about taking care of the foal, Mandy stood facing him. The steps were wide enough for two, but she'd have been shoulder-to-shoulder with him and she decided against that. She found it easy to talk while he chewed on the venison she'd roasted slowly to make it tender.

"Thanks, ma'am." When the food was gone, Tom stood and Mandy backed up too many steps but couldn't stop herself. "Mighty tasty. A sight better than jerky, and that's the honest truth." He went back to his bucket of clay. Hoisting it, he rounded the cabin, set it down, reached in, and picked up the thick, sticky mud.

"Tell me how the clay works. Did you add water to get it like this?" Mandy reached in and got a handful for herself, forgetting awkwardness as she played with the pliable soil.

"Nope, dug it out of the ground that way. It's not far from the spring and it's already well soaked. I didn't bring more because

251

it'll dry out fast. You'll be hauling heavy buckets for days if you use this stuff. You'll wear yourself out toting it home. So I'll do as much of that for you as I can today."

"Mr. Linscott, I—"

"Call me Tom, ma'am. Seems strange to be called mister out here. Makes me feel like I'm the new schoolteacher or somethin'."

Mandy laughed. She couldn't imagine Tom Linscott standing in front of a classroom with a ruler. "All right, it's Mandy then, not ma'am."

They worked over the heavy clay for hours in near silence, only talking when Tom said he was running for more clay. He did the highest parts of the walls, where Mandy couldn't have reached without a ladder, and he was fast enough he did most of the lower walls, too. That required being on his knees. Mandy did the middle and would have done more, but she could barely keep up with him as it was. She sighed with gratitude to think of all the work she'd been spared by not having to carry those heavy buckets.

As they neared the end of the task, Mandy looked down at Tom, working on his knees about five paces to her right. "This is way faster than mixing the mud, and it's not as runny."

"Yes, it packs in tighter, too, and lasts longer." Tom had rolled up his sleeves and had clay nearly to his elbows. He scratched at his nose and left three stripes of red clay on his cheek.

"You look like you're wearing war paint," Mandy laughed.

Tom finished filling the last crack between two logs on the foundation of the cabin. He turned his head sideways and smiled up at her.

"Thank you for thinking of the clay and helping me mud these walls." As she said it she realized the day had worn down. "Will you need a place to stay tonight?" Her light heart gained some weight.

"Um. . .I suppose I didn't figure on it. I could stay and finish splitting the wood, and I could put another coat of mud on a few spots tomorrow. Is—that is, I'd like to"—Tom's brow furrowed and a look of distaste turned his lips downward—"meet your husband. I'm surprised he left you here alone. And with all this work needing doing. Where is he?"

He quickly glanced at the pile of kindling he'd split. Mandy realized she'd forgotten all about her husband for the last few hours, and Tom knew full well that the work he was doing was work she'd have had to do, not Sidney. Which meant he was doing this out of pity.

Mandy carefully added the last patch on the cabin. It might need a few places filled in tomorrow, after the clay had thoroughly dried, but for now it was done. She couldn't decide how to respond to Tom's question. The simple truth was, "Sidney knows I can take care of myself. He had errands in Helena."

"My wranglers told me the Hardens left you pretty well supplied."

Tom knew far too much about her business and Mandy burned with the shame of it. She couldn't bring herself to admit Sidney was on his second trip to town, and both times for supplies for his gold mining. "I don't know when he'll be home. Soon, I'm sure. The Hardens were very helpful to us. There were just a few things we needed before winter set in."

Tom rose, to tower over her, and she looked up into blue eyes, kind but worried, too, and maybe just a bit too interested.

She turned and strode toward the water trough where she could rid her hands of the sticky red clay.

He came up beside her and washed vigorously in the wooden water trough.

The Hardens had found this rotted log and brought it in and set it up to hold water. Someone had done nearly everything for her, all the things that should have fallen to her husband. It stung.

"I'm sorry, Mandy. I didn't mean to speak out of turn."

Nodding, Mandy paid far too much attention to the red under her fingernails. "That's quite all right, but I think you need to go now, Mr. Linscott."

"I think you're right." Tom turned and headed for the corral. Mandy watched him catch his rogue stallion with quiet competence that she couldn't help but admire. As he rode out of the yard, he came close to where she'd mindlessly stood watching him. "Thanks for your help with the foal. He's in good hands; that's a comfort to me. I thank you for letting me repay you in this little way." He touched the brim of his Stetson and rode away without waiting for her to respond.

Which was good, because she was speechless. He was just the latest in a line of people who had helped so much and somehow made it seem like they were indebted.

God, when I asked for protection, You responded beyond my dreams. Thank You, Lord. Thank You.

Sidney got home at a decent hour with his gold pan. No whiskey on his breath, though Mandy felt as if it was outside the bounds of honor to check closely, and to ask would be to accuse him of lying.

Sidney made no mention of the split wood, even though Tom had stacked a neat pile of it by the front door and the rest was lying in a jumble by the chopping block. And he didn't comment on the fact that their house had turned a dull shade of brick red from all the clay.

Mandy couldn't decide if he thought she'd done all that work today and accepted it as her doing her rightful chores, or did the man really not even notice. How did he think a house got heated and a meal got cooked anyway? Maybe he had no idea how much work was involved in mudding a cabin.

Though she wasn't sure why, Mandy didn't tell Sidney that they'd had company.

They sat at the rustic table Silas Harden had built out of split saplings. They ate deer meat shot by Emma Harden and butchered by Mandy. And they sat in a house much warmer because of Linscott's hard work, and cooked that deer over a fire fueled by kindling Tom had split.

There was a dry sink made from a hollowed-out, split log. That and the bedstead, which she'd finished, was all the furniture they had. But it was a good start.

They enjoyed the stew, cooked in a pot that was among the things stowed in the crate from her parents. The Hardens had left some of their camping gear in the form of tin plates, knives, and forks. They claimed it made a lighter trip home, but Mandy wondered what they'd be short of next year for their drive.

Mandy was so relieved to have a solid roof over her head she didn't think of wanting more. Anything else, she'd build through the winter. Sadly, she now knew she'd have to do all of this herself. Sidney didn't have the skill to do it—there was no shame in that. But that he didn't have any interest in learning was shameful indeed.

As they sat surrounded by comfort, provided by others, all Sidney could talk about was his gold pan.

Mandy nearly squirmed with her own shame for comparing her beloved husband to another man. She needed to bridge the gap she felt between them. "Tell me about your childhood, Sidney. Did you have brothers and sisters?"

Sidney straightened a bit. He'd been slumped in his seat, looking exhausted. "Not much to tell really. I was an only child. My father died in the Civil War when I was a youngster. Don't even remember him."

"Really?" Mandy found this glimpse of her husband's young life fascinating, which made her realize how little Sidney talked about himself. "My pa was in the War, too. Where'd your pa fight?"

Shaking his head, Sidney said, "We didn't ever hear many stories about Father. He died a hero, my mother used to say. Died in the Battle of Shiloh."

Mandy gasped. "My pa fought in the Battle of Shiloh. What's

your father's name? Maybe they knew each other."

"It's. . .uh. . .J–John Gray." Sidney's eyes flickered to Mandy's and away. "Mother and I ended up living over a—a store. She took in. . .washing and such. I left—that is, I *didn't* leave school although I *wanted* to. I wanted to help support us, but Mother always lamented her lack of a good education. She believed things would have been easier for us after Father died if she could have been a schoolteacher. So, she pushed me to stay in, and I worked as best I could after school to help out. She died the year I started studying at Yale Law School in Boston."

"I'm so sorry you lost your parents so young. My pa, the one you know, isn't my real father. Ma was married to my pa's twin brother and she was widowed. So, I know how sad it is to lose a father. And you lost your mother, too. . ." Mandy shook her head. No wonder he didn't talk about himself much. "So much sadness."

"Really?" Sidney asked. "You've never said that before. I figured Clay McClellen was your real pa."

"He is. I mean he's *real*. He's a wonderful father. And all my little brothers came after Ma married him. It's too bad your ma didn't remarry. Times were real hard for us after Ma's first husband died. Having a father makes such a difference, and I'd think for a boy it would be even more so."

"She knew a man or two." Something dark passed across Sidney's expression that Mandy found frightening. She'd never seen even a glimpse of the cruelty his expression clearly said he was capable of. Then he closed his eyes and took a deep breath, and when he opened them, he was her Sidney again. "I was always glad to see them go."

"You said your parents were gone, but you never talk about them." Mandy wished she could say the right thing to make up for all Sidney's losses.

Then she remembered something else. "Beth lived in the East for a few years and she wrote home often. She spoke of Yale.

Isn't it in Connecticut?" Mandy had never gone to college. She'd finished high school and gone home to the ranch and lived with her family and helped run the household. But that didn't make her stupid.

"Oh, sorry." Sidney gave her a sheepish smile. Charming, sweet. "I meant Connecticut. Slip of the tongue. New Haven, Connecticut. Harvard is in Boston and I considered going there, almost chose it. Well"—Sidney stood quickly and his chair slid back hard and almost fell over—"it's been a long day. I'll turn in now."

It had been a long day for her, too, and it wasn't over yet. "So tomorrow you'll try panning for gold then?"

"Yes, I'm hopeful that the spring might show some color." Sidney suddenly looked very young and nervous.

Mandy's heart turned over to think how far this life was from the big cities back East. He'd have been rich and comfortable if he'd stayed in Connecticut to be a lawyer. But he'd chosen Texas. He'd never really explained why. And now he'd come to yet another wilderness. It had been his idea to come, but he hadn't really known what he was getting into.

She lifted the plates off the table and carried them to the sink. A door shut and she turned to see that Sidney had gone on to bed. Mandy finished clearing the table then decided to go see how Sidney liked the new bedstead.

She swung the door open and decided he must like it. He was already asleep. Then she stared at his back and decided maybe he was just a bit *too* still. She doubted he could have lain down more than two minutes ago, so how could he be asleep?

She thought of Tom Linscott chopping her wood and sealing her cabin. She should have mentioned the visit. No reason not to. She could say something even now. Then she decided if Sidney wanted to play possum, she'd embarrass him by speaking, acknowledging he was faking it. It suited her not to tell him about her day anyway. Maybe tomorrow she'd bring it up. Or maybe he'd notice all the work and that would start them in talking.

She slipped back out to finish cleaning the kitchen.

Alone.

★ Twenty-eight ★

What had looked like a long hard trek over rugged dry ground was easy with Pa's horses.

Beth didn't mind that it wasn't hard, but she wished desperately it was still long. "I think it's time to camp for the night." Beth lifted her hand to her head, feigning weakness. The act was completely beneath her—playing dainty, fragile woman. But at this rate, they'd make the fort by nightfall.

"You're fine." Alex arched his brows and refused to take her seriously.

She should have taken some class in the theater when she was back East. She had minimal skills as an actress. She was fine. She'd whined around until they'd stretched their time out resting from their wounds for about three days too long. She'd healed so thoroughly, her stitches were nearly ready to come out for heaven's sake.

She'd have stayed longer if they hadn't gotten weary of that whining pig, Cletus Slaughter. Of course they couldn't let him go, but it wasn't in Ma's makeup to just shoot him like a rabid skunk, so they were hauling him along back to the fort, too, draped over his saddle for the most part, since he was given to escape attempts.

That had gotten old by the middle of the second day. Now they just put him on his horse and hauled him along like he was part of their supplies.

Pa had picked up sign and led them to the Santa Fe Trail and they were making good time. Too good.

Alex had fallen silent for more than a day now. Beth couldn't get him to say more than a rare word. He looked ashen but determined. He was riding to face a firing squad. And he was doing it to protect her.

The trail grew wider and more obviously well traveled. Fort Union couldn't be far ahead.

Beth and Alex rode side-by-side in the lead. Pa and Ma brought up the rear, with Cletus draped over his saddle on a horse being led by Pa and a pack animal tied to Cletus's horse.

The sun was low in the sky, but there was plenty of daylight left. It was way too early to camp and Beth knew it. She guided her horse so she was within whispering distance of Alex. "There must be another way."

Turning as if his neck was rusty, Alex looked her in the eye and was silent for a long time. "God bless you, Beth honey, for wanting to save me and protect me. But it's settled. I'm going to do the right thing."

"Even if it kills you?"

"*Especially* if it kills me." Alex's voice rose. "I got myself messed up in a killing business by being a coward. Slaughter proved that to be a plain fact." Alex jerked his thumb in the direction of the bounty hunter dangling over Pa's saddle. "If I have to die to save your life, then I'll do it willingly."

"I'll still collect the reward on you, Buchanan." Cletus had been riding with a kerchief tied over his mouth, but he must have slipped it off. "You're hauling me in as a captive, but I'm on the side of the law."

"Shooting at my wife and daughter puts you on the wrong side, Slaughter." Pa spoke in a voice that would have made Beth quake in her boots if it'd been aimed at her. "I'll make sure they understand that when you try and collect your bounty."

Slaughter wasn't so smart. "That's *my* money. You're all thieves. You're all as bad as the man you protect. I'll see to it the lot of you gets locked up—"

A dull thud ended his tirade. Beth looked back and saw Cletus now hanging limp. Ma spun her pistol in her hand, having obviously just used the butt end of it on Slaughter's hard head.

She looked a little embarrassed. "Sorry. I should have just put the gag back in his mouth, but I am worn clear beyond my last bit of patience with this fool." She holstered her gun with a quiet shush of iron on leather.

Pa grunted and it sounded like satisfaction. Beth wouldn't have minded using the butt end of a pistol on Slaughter herself, so she knew how her parents felt.

Beth wanted to continue pleading with Alex but instead turned to face forward. She let her eyes fall shut, trusting her horse to carry her along with the others. She couldn't bear to think of what lay ahead.

A rider coming fast from behind caught up. It was a cavalry officer.

"How far to the fort?" Pa asked as the man slowed up alongside.

"I'm hoping to make it in time for supper. But unless you push it, it'll be full dark when you get there." The officer jerked his head at their prisoner. "He dead?"

"Nope," Pa said, "we're bringing him in for shooting me and my daughter." Pa lifted his arm to draw attention to the sling Alex had fashioned to make the trip more comfortable. "We bested him and now need a place to lock him up."

"You want me to take him on in? He'll be uncomfortable moving at a gallop, but I'll do it."

"Nope, go along. We'll make the fort when we make it." Pa

touched the brim of his Stetson, and the officer nodded, clearly delighted not to have the man on his hands, and rode off.

Pa maneuvered his horse until he'd ridden up between Alex and Beth. He turned to Alex. "If you want out of this mess, we'll help you. You can ride off, start over somewhere."

Alex and Pa exchanged a long look. "There's more to that offer, isn't there, Clay?" Alex's words were husky and raw, as if Pa hurt him somehow.

Beth wasn't sure how. She held her breath hoping Alex would say yes and she and her husband could cut off from this trail and make a run for California.

"You know there is. I'll help you, but I won't let Beth go along. Not while there are varmints like Slaughter gunning for you."

"Pa!" Beth grabbed his arm. "My place is with my husband." The fear Beth felt was yet a new kind of worry. Fear of being separated from Alex. Because she loved him. She had already figured out that she cared about Alex. She was committed to him and respected him and even loved him, but not until this moment did she realize how deep it went. She had fallen completely and deeply and forever in love with Alex Buchanan.

Pa didn't answer Beth. Instead he kept his attention on Alex.

Beth was terrified Alex would ride off into the sunset, leaving her behind.

"You know I can't do that, Clay. I can't ride away from this. I've tried that before and it's only brought harm to the people around me." Alex gave Pa's arm a significant look then studied the bandage on Beth's head.

"I'll go with you, Alex. We can head anywhere you want. Maybe we could go north and find Mandy and her husband. Leave this behind." A firing squad, that's what Beth had pictured, though maybe they'd hang him instead. Beth wondered if the condemned got to choose.

"You did bring this trouble on us, Alex. But you saved Sally. Nothing about your past brought on those bee stings. Pure and simple, if you hadn't been there, one of my daughters would be dead. You cared for Beth when she was so badly hurt. You bandaged me up when I got shot. All those things put me in your debt and I pay my debts. I'll tell 'em you made a break for it, got away clean. You're a good man and a gifted doctor. The War broke a lot of men, and broken men don't deserve to die."

Beth looked from Pa to Alex, knowing that if Alex rode off, she'd go with him. Pa could grab her and hold her back, but he couldn't hold on to her forever. She was tempted to shout that right out loud, but if she did, Alex wouldn't go. Protecting her was more important to him than living. She felt the same way.

"I appreciate that, Clay. I sincerely do. But I won't let you dishonor yourself, nor Sophie and Beth, to protect me. And letting a guilty man go free isn't honorable. If I die at the end of this, knowing I did some good for your family and the others I doctored in Mosqueros will make it easier to bear. I'll always be grateful for the time I spent being part of your family."

That was the end of it, and the only reason Beth didn't scream and cry and punch Alex in the face to make him go was because she knew it wouldn't work.

They rode on as the dusk settled on the land. Her folks dropped back to ride side-by-side again. They were silent, increasingly grim. All of them knew full well what they rode toward.

In the waning light, Beth caught her first look at the American flag waving proudly over the fort, still at a distance but closing fast. Her time with her husband was nearly up.

Pa and Ma rode up so they were four abreast on the well-worn trail as the sun dropped over the horizon.

Only a lifetime of discipline kept Beth from using her own gun butt on Alex's mulish head, throwing him over his saddle, and running off with him.

"I was a major in the army during the War Between the States, Alex. I still know a few people from those days. When we get there, I'll send a wire or two, insist that you be given a fair hearing."

Alex shook his head. "I want to face this, sir. I want to take my due punishment."

"You will." Pa kicked his horse so he moved ahead and Ma went along.

Just as the stars came out, they rode through the gates of Fort Union.

"Luther!" Mandy lost every bit of decorum she'd ever possessed, and being raised in a wild land, she'd never had all that much. Laughing, she threw her arms wide and ran down her steps toward her old friend as he dismounted. She flung herself into Luther's waiting arms.

He lifted her clean off her feet with a familiar chuckle. "Good to see you, girl. Good to see you're doing well." Luther nearly hugged the stuffing out of her.

"Buff, you came, too." Mandy welcomed Buff just as enthusiastically.

Buff's cheeks turned pink behind his full beard and he had a mile-wide smile and a sturdy hug, but he didn't say a word. Buff wasn't one for much chitchat.

"Come on inside and I'll get you some coffee."

Luther and Buff followed Mandy into the house.

She wondered if she could get ten words out of the two of them.

"Where's Sidney?" Luther asked.

Mandy was struck by the strangeness of the question. Luther wasn't one for small talk, so why would he say such a thing? Luther's way was to look around, see that someone wasn't there, and figure it all out for himself.

"Panning for gold." Mandy wasn't sure why that made her feel warm, like maybe she was blushing.

As Luther and Buff sat down, Mandy nearly laughed aloud with delight that there was a chair for each of them. Thanks to the split wood and only needing to touch up the cabin with a bit of clay, she'd had the time to contrive two more chairs. She'd also tanned both deer hides, hunted up another buck and smoked that meat, and gone a long way to gentling the foal. There'd been a light snow in the night after Tom's visit, and she felt the winter pressing on her harder every day.

"So, tell me why you're here, Luther. You're not leaving Pa's ranch for good, are you?" Mandy noticed she'd twisted her fingers together until it maybe looked just the least little bit like she was begging Luther to say he'd moved up here and planned to stay. Near her. The bitter homesickness was such a weakness Mandy felt shame.

Luther didn't answer. He'd hung his fur hat up and now he seemed fixated on smoothing his hair. Not likely since he didn't have much. But his hands ran over the top of his head and the silence stretched.

"Best to just out with it," Buff said.

That was a lot of talking for Buff. And it didn't miss Mandy's notice that the talking was to make someone else do the talking.

Luther nodded then leaned back a bit in his chair to straighten his leg and extract a battered-looking, overly fat letter from his pocket. He extended it to Mandy.

She reached eagerly for it. "A letter from home? From Ma?" She felt like singing. When she grabbed the bulging envelope, Luther didn't let go. Mandy looked up smiling, thinking he meant to tease her. She saw something in Luther's eyes she'd never seen before—a look of fear and regret and maybe even pity. The smile melted off Mandy's face and she braced herself for bad news.

"There's such in that letter that's gonna upset you, Mandy girl. It's from your pa and it explains everything. There's even proof. I'm sorry for it."

Mandy tugged, less eagerly but more deliberately.

Still, Luther held the letter.

"Is someone sick?" Mandy felt her heart beat faster. She nearly choked on the only question she could think of. "Is it Beth? Was she hurt on the trip—"

"Nope, she wasn't hurt. No one of your kin is hurt. But—but there was an accident all right. A stagecoach overturned. Beth came upon the wreck and—and—"

"And she had to go to doctoring. That's why she missed my wedding." Mandy well knew her little sister's healing ways and compassionate heart. She could never walk away from someone in need.

"It's gotta be said." Luther sat up, squared his shoulders, and faced her head-on. "I'm sorry to be the one saying it."

"What, Luther? Tell me."

"There was a young woman about your age on that stagecoach. Name'a Gray. Celeste Gray."

Mandy frowned, and her hand on the envelope turned white at the knuckles from fear. "Some family of Sidney's? A sister? No, that can't be. Sidney said he doesn't have any sisters, or brothers either. He's never mentioned any family. Maybe a cousin coming to the wed—"

"Not a sister, Mandy girl." Luther looked sideways at Buff. "Not a girl cousin."

Buff shook his head.

"Tell me what's going on right now!" Mandy was ready to explode from the tension.

Luther rubbed one big rough hand over his face, still doggedly hanging on to the letter. "It was his wife."

Mandy shook her head and almost smiled. What he said made no sense. "*I'm* his wife."

Mandy saw Luther swallow so hard his whole beard quivered. "Sidney was—girl, he was married already."

"B–but she's dead?" Mandy heard her voice, but it sounded like it was a long distance away. "Sidney is a widower? When did his wife die?"

"Near as we can figure, a few hours before he married you."

"A few hours?" Mandy shook her head, thinking that she must be addled.

Luther held her gaze.

She'd known Luther all her life and he'd never been one to joke around. So why was he doing it now?

"B—but he'd been sparking me since he came to Mosqueros. He proposed to me. He couldn't have—"

The cabin door swung open and a very beleaguered Sidney stepped inside, his gold pan hanging dejectedly from his fingertips. "Is dinner ready?" His eyes focused on Luther and Buff, and his eyes widened in recognition. He narrowed his eyes and turned to Mandy and scowled. "We've got company from Mosqueros? Already?"

Mandy's eyes went to the letter she still shared with Luther. With sudden strength she jerked it out of her old friend's hand.

★ Twenty-nine ★

Fort Union wasn't like Alex expected. It had no stockade surrounding it. No intimidating row of logs standing shoulder-to-shoulder, sharpened to points on top.

Instead, the fort looked, in the moonlight, like a frontier village with broad streets meeting at squared-off intersections. The line of buildings visible were adobe. They looked well-built and well cared for.

There were no apparent bristling weapons, no alert guards. It was a quiet village. Even this late at night, it seemed that there should be some activity.

Clay led the way into this placid military outpost and went up to a man strolling along the front of a row of buildings. "We want to see the officer in charge."

Alex thought of the battles, the death, the danger, the blood. And here he stood in the midst of almost complete peace. A coyote howled in the dark night. A breeze blew quietly as the heat of the day eased until it was nearly too cold, as the desert was apt to do. His stomach twisted as he wondered if he'd end up dying in this peaceful place.

He'd lost the best part of himself in service to his country. But that lost part, the caretaker, the healer, had recently been resurrected. Alex almost regretted that. If they'd have locked him up and shot him at dawn before he met Beth, a part of him would have welcomed it. The end of his living nightmare. But now he had so much to lose.

But resurrecting himself included his faith. If he entered into eternity, he'd spend it with God.

God, forgive me if I don't welcome that closeness to You. I so wanted to have a life here with Beth. Thank You, though, for giving me a chance to heal my relationship with You.

The sentry straightened and saluted Clay. "The colonel ain't here, sir. Rode all the way back East to meet face-to-face with President Arthur." The sentry made that announcement wide-eyed, as if stunned by knowing his commander could speak to someone so lofty.

Alex had to admit that this dusty outpost seemed a world away from the president of the United States.

"The lieutenant handles things while the colonel is away, sir."

Beth swung down off her horse.

Alex hesitated, as if once he touched this military ground his fate would be sealed. Reluctantly, he dismounted, too.

Beth came to his side and clutched his hand. Her strength propped him up again, like always.

Sophie went to stand by her husband.

The guard's respectful reaction to Clay made Alex aware of his father-in-law's military bearing and former rank.

"No need saluting me, son. I took off the uniform years ago." Despite his words, Clay fell into the authority without trying and made it known he was an officer to be obeyed. "We'll see the lieutenant then." Clay slipped his gloves off as he spoke and touched the brim of his Stetson in a casual salute.

The man shook his head frantically. "Lieutenant Deuel's gone to his quarters for the night. I can't wake him." Alex saw fear in the soldier's wide-eyed refusal to get his commanding officer.

"Where are the sentries?" Clay asked. "Does the whole fort just go to sleep at night? Are things that secure?"

"I've seen no danger in the year I've been posted here," the young soldier said. "We don't even have many men stationed here anymore. We're always hearing rumors that they'll close the fort up and move us somewhere else. I guess I'm the closest we've got to a night watch. I take a shift then hand it off to someone else. It's pretty peaceful."

Sophie came up and smiled at the young guard.

The man forgot Clay and looked first at Sophie, then Beth. From his fascinated reaction, Alex wondered how long it had been since the young man had seen a pretty woman.

"Go get the lieutenant," Clay ordered. Alex suspected Clay didn't mean to start giving orders to a soldier. He just couldn't quite control himself.

The young soldier tore his eyes away from Sophie. "The l– lieutenant, he won't see no one now 'til mornin', sir."

"We don't want to put this off." Despite his assurance that he wasn't an officer, Clay made that sound like another direct order.

The guard was sunburned and looked about fifteen years old. Alex wondered if he'd looked that young when he'd first joined the cavalry. Now the barely grown boy shook his head, looking genuinely sorry. "Lieutenant Deuel don't do nothin' he don't hafta do. He won't come out for you. Not even to see to a prisoner." The young man gave a significant look at Slaughter then went back to fixing his fearful eyes on Clay, as if he expected to be court-martialed for disobeying. "In fact, were I you, I'd ride right on out of here and come back when you hear the colonel's returned."

Clay sighed. "We're not going to ride into the hills and wait for the colonel."

The sentry came right up to Clay and whispered. Alex leaned in to catch the words. "Lieutenant Deuel's got a—a streak of—

of—" The young man looked over his shoulder as if he might be observed. "Sometimes he's of a mind to make rulings just because someone bothered him. They don't make a whole lotta sense."

The man glanced around again and stood straight and spoke loud. "He's a fine man, the lieutenant."

Furrowing his forehead, Alex tried to figure out what the soldier was talking about. He'd said two almost exactly opposite things. Then Alex noticed another soldier just rounding the end of the building row. So what this soldier whispered when he was alone was different from what he'd say for all the world to hear. Apprehension tightened Alex's gut. What kind of fort was this? And what kind of decision could he hope for from this temporarily in-charge officer, Lieutenant Deuel?

"Have you got a place we can sleep for the night? And a place to lock this varmint up?" Clay jerked his head at the bounty hunter. He either didn't catch the undercurrent of the soldier's words or, more likely because Clay didn't miss much, he thought he could handle what lay ahead.

"The prisoner is named Cletus Slaughter. He shot me and my daughter. He claims he's a bounty hunter and attacked us all because he was after my son here." Clay jabbed his thumb at Alex.

A place warmed in Alex's heart that he hadn't known was cold. When he'd broken with his father, even though Alex still believed he'd done the right thing, the hurt had gone deep and never healed. Now, to have Clay McClellen call him his son. . . Alex was shocked at the urge to cry.

Alex wasn't sure what had caused this strange compulsion toward tears, but he desperately wanted it to stop.

The sentry shook his head. "Yes, sir. I'll have him locked up, sir. But seriously, you should just ride out. Go to Santa Fe and turn this guy in. Or go to Santa Fe and hide. I mean. . .uh. . .wait until the colonel comes back."

"We're staying," Clay glared at the man.

The nervous soldier nodded and hollered.

Three more recruits came out of a nearby building with the leisurely movements of men who had never been in battle and didn't fear that one might be starting up.

Alex envied them.

"Lock this prisoner up."

Two of the newcomers lowered Cletus from his horse and untied him.

Slaughter grabbed immediately for the kerchief that had kept him mercifully silent. "I'm not the one who should be arrested here." Slaughter's eyes were bloodshot and the corners of his mouth were foaming white. He looked for all the world as if he had rabies. "I'm a bounty hunter and I've worked with the colonel a lotta times over the years, bringing in the cowards that desert the army." Slaughter jabbed a finger straight at Alex's chest. "That man is wanted. Arrest him."

The sentry looked between Slaughter, Alex, and Clay. "Your son, you said?"

Clay nodded. "And we're here to straighten this out. We rode in, didn't we? And we had that would-be bounty hunter tied down. We'll answer all these questions when we talk to the lieutenant."

The soldier swallowed visibly, even in the dim moonlight, at the mention of the lieutenant.

"If you want me locked up, I'll go quietly." Alex stepped forward. He needed to take his punishment right from the first.

"Nope, I'll trust you folks. You rode in and you didn't hafta." The sentry ordered Slaughter taken away, still fuming and raving. The other soldier took the horses to bed down for the night.

"Do you folks need to see a doctor? If you've been shot, maybe you oughta have him look at you." The sentry gave the sling on Clay's arm a long look. "The doc'll get outa bed in the night for you." An obvious commentary on the lieutenant refusing to work after hours.

Clay looked at Beth, then Alex. Both shook their heads. "I think we're good. We've been doctored up enough. A place to sleep sounds good, though. I don't suppose there's a meal to be had here?"

"I think I can find some stew left from supper, still simmering. The cook makes enough to last a couple'a days usually and it tastes like slop from the first day to the last. It's filling though, keeps the front of your belly from rubbin' against the back. I'll bring some over." The guard pointed to another man approaching them. "He can show you to your quarters."

As they were guided to a long slender building, Clay asked, "Isn't this a barracks? Our womenfolk aren't going to bunk down with a bunch of soldiers."

The man escorting them shook his head rapidly. "Oh no, sir. We'd never do that. We have plenty of empty beds. No need to share. We've been a warehouse for supplies for all the Western forts and a place to watch over the Santa Fe Trail. But the trail don't need no watchin' over since the trains went through. And that goes for supplies, too. They're all sent by train these days. And there's no warrin'. It's plumb peaceful. Since the Indians lost the last war, they've all gone to the reservation. We barely even think of fighting."

"The Red River War," Alex said quietly. The Indians had indeed gone to the reservation. But not without a lot of killing first.

"Yep, I didn't sign on here until that was ended. Now they've cut back on the number of soldiers housed here at Fort Union until we're almost empty."

"All right, soldier. Sounds fine." Clay reached for the door, but the escort beat him to it. Alex noted the obedient tone of all the enlisted men to Clay.

The line of buildings had a porch stretching the length of them.

"Your food ought to be here shortly." The soldier grimaced and Alex wondered just how bad the food was going to be. "You can eat together in this room, and I'll unlock the door to the next room so you can have private sleeping quarters. Both are cleaned and set up for visitors. We never have many, though."

The soldier's glum claims of a boring military life sounded blissful to Alex. Why couldn't he have been the company doctor of this place?

They entered the long thin building and there was a main room, with doors leading off to the side.

"This room used to be set up for visiting officers so there's an actual bedroom. Same next door," the young recruit told them.

"Thanks." Clay pulled his Stetson off.

Alex hadn't heard so much as a word of complaint from Clay or Beth all through this long ride to the fort, but they had to be hurting. Clay had lost a lot of blood and had a bullet wound that was a long way from healed. Beth's injury hadn't been as serious, but she'd taken a hard blow to the head and she had to be suffering from it after these long days in the saddle. Alex thought he saw lines of fatigue and pain on Clay's face, but maybe it was just lines burned by living in Texas. He had a few of those himself.

The soldier lit two lanterns that sat near the door then left just as the other soldier came in with a pot of stew and some tin plates and forks. "I scared up some biscuits, too."

"Obliged." Clay took the food.

Sophie relieved him of it and had the table set and the stew on by the time the young soldier had said good night.

The stew was rank; a brown paste that showed no sign of beef or vegetables. The biscuits had the appeal of chewing on a piece of adobe that'd been drying in the sun for a hundred years.

Alex choked down enough food to stave off starvation, fearing for his teeth the whole time.

The four of them ate silently, too hungry and tired for talk. At last, the meal could be called to a halt, leaving them longing for the days on the trail when they'd lived on hard tack and beef jerky.

Alex stood to escort his wife next door. He rested his hand on Beth's back to guide her. "You need some rest."

"Hold up." Clay's voice stopped them cold.

It occurred to Alex that he was obeying Clay's orders, just like everyone else.

"Beth, you oughta stay with your ma and me."

Alex turned, surprised. "No." Alex squared off against Clay. "Why don't you want her to stay with me?"

"Pa!" Beth protested and wrapped two arms tight around Alex's waist. She clung to him now, when so recently she'd been holding him up. She really did care about him. She was truly his wife in every sense of the word.

Alex didn't want her upset. She was walking wounded, too. But after he faced the charges against him tomorrow, he might never have his wife in his arms again. He wasn't giving her up tonight. His chest tightened until he could barely breathe. He was surprised how hurt he was by Clay's effort to separate him from Beth. "Not an hour ago you called me your son."

Clay held Alex's eyes. What passed between them was beyond words, but Alex saw it all. Clay's gratitude for saving Sally's life, the respect Alex held for Clay's strength of will, the fear Clay held for his daughter, the regret for all Alex would put Beth through in the near future. It wasn't even the future. He'd already begun slowly, surely, breaking her heart.

Sophie's hand came up and rested on Clay's. "Let it go. Let them be together for the night."

Clay looked down at his wife's hand then back up at his daughter, also hanging on to a man—but not him anymore. Clay shook his head. "Fine. I'm sorry. I just—" He shook his head again, harder. "You're going to hurt my girl. I'd do anything to stop one of my daughters from suffering a moment's sadness. And every minute you're together, the hurt's just going to get deeper. I think you should—make your break from each other now. Get on with it."

Alex knew Clay was right.

"You're wrong, Pa. It doesn't work that way." Beth let go of

Alex and stepped toward her father. For a terrible, grief-stricken moment, Alex was afraid she was leaving him, even though he knew she probably should.

"No, he's not." Alex felt his hands slip from around Beth as she stepped toward her parents. "No matter what punishment they hand out tomorrow, you're going to have to leave me behind here. They'll lock me up for sure."

Beth turned to him and placed both hands on his chest. "He's wrong because it's already too late. If they take you away from me, I'm going to be as sad as I know how to be. One more night won't make it any worse."

Alex looked into those strong, wise, beautiful blue eyes, and though he found strength there as always, he didn't find the strength to let her go. He kissed her, right in front of her parents. "Come on then."

Sophie took one of the lanterns and, still holding on to Clay, left the room without looking back.

The other lantern lit Alex's way as he pulled Beth outside and into the next room. It was clean and had the same front living area as the room where they'd eaten. They passed through it into the officer's bedroom on the north.

Once the door was closed and Alex had her with him, he could breathe again. How was he going to manage when they locked him away? With grim amusement he knew it wouldn't be for long. The firing squad would limit his time for suffering.

"You're sure you don't want to go with them, Beth honey? I'm sorry. I want you with me, but that's not fair to you."

"I'm staying, Alex. And I'm exhausted. I just want to lie down." Beth's blue eyes met his in the dimly lit room. The lantern flickered and it seemed to Alex that the light went deep into Beth, until her soul was visible. Her beautiful, gracious soul.

When they lay next to each other, Beth's head resting on Alex's shoulder, he couldn't hold back the words, though he felt like laying them on Beth only added to her burden. "I love you, Beth."

"I love you, too, Alex." She nestled closer.

Rising up on one elbow so he could look down at his precious wife, Alex leaned down to kiss her gently. "I almost wish you didn't. If you love me, then what happens to me tomorrow is going to hurt you terribly. It's a scar on my soul that I've brought this pain to you. One more thing I need forgiveness for."

"Okay, I forgive you." Beth lifted one of her strong, healing hands and rested it on the rough stubble of Alex's face.

He hadn't bathed in days, unless he counted muddy floodwater—and he didn't. "I shouldn't be near you. I've got no right to touch someone as wonderful as you. I shouldn't let you touch me. Your pa was right."

The room was dark with the lantern extinguished, but the moon washed the room in silver. Alex saw Beth, her skin cast midnight blue. Her eyes sparkling like stars.

"It'll be settled tomorrow, Beth. And I will face whatever punishment they have for me. I am so thankful for the short time I've had as your husband."

"Hush." Beth rested her delicate, healing fingers on his lips. "We'll figure it out, Alex. Don't talk like it's settled. Don't give up hope."

"I wish I could give up hope. It might hurt less if I didn't have any."

"Well, don't ask me to give up. Because I will never give up on you, Alex. Not as long as there is a chance." Beth pulled his head closer.

Alex resisted, feeling like he sullied her even by holding her close.

But Beth had been stronger than him from the beginning. She got her wish for closeness.

Alex didn't get his wish to give up, because having Beth in his arms gave him a hope that would not die.

"Mandy, I'd like to talk to you outside, right now." Sidney glared between Mandy and their guests belligerently.

"Care to tell me who Celeste Gray is?" She met his eyes.

His arms came uncrossed and the look on his face changed. Mandy wasn't sure what she looked like exactly but it must have been fearsome because Sidney backed up a step. "C–Celeste?" Sidney's stuttering told Mandy all she needed to know.

"Yes, she's dead by the way. But then, I bet you're not going to mourn your *wife's death*, are you?" Mandy rubbed her thumb over that little callus on her trigger finger.

"Celeste's dead?" Sidney had the wide-eyed look of a deer who knew he was shortly going to be venison.

"Yes. In fact it sounds like she died in time."

"In time for what?"

"In time for our marriage to be legal."

"Who told you about Celeste?" Sidney's eyes went from Luther to Buff. He tried for a scowl, but it wouldn't stick on his face when he confronted the two extremely serious men who now sat at Mandy's table.

"What kind of a sidewinder courts and marries a woman when he's already married?" Mandy couldn't believe she'd said those words aloud. "It was all lies, wasn't it? The chance for a job in Denver. You must have known we were leaving Mosqueros long before you announced it to me."

"No. Mandy, I don't know what you've heard, but Celeste and I were never married. I knew her. But she. . . If she claimed we were married she was lying."

Mandy held the letter up to show Sidney. "I wonder what my pa wrote in this letter he sent along with Buff and Luther." She waved the letter. "It's fat. Room for lots of details. Maybe even proof. My pa has never lied to me. Luther and Buff have never lied to me." Mandy stood so suddenly that her chair toppled over backward with a loud clatter. "In fact, I've really never been lied to much in my life. That's why I didn't recognize it when lies started pouring from your dishonest lips." Mandy ripped the letter open with a vicious wrench of her hands. The envelope split with a loud sizzling hiss.

"No, Mandy. Don't read that. You've got to give me a chance to prove I'm telling the truth."

Mandy pulled a heavy sheet of folded paper from the envelope, along with a thin letter. She unfolded the heavy document first and read it. "A marriage license." She looked at the next thing contained in the envelope. A picture of Sidney sitting, dressed formally. Behind him stood a pretty, dark-haired woman in a gown that looked white. Both of them looked terribly serious.

"Those were found among her things." Luther had such regret in his voice that Mandy felt bad for Luther. He understood how badly this made Mandy feel, and in his whole life, Luther had never caused anyone in her family a moment's pain. "Your pa wrote a letter explaining everything. We're here to take Mandy home."

Raising her chin, she stared at Sidney.

Letting him see her anger.

Her sense of betrayal.

The—she faltered over it—the pain. It was as if her heart broke in half. She physically felt the agony in her chest.

"Mandy, please, you've got to listen to me." Sidney was across the room in two long strides.

Scraping chairs drew Mandy's attention, and she saw Buff and Luther standing, wary, ready to step between her and Sidney.

The humiliation.

Everyone knew about this. She looked back at Sidney. "You have disgraced me. Made a fool out of me." Her eyes fell shut under the weight of it. "I can't believe anyone is possessed of such a lack of honor."

Sidney took the marriage license from her hands and she didn't fight it. Why bother?

Mandy forced her eyes open to watch her husband squirm.

Sidney studied the parchment for far too long, and Mandy

knew he was spinning his lies, testing them in his head before he spouted them at her. "This is a forgery." He glanced up then away. Then he looked back, his gaze strong, his shoulders square. The man had learned how to lie very well, which spoke of much practice at the sin. "I'm telling you, this isn't true. We had this tintype made. I can't deny I knew this woman. But I never married her. You and I are married, legally married. I love you and I thought you loved me." Temper flashed in his eyes. "I expect you to trust me."

"Over my father? Over Luther and Buff, whom I've known and trusted all my life? Over my own perfectly good two eyes?" Mandy hated Sidney's sincere tone, that injured anger. It broke Mandy's heart yet again to know she couldn't tell if this was the truth or another lie.

"No, I'm not saying they're lying. They got this and they believed it. I don't blame them. And your friends rushed up here to protect you. I respect all of that. I'd have done the same for my own daughter." Sidney reached out and grasped Mandy's wrist. His words were a stark reminder that they could indeed have a daughter on the way. Or a son. That was the way of married life.

"But they were fooled by this woman. Just like I was. I knew her, and for a while I thought we might be in love. But I found out she was a dishonest schemer and left her. She's followed me before and caused trouble for me. Nothing like this, but it's true that part of the reason I came West was because of her—her obsession with me. That's the only word I can use to describe it."

Mandy just didn't know.

"That's an official marriage license." Luther spoke from his spot on the table.

Sidney gave Luther a single furious glance. "She's very good at what she does. And she has enough money to pay dishonest men to do fine work for her."

"A judge has signed it and it bears his seal." Mandy could see that Luther still didn't trust Sidney a whit.

Well, now neither did Mandy. How could she be sure of anything he told her, ever again?

Shaking her head, Mandy stood and stared at her husband, trying to see inside Sidney's head.

The corners of his mouth turned down, his eyes shown with hurt. Yes, hurt. She'd hurt him by not trusting him. Or else he was a very good liar.

"There's a way to find out." Luther pulled Mandy's attention again and she could see that Luther knew her mind. Knew her doubts. Knew her hurt and love and betrayal and wasn't going to stand for her taking Sidney's word for anything.

"How?"

"You stay out of this." Sidney turned a grim face to Luther. "You come in here with your lies and—"

"How!" Mandy spoke loud enough to shut Sidney's mouth.

He turned back to her, forbidding and annoyed.

Mandy felt a strange kind of power in no longer worrying about making Sidney happy. He'd been prone to sullenness, and she'd worked hard trying to please him. Well, no more. It was now his turn to do some hard work.

"There's a judge's name affixed to that license and it's from Boston," Luther said. "We wire him and ask if he really signed this document. This looks mighty official to me—"

"Celeste is a skilled forger," Sidney interjected.

Luther talked right over him. "And it's not some small wedding in a church in the middle of West Texas, where the parson might be a circuit rider and have moved on and the witnesses might be few. Wire the city and have 'em check the records."

Mandy turned to Sidney. "That sounds fair."

"No, it's not fair." Sidney stepped so close he was nearly plastered against her. He loomed over her, bending down to glare until their noses almost touched. "You should take my word for this. You should *trust* me. We took vows, love, honor, and obey. You are *not* honoring me, Mandy Gray."

Mandy almost laughed in his face. "I'm not honoring *you*? Even if you're telling me the truth, Sidney, you should have told me about this woman. You've never told me *anything* about your life. You know what? That's the reason I doubt you now. Because I know nothing about you. Why is that, I wonder?"

"I haven't had an easy life. I don't like to talk about it." Sidney sounded pouty. Well, his pouting days were over if he wanted to clear up this mess.

"Maybe your life was hard." Mandy didn't bother to point out that she'd lived with her mother and sisters in a thicket for a few years after her first pa died. They'd had a tiny, rickety shelter and they'd lived on rabbit and fish and greens. Her life had been hard, too. And she'd told Sidney all about herself. "Maybe you don't like talking about it and maybe you've kept quiet partly because of this woman, but what it adds up to is I don't really know you. I spent the last two months listening to you be charming and sweet and flattering, but I didn't hear a word about who you are. If you'd talked with me about your growing-up years, including the trouble you've had with some obsessed woman, we wouldn't be in this spot right now, would we? To my mind that makes you a liar. Whether a liar about being married or a liar about who you really are, I'll decide for myself after the judge writes back. For now, you're going to have to sleep in the barn."

So many things flickered across Sidney's face Mandy could barely keep up. Anger, hurt, disdain, contempt. Love. He might really love her. And he was really married to her. But what kind of tragic excuse for a marriage did they have with all this unknown between them?

"I'll do it, Mandy. I'll move out of the house and we'll send your wire and wait for your answer. I'll do it all because I love you. But when the truth comes out, I'm going to make you *beg* me for forgiveness." Contempt won over all Sidney's warring emotions. He stormed out of the house.

Mandy realized he'd always looked down on her. He'd done it

282

in subtle ways, but she knew now he'd made her grateful that he loved her. While he'd been charming her, he'd let her know in a hundred little ways she was lucky he'd chosen her.

Pa had known that. He'd never forbidden Mandy to see Sidney, but he'd pressured them to take more time before they married. And when Mandy wouldn't listen, he'd pressured them to stay in Mosqueros, probably knowing it would fall to him to take care of his daughter once Sidney's true nature was revealed.

But Mandy hadn't listened to the wisest man she'd ever known, a man who loved her with all his heart.

And once she realized that, Mandy held herself in contempt.

Thirty

The four of them had plenty of time for breakfast—more dreadful stew. Then they had time to sit. Alex wound up tighter and tighter.

Clay had gone early to find the lieutenant and returned to say he wasn't in his office yet and no one would dare bother him at his residence. He'd also sent a wire to someone back East he'd known during the War.

At Sophie's urging, Alex cleaned himself up after breakfast. He shaved and washed up good. Clay even found a store on the base and, with Sophie along to advise, got clean clothes for Alex and himself.

Alex felt like a fool getting gussied up to go face a hanging, but the hours were creeping by so slowly, Alex agreed more to keep moving than for any other reason. Back in his room, Alex poured water from the ewer into the painted china bowl then removed his shirt.

Beth gasped. "What happened to you?" She came up behind him, where he stood in his undershirt with his hands cupped in the water of the water basin.

Alex let the water flow back into the basin as he looked over his shoulder.

Beth touched his upper arm, beside the strap of his sleeveless undershirt.

"A scar from the war." He wished he'd never let her see it. He forgot about those scars for the most part. It was the scars inside his head he couldn't forget.

Beth pulled the shoulder of his shirt aside then pulled down on his neck. Another gasp followed as she looked at his back. It was ugly. He'd neglected his wounds until they'd festered. He'd nearly died from them. They were rough and they covered his back and his neck, and there were more above his hairline and below his belt.

He turned to face her. "Forget the scars, Beth. They're nasty but they're all healed up, have been for years."

Beth's brow furrowed. "You told me you'd been wounded, hit by shrapnel, but I had no idea it was this bad."

Shrugging, Alex said, "I didn't know it either. Never have given it much thought. The wounds were long healed up without much attention from me. It's the nightmares that came with the war that are my real scars."

Beth pulled him close.

He wrapped his arms around her waist. "I'm so sorry I got you into—"

Beth silenced him with her lips. He felt her arms around him, touching his back and the deep ridges and gouges of his wounds. One more burden he'd laid on his precious wife.

When he pulled away, he hated to turn his back, knowing the scars would bother her.

She seemed to know it, with the sensitivity she showed in everything. "I'll go wait with Ma and Pa."

He nodded and she left the room, then he got back to cleaning up.

The noon meal had come, stew again, this time with the added bonus of being cold. There was coffee that tasted—crunchy.

Alex did his best to cover his nerves, to put on a good front for Beth.

"I've sent a telegraph home to Mosqueros tellin' the family where we got to." Clay grimaced at the coffee but kept drinking. "And I've asked the telegraph office there to forward any wires that came from Luther."

"I wonder if he's found Mandy," Sophie said.

Alex had heard just enough about the man Beth's sister had married to wonder what was wrong with these McClellen girls to use such poor judgment picking husbands, himself being the prime example. The fact that Beth loved him only made him wonder the more.

Clay shook his head. "I reckon he'll let us know as soon as he catches up to her."

A sharp rap at the door drew their attention, and Clay went to answer it.

An older soldier waited there, his hair gray where it showed beneath his cap. "The lieutenant will see you folks now."

"It's about time," Clay snapped.

Alex knew he was wound up like a fifty-cent pocket watch, but Clay had acted pretty calm until now. Maybe it was the same act Alex was putting on for Beth. Most likely all four of them were putting on acts.

"Didn't see no sense in hurryin' you along." The soldier, his face clean shaven and his uniform clean and sharply pressed, looked worried. "You're not gonna like the lieutenant. In fact, were I you, I might just forget this whole thing and head for the hills. You rode in, you know. No reason you couldn't just ride right back out. Wait a while 'til the colonel comes back."

"Let's get going," Clay ordered. "We're not running."

The soldier shook his head with what looked like genuine regret and escorted them across the yard to the commander's office. They walked past a man sitting at a secretary's desk and heard a loud voice ranting in the next room—Cletus already spewing his lies.

As they entered, Cletus glared at them without taking a break in his complaints. "I was attacked by the doctor and his cohorts. I had a right to bring him in, and by fightin' me, they threw in with him and committed their own crimes. I want the lot of them locked up."

The lieutenant's eyes shifted from Cletus to them. He had eyes so light blue they looked gray. His uniform was so posy fresh Alex wondered if he changed it several times during the day, not a bit of this desert dust anywhere. He had a white plate in front of him, half-full of the mess they'd had for dinner. He was chewing as if every bite nearly killed him. The lieutenant ate his on thin fine china, with a long-stemmed goblet that looked like crystal to Alex. The silverware was placed in almost painful precision above the plate.

The lieutenant quit eating, leaving most of the food behind, then lifted a napkin from his lap and dabbed at his mouth as if he wished he could wipe the whole meal away. "Take the table service away, sergeant. And when I'm done with these folks, bring me that cook. She's fired."

"Yes, sir. I'll have the cook brought in as soon as this meeting is over." The older man moved quickly to lift the dishes. "But, sir, I don't think you can fire the colonel's wife. I mean the colonel's gonna come back sometime and he might not like it."

"Bring her in here!" Lieutenant Deuel roared.

Alex and Beth exchanged glances.

The soldier toted the dishes out, and two other uniformed men stood stiffly at attention. They were positioned on either side of the lieutenant behind him, posed so rigidly they matched the flagpoles standing proudly beside them.

Lieutenant Deuel shifted his solemn gaze from Cletus to Alex. "Sit down. I'm Lieutenant Deuel. Mr. Slaughter has made some serious charges against all of you."

Clay introduced himself and the rest of them then said, "We've got charges of our own, sir." Clay saluted as was proper, officer to officer, even if one of those officers was long separated from the service. "I'm Clay McClellen, formerly a major in the Union Army. We came in to get this cleared up."

Alex should have saluted, too, maybe. He was afraid the lieutenant would take it as an offense considering he was a deserter. Except maybe if he *didn't* salute the lieutenant would take it as an offense. Unable to decide, Alex remained still. He'd never been very good at military things.

"You speak as if deserting one's post is something easily resolved, Mr. McClellen. I assure you it's not."

Someone had lined up five chairs in a painfully neat row across the desk from the lieutenant. Cletus sat down hard on the one farthest to the left and scooted it back a few inches.

The lieutenant flinched like the misaligned chair created a disorder he found unbearable. Slaughter didn't notice, but Alex did and resolved not to scoot under any circumstances. He'd known men like the lieutenant and the oddest things could set them off.

Cletus leaned back in his chair, dirty and grizzled with his sparse beard.

Alex's efforts to clean up, hoping to look like a respectable citizen, seemed dishonest next to Cletus's grime. He'd hoped that would make the lieutenant trust him, but somehow now, to Alex, it seemed like he'd put on a false front while Cletus was presenting himself as a hardworking, decent man. The lieutenant might be partial to cleanliness, but surely no one would pronounce a sentence higher or lower based on a man's clothing.

Clay caught Alex's eye and jerked his thumb at the chair farthest to the right. Beth, with a bandage still on her head, sat next to Alex. Sophie sat by Beth. Clay, with his arm in a sling, took the chair beside Cletus.

The lieutenant was young. Younger than Alex in fact. He had

288

a baby face that didn't look capable of growing whiskers. How did such a young man come to be in charge of a fort? But then, despite its size, Fort Union wasn't much of a fort these days.

"Now"—Lieutenant Deuel folded his arms on the desk in front of him and nearly stabbed Alex to death with those gray eyes—"Mr. Slaughter accuses you of shooting him, taking him prisoner, and assisting an army deserter."

Clay stood. "We defended—"

"Sit back down." Deuel talked over top of Clay and raised his hand to ask for silence. "I didn't ask you. And I know some of that is a lie. It is obvious to me that you've been injured."

Clay sat back down.

"Mr. Slaughter would have me believe he was just defending himself when he shot you and your daughter, Mr. McClellen, but no woman would shoot at a man, so seeing a bullet wound on you, Mrs. Buchanan"—Deuel looked at Beth—"puts a lie to at least part of his charges."

"That woman—" Cletus stood and stormed toward the young officer.

Both soldiers behind Deuel stepped forward.

"Stop or I'll have you removed and locked up, Mr. Slaughter." For his youth, the lieutenant had considerable power in his voice.

Though he was fuming, fists clenched tight as his jaw, Cletus sat back down. He made Alex think of a snapping, snarling wolf.

"Now, what I see here is a deserter." The lieutenant turned those cold eyes on Alex and the little bits of hope he'd nurtured faded. "What was your rank, Dr. Buchanan?"

"I was a captain."

The lieutenant arched his brows.

Alex felt his collar tighten, wondering if the man would feel some satisfaction in ruling against a man who'd outranked him.

"Well, Captain Buchanan, as you know, the punishment for desertion can be execution."

Lieutenant Deuel watched him with sharp eyes.

Alex couldn't quite control a gulp. "Yes, I'm aware of that. I've come in to face whatever punishment you deem necessary."

One of the men behind Deuel caught Alex's eye and gave his head a tiny, frantic shake. Alex ignored the man.

Deuel nodded. "I will take the fact that you came in on your own into consideration. But that doesn't change the fact that you've confessed and it won't require any trial to find you guilty."

Alex wanted to protest but he fought the impulse. "I *am* guilty, Lieutenant Deuel."

The soldiers standing at attention exchanged looks. One of them rolled his eyes.

"However, there's more than that. If what Mr. Slaughter is telling me is true, then the group with you has committed crimes."

The lieutenant's eyes skimmed down the row, running past Beth, Sophie, and Clay.

Alex's stomach twisted at what he saw in those eyes. Then he looked closer at the lieutenant. There was something—

"I'd like to respond to that, lieutenant." Clay spoke politely but with that same authority that seemed to be part of him, but more apparent here in military surrounding.

"I'm sure you would, Major McClellen. But right now it's *my* turn, and the only speaking *you'll* be doing is to answer my questions."

Clay's jaw tensed but he nodded. "Yes, sir."

Lieutenant Deuel definitely had a hostile attitude toward Alex and he was extending that to the McClellens. But then based on the soldiers behind the lieutenant and the way the man was treating Slaughter, it was possible the guy was hostile to everyone.

"Now, how long ago did you desert, *captain?*" Deuel laced the military rank with venom.

"I served with Colonel Miles out of Fort Dodge. I—let's see—" Alex had done his best to forget the details, which left him only with vague haunting memories of blood and death. "It was the summer, or autumn maybe, of 1874. I—I rode with the supply wagons Colonel Miles sent under the command of Captain Lyman to Camp Supply in Indian Territory. I was supposed to restock bandages and make sure Colonel Miles's new camp on the Red River had whatever I thought necessary. We fought a battle with the Kiowas and Comanches on that trip that lasted—I can't remember how long—days. We were surrounded." Alex rubbed his head wishing he could wipe away the nightmare.

He felt his vision widening as the room faded and the rifle fire cut through day and night.

"There was a terrible rainstorm." He could feel the mud everywhere, hear the report of guns. Horses wounded and screaming in pain. Men dead and dying. He smelled the blood, even in the downpour. "There were around a hundred men and only ten or so armed. Captain Lyman had us dig in, but the Indians had us under siege and they meant to keep after us until we were all dead."

Fingernails sunk into his arm and he pulled himself back to see Beth leaning toward him. He looked in her eyes and they steadied him.

"Give us strength." He heard her whispering, her lips barely moving. Strength. She asked God for enough strength for both of them.

He asked for strength, too, as he tried to remember what happened after that siege.

"We—we got out. Someone came. Then I had to tend the men hurt in the Battle of Buffalo Wallow. They'd just been brought in when we were rescued. Those men had barely been given a week to heal, and we had wounded from the battle near Camp Supply. Some of them were still terribly wounded when a new battle broke out in Palo Duro Canyon. The colonel ordered me to the site. I told him—" Alex looked up into the lieutenant's eyes. "I—I couldn't do it. I couldn't face more death. I had men still trying to decide which side of the Pearly Gates they were going to end up on right there in camp and I was shaky. My hands wouldn't quit shaking and I—I hadn't slept since the siege. I had nightmares if I even dozed off. I was barely able to keep up with the job I had there. But the colonel said they needed me and I had to go."

Alex remembered refusing, maybe begging. It was all a blur. "In Palo Duro, it was Colonel MacKenzie's Fourth Cavalry that took on Iron Shirt and his Cheyenne, and there were Comanches and Kiowas there, too. The cavalry captured a whole village. There were a thousand or more people in that village. Most of the women and children were fine, but a few were hurt. I tried to see to them, but I was ordered to tend the cavalry first. Women and children suffered and died while I bandaged scratches."

Alex ran a shaking hand deep into his hair. "And there were a thousand horses. We slaughtered them to keep them from the Indians. I heard the shots where they were killed and the screaming of the horses. And the wounded kept coming. I saw them fall on the battlefield and I went to them, trying to bring them back behind infantry lines. Then I—I was hit. Shrapnel from somewhere. It wasn't a bullet wound, I don't think. The scars on my back don't look like bullets. I didn't even know I'd been hit until later. But I was tending a man. . ." Alex's voice faded as he saw that man dying under his hands, trying to put himself back together, and the blood and entrails dangling from Alex's doctor's bag.

Alex dragged himself back to the quiet room. "Death everywhere."

Give me strength, Lord. Give me strength.

"I ran. Or I suppose I ran. I don't remember it very well. Someone told me later I'd been shot and that man did what doctoring he could. I don't know where I was. Far from the battlefield by then. I don't know if it was hours or days or weeks later." Alex looked up. "I did it, sir. I cracked under pressure and ran like a coward and never went back. I couldn't do it anymore. I couldn't be a doctor. I couldn't have any more blood on my hands. And the army wouldn't let me stop."

"So you were shot in the back while you were running away?" The lieutenant sounded as merciless as that battle.

"No, sir, I don't think so. I think it was from our own side. Maybe a ricochet. Like I said, I didn't even know I'd been wounded until later. I had to wade out into that battlefield to help the men who were down. I was ahead of our troops. It was our own cavalry weapons. It happens in war. It's madness."

Trying to bring himself fully back to the room, Alex found Beth, holding his hand in a viselike grip that hurt now that he was aware of it. He reached with his free hand and caught hold of her, two of his hands entwined with one of hers. "Beth honey, I'm so sorry. I'm sorry you found yourself bound to a coward."

Her grip eased. She'd been using the pain of her grip to drag him back to the present.

Alex wondered how much of his cowardice had shown in this room.

"You were with Colonel MacKenzie at Palo Duro?" Deuel asked, his voice sounding tight, strained. His face flushed red.

"Yes, sir, I was." Alex's heart sped up at the rage boiling out of the lieutenant.

"My brother was with the company on that supply train. He'd been mending, but after Palo Duro, he had no medical care. He died a few days after Palo Duro." Deuel's words landed like stones on Alex's already battered conscience.

Another person died because of him. How many had he failed *before* he'd run away? How many *after*?

Beth's grip on his hand tightened.

Alex swallowed, but it felt like something hard and unmovable had lodged in his throat.

"My brother died for want of your medical attention."

Silence held firm in the room. If Alex had a chance when he'd entered the room, that chance had just died as surely as the lieutenant's brother.

"I find you guilty, Captain Buchanan." The lieutenant's fist slammed on the desk with the force of final judgment. Without taking his burning eyes off Alex, Deuel said, "I'll decide your punishment by the end of the day. If I have my way, you'll be facing a firing squad with the sunrise, doctor."

Lieutenant Deuel's words hit as hard as the shrapnel that had been the final blow to Alex on that long ago day.

"No." Beth threw her arms around Alex. "You can't do this."

Alex pulled her tight against him and felt her hot tears brush against his face as he held her.

"Lock him up," the lieutenant shouted.

Someone grabbed Alex's arm and he let go of Beth.

She clung to his neck, crying.

"It's all right, Beth. Don't cry. Don't waste your heart on me."

"And lock the rest of them up, too." The lieutenant snapped his fingers as if he held the power of life and death over all of them and delighted in using his power—and abusing it. "All of them. Slaughter and all three of the McClellens."

"Th–the women, too, Lieutendant Deuel—sir?" The man holding Alex's arm stuttered, and Alex saw a surprising amount of fear in the young man's face. Not the respect and obedience expected toward a superior officer, but cold, trembling fear.

"Yes, the women, too. And you carry out those orders without further question, private, or I might just throw you in with them when I line the lot of them up in the morning."

"What?" Alex erupted.

Beth gasped.

"Calm," the private whispered to Alex. "Obey him."

The private pulled Alex so they were headed for the door. With their backs turned to the lieutenant, he whispered, "He won't do it. At least he don't mean it about the McClellens being shot."

Both men holding Alex nearly dragged him out of the office. He looked and caught Beth's eye.

She'd risen to her feet and now looked anxiously after him.

He needed Beth. In the second their eyes held, he realized that, yes, Beth had stayed by his side during his doctoring, but she'd been close every moment.

He thought of that first night in Clay's bunkhouse. The first time he'd tried to sleep after Beth stormed into his life and forced him to use his healing skills. The nightmares had come when Beth was gone.

He'd never spent another night alone. Nor another day. It wasn't just during medical treatment that he was one wrong thought away from sinking into his nightmares. It was all the time.

Knowing he was going to be locked away from her twisted inside of him, unlocking his nightmares. Blood, horses screaming. "No! Beth!" He heard himself shout but wasn't sure if he spoke the words aloud or if the cry came only on the inside.

He wrenched away, but the soldiers had too firm of a grip on him. They dragged Alex out, and the door slapped shut behind him.

They were in a small outer office, with a soldier sitting with his hands clutched together at a secretary's desk. "What'd he do now?" the lieutenant's aide asked.

"He ordered this man executed," the private said.

Alex fought to listen, fought to understand the words being spoken.

"Get a wire off to the nearest fort with a commanding officer who outranks him," the private said. "Do it quick before he can stop you."

That made no sense. Alex shook his head and heard the bullets whizzing past.

The man behind the desk dashed out of the room. Alex's two escorts followed.

"My wife. I need Beth." Alex hated the sound of his voice. Desperate, cowardly, broken.

God, I'm broken. You heal the brokenhearted. Help me, Lord Jesus

Christ. Give me strength.

Once they were outside, the men said, "He's crazy."

Jerking his head up, Alex hated it that they knew. "I'm crazy?" He needed to beg them to forgive him, beg the men he'd killed to forgive him. Beg Beth. Beg her parents. Beg everyone to forgive him.

"Not you, Doc. We mean the lieutenant. He's crazy on the subject of his brother. And it's gone straight to his head bein' in charge of this fort. He's been throwing around any orders he can think of since afore the dust settled on the colonel's trail. We'll do somethin', Doc. We can stop this."

"Stop this?" Alex only barely understood what they were saying, but he struggled to keep his nightmares at bay.

"And that Cletus Slaughter, the colonel hates him. He's brought in more deserters draped over his saddle than any other man in the West. Decent men who'd just had enough or had trouble at home. War can break a man, Doc. You're not the first. I ain't seen much fightin'."

The man escorting Alex was younger, but he had the weathered skin of a frontier soldier. Kind eyes, but smart, like he'd seen a lot of hard living. But he'd let it make him wise instead of broken.

"But I've seen a bit of it. And I think—I think. . ." The man fell silent and the silence drew Alex, helped him get a better grip on the here and now and pull him out of the past. "I think many's the man who—to break—to reach a breakin' point and walk away—well, sir, I think that might be a kind of courage some of us never find."

Shaking his head, Alex said, "No. I ran. I was a coward. Men died."

"A lot of men ran. They don't deserve to be shot in the back by the likes of Slaughter. He's been makin' good money with the army's rewards. If the colonel was here, I'm not sayin' he wouldn't punish you, but this is crazy, crazy. Not even a proper military trial. And to threaten your family, who brought you in. Two of 'em shot. The lieutenant's mad as a cornered he-coon when it comes to his brother. If you'd have been brought in for somethin' else, he might'a just let you walk right out. That ain't justice. Not to my mind."

The men hustled Alex down the long row of buildings until they came to one with bars on the windows. They took him inside and had him inside a cell with the doors clanging shut before he could comprehend all they'd said.

"What about my wife?" He turned, the panic that Beth could be hurt by this insanity making him desperate. Even more desperate than his separation from her.

God, please, please, please, give me strength.

"We'll try to fix it, Doc. If nothing else, we'll break you out tonight and hide you somewhere until the colonel comes back."

Shaking his head, Alex said, "That's insubordination. Maybe even treason to aid an arrested deserter. I can't let you commit a crime to protect me." Alex was now possibly going to *escape* from prison? The only clear thought that came to his muddled head was to wonder what the punishment was for that stacked on top of being a deserter?

"We'll see that your family is treated right, Doc." One of the men opened the door to leave Alex alone in the cell.

The world faded around him. The jail cell, the walls, the hard cot. He heard horses neigh in pain, rifle fire split the air. Clinging to this awful place he asked, "Will my wife and her parents be locked up in here where we can be close?"

If only they'd come, he could hang on. He could stay here, away from his nightmares.

"Doubt it," the soldier who'd done all the talking said. "The lieutenant might see that as being too kindhearted. And this fort is mighty empty. We've got plenty of empty lockups."

Alex's knees gave out as the two men left and he sank down on his hard cot. He saw a man already dead but still too dumb to know it, trying to put his eviscerated body back together. Blood everywhere. Horses screaming and dying. The impact of bullets hitting his back. He fell forward onto the stone floor of the cell.

And now he was alone. He looked down and saw his hands crimson and dripping blood.

God, please give me strength.

And he saw Beth and the crimson faded.

Alex clung to that vision of her, knowing it was given to him by a loving, compassionate God.

★ Thirty-one ★

Mandy, I want to talk to you. . .just you." Sidney threw a scalding look at the men watching them fight.

Protect me, dear God.

Mandy was humiliated by the knowledge that she'd married Sidney and didn't know him at all. But they did have to make a decision. Mandy's first instinct was to simply walk away. She knew Luther would escort her home, back to her parents.

She also knew that she was a married woman. She'd taken those vows before God. She'd meant them with all her heart, a vow to forsake all others and cleave only unto her husband. Until death do them part. She had a sudden, very satisfying fantasy about Sidney being parted from her by death—she was doing the *parting* using her bare hands.

Glaring at him, she pulled herself back to the problem of the moment. "Yes, I think that's wise."

Turning to Luther, she saw the stubbornness that had brought Luther to an old age fighting in Texas and before that in these rugged, beautiful Rocky Mountains. He was a hard man to budge.

"Please, Luther. Sidney and I do need to have this out, and we need to do it in private."

Rebellion shone out of Luther's eyes. For a second, Mandy wondered if he'd take this decision out of her hands and haul her home against her will.

She almost wished he would. Being an adult and making her own decisions was proving to be vexing beyond belief.

If she walked away from Sidney, she could never again marry. After all, she had a husband. And that meant she could never hope for a family of her own. Which brought it fully into mind that she could well have the beginning of that family already. She only resisted resting her hand on her stomach by sheer willpower.

And the next thought followed perfectly after that—if she did have the beginning of a baby, that baby would have a pure weasel for a father. What kind of thing was that to do to a child?

She held Luther's gaze.

Finally, scowling, he rose from his chair. "I'll let you talk." Luther turned those hard eyes on Sidney. The heavy graying brows lowered. "But one thing I won't do, whatever you decide, is leave. You can talk to her all day long, but the way I see it, Mandy is gonna need help until she's ready to head home without you. Or, if you talk her into stayin', she'll need help teaching you how to be a man. And I reckon it falls to me to be that help whatever she chooses."

Luther went to the door and opened it, but he turned back to Sidney. Mandy saw a trace of kindness in Luther's expression. "Instead of mining for gold, Sid, you need to learn hunting. Learn to build furniture and cut firewood. Learn to tan a hide and bust up ground for a garden. Or you need to go into Helena and start up your lawyering, if you really *are* a lawyer. Whether you are or not, there are jobs for a man in a rugged country like this, if he's not afraid to work."

Luther's tone said very clearly he expected Sidney to be afraid. "Either way, you've got some growing up to do, boy."

Sidney flushed and looked away with his usual sullen expression.

Mandy's heart sank to think of just how much growing up her husband had to do. She wasn't sure he had enough time, even if he lived to be ninety.

Buff followed Luther outside and shut the door quietly.

Mandy turned to Sidney, and they just looked for a while, staring into each other's eyes.

Mandy had so much to say she didn't know where to start.

She wished Sidney would do the starting, but she realized he never had. He'd listened and shared his dreams, and he'd poured on the charm, but he'd never done much talking about important, sensible things.

And Mandy was, at the very root of her soul, a sensible woman. "I guess you've got nothing to say to me about this woman? Is that right, Sidney? Is that what I can figure out from your silence?"

"I've told you the truth. That woman is just someone I knew back a few years. I did not marry her. She's crazy. I knew she kept following me around. That's part of the reason I came West— to leave her behind. But I had no idea she was crazy enough to follow me all that way, fake those papers." Sidney glowered at Mandy as if daring her to doubt him.

"So if I do as Luther said and send back East for details on Sidney and Celeste Gray, the names on this marriage license, with dates and the name of the judge and the courthouse where you said your vows, I'll find out there was never any such marriage, is that right?"

"That's right." Sidney's eyes shifted to the side and Mandy knew he was bluffing. A bit nicer word than *lying*, but really no different.

Mandy nodded, silent, as she let the pain flow over her. "Okay, well, that's what I'm going to do. So, until I hear word back from the East, we will not live together as man and wife. We'll stay here and run this homestead and wait for word."

"You owe me your loyalty, *Mrs. Gray*. You swore *vows* to me, standing before *God*, and the first time you have to choose between me and your family, you pick *them*. What kind of vows are those?"

"I owe *you* loyalty?" Mandy would have laughed in his face if the pain hadn't been so great. "What kind of a husband are you? What kind of vows did *you* swear to? You've *never* told me about your childhood. Or what little you've told is vague and probably half falsehood. You know everything about me and I know nothing about you. Was your father really at Shiloh? Did you really go to Yale?"

"I have no idea who my father is." Sidney flung his arms wide and whirled away from her. "My mother was a *dance hall* girl. She didn't work above a *store*. She worked above a *saloon*! My father could have been a dozen men, maybe a hun—" Sidney's voice broke and he sank into a chair. Sobs broke from his throat and his head hung as if it weighed a hundred pounds and his neck couldn't bear the weight.

Mandy was aghast. Her husband was *crying*. She'd never heard of such a thing. Men didn't cry. Compassion for her husband welled up in her. She did love him. Love didn't die in a day. It could be badly wounded, the pleasure could turn to pain, but the love was still there.

But she was a sensible girl—no, woman. All the compassion in the world couldn't make her close her eyes to her husband's treachery. She went up to him and rested her hands on his heaving shoulders.

He was quiet now, a shudder racked his body.

"Know this, Sidney Gray, I am giving you a chance, right now, to tell me the whole truth. I love you and we can start again from this point with honesty between us. But if you've lied to me, I'm not talking about before today, if you lie to me *today* about being married to that woman, our marriage is over. I'm giving you a chance to tell me the plain, flat-out truth and nothing but. But if you persist in your lies until we get word from Boston—"

"I was married to her." Sidney's voice was so low, Mandy could hardly hear it. But she heard. Oh yes, she heard the words that slit her soul deep. "Yes, the truth is I was married to Celeste. She's all the things I said she was and our marriage was a terrible mistake. She was crazy, dangerous. I left her. I ran away nearly three years ago, and I've been wandering ever since." Sidney lifted his head and twisted in his chair to look at Mandy.

"She pursued me in the East until I finally headed to Texas to escape her for good." Sidney took her hands where they now rested on the back of his chair. "It's not fair that I'm bound to her for life. I don't love her. I can't be held to a promise I made without knowing what I was promising."

"Like I was," Mandy said quietly.

Sidney's eyes fell shut. "I love you, Mandy. I never knew what love was until I met you. I love your decency, your kindness, your faith."

"My faith?" Mandy asked.

Sidney had always accompanied her to church. She had assumed he shared her faith. But why would that be the one area where he'd told the truth?

"Yes." Sidney pressed a kiss on her hands, where they were entwined with his, then rose to stand before her. "I learned something from sitting with you in that church. I learned about God in a way I never had before." His eyes met hers dead-on. "I'm a changed man, Mandy. I did a lot of things in my growing-up years I'm not proud of. But I've asked God to forgive me for them. Celeste was so far in my past—"

"You married me knowing you were already married?" Mandy felt dirty and stained.

"And my life was so new. I felt forgiven even for my foolish marriage. Please, Mandy, please give me a chance to be the husband I can be. I've felt so awful with the lies I was holding inside. Now that the truth is known, I can really share my life with you and be closer to you." He slid one arm around her waist.

"We truly are married. You can no more deny that than I could honestly deny my own marriage. Please give me a chance. Say you still love me enough to try and go on together."

She felt stained—like a sinner. She needed to forgive Sidney just as God had forgiven her. But how could a woman forgive such a thing?

"Judge not, and ye shall not be judged: condemn not, and ye shall not be condemned: forgive, and ye shall be forgiven."

Mandy knew that verse well. And she knew, to the extent anyone could know, that Sidney was speaking from his heart. But how could they go on? How could she feel any affection for him?

Sidney wrapped his arms around her and she felt a frisson of dread, but she let him pull her close. She tried, with considerable might, to forgive him and find a way to go on with her marriage.

Protect me, Lord. Protect me from all of this, what I feel for him and what I don't feel. Help me know what to do.

At last she got control of the turmoil in her mind and she straightened away from her husband. Looking him square in the eye she said, "If you mean what you say about honesty, then I will stay with you. But we are going to have to *both* be honest."

"Wh–what do you mean? Have you been dishonest, too?" He looked almost eager, as if hoping he wasn't the only sinner in the family.

"Yes, I have been dishonest. I've been very unhappy with you since we've gotten married, and instead of telling you, I've ignored it and acted content. But that's over now. Now I start telling you exactly what I think. And you are going to *listen.*"

"What you think?" Sidney's brows arched nearly to his hairline.

"Yes. I know this life is new to you, but there are things a man needs to do on a homestead and you're not doing them. I'm going to teach you how to live in a cabin on the frontier and you're going to learn."

That sulky look crossed Sidney's face.

"No! Stop that right now."

"Stop what? I didn't say anything."

"I can see you being annoyed. I can see you taking offense at my words. Well, too bad. You're going to let me and Luther and Buff teach you the skills you need to survive a Rocky Mountain winter. And I expect you to cooperate and learn. I think we've already proven that you're not doing all that well making your own decisions. Mining for gold is a waste and you're going to have to do it in your spare time. Chores come first."

"What chores?"

He honestly didn't know.

"Didn't you notice all the wood that's been split? Didn't you notice there's no breeze in our cabin anymore?" Mandy swallowed hard, but honesty worked both ways. "A man rode in to look at the foal. His stallion sired the little colt. That man, Tom Linscott, said he appreciated that we were taking care of the little guy and in thanks he chopped a winter's worth of wood."

At that moment the strike of an ax rang out. Mandy knew without looking that either Luther or Buff had gone to work on the remaining cords of wood. The two of them were unable to stand around idling when there was work to be done.

"What do you say, Sidney? Are you going to be a real husband? A good husband? Or are you going to run off on me, like you did Celeste, and go find someone else to marry?"

Sidney stared at her, his lips curled in discontent. But he didn't leave and he didn't sulk. Finally, he said, "Yes, I'll do what you ask. I'll try harder to be a good husband. I know nothing of life out here—hunting, building, caring for animals. But I'll learn. You have my word on that. And right now, my word is worth nothing. But I do love you, Mandy, and I promise you'll never regret giving me this chance."

Mandy nodded and let Sidney pull her back into his arms, though she disliked his touch and was tempted to say so. But she didn't. And well, she realized that not saying so was a kind of lie. But she didn't tell the truth that pressed to escape her lips.

And then another truth made itself known and remained unspoken.

She already regretted agreeing to stay with her husband.

★ Thirty-two ★

Thank you, Lieutenant, for getting him away from me." Beth turned, wearing a smile she hoped looked genuine.

Ma gave a tiny gasp of surprise, but Ma was quick. She suppressed the noise and simply nodded her head. "Terrible mistake to let that troubled man into the family. I can't imagine he was much good to the war effort."

Both of them had been around men all their lives. Beth recognized the lieutenant's type. Well, she'd just see if she could use the man's taste for cruelty to her advantage.

Beth turned calmly back to face forward and lowered herself smoothly into her chair, folding her hands as if she was settling in for a tea party. The truth was just the opposite. She'd seen Alex. Knew he was on the brink. He needed her. And she needed him just as much. "It's true we're married, sir, but I didn't know his nature when we were wed."

The lieutenant's odd, light-colored eyes focused on her with a hungry look, as if he'd found a new repository for his sadism.

"I'm relieved to finally be free of him." Beth shuddered. It wasn't even fake. Lieutenant Deuel's eyes were enough to make a snake shudder. "Thank you. If you're going to lock me up, please, I'm begging you, don't put me anywhere near that awful man."

The door clanged shut with a metallic bang, Beth locked in with Alex, just as she'd known that sadistic jerk would do. Beth stood pressed against the bars, as far from Alex as she could get, until the soldier left them alone. "Alex, I'm here." She rushed to his side, dropped down, and wrapped her arms around him.

He was on his knees. It took mere moments for him to respond. "Beth honey?"

The gray pallor of his skin and haunted eyes nearly broke her heart. The more she heard about what he'd endured during the war, the more compassion she had. She knew her own backbone. It was pure iron, and she strengthened it with regular prayer. But his tales of blood and death and exhaustion, in a man so tuned to healing, made her wonder if she wouldn't have broken, too.

She noted how quickly he responded to her. He'd not been as lost in the past as other times.

"Alex, they're locking us up together."

"I was praying." Alex's eyes fell shut and he shook his head as if trying to throw away the traces of his thoughts. "I think—I think I'd have been okay. It was pressing against me, the nightmares, but I kept praying and kept thinking of you."

Beth cut off his words by kissing the daylights out of him. She was still kissing him when she heard a throat clear loudly. She lifted her head to see her parents standing in the nearby cell, their arms crossed. Ma's toe tapped impatiently.

"He okay now?" Pa asked.

"Yes." Beth looked at Alex and she saw the strength there. He was still connected to her in that strange and wonderful way. But he wasn't trying to draw on her strength. He had his own.

She stood and helped Alex to his feet. Then the two of them sat on the single cot, and Ma and Pa did the same on their side of the bars.

"Now, you wanted us locked in here with him, isn't that right?" Ma asked.

Beth managed a smile, though she couldn't put much of her heart into it. "Yes, I did."

"How'd you manage that?" Alex asked. "The lieutenant looked like he'd delight in denying any request."

"I saw that, too. That's why I told him I was thrilled at the thought of your being locked away from me." She smiled.

Alex rolled his eyes and wrapped his arms around her. "Great. So now he thinks I'm so awful my wife hates me."

"Well, admit it, Alex, the man had already decided to stand you up in front of a firing squad at sunrise. His opinion really couldn't have sunk any lower."

"So the extent of your plan was just to get us locked up in here?" Pa asked.

Beth shrugged. "I was pretty sure Alex would need me."

"I thought maybe you'd figured out a way to get us out of this mess."

Shaking her head, Beth said, "Nope."

Then Ma stood from the cot and walked over to grab the bars that separated them. Beth had seen that gleam in her ma's eyes plenty of times before. It was always a good sign.

"Then it's a good thing I've got an idea." Ma smirked.

"I have married myself a wily woman." Pa came up beside her and slid an arm around her. "Tell me how we're gonna set a booby trap for this guy from inside our jail cell."

"First, we need Beth's doctor's bag." Ma looked at Pa.

"I got the feeling the soldiers who are serving under the lieutenant aren't real happy with him." Pa turned toward the door.

"One of them offered to help me escape," Alex said. "Then do a real bad job of hunting for me until the colonel gets back. So, I'd say you're right about that."

"Really, escape?" Beth asked. "But then you'd be a wanted man for something new."

"Yeah, that's all I need." Alex shook his head.

"Besides putting any soldier who helped you at risk," Sophie added.

"I had the same thought, which is why I didn't tell him I'd do it."

"Well, if that disgruntled soldier will help you escape, then he ought to be willing to bring Beth's bag." Ma quirked a smile. "And he'd probably let me and my poor mistreated daughter out of here and allow us to help the colonel's wife cook supper."

Alex saw matching looks of disgust to think of the food they'd been eating. "It sounded like she might be fired before supper."

"No, I met her in the hall, when we were being taken out, and talked to her for a minute. She's an excellent cook. Or so she says. She apologized for the food we've gotten. The man escorting us to the jail agreed. He said we got the wrong meal. Leftovers from a meal she'd prepared strictly for the lieutenant. Since he's the only one who doesn't come in to eat, instead insisting a meal be delivered to him, they dipped ours out of the same pot as his."

"I saw you whispering to her," Clay said. "And the soldier said something about the food. Why's she cooking bad on purpose?"

"Lieutenant Deuel growled at her over a dirty fork the first day after her husband left. She's been torturing him with dreadful food ever since."

Beth smiled. Alex would have, too, if he wasn't facing a firing squad at dawn.

"And now you're going to help her cook for that arrogant little pup to try and cheer him up?" Clay arched a brow at his wife.

"No, I'm thinking of what Beth said when Laurie handed her Dover's Powder, when Alex was ready to cut Sally's throat."

There was an extended silence. Alex could barely remember operating on Sally.

Clay broke the silence. "That is a sneaky thing to do, Sophie McClellen." He didn't sound that upset, and the smile on his face took all the bite out of his words.

"I know, Clay. I'm so ashamed of myself I can barely stand my own company." Sophie sounded like an extremely repentant Southern belle. Beth knew her ma was neither Southern nor a belle, and she didn't have a repentant bone in her body, at least not about this.

Clay smiled. "So, what can I do to help?"

"You can't give him Dover's Powder. That'll make him sick as a dog." Alex shouldn't have bothered to say that out loud, since that was obviously the whole point. But he was a doctor. He'd sworn an oath to do no harm.

Still, it wasn't as if the lieutenant would be sick all that long.

"If we're lucky." Sophie gave Alex a fond—if slightly evil—smile. "Then you, the only doctor for miles around, will jump in and save his worthless hide."

"Hey, I'm a doctor, too," Beth protested.

Sophie glared at Beth.

Who immediately figured out what her ma wanted. "Except tomorrow I'm going to be a helpless little female, one who couldn't hold her own in a pillow fight, let alone a gunfight, and who would faint dead away if asked to tend the tiniest scratch." Beth felt a little Southern belle-ish herself.

Sophie nodded.

"I can't *save* him from Dover's Powder." Alex wondered at his new mother-in-law. "He's just gotta throw it all up."

"When I was growing up, there was a neighbor lady who called herself an old-timey healer. She did a fair job, too. I remember her bringing us a cure every time we got a bad cold."

"There's no cure for a cold." Alex crossed his arms, impatient with quack doctors.

Sophie moved closer to the bars. "It worked every time."

"What did she give you?" Alex felt his pulse speed up. Had someone really found a cure for the common cold? It would soothe the ills of thousands of people. It would—

"She'd leave this nasty-tasting, gluey paste, and we'd take it faithfully three times a day. She also ordered us to rest and stay warm and drink plenty of fluids. And we'd be well in a week or ten days."

Alex coughed then laughed. It felt good considering the dire situation.

Sophie's smile got a bit darker. "No one says your cure will be instantaneous. And while you're *curing* him, he'll be so busy casting up my perfectly tasty dinner, he'll be too busy to issue any execution orders at sunrise."

"He might even decide he owes you his life." Clay ran his hand down Sophie's back.

Alex went to the window of his cell—which he noticed at that moment was standing slightly open. There were bars, but a heavy key was set into the lock.

He caught the eye of the soldier who withdrew his hand from the key quickly and turned to look away as if he hadn't noticed a thing.

"I'm not escaping." Alex pushed the window wider so he could talk with the soldier.

"Didn't say you were, sir." The recruit tried to look innocent.

"You can take the key back now."

"What key?" the man asked, looking straight at the key.

"But if you wanted to save my family a lot of grief, you could let my wife and her ma out of here. They'd be willing to help with the cooking."

The young man furrowed his brow for a minute. Then his expression cleared. "They want to cook for the lieutenant just like the colonel's wife does, huh?"

"I didn't say any such thing."

The soldier grinned, took the key out of the bars, still standing open, and quickly came around to enter the jail. "I think I'd be within my rights to. . .assign these two ladies to a. . .a. . .work detail. Give 'em hard labor to punish them for their crimes."

"Quite right," Sophie said. "And if it's no trouble, we'd

appreciate stopping by our rooms. We have need of my son's doctor's bag, too."

"Why, no trouble at all, Miz McClellen." The soldier turned the key in Alex's cell door to let Beth out. He then turned to the cell holding Sophie and Clay. The young man didn't even pretend to relock either door. He hung the key on the wall in plain sight of his prisoners, too.

Alex rolled his eyes.

"I'd be glad to let you pick up that bag, ma'am. Is there anything else you'd like?"

"Well, you could tell us exactly what the lieutenant said to the colonel's wife to inspire the meals we've eaten since we arrived at the fort." Sophie left the room, with the eager soldier at her side.

Beth turned back, looked at the jail doors swung wide, shook her head, and followed after her mother.

★ Thirty-three ★

Not so much, Ma."

She watched her mother pour the Dover's Powder into the stew the colonel's wife had concocted for the lieutenant. Ma mercifully only treated Deuel's food, sparing the rest of the camp.

"Now, lassie, we don't want to give him too little either. I'd be after usin' a heavy hand." Colonel McGarritt's wife had also proved to be an eager co-conspirator. "Why, there's opium in that, you say? He'll need to be ridding his stomach of the vile stuff."

Beth was utterly unsurprised at the woman's opinion. She'd done nothing but rail against Lieutenant Deuel since she and her ma had come in. Plus the whole idea of cooking swill for the lieutenant revealed a cruel streak. Not that Beth didn't agree with the woman.

"I still don't see why we had to waste good food on that'n." Paula McGarritt had proved to be a kindred spirit. "Waste of good meat it is."

"He'll be more likely to eat it. He didn't finish his dinner." Sophie looked up from her witch's brew and smiled. "I reckon your feelings were hurt by that."

Paula started laughing. Beth was very glad the woman wasn't mad at her.

They stirred the powder in, and Paula called out to the waiting soldier, "Take the lieutenant his food."

Beth insisted on carrying the food in to the lieutenant, feeling that, since she was breaking her oath as a doctor, not that she'd been allowed to take it but in her heart she'd embraced her healing vows, then she ought to face up to the bad feelings that might come of this.

Sophie accompanied her.

"What are you two doing out of your cells?"

"We got put on work detail, Lieutenant Deuel." Ma acted put upon, like she'd been chiseling hard rock all day.

"Hmph." Deuel sniffed. "Well done. I'll have to remember to congratulate my jailer."

Then he saw the food and his eyes widened and he smiled. "Well done indeed." He took his first bite with gusto.

Beth's heart beat a little too hard.

"By the way, ladies, I apologize for my actions before." He plowed through the meal as if he hadn't eaten in weeks. Which was very possible.

"Apologize?" Beth quit watching the food go down his gullet. "What for?"

"Why, for losing my temper with your husband of course, Mrs. Buchanan. I was so furious about his possibly neglecting my brother."

Half the plate was empty now, and the lieutenant showed no signs of slowing down. How much of that *had* Ma poured in?

"I, of course, have no intention of having him shot at dawn."

Ma's hand shot out and she stopped the fork before the lieutenant swallowed another bite.

"Beth, I see a…uh…a fly in the lieutenant's plate." Ma grabbed the plate, thrust it at Beth, and said, "Get some fresh food."

"No." The lieutenant made a grab for the plate. "I saw no fly. It's fine. It's delicious. In fact, you can have the job of cooking from now until we sort this business out with the doctor. And naturally none of you will be charged with a crime. You brought the man in. In fact, I suspect you'll be given the reward. Dr. Buchanan will have to sit through a regular military court and we'll need to wait until the colonel comes back."

The lieutenant paused in his efforts to retrieve his plate. His hands went to his stomach. "How strange. I may have—" The man stood from his place at his desk and rounded it.

Beth had a pretty good idea where he was heading.

"Excuse me, ladies. I believe I ate my food a bit too fast." He bolted from the room, holding one hand over his mouth and the other clutching his midsection.

"You follow him," Ma ordered Beth. "I'll go get the doctor."

Ma rushed out, then when Beth followed only steps behind, they heard the sound of retching from around the corner of the building.

"That stuff couldn't kill him, could it?" Ma asked.

A terrible groan of agony rang in the settling dusk.

Beth shook her head. "No. Impossible."

"Help. I'm dying!" Deuel nearly screamed. Then the retching started again.

Ma shouted, "My son is a doctor. He'll save you." She turned to look at Beth and shrugged her shoulders and whispered, "Well, he will."

Ma could have shouted her little comment to Beth since the lieutenant was so loud a herd of rampaging buffalo could storm by and no one would notice over the ruckus Deuel was causing.

"Just go get Alex."

Beth ran in the direction of the lieutenant, but she was careful to round the corner cautiously. No sense getting too close to a vomiting man with a full stomach.

Alex spent the next week treating so many small complaints at the fort that he about decided the cavalry was comprised exclusively of a pack of whiners. Either that or the soldiers all wanted a peek at Lieutenant Deuel lying prostrate in bed.

But the lieutenant was up and about finally, and Colonel McGarritt summoned Alex to his office. It was time to face justice. Dreading it, but also glad it was over, Alex washed up from sewing up Mrs. McGarritt's thumb. She'd cut it slicing potatoes.

"Let me help straighten your collar." Beth fussed over him and the colonel's wife did her share of advising, too. She'd taken an immense liking to the whole McClellen/Buchanan clan since they'd pulled her into their Dover's Powder conspiracy.

Mrs. McGarritt went ahead to summon Sophie and Clay. Alex and Beth met them at the door to the colonel's office. The four of them walked in, in time to hear Cletus Slaughter haranguing Colonel McGarritt with his charges against Alex and his family.

"Sit down, Mr. Slaughter. It's best you know that every word out of your mouth makes me more determined to find an excuse to lock you up."

Growling like a whipped dog, Cletus settled into his chair on the far left. The setup was the same as before, but the chairs were simply shoved into a line. If one chair was at an angle or a few inches farther back, no one seemed to notice or care.

"Hello, major." The colonel stood and extended a hand to Clay. The man's full head of white hair surrounded a weathered face with lines that turned up when he smiled. "I was with McCook's Army of Ohio at the Battle of Shiloh. Doubt you remember. I was a sergeant back then."

"I was with Grant. You and Buell's men saved us from a terrible defeat." Clay shook the man's hand with real warmth, and Alex wondered how anyone could come away from war as steady as his father-in-law. Hopefully, McGarritt was just as steady.

Give me strength, Lord.

Alex prayed as he sat down, and he happened to glance at

Beth and see her lips move in the same prayer he'd just sent heavenward.

She was thinking the same thing and her eyes flashed with love and encouragement and strength.

"Now, I've been somewhat apprised of the situation, gentlemen, through the report of Lieutenant Deuel. And. . .uh. . .well, my wife told me her version. The two stories are quite different." Colonel McGarritt sat down and folded his hands together on papers on his desk. He turned blue, piercing eyes to Alex.

Swallowing hard, Alex knew that from this man he would get fair treatment and justice. But justice might be very harsh.

"You were at the siege by Camp Supply and the Battle of Buffalo Wallow and Palo Duro?"

Alex nodded. "Yes, I ran. In the middle of the fighting at Palo Duro, I—I just snapped. I ran. I deserted, sir. I admit it and will take whatever punishment you deem necessary."

"But Palo Duro was the end of it. There were no more battles after that. And you'd put in your time and then some. Stayed on because of the need, I see from your records."

"You have my military records?" Alex frowned. "I didn't serve here."

"No, but my wife wired Fort Dodge and they sent your records here. They arrived a day or two ago. If you'd have just ridden back to the fort, they'd have probably mustered you out on the spot. Or soon after."

Alex didn't understand what that had to do with it. "I didn't ride back. That's the whole point."

Colonel McGarritt turned to Slaughter. "And you were going to bring him in dead, is that right? Did you even attempt to arrest him? He's obviously shown a willingness to cooperate."

With a snort of disgust, Slaughter said, "Nothin' on that poster that finds any fault with the dead part of 'dead or alive'."

"Well, there's something pure wrong with you shooting two law-abiding citizens from cover. You're going to jail, Mr. Slaughter."

"No!" Slaughter lunged at the colonel.

Clay stopped him in his tracks. Two men standing sentry leapt forward and forced him, howling, back into his chair.

"I have been forced to put up with your cruelty with deserters." The colonel rose from his seat and jabbed a finger at Slaughter. "But I will not stand by while you shoot a young woman and her father just because they're standing close to a man you want to arrest." The colonel looked at his sentry. "Take him away. We'll decide on a sentence later. But I'd like to see him burn in Yuma for the rest of his life."

Slaughter roared and struggled against the ruthless grip on his arms. They could still hear his shouting as he was dragged away from the building.

"Colonel, I'd like to say something before you go on with your questioning." Beth's voice echoed with strength and kindness and compassion. Even in this situation, Alex felt soothed by her miraculous voice.

"Of course, Mrs. Buchanan." The colonel relaxed back into his desk chair.

"I don't know exactly the rules about desertion, but I know my husband has mentioned being hit by shrapnel. I don't think anyone, including Alex, understands just how badly wounded he was."

"Beth, no." Alex touched her arm. "I won't let you make excuses for me."

Beth patted his hand. "No one in the room, except me, has seen his back. He believes he ran off, deserted. But he also admits he doesn't remember anything for some time after the last battle. His wounds are far more grievous than he lets on. I don't believe he made a thoughtful decision to desert. I think he staggered off the battlefield, shot and bleeding. There are scars on his scalp. He probably had a concussion. I don't think he made a choice to leave. The only crime he's guilty of is, much later, when he came to himself, haunted by what he'd survived, he didn't come back.

That may be desertion, but you need to understand he didn't run off, afraid of battle."

"Let's see these scars, doctor." The colonel's eyes narrowed as if he thought Beth was lying.

Reluctantly, but to support his wife, Alex stood, turned his back on the gathering, and unbuttoned his shirt.

Then Beth moved behind him and lifted his undershirt up from the waist.

Alex heard Sophie gasp. Even Clay and the colonel drew their breath in hard. Alex looked over his shoulder and saw horror on the colonel's face and sad resolve on Beth's.

"Are they really that bad?" It was a plain, bald fact that Alex had never spent much time trying to see his back in a mirror.

"They're deep and there are dozens of them." The colonel nodded his head. "It's not even mentioned in the report that you were wounded, not a single word about the shrapnel."

"If he hadn't stumbled off and kept going, he'd have been in the care of a doctor rather than being a doctor. I doubt he'd have been able to treat anyone." Beth's strong, gentle fingers brushed over his hair just above his nape. "If you'll look closer, there are a half dozen more scars on his scalp."

"No, I'll take your word for it, ma'am." Colonel McGarritt leaned back in his chair, rubbing one hand over his clean-shaven chin. "Give me a minute to sort this out."

Alex donned his shirt and did his best to tuck it in and return himself to a tidy state. He sat, holding Beth's hand, feeling as if the Sword of Damocles was dangling over his head by a single, slender horsehair. He watched the perplexed colonel and wondered exactly what his back did look like.

At last the colonel lifted his head, his expression grim. "I think that to let you walk away from this would not be justice, Dr. Buchanan."

Beth exhaled sharply. "Colonel, please—"

The colonel lifted one hand sharply to cut her off. "Let me

finish. I can see the weight of the guilt on you, doctor. I think to let you walk away would leave you bearing this guilt. I am going to insist that you spend the next year—"

Alex stiffened his spine as his heart plunged. A year in prison. He could do that. He'd willingly pay the price for his cowardice. But the shame he'd bring on Beth and her family was terrible. He could never ask her to wait. He could—

"—serving as the doctor on this base."

Alex's hopes soared. "Yes, I'd serve you well, sir." Then Alex grimaced. "There. . .uh. . .there are no more wars looming, are there?"

The colonel's stern face lifted into a smile. "No, things have gotten purely peaceful around Fort Union these days. Unless my wife doesn't get the ingredients that she needs to do her baking. Then there's shooting trouble."

Alex smiled. Then he laughed. "Well, I'll be glad to make runs with the supply wagon to prevent that from happening."

They all laughed, more from relief than from the quality of Alex's joke.

A loud rap on the door brought the laughter to an end.

"Come in," the colonel called out.

"I've got a telegraph, sir." A young soldier entered, saluting smartly. "It has to do with this case, so I brought it in."

"Let me see it." McGarritt extended his hand.

The private rushed forward and handed the slip of paper to the fort commander.

Reading quietly for a few seconds, McGarritt raised his eyes and studied first Alex then Clay. At last, focused on Clay, he said, "Well, whom exactly did you send that wire to, Major McClellen?"

"I sent several wires, including—well, I served for a time with Colonel Miles in the Civil War. He's the man who gave me the battlefield promotion to major. I've kept in touch with him over the years."

"And Colonel Miles has kept in touch with many other people. Including the president—the man I was just back East to visit. This is sent directly from President Arthur. Captain Buchanan has been given a full pardon."

Beth gasped and flung her arms around Alex's neck. He couldn't take his eyes off the colonel, waiting for the man to overrule the president.

"It says here that President Buchanan was a distant relative of yours, too, young man. I see no notice of that on your military record."

Alex looked from the colonel to Clay. "I never talk about that. I didn't know him. And I was too young to vote for him. But I know for a fact that my dad didn't vote for my great-uncle James. Father always said it was his uncle's fault we fought the Civil War."

"Your father, who owned a railroad?" The colonel lifted the papers from his desk and waved then at Alex.

Beth jerked in surprise and turned to glare at him. "Your pa owned a railroad? You've never mentioned that."

Alex shrugged. "I defied him to become a doctor. He wanted me in the family business. He made it so hard for me, with all his connections, I couldn't find work. So I joined the army and headed west."

"Well, your family is looking for you, and there's a part of his company waiting for you back East."

"I don't want it, and I don't want to trade on my father's wealth or my great-uncle's political connections or even my wounds to avoid taking responsibility for what I've done. President Buchanan was something of a family embarrassment anyway. My father always called him a muttonhead."

The colonel gasped and Alex winced.

Why had he said that? What if the colonel was friends with Uncle James? What if—

"I was in the military when President Buchanan was in office, young man." The colonel's eyes flashed and Alex's stomach sank. Then the flash turned to a twinkle. "He *was* a muttonhead."

"I asked a few questions in my telegraphs," Clay said. "I found the truth and I didn't see any harm in mentioning that your family had served this country honorably for generations. And that includes you, son."

"I'll take whatever punishment you think is fair, colonel."

"Are you sure you don't want to go back and claim your share of the railroad, Alex?"

Alex smiled at Beth and lifted her fingers to his lips. "I don't want to run a railroad."

"Why not?" Beth looked from his eyes to where his kiss brushed her hand.

"Because I'm a doctor."

★ Thirty-four ★

Luther swung the ax and the cord of wood snapped in half from that single blow.

Mandy watched out her front door and resisted the urge to take the ax, apologize again for her husband, and chop the wood herself.

Sidney had tried over the winter. Never with a very good attitude, but he'd managed his share of bleeding blisters. He still wasn't easy about the job like Luther and Buff, but for a while Mandy had thought he was coming along.

Then spring had arrived and Sidney had gone back to mining.

Too often he wasn't here. He didn't ride into Helena anymore, but he'd taken to leaving for days at a time. Mandy had never seen the hole her husband was digging. Sidney was secretive and hostile if Luther or Buff offered to come along.

Mandy was fed up with his meager efforts to be a homesteader. The life didn't suit him, and it was time he admitted that and admitted there was no gold.

It was time because—Mandy rested her hand on her still-flat

belly—because if they left now, they could be back in Texas before she got so big it was uncomfortable to travel.

She looked into the woods, wondering how long he'd be gone this time. It was already nearly a week.

When he returned, she'd tell him about the baby and then she'd tell him she wanted her ma. The spring had brought several letters including news of Beth's marriage and that Beth was living at a fort with her doctor husband.

Mandy wanted to hear the whole story. And she wanted her sister to deliver her baby.

The little colt, now six months old, galloped around the corral, so black he gleamed, so big and graceful it made Mandy's breath catch to watch him. It made her think of the colt's sire. She could see a perfect copy of that magnificent stallion in the little guy. Except this little one was a friendly cuss. Mandy had gentled him and coaxed him into good behavior.

And it made her think about the stallion's owner. Tom Linscott. He wouldn't come for the baby. Belle Harden would. But the fact that Mandy occasionally caught herself longing for Tom to come, and swamped with guilt at the very idea, was a powerful reason to get far away from this country.

Belle would be here soon to take her baby home. Mandy would wait for Belle, and then she and Sidney would head for Texas. If only Sidney would agree.

Mandy knew that Sidney didn't want to go back. Mainly because he was afraid of Pa. But eventually Sidney would come around. And maybe the baby would be the thing that would finally persuade him. After all, nothing held them here.

Fretting to think of the job she had ahead of her to coax Sidney back toward Texas, Mandy looked away from Luther so he wouldn't see her scowl.

And that's when she saw Sidney racing out of the woods on horseback, a huge grin splitting his face. Sidney swung down from his horse and ran toward Mandy, jumping and yelling while he ran. He looked as happy as a man who'd just found—

"Gold!"

Mandy heaved a sigh of relief, glad to see that beautiful smile on Sidney's face. "Yes, I know you enjoy hunting for gold, but—"

"I found gold, Mandy." Sidney kept sprinting and grabbed her around the waist, hoisted her into the air, and spun her around.

In her whirling vision, Mandy saw Luther watching. Luther knew how badly she dreamed of going back to Texas. Luther wasn't all that fond of the brutal cold either. He'd promised to drop hints to Sidney about Texas. In fact, he'd promised to take Mandy if Sidney wouldn't.

"Y–you're saying you found a gold mine?"

"We're rich, Mandy." Sidney's smile faded and he glanced over his shoulder as if he suspected Luther of overhearing. "I'm not going to take anyone with me. I'll ride out and do the mining on the sly until I've—I've. . .uh. . .dug every ounce of gold out of that mine. Then I'll make one fast trip with it. I'll find a secure bank. Somewhere settled."

Sidney's eyes shifted left and right. He reminded Mandy of a rat she'd cornered in the barn one cold morning. "I don't want to tell anyone until the gold is safe, or others will come for it. Steal my gold."

Swallowing hard, Sidney suddenly looked straight at Mandy. "I probably shouldn't have even told you." His arms dropped from around her waist and he stepped back. "I should have handled the whole thing, gotten the gold somewhere safe, and then told you about it."

"Sidney, I won't tell anyone. Who would I tell?" Mandy thought of Belle Harden. Quite possibly the only person Mandy would see all year. She hadn't even ridden into Helena since the day they'd ridden out here with the Hardens.

"Yeah, yeah sure. And you're my wife. You can't steal my gold. A wife belongs to her husband. So whatever you have is mine anyway."

"So, once you get the gold mined and take it to wherever you decide, I think—" Mandy knew he wasn't going to like this. "I think we should go back to Texas, Sidney. I–I'm going to have a ba—"

"Texas?" Sidney shook his head and sneered. "No. This is my state. I can be a powerful man in this state. I can *own* this state if I want."

"You mean like buy a ranch? We could buy a ranch back in Texas. I'd like to see my folks. And if you get all the gold, then there's nothing left here for us. Texas—"

"I said no." Sidney glared at her.

"Maybe I could go alone then."

"You're not going anywhere."

"But you're not here anyway, Sidney. You could come when you're ready. You could join me."

"You'll do as you're told." Sidney grabbed her forearm and jerked her against him. "You'll be a decent wife. You'll make me proud for once in your life. Get some clothes that don't shame me."

He'd always been petulant. Even childish. And she saw that expression, one she hated. But there was more now. Arrogance she'd never seen before. Greed. A feverish gleam in his eye.

He'd been so happy when he'd ridden in here. She felt as if his anger now was her fault. But it *wasn't*. That suspicious look, the greed, those had come over him before she'd said a word. This wasn't her fault.

"This is our place." He jabbed a finger toward the ground that separated them.

Suddenly, to Mandy, it was a chasm.

"This is our land." He spread his arms wide, his eyes hungry as he looked around, as if he wanted to own it all. "We're staying." One slash of his hands ended the conversation.

He wheeled around and headed for his horse. As he swung up, the horse sidestepped and Sidney clung to the saddle horn, still

327

not comfortable in the saddle. "I'm the head of this house, Mandy. I expect some obedience from you. Some *respect*. A little *gratitude*. I'll be back, and you'd better be here, wife."

Mandy caught herself rubbing the little callus on her finger. She had her rifle on her back as always. The coldness that came over her in times of trouble, or when she was on the hunt, sleeted through her veins. She hated the cold. Truth was, she was terrified of that cold.

Someday it might freeze solid and never thaw.

"We're rich!" Sidney laughed and spurred his horse in the direction of Helena.

Mandy had no idea where he was going. And only in the most dutiful way did she even care.

Mandy hugged the cold tight to her soul, fearing it and also glad, because she was sure the instant the cold left her, the ice in her chest would melt and she'd be left with a broken, bleeding heart.

★ Thirty-five ★

Mosqueros, Texas, 1880

The driver shouted over the thundering hooves of his four horses. He'd been shouting at the poor horses for days.

Beth was tempted to swing out the door, clamber onto the top of the stage, and beat the man to within an inch of his life for the way he pushed his horses. And it didn't pass unnoticed that Beth was contemplating violence against every man within her reach.

It had been a long trip home.

She glared at Alex, out like a light on the seat across from her. They were alone in the stagecoach, which was a mercy. The man hadn't bathed in days. Neither had she in all honesty. And they both reeked.

They'd planned to take the train all the way to Mosqueros, but there'd been a derailment, and the train was stopped for a time. Riding home on the stage had seemed like a wonderful idea, fresh air, sunshine, horses,

She realized with a sudden start that the stage was picking up speed on the downward slope. Not a good sign. She also realized she hadn't heard that loudmouthed driver holler at the poor horses for a full minute. That was a first for this ill-advised trip.

She looked at her sleeping husband and shook her head. The man was at the end of his rope, and that was a fact. He'd hardly slept for the last month as he'd dealt with all his father's business in Boston and done a fair job of reacquainting himself with his ridiculously large family.

Beth had loved every minute of it. But even more, she loved getting to come home to Texas.

She'd given serious consideration to postponing her arrival in Mosqueros by a long time, with a side trip to see Mandy. Beth had heard that Mandy's baby girl would be all the way grown up by the time Beth got to see her. And Mandy had built a nice new house. Beth didn't know much more than that, but there was an undercurrent of unhappiness in Mandy's letters. They were well disguised, but Beth could read between the lines of the cheerful letters. Mandy was lonely for family. Alex had forbidden the trip and Beth had gone along, being a practical, intelligent woman. She was in no condition to ride all the way around the country.

The stage picked up more speed and there was only silence from the brute of a driver. There must be trouble.

Deciding to let Alex sleep, since she was better equipped to help in the event of stagecoach-related trouble of any kind, she fought with the latches on the stagecoach window and poked her head out the door. . .to see the lax arm of the driver, hanging over the side.

The man was obviously incapacitated. Which meant, on this long downhill run, along a narrow twisting trail with cliffs at nearly every turn, no one was driving this stage.

She didn't give it a second thought. She slipped out the window, grabbed the roof of the stage, and swung herself up. She landed with a thud on the top, annoyed at how graceless she'd gotten with the passing months. Well, that couldn't be helped.

She scooted to the front and, with a scowl at the unconscious driver who lay sprawled across the seat, grabbed him by the neck of his sweat-stained broadcloth shirt and hauled him onto the roof. She slid into the driver's seat, caught the reins, which had mercifully not fallen to the ground, and shouted, "Whoa!"

The horses tried to oblige, but the stage was rolling along at a fast clip.

Beth threw on the brake, putting all her strength into leaning on the long wooden handle. Shouting, calling to the horses to fight the weight of the coach.

They began to make progress slowing the fast, downward motion.

Dead ahead, Beth saw a hairpin turn skirting the bluff, falling away to a sheer cliff on the right while it rose up straight on the left. They'd never make the turn on this narrow road at this speed.

Beth shouted louder at the poor horses. Maybe they were so used to being shouted at they didn't respond to anything else. But she liked to think she had the most soothing shout of anyone in horse-dom.

She twisted the reins around her wrist to take up the length and put her now considerable weight into braking the stage. They weren't going to make it. The trail narrowed. Their chance to throw themselves out before the stage went over the cliff was going to be past. She sucked in a breath to yell at Alex, when suddenly she had the strength of ten.

Alex's arms came around her as he dropped onto the seat from behind her.

"Which one, the brake or the reins?"

She knew exactly what he meant. "The brake."

He took over and had a lot more brute strength to donate to the cause. The stage immediately lost some of its forward momentum.

Beth was able to work the reins better, urging the horses to cooperate until they were nearly sitting back on their heels, fighting the heavy stagecoach.

The stage slowed. . .then slowed again. The curve ahead came nearer and nearer. They were still going too fast.

One of the horses neighed in panic as the sheer cliff had the horse looking straight out over space. The horses and Beth, Alex on the brake, took the corner. They could make it, if only the coach didn't tip.

Beth sawed at the reins, and all four horses, their heads up, took the curve, staying so close to the left side the stage door scraped against the wall of the bluff.

Skidding and sliding, the stage careened, tilted to the right. The wheels on the left lifted up off the ground. The coach canted.

"We're not going to make it." Beth prepared to grab Alex and somehow the driver, too, and jump.

"Throw your weight left!" Alex shouted, pinned to the right side by his need to hang on to the brake.

Beth leaned so hard and fast to the left she nearly lost her seat.

The stage wobbled, yawed upward right, then suddenly snapped down onto all four wheels. The curve straightened and leveled off. With the growl of wooden wheels scraping on rocky soil, they brought the stage to a halt.

Dust swallowed them up. Beth concentrated on breathing for just a second and swallowed a lungful of dirt.

In the blinding cloud of Texas topsoil, Alex rasped into her ear, "Why didn't you wake me up?"

Beth turned and was close enough to look right into her husband's eyes.

He was only inches away, surrounding her, his legs along the length of hers. His arms, now that the stage was stopped and the brake locked, wrapped around her. Although, judging from the fire in his eyes, this might not be a hug so much as a handy chance to throttle her.

"I didn't realize how serious the situation was until I was up here."

"And you got up here how? Exactly?" Alex scowled.

"I just swung myself up. You know I can do that."

Alex's arms slid from where they were wrapped around her shoulders, down to her protruding belly. "I didn't know you could do that now that you're almost ready to have a baby."

"It was a little more trouble than usual, but I managed." Beth realized several things at once, primary among them she wasn't in the mood to be scolded by her husband. She leaned forward and kissed him. "I'm sorry. I should have at least told you the driver was in trouble."

The next thing she realized was that the stage driver needed help. "I wonder what happened to him." Beth studied the man who was stirring. She saw a trickle of blood on his head that looked like. . . "Is that bruise on his face in the shape of a horseshoe?"

Alex released Beth and clambered up to examine the man.

Beth looked at the team. "I suppose one of the horses threw a shoe and it knocked him insensible."

And the last thing she realized was that she was going to have this baby a little sooner than she'd expected. "Can you handle things up there on the roof, Alex? It's not that far to Mosqueros and I'd like to get on into town." Truth be told, Beth was seriously tempted to turn the stage off the trail and head overland to her ma's house. But it might constitute a crime, what with the mail pouch and all.

"Go ahead. I'll just stop the bleeding and we can ride up here. It's only a couple of more miles and he can lie flat out here better than inside anyway." Alex didn't even look at her, as he was so busy tending the man. And he wasn't looking to Beth for strength either. He had his own these days. Strength of will, the strength of his health, and strength of soul. He'd made his peace with God and man, the past and future and—himself.

Beth loosed the brake and called to the horses, which all four moved out with a good will, considering what they'd been through in the last few minutes.

It was only minutes later that Beth heard stirring behind her and glanced back to see Alex easing the awake but groggy driver through the open door of the stage.

Then Alex came up and sat beside her on the narrow seat. "So how far apart are the contractions?"

Beth smiled. The man was too sensitive for his own good. "I just had the first one a few minutes ago. My water broke, though. I guess it's time."

"It's a little early." Alex didn't sound too worried. The baby wasn't early by much. "I know you're tough, but you really should have sent me up here to do this job. You're going to have to cut back once the baby's here."

"Of course I'll cut back. I've been cutting back since we first found out I was expecting, haven't I? Just like you've told me to?"

Alex snorted in a completely rude way, but Beth didn't take exception, since, if anything, she'd been working harder than ever before.

Then they drove into Mosqueros.

Beth saw the parson first thing. "Hi." She shouted and waved.

Parson Radcliff made a beeline for them, his arms loaded with his now almost two-year-old son, the one Beth and Alex had delivered their first second back in Mosqueros. "Beth, Alex, welcome home. We have missed you."

"Parson, could you find someone to ride out to the ranch and fetch my ma into town?" Beth rested one hand on her currently rigid stomach. "The baby's coming and I'd like Ma to be here for it."

The parson looked momentarily stunned, then nodded. "Can I help you down from there?"

Alex had already jumped down, rounded the stage, and was reaching up to assist her. "I've got her, Parson. But the real stage driver is inside the stage and I need to get him and Beth to our office."

As the parson hurried off the do their bidding, Alex turned suddenly. Since Beth was just ready to let him catch her, she almost fell to the ground. Fortunately, she had kept a firm grip on the seat and was able to scamper down herself with little trouble.

"Is the office still there?" Alex looked at the row of buildings lining the town. Beth's eyes followed in the same direction and she smiled to see that, yes, Mosqueros had saved the doctor's office for them.

Alex turned back, reaching up, looking up to help her, then started and dropped his eyes to where she stood beside him. "You should have waited for me to help you down. You could have fallen."

Beth didn't roll her eyes through sheer practice, born of being married to a man she reckoned. "You get the driver." She patted Alex on the arm. "I'll go see to finding a place to rest him and myself."

Alex nodded and Beth walked on. She realized that while Alex liked to observe the niceties of manners and liked to scold her for overdoing, the truth was he treated her with more respect than Beth had ever known possible. He didn't even hesitate to let her walk off alone. He knew she could handle most anything and, perhaps more importantly, knew that she'd be honest if she couldn't handle it.

She walked toward home, pausing to let another labor pain come and go. Probably not even five minutes between them. This baby would come fast, and Beth had a lot to do before she could lie down.

Alex caught up to her before she reached the office and, with one arm slung around the bleeding stage driver, who leaned heavily, beat Beth to the door and opened it for her, allowing her to proceed.

She smiled as she passed him.

And he smiled back.

She'd never seen one second of regret that Alex had sold his share of his father's railroad and walked away from his chance for a vast amount of power. He'd done it now, just as he'd done it in his youth, to meet the calling God had laid upon his heart.

Her husband had survived torment and nightmares and emerged a strong, wise man of faith.

A man with his own strength, who knew hers, who accepted and loved his wife and worked joyfully beside a doctor in petticoats.

Discussion Questions

1. Women have very different expectations today than in the 19th century. Talk about Beth's wish to be a doctor. How often did women back then really go against societal expectations?

2. Alex Buchanan had Post Traumatic Stress Syndrome. Did you ever know anyone from WWII or the Korean War who was "shell shocked"? Talk about how differently we handle mental illness now.

3. Did Alex's journey to mental health seem reasonable? Explain.

4. 4. Alex drew strength just from looking in Beth's eyes. Have you ever had someone in your life that made you feel like a better person, who lifted you to a higher place, mentally, spiritually, and physically?

5. You didn't expect Sophie McClellen's daughter to grow up to be quiet little things, did you? If you read *Petticoat Ranch*, talk about what you remember about the girls in that book.

6. Did you like switching to Mandy's story and back to Beth's? Is that a style of storytelling you enjoy? If not, explain.

7. Which story did you like more, Beth's or Mandy's? Why?

8. If you've read *The Husband Tree*, or any of the books from the Montana Marriages series, did you like it that Belle Tanner and her family made a cameo appearance in this new series? What do you like or not like about Belle?

9. Was Alex too weak at the beginning? Does such a deeply troubled hero appeal to you? How does your ideal hero behave?

10. Do women have a need to "save" troubled men as Beth did Alex? Do you think this particular storyline is maybe not such a good one for women, even though it's fun? How should a woman approach a relationship with a flawed man?

11. There really were bounties on deserters from the army, and death was a possible punishment. Desertion was mostly overlooked though. Talk about some of the scars left on this country from the fight to settle the West.

Wrangler *in* Petticoats

One

Montana Territory, 1882

Sally McClellen fought to control her temper and her horse.

But her horse wasn't the problem. It was her temper upsetting the horse. He wouldn't have been acting fidgety if it weren't for her testy grip on the reins. So any trouble Sally had was all her own doing.

"None of this gets me one step closer to Mandy. She needs me." Sally was so anxious to get on down the trail she thought she might explode.

They rode around the curve of a steep mountain trail and in the distance caught their first glimpse of a river lined with high banks of stunning red rock.

"Sure it's a pretty sight, but—"

"It's more than pretty. It's *beautiful*." Paula McGarritt, Sally's traveling companion, looked at her and smiled. "Admit it. It was worth riding out here."

Mrs. McGarritt knew full well how impatient Sally was, but

341

Mrs. McGarritt, sweet and friendly as she was, didn't let anyone push her around. The colonel's wife sat her horse sidesaddle in a proper riding dress. She had made her opinion known early and often about Sally's manly riding clothes and her habit of riding astride.

"It *is* beautiful." Sally stifled an irritated sigh. They were here now, staring at the rocks. As if none of this group had ever seen a rock before. They all lived in west Texas or New Mexico. Their whole world was pretty much made of rocks.

Sally relaxed her grip on the reins to spare her restless horse. They'd be at Mandy's in a few days. Less because they'd abandoned the trail and gone cross country. But Colonel McGarritt had agreed to the shortcut because he had a hankering to get out of the train and see some wild country. When Pa had asked if they'd see Sally safely to Mandy's house, the colonel had studied the area and decided he'd like to see several places along the trail—this canyon among them.

He'd have just stayed on the train, though, if it wasn't for Mandy living in the middle of nowhere with her no-account husband. So, Sally took the detours that interested the colonel and his wife in the best spirit she could manage. Griping didn't help and it made everyone else miserable.

Which wasn't to say she hadn't done plenty of it. But still— the group had voted. She'd lost. This was America. "Thank you for insisting we ride out here."

"You're welcome." Mrs. McGarritt grinned at Sally, not one bit fooled by her forced politeness. The older lady reached out her hand and Sally clasped it.

"Spectacular," Colonel McGarritt said. "Absolutely stunning."

Sally tore her eyes from the view to intercept Mrs. McGarritt's smug look. Paula was too polite to say, "I told you so." But Sally caught the superior look and didn't even mind.

Much.

The crimson bluffs were magnificent. But was it worth the

time they'd wasted abandoning the most direct path? When Mandy might be in trouble? She was at least suffering from terrible homesickness. Her last letter had been a poorly concealed cry of loneliness. But with a third baby on the way and no womenfolk within fifty miles, she really needed the help as soon as possible.

No, this wasn't even close to worth it.

Only by sheer force of will did Sally keep her hands loose on her reins and a smile on her face. They had plenty of time to get to Mandy's before the baby came. And Sally knew, from the map Mandy had sent, that the site of her new home was going to take this party a long way out of their way, and the group had all gone along with it; and they'd been a sight more mannerly about it than she was being.

Mandy would soon have her third baby in three years of marriage. She needed help. A woman's help. Luther and Buff did what they could, but they had no place at the birth of Mandy's baby. Sally offered to go.

Ma and Pa had a dim view of Mandy's husband and they'd relented, though they'd made a fuss over losing another daughter to Montana. But Sally had promised not to let Montana keep her. She'd promised it wouldn't be forever. A year at most. Sally would help with the babies. Probably end up spending the winter with Mandy and no-account Sidney, then head home.

And now, instead of making the best time possible, here she sat staring at the admittedly beautiful canyon and river God painted with a blazing crimson brush.

She and Paula McGarritt rode with six men. All but Sally were making their way to Seattle. The group had been forming before Sally had gotten the idea to travel to see Mandy.

Pa would have never allowed Sally to travel so far alone. But once Pa had heard of this group of sturdy men, and the stalwart Mrs. McGarritt who would act as chaperone, he'd relented. Now the travelers were slowing Sally down.

She was well aware she should be ashamed of herself. Then

she noticed she'd tightened her hands on the reins again and her horse was tossing its head. Sally relaxed and sat with the most patience possible beside Paula, who wore a prim riding skirt, her gray hair neatly hidden beneath her bonnet, her spine ramrod straight.

Sally knew about tough and considered herself as tough as they came. But she had to admit, the nearly sixty-year-old Paula McGarritt could keep up with her. Maybe not in a footrace, but the woman was frontier born and bred, and she was at home in rugged conditions. And these were rugged indeed.

Though Mrs. McGarritt had clung to her proper clothing to take this ride, Sally had slipped away once they'd left the train and changed into her wrangler clothes. Mrs. McGarritt had scolded, but Sally, already chafing under the delay, refused to change back, so Mrs. McGarritt had relented and allowed Sally to wear chaps and ride astride with a rifle strapped on her back.

Sally had won that small battle but lost on the sightseeing trip. Now here they were looking at pretty rocks when they should be making tracks for Mandy's house.

Mrs. McGarritt said, "Let's ride down closer. I want a better look."

Sally didn't like it, but she said nothing, resigned to the delay. Now she rode along to take a closer look than their bird's-eye view from a mountain crest. They funneled down the narrow trail.

The trail made its serpentine way down the mountain. Sally admitted it felt good to be on horseback again after the long train ride. They wove around a curve.

Sally looked at the sheer drop to her left and swallowed hard. They were as far out in the wilderness as a body could get. And this side trip down to those red rocks served no purpose. Food to hunt, cattle to round up, fine. But to stare at rocks, no matter how pretty? Sally shook her head but remained silent.

The land dropped off for a hundred feet on her left. The horses' hooves scratched along on the loose dirt and round pebbles. The trail was a steep slope downward, which meant slick even on this bone-dry day in June.

As the trail twisted, Sally saw the end of this dangerous stretch only a few yards ahead and breathed a sigh of relief to pass this particularly treacherous section of the trail. Now with only a few more tortuous yards to cover, Sally relaxed. "Mrs. McGarritt," she called out, wanting to tease the dear lady again about dragging Sally along on her joyride.

Paula, below Sally on the trail, gained nearly level ground. The cliff no longer yawned at her side. She turned in her saddle, smiling. "You can thank me later, girl. When you're dressed like a proper young lady again."

Thank her? Not likely and well Mrs. McGarritt knew it. The two of them exchanged a warm smile. Mrs. McGarritt really was a sweetheart, for a tough old bird.

Once she looked away, Sally gently brushed her fingertips over the front of her broadcloth shirt and felt the ribbon beneath the rough fabric. No one knew of Sally's fondness for ribbons and a bit of lace. She went to great lengths to keep her little bows and frills hidden, pinning them on her chemise when no one was around, removing them before laundry day so even Ma wouldn't see.

Admiring pretty things felt dangerous to Sally, so she didn't speak of it. Pa loved having her at his side on roundups and working the herd. For some reason, Sally felt certain that if she went girly on her pa, he might not love her as much. Oh, he'd always love her. She trusted in her pa's love. But he might not love her in the same way. With Beth and Mandy gone, Laurie owned Pa's heart as the princess. Sally's place was beside him riding the range.

Trusting her horse to manage the steep trail, Sally pondered this spark of womanly weakness that drew her to lace and frills and such nonsense. Her foolish daydreams ended with the sharp crack of gunfire.

Paula McGarritt slammed backward off her horse.

Sally's world slowed down and focused sharply as it always did in times of danger. Her hand went to her rifle before she spun to face the shooting.

Another bullet sounded, from above. Someone shooting from cover.

Smelling the burning gunpowder, hearing the direction of the bullets, Sally's gun was firing without her making a decision to aim or pull the trigger.

Mrs. McGarritt landed with a dull thud, flat on her back, behind her horse's heels, a bloom of red spreading in the center of her chest. She bounced once, kicking up a puff of dust, then lay still, her open eyes staring sightlessly at the sun.

Sally raged at the fine lady's death and focused on an outcropping of rocks hiding one of the outlaws. Her rifle fired almost as if it had a will of its own. The rock hiding the assailants was in front of other, larger rocks, and Sally consciously aimed for a ricochet shot, hoping to get around the stone.

A barrage of gunfire kept coming at her.

She dragged bullets from her gun belt as she emptied her weapon then reloaded as bullets whizzed by her head close enough she felt the heat of them.

They came from a different spot. She aimed in the direction of the shot and pulled the trigger as a second member of the colonel's party was shot off his horse, then a third.

Her horse staggered toward the cliff side, hit. Sally dived to the ground, throwing herself to the cliff side of the narrow trail, with only inches to spare between her and the edge. Her horse went down under the withering fire and fell toward her, screaming in pain.

Gunfire poured down like deadly rain.

Sally was now sure there were three of them. They'd lain in wait like rattlesnakes, attacked from the front, rear, and directly overhead, and were picking them off with vicious precision. Cold-blooded murderers.

Rolling even closer to the cliff, Sally avoided the collapsing horse. Raging at the senseless killing, she used her mount's thrashing body for meager shelter.

Fighting her terrified, dying horse, Sally rolled to her left just enough to twirl her rifle in her right hand, cock it, aim, and fire. She'd yet to see any of the coyotes who were attacking them, but aim was instinctive and she trusted it.

The men around her, the ones who hadn't died in the first hail of bullets, battled with her against the dry-gulchers shooting from cover. Sally saw Colonel McGarritt take one agonized look at his wife lying dead and turn back to the assault from overhead. He had a rifle in his right hand and a Colt six-shooter in the left. A constant roll of fire came from him as if his rage and grief were blazing lead.

A quick look told Sally only four men had survived the first shots. The cover was bad. Another man jerked backward, struck the ground hard, and collapsed on his back.

A cry from overhead told Sally somebody's bullet had found its mark. There were three shooters. With the cry, one of them quit firing.

Another of her companions collapsed to the ground. There just was no shelter. The horses weren't enough. Sally's horse neighed in pain and made a valiant lurching effort to regain its feet. The movement sent the horse—and Sally—dangerously close to the cliff. Bullets whizzed like furious bees from two directions. Sally aimed at the source of that vicious raining lead and fired as fast as she could jack another bullet into her Winchester.

Another yell from overhead and another of the three rifles fell silent. One was still in full action and she aimed in that direction.

A shout from behind told her Colonel McGarritt was hit, but his gun kept firing.

A bullet hit the trail inches from her head and kicked dirt into her eyes, blinding her. It didn't even slow her down because she was aiming as much with her ears and gut as with her vision.

The remaining shooter switched between Sally and Colonel McGarritt with a steady roll of gunfire.

Sally clawed at her eyes to clear her vision in time to see Colonel McGarritt drop his gun and fall limp on his back. She was the last one of their party firing. Everyone was either dead or out of action.

God, have mercy on all of us. Have mercy on me. God, have mercy. God, have mercy.

Her trigger clicked on an empty chamber and she shifted to reload her Winchester. A bullet struck hard low on her belly. Her arms kept working so she refused to think of what a gut shot meant.

Praying steadily for mercy, for safety, for strength to survive the horrible wound, she squinted through her pained eyes to see her horse, riddled with bullets, kick its legs and make a hopeless effort to rise. Furious at the death and destruction around her, Sally was too disoriented to know left from right.

The dying horse staggered up then fell toward her. Sally rolled aside but not far enough. The horse slammed her backward. Clawing at the rock-strewn trail, she felt the ground go out from under her.

She pitched over the edge of the cliff and screamed as she plunged into nothingness.

"We got 'em," Fergus Reynolds yelled and laughed when the last one went down. He pushed back his coonskin cap and scratched his hair, enjoying the triumph. "We earned our pay today. Let's go collect."

He rose from the rocks he'd chosen for their vantage point on the trail and headed for his horse. Swinging up, he thrust his rifle in his scabbard and kicked his chestnut gelding into motion.

That's when he saw his brother. Dead. Curly Ike, with that same weird streak of white in his hair that Fergus and Pa both had. He lay sprawled in the dirt, his chest soaked in blood.

Fergus tasted rage. No one killed one of the Reynolds clan without punishment.

He, Tulsa, and Curly had a habit of keeping their ears open in town. This bunch had gotten off the train and talked of the trail they'd take, straight out in the wilderness. There was some sight out the way these folks were riding that drew a small but steady stream of sightseers, so Fergus knew right where to lie in wait.

Fergus and his gang had gotten to their vantage point and been ready. Only after they opened up on them did Fergus realize that they'd taken on a salty bunch. Most of the folks that rode this trail were easy pickings. But not this crowd. They'd fought back hard, thrown themselves off their horses and scrambled for shelter, their guns in action almost instantly.

"That cowpoke who went over the cliff shot me!" Tulsa came down the trail toward the horses, raging. "Creased my shootin' arm."

Fergus looked at his saddle partner and wondered bitterly why Tulsa was alive while his brother was dead. Fergus remembered from his youth that his family had been one for feuding and fighting for family. It burned him now that his brother was dead. But those who had killed him were beyond paying for that. The family sticks together.

Fergus even thought of his name. His real name. One he'd left behind long ago. "Curly's dead."

Tulsa fumbled at his blood-soaked arm, trying to stop the bleeding. He barely spared a glance at Curly, and that made Fergus killing mad. "I put a bullet in the gut of the one who went over the side. He was still aiming and shooting when he was gut shot. He was dead while he was still fightin'. He was just too stupid to know it."

Fergus could taste the rage and the need for revenge. But how did a man avenge himself against someone who was dead?

"He got off a lucky shot." Tulsa flexed his hand as he rolled up his shirtsleeve.

No luck, nohow. Skill. Cold-blooded warriors. Fergus and his saddle partners had never had much trouble finding a few travelers who could be separated from their money. They'd loiter around town, watch for people heading out into the back country, then ride ahead and lie in wait. They picked folks who were passing through so no one noticed when they didn't come back to town, and wherever they were going, if people there missed them, they didn't know where to start hunting.

But today they'd bought into the wrong fight and it had cost his brother's life.

Tulsa's arm worked, and no bones looked broken. But a shot like that would keep Tulsa laid up for a few days. He wouldn't be any good for shooting for a while. And Tulsa was a crack shot. With Curly dead, they were out of action for a while.

"The one you're talking about, that went over the cliff, had himself a mighty nice Winchester," Tulsa muttered. "We won't get to strip nothin' offa him."

"He screamed like a girl when he fell." It fed a hungry place in Fergus's gut to listen to a grown man scream.

"I don't like him getting away with his gun, even if he did die for his trouble." Tulsa pulled out a handkerchief and tried to tie it around his bleeding arm, his eyes blazed with hate.

Fergus thought of his brother. They'd been riding the outlaw trail together for near twenty years. "I want to go down there and make sure he's got nothing left. Not a dime in his pocket and not a bullet in his belt." Fergus ran his hand over the bandolier belts he strapped across his chest and kept filled with bullets. There were empty spaces now, but Fergus would refill them soon. He liked having a lot of firepower close to hand.

Fergus turned from the people they'd killed, sprawled on the ground, including a woman, and looked at the cliff. They haunted this area and they'd turned the bottom of that cliff into a graveyard. If they wanted that sharpshooting cowpoke's rifle and money, they'd have to climb down to get it. A chill rushed up

Fergus's back when he thought of going down there. Death wasn't something Fergus worried about much. Not his and not anyone else's. But he didn't want to wade into a graveyard where nobody'd bothered to dig holes.

A graveyard he'd created. They'd been throwing their victims over that cliff for three years.

The sick fear made Fergus feel like a yellow belly, and that didn't sit well. So maybe he ought to go down and see his handiwork. "We'll have to go a roundabout way to get down there then hope we find the cowpoke's body. Some of that drop is sheer, but there are enough trees his body could have snagged anywhere."

They made their way down to where their day's work lay bleeding into the dirt. The three of them had made a good living on the fools who passed this way. Now there were only two of them.

There was talk about sending armed men into Yellowstone to protect the visitors, and that would settle the whole area. But nothing had come of it so far. And while they dithered, Fergus lived mighty high on the hog.

But he'd just paid one ugly price for his easy living. His brother was dead.

Two

Sally slapped into a branch. It scraped her belly and she clawed, but the branch snapped.

On. Falling.

Down. Slowed by the tree but not stopped, just beaten and dropped. Slapped and let go. Battered and bleeding and falling, hurdling, plunging.

That cliff had been sky high. Now she'd return to earth. Trees grew parallel to the cliff. She skidded between tree and stone, slashing through the skinny top branches, slamming into thicker ones, only to hit the top of the next trees and their frail upper reaches.

Twigs stabbed at her face and neck. She clawed at the trees, trying to find a way to stop, save herself. The branches she managed to grab broke, not even slowing her down as she plummeted toward the rocky ground far below. Another hard blow, this time to her back, as she tumbled. Then another and another.

She rolled and slammed her stomach into a thicker branch. For a second she stopped. A pine tree—tougher than the aspens—snagged on a buckle. She fought for a hold. The branch tilted. The needles tore at her flesh. The sheer cliff was within her grasp, but too smooth to find a handhold.

Sliding toward the rock wall, for a second she was pinned. Solid, sheer rock on one side, bristling pine bowed but unbroken.

Her head swung down as she hung from her belly. Her hands scrambled for a solid hold on the tree or the granite. Fingernails ripped at unforgiving rock. Her flesh shredded on prickly pine.

As she dangled, her eyes blinked open and she looked straight into the startled face of a man. A man perched in a nearby tree like a two-hundred-pound squirrel.

The horror on his face told her, even in an instant, that he'd seen her fall. He knew he was watching someone die. He shouted and reached for her. But he might as well have been a mile away. There was too much distance between them.

Sally had one heartbeat to know he wasn't part of the shooting from overhead. Her second heartbeat held pity for him. He was watching something ugly. Something no rational human being would want any part of.

She knew she didn't want any part of it.

"God, have mercy," she cried out to the Lord and also to this man. It was almost as if their souls touched in that single look.

In those fleeting seconds she let herself be completely alive. Looking into the man's eyes, probably the last human being she'd ever see, was as powerful as any moment of her life.

Even as she clawed at the branch, it slipped through her buckle. She knew unless she got ahold of something solid, she was going to be with God this very day in heaven, because she still had a long way to fall and a hard meeting with the ground.

With her eyes, she told that man good-bye, told the whole world good-bye. She regretted knowing how her family would grieve. Pa would blame himself. Ma would hurt nearly to death. Mandy would have no one to take care of her. Beth would relive this and want so desperately to help. Laurie would cry. Her little brothers would want to.

Her weight tore her loose from the ponderosa pine and she plunged. She hit sturdier branches with a sickening thud, face down. The air slammed out of her lungs. The tree gave again and she fell, hit and fell, hit and fell. The rock on her right grated her skin. The tree on her left seemed to take pleasure in its slapping leaves, occasional sharp needles, and harsh, scraping bark. The world set out to do every bit of harm it knew.

She had no idea how far she fell, if it was for a long time or if the world had just slowed down as she plunged to her death. And then the ground, rushing toward her. Nowhere left to fall.

A sudden blow wiped it all away.

Logan McKenzie slapped one hand to his Colt six-shooter when he heard the gunfire.

Of course it was gone. Left on his horse rather than climb a tree with it. Nothing much to shoot in a tree.

He looked up, not sure what he'd do with the gun from here anyway.

The shooting went on and on. He was no hand at such things, but he knew there were a lot of guns. Something terrible was happening up there.

A sudden, terrible crack of branches drew his eyes still above him but lower. Something coming straight for him.

He caught the branch of his tree and swung himself aside only seconds before a huge form hit right where he'd been sitting.

As it plunged past, he recognized it. A horse.

Dear Lord God, what is happening?

More shattering branches. More gunfire.

This time, whatever fell wasn't so close. He turned to face whatever was next.

Another horse. It whinnied, terrified. Horrified.

The sight of that huge brown body plunging past him was

sickening, shocking. A sight burned in his brain he would be forced to live with for the rest of his life.

Logan's prayers grew and spread.

The gunfire went on.

No way to go up without going down first. Logan dropped his sketchbook and pencil and rushed, hand over hand, to the ground far, far below. He'd descended no more than a dozen feet when he heard something else falling toward him and turned to see, to dodge.

A woman slammed into a branch of a tree next to him. Only a few yards away. Her belt snagged on something and she hung, stopped in her fall for a precarious second. The space between them wasn't far. . .just too far. There was no way to reach her.

Logan cried out in anguish, and she looked right into his eyes.

A terrified, beautiful woman. Long blond hair trailed and tangled with the branches. All of her terror passed between them.

The world stopped spinning. She let him into her soul through her eyes. Shared her pain, terror, regret.

The connection was unlike anything Logan had known. She handed her life to him in that frozen moment. Endowed him with her beating heart and her gasping lungs. Left them to him like an inheritance as if she knew, seconds from now, she'd no longer need them.

She even somehow let him know she was sorry. Sorry to be dying and sorry he'd been forced to witness it.

He moved to get to her, save her—though the space between the trees made it impossible. He knew it. She knew it.

Farther down maybe. If she hung for a few more minutes he could get across.

The limb that held her snapped and she fell.

"No!" Dropping hand over hand, he raced down the tree. It cut at his hands and tore at his clothes as if the tree itself was trying to stop him. He tried to follow the woman with his eyes.

She'd vanished after the horses.

The tree clawed his hands. Like all of nature, it could punish someone who wasn't careful, and he wasn't at all. The urgency was too huge.

His prayers weren't words anymore, just groans too deep for words. Screams of regret that he didn't utter aloud. Desperate longing that he could get to her. Save her. But it was too late, far too late.

He tore a layer of skin off his right forearm as he went down and down and down. The branches got wider and sturdier. He noticed but ignored the fire in his hands from the scraping bark.

When he hit the ground, he skidded along the steep ground, mostly on his backside, descending, slamming into the tall, slender aspens that covered this mountainside. Looking everywhere for the woman.

Because he skidded right past it, he grabbed at the sketchbook he'd dropped, barely aware that his hand had closed over it.

There she was! Covered in blood. Lying motionless—certainly dead—against a pile of talus rock gathered by avalanches over centuries.

Swallowing hard, shocked by an urge to cry, mourn her, Logan kept moving, the sight of her terrified eyes burning in his head like a red-hot iron. He felt bound to her, even in her death. Their eyes meeting was the most intimate thing Logan had ever shared with another human being. He'd be haunted by that unspoken scream for help—help he hadn't given—for the rest of his life.

He needed to see to her burial. As he slid and ran toward her, he planned to see if she carried anything with a name on it. He could tell her people what had become of her. Try to explain what had happened to her, though he had no idea.

He ran, slipped on some loose rock, and ended up sliding, head first, belly down, right up to her side. He rolled sideways so he wouldn't skate into her, careened into a pile of rocks, and came to a sudden, stunning halt. He scrambled on his hands and knees to her side.

356

Her face was covered in blood. She had on chaps and a leather jacket. Men's clothing. Shredded and tattered but protected by the rugged clothing far more than she'd have been in gingham and petticoats.

God, the poor soul, bless her. Take her into Your arms.

He reached a shaking hand to press against the blood-soaked front of her shirt, to feel for a heartbeat. Before he even touched her, her chest rose and he snatched his hand back. She was alive.

Logan looked up—forever—to where she'd fallen. The top of this cliff wasn't visible with the many trees in the way. Logan remembered the gunfire. It was well no one could see down here.

He turned back to her. She lay flat on her back, arms outstretched. Her hair spread wild and white-blond in all directions. Her face was covered in blood. He thought of Wise Sister, his housekeeper. She knew healing, but he was miles and miles from his home and Wise Sister's help.

Stopping her bleeding was within his skill. Logan stripped off his buckskin jacket and cast it aside, glad for the warm day. Then he tore his shirt off so fast he popped a few buttons. He tried to rip it in half, but the sturdy fabric wouldn't give.

He snatched the knife out of his boot. As he did, Logan noticed a fetid smell. For some reason the smell poked at him like a warning of danger, as if he wasn't already enough on edge.

He shook off the strange tension caused by that scent and cut through his shirt's tough bottom hem, then ripped it in two up to the back of the neck. He needed the knife again to get through that. Then he formed a pad of cloth. Because the woman was so still, he spoke, if only to keep himself company. "I'm going to just press on the fastest bleeding wound on your forehead."

Pausing, he knew he was wasting time speaking to her. But it pushed down his fear of harming her. "I won't move you at all. Just let me staunch the blood. We don't want you losing any more, now do we? I'd say you've got the amount you need in your veins and we shouldn't waste a drop of it."

A second rivulet appeared out of a spot farther back on her head. He used a corner of the cloth pad to stop that.

The woman was wearing an outlandish getup—men's clothing from top to bottom—but Logan thanked God for whatever had prompted her to dress this way. The top button of her broadcloth shirt was torn away, and he caught a glimpse of pink ribbon right at the hollow of neck. Somehow that pleased him, though he had no idea why it should.

A closer look and he saw a little scar, tiny but nasty looking, right at her throat, as if someone had stabbed her in the neck. What in the world had caused that? And how had she managed to survive it?

As he knelt there, pressing gently but firmly on the worst of her cuts, he had time to study her and saw a rifle on her back. He noticed the strap holding it there and that the buckle, right at gut level on her left, was smashed. A flattened bullet protruded from the metal. A bullet that would have killed her if the strap hadn't stopped it.

A small breeze kicked up, swirled around him, and stirred up that smell again. He looked around while he pressed on the woman's wounds. There were dense woods all around the pile of avalanched rocks. The smell seemed to come from everywhere and nowhere.

Death.

Old death.

How old was this avalanche? There were slides like this all over in the mountains, and it was a normal thing to come upon shale slides blocking a trail. Logan had done enough reading about land formations in the Rockies that he knew it was called talus. Most likely this slide of broken rock fragments was recent and it had killed an animal as it swept down.

He did his best to ignore the stench and fussed with the wounds until he'd stopped all the bleeding he found. He'd been forced to work at his father's side as a child and knew a bit about doctoring. She should have stitches on these largest cuts, and a quick check showed him no broken bones that he could find. As for her insides, her spine, her neck, who could say what damage had been done?

"I'd say you're all fixed up now, except you're still out cold." Kneeling by her side, he watched her breath, and then he watched some more.

"I don't think I dare to move you. But then I don't really dare leave you lying here, either." He glanced up that cliff. No more gunfire. His fingers itched for his Colt and he took an oath then and there to never walk away and leave it in his saddlebag again. But he had her rifle if there was trouble.

"My horse is just down the hill a ways, picketed on grass. This hill turns much flatter about a hundred yards down past these trees. I could take you home." Her chest rose and fell a bit more deeply. He pressed a hand against her wrist and found a steady pulse. He'd been trained to the extent his father could jam knowledge into his stubborn head. But for the most part back then, he'd daydreamed about the great outdoors and wondered about the next picture he'd paint. And now, when doctoring skills might save a young woman's life, he was stuck here with a sketchbook and little else.

"If you've got parts inside broken up, you'd be getting weaker, and you don't seem to be." He didn't know what he was talking about. Still, it stood to reason. "You seem to be all in one piece. No unnatural twists in your arms and legs." Of course her arms and legs were completely covered. "I'll bet you'd be fine if I hauled you on a long horseback ride."

Her response was as expected. Total silence.

Logan stared at her, willing her to come back to him, answer him. Praying she would. He really wasn't much good for anything but drawing pictures. And, though he definitely excelled at that, it was a foolish mission in life, or so his father said. And in many ways Logan agreed. The only real reason he didn't stop was because he couldn't.

"I think, from the look of you, you'd consider my drawing as foolishness, too. Although I suppose your clothing is a bit foolish for a woman, so maybe you understand someone who's a little different. Of course you've chosen clothing that is, above all else, practical. So I suspect you're dead set on being practical." Logan sighed. She'd be as annoyed with his painting as Father.

He could do nothing other than stay, keep a vigil over her. She'd wake up or she'd die. The thought hurt deep in his chest, and Logan prayed silently for a long while, hoping up here in the mountains they were just a bit closer to God in heaven. That was foolishness, too, because God was right inside Logan's heart no matter the altitude.

"What happened up there, anyway?" Logan looked up, up, up. There'd been no shout from above. No one climbed down to search for this young woman. Of course, who could scale that slope to come down and check?

And if someone did come, well, would that be good or bad? There'd been a lot of gunfire up there. "Which usually means good guys and bad guys. No way of saying whether someone coming down here had it in mind to make sure you're dead or to save you if you're alive."

Although if someone was worried about her being alive, there should have been a shout or two. Calling her name. It didn't bode well for whoever had been with her. He looked down at her.

Her eyes flickered open.

He scrambled on hands and knees and bent over her.

"All dead."

He read her lips more than heard her. He leaned down to within an inch of her, hoping to catch any other words she uttered.

"Shot. Dry-gulchers. God, have mercy." The young woman reached to her side with a trembling hand and fumbled for the muzzle of her rifle. The muzzle barely showed by her right hip. The butt was visible above her left shoulder. She'd fallen all that way, was only semiconscious, yet her first act was to reach for her weapon.

"I'll protect you." He said it and knew it was an oath before God. "I'll take care of you and see you get home."

Logan was no gunman, no cowboy, no mountain man. He hunted elk. . .to draw them. He would rather sketch a grizzly bear than shoot it for its hide. The wild things seemed to know that and leave him alone. But he'd been living in a hard land for three years and he'd learned a few things. Wise Sister and her husband, Pierre Babineau, had seen to it.

Wise Sister, the wizened Shoshone woman who tended to his home, was in charge of putting meat on the table, and she did her job well. Logan didn't concern himself with how.

"Can you move?"

The young woman blinked at him, and her beautiful blue eyes focused a bit as if she were trying to force herself to understand.

Logan pointed upward. "You fell from way up there. I can't get you back up there, not without about a full day of winding around. If I did get you up there, we wouldn't want to see what happened. And there might be danger if we rode that way." Logan would have faced it if he'd been alone. But with this young woman, so injured, there was no possible way.

The woman stared at his lips as if focusing every ounce of her efforts on comprehension.

It made Logan overly aware of his lips for some odd reason. "I'm going to take you to my cabin. It's a long ride. We'll be pressed to get there before dark. But it's the opposite way from whatever trouble happened up on that mountaintop. I've got a woman at home who is a Shoshone healer. She'll help take care of you."

"Help?" The woman lifted the hand that had reached for her gun and rested it on his upper arm.

Logan smiled at the life that seemed to burn like blue fire out of her eyes. She was a tough one, all right. Maybe she had been up there alone. Maybe that's why no one had come. Dry-gulchers, she'd said. All dead. Maybe she'd been referring to her horse. Horses, there'd been two. But maybe one was a pack animal. He glanced around and didn't see either of them. Either they'd fallen farther down the mountain or gotten stuck higher up.

Such violence, such a waste of life. He knew that nature was full of violence. Bears ate fish. Mountain lions ate deer. Wolves ate rabbits and a pack could pull down an elk. Yes, there was violence out here and he respected that as the way of nature. But only man killed senselessly.

"I'm going to carry you to my horse now, miss." He looked down at her and wondered if she could think clearly enough to tell him her name. "I'm Logan. Logan McKenzie."

"Logan?" Her eyes blinked slowly and she stared at him as if her vision was blurred and nothing she saw made sense.

"What's your name?"

She might have been carrying papers in one of her manly pockets. Those would tell her name. But Logan hadn't gotten around to searching her before she awoke, and now that she was conscious, he certainly wasn't going to be frisking her. She just might be able to get to that gun. He didn't underestimate her.

"S–Sally."

She definitely sounded like the West. Her few words carried a drawl that was in stark contrast to the clipped tones and upper crust accent and snooty vocabulary he'd been raised with in New York City. His voice set him apart and he'd been trying to learn Western lingo. Learning the culture fed his art.

"I'm Sally Mc—"

A low growl cut off her words and pulled Logan's gaze up.

Wolves. Three of them, crouched low, barely visible in a clump of quaking aspen trees just across the talus slide.

Ah yes, violence in nature indeed. They smelled the blood. Or they smelled whatever scent of death lingered at this place.

"Rifle. Get my. . .my Winchester."

Logan was more inclined to get his sketchbook. They were beautiful creatures. But one of the wolves inched forward, ears lying back, looking ready to attack.

Logan slid his hand behind her neck and lifted her carefully to ease Sally's rifle off her back. She reached for it but he stood, the heavy iron steady and familiar in his hands. He realized just how much he'd learned in his years in the wild and how little he fit with the people back East, where he spent his winters.

"Are there more of you?" He raised his voice, hoping the wolves would back off. Wondering if there might be more than these three. Hiking and studying nature had taught him that a pack was usually larger. Although in the summer they weren't as likely to gather in large groups.

The wolf wasn't impressed with his shouting and inched closer.

He cocked the rifle, a Winchester '73 like Babineau favored, aimed at the nearest really fat tree, and pulled the trigger.

The animals vanished as swiftly and silently as wraiths.

Wise Sister had scolded him when he'd admitted he often left his Colt in his saddlebag. This proved her right. He should keep it close to hand. Of course, he usually didn't hang around in the forest soaked in blood.

"You missed." The woman, Sally Mac, tried to sit up, levering herself forward with one elbow as if to wrest her rifle from his hands.

"No reason to kill them." He admired tenacity, and Sally had a bundle of it.

"They're wolves, what. . .other. . .reason d'you. . .n–need?"

Logan smiled. "You seem to be recovering." He remembered how she'd carried the weapon. He'd do the same. He slung it over his own shoulders, adjusted it like she'd had it, then crouched and eased his arms under her.

He hiked long miles and was prone to climbing trees and rocks and wading in fast-moving streams to experiment with angles on a painting, so he was fit enough. And she didn't weigh much anyway. He carefully lifted.

She gasped in pain.

"I'm sorry." He looked down at her and she quickly suppressed the sound, closing her eyes as if she'd shamed herself with that sound of pain. He began walking, careful to jostle her the least possible amount.

He skirted the avalanche, taking a longer but more easily hiked path to the lower grassland where he'd picketed his horse. As he reached the end of the talus, he passed through a thick stand of trees and kept his ears and eyes open for any sign of the wolves. None jumped him. And then he stopped, the shock so sudden he jerked poor Sally Mac and squeezed another gasp out of her.

Her eyes flew open. "What?" Then she looked in the direction he was staring, shouted, and struggled against his grip.

"No, stay still. There's nothing we can do for him." If it was a him. A. . .skull. A human skull, someone obviously long dead. Logan thought of the wolves and looked more closely at the skull. It was possible it hadn't been so very long.

"That one?" Sally pointed away from the skull Logan stared at.

Logan gave her a startled glance then followed the direction of her eyes and saw another skull. As his vision widened, he saw a bone. . .likely a human arm but possibly not. Logan didn't want to believe he stood in the middle of a ghastly burial ground.

Then he looked back, all the way up to where he'd heard the gunfire.

Three

I'm not riding down there." Tulsa rubbed his arm. The man was always moving, nervous, with weasel eyes. Fergus got tired of it, but Tulsa didn't miss much and that was a worthy skill. But without Curly around, Fergus found Tulsa wearing on his nerves worse than usual.

Fergus had torn strips of cloth off the dead woman's skirts and saw just how deep that gouge was that cut Tulsa's forearm. No doctor around to make pretty stitches so Tulsa was going to have an ugly scar to remember taking his first bullet, and that was if the wound didn't turn septic and kill him.

"I am. That cowpoke killed my brother. I'm hunting up what's left of him and taking it for myself." Fergus was so sick of Tulsa's whining he had a very pleasant daydream about putting a bullet in the man. He restrained himself. He didn't want to ride these hills alone. Three had been the perfect number for waylaying those who came riding through.

"Long trip down for a rifle." Tulsa turned back to stripping their victims of valuables. Tulsa was skin and bones, except for a

potbelly. His legs were so bowed no one had to say out loud he'd
been next thing to born on horseback and wasn't a man to walk
when he could ride. He was a hard man for all his whining, and
a dead shot. He'd never been so much as scratched before. That
creasing bullet had cut into his pride as much as his arm.

Fergus could use that. "If you ain't in, I reckon I'll meet up
with you in town later. It don't sit right to not take somethin' back
after that no-account killed Curly Ike and shot you. He might
have a few dollars in his pocket."

"Lookee here." Tulsa pulled a fat envelope out of a saddlebag.
Money, paper money, spilled out and Tulsa hurried to grab it.
Then he looked up at Fergus. "Two horses went over with that
cowpoke."

The horses that had lived had run off. Fergus saw one far
down the trail that had stopped to graze. Those saddlebags looked
fat, too.

"It's a rich group." Fergus's eyes narrowed as he added up the
wealth he'd have if every saddlebag had this kind of money. "By
the time we round up that horse down there, we'll be halfway to
the bottom of this cliff anyway. I say we go down there and have
a look around."

Tulsa frowned, greed warring with his desire to do as little
work as possible. Then a gunshot rang out from far below.

They both rushed to the edge of the cliff but could see nothing.

"Whoever you shot must have survived the bullet and the
fall." Tulsa scowled. "We've never had anyone live to go to the
sheriff before."

Fergus looked at the dead horse beside him. "We can't hoist
this horse over the ledge, so someone's gonna see we've left trouble
on this trail."

"We have us a stake, 'specially if we find good money in the
other saddlebags." Tulsa's eyes slid back and forth like a sneaky
ferret. "We might want to move out for a while. Take it easy. We
might have enough to have an easy-livin' winter in San Francisco."

"And we'll let this trail cool down for a while." The bitter loss of his brother was almost forgotten as Fergus counted the money he might well find in the saddlebags at the bottom of this cliff. "When our cash runs out, we'll come on back. Plenty of curious folks comin' into the area. Most head for those geysers in Yellowstone, but there are always a few fools that come up here."

The two men exchanged a harsh, greedy laugh.

Tulsa shoved the last sightseer toward the edge of that cliff. Then they both set out to take a much longer but less deadly way down.

Logan heard something coming. Falling.

It stopped overhead and there was no more sound. But he suspected it was another member of this woman's party being tossed over the edge. Only the fact that she'd fallen had saved her life. If she'd been up on that trail, wounded, they'd have finished her off and cast her over. "Were there many with you up there?"

"Yes. All dead. All but me." Her head sagged against him, her cheek resting on his chest, as if the last of her strength was spent.

Logan needed to stay and bury the dead. A white bleached bone was only a few feet away from him on this crude burial ground. The men who had attacked Sally were savages worse than the most vicious wolves.

Logan knew he had no choice about walking away. He had to see to the living. Between the wolves and the wounded woman, Logan could do nothing but go on. He knew now why the wolves stalked this area in a pack. There was an unnatural supply of food.

Sickened, Logan began walking with his delicate cargo. He'd come back. Identify these bodies if possible and inform their families. Then report this to the authorities.

What authorities? There was no law out here. The place was almost completely empty, though travelers to Yellowstone had increased the chance of a few wanderers coming down these mountain trails. A fact evil men had no doubt discovered.

Logan suspected these men loitered around town and followed sojourners into the wilderness. That would explain how they knew where to position themselves to waylay people.

A perfect place for lawlessness of the worst sort.

He picked up his speed, heading for his picketed horse. Hoping he wasn't hurting Sally. But considering the wolves, both animal and human, which would have definitely been on her had she been alone, getting out of here was about the only real choice he had.

Settling in to take the long strides he'd learned while hiking miles and miles in these rugged, beautiful, wooded mountains, he glanced down and saw that her eyes had closed. Passed out again.

Regret hit him hard. He'd hurt her. Holding her closer was his only way to apologize. He walked along with painful care and prayed over her, and for the others who had died here.

They were beyond help. She had a chance.

A wild cry overhead pulled his eyes upward and diverted him from the brutal ugliness he'd just encountered. He stopped to drink in the eagle soaring, playing on the wind, lifting and falling, wheeling and diving. Majestic and free and glorious.

Dear Lord God, bless the souls of those who died here. Help me protect this young woman from the dangers in this beautiful creation of Yours.

His throat ached with the beauty of it. With the beauty of this entire, spectacular corner of the earth. He could stay here and draw forever. And he just might.

Looking back down at the battered woman, he saw past the blood to how perfect her face was. Bone structure that sang to his artist's heart as surely as the victorious eagle above. Blond hair that had fallen out of a braid. That little pink bow peeking out. The cruel scar at her throat.

Why was she dressed like a man? He wondered about it, but he didn't object to it in the least. He believed in letting people live their own lives, in their own way. It's what he'd wanted desperately from his father.

He reached the clearing and breathed a sigh of relief to see his horse, a sturdy brown gelding, still there, cropping grass. A vision of peacefulness in this valley of the shadow of death. Beyond the horse he saw the white-capped mountains.

A flicker in his artist's heart made him wonder if he should paint the ugliness of nature, too. There was no power in art if it wasn't honest. Logan wanted to do work that mattered, that lasted. But the ugliness of what he'd seen back there in that talus slide was a depth of ugliness Logan didn't believe would fit in the artistic world. He'd consider it. Wolves, death, murder. It would be drawing tragedy and sin and hate. Did God give him this gift and hope he'd use it in such a way? Logan couldn't decide.

His father's oft-repeated opinion that Logan was wasting his life echoed and taunted. His father saw death, fought for life, and even if he lost, went on to fight again.

Was Logan less courageous than his father? Was choosing to draw his pictures a way to run from the ugly side of life? Logan had always believed he was showing courage to follow this leading from God, but maybe he was, in fact, a coward. All of this doubt assaulted him as he approached his horse in this wild setting.

Logan looked back at the perfect beauty of his sleeping patient. How his father would tease him about trying to doctor someone after Logan had turned his back on the profession. Now Logan wished he'd at least listened more. Then he'd know better what to do. Instead, he'd spent his childhood with his head in the clouds. Drawing and dreaming. And now, when a bit of medical knowledge would possibly save a life, he had none.

He let her beauty pull him away from the ugliness he'd seen. He wanted to paint her. Use his precious oils to catch the color of her white-yellow hair and sapphire eyes and the depth of the soul he'd seen as she hung in a tree just past his reach.

Later. But it would happen.

He would paint her face. He rarely did portraits, but this one he must do.

He laid her down on the ground carefully, saddled his gelding, and mounted with Sally cradled in his arms. He gave the animal a gentle kick.

The horse knew the way home, even though it was hours and hours away. The old boy was fat with grass, but he knew there'd be a bait of oats waiting so he moved along with little guidance.

Which left Logan free to give all his attention to the beautiful Buckskin Angel that had fallen from above to land in need of his care.

The Rocky Mountains truly were a land of contrasts.

Near miraculous beauty. . .and murder.

Four

Where's Sally?" Mandy's heart sank as she saw Sidney alone in the buggy.

She'd expected Luther and Buff back days ago with her little sister. Sidney tended to make his trips to town stretch to a week. Luther and Buff could make it in two brutally hard days. Now, after days of tension that had stretched her temper tight as a fiddle string, Sidney had returned with no Sally and no Luther and Buff.

Mandy looked at the two men who rode behind Sidney. His bodyguards. Bodyguards were as ridiculous as the house Sidney was building.

She ignored the hammering going on behind her. Men were hard at work building Sidney's ridiculous mansion, thanks to all that ridiculous gold.

"Sally wasn't there, but there was a message from her." Sidney, who'd gained weight steadily since he'd found his gold, lumbered down from his ornate buggy, its sides gray instead of proper black. Just as Sidney's suit was gray and Mandy's dress. The gray was custom-made and far more expensive than a black buggy. It was like the man was *looking* for someone to overcharge him. "Luther and Buff left town ahead of me to meet her. There was a note saying they'd left the train and would be coming from a different direction. I expected to find them all here."

Mandy had to fight back a cry of disappointment. "It's not like Sally to let anything delay her."

"There was a letter from Texas. From your ma and pa." Sidney smiled his superior smirk that told her how little he cared for her parents. Then he reached his plump, dimpled hand into the inner pocket of his suit with deliberately taunting slowness and produced a tattered envelope. Opened.

It was all Mandy could do not to go after him with the butt of her Winchester. Just like every day.

She controlled the urge with little effort. With practice, a woman could learn to do almost anything. "Does the letter say she'll be late?"

The letter Sidney carried had been written to her and her alone. Her parents always wrote the letters with only Mandy's name on the outside. Their way of being stubborn about the fact she'd married a man who already had a wife. . .almost.

Not that Mandy had known that at the time.

And the wife had, after all, been dead.

Not that Sidney had known *that* at the time.

Still, even without his name on the letter, Sidney always opened it and read it on his way home from town.

Mandy had her teeth clenched behind her smile.

"The letter is old, sent before Sally started out. We have worthless mail delivery out here." Sidney shook his head and sniffed in a way that made people dislike him. People including her.

How could Sidney think they'd have mail delivery when he picked a house site at the top of a mountain slope? He didn't expect it, not really. He just liked sneering.

Sidney tossed the reins of his team of grays to the taller of his two bodyguards. Bodyguards, what nonsense. A man guarded his own body out West.

These two were tough men, Mandy had no doubt, but they rarely spoke, and she didn't like what she saw in their eyes, cruelty and arrogance and sometimes, when they fastened on her, something ugly. Something that made her keep her rifle close to hand day and night.

"They'll be here soon. It'll be nice to have some company." He might even mean it. Sidney rarely covered his feelings. A fact Mandy deeply regretted.

A stiff upper lip sounded like heaven. Rather than jump up and down and start screaming and fretting over the delay or worrying over her missing little sister, Mandy just kept smiling. Sidney didn't like her all worked up. Pleasant, calm, polite, restrained. Above all restrained. She'd become a master at restraint almost equal to her sharpshooting.

And at night, if she had the occasional dream about her hands wrapped around Sidney's flabby neck, well, she never actually touched the man, so no harm was done. In fact, it was possible that's why God had created dreams.

"Pa's home!" Little Angela came charging out of the cabin. Just past two, she was a fireball. Lively and bright and full of sass. And dressed in gray.

She reminded Mandy of her sister Laurie so much it was like a constant ache in her throat. Mandy had a big hand in raising Laurie, so turning all her love to this little tyke was a simple task indeed.

Angela ran straight past Mandy to her pa.

Sidney caught Angela up in his arms with a grunt of effort. "Hello, sweetie. I've got a surprise for you from town." Being wealthy had agreed with Sidney to a certain extent. Being a king—at least in his own mind—suited him right down to the ground.

A loud cry from their cabin turned Mandy's attention. She looked over her shoulder at the small but adequate cabin Sidney had paid someone else to build before he figured out just how much money he really had.

Little Catherine was awake. Hungry no doubt. Mandy needed to get her weaned before the next one came. But with both of their milk cows dried up, waiting to calf, milk was scarce up here in the high-up hills where Sidney seemed determined to live.

Luther and Buff would have brought supplies from town, but they'd been focused on picking up Sally. Then, since she hadn't arrived, it appeared that they'd turned their attention to figuring out why.

Which would leave the supplies to Sidney. Who came home empty-handed.

He stood Angela back on her two wobbly feet, handed her a licorice stick, and shooed her away like an unwelcome fly. But he had hugged her nicely first.

"Can I read the letter, Sidney? While I see to Catherine?" Mandy used exactly the correct tone. Not over eager. Pleasant, restrained, restrained, restrained.

Mandy adjusted the rifle strapped on her back. She'd begun to leave it off occasionally after their first year out here. Hung it over the door in the tidy little cabin. Then Sidney had struck it rich and hired his bodyguards with their watchful, hungry eyes, and she'd clung to it, either within grabbing distance inside or strapped on her back outside. She even slept with it beside her bed.

The taller of the two men gave her a long look behind Sidney's back, and Mandy was grateful that she was in an advanced state of pregnancy. Sidney had kept her in that state ever since they'd gotten married.

But Mandy didn't mind. Her daughters were the best part of her marriage. No contest.

God protect me. And protect Sidney from me.

She shouldn't ask. It wasn't properly restrained. But she couldn't stop herself. "Sidney, did you remember to bring supplies from the general store?"

Why they needed supplies when they were surrounded by mountains teeming with food was beyond Mandy, but she knew with Luther and Buff riding out to meet Sally and bringing her the rest of the way, there was only the food that she fetched with the business end of her rifle, or what Sidney brought from town. And going hunting when she was eight months into her confinement, with two toddlers in tow, was a bit much. Not that she hadn't done it. The hunting was hard enough, but bleeding and gutting a deer, then hauling her catch home and butchering it taxed her right to the limit.

Luther and Buff had left plenty of food. But that was before any of them knew about the men coming to build the new house even farther up the hill.

Sidney, not a practical man at the best of times, had neglected to mention the work crews, who had arrived shortly after he left. All Sidney knew was there was always food on the table somehow and he ate his share and more with great enthusiasm. He had no personal curiosity about how it got there.

"No, I didn't have time for that, Mandy. I had business to see to. Important business." Sidney came into possession of his kingly voice with little provocation. Mandy would have liked to shove that attitude of his right down his throat.

"As if eating isn't important?" Uh-oh. That was definitely not properly restrained.

The baby cried again, louder. Mandy needed that letter before she settled in to feeding Catherine.

Sidney's eyes flashed in his puffy, pallid face—temper, always sullen, pouty. One more word from her, and he'd probably not speak to her for days. Oh, she was tempted. She was more than tempted.

"Sidney, how am I supposed to feed five workmen, your

bodyguards, plus our two children and you without food?"

Sidney crushed her letter in his hand. Mandy felt as if he'd physically crushed her heart. What if he destroyed it? What if there was news? Beth was expecting a baby and Mandy knew it might have come by now.

She thought about her rifle on her back in such a sinful way she was horrified. Restraint.

God protect me from my temper. And mostly, protect Sidney from it.

"I do everything around here." Sidney lifted his fist, holding the letter in a tight ball, but Mandy could smooth it out easily. "I provide you with luxuries your *father* never dreamed of."

Sidney pulled a match out of his pocket. The man had taken to smoking expensive cigars since the gold mine had come in. So a match didn't necessarily mean disaster. He could be planning to smoke.

"I will not put up with your constant nagging." Sidney struck the match and held it to the paper.

"I'm sorry, Sidney. So sorry. I will never speak like that to you again." She held her breath. Prayed. Her fingers had an actual itch on the tips and it would scratch them very nicely to grab her rifle. She wouldn't shoot him of course. But just one well-placed butt stroke to the head—

"See that you don't, woman. And get in the house. It's not proper for you to flaunt yourself in front of the workmen. Will you never learn decent manners?" He very deliberately dropped the letter to the ground and stomped on it as he walked past her without looking at her.

"Yes, Sidney, I'll be right in." She rushed for the letter and snatched it up. She looked up to see the bodyguards smirking at her.

One, Cordell Cooter, who held the horses, was tall and thin and young. The other, Nils Platte, was stocky and older and hard. Both treated her with disdain to match Sidney's. Although

Cooter's disdain was different. Mandy saw contempt in the eyes of both men, but Cooter's contempt had more to it. Mandy couldn't define it, but she knew it wasn't decent and she knew she'd never want to be at Cooter's mercy. Of course, she'd prefer not to be at Sidney's mercy either, and here she was. It crossed Mandy's mind that the two might one day be forced to protect Sidney from her.

Angela grabbed onto her leg, and Mandy tried her best not to look devastated by Sidney's humiliating treatment. But one look at little Angela's expression told Mandy she'd failed. Her precious daughter had tears brimming in her eyes. She looked to her mama for comfort, and Mandy could barely find the strength to hold a frown off her face. She picked up her daughter and hugged her tight, smelling the fresh scent of her recently washed blond curls.

Restraint. She had to learn restraint. Sidney knew too many ways to make her regret it if she didn't.

"Protect me, Lord," Mandy whispered against her baby's smooth, pretty pink cheeks. "Protect us both."

Catherine wailed inside. The baby kicked in Mandy's belly. Angela's tears spilled over. And Mandy restrained her temper, shoved the letter deep in the pocket of her gingham dress, and tried to figure out how to feed eleven people with bare cupboards.

She was a good shot. And she had a vigorous garden. She'd manage.

Being rich had turned out to be terribly hard work. Being married to a man who thought he was the King on the Mountain had turned out to be a nuisance.

"We shoulda met 'em by now." Luther looked sideways at Buff. Worry was riding them both hard. So hard Luther had spoken aloud what they both knew without words.

"Just keep headin' to meet 'em. All we can do." Buff pulled the crude map the colonel had sent along with the train, along with a note from Sally saying they'd cut days off the trip by heading cross country rather than riding all the way to Helena.

"Could we have missed 'em turning off the trail somewhere?" Luther reached for the map and studied it. "Or missed the place where their trail intersected with the trail from Helena to Mandy's cabin?" Luther wasn't much of a one for talking, but this needed to be hashed out before they rode another step—maybe in the wrong direction. They were already inching along, studying sign. Sally should have been here by now.

"Reckon they ran into trouble." Buff stared down through the rugged country the colonel had said they were riding through to get a look at some of the scenery along the trail Lewis and Clark had ridden so long ago.

"Only reason for 'em to be this late." Luther folded the map and kicked his horse forward, his stomach stomping on his guts as he thought of all that could go wrong in country this wild.

Five

Logan barely paid attention to where they rode. The horse knew the way after all. Instead he focused on the woman in his arms.

They'd been riding for hours when they finally reached the carefully concealed trail that led home. He still had a long stretch to go, but now they were on the final leg, climbing to the heavens. Logan's heart beat harder as he thought of what was waiting up there—the glory of God's creation.

He looked down and saw Sally's eyes flicker open. Blue eyes. Magnificent. Like God had mixed the colors Himself and taken long hours to get a once-in-a-lifetime shade of pure, vivid blue.

Her eyes narrowed. "Who are you?"

"My name is Logan."

"Logan?" Confusion dimmed her expression for a moment.

"Logan." He smiled. "Logan McKenzie. Don't you remember from earlier?" Logan tried to think how to ease her worry. "You fell. I found you unconscious, but you woke up for a while. Long enough to tell me your name is Sally. I'm taking you to Wise Sister, the Shoshone woman who cooks for me and looks after my house. She knows medicine. We weren't safe back there."

"You're the mighty wolf shooter." She frowned and her eyes slid to his shoulder where she could no doubt see the butt of her rifle. He wore it just as she had, strapped across his back.

Since he'd deliberately missed the wolf, Logan didn't take offense. "Yes, I scared off a pack of wolves. Can you tell me if anything hurts particularly? I'm no doctor." Something he'd never regretted until now. "I couldn't leave you there, so I'm taking you to Wise Sister." He spoke slowly, clearly, hoping she could remember this time.

Sally pushed at his shoulders and tried to sit up. She cried out in pain. Her well-tanned skin turned an alarming shade of gray.

"What?"

"Something's wrong. My—my—" Her left arm was tucked between their bodies, but her right arm was free, and she clutched her chest with a gasp of pain.

"You fell a long way. I couldn't see any obviously broken bones, but I wouldn't be surprised."

"And my leg. My right leg."

"I'm sure being moved is agony, but I couldn't leave you and you needed care. Lie still." He lowered his forehead so it rested on hers, trying to soothe her. "We'll get there."

He didn't say it would be a long time yet. He'd set out yesterday and intended to stay out overnight tonight and maybe longer. He wanted to do a thorough sketch study of the crimson rocks he'd found in that area. He'd planned to sleep out. He'd never expected to turn around and ride all the way back home only an hour after he'd perched in his tree. "Can you go back to sleep? That would make the trip pass more quickly for you."

"I—I don't think so. My leg is on fire. God, have mercy."

Logan pulled away from her to look at her leg, completely covered by her buckskin pants and, below that, the heavy Western boots she wore. He carefully reached down and lifted a bit of her pants leg. The pants weren't overly tight, and he could see that

380

her boot was firmly in place. He inched the pants leg up with one hand until he found the top of the boot and his stomach twisted.

Her leg, right below the knee, was swollen until her skin sagged over the top of the boot. It had looked fine during his early inspection for wounds, but now it was an awful sight. There was no sign of bleeding or a protruding bone, but the boot had to be cutting off her circulation.

He prayed silently as he lowered the buckskin. *God, give me guidance. Speak to my heart, put wisdom in my head.*

Overhead the scream of an eagle drew his attention. Logan looked up, not to watch the magnificent bird, its white head gleaming against the blue sky, but to reach out for God and acknowledge man's lowly place and God's ruling hand.

He looked at her and saw she had a knife in a sheath at her waist. A knife to slit the boot? Though he felt pressed to get to Wise Sister as soon as possible, he had to do something about that constricting boot.

Urging his horse forward, he sought a likely place to dismount. When he found it, he stepped off onto a stirrup-high, flat stone and lowered Sally to the rock.

She gasped as he eased his arms from around her.

"I'm sorry."

"My chest feels like it's being chawed on by that pack of wolves you missed."

Logan controlled a smile. Which wasn't hard. All he had to do was think of her leg.

"I'm going to cut your boot."

"No, don't touch me, please." Sally made a single forward motion then gasped in pain and subsided.

"I'm sorry. I've got to loosen it. Your leg is so swollen I'm afraid the circulation is cut off. You could lose your leg."

The pretty jawline firmed. Her teeth clenched so hard, Logan was afraid she'd grind them down flat. She kept her eyes wide open, looked straight up at the sky, and gave a single nod of her head. "Do it."

"I'll be as gentle as possible." He raised her pants leg just past the top of her boot and pulled his knife out of his boot. He kept it razor sharp at all times, but boot leather was tough.

"Is it broken?" Sally stared at his face but stayed flat, making no attempt to see her leg.

Logan thought that was more because it hurt to move than a sign she had any faith in him. "It must be, Sally. I'm sorry to say that, but it, well, it's bad, broken or sprained, either one." Logan couldn't imagine a sprain swelling like this. "I'm going to have to"—Logan swallowed hard—"get my finger between your leg and the boot."

"Quit talking and get on with it," Sally said between her teeth.

Sliding his finger in was a terrible business. He had to do it or he'd cut her. He got the slightest fraction of an inch pulled away and touched the boot with his knife. The tough leather cut, but not easily. He fought it, inch by inch, doing his best not to move her leg. Sally wore a heavy, manly sock under her boots and that gave her a bit of protection against a slip of the blade.

The swelling didn't let up; in fact, as they got to what Logan hoped would be a slender ankle, the boot only seemed tighter. Sally cried out when he touched her ankle and then went limp. He looked at her quickly. She appeared to have fainted, which was a mercy for her. Hadn't she asked for God to have mercy?

Still careful, even with her unconscious, Logan cut all the way to a thick seam near the boot heel. It wasn't so tight there, and with a sigh of relief, he decided it was enough. It gave him a partial view of her stocking-clad leg, which showed no signs of bleeding; and it didn't look like the bone was displaced. What was left of her boot made a good support for her ankle, so he didn't remove it.

His stomach twisted as he took one careful look at her gray complexion. He'd hurt her terribly. Unable to resist, he ran a finger down the soft curve of her cheek, drawn to the delicate beauty in the buckskin outfit. The combination spoke to his artist's heart. How he'd hated hurting her.

Sheathing his knife, moving as cautiously as possibly, he gathered her back in his arms, climbed on his horse, and rode on. After three years out here, he'd learned to be savvy about a trail, leave no tracks. He'd never felt threatened—until today— but Pierre and Wise Sister were knowing people and he took their advice to heart, if for no other reason than because a man being out here in the wild might scare off wildlife and he didn't want that.

Now he approached the well-hidden trail to his cabin on rocky ground where no hoof prints would show. His sure-footed horse had taken this same path many times, and he did most of the work, picking his way up the steep, rocky path.

When Logan finally crested the top of the mountain, he breathed a sigh of relief to see Wise Sister walking up to her cabin from the west, her bow slung over her shoulder, a quiver of arrows on her back. She spent time hunting many days, and he'd feared he might wait hours for her to come home and help.

It wasn't the first time that she'd been exactly where he needed her at a crucial time. He'd never really figured out how she did that.

Wise Sister wasn't one to let someone ride up on her by surprise. From the moment he saw her, she was watching. He couldn't even see her expression from this distance, but she must have taken everything in, his unexpected return and the woman in his arms, because she rushed to her cabin. By the time he rode the rest of the way home, smoke was streaming out of her chimney and he could smell something herbal in the air.

Then Wise Sister came out of the cabin, her long hair, more white than gray, in two braids that hung down her back. She came to him and reached up her arms. Logan knew she was uncommonly strong for a round, old woman.

"She fell. Mind her leg. I think it's broken. Her ribs, too."

"Hush." Wise Sister gave him a look that would have shut him up without the single word.

Wise Sister spoke broken English and Logan knew a lot of Shoshone words. They managed somehow. When Wise Sister's husband, a French fur trader, Pierre Babineau, had been alive, he'd interpreted for them. Babineau had also, working with Wise Sister, built a cabin just for Logan and hunted food. Logan paid them generously, one of the perks of having a good market back East for his paintings. They all got along well.

But this year, when Logan had come back in the spring, as he'd done each year while he worked on sketching the scenery in the area, Wise Sister had been alone and there'd been a grave dug beneath a towering pine tree marked with a rustic cross. Since then she'd quietly and competently seen to Logan's needs alone.

The honest truth was, though he trusted her with his life, Logan considered her a formidable woman and a little scary. So he handed Sally over without protest.

She took Sally into her arms and, in her quiet way, took complete charge. She hurried into the cabin, leaving Logan to tend to the horse.

Six

Logan turned his gelding loose in the rough corral Pierre had built. The horses Logan used to pack in all his painting supplies in the spring looked up and snorted at their friend as it trotted into the pasture.

He hung up the saddle and bridle in a little shed with quick, practiced motions, his mind on Sally. He'd grown up with horses. Saddling a Western animal was a bit different, but it came easy.

Rushing in the gathering dusk, he headed straight for the small cabin behind his, but he realized with a pang that it bothered him that Wise Sister had taken Sally into her cabin rather than his. Of course she had. It made sense. It would be improper to care for a woman in his house, since Sally might well be laid up for a long time. But Wise Sister's cabin was half the size of his. The women should live in his cabin and he should take the small one. And besides, knowing it was ridiculous, Logan couldn't help but feel like Sally was his.

As he reached Wise Sister's door, he paused, not wanting to burst in and catch a glimpse of an exposed limb. Swallowing

385

hard as the exposed limb notion flickered through his head, he admitted that he hadn't thought much about women since he'd started working on painting the scenery in the Rockies. He picked the wilderness and there weren't any women here, so he didn't bother thinking about them.

But right now, there was no denying he had himself some thoughts. A woman, whose limbs might be exposed, had been dropped from the heavens into his arms. That made her a gift from God straight to him, and he was strongly inclined to accept that gift. With a grin, he decided he probably needed to consult Sally on that. Then he knocked and waited a moment.

"Come." Wise Sister wasn't for saying a sentence when a word would do.

Logan entered the cabin, always amazed at the lifetime of beautiful things Wise Sister had gathered. She was above all a practical woman, but her home wasn't practical. It was beautiful. . . and rich in sentiment.

The artist in him loved the beaded dresses, furred window covers, woven baskets, and dyed and knotted wall hangings. The one-room cabin sang to Logan's heart. He always wished for time in here to touch the textures, study the vivid colors, learn this different kind of art than what he was used to.

All of it soothed his soul, but none of it pleased him as much as the picture Wise Sister hung in a place of honor. He took one second to look at the portrait he'd painted of Wise Sister and Babineau. He'd done well with that one, capturing Wise Sister's calm and her deep, dark, patient eyes. And he'd found the wild man in Pierre Babineau and put him on the canvas. He was a perfect match for Wise Sister's quiet strength. The contrast between the two shone out of his picture, and Wise Sister had honored him indeed to hang it among her lifetime gathering of precious, beautiful things.

Logan moved to the foot of the bed where Sally lay flat on the large bedstead in Wise Sister's cabin, wearing a nightgown he recognized as his housekeeper's. It covered Sally from neck to toe. No limbs exposed anywhere.

Sally's gaze rose to his as Wise Sister stood beside her, tearing a sheet into strips. "I reckon I've got you to thank—" She stopped, obviously not remembering his name. He'd told her twice already, but she'd had a bad day.

"Logan."

"Thank you for seein' to me, Logan." She spoke as if moving her jaw was painful. Logan suspected there was nowhere on her that didn't hurt. "Wise Sister says I have a broken leg and some badly cracked—if not broken—ribs."

"Wrap leg now." Wise Sister lifted the cloths she was tearing.

"Let me help." Logan stepped forward, closer to pretty Sally.

Wise Sister pointed to a thin, flat board, about four inches wide and ten inches long, lying on the floor by her feet. "Cut in half." Wise Sister reached for the board, lifted it, and drew a finger across the board.

If Logan cut it correctly, it would be two boards, each five inches long. He took the wood outside to the chopping block and whacked it in half with a single, well-placed blow.

When he got back, Wise Sister shoved two socks at him. "Wood in socks."

He understood her order. It made no sense, but he understood.

As he covered the boards with the socks, Wise Sister set aside her pile of cloth strips and turned her attention to Sally's leg. Sally lay with her eyes closed.

Logan noticed two boots on the cabin floor, one cut nearly in half. On a chair next to the boots he saw Sally's clothing. Chaps—of all things for a woman to wear. A fringed leather coat. Broadcloth pants and a shirt with an ugly splatter of blood across it. There was also her chemise, bloodstained and ruined. It lay in a heap on the floor and looked as if Wise Sister had cut it off. He noticed a feminine pink bow on the front of that chemise. It looked almost silly lying amidst the mannish clothes. There was no blood on the ribbon. He didn't know that much about women, but his mother had liked frills and ribbons. He was glad this bit of frippery had survived for Sally.

Wise Sister gently eased a long sock onto Sally's badly swollen foot.

Logan turned to watch Sally's expression. His teeth gritted in sympathy for her pain.

Sally's neck arched back, pressing her head against the pillow. She never made a sound, but the color leeched out of her face. Her eyes closed and cords stood up in her throat. Her clenched jaw told Logan she was in agony.

"I'm going to pray while we work, Sally." Logan lifted her hand and saw white knuckles and an iron-hard fist.

Sally nodded almost imperceptibly. "God, have mercy."

He was surprised she could get words through her tight jaw. Logan spoke aloud to God, asking for the pain to end. Asking for healing and safety from those men, whoever had attacked her. He felt God come very near, as so often happened out here.

Once he ended the prayer, he began to talk, hoping the sound of his voice would be a comfort or at least a distraction. "I feel as if the mountaintops put me close to God. This corner of creation is God at His most miraculous. I think of this place, especially Yellowstone—I go in there for a few weeks every year—as being a gift from an artist God."

"I need your hands, Logan." Wise Sister gently positioned the sock-covered slats on the sides of Sally's terribly swollen ankle. "Hold."

Letting go of Sally wasn't easy, but Logan slipped his hand free and helped Wise Sister.

Sally swallowed hard and her jaw relaxed just a bit.

Hoping it distracted her, Logan went on while Wise Sister began her wrapping. "At the creation, the heavenly Father used these mountains as His canvas," Logan continued, trying to express in words what he couldn't get so many people to understand. Why he spent his life out here painting. "When I ride into Yellowstone, I paint the waterfalls and rugged canyons, the blasting geysers and primordial woodlands, the boiling mud pots and steaming hot springs. To me, all of that is an expression of God's love for the world He created."

Her tight jaw relaxed just enough for a smile to creep onto her face.

"There are pools of water in Yellowstone that are unlike anything I've ever seen before. It's so colorful, like a rainbow in the water and sometimes in the air above the water, too." Logan was doing his best to help Wise Sister and pay attention to Sally's expression at the same time, to call a halt if she appeared to hurt past what she was able to bear. She seemed to be listening, so he went on. "The geysers are so strange and beautiful. It's hard to believe they even exist. I've never seen anything like them before. Water, just spouting right up out of the ground. And there are a whole bunch of them. Some of them just come and go whenever they want. One they call Old Faithful."

Sally's mouth barely moved as she responded. "I've heard of it."

Logan saw Wise Sister wrapping around and around. Sally's ankle was now so thick with the white cloth that it should hold the bone steady enough to heal.

"Keep talking." Sally's request was more of an order.

"It fires off a spray about once an hour. And it's so hot you have to stay well back."

Sally's eyes were open a slit, boring into Logan as if she were trying to climb out of her body and into his. Which Logan couldn't blame her for. She couldn't have been real thrilled with her current condition.

"I stay there a few weeks and paint. Then I come back here. Wise Sister and her husband Pierre have lived here for years. I met Pierre when I first came into the area, and Pierre acted as my guide. He told me he lived in a spectacular place. We came up here, where he'd lived with Wise Sister for years. I asked if they'd stay on, work for me, help me find my way in these mountains."

Logan glanced at Wise Sister, who caught the look and shooed his hands away from Sally's ankle, then nodded encouragement for him to keep talking. Holding the limb motionless seemed to be helping because a bit of color returned to Sally's cheeks.

"For three years I've been coming back here." Logan went back to holding Sally's hand. "Pierre and Wise Sister built my cabin for me, with huge windows to let in the light and the view. And as I got to know them, Pierre the rover, Wise Sister the homemaker, I came to love it here. I hope to come back every summer for the rest of my life. Or at least until I've painted it all. Which should take the rest of my life, so that's the same thing."

Sally caught hold of his hand so tightly Logan wondered if he'd be able to paint when this was done. He found he didn't really care enough to let go.

"I've had the notion that maybe this is where God had the Garden of Eden."

A soft sniff of humorous disdain sounded from Sally, and she wrinkled her nose and spoke through gritted teeth. "Too hard of a land for the Garden of Eden."

If she could laugh at him, it was a good sign she was listening... and maybe not hurting so badly.

"It is that. True enough. And it sounds to me like the Garden of Eden was an easy life. But the beauty makes up for it. It's staggering. The sun rises from the east in a splash of glory. It's often blazing red in the west at night. There are majestic elk, powerful buffalo, towering lodgepole pines, and soaring eagles. God has created many beautiful things, including—" Logan checked himself before he mentioned Sally. She was so lovely. "Surely God never has created anything more beautiful."

Wise Sister worked quickly, gently binding Sally's leg.

Sally swallowed convulsively but never once cried out. Logan was impressed beyond words.

When the leg was tightly bound, Wise Sister brushed Sally's hair back from her face. "Ribs next."

Sally gulped audibly.

"You." Wise Sister looked at him and he straightened, ready to do whatever would help most. "Go." Wise Sister jerked her hand toward the door.

"But I—"

A threatening grunt erupted from his housekeeper's throat. "Woman. Only women."

Logan knew wrapping ribs was the usual treatment. And that no doubt needed doing without the nightgown in the way. He wanted to stay and help. But as usual Wise Sister was terrifying, also undoubtedly right. He left, but he didn't like it.

He paced, went into his cabin, twiddled his thumbs, and went half mad with worry and impatience before he remembered he knew how to draw. "I can sketch her face." He slapped his shirt pocket. No pencil. He'd lost it when he'd dropped his sketchbook. He was always scrupulously careful with his equipment because of the work it took to haul it in here. But a woman had been plunging past him after all.

It didn't matter, he had another pencil. Rushing to the trunk he hauled in here every year, he threw open the lid. "Got to get her face down on paper." It burned in him. To think he'd forgotten.

He pulled out a fresh sketchbook. "Can I do it? Can I capture her beauty and courage?" He only knew he'd never be satisfied until he'd given it every ounce of his talent and effort.

Each spring, he also brought canvas and as many pots of oil paint as he could carry. Then he steeped himself in this magnificent place and immersed himself in art all summer.

The winter began threatening in September. Leaving would have torn Logan's heart out except it was about the same time he ran out of canvas and oil paint and sketchbooks. So, he hauled it all home, sold what he could bear to part with, and spent the winter in his parents' house in New York City painting, using his sketches and memory to supply the colors.

He took his first stroke of pencil on paper and felt all his nervous tension melt away as it always did when he let himself get lost in his art.

What would his family think of Sally's portrait? His doctor father and four doctor brothers loved him and admired his work, all while telling him good-naturedly that he was out of his mind to spend his life drawing pictures.

They'd calmed their teasing some since he'd started making a solid income with his painting, squeaked his way into a few museums, and appeared in the pages of *Harper's Weekly*. They were almost used to his scenery. But they'd never seen a drawing of a woman he'd done. Even the one portrait he'd done of Wise Sister he'd left behind for her.

Sally's face appeared on the paper as if it flowed out of his fingertips. He didn't hesitate for a second. The ability to draw and paint was something he'd been born with, and even he didn't understand it. But with or without understanding, he was completely confident when he was creating.

He filled the first sheet with a profile, another one of her sleeping, another one of her in his arms. As he drew that, it struck Logan that he'd never attempted to draw a picture of himself before. He just let the image come, but wondered if that was what he really looked like. Could a person have an honest image of himself?

Next he caught her terror during the fall and lived that horrifying second again, when she'd caught on that branch and their eyes had met and he'd reached out but not far enough. The picture was awful. Drawing her fear was like living it through her. It was an honest picture, but painful to see and too personal. Logan tucked it into his trunk, not eager to see it again.

He drew her from the back, with that rifle in place. He drew her in chaps and wrote the words "Buckskin Angel" across the top. Then he thought of that tiny ribbon and used his imagination to put her in a dress.

Wise Sister pushed the door open, looked around the cabin, and made an unbelievably rude noise. "Done. Go."

She waved a shooing hand at him, then hustled to his fireplace and began building a fire. Only then did Logan realize night had fallen. A lantern was lit. He supposed he'd done that at some point.

Shaking his head, he made a pile of his drawings, amazed at the number he'd done, and put them off to the side. He saw the fire catch, then Wise Sister—as she always did—stopped to stare at Logan's favorite painting—*Blazing Land*.

He'd done it the first thing when he'd come back this spring, of the view outside his window. A brutally beautiful sunrise, the snowcapped peaks in the background and churning water in the foreground. This was a picture of the spectacular place he'd chosen to build his cabin, at the most glorious moment he'd ever seen.

The color of the sun that morning had turned everything outside his window into dancing fire. Logan hadn't done a bit of sketching. He'd just stretched his canvas and started painting. He hadn't been able to confine *Blazing Land* to a smaller canvas.

It was a foolish picture, Logan knew. First of all, huge. What had possessed him to use so much of his precious canvas on one painting? And the style, not his usual.

He'd had it churning to try his hand at a new style they were calling Impressionism. He'd studied it during the winter, and that perfect sunrise had demanded to be done in that style. He wanted the strong, undiluted colors. He wanted to paint in the outdoors and try to capture a moment and a feeling and a flash of sunlight, rather than go out to sketch and come back inside to create.

He'd done lots of sketching outdoors in his earlier years, especially tramping around Yellowstone. Who could stay inside in this stunning wilderness? But now he was doing the actual *painting* outside. He loved the slash of the paint knife and the thick colors until the painting was almost three dimensional. But such a huge picture. . .it reached the ceiling of his cabin, and the walls were eight feet high.

But he hadn't worked outside with *Blazing Land*. If he'd painted it outside, he couldn't have gotten it in the door to his cabin. Now he couldn't get it out. If he did get it out, he couldn't pack it on horseback to the nearest town. If he could figure a way to pack it to town, it wouldn't fit on the train.

If he somehow found a train car that could handle it, he couldn't find a home or museum anywhere that could get it inside *its* door.

Add to that, the Impressionist style was still controversial and often rejected by museums outright. No museum would want it.

It had been pure indulgence. A foolish picture indeed. And yet he couldn't stop himself from doing it just the way he had.

Logan seriously suspected that Wise Sister thought he was an idiot. But as Wise Sister studied that painting, the feeling bloomed like the most glorious flower that she understood, at least a little, that art could have value.

Her scowling, taciturn expression softened, and Logan knew that, as much as Wise Sister scolded, she approved of him in a way that defied her own common sense. He was surprised to realize it meant more to him than the highest compliments of the art critics back in New York.

He smiled as he hurried out to visit his Buckskin Angel.

S e v e n

Sally hurt like she'd been thrown off the back of a bucking bronco, then stomped on by a longhorn bull, then chawed on by a lobo wolf.

Worse yet, God, have mercy, she was feeling a lot better.

It had been a *pack* of wolves chawing while Wise Sister had splinted her leg and wrapped her ribs. Besides the breaks and bruises, she'd taken several blows to the noggin, and her vision was blurred. She'd sworn Wise Sister was three people at one time. But maybe that's just because the quiet old woman hurt her as bad as three people. Three people with wolf teeth.

She'd finally—almost fully—remembered what had happened, and her heart was hurting as bad as her body. Mrs. McGarritt—dead. The sight of Paula McGarritt, lying dead, on her back on that trail—Sally'd had one brief heartbeat to see her and the sight haunted her now every time she closed her eyes.

Colonel and Mrs. McGarritt had been close family friends. They were honorary grandparents to Beth and Alex's baby. The others riding with Sally were solid, knowing hands. Soldiers almost to a man. Tough, competent, trail savvy, and they'd been mowed down by yellow-bellied cowards.

Sally had done her best to put a bullet or two into them. The others with her had done their share, but Sally had heard the wrong guns still firing as she fell. The dry-gulchers had won. Sally had to figure everyone with her was dead. The members of her company would've come if they were alive.

As vague memories returned, she knew there'd been no sounds from above, except what she knew were bodies being thrown off the trail. From the bones she'd seen, Sally knew for a fact those coyotes had done this before. They were making a living at it.

But they'd made a mistake this time. The colonel was an important man with important friends. He came from a well-respected family that owned a big chunk of land in New Mexico. The colonel wasn't going to be shot to doll rags, tossed over a cliff, and forgotten. Folks would come hunting and they'd stay on the hunt until they had answers.

Someone would come for her, too. Sally had sent that letter on to Luther and Buff, who were to meet her train and guide her out to Mandy's. She'd be discovered missing within days.

Luther was smarter in the woods than Pa, even Ma. Maybe not Beth, but no one was better than Beth. Luther would be back-trailing her as soon as she didn't make the place where this shortcut crossed the trail to Mandy's.

If the man—Logan—who'd found her hadn't hauled her a day's ride away from that hill, Luther might be there to find her already. But Wise Sister was certain Sally had needed doctoring, so it was as well Logan had done what he'd done.

Didn't matter nohow. Luther'd still come, just take him longer. Luther and Buff could read sign like the written word. They'd come and find her, and she'd be on her way to Mandy's.

Urgency pressed on Sally when she thought of Mandy with a baby on the way. The last letter they'd gotten from her was as polite and perky as all Mandy's letters, but Sally had heard a thread of desperate loneliness in Mandy. Ma and Pa must have, too, because they agreed to let Sally come north and stay.

Suddenly Sally wanted to see her pa so bad it was the worst pain of all. She'd tried so hard all her life to be special to him. And she knew he loved her dearly, especially if she rode at his side and worked the ranch hard. Why had she ever left home? To her horror, she burst into tears.

The door swung open and her rescuer walked in. He saw her tears, and Sally waited for him to run.

Fine with her. She couldn't seem to stop crying and she didn't need to shame herself in front of a strange man.

"Sally." He said her name like a prayer and closed the door—with him on the inside. He hadn't run? What kind of strange behavior was that for a man?

Instead, he hurried to her side, just like she wasn't bawling like a motherless calf. Pulling up a chair with a scratching noise that made her head ache, he sat beside her and lifted her hand with such gentleness she only cried harder.

She swiped at the tears streaming down her face with her free hand but decided it would hurt too badly to pull free of his grasp. Besides, it felt nice.

"What can I do to help you?" Logan leaned close and whispered. "I'm sorry I left. Wise Sister threw me out. I wanted to stay and help but"—he smiled sheepishly—"I'm kind of afraid of her."

A ripple of laughter broke through Sally's shameful tears. "Nothin' you can do. I reckon I'm just beat up is all."

"Beat up." Logan produced a snow white handkerchief and handed it to her. "Broken leg, knocked cold, fell off a cliff, shot. Yeah, I think *beat up* about covers it."

"I'm seeing two of you." She mopped at her eyes but kept a hold on his hand. It made the world spin just a little less.

"A concussion."

"What?"

"Doctor talk." Logan smiled.

Sally felt an ache in her chest that wasn't the same as her battered ribs at all. Still, what else could it be? His eyes, a warm brown that matched his unruly hair, seemed so full of sympathy Sally clutched his hand even tighter.

"My father's a doctor." Logan rubbed his thumb over her palm, like a caress, and it distracted her from her tears. "It's what they call a hard whack on the head that knocks you unconscious and makes you see double."

"Or triple."

"Ouch." Logan winced. "It'll clear up in a day or so."

"My sister's a doctor, too."

"Really?" Logan sat up straight, eyes wide with surprise. "A woman doctor? I've heard of a few of those, but not many."

"Well, to hear Beth tell it, they weren't real nice about it. But she managed to find a doctor who'd let her study with him. And now, in Mosqueros—in Texas where I'm from—we only have her and her husband to do all the doctorin', so folks let her help them—some—as long as Alex is there, too. Makes her cranky, but she puts up with it."

"It made me cranky when my father tried to *force* me to be a doctor."

"Instead you live in the middle of nowhere on a mountaintop?" Sally narrowed her eyes as she tried to remember and that made her headache worse. "We did ride to a mountaintop, didn't we?"

"Well, I suppose, though there are higher mountains around it, so maybe not the very top." There was a look in his eyes that drew her—warmth, depth, kindness. He was different than any man she'd ever met.

"No one for you to doctor around here."

"Except for the occasional woman who falls out of the heavens." Sally was surprised she had the strength to make even that weak joke.

He flashed a smile full of even white teeth, a generous and

easy smile that made her want to see it again. She tried to think of something else funny to say, but that also made her headache worse. In honesty, breathing made her headache worse.

"First time I've ever wished I'd paid closer attention when Father was trying to wring a little help out of me." His nice smile faded, replaced with regret. "I know I hurt you bringing you up here, but we couldn't go up the way you came down. Those men, whoever shot you, were still up there, or they could have been. I felt like you had to have care. Wise Sister knows everything."

"Everything?" It made Sally think of her ma, and she almost started crying again.

"Well, maybe not *everything*." Logan studied her and his thumb rubbed her palm again as if he could see her struggle. "So far she hasn't taken up painting and bested me there." Logan looked at a woven mat hanging on the wall. "Although she made that, and to me that makes her an artist, even though it doesn't require paint."

Sally hadn't paid much attention to her surroundings, but she'd noticed this mat of knots and dyed string, beads and bits of feather and fur. As she studied the wall, she saw more. She saw carved leather and a soft, beaded dress that made her heart ache a little. There was a painting, too. And Logan had said Wise Sister didn't paint. That must mean that he did it. And thinking about a man paying attention to the beauty of a woven mat made her headache much worse. And had he said Wise Sister hadn't bested him at painting?

"But she's better at everything else." Logan diverted her with his story and his strong, callused hand. "As soon as you're healed, I'll take you back to town." Logan frowned. "The trail isn't safe, though, I guess. Judging from the other bodies we found." Logan looked warily at her. "Do you remember that?"

Sally nodded. "Awful. Those men have killed before. That's not a heavily traveled trail, but it gets a few people passing through. Pretty clear those back shooters watch the trail for riders."

"I know the dangers of the wild, steep trails and grizzlies and landslides, but for some reason I thought I was safe out here from man." Logan gave a brief, humorless laugh. "I found out today that's not true."

His eyes widened. "You know, I ride in on that trail when I come in the spring. I'm lucky they haven't shot me."

"Come? In the spring? Why?"

Logan leaned closer and Sally saw a light in his eyes that was almost frightening. She hadn't considered him anything but sweet. Until now. Maybe a mite stupid to have hauled her so far from where Luther'd come huntin'. A knowing man might reason out that if someone came trailing her, he oughta make it easy for them to find her. But besides that, he'd been sweet. Now he looked, well, just a bit shy of loco.

"I'm painting the Rockies."

All Sally could think of was the whitewash Pa had brought home to use on the cabin back home. "Painting the Rockies?"

"Yes. I'm an artist. Oil paints, pencil sketches. I'm going to start sculpting, too. I've been studying up. I think I've got it figured out."

"An artist?" Sally wondered why he didn't just say, "I'm a no-account bum." How could drawing a picture put meat on the table?

"I've discovered this miraculous land, and I'm going to spend every summer here until I've explored it all."

Exploring made some sense. After all, pioneers were explorers in a way, and Sally's ma had been a pioneer in west Texas. So, if he was looking for new trails for cattle drives to the west, or rich hunting and trapping grounds, or crop land, or a grassy valley to run a herd on, or even a place to dig for gold, she could understand it.

"Yes, I'm finding every beautiful site in the area. I go out to places like that canyon where you were, and I do a study of it."

"You study?" Like a school boy?

"A study." Logan nodded cheerfully as if he hadn't just admitted he was a bum. "I do a fast draw—"

"I'm a pretty fast draw myself." He'd finally said something that made sense.

"You can draw?" Logan perked up.

Truth be told, so did Sally. If the man was good with a gun, he couldn't be completely worthless.

"Yep, I can get my rifle into action faster than almost anyone, except my sister Mandy. She's the fastest draw in our family. Maybe in the whole West."

"Oh no. I mean I do a fast drawing of an area. A drawing, like with a charcoal pencil on paper? That kind of drawing."

Sally's headache was getting worse every second he talked.

"I've found my calling. Some of my work is—" He shrugged as if regretting he'd started that last sentence.

"Is what?" Sally tried to remember the last time she'd drawn a picture. There'd been a few stick figures sketched into the dirt. . . when she was five.

Of course, the colonel had drawn a map to send on to Luther.

"Well." He shrugged again, almost as if he were embarrassed. Which Sally could well understand. "I've been hung in museums."

"Hung? Like you stole a horse and a posse caught up with you and—"

"No." Logan smiled and it had the odd effect of easing some of the headache his nonsense had caused. Didn't do a thing for her broken leg, though.

"Hung like they bought a painting from me and hung it on their wall." He actually blushed just a bit.

"Oh." Now Sally could understand the blush. It was embarrassing to admit to spending his life painting. Such enthusiasm to waste over something so useless. Although the barn had looked mighty nice after it'd been whitewashed.

"How do you have time?" Sally shook her head and instantly regretted moving. "On my family's ranch, it takes all of us working

401

hard to keep the ranch going and hunt game, tend the garden and haul water. You don't have a herd, I s'pose." She felt some pity for him but tried to conceal that.

"Wise Sister does all that. Well, not ride herd, since I don't have one." Logan smiled.

Sally frowned. "She can't do it alone."

"Sure she can. She always has."

"Always?"

"This is my third summer out here." Suddenly Logan looked over his shoulder, as if he could see through the door to Wise Sister. "Her husband was alive until this spring, though." Logan looked back at Sally. "Is it a lot of work to keep a cabin going? She's never complained."

Sally remembered a few words of complaint just in the time Wise Sister had been tending her. Of course, Logan might be too busy drawing his pretty pictures to hear the fussing. And Sally had to admit, Wise Sister was quiet in her complaints.

In fact, she'd said little or nothing, but Sally, knowing the way of the West, had apologized for making so much work for Wise Sister and putting her behind. Sally knew Wise Sister was now going to have to work twice as hard and three times as fast to get a meal on for supper. Especially since Logan had left yesterday with no plans to return for a while.

"Yes, it's a lot of work." Sally narrowed her eyes. "You really don't know what all needs to be done every day to run your property? You really don't help at all? You don't do the huntin' at least?"

"I don't hunt much. It would scare the animals away from the cabin. I don't want that."

Sally's mouth gaped open but no words emerged.

"Maybe you'd better tell me what all there is to do." Logan planted his elbows on his knees.

He sounded like he cared. Just because he was ignorant didn't mean he was stupid. Sally knew the difference. He'd asked; she'd tell him.

"She has to hunt for your food. Hunting takes a long time. Maybe she sets snares. Do you have chickens?"

"No."

Sally sighed. "Do you eat a lot of rabbit and—" Hesitating, Sally said, "I don't rightly know what wild chickens you've got around here. Back home we've got pheasants and grouse and some wild turkeys. But mostly we eat chickens, raise 'em right in the yard. Saves a lot of time."

"Well, there are beautiful birds and animals in the mountains. Geese and ducks in many different species. Ptarmigans, pheasants, grouse, and wild turkeys. The bald eagles and golden eagles are the best."

"Best tasting?"

Logan jerked and sat up straight, glaring. "No, not best *tasting*. The best to *draw*. They're beautiful, and the way they soar on the wind and play—"

Sally snorted. "You don't have a lick of sense, do you?"

"I've heard that before, believe it or not." Logan tilted his head at her.

Sally would have rolled her eyes heavenward, but she was pretty sure it'd hurt. "No surprise there."

"I want to paint you." Logan leaned closer, and he quit looking her in the eye. Instead he focused intently on her.

She felt as if he'd forgotten about her and only saw the pieces. It was an unpleasant feeling, and she resisted—only due to the pain she was sure would follow—shoving him back. "Paint me." She knew he wasn't talking about whitewash now. He'd better not be.

"Yes, I've already started. I made sketches, but I'll want you to pose, too, and—"

"I'm leaving as soon as I'm seeing only one of you, so don't bother getting out your paintbrush."

The door swung open and a gust of wind came in with Wise Sister, her hands full. "Storm." She wrestled the door closed without Logan offering to give her a hand.

Sally scowled, and that hurt, too.

A rumble of thunder accompanied Wise Sister's word. Distant, but Sally realized it had gotten dark, fully dark. She'd thought it was sunset. She'd lost all track of time, but now it appeared clouds were the culprit, or part of it. "There goes any trail we left." Sally looked at Wise Sister.

"Someone will come?" Wise Sister carried a pot with her, steaming and savory.

Sally wasn't sure she could keep anything down. Her headache made her stomach swoop around. But she hadn't eaten since breakfast, and she knew bones and bruises knit best on good food. "Yes, I have friends who'll be searching. How far is this from that trail?" Sally looked at Wise Sister, figuring her for the person in possession of good sense in this room.

Logan answered. "We rode nearly all day. Not fast, though. It's a long, treacherous climb down to that canyon."

Sally did her best not to groan. She reckoned her best wasn't that good.

"Bad trail." Wise Sister set a plate on the table as the sky opened up. "And now the rain washes it clean."

Sally accepted that. She also knew Luther and Buff. They'd read what happened on that trail. They'd look for her body. When they didn't find it, they'd search. Her heart warmed to think of the strong men who loved her. Which made her think of Logan—the fastest draw in the. . .museum.

"I have to go back." She glanced at him but mostly just focused on Wise Sister.

Logan jumped as if she'd poked him with a branding iron. "Not until I've painted you."

"Not until your head clears and your leg is fit to ride." Wise Sister looked at the leg, which lay propped up on a rolled-up blanket. "Two weeks. Much hurt. Much harm to you if you go sooner. Four weeks better."

A month? "No, I can't do that." Sally looked at Wise Sister. She just couldn't add another job to the older woman's day, so she turned to Logan. "You're going to have to go get them."

"Get who?"

"Luther, a friend. Luther and Buff will come hunting."

"Buff?" Wise Sister seemed distracted for a moment but didn't speak.

"Yes, they're friends of mine who were meeting me in Helena. I sent a note that we'd left the train and I'd most likely beat 'em to Mandy's house. They'll ride to the spot we were supposed to cross the trail, and when we aren't there, they'll start heading out to meet me. They'll find the spot where the ambush happened and start hunting me. You're going to have to go out and find them and bring them back here. I can't leave them riding all over this wilderness for a month."

"The trail isn't passable in this weather." Logan looked at the window, peppered with hard, driving rain.

"Smoke signals," Wise Sister said.

Sally nodded. "Yes, good. How deep in the woods are we here?"

"The trees get deep behind the cabin," Logan said. "But in front it's clear. It's a spectacular view."

Sally couldn't imagine what that had to do with anything. "Okay. Luther might be here already. If not, he'll be on my trail within days. We can start a signal fire and—"

"What if those men see the signals?" Logan asked, shaking his head. "Smoke will signal anyone, good and bad."

Sally felt a flare of irritation that Logan didn't deserve. He was right. And she didn't want to hear about it.

Wise Sister scooped some stew onto a tin plate and tapped her metal spoon with a harsh click. "Time now for food and rest. Tomorrow we plan."

Sally fell silent. Wise Sister brought her the plate, pulled a fork out of the pocket of her beaded buckskin dress, and handed it to Sally.

"I'm—I'm not sure—" Sally gulped. "I might not be able to—to keep it down. I'm feeling sorta sick." She looked up at Wise Sister.

"One bite." Wise Sister urged the plate on Sally, and the rich smell of stew teased her and settled her twisting stomach a bit. "Then rest. Then one more bite." The woman's face was lined with deep wrinkles. Her dark skin fell in somber lines, but there was understanding and kindness in her black eyes.

"Thank you." Sally's eyes filled with tears again. What was wrong with her?

"Good girl. One bite. Then you rest." Wise Sister brushed Sally's hair back. Wise Sister was a short, round woman, her long, dark braids shot with gray. Though there was no physical resemblance, her strong, competent hands reminded Sally of her ma. Which made her think of Beth and what a skilled doctor she was. Which made her think of Mandy and how much she longed to see her big sister, meet her babies, help her when the new one came.

Logan leaned in and drew Sally's attention. "I'll ride out to meet your friends, Sally. I'll give them another day to get to the area, if you think your friend Luther is that close. The rain will let up and the trail will dry and I'll go."

"Helpless as a pup." Wise Sister frowned at Logan.

A flare of lightning flashed in the window, followed by a clap of thunder. Sally's stomach clenched from the thunder and worry about Logan out there with those back-shooting yellow coyotes. And her headache pounded like a drumbeat. "You can't go out there with those men." Something turned over deep in Sally's heart to think of Logan riding that dangerous trail. She remembered little of it, but she'd gotten an impression of it, and Wise Sister's furrowed brow told her everything else.

"I ride that trail out of here all the time. I may not go all the way to town, but I've never had trouble wandering this land." Logan's expression went grim. "Your friends are in danger if they're coming for you."

Sally wanted to deny it. "Buff and Luther are tough, knowing men. They'll ride careful." But the colonel was a tough man, too. Luther would ride wary. Still, the thought of him and Buff dying on that trail, cut down like the colonel and his wife, made her eyes burn again with those shameful tears.

"Eat now." Logan didn't run from her tears, again. Sally was amazed and, though it shamed her to admit it, a bit pleased. Never once crying—well, almost never—for her whole life had proved to be a burden.

"I can't go in the rain so we have time to think of something." He gently gripped her hand, and their eyes met and held for long seconds.

Sally had already decided he was a useless, no-account kind of a man. But something in those warm brown eyes seemed to give her strength. And how was it that a no-account man had strength to share?

But he did. And right now, Sally needed every bit of it.

With hands she couldn't quite control, she took the plate and fork from Wise Sister and ate a shaky bite of the stew. For a second she didn't think she'd be able to swallow it. The meat—she recognized venison—was tender, and there were carrots, potatoes, and onions in the thick gravy. But even with everything cooked to melting tenderness, it worsened her headache when she chewed.

Logan rested a hand on her shoulder as if he knew, and Sally remembered the many times her parents had seemed to almost read each other's minds. She looked up at the concern in his eyes. That hand and the worry steadied her and she found she could swallow.

Wise Sister came on her other side and took the plate, as if she knew the weight of that small, tin dish with its bit of food was more than Sally could handle.

Coddled and surrounded by their concern, Sally, who took great pride in her toughness, let the bite of food settle, and she found it did awaken her appetite and make her feel stronger. Her vision even cleared until she was only seeing one of each of her new friends. She ate steadily. "This is delicious, Wise Sister." She managed a smile and shared one with Logan, too. "Thank you both for all you've done for me."

They both smiled and murmured kind words.

Sally had nearly finished the plate when a wave of exhaustion swept over her. "I think I need to sleep now." Sally's eyes drooped.

They flickered open when Wise Sister took her fork out of her hand. She saw Logan pull the blanket up to her chin.

"Thank you." Her eyes fell closed again.

Tearing through treetops. Certain death, pain, terror, falling, falling, falling.

A tight scream from her own throat jerked her awake just as she'd have hit the rocks at the base of the cliff.

Logan was there on one side, Wise Sister on the other. Neither had moved. Both were staring at her, worry cutting lines into their faces.

She hadn't even gotten fully to sleep and now she was afraid to close her eyes again. Would she face this same nightmare every time she slept? Maybe for the rest of her life?

Fergus heard the first wolf and whirled around, expecting to see the brute charging him out of the scrub. That's how near it sounded.

The howl was answered by a pack...close at hand. All around them.

Fergus clawed at his Colt and brought the gun up, but with nothing to aim at. The howling went on, echoing, eerie, so wild it sent chills up Fergus's backbone. The howling bounced off the mountains, surrounding them until it sounded like a hundred wolves.

His gun still drawn, Fergus noticed his hand shaking, and he would have ridden away if it hadn't been pitch dark. And if he hadn't needed to pretend like he wasn't a skeered rabbit.

It had taken the rest of the day to find their way across broken ground to the bottom of the cliff the cowpoke had fallen over. First they'd chased down the horses and stripped them of cash. That had taken awhile. Then they'd found it hard going to recognize the bottom of that cliff. Things had looked different down here.

What had finally told them they'd found the right place was the smell of death. Dead men, dead horses. And not just those who died today. Older. Rotting. And those demonic howling wolves had eaten the flesh of men before. That's why they hunted in this area most likely. And they might want more. They might have learned boldness.

Even that smell hadn't driven him and Tulsa away, because they'd found a lot of money in the saddlebags. And two horses had gone over the cliff. And that cowpoke had killed his brother. Fergus ran one unsteady hand deep into his hair, over the white streak that he'd always had in his black hair. Right at his temple. He'd heard that gunshot from down here. That cowpoke must have lived. If he had, where was he? Somewhere out there, armed and more dangerous than the wolves?

Besides killing his brother, the cowpoke was a witness. He'd seen nothing, hadn't he? How could he have? Fergus had never broken cover. But had Curly or Tulsa? They all three had that matching streak of white. Fergus might be picked out by that single feature.

"We ought to pack it in." Tulsa had whipsawed back and forth between wanting the money and wanting a soft bed. Now he sat by the fire, foot tapping, fingers running round and round on his Winchester while they listened to those ghostly howls. "What's say we head for town in the morning?"

"Go if you want. That cowpoke killed my brother. And if we find enough money in those saddlebags, we'll be walking in high cotton for a long time." Fergus knew the money was a bigger draw than avenging his brother.

Tulsa was a cousin, not a brother, so he didn't care much what happened to Curly. Now Tulsa reached under his coonskin cap and rubbed that funny strip of pure white hair. Same spot as Fergus's.

He didn't think worse of Tulsa because of his caring about the money and not Curly. That was normal, and Tulsa'd throw in because of it.

Tulsa grunted his agreement, and Fergus knew the money was a stronger pull than the bullet hole in his saddle partner's arm. They weren't quittin'.

Fergus lay awake, his Colt six-shooter clutched in his hand, his bandolier refilled and within reach, listening to those haunting sounds as the wolves talked to the moon. He thought of that single gunshot they'd heard. Someone was definitely alive down here, but it couldn't be that puny cowpoke. Fergus had seen his bullet strike. But if it *wasn't* him, then who?

Whatever happened down here, Fergus had to track it down and make sure it wasn't going to cause him trouble down the line. Fergus prided himself on being a thorough, careful man.

The next morning, it didn't take ten minutes to find trouble. Fergus crouched by one of a thousand paw prints. "Those wolves weren't here just by chance. This place is thick with wolf sign."

A curl ran up his spine. The wolves were used to feeding on human flesh. They lived right down here. Waiting, probably, for food to come falling from the sky. Fergus had been feeding a wolf pack. Now they were prowling close by and not of a mind to be kind to the man who fed 'em.

"Look at that slope." Fergus was daunted by what they were up against. He pointed up at the trees that seemed to grow straight out of the side of the mountain, point upward, and grow hugged up close to the rock face. "I don't see the cowpoke or any sign of the horses. They could be snagged on that slope anywhere. We'd have to be mountain goats to find 'em. And that's if the wolves didn't drag them off."

Tulsa snarled, as likeable as the wolf pack, and started scouting.

They found bodies all right, some they'd tossed down yesterday, some a lot older. Fergus kept looking up at those trees. The bodies were up there. Between the heavy woods and the wolves, it was looking like a long, hard job.

All day they worked, scaling the cliff a long way up.

"There's nothin' here, Fergus."

Then Fergus spotted a horse. With a shout, he scrambled toward the dead critter and found a rich stash in the saddlebags. Waving the money over his head, he yelled, "This is enough to keep me on the hunt."

They spent all day finding both horses and the rest of yesterday's victims, but there was no sign of the cowpoke nor his rifle.

As sun began to set, Tulsa and Fergus set up camp again.

"Could he have survived, Fergus?"

"I gut shot him. He's dead. Even if he survived the fall, the bullet I put in him would have finished him. Wolves must've drug him off."

"Then who fired that gun?"

"Maybe he lived through the fall and got a shot off. A signal for help or something. But he can't have lived. It's still the wolves."

Tulsa grunted and twitched. "Reckon. We'll hunt farther down the cliff tomorrow. No wolf is going to drag a body far."

Fergus tried to settle in to sleep, but the quiet started him into twitching as bad as Tulsa. Yes, they'd found enough money to make their day's work worthwhile. But searching the ugly burial ground gnawed at his gut. He felt his sins crowding in on him as he saw the death he'd visited on people. Hunting for a dead man spooked him. A dead man who'd vanished.

"Let's get out of this boot hill to sleep. Those wolves think they own that stretch of hill." Truth was, Fergus wasn't afraid of a few wolves. It was the ghosts that seemed to haunt this land. Not that he believed in ghosts, but if there was such a thing, then this would be the place for them.

Tulsa nodded and they rode off from the unholy graveyard.

They slept and went back to their search the next day. It was almost sunset when they finally found something that made no sense.

"What's a pencil doin' out here?" Fergus held it up. A pencil sharpened and showing no sign of being weathered.

"It just fell out of the pocket of one of 'em we shot, Fergus." Tulsa kept working around the ground, moving farther and farther downhill.

"None of 'em fell here. Not all the way down this far."

Tulsa looked at the cliff then at the pencil. "A wolf carried it away?"

"No teeth marks I can see. And no wolf tracks here. If a wolf dropped it here, it could have only been a day or two ago. There was a storm before that, and there'd be tracks if it was after the rain."

A pencil? A strange pencil with thick lead. Fergus studied it then started looking for sign that someone else had been here.

"Down here, on the flat," Fergus called over his shoulder.

Tulsa headed down. "A horse was picketed."

Someone had ridden away from here.

Crouching to the ground, Tulsa pointed to a single set of footprints. "How could our cowpoke have ridden away? And how could he have a horse handy?"

"Looks like whoever it was carried a heavy load." Fergus looked up that long, tree-covered mountainside.

"No one could survive that." Tulsa stared and scrubbed his hand over his bristly face and felt his stomach growl.

"Nope. I know where my bullet hit. But maybe whoever was down here took the man off to bury him."

"Why not just bury him here?"

Fergus shrugged. "He was carrying something heavy and the

tracks are right to've been made the day we hit those sightseers. Even if it don't make no sense, he must've taken that cowpoke off to bury him. And if he did, he stripped the gun and any money from the guy. That means he took what's ours." Fergus liked the idea of someone to hunt, someone to hate. He liked the wild places. And now, with someone to hunt, he felt like a wolf again... instead of a haunted man.

"Whoever took that cowpoke has his gun. He owes me." Tulsa looked at his bandaged arm. "That means I've still got a chance at some payback. The tracks go off to the west in a straight line."

"Two days' head start."

Fergus didn't care, they could catch up.

A smile cracked on Tulsa's face. "A slow-moving horse carrying a heavy load."

A sudden rustling in the woods drew Fergus's attention to the gleam of a pair of yellow eyes.

Wolves. Looking at him. Wondering if he'd make a good meal.

Fergus pulled his six-shooter. The wolf must have seen one before, because it darted from sight before Fergus could take aim. He shot in the direction of the wolf anyway but didn't hear a yelp.

Too bad. It would have felt good to kill something.

Then, knowing just how the wolf felt when it locked eyes on prey, Fergus turned to Tulsa. "Let's track that rider down."

They mounted up and headed west, setting a fast pace.

Eight

Mandy shouldn't have asked Sally to come. What had she been thinking? Mandy had to accept her life, and wanting her sister—any of her sisters—around was pure selfishness.

When she'd gotten the letter saying Sally was coming, she'd been so thrilled she'd had her hands full keeping her usual restraint in place. And the letter had come too late to stop Sally, which Sidney would certainly have done. But by the time word arrived, Sally was already on her way with the colonel and his party as escorts and the directions to Mandy's mountaintop home in hand.

Mandy thought of Sidney's bodyguards, Cooter and Platte. Sally might not even be safe. Although with Luther and Buff close to hand, no one would hurt Sally or Mandy. But her old friends weren't here now. Mandy had always disliked and distrusted the men Sidney hired, but she'd never really feared them because Luther was always nearby.

Mandy suspected being far gone with child kept the guards away, and though she didn't like all the workmen, they'd shown no signs of ugly intentions toward her. But she was coming close to the time of birthing her baby.

Her condition kept Sidney away, too, for which she was profoundly grateful. He still wanted her right beside him in the night. Said it was her place, and she reckoned it was. But mercifully, her rounded body didn't inspire his husbandly attentions.

She could barely stand to be close to him. She'd gotten to spending most of the night drowsing in her rocking chair. The children often woke up, which irritated Sidney something fierce if they disturbed him. This way she could see to them better, and the distance from Sidney was better for her chances to sleep anyway. Nightly, Mandy waited until Sidney fell asleep and began his raucous snoring then slipped out of bed.

Now, she settled in her rocking chair, made as comfortable as possible with blankets and a stump pulled in for a footstool, and regretted writing and inviting any of her family to come. She'd even managed to sneak the letter out to the mail, which had been no small trick because Sidney always read any letters she wrote.

But Luther had taken this one to town and mailed it for her, and now Sally was coming. And Mandy had put her little sister in danger, both on the long trail and here once she arrived—if she arrived.

Mandy looked down at the rifle that lay on the floor beside her chair and knew neither she nor Sally would be easy women to hurt, but where was Sally?

She was in danger certainly. Although perhaps Luther had found her already and was heading here. There was no way to send word, living up at the top of this treacherous mountain, a long, long ride out from Helena.

The new house was going to be nothing short of a mansion. Mandy marveled at it as she watched it being built. They'd used dynamite, the explosions terrifying, to clear a road to pull in timbers and stone. Gray stone. Sidney had been so excited when he'd told her it would be gray. Like his name.

He'd even named it. Gray Towers. Mandy had heard of such

things, and a person often named their ranch, but a house? It just seemed plain boastful, and she knew Sidney meant it just that way.

The trail as it was now was steep, with high sides cut away by the blasting. Those trails were impassable last winter when they'd stayed here in the cabin, and before the blasting, they'd only come in and out on horseback. Now they were wider, but not much.

Sidney had his shiny buggy. Maybe, if she got lucky, the house would be finished and Sidney, with his bodyguards, and all the workmen would ride to town just before a big snowfall and end up locked away from her for the winter.

Mandy smiled at the very thought. And he couldn't even blame her. She'd warned him of the certain winter blockage. And they'd lived it last winter. But instead of moving them down closer to Helena, he'd widened the trail leaving it even deeper and more prone to being cut off. Even widened, it was a dangerous trip down to the perfectly nice cabin they lived in before the gold strike. Worse yet, they were moving farther uphill even from the cabin they were in now. It was another mile up a path that would give a mountain goat the vapors, on a trail skirting sheer cliffs, to reach the new house site.

Mandy went out and looked at the slowly rising house every day, stunned by the site of it. They'd rattle around inside that monstrosity. How would they keep it warm? Did Sidney expect Luther and Buff to cut enough wood to fill that whopper of a house with heat?

A cry pulled her out of her dark thoughts and she rose quickly. Catherine was awake. She should want the little girl to sleep through the night, but Mandy always felt relief when Catherine cried. Now if Sidney came out and checked, it would be obvious that Mandy had been forced from their bed.

He liked her right there beside him. Like the idiot didn't leave her alone for days at a time when he went to town.

Mandy hurried into the girls' room and scooped her pretty

baby out of the cradle Luther had built. She quickly carried Catherine back to the rocker Buff had built and settled in by the potbellied stove Luther had hauled from town. Then she settled in to sing quietly and nurse her baby. The little one barely fit around Mandy's expanded stomach, but they'd learned to manage.

Mandy hoped the cow calved before the baby came. It should. Otherwise she'd be nursing both children because there was no milk. As it was, Angela was doing without. Not a good situation for a two-year-old. Not a good situation for an expectant mother. For a rich person, Mandy had quite a time feeding her family. Sidney might manage to get fat, but Mandy and the children were lean and now, with Luther and Buff away, downright hungry.

Mandy turned her thoughts away from her worries and brushed her hand over the bit of dandelion fluff that was Catherine's hair. Catherine was soon done eating and fast asleep in Mandy's arms. She just held the baby and rocked her for the pleasure of it now. The baby's hair was white and fine, very much like Angela's had been. She wondered if this time she'd have a son. Resting her hand on her middle, she pictured a rambunctious little boy around the house and almost wept for how much she missed her little brothers.

Sidney didn't comment much on the children, but he seemed to think it was fitting that Mandy remain constantly in a family way. Except for the unpleasantness involved with becoming so, Mandy didn't mind the babies either. Her life made sense when she held her girls in her arms.

A sharp squeak came from the porch that ran along the front of the little cabin, right near the window that was beside the door.

Mandy's blood ran cold. She moved without even thinking. She had the rifle in one hand and the baby in the other. She rushed, silently, into the girls' room and laid sleeping Catherine down, praying silently that the little one would stay asleep.

Then she stepped back into the main room, her nerves cool, her ears focused on the outside. She swung the door open to her own bedroom. "Sidney," she said, keeping her voice low so whoever was out there wouldn't hear. She heard her husband mutter and snort. She hissed, "Sidney, get up."

It didn't sit right to go on into the room. She wanted her own body between whoever was out there and her children. But Sidney wasn't going to respond without some encouragement. She walked to his side and shook his pudgy shoulder. "Wake up!"

"What? What's going—"

Mandy slapped her hand over his mouth, and even in her desperate hurry to get back to investigate that sound, she might have slapped a bit too hard and enjoyed it a bit too much. It almost pushed back the cold because of the heat of that bit of violence. "Shhhh. Quiet." Her eyes had adjusted to the dark enough that she could see him looking at her. "There's someone outside our door."

His eyes narrowed and he jerked his chin to show he understood her.

She removed her hand, resisted the urge to wipe his touch off her palm, jacked a shell into the chamber of her Winchester, and left him. He needed to know, but she honestly doubted he'd be any help.

She went out into the room she'd left only moments before and moved quickly across the split log floor. Pressing her back against the wall, she positioned herself with the front door on her left and the window where she'd heard that footstep on her right. Their table stood in front of the window. She held her rifle in two hands, against her chest just above her round belly, barrel pointed up, her finger on the trigger.

The curtain was pulled shut. She was always careful about that because of the workmen and the two bodyguards who stayed in the bunkhouse. She hated the idea of their walking past the house and looking in the window at her.

Her senses were alert. Her nerves like steel. Steady as a rock. And cold as death.

She looked to her right, at the window, but she listened the way she and her sister Beth had learned to listen, with total attention, eyes and ears and nose focused. Her hand was steady on the trigger, trusting her instincts. Instincts could be a simple whisper of warning from God. Mandy was always open to that.

Who was out there at this time of night? The workmen and Sidney's guards slept in the bunkhouse closer to the new house.

Sidney came to their bedroom door and she was surprised to see a six-gun in his hand. And he looked comfortable holding it. "Where?" He moved his lips but Mandy understood.

She jerked her head at the window.

Sidney came across the room to the other side of the window, the table between them, and pressed his back to the wall just as Mandy had. His belly stuck out almost as far as Mandy's did, too. To Mandy's surprise, he was taking her very seriously. Mandy had never seen him like this. Sidney was a pouter, a city boy. He hired people to defend him—bodyguards.

Mandy supposed, in their way, Luther and Buff were her bodyguards, though no one had ever called them such. She knew Sidney tolerated them simply because he couldn't get rid of them. Luther had made it clear from the beginning that he wasn't leaving and that was the end of it. And Sidney didn't fuss much. After all, Luther and Buff did almost all the work a man should do to run a home—hunting, skinning and tanning hides, cutting firewood, making shoes, doing the heavy work in the garden, and caring for the livestock.

Mandy wished so much that it was them making that noise. That in a few moments a knock would come at her door and Sally would call out, with Luther right behind her, both of them grinning, safe and happy to see her.

No knock sounded. No shout of hello.

She should have felt fear. In a detached way, Mandy knew that. But instead all she felt was calm, nearly irrational calm. Her eyes met Sidney's. A lot passed between them with a look. Who

419

was out there? They'd never had trouble with thieves.

Sidney was very crafty about his money. Mandy had often thought that her husband had wiles unbecoming an honest man. There was no stockpile of gold here at their home. He kept the bulk of his money in a bank in Denver—a bank chosen specifically for its tight security. When Sidney needed more, he traveled to Denver, made his purchases, and returned, with a bit of cash but no gold, ever. Mandy had never seen it and she'd never been to Sidney's mine.

The noise didn't repeat itself. When minutes ticked by and there was nothing else, Mandy finally felt her instincts relax, and as before, she trusted them. She straightened away from the window.

"Whoever was out there is gone."

"You're sure you heard a man, not a deer or the wind rattling branches?" Sidney had that look on his face. Sneering. As if the sight of her with the rifle was a disgrace.

The insult was too much with the tension of the moment. Another time she'd ignore it, but right now she wasn't able to let her husband get away with. "I know the difference." The venom in her voice surprised even her. Maybe she wasn't as calm as she'd thought. Her tight grip on her rifle scared her a little. "We'll talk about this tomorrow. Go back to bed." She spoke like a general ordering a private around. She never, ever took that tone with Sidney.

He looked from the rifle to her eyes and back. Mandy wasn't sure what he saw, but for once he didn't make a snide remark. Instead, he swallowed hard, then went to his room and quietly closed the door.

She settled into her rocking chair with her Winchester on her lap. After a few minutes, she calmed enough to let go of the icy chill that had helped her be the fastest shot most anyone had ever seen. She began rocking.

Mandy could have gone back to bed, she knew, but instead she stayed in her chair and had a fierce little talk with Sidney inside her head. She decided that this was the last time she was going to keep the words to herself. Restraint wasn't getting her anything.

Tomorrow morning, she'd see if Sidney could handle the unrestrained version of the woman he'd married.

"We're not gonna find those tracks now, Tulsa." Fergus settled into the hideout they'd skedaddled to when the clouds started to build up. The trail had been simple to follow for a long time, but now they had no direction.

"I've been thinkin'." Tulsa tore a chaw of tobacco off with his teeth.

Fergus resisted the urge to ram his fist into Tulsa's face. They were cold and wet and a long way from easy food and the comfort the money bulging their pockets could provide. " 'Bout what?" Fergus didn't let any of his mad sound in his voice.

"We both know that rider was hauling too big a load."

Fergus couldn't help but listen. Tulsa had a lot of bad qualities, but he was a crack shot and he was a hand at reading sign. Fergus knew better than to talk when Tulsa was thinking about a trail.

"I think whoever you shot off that trail lived."

Fergus shook his head. "He was gut shot. I saw the bullet hit."

"I know you hit what you aim at, but it's not the first time a bullet ricocheted off a belt buckle. That rider is carryin' a double load. We saw those horse's tracks coming into that clearing, and where he'd been picketed was clear. Then on the way out, the hooves dug deeper."

The rain peppered outside this overhang they'd found along the base of a cliff. The two of them knew a few bolt holes in this country. This was a good 'un, the kind of place a posse would ride right by, but it wasn't so good for getting out of the rain. The rain wasn't falling smack on their heads, but every gust of wind blew a face full of water in. They sat and listened to the pouring rain and the occasional crack of thunder and considered what it all meant.

"Even if he lived, he never saw us," Fergus said. "He's no danger to us."

"Sure he is. We've had a nice quiet little business riding some of the back trails in here. There's no law, and as long as we kept moving around, no one even seemed to notice. A few greenhorns turn up missing, no one thinks much of it. They was ridin' into a rugged country to see the sights, hoping for a closer look at some mountains. Bad things happen in rough country so who's going to care? But we've never had no one live."

"Nope." Fergus stared into the black night. A blaze of lightning lit up the sky and Fergus thought it was the most desolate sight he'd ever seen. This was a strange land and it had more than its share of things to draw the eye. He understood why people might want to hunt around out here just for a look-see. Even if he thought 'em fools for doing it. But right now, to Fergus, it was the most godforsaken place on earth.

"No sheriff out here in the wilderness so we've been left to ourselves. But if someone went in and told that he'd been attacked and his party went missing, a U.S. marshal might get sent in here. We haven't been that careful in the towns around here. It wouldn't take much of a marshal to figure out we've been spending money with no sign how we earned it. We've even sold a few stolen horses too close to town. If that man you shot lived, we either need to shut him up or quit the country." Tulsa turned to stare at Fergus, and a slash of lightning lit up their damp little corner of the cliff.

Fergus stared at Tulsa then turned back to the storm. "It's the best I've ever had it. Easy money. Plenty of it. No lawmen to be seen anywhere. I'm not ready to quit."

They sat quietly as the storm raged on. Fergus knew without asking that they'd made a decision. He figured Tulsa read things exactly right. Hard as it was to believe, that skinny wrangler had lived and found someone to care for him.

Pure blind bad luck for Fergus. "You've read it right, I reckon. We got nothin' else to do. We might as well see if we can pick up his trail. The way he went don't lead to any town. He's going up into the highlands. That cuts down on the land we have to cover. A mountain man must have come down out of the high-up hills and been passing through. If he found the wrangler I shot and took him in, then we'll have to kill the mountain man, too."

"A man who survives that fall after he's been shot is a tough man." Tulsa spoke quietly, but Fergus heard the hunger in his voice. Tulsa was a man who liked to kill. "And a mountain man ain't one who's easy to sneak up on, neither."

"So we ride careful." Fergus rested his head against hard, damp rock and longed for a dry bed and a hot meal, but he didn't say the words that might persuade Tulsa to quit the search. Right now, wet, cold, miserable wasn't so good, but this was the easy life, and he wasn't giving it up. "A little rain won't stop us from finding them."

Nine

It took Sally three days to snap.

"I've got to get out there." Sally threw her blanket off. "Luther and Buff will be hunting. They're in danger. All I've got to do is get down to the lower valley and they'll find me."

She was swathed in a thick nightgown from neck to ankle. She had one of her thick socks on her healthy foot and a huge bandage on her broken one. But still, she should have remained demurely covered.

Wise Sister gave her a quiet look that almost made Sally settle down.

Of course Logan didn't use *looks*. He'd rather talk a thing to death. "You stay in that bed." Logan hurried to cover her again.

"I can't lie here like this. I can't stand it. I'm losing my mind." Her behavior was outrageous. Even with Wise Sister here it was improper to push back her blankets in front of Logan. She knew it but she couldn't control the burn that she had to *do* something. And her clothes had vanished so it was the nightgown or nothing. Honestly, she felt like a fox with its foot caught in a trap, and she was ready to start gnawing. Her foot even hurt enough to make that seem real.

She wrestled with Logan over possession of the coverlet and managed to get her feet swung over the edge of the bed. She only did it because Logan was afraid to stop her. He worried about her pain all the time so she knew he was fully aware that she hurt in every inch of her body, and he was too careful with her to grab her anywhere.

She sat up. Her broken leg bent at the knee and her foot dropped to the floor. Pain shot like burning arrows up her body and met up with her battered ribs, and the two joined forces and attacked her fragile skull.

"You can't go anywhere." Logan glowered.

"Too soon." Wise Sister came up beside Logan.

"You've been saying that for three days."

"And we've been right for three days. And we're *still* right." Logan spread his arms wide as if he was going to herd her back into bed.

How often had she used the same approach with a stubborn cow? And she didn't appreciate that the comparison had occurred to her.

"I have *got* to get out of here." She scooted forward, hoping to stand on her good leg and—what? Hop down the mountain? Even scooting was too much. She couldn't bite back a gasp of pain when she put the least bit of pressure on her foot.

The fact that it was all impossible didn't deter her. "Now what have you done with my clothes?"

"It's still raining, Sally." Logan stepped back, tidy in his black pants and vest. The sleeves of his white shirt were rolled up to just below his elbows. The man never worked harder than lifting a pencil. Or leastways, she'd never seen him.

Wise Sister had some traps and they'd had muskrat stew for the noon meal. Logan, well, she'd never seen him do a thing but draw pictures.

Wise Sister turned and picked up what looked like folded, tanned leather. "You go soon. Not today. Not in the rain."

Jerking her head around to glare at the window, Sally saw the dreary rain that had fallen off and on for days. There'd even been snow one night. Sally had awakened in the dim light of morning to see the window coated with it.

"Luther is out there by now. He'll be so worried." Desperation reared up until she felt like she was trying to stay on the back of a wild stallion. She couldn't let her old friend wander those hills searching. She felt the guns of those outlaws drawing beads on Luther's back. She could close her eyes and imagine Buff shot, bleeding, dying. . .like Paula McGarritt.

Every time Sally closed her eyes, Sally saw Mrs. McGarritt being slammed out of her saddle. She'd been awakened by nightmares every night. Wise Sister would be awake and soothe her and help her relax back into sleep.

And now, today, she was done letting Luther and Buff risk everything to find her. But there was no way to walk out of here and she didn't have a horse. Logan did, though, and she wasn't above stealing one. Sure that was a hanging offense as well as a sin, but it wasn't like she planned to *keep* it.

Wise Sister knelt on the floor in front of Sally and unfolded the leather.

"What's that?"

"Moccasin. Much tough buckskin. Protect leg on long ride."

Sally flinched, knowing it was going to hurt to put that on no matter how gentle Wise Sister was.

Wise Sister looked up from where she knelt, and Sally saw the sly expression. Sally got the message. There was no need to say it out loud.

"If it's too painful for you to let her pull on that moccasin," Logan went ahead and said it out loud, "then how do you expect to ride down the mountain, then travel for a long, rugged ride in a rain storm?"

Sally fought back the urge to slug him. It helped that just forming a fist hurt like the dickens. "Just fasten the moccasin. A body's gotta do what hurts sometime. Give me my rifle. I feel edgy if I can't grab it."

Sally looked from Logan to Wise Sister and back. She didn't like what she saw in either face. Not that they were going to stop her, but that they didn't believe they'd have to when it came right down to it. She was sorely afraid they were right. "I've got to try."

Wise Sister nodded.

Logan shook his head.

"I'll do it without you if I have to." Sally would dearly love some help. "Ouch!" Sally's leg caught fire, and though she'd like to blame that on Wise Sister, the elderly woman had been terribly careful while she adjusted the soft boot.

Wise Sister finished lacing on the knee-high moccasin, then got the rifle and leaned it against the bed.

Sally felt some muscles unknot, knowing she could fight if she had to.

"If you're going to be stubborn, we can try." Logan came close on her left, slung the rifle over his shoulders. He did it smoothly, which didn't match with what she knew of him, that he was a citified sort of man, not given to the outdoors or manly ways.

Sally would have preferred the gun in her own grasp, but it would have hurt her chest too much.

Wise Sister stood on her left. They gently took her arms. Lifted. Wise Sister looked grim. Logan grimaced as if he felt Sally's pain himself. In fact, the way he watched her face, she suspected he was just mimicking the expression on her own face, though she fought hard to keep her pain from showing.

Sally rose. Every inch she gained burned like fire, on her leg, through her chest, in her head. She had bumps and bruises all over her body, including an ugly, blackened bruise low on her belly where that bullet had struck her belt. It hadn't penetrated her skin, but it had slammed into her hard. Her arms were bruised but her shirt had spared her cuts and scrapes. Her hands were awful to look at, her nails broken, her palms raw from where she'd tried to catch hold of tree limbs and the rock wall she'd fallen past. She'd been spared a mirror, but she could feel the scratches and bruises on her face.

And Logan still wanted to paint her. Ridiculous.

A lot of her wounds hurt bad enough to put her in bed, but it was hard to even notice them with her leg screaming at her to lie back down and her chest punishing her for every breath. She didn't let a single squeak of pain loose. "Let's go." Sally spoke through clenched teeth. "I've got to find Luther. I can't just lay here in bed while he's out there searching, putting himself in danger."

A look passed between Wise Sister and Logan that clearly said they thought she was an idiot. Well, she wasn't. She was desperate.

They made it to the door before Sally's vision started to tunnel and go black.

When she woke up she was back in bed. She didn't know how much time had passed.

Wise Sister said, "I'll go."

"No, I'll go," Logan cut in. "You've got to stay here and see to Sally."

"I leave sign for a knowing man. Buff. I know this man. I know how to tell him of you."

"You know Buff?" Sally asked.

Rather than answer, Wise Sister said, "I know wild places." Wise Sister looked with some compassion at Logan. "Better than you."

"Yes, you are better than me, but the ride down this mountain is too dangerous." Logan crossed his arms. "I won't let you ride out of here, and I can't stay alone with this young woman. She would be ruined. We'd have to marry."

428

That gave Sally a jolt that had nothing to do with a broken leg.

"I'll be gone only one day. Back by nightfall. No harm to Sally. No need to marry."

That sounded like Wise Sister thought Sally needed saving from such a fate. Well, it was a fact that marrying the strange painting man wasn't the way she saw her life going.

"I go afoot."

"In the cold and mud?" Logan's jaw got hard.

"So, I get cold. I get muddy. What is that to me?" Wise Sister looked at the window, sheeted with rain.

Sally's guilt was flooding worse than the weather.

"No." Logan slashed his hand to make it final. "I'm going."

"You can't move quiet." Wise Sister snorted at him. "Bad men find you. Hurt you. Force you to lead them to Sally then kill you, then come for her."

"I ride out of here all the time."

"Not in this weather." Wise Sister sounded wise, stubborn but wise. "Not with bad men around."

"Those killers have been around a long time. We saw evidence of that at the base of that cliff." Logan looked at Sally, and she saw how sickened he was by the proof of her attackers' ruthlessness. She wanted to think of him as weak for it, but truth be told, it was sickening to her, too.

"Better then that I go." Wise Sister's round face lined in downward curves as she frowned.

Sally looked back and forth between them until her neck protested and her head started to ache. She was still the best one for the job.

True, she had broken ribs. And an aching head. And a leg that wouldn't hold her up. And she'd fainted the first time she'd stood upright.

But except for that, she was the best one for the job.

"I won't let you risk it." Logan crossed his arms.

429

"And I won't let you be hurt." Wise Sister jammed her fists on her rounded waist. "You paint good. Important for you to be safe. I go."

The last drew Sally up short as she tried to keep up with the argument. Wise Sister worried about Logan's painting? Wise Sister seemed so sensible. Although, as Sally looked at the cabin, a lifetime of pretty things filled every inch of the wall, every corner. Everywhere Sally looked the cabin was touched by beauty. She thought of the pretty ribbon she'd had on her chemise and knew beauty could live alongside common sense.

"And I won't stay here"—Logan jabbed a finger toward the floor—"warm and dry and safe while you risk—"

"Stop!" Sally yelled—which hurt her face.

The two nursemaids turned from bickering with each other to face her.

"Neither one of you is going. I am."

Matching stubborn scowls appeared on their faces. Sally was annoyed to realize that, whatever their squabbling, they did agree on something. Keeping her corralled. Great.

"But not today."

Logan's shoulders relaxed.

"Best to wait." Compassion appeared on Wise Sister's face. "Your friends will ride careful."

They both seemed to get over their earlier upset instantly. Sally got the sneaking suspicion that making her feel guilty was the whole point.

It didn't matter. They were right. No one, least of all her, was going anywhere today.

"I get food as soon as you're comfortable." Wise Sister straightened Sally's blankets with quick, gentle movements.

While Wise Sister fussed over her, Sally looked at Logan. "Your painting is important? Wise Sister thinks so." Sally could not imagine how a sensible woman like Wise Sister could be so foolish.

Sally did her very best to keep her expression bland so as not to let Logan see that she thought he was an idiot.

It was obvious Sally thought his painting was a waste of his life.

"It's the highest compliment anyone has ever given me. Wise Sister not just *liking* my paintings, but believing there's value in them." Logan nodded to Wise Sister. "She has an artist's soul. The dye she's used to color her weaving, the porcupine quills to create pictures in a basket, the softness of the furs and the supple leather she works with, all of it is art. It's not practical, but she can't deny her love for making things beautiful."

Wise Sister sniffed.

Logan studied Sally for a few seconds. "I want you to see some of what I've done. You thought you were up to a long ride in the cold rain. How about a fifty-foot walk across to my cabin?" And if it hurt her, it might calm her desire to go anywhere for a while.

"Okay, I reckon I'd like to see what whiles away your time, leaving all the work for Wise Sister."

It pinched, but Logan was able to smile at her. He'd had plenty of practice at smiling through insults. "Can we take her over to the other cabin?" He glanced at Wise Sister.

She was silent for a moment—but then, Wise Sister was silent for most moments. "We try." Wise Sister picked up a slicker, one left from Babineau, and slipped it over Sally's head. With the slicker in place, Wise Sister pulled Sally's blankets back.

The slicker was large enough to cover Sally from her neck to her moccasined foot. Sally began to inch off the bed.

"Don't move." Wise Sister jabbed a finger at her.

"Now do you get why I think she's scary?" Logan whispered, not even pretending to be quiet enough to keep Wise Sister from hearing him.

Wise Sister rolled her eyes.

Sally smiled.

Logan's fingers itched for his pencil to capture the gentle curve of Sally's lips.

"Tell me to stop if it hurts." Logan eased one arm behind Sally's slender waist and another under her knees, cautious about every move. He kept his eyes on her face, knowing her well enough already to understand that she wouldn't admit to pain. She'd fainted from it without a word of protest only moments ago. Gently, he lifted her in his arms. She didn't cry out, didn't even flinch, but he saw lines deepen around her mouth. "Are you sure you want to go?"

Her jaw was clenched so tight, Logan didn't think she was up to speaking. But she nodded, the faintest of motions. Then, an inch at a time, she slid one arm up and wrapped it around his neck. For a second their faces were close. . .very close.

"Are you sure?" He hadn't meant to whisper. But on the other hand, no sense yelling when someone was only inches away.

"Sure about what?"

Their eyes held and Logan found something for the first time in years that seemed more important than painting. Sally's arm around his neck moved restlessly and Logan felt himself pulled closer.

His gaze flickered to her lips and back to her sky blue eyes. "You're so beautiful."

A tiny smile perked the corners of her lips. "I am?" The words were little more than a sigh.

"More beautiful than the mountains and waterfalls and soaring eagles."

The moment eased a bit when Sally's smile stretched wide. "I'm prettier than jagged high-up hills; running water; and a hook-nosed, bald bird?" The smile turned to a laugh. "I reckon you think that's flattery, don't you?"

Somehow, put like that, it did seem less than a compliment. But her laugh took the sting out of his usual incompetent ways with people, women especially. Despite his upbringing, Logan knew he had an uncivilized streak, especially when good manners came between him and his art. He belonged out in these mountains alone. "Wait'll you see more of the Rockies. I'd love to take you and show you Yellowstone. You'll know I've just given you the highest praise."

"I've seen enough. Rich hunting land and good grazing, but too rocky to grow a crop. I reckon a body would find a spot for a garden here and there."

Wise Sister draped Logan's coat over his shoulders and dropped his Stetson on his head. He'd have walked outside without either if the elderly woman hadn't thought of it.

He moved slowly in the rain, leaning forward so the broad brim of his hat sheltered Sally. Maybe he should just give it to her and let the cold water soak in and cool his overly warm thoughts about this pretty woman.

Wise Sister went ahead. The two of them lagged behind, protected and dry in the soaking rain until Logan felt like they were in a cocoon, wrapping them away from the rest of the world.

He had to round the cabin to go in the front door, and he stopped under the wide eaves of the house. "I like that you've come out to my land, Sally." Logan's whisper wasn't necessary now. But his voice wasn't working just right and that was all he could manage.

"I was passing through, heading to see my sister is all." Her arm flexed on his neck and seemed to pull him closer.

"I'm so sorry you were hurt. It's nothing short of a miracle that your buckle stopped that bullet and you fell all that way and survived." Logan's throat swelled as he thought of what a close thing it had been.

"And that you were there to find me and care for me." Her fingers shifted and slid up his neck, touching his hair.

He'd let it get ridiculously long since he'd come out here. "It wasn't your time. God wasn't ready to take you home yet."

Sally nodded, almost imperceptibly, but Logan saw it and

liked that she had a solid acceptance of life and death.

It would be so easy to lean just a bit closer. To see if Sally's smile tasted as pretty as it looked. Logan closed an inch and then another. Sally did some closing of her own.

A sudden gust of wind blew water straight into Logan's face, and it worked as well as if Sally had slapped him. He straightened. "What am I doing?" He shook his head as if he were a wet dog. "I can't get involved with a woman out here."

Stiffening in his arms, Sally said, "Involved? You think I want to get involved with a man who paints pictures instead of doing proper work?"

"Just because he saved your life?" Logan relaxed and smiled. He actually liked her in a safer kind of way—when she insulted him. He understood insults. They were so common. It was Wise Sister's approval that confused him. Sally's pretty smile confused him more.

"Well, yes." She sounded less belligerent. "You did do that, didn't you?"

"Yes, I did." An impulse made him do the very thing he'd already decided not to do, thanks to that God-given splash of cold water in the face. He leaned down and kissed Sally right on the lips.

He lifted his head. Their eyes met and held.

"You are way, way prettier than a hook-nosed, bald bird."

"Thank you." Sally smiled and the intimate moment passed.

Gone but not forgotten, Buckskin Angel.

Logan moved on toward the cabin.

Wise Sister had already thrown a chunk of wood on the burning embers. She moved to grab a pot, fill it with water, and set it on to cook. Wise Sister never seemed to move quickly, but she got everything done with almost frightening efficiency. She looked up from the fire and smiled.

It took Logan aback some. Wise Sister didn't show much of what she was feeling. As far as he could tell, she'd never pined for her husband. If she missed Babineau, Logan didn't know. She'd never once complained. Of course the man came and went some, prone to heading for the hills a few times every summer. Maybe she was used to his absence.

For the first time, Logan felt bad about the way he'd treated Wise Sister. He considered her far more than a cook and housekeeper. He thought of her as a fellow artist and his friend. But he hadn't been a very good friend. He was just so used to her not talking much. It had never occurred to him to try and draw her out.

"She needs rest." Wise Sister went to the dry sink and began skinning potatoes. Wise Sister was a genius at drawing food out of this rugged land.

There were papers and pencils, paints and paintbrushes all over. Noticing how cluttered it was, Logan felt embarrassed at his housekeeping, but he wasn't negligent of the things that mattered. All the brushes were carefully cleaned, all the pots of paint meticulously sealed. He knew he'd need every drop of the paints and each bristle in his brushes. They could be ruined so easily.

Logan settled Sally on the chair next to his kitchen table. He took a moment to be glad that he had a separate room for his bedroom because it would feel awkward to bring Sally into the place he slept.

Logan cautiously slid his arms away from her, watching for any sign she might not be able to sit alone. He hurried to get his other chair and carefully propped her foot on it. "Are you all right?" He put a folded blanket on the chair to cushion it.

"I'm fine, but why did you—" Her eyes went past him and landed on *Blazing Land*.

The shutters were closed on the oversized windows that covered most of the front of the cabin, one on either side of the cabin door. There was no glass in them. Glass would have been hard to get in here without it breaking.

435

Besides, Logan wanted lots of natural light and he wanted to hear and smell the outdoors, as well as see it. When the shutters were open, it was almost like the whole front wall was missing. Babineau had thought he was foolish to ask for those huge openings, but the man had grudgingly followed Logan's instructions. Now, as Logan always did when the windows were closed, he'd moved *Blazing Land* to lean in front of the window on the left side of his door. It brought the outside in for him.

Other, smaller paintings leaned against the wall, surrounding the room. Logan had worked feverishly since he'd arrived in early May. The desire to capture the unspoiled beauty here drove him like nothing ever had.

He thought of the murder he'd happened upon and the evidence that it had happened before. Logan had ridden that same trail to come into the area in the spring. Yet he'd had no idea of the danger.

Babineau had often preached to him about it being a lawless place. And Logan had learned to be mindful of the world around him. But he'd never caught a hint of danger beyond what was normal—grizzlies, mountain lions, rattlesnakes, and steep trails. Logan trod the trails carefully and wisely, and because of that, he'd believed he had no cause to fear this land. It saddened him to know those days were over.

Sally studied the painting, and Logan waited, hardly aware that he'd quit breathing. For some reason, having Sally believe in him meant everything.

"That's it? That's what you've spent your time doing when you should have been helping hunt for food?"

Maybe it meant a bit too much. "Well, I *have* done other—"

"Quiet," Wise Sister cut Logan off. She said to Sally, "Look again. Give it time."

Sally glanced at Wise Sister and something passed between them that Logan couldn't interpret. He was never much of a hand with women. In fact, he'd never been much aware of anyone around him. His head was in the clouds, always searching for beauty so he could express it through his paintbrush.

Sally turned back to the painting with a shrug. Logan decided maybe she needed a *lot* of time. Hours. Maybe days.

Remembering how Sally had chastised him about his treatment of Wise Sister, he left Sally and went to Wise Sister's side. "Can I help you?"

She dropped a whole potato in the pot and splashed hot water on the front of Logan's shirt.

He stepped back, waving a hand at his shirt, pulling it out from his stomach.

"Sorry." Wise Sister studied him a few seconds then must have decided he'd live. "Help?"

"Yes, help you make supper. I never help around here, and I'm sorry for that. I didn't realize quite what a huge job I'd given you, without Pierre around. That was unkind of me."

"Can you cut up a parsnip?"

"I don't even know what a parsnip is."

Wise Sister jerked her head in the direction of several whitish vegetables lying on the table.

"I—uh—suppose I could learn."

"Thank you." Wise Sister gave him a smile that was a bit sad around the edges. "Some days, yes, help. Not today. Easy meal today."

Logan stared at her and she looked back, solemn but kind and serene. Finally he shrugged. "Okay, but I'm serious. I'm going to start helping more."

"Rain has slowed. Open that window." Wise Sister pointed at the shutter on the right side of the door, the side that didn't have Logan's painting leaning on it. Logan thought that might qualify as helping. He didn't remember Wise Sister giving him very many orders before. Well, occasionally she ordered him to get out of the cabin. But this was different.

He obeyed her quickly, going outside to work under the broad eaves. The shutters hung from leather straps and they were heavy to swing open. Wrestling with them, Logan got one side open and looked in to see Sally still looking at *Blazing Land*.

He finished quickly then came back inside. Even with the day overcast and rain dripping heavily, the gloomy cabin was considerably brighter when the shutters were open.

Maybe Sally would like the painting better in good light. Logan couldn't stand the suspense, which was really stupid of him. Why be in a hurry to have this pretty woman cut his heart out?

He pulled up the one other chair in the room and sat beside her. She cast him a look out of the corner of her eye then went back to *Blazing Land*. He couldn't decide if that was because the picture drew her back or because she was obedient to Wise Sister. He was sadly afraid it was the latter.

"Ever since I was old enough to pick up a pencil, pictures have come out of me." Logan felt compelled to try to make Sally understand. "My mother says I was drawing dogs and kittens when I was three years old."

When would he learn it was useless to try to explain? But, like a fool, he kept trying. "I don't know why. I only know it's a gift God gave me. Not just the talent for it, but a love for it, too. I feel more alive when I'm painting than any other time. I can't claim any credit for it because it was simply mine from birth. Colors and shapes almost shout out to me, asking me to capture them on canvas. I see a color I love, and I start mentally mixing the paints, trying to figure out how to get that exact shade."

Logan rarely tried to make anyone understand. His family on occasion. They loved him and worried about him. Wise Sister seemed content to go about her life, doing her job, caring for Logan and his home, without making much effort to understand him. But he wished wildly that Sally would. "Painting isn't something I *do*."

Sally turned from the painting, and Logan regretted he'd

distracted her. "What's that mean?" Her brow furrowed. At least she was listening.

"It's something I *am*. It's how God created me. He gave me a love for art and a longing to draw and paint that is almost like— like thirst. Not many people understand. They think I should do something more. . .useful. The simple truth is I can't stop any more than I could stop drinking water. I know it's not a practical way to spend my life. If I could stop, I would. It would be much more comfortable to live on a doctor's income, in a modern house back East, with easy access to water and food. I've got four brothers and they all followed my father into the medical profession. They all live in warm homes in New York City. I miss them."

"Lots of hills and trees to paint back East, aren't there? Why here?"

"A good question." Logan smiled. "I read about it. The geyser in Yellowstone, Old Faithful, is what drew me to begin with. They mostly write about that in newspapers back East, but there were several articles that talked about the unusual sights. I just had to see them. Then I got here and, yes, it was spectacular but there was more. I wanted to get into the mountains. I met Pierre, and he brought me to this place where he'd lived with Wise Sister for years, said it was the most beautiful place he'd ever seen. That's what you were doing out here, wasn't it? Looking at the scenery?"

"The group I was with was excited about the scenery. I only wanted to take the shortest route to my sister's house. One of the men in our party used to scout in this area and he knew about those red canyon walls, and the colonel and his wife wanted to see them. I didn't want to veer right nor left on my way to Mandy's house." Sally's expression closed and Logan thought of the people who had died with her. "I thought it was foolishness. I need to get to my sister. She's gonna have a baby anytime. My folks said I could go and stay with her awhile. My ma thinks she's married to a no-account man."

"No-account because he doesn't work the land, hunt for food...because he doesn't provide well?" Logan had just described himself. Sally's parents wouldn't approve of him either.

Not that it mattered. Despite that kiss under the eaves, that moment of closeness that was more than he'd ever shared with another human being, this wasn't a life any woman wanted to share with a man. He accepted that.

"Sidney's rich, for a fact. But there's lotsa ways to be no-account that don't have a thing to do with money. And by all reports, Sidney is all of 'em."

For some reason, that came as a relief to Logan. It sounded like Sally had a good grip of what really made a man "no-account." If only he didn't rank as one. . .

Sally's eyes wandered to *Blazing Land*.

"I know this isn't a...a...normal painting." Logan looked back at his much-loved creation. "I've got lots that are more traditional. But this is a new technique. I studied it over the winter. Some people are calling it Impressionism. It uses the sunlight, how it shadows things at the exact moment you're painting. Instead of mixing colors to make a shade, you put the colors side by side. It's bolder. The paint is thick in places, translucent in others. I use a knife for most of it instead of a paintbrush. I'm trying to catch more than a view. I'm trying to put—right on that canvas—how I *felt* as I watched that sunrise."

"But it's not the way it really looks," Sally protested. "A painting oughta show the way things really look, seems to me."

Logan nodded. "Many would agree with you. But it's an interesting way to look at the world. I enjoyed doing it." Logan turned from his painting and smiled at Sally. "I appreciate that you took the time to really look." Then, with only the smallest hesitation, he reached up and rested one finger on Sally's chest. "Art is in here."

Sally frowned. "What's that mean?"

"It means if *you* like it, then it's good—for you. If you don't like it, then it's not good—for you." Logan tapped on her chest gently. "You get to decide. No one tells you if you're right or wrong."

"Well, it's a strange painting, but I won't say flat out I don't like it. I suppose it's just too *different* for me to know what to think, leastways right now. But it does give me a feeling of what it must have been like to see all those colors splashed across the sky."

Logan lowered his hand, satisfied. His eyes slid from the painting, which he loved, to the view through the open shutter, which he loved more. His breath caught.

At his gasp, Sally turned and looked. "Elk."

"Elk." Logan saw that their antlers were sprouting fast. He wanted to draw them in all stages of growth.

"Beautiful." Logan reached for his pencil.

"Supper." Sally reached for her rifle.

Logan almost lost the gun slung across his back because he hadn't been ready, but he managed to keep her from disarming him. "Hey, we can't shoot them."

Sally tore her eyes away from the elk, almost as if it were painful. "Sure we can." She tugged on the rifle and groaned in pain.

Wise Sister moved fast, for a slow-moving woman, and put herself in front of the window. "Can't shoot from cabin."

"Why not?" Sally looked at her rifle again and glared at Logan.

"His rule." Wise Sister jabbed a finger at Logan.

Sally shifted her glare from Wise Sister to Logan. "Why would you let food wander right up to your back door and then not shoot it?"

"Because they won't come back."

"What?"

Wise Sister sighed. "True. Gun scare elk away."

"We can eat for maybe a month on one. Who cares if they run off after we shoot one?"

"He cares." Wise Sister jerked her thumb at Logan.

"I want them to feel safe here." Logan smiled. "They won't if we shoot one. That is so obvious."

"That is so stupid."

"But, if they find out this is a dangerous area, then I can't draw them from the cabin." Logan looked out and saw that they'd come within one hundred yards of the cabin. He wished they'd feel safe enough to let him touch them. He also wished Sally's mouth wasn't gaped open with no words coming out.

"Give up," Wise Sister muttered and exchanged a look with Sally.

Sally closed her eyes and sagged back in her chair.

"Supper soon." Wise Sister looked at Logan. "Plates. You put plates on table. And get my chair. In my cabin."

That perked Logan up considerably. Wise Sister was going to let him help. He adjusted Sally's gun across his back.

"Hey, leave that here." Sally sat up straighter but it hurt.

Logan saw that clearly in her face, though of course she made not the slightest noise at the pain.

"I think I'll take it with me. Just in case."

"In case what?" The fire flashing out of the pretty little woman's eyes nearly burned a hole in his shirt.

"In case you get hungry in the one minute I'll be gone." Logan left the cabin. It hurt for her not to understand him. Of course he expected it, but he'd hoped. Still, seeing her frustration, her annoyance, laced humor in with his disappointment. She really did think her way was best. Strange place this West. Too many guns, not enough respect for nature.

Of course, he'd scoot his chair up to an elk steak as quick as anyone. Wise Sister had brought down at least one elk since he'd arrived in the spring with her trusty bow.

She didn't like guns, he'd learned. She could do whatever needed doing with her swift, silent arrows. How far had Wise Sister hiked to get that elk? How far had she hauled it? How had she lifted the carcass to cut it, bleed it, and butcher it? He'd never asked. He'd just picked up his fork and enjoyed.

He went into Wise Sister's cabin and picked up a chair. Wise Sister had one, Logan had three, all four built by Babineau.

Everything was built by Babineau or Wise Sister. Everything in this cabin, keepsakes and bits of beauty, had been collected or created over a lifetime in these mountains. Logan saw his picture amidst Wise Sister's things. As always, he was deeply honored he'd rated a few square feet of her precious space.

She did like him and she even respected him. But he wasn't taking on his fair share of the weight of living in the West. He'd definitely change that and start doing what he could to ease Wise Sister's workload.

As he exited the cabin, he paused to study that small herd of elk. It might be conceit but he thought he recognized them. Of course the bull—there was only one of them—but even the two dozen or so cows and their spring babies each had a personality. The yearlings were sprouting modest racks of antlers. One adult bull, still a youngster, snorted at that old king on occasion, but he always backed down.

Logan loved trying to sketch that tension and the power in their little skirmishes. Logan was sure it was the same herd as last year.

Reasonably sure.

He'd already sketched the bull elk that stood so proudly on an overlook—on guard, remote, proud. The big animal was well gone on this year's magnificent rack of antlers. By autumn they'd be spectacular. He'd stand up there with his chest thrust out, his head held high, protecting his family.

Logan thought of wounded Sally and could understand just how the bull felt. But he couldn't imagine shooting at them. In Sally's mind that probably made him a no-account weakling.

He thought of that kiss they'd shared and wanted another. But it wasn't a wise thing to do, kissing a woman who called him stupid with nearly every breath. Even if she didn't say it out loud.

MARY CONNEALY

Logan wasn't incompetent. And he could shoot an elk if he had to. He wouldn't starve for his art. He'd gotten used to the wild country. And he wasn't as good slipping around as Wise Sister, but he'd learned to move quietly, without drawing attention to himself, so he could ease up on some shy critter. He didn't mind hiking, and he was comfortable sleeping on the ground in a bedroll. He'd taken to the Western land well, learned his way with a gun and a campfire and a rugged trail. He wasn't afraid to sleep outside.

He and Babineau had spent most of the first summer camping in Yellowstone. When he'd returned in the spring, he'd met Babineau and gone into Yellowstone again, but only for a few weeks. Then they'd come here for the rest of the season. And Logan had found he had his own elk herd and persuaded Wise Sister not to use it as a food supply.

Logan grinned when he thought of that confrontation, translated by Babineau. Wise Sister had chalked him up as a complete fool. Logan tried to explain that a man couldn't always find an elk to draw when he wanted one. It made no sense to scare off a handy herd.

Even then, when she'd thought he had no common sense, she'd liked his paintings. He'd painted the portrait of her and Pierre, and she'd given it a place of honor. And best of all, she'd agreed, grudgingly, to hike away from the cabin to hunt for food.

Logan needed to keep Sally disarmed until she saw the light. Logan looked at the elk and the elk seemed to look back and even, maybe, be thankful that Logan was willing to annoy the woman he found so fascinating.

"You're welcome." Logan gave his four-legged friend a nod of understanding and thought the elk got it, however fanciful that notion. "You should be flattered, old boy."

The elk lowered his head as if to threaten Logan and ask why.

"Because she's really cute."

Ten

Luther jerked back on his reins so hard his mount reared and snorted. "That's Sally's horse."

Kicking his chestnut gelding forward, he galloped toward the carcass of a dead horse. He swung down, crouched low to see the McClellen brand. Even with the rain, Luther could see what else had happened here.

Death.

Luther looked at the steep rock wall that lined the trail and saw, in a few spots sheltered from the rain. "Blood. Lots of it."

His eyes met Buff's and they both knew without speaking. Too much of it.

Luther's jaw got so tight he couldn't force words through. He and Buff went over the trail carefully until it had given up all its secrets. They found spent shells where someone had shot from cover and left one of their own behind, not even bothering to bury him. Then they looked over the cliff.

"If she went over this she's dead," Luther said, not because it helped to talk but because saying it out loud was almost necessary, to force the possibility into his brain that he could have lost one of his precious girls.

"Let's go." Buff swung up on his horse and headed down with no further words.

It was a long, long way down the trail. Then they had to wind through a land so rugged it was almost impossible to get to the bottom of that cliff.

It was a day's work studying the carnage at the bottom of the trail. They didn't know how many people had traveled with Sally, but they found enough death down there to account for a good-sized group. The one thing they didn't find was any trace of Sally.

Luther knew it wasn't reasonable to hope Sally had lived through that turkey shoot up on the trail, or lived through falling over a cliff. But she wasn't here and that meant she was somewhere else. He couldn't stop himself from hoping.

About nightfall, they found where a horse had been tethered; and in a spot sheltered from the rain, they studied the sign.

"Two riders. Same tracks of the coyotes who mowed down the colonel and his party. Leading extra horses. Horses they stole from Colonel McGarritt." Luther's gut burned hot. "Dry-gulchers." Sally's party had been hit hard. Luther had seen what had happened on that trail above. Sally, his little cowgirl, had to've been right in the middle of it.

They hadn't found her body. Nothing could tie these tracks to Sally, not well enough for a judge to find them guilty. But Luther knew what he knew. He could find the men who'd done her harm. Right now there were no tracks to follow, but Luther could make out which direction they headed, and the lay of the land made only one direction possible. Luther would find them. And when he did, he and Buff would get answers. "The colonel had friends. Won't be just us who comes a-runnin'."

"Clay might head up, too. Not one to leave his little girl's safety to someone else." Buff grunted and chewed on a chunk of beef jerky as they mounted up.

That sounded like hope to Luther. A little girl's safety meant a little girl who was in danger, which meant a little girl who was still alive.

"We're heading into a mighty wild land." Luther kicked his horse and went forward on the wet ground. The men they were tailing were heading for high ground.

"Best get after Sally." Buff was obviously impatient with Luther for his chitchatting.

They rode on, through woodlands and shale slides, down ravines and along treacherous slopes. Spreading out, checking side trails, as the day wore down they finally picked up the hoof prints of the men who'd done the shooting. They followed as they lost the light and could see the men they were after meandering, like maybe they were searching for something.

Searching for Sally.

The tracks they followed turned and headed for a gap in the mountains. "Leave a marker for anyone coming after us." Luther jerked a thumb at a small sheltered spot in the treacherous trail, just a few yards from a meandering creek.

"Good spot to camp." Buff swung down and Luther did the same.

"I itch to keep going, but this land will break a horse's leg easy as not." Luther began gathering firewood as he wondered at the land around them.

"Mind that itch. Could be more than frettin' over our Sally." Buff laid out the pile of stones for Clay. "Had a hankerin' to see her again. Been too long."

"Didn't like leavin' Mandy with that no good husband of hers neither." Luther built a fire small enough to fit in the crown of his Stetson. No sense tellin' the outlaws where they were camping.

"Money didn't do that polecat no good." Buff stripped the leather off his horse.

Luther shook his head. "Had a chance I think, till he found that gold. Might've come around to being a decent man. Now

447

he just needs someone lookin' out for him all the time." Luther stopped and turned to Buff. "I don't feel right about huntin' Sally and lettin' Mandy stay home alone."

"Woman oughta be safe in her own home. And Mandy is a pure pleasure to watch with that rifle. Never knew no one who could best her—man, woman, nor child." Buff smiled like a proud papa.

Luther knew how he felt. They'd had a hand in raisin' the McClellen girls and were happy with the way they'd shaped up. Women fit to tame a wild land.

"Mandy needs us, no use denying it. But she can watch her back for a few days, especially with Sidney back home. He's not gonna be able to beat anyone who braces him, face-to-face, but he's hired hisself a pack of coyotes. None of 'em'll come at Mandy directly, not while Sid's around. We just gotta get back before he takes off for another one of his weeklong trips to town."

Luther took the coffeepot off his pack horse and turned to dip it in the stream they'd chosen to camp beside. "Look at that, Buff."

A huge grizzly lumbered out of the woods on the far side of the fast-moving water. Luther heard Buff's gun cock a second after his own. The bear looked them over, woofed at them a few times, then kept coming over the broken land that sloped downward to the rushing creek. Two cubs frisked out of the forest behind her.

"She's never seen a man before, nor a gun." Luther glanced at Buff, who'd come up beside him. "Doesn't know to be afraid."

"How deep is that water?" Buff asked.

"Hard to say. I hope she stays on her side."

They watched the massive bear and her rollicking babies drink long and deep. The animal acted like exactly what she was—the biggest, meanest animal for a thousand miles. She wasn't afraid of anything. She'd never seen a man, never seen the damage a Winchester could do.

Luther had just a few minutes to feel bad about encroaching on her kingdom, knowing flying lead would knock her off her throne in a heartbeat.

She drank as the sun lowered, and finally, her thirst quenched, she turned and waddled back toward the thick growth of pine and aspen, her cubs wrestling and gamboling along behind her.

"We'll stay here and eat, but I think we'd better move away from the water to camp. If one mama grizzly drinks here, others, not quite so friendly, might." Buff turned back to his fire while Luther filled his coffeepot.

While they ate, a herd of elk came down to drink. A golden yellow cougar with four cubs came, too. And a couple of deer, a pair of wolves, and a lone moose, with a short growth of antlers. Other, smaller animals passed by, too, before Luther and Buff finished their quick meal and moved on to a better, less popular spot.

"If our girls had only those animals to face they'd be just fine." Luther spread out his bedroll and contemplated two-legged critters and how much more trouble they could be than the four-legged variety.

He was worried sick, but he ended the day a lot better than he'd begun it, with the discovery of Sally's dead horse.

This morning he'd known she was dead. Tonight he had hope.

If she'd somehow survived that fall, then she had a fighting chance of surviving until they could get to her. He'd helped raise those McClellen girls. He knew what they were made of. He figured they'd be fine if they were ready for trouble.

Except maybe Sally wasn't fine.

That made him sick, and as he lay down, he wished a grizzly would charge him to give him something more pleasant to think about.

Mandy didn't normally speak to her husband if she could help it. That had been her policy for the last couple of years. But last night she'd finally figured out that it wasn't a good strategy for a marriage.

"There was someone outside last night." Mandy put her fork on the dinner plate with a sharp click of metal on glass.

With Sidney's suspicious nature, who knew? He might actually decide they shouldn't live all the way up on this stupid mountaintop. They were a long way from the law up here. A long, long, long way.

"So you say. I didn't hear anything." Sidney shoveled a massive amount of food into his mouth three meals a day. Mandy noticed the blotches of grease at the corners of his mouth and had to force herself not to grimace. Sidney set his fragile coffee cup down on its fussy little plate. Sidney had insisted on buying the glass dishes.

Mandy admitted they were pretty, but she missed the duller click of tin on wood. "Well, I did, and I trust my judgment a lot better than yours." Those were fighting words, Mandy knew it, but it was fine with her. She and her husband were about two years overdue for a good fight.

Sidney's eyes narrowed. Mandy pushed her plate back, crossed her arms on the table, and leaned forward. They were on opposite ends, much like where'd they'd stood last night. Armed, working together on something for once.

She did her best not to start yelling. That wasn't going to help. Although she held the idea in reserve in the event she needed it later.

"What exactly did you hear?"

Mandy prayed to God that, despite showing all sorts of signs of being a halfwit, Sidney would know enough to trust her on this. "Someone stepped up on the porch. Right by this window." The window the kitchen table sat in front of. "It was a man, I'm sure of it, not an animal or the house settling or the wind. Someone snooping around. I turned the lantern on when I got up with Catherine. I think, whoever it was might have been thinking of coming inside."

Mandy shivered, remembering how she'd felt—watched. The windows had curtains but the fabric was thin. A man could watch through the windows and see pretty well inside. At least make out her form in the rocker. And the glass and curtains certainly wouldn't stop a bullet.

Sidney seemed to take her very seriously. Mandy was grateful for that. . .for his sake.

His eyes shifted as he frowned. "I've regretted a few of the men I hired to build the house."

Mandy sighed with relief, though she didn't let Sidney see that. She was no longer going to twist herself into a knot hoping for Sidney's respect. Starting today she was going to demand it.

"And what about the two men who ride with you? I don't trust them either." Mandy had never gotten Sidney to listen to a word against Cooter or Platte. Of course, Mandy rarely spoke to Sidney, so it's not like he'd had a lot of chances. And why wouldn't he be suspicious? So far the only people he hadn't suspected of wanting his gold were Catherine and Angela. And he'd probably get around to that when they were a few years older.

Sidney did what he did best: quietly blamed the whole world for trouble of his own making. "I hate to fire any of the men because the house is a big project and it needs a lot of workers. But I'll look into it, see if anyone admits to being out for a walk last night."

That wasn't good enough but probably all Sidney was capable of. She'd protect this family herself.

"Why did you build up here?" Mandy expected little but criticism from him. But Sidney was talking a bit, and she was genuinely interested. She hoped he could tell. "I would have thought you might want to go back East, to a more comfortable life. The living is hard out here."

Mandy didn't mention train travel and the fact that she could occasionally go visit her family if they lived nearer civilization.

She could go maybe twice a year, for six months each time.

She remembered that, at the beginning, when Sidney was more vulnerable to her opinion, before gold had made him believe he was royalty, he'd admitted his mother had been disreputable. It was possible there was something back East that Sidney wanted to stay far away from.

Sidney, maybe distracted by his paranoia, didn't snap at Mandy. "There's just something about that spot, up on the mountaintop." He pushed back the curtain and looked out the window up at his monument to his own greatness. "When I first hired my assistants"—only through sheer willpower did Mandy keep from rolling her eyes at Sidney calling Cooter and Platte his "assistants"—"we scouted around looking for a building site. I loved the view from here, and this cabin seemed adequate to our needs. But now, with the children coming. . ." He gave Mandy's stomach a satisfied look that made her uncomfortable.

She had a feeling Sidney thought to keep her in the family way for most of her life. She loved her children, but she wasn't a bit fond of Sidney. And some. . .closeness to him was required for all those babies to come along.

"We need more space, and once I was up here, I looked around and realized the view was even better from up there."

Mandy had a sudden image of Sidney getting into that house and realizing there were even higher peaks around. It was high up, but it wasn't the very top of the world after all. They'd have to move again and again, higher and higher. Maybe he'd think the house had to be bigger every time, too. Pretty soon she'd be living in a castle atop a snowcap.

Since he was talking pleasantly for a change, she carefully kept from snorting in disgust.

"We'll be happy up there, Mandy. You wait and see."

The way he said it pinched Mandy's heart. She really was fed up with her husband and, because of that, didn't spend much time trying to understand him. She thought, in fact, that she *did* understand him. He was an idiot, she understood that completely. But he sounded sad when he said that. As if— "Aren't you happy now, Sidney?"

His head came up, his eyes wide, as if her questions startled him.

Knowing how moody he was, Mandy told herself she probably shouldn't pursue it, but it didn't hurt to try to have a good relationship with her husband. It was probably a waste of time, but it didn't hurt to try. "You're healthy. We're all healthy. We're rich. We have beautiful children. Why wouldn't you be happy right now?"

"I—I *am* happy, I suppose, but I could be *happier*. I just need to get our lives in order and then we can finally settle down and live in contentment. I can have what I need to be happy and you—you can put down that rifle you always keep at hand and be a proper woman."

The part about her being proper wasn't new. She leaned forward, restraining her temper. "You don't know me at all, do you, Sidney?"

Scowling, Sidney said, "Of course I know you. Don't be ridiculous."

Praying for the right words, Mandy said, "You want to find happiness for yourself. You think you'll find it with the right house and the right view and the right amount of money, and I hope you do. I hope you find whatever it is you're searching for. But you owe me the same thing. I'm a woman born and raised on a Texas ranch. I lived with my ma and little sisters, a real hardscrabble life, for two years before she married my pa. I learned—"

"I know all that." His expression closed up.

Mandy kept trying. "The thing is, you want contentment and happiness, and I want them for you. But do you want *my* contentment? Do you even know me well enough to care if I'm happy?"

"What have you got to be unhappy about?" The growling was starting.

"I was the best sharpshooter on the McClellen ranch, Sidney. Do you realize that?"

"I've heard you say you're a good shot."

"Not a *good* shot, the *best*. One of the best in all of west Texas, my pa used to say. I use my rifle to feed *this family*, but it's more than that. It's a talent I have that I'm proud of." And a little scared of, but she didn't say that out loud. "It's not something I do for lack of womanly manners. It's a big part of who I am, the skill that came from needing to be accurate, from living a rugged life where we needed to put food on the table to survive, then later from competing with my sisters and Pa and Ma."

Sidney stared at her as if wishing she'd say something that made sense.

"Your contentment seems to require making me over into a wife you can be proud of, but you owe me the respect of being proud of me *right now*!" Mandy saw her fists clenched and forced them to open.

Lord, protect me.

Right now she needed the Lord to protect her from her own temper. She felt the cold that came over her when she was shooting. The icy cold that steadied her hands and calmed her nerves. Her eyesight seemed to sharpen. The world slowed down. It was always in the back of her mind that one of these times, when she held her gun, her blood flowing like sleet in her veins, she might not come back from the cold. This time she might stay frozen forever.

Above all, she knew that this fighting fury, calm and deadly, had no place in this talk with her husband. She tried to push the cold away.

"I hope and pray for your happiness and want you to be content, but you owe me that right back. Instead of *fixing* me, you need to take pride in having a wife that can outshoot, outrope, and outride almost every man in these mountains." Leaning forward, trying to pierce Sidney's cloddish opinions, she added,

"When am I going to get that from you?"

"Get what?"

"Get *respect*." She slammed a fist on the table, and when she did Sidney's eyes focused on her.

Until this moment, he'd quit listening. Was she surprised?

Sighing, Mandy leaned back. "Get you to embrace what I *am* instead of trying to mold me into whatever twisted vision of perfect womanhood you have inside your head."

"I respect you, Mandy. I just wish you were more refined. You were brought up in a wild place."

Mandy's eyes went out the window to the back of beyond where they lived. There was no place wilder than this.

"I respect who you are, but that doesn't mean you can't learn more womanly ways, better manners."

Better manners? Maybe she'd say "please" when she took the butt of her gun to his head. And "thank you" after he passed out on the floor. She fought down the cold. It seemed like when a woman tackled a big old fight with her husband, she ought to at least be fiery hot with rage.

"Look at how I've changed since I found gold." Sidney touched his chest with his widespread fingers, flashing his stupid ring at her, caressing his dark gray suit and white silk shirt with the foolish string tie that only had a use, as far as Mandy could see, if Sidney suddenly needed to brand a fractious calf. "I dress better, ride in a better carriage, conduct myself like a wealthy man ought. That's all part of finding contentment."

And what about finding your teeth when I knock them out, huh, Sid?

"Oh, before I go up to see how the work is progressing on the house, I forgot to mention that I bought a team of horses when I was in Helena."

Spending money like it was fresh milk he was afraid would go sour if he kept it around too long.

It was a shame there was so much of it, because if it ever ran out, Sidney might stop being such an arrogant halfwit.

"We could use a couple for the girls." Mandy allowed him that. Buying horses wasn't a pure waste. "They'll need gentle saddle ponies. Did you—"

"I didn't get *ponies* for the children to ride, for heaven's sake." He looked at her like she'd lost her mind.

Well, considering the man she'd married, he might have a point.

"It's not ladylike for a woman to ride a horse. I bought a new carriage and need a matched pair to pull it. I would have preferred grays of course. But these are the best so I bought them. I found a breeder over by Divide who, the word is, has the prettiest pair of black thoroughbreds anyone in these parts has ever seen. They're two-year-olds, out of a black stallion he owns that seems to be famous through the whole state. I bought them, and he's delivering them as soon as they're thoroughly trained to pull a buggy."

"Divide?" Mandy's stomach swooped. "A black stallion?" That could only be—

"Tom Linscott." Sidney pushed back from the table. "He was in Helena delivering his herd. I'd asked about horses and they pointed me in his direction. He seemed really interested in our new house and where we lived. He'd heard of me, in fact. I suppose I need to get used to being an important man."

He'd heard of Sidney all right. When he'd come to visit and Sidney wasn't home—the summer she and Sidney had gotten married. Tom had wanted to see the little foal Belle Harden's mare had delivered out of his stallion. And he'd stayed all day and done the work a husband should have done. By the end of that day, he'd known exactly who. . .and what. . .Sidney was, without Mandy saying a word.

"He'll be a month at least delivering them because I insisted he not try and unload inferior, badly trained animals on us."

"Did you say that to him?" Mandy swallowed hard, remembering Tom could get cranky, especially about his horses.

"I told him my expectations, of course."

And he let you live? Mandy didn't say that out loud, but she was impressed with Tom's restraint.

"I told him where we lived, and he said he'd come on up. Remember, we raised a foal out of his stallion that first year we lived out here?"

"I remember," Mandy said faintly. She also remembered that Tom Linscott had touched a very tender place in her heart at a time when she wasn't very happy with her husband. She'd been glad not to see Tom again.

And now she would. And she was even unhappier with her husband now than then.

At least she wasn't cold anymore.

She ran her hand over her stomach and was grateful Catherine cried from the bedroom. She didn't have good control of the expression on her face and wasn't sure what Sidney would see.

She rose from the table, but before she turned to fetch her little girl, the itching of guilt made her more forgiving of her husband. "I want you to be contented and happy, Sidney."

She wanted it for herself too, badly, because right this moment she was as restless and discontented as any woman who ever lived. She thought of Eve in the Garden of Eden, reaching for that apple, and knew how a woman could be wildly tempted to do something she knew was wrong.

"It's something I pray for—your happiness." And she was going to start praying harder, for all of them. "But contentment isn't going to come from gold or a fine house or the best horses or a grand view from a mountaintop."

She thought her expression was one she dared to let Sidney see now. She hoped. Turning to him, she spoke kindly, with her whole heart. "Happiness is inside of you. It comes from being at peace—with yourself, and mostly with God. It usually grows best when you're *giving* rather than taking. We're so far out we can't attend a church service, but I worship with the children on

Sunday mornings. You could join us. You could—"

"Mandy," Sidney cut her off in that arrogant voice that made her think of the weight of her gun on her back.

She realized that she'd just asked Sidney to accept her and respect her. Now here she stood trying to change him.

"Don't start that." Sidney waved his hand impatiently, dismissively.

Mandy noticed again that ring on his hand. It fit, which must mean it was new because his fingers had gotten fat along with the rest of him. It was a large, rather ugly ring that looked like he'd had a gold nugget made into a piece of jewelry. He might have been wearing it for quite a time. Mandy realized that she'd gotten into the habit of ignoring him whenever possible.

God, please protect my husband from that day when I really explode.

Mandy was genuinely afraid that day was coming soon. She'd seen and heard the explosions when they'd blasted a trail up to this pass. She sometimes imagined her own temper detonating.

Boom!

And from now on she was going to quit fearing that. She was no longer going to be the wife Sidney wanted her to be.

Sidney stood from the table and headed for the door. Going to check on his mountaintop castle.

Starting right now. . .in fact, she'd already started. . .she was going to be herself, no matter how much Sidney disliked that.

Another thought struck Mandy hard. It was so obvious she almost smiled. She had never succeeded in being *good* enough for Sidney. All her efforts and they'd been a waste of time. Oh, sometimes for a few hours she'd been able to please him, but she'd never been proper enough, restrained enough. And that wasn't for lack of trying.

It was just the cold, hard, dirty truth that Sidney's unhappiness was something that had nothing to do with her. Though he blamed her, it had everything to do with him.

So she couldn't even say she was failing. The truth was she was wasting her time trying to suit him, trying to be restrained enough for him to be happy with her. Mandy vowed to herself that she wasn't doing it anymore.

She watched Sidney leave, wondering what the future held for her and her unhappy husband.

Tom Linscott's face immediately came into focus, vivid and clear, every feature etched in her mind. Which was frightening because she'd only seen him once, and that had been over two years ago.

She turned her thoughts back to violence against her husband, which somehow seemed far less sinful. If she lost her temper—truly, horribly lost it—Sidney might be finished with her, and she might get herself sent down the road. . .all the way home to her parents in Texas.

Mandy tried very hard to convince herself that would be a very bad thing.

Eleven

Seven days since she'd fallen off a cliff. Sally hadn't gotten free yet, but this was it. Now it was time.

Sally watched Wise Sister clean up after breakfast, waiting impatiently for the sweet lady to go away.

"This is for you." Last night Wise Sister had sewed busily for the entire evening, and this morning she'd laid out a beautiful doeskin dress, tanned nearly white. Now she presented that dress to Sally.

"Really?" With a gasp of pleasure, Sally reached out and touched the beautifully tanned dress. Somehow that dress seemed to bring all the parts of Sally's nature together. It was practical and tough. But it was beautiful and so lovely to touch. Sally realized as she took the dress from Wise Sister that her heart had longed for the creation Wise Sister was working on.

"Your clothes are ruined. Ripped. You need something." The kind Shoshone woman slung her quiver on her back. "Get dressed."

The elderly woman headed out to hunt so Sally had only

Logan to contend with.

Her leg was still as broken as it could be, no denying, though the swelling had gone down a bit, and Wise Sister had tightened the splints and the leather moccasin to fit. But her ribs were feeling a lot better. Now, every time she moved or breathed, it felt like being clubbed with a dull hammer rather than like wolves gobbling down her chest. A big improvement.

Her headache was gone. That gave her the most hope. She'd been practicing sitting up whenever she got left alone for a minute, and all day yesterday she'd managed it without the room spinning. She'd stood one-legged a few times, too, clinging to the bed carefully so she wouldn't fall and make her injuries worse.

And now she had clothes. That had been a big problem holding her back. Sally ran her hand over the fringe along the arms and skirt and a few rows of beads that Sally would have protested about if she'd realized who Wise Sister was making the dress for. It was a shame to waste such fussiness on Sally. Such pretty fussiness.

Her Winchester was there, too.

Sally chafed to think of her chaps and broadcloth pants, but she'd seen herself that they were destroyed. She thought of what Ma would say if she knew Sally had changed into her manly clothes after she'd left the train. Ma would be annoyed at her behavior, but those clothes, tough and protective, had helped save Sally's life. Ma would forgive all Sally's outrageous behavior and give thanks because of that.

A tiny twist of pleasure forced Sally to admit it would feel good to wear the doeskin dress. And it would be much easier to put on, considering the sorry state of her ribs and leg. Eyeing the doeskin, Sally knew that this morning she was going to get dressed and get out.

So what if she was on top of a mountain? She'd scoot downhill on her backside if Logan wouldn't give her a horse. One way or another, she was going.

Sally figured to dress then go find herself a sturdy crutch. She knew she'd never get far without being caught, but if she could get up and prove to Logan and Wise Sister that she was capable, they'd lend her a horse and let her get on with it.

This was the West, and out here, just like in Texas, people forked their own broncs. This was Sally's problem, and she'd solve it.

She moved slowly, careful not to jar her aching leg. Standing, she had only two hops to reach the dress. She made that with only a token protest from her battered body. She sank into a chair and took it slow and easy pulling on Wise Sister's gift.

The tanning had taken a lot of time and was already done before Sally had come crashing into Wise Sister's life. Sally wondered what Wise Sister had been planning for the lovely piece of goods.

Studying the cabin, Sally knew Wise Sister might have had grand plans to decorate the leather and use it in her home somehow.

Sally listened carefully as she pulled her dress into place. Once it was on, she also noticed the bit of ribbon that had been on her chemise. It had been lying on the table beneath the dress. The pin she used to keep it in place and remove it to be hidden at the end of the day was there, too. Not a speck of blood on her secret, womanly indulgence. She picked up the bit of foolishness and, with care, found a seam inside the soft dress and pinned the ribbon in place, out of sight.

She hurried to finish dressing, worried that Logan might come to the cabin. With her ears peeled, she prepared to yell out for him to wait until she was decent. When he saw her dressed, she fully expected him to start yelling right back.

She wasn't interrupted and was soon fully dressed, even getting her remaining boot on her good foot. That made her feel steadier. She sat, gathering her strength, wondering exactly where she'd have to go to get a crutch, when she heard a footstep at the door.

There was a knock, which there had never been before, but then Sally realized how rarely she'd been left alone. One of her two caretakers was always with her. Humbly, she had to admit that they'd taken good care of her.

"Come in." She squared her shoulders, bracing for the fight she intended to win.

The door swung open and Logan stepped in and smiled. "We knew you were ready to get dressed. I see you've finished."

It irritated Sally to find out her scheming and plotting had, instead, been predictable. "I'm dressed and ready to go." Sally crossed her arms, delighted at how little that hurt.

"Wise Sister has already gone to scout for your friends. Your breakfast is ready over in the other cabin. Shall I carry you over there or bring it here?"

"You made me breakfast?"

"No, of course not." Logan shuddered. "I want you to get better. What I'd cook might well set you back. Wise Sister made it before she rode out."

"She shouldn't go out there. It's dangerous."

"She's only going for a few hours. She said something about Buff, but I didn't understand it. Just that Buff would read her sign. Does your friend speak Shoshone?"

"Not that I know of."

Logan shrugged. "Wise Sister is sure she can leave a sign your friends can follow but stay clear of anyone else who might be prowling around. We talked about it, and she convinced me I'd only make things worse." Logan smiled.

He wasn't a very normal sort of man. Her pa wouldn't have been happy about a woman doing a job he saw as his. And most men wouldn't laugh at themselves. Sally found that the attitude was refreshing. But Logan was strange, with his odd painting. Maybe he'd learned to accept others in hopes they'd also accept him. She wondered if he liked her pretty new dress.

"Wise Sister left some heavy branches. She said she thought

you'd be able to fashion yourself a good crutch with it." Logan came up beside her, swung *her* rifle over *his* shoulders and scooped Sally into his arms.

Whatever kind of bad job he was doing of caring for himself, Sally had to admit the man was strong.

He lifted her with ease and smiled down at her. "Let's go. You can eat, and I can paint you."

Sally felt a very strange twist in her gut that she didn't understand, and her arms seemed a bit too natural wrapped around Logan's neck.

Logan stopped. "Do you mind getting the door?"

Sally grinned. They got into his cabin the same way.

He settled her at the table with such gentleness Sally couldn't stop from whispering, "Thanks."

Logan paused as he slid his arms free of her back and knees, his face too close. His eyes were an odd shade of deep brown, and this close she could see they were shot through with an almost golden yellow stripe. Though he acted gentle, those eyes made her think of the eagles that soared overhead in this strange land. Predator eyes, strong, dangerous. There was a depth to them that made no sense. The man painted when he should be chopping wood and hunting for supper.

But, though she didn't understand the way he lived, she saw in him patience, confidence, an assurance that, though he knew he didn't exactly suit the world, he suited himself. It was amazingly attractive.

It reminded her for a fleeting second that she dressed like a man and worked a man's job. And yet she apologized to no one for her behavior. Could it possibly be that deep down, she and Logan were a lot alike?

Then his eyes changed. Where once there was kindness and concern, the depth now held warmth. More than warmth. . .heat.

He kissed her.

He certainly shouldn't be doing that. She pulled back to tell him to stop, but he followed along, and she forgot what she was going to say.

His hands touched her face, and he tilted her head gently and deepened the kiss.

Her hands came up to rest on his wrists. To hold on. Tight.

She wondered at his talented, strong hands and how gentle they were.

Something awoke in her that she hadn't known was sleeping. An affection for Logan bloomed that was a mismatch for her opinion that he was a no-account kind of man.

He raised his head so their lips separated, and Sally followed after him and brought him back to her, back to that kiss.

Logan straightened away, his eyes on her as if she were the most beautiful thing he'd ever seen, even better than a hook-nosed bald eagle. "Let me draw you, exactly like that."

Scooting her chair close to the table, he sat around the corner from her, only inches away. His sketchbook was laying right there, and he picked it up. It was never far from his hands. He began drawing while Sally wondered what he saw in her that he found so fascinating, that made him share a kiss then grab a pencil.

"You can move if you want." He looked up from his drawing but it was a studying kind of look.

"Really? I thought you'd want me to sit still." So that meant she was obeying him, even while she was still planning to tell him he had a lot of nerve to just announce he was going to draw her picture.

Not to mention kissing her.

And he *hadn't* mentioned it once he pulled back. She'd noticed that clear enough.

God, have mercy. I want him to kiss me again.

"No, moving is good for me. I can see different angles of your face, catch the way your bones and muscles work together. I can catch shadows from the light coming in through the window." He reached past her and pulled a red-and-white-checked towel off a plate on the table, revealing scrambled eggs, a slab of venison, and a square of cornbread covered with honey. "I'll pour you some coffee."

Logan set his sketchbook aside as if it hurt him to let it go, grabbed the coffeepot off the stove, poured a black tin cup full of the steaming liquid, then hurriedly returned the pot with a clank of metal on metal and rushed back to sit beside her and resume drawing.

"You hadn't oughta kissed me like that." Sally hated saying that. Hated knowing she could never let him do it again. He'd done it before, and she'd thought that was the end of it. Now he'd sneaked past her again. "It's not proper."

He looked up from his drawing, but his expression showed no agreement with her or regret that she'd just told him he couldn't kiss her again. Instead he just studied her for long quiet moments with those deep, probing eyes. It seemed like he was trying to see inside her head.

Which she sorely hoped he couldn't, because she didn't want him to know how much she'd thought of their first kiss. How often she'd imagined having another. . .which she just had. . .and how much she regretted that she had to call a halt to such nonsense.

Finally, he went back to drawing.

Sally decided not to mention the kiss again and invite another such long look.

She ate quietly, savoring the meat and eggs. She'd seen no chickens, but maybe there were ducks and pheasants around. Wise Sister would know how to rob their nests.

She stared out the windows, wondering about the kiss and Logan's single-minded painting and the work a lone woman would have to do to provide this meal, when she noticed how far and wide she could see. "You've got both your shutters off today." The south wall of his cabin was almost completely open.

She sought out the huge painting, now leaning on the east wall. "What made you paint it in such an odd fashion? It doesn't look real. I thought a painter's skill was judged by how much his pictures looked like what he was drawing."

Logan smiled, looked up from his sketchbook, opened his mouth, and then stopped. "I need you to take your hair down, catch the light on all that yellow gold."

Her hair was in one long braid that had swung over her shoulder and hung down nearly to her lap.

"I'll do it." He reached over, without asking so much as a by-your-leave, and tugged on the leather thong Wise Sister had given her to contain the braid.

"What are you—"

"Got it. Thanks." He tossed the strip of leather onto the table next to Sally, set the sketchbook beside the hair tie, and with quick movements undid her braid then pulled her hair into disorder.

"You—wait—I don't—" Sally sputtered, shoving at his hands, but it was too late to do a thing.

His hands lingered on her hair far longer than Sally thought was necessary. Their fingers were intertwined. She ought to stab him with her fork, but her breath caught as she saw his eyes slide from her hand, tangled in his fingers, to her eyes.

With a shake of his head, he let go of her and went right back to drawing. "*Blazing Land* is the name of the picture. It was"—he looked up from his drawing and smiled—"pure indulgence that I painted it. A waste of paint and canvas, a huge picture impossible to take home."

He looked at the wall-sized painting behind his back. A rueful smile bloomed. "But it was like I had that inside me. I couldn't do anything else until I—got it out—got it out of the way." He stared at the picture, then shrugged his shoulders and went back to drawing.

Then she looked a bit farther and saw a smaller painting. The big one demanded attention, but the smaller one. . . "Is that—me?" She sat on a horse, dressed in pants and her buckskin jacket, the horse in motion under her while she focused completely on something beyond the picture. She held the reins in one hand, a rope coiled over her head in the other, a lasso she was almost ready to throw.

Logan looked up, followed the line of her vision, and smiled. "Yes. Another thing I had to get out of my system." He looked back at her. "Except, I don't seem to have quite done that yet. I get up in the morning thinking to capture another sunrise, and all I can do is study sketches of you."

He made a move that looked like he was going to touch her hair again, then stopped and jabbed his pencil at her plate. "Eat. You need food to knit your bones. That's what Wise Sister said."

"You've never even seen me on horseback."

"Well, not while you were conscious."

That's right. He'd carried her home. Just swept her up and whisked her away, like one of his eagles carrying something back to its nest. Eagles did that with food.

She shook off that thought and studied the painting he'd done of her. The picture seemed to move. It was alive, dust kicking up, the horse wheeling, obeying the pressure of her knees. She could feel herself—in the painting—riding, concentrating, aiming that rope. She could smell the sweat a person worked up and the horse, the dust, the cattle she'd have been working. "That's—that's— you're really good."

Logan looked up and grinned. "Well—it's not humble to admit it, I suppose, but, yes, I am really good."

He reached for her again, this time not checking himself, and stroked one finger down the side of her face, around so he touched her chin, staring at her in that intense way. Frowning, he said, "It's not a normal pastime, painting. But since I can't seem to stop and can't focus on anything long enough to find a more useful career, I'm just giving it all I've got."

Logan quit touching her then looked over at the painting of her for a minute. He snapped his fingers and lunged out of his chair toward the other side of the room where a square of cloth covered something on a table. He pulled the cloth away, and Sally saw another picture of her, dressed in buckskin again. A twinge of embarrassment surprised her. He'd never seen her in women's clothes until today, and he'd yet to comment on Wise Sister's gift.

She thought of the way he'd kissed her. She'd never considered kissing much. When she was around men, it was either her father or brothers or men she was trying to outdo in some way. She wanted the cowhands on her family ranch to respect her. And there was no place for kissing in that. Nor had she ever wanted there to be.

It hit her suddenly that she spent most of her life proving herself to men and when, as she always did, she proved herself better, she looked on them with pity. So, if a tough Texas cowboy couldn't win enough respect to awaken some affection, how could a man who painted pictures?

Simple answer was he couldn't. And if she didn't respect him, then she shouldn't be kissing him. She thought of her big sister Mandy, married to a man her parents loathed. . .Luther hated. Sally suspected Mandy hated him, too, once she'd gotten over being addle-headed in love with him at first.

It could happen. A woman could fall for a no-account man. Or a man could appear to be of some account then prove himself later to be a scoundrel and a liar, as Sidney had.

Sally knew that lesson from hearing about her big sister, mainly through letters they received from Luther, but some of it had sneaked into Mandy's letters, too. Mostly she knew how Mandy felt just because of the complete lack of any affectionate mention of Sidney.

Mandy was the smartest, toughest big sister a girl could have, and she'd been tricked into marrying a man who was busy night and day wrecking her life. Now it looked like Sally might have that same inclination. In fact, as she thought about it, Sally remembered the stories she'd heard about her own pa, the first man Ma had been married to. Though Sally could barely remember him, her sisters claimed he was a hard man to have around. So even her ma had been lured into a bad marriage.

And Beth—well, Alex had turned out to be okay, a fine man in fact. But that was just pure good luck. When Beth married him, it didn't look like she'd done one bit of a good thing.

Sally stroked the tiny scar on her neck.

"What is that?"

Abandoning her dark thoughts of no-account men, Sally touched the bit of redness that was never going to fade. "My sister Beth's husband—"

"The doctor." Logan supplied, drawing away.

"Yes, he. . .well, he did a little bit of surgery on me."

"On your throat?" He looked up, horrified.

"Yes, it was the day he married my sister. They'd only met a few hours before. My throat swelled shut when I was stung by a swarm of bees, and he cut here." Sally drew one finger down that tiny scar and thought kind thoughts about Alex. Maybe Beth *had* known what she was doing.

"He made a hole into my—well—my lungs, I guess. I don't reckon I know exactly what he did. But he cut here, below where my throat was swelled shut, and blew through a tube to keep me alive until the swelling went down."

"I've never heard of that." Logan shook his head as if denying it and studied her neck more closely. "I don't remember much about my father's doctoring advice, but I know a person can't be having his. . .or her. . .throat cut."

She saw a flash of anger on Logan's face, as if he were mad about Alex cutting into her. As if he'd like to protect her from any such violation. His concern and anger appealed to her in a way she couldn't describe, since she'd never felt such a thing for a man before. "Alex knew what he was doing, I'd say. Though I was unconscious, I suspect I was grateful enough for the air when it started flowing again."

Sally was warmed by Logan's protective anger, and she could

see how a woman could be lured toward a man who wasn't what she wanted. It happened too much, too easy. And maybe especially her family seemed apt to make stupid choices in men.

Which explained why she was thinking about Logan's kiss. And even worse, wondering how she could get him to kiss her again. It was probably in her blood to do stupid things when it came to men.

It was almost a comfort to decide what she was feeling wasn't her fault. In fact, it cheered her right up to blame this on her mother.

Twelve

Logan slashed at the canvas with a kind of victorious violence.

He loved painting like this, with a knife instead of a brush. Thick paint, vivid colors. Sunlit scenes. . .and faces.

He'd brought a lot of supplies with him this year, thinking to ride into Yellowstone with Babineau as he had last year. The agreement he'd made with Babineau was the same as the year before. They'd meet at the train station. Logan would leave half the supplies stored at the train depot and Pierre would help him haul the rest into Yellowstone. Logan would paint there for three or four weeks then they'd take his finished work back to the train, ship it home, pack the stored canvas and paints, and ride to the cabins, where Wise Sister waited. She never followed after Babineau when he went wandering.

Except Logan had arrived and waited. Waited several days. Precious days of the short Rocky Mountain summer. But Logan finally had to admit that Babineau wasn't coming. He'd left word, bought some pack horses, loaded his supplies, and gone into Yellowstone himself. He'd survived somehow. In fact, he'd gotten lost in his work.

While he was in Yellowstone, he'd painted Old Faithful and a dozen other geysers. He'd spent an entire week doing sketches of the waterfalls and the Yellowstone River. He'd also painted the new bridge spanning the river and the tent city that had grown up around Yellowstone like an ugly sore on the beautiful land. These he might be able to sell to newspapers or magazines. He might write about the people coming to Yellowstone, too, try his hand at a bit of storytelling to go with his art.

He'd done it all alone and found pride in knowing he could handle it. Then he'd packed the paintings back to the railroad station, crated them, and shipped them home. Then he'd picked up his stored supplies and set out for the cabin. He'd ridden there several times with Pierre and he'd known where he was going. He'd hoped.

He'd also hauled in the supplies he'd known were needed for the summer at the cabin. He'd found his way easily, wondering where Pierre had gotten to. He'd found Wise Sister alone, with a fresh grave that told its own story.

Wise Sister had gone on with her life and taken care of Logan's house, and Logan had let her. He'd never considered that he was asking too much of the woman.

He'd wanted to load six or even ten horses with canvas and paint. In fact, he'd planned to do just that next year if he sold enough of his paintings. But the grass was sparse up here, the corral small. Wise Sister took the horses daily to graze and drink water, and now Logan realized how much work that was. He couldn't add more horses to her daily chores.

But this style of painting was going through his supply of paints fast. Soon he'd have to be content with sketches. That chafed like wool on a sunburn. Maddening to know that, for lack of paint, he'd have to give up on this task that burned him alive with passion and pleasure. Next year he'd bring more. He had to, somehow.

As he painted, the sun lowered in the west. The mountain peaks would swallow it up long before true sunset. He felt exhilaration in the movement of his muscles and the emotion that flowed out from him onto the canvas. And as those emotions rose, another painting nudged him, haunted him until his mind wouldn't stay on this canvas.

Before he lost the light, he set his paints aside for a blank canvas and returned to his more traditional style of painting. Slowly Sally's face emerged. Her expression was perfect, the exact way she'd looked after he kissed her. It was the face of a woman in love. He doubted that she was, at least not in a deep and lasting way. But at that very moment, when she'd been in his arms, maybe there was a trace of truth in it. What would he give to have Sally look at him like this every day for the rest of his life?

The painting drew him just as powerfully as his slashing knives and violent red sunsets. It awakened something in him that burned in a different way than the pleasure of painting. But burned just as hot. Nothing—no one—had come close before.

He looked away from his work to watch her fashioning a crutch out of the sturdy forked branch Wise Sister had left behind. Practical woman, handy with a knife. She'd been at it all day, whittling at the wood and stitching a leather pad for her arm. She was an artist in her own way, though she'd probably punch him for saying such a thing.

She glanced at him, as if she were aware of his every move, even with her attention firmly fixed on her carpentry work. Then her eyes went past him to the painting.

He watched the play of feelings cross her face and wanted to sketch every one of them. Annoyance, unwilling fascination, curiosity, he thought maybe he even saw just a flash of respect. He loved her expressiveness. She hid nothing of what she felt, a completely open and honest human being.

"That is a stupid painting."

Painfully honest.

"You made me look dumber than an empty-headed maverick calf."

He'd made her look like a woman who'd just been kissed and wanted to be kissed again. And maybe, from her point of view, that equaled dumb.

"I paint what I see, Sally. I saw that look in your eyes the moment after I kissed you."

She pointed the razor-sharp knife she'd brought over the cliff with her at his nose. He was glad he was a few steps away.

"We aren't going to talk about that. We agreed."

Smiling, Logan looked at what he'd created, what he'd found in her. His heart ached as if he'd taken that knife right between the ribs because he knew Sally would never stay here with him. She thought he was a fool.

Not only did she not want him, he didn't want her. Not really. He'd be a bad person to tie in with. He was obsessed with painting. Look at poor Wise Sister; she'd been working like two people and he'd never noticed. He got so caught up in his painting he was thoughtless of everyone else.

"I'm too selfish of a man to ever kiss a woman." Logan didn't look at her. He was afraid of what he'd see. Despite her anger, he knew she longed for there to be more between them. But despite that longing, she'd leave. It wouldn't take much for him to be on his knees begging her to stay. "I—I shouldn't have done that. It's dishonorable to give you hope there could be something between us."

"I have no such *hopes*."

The anger in her voice made him look.

"My *hope* is to get out of here." She glared, that wonderful expressiveness, those blazing eyes, that perfect, silken skin. He'd never seen anything more beautiful, and while he drank her in, he saw her hand tightened on the knife. "If you think I'm *hoping* you'll decide I'm *worthy* of the great artist—"

"I know you're leaving," he cut her off. Logan was tempted to smile, but mindful of the knife and her temper, he didn't. He loved her spirit, her strength, even her honest disparagement. At least he could trust her to say exactly what she thought. But he thought it was fair to at least fight for her good opinion of him. "That day you went over the cliff, you were dressed like a man."

She didn't stab him, so he continued. "That's what you like. That's how you're happy."

She arched her brows, as if surprised he knew that and accepted it.

"That's odd behavior for a woman, but I find I like it well enough. It makes sense to me that you'd dress in a way that's comfortable and, even more importantly, safe."

"My thinking exactly." Sally sniffed and turned her knife back to working on her crutch.

He knew it would soon be done. Then she'd either walk out of here or her family would show up and take her away. Whichever happened, the end was the same. The prettiest, most fascinating woman he'd ever known would be gone.

What's more, he didn't want her to stay. He knew himself well enough to know that she'd come to hate him. The sun would be coming up, or setting, and the land would be ablaze with violet light or a crimson glow, and he'd ignore her and race against the movement of the sun and the fading of the day to catch the color and depth of it.

She didn't have much respect for him, but she didn't hate him. If she stayed, if he begged her and cajoled her and made promises that might be beyond his ability to keep, she might be persuaded. A few more moments in his arms and all the pretty words a man could say, and he might catch himself a wife. But she'd end up hating him. The very thought broke his heart.

"So, why can *you* be different, live to suit yourself, turn up your pretty little nose at conventions and I can't?" Logan quit talking and waited.

She set her knife on the table. "It's different, what I do."

"How?" He set his own knife aside.

"What I do makes *sense*. I may be different but I'm practical. I dress like this to get my work done."

"So, I live out here and paint because that's *my* work. I don't see how you can disdain what I do while you go around doing exactly as you wish, even though it's not a bit normal."

Glaring as if she could burn a hole straight through him, Sally sat, her jaw clenched into a tight, straight line. At last she leaned back in her chair and relaxed. "I suppose that's fair. Though I don't see how drawing your pictures puts food on the table. I help take care of my family. You do nothing but draw."

"You said you have a sister who's a doctor, right?"

A smile curved Sally's lips, and Logan could see how fond she was of her family. "Beth's a doctor, that's right."

"Well, how does doctoring put food on the table? Does she go hunting after her workday is done?"

"They buy food at the general store."

"I buy food with the money I earn painting."

"No, you don't. You make Wise Sister go hunt it for you."

"But I pay her to handle that. If she's working too hard, I didn't realize it, and she's never come out and said it's too much for her. I can fix that. I can help her more or hire someone else to help her. But hiring her is the same as your sister, Beth, and her husband going to the general store."

Sally stared at him. Then her eyes went to the picture he was painting of her and slid on past it to *Blazing Land*. "You think you'll find someone to pay you money for that picture of me?"

Logan would never part with this one, not for any amount of money, but he decided not to tell Sally that. "I've found a good, steady market for Western art back East. I'll load my work onto my packhorses in the fall, before the winter closes down on me, take the train back to New York, spend the winter painting from my sketches and my memory, and sell the finished works. I'll make enough to come back next summer."

"And that's it? For your whole life? No family, no children?"

The thought of no family and children, while pretty Sally sat there, was an ache in his chest. "This is my calling. I feel it as if God had carved it into a stone tablet." He looked out the wide-open windows and saw the herd of elk, *his* herd of elk, wander out of a draw about a hundred yards away. "And I'm—I'm self-centered. You've convinced me of that. I'd make a bad husband, a worse father, because if the light was right, and the clouds were a perfect shade of red, I'd pick up my paints and work."

He thought of how he'd been able to ignore his father. Logan could never have been a doctor, he knew that, but that didn't mean he had to be disrespectful of his father's wishes and wisdom. "I'd pick my art over my family every time. God may judge me for a sinner, but He also gave me this passion, this burning need to put the world on canvas."

"You could be less selfish. You could put the sin aside and live a better way and still paint."

"I can't." Logan studied the bull elk as if he held the meaning of life. "I've known myself long enough to know I can't."

The young upstart in the herd lowered his antlers and pawed the ground, and the bull turned to face the challenge yet again.

Seeing the elk pulled Logan's attention to the table in the corner. Yet another type of art he was attempting. He stepped toward the object covered with a wet towel.

"Can't or won't?"

Her voice stopped him and made him realize that once again his art had come before someone's needs. She sounded sad, which made him want to comfort her, and that reminded him of their kiss. She had a right to believe he wouldn't be kissing her if he couldn't have an honorable interest in her. And he'd just admitted he didn't.

"Can't or won't, in the end, the result is the same, Sally. A wife would end up being hurt. That's reason enough to never take one." To take his mind off the unruly image of Sally being his wife, he strode to the table and lifted the damp cloth to reveal an elk, fashioned out of clay. The animal stood proud, its chest out, its antlered head tilted nose up, mouth open, bugling to the sky.

Logan had found clay along a riverbed last year, so this winter he'd studied with a sculptor in New York and had come to love the touch of the clay on his hands. He studied the statue, nearly a foot tall, including the elaborate antlers, then went back to studying his living subject out the window. The bull and his young adversary circling each other. Sparring, charging, angry, violent. Logan wanted to capture it all.

A slow, quiet sigh pulled his attention away from the elk. And he lost all interest in the struggle of the two strong male creatures and turned to something a hundred times more interesting.

Sally.

Their eyes met and that kiss was between them like a living, breathing, burning thing.

"I reckon then," Sally said after far too long, her voice unsteady, "you'd better not kiss me again. You'd better stay away from me."

Logan nodded and moved closer to her. "You're right."

Their eyes held. The moment stretched.

Reminding himself that art was truth and he needed to be as honest in his life as in his art, Logan said, "I think I probably will kiss you again, Buckskin Angel."

His determination to stay away battled the force of his attraction and made him think of the mountains, made of stone, and the fact that they weren't all that solid. In fact, there were avalanches all the time. "I'm not sure if I *can* stay away from you."

Shaking her head, Sally turned her attention to the elk statue. "You made that, too?"

"Yes." Logan heaved a sigh of relief at the new subject. "I've been studying sculpture. I wanted to try and get all the sides of a subject instead of the flatness of painting."

"So it dries and you haul it back to New York, too? It's made of clay, isn't it? That isn't very strong, especially not the antlers.

You'll never get it all that way on a train without breaking it."

Logan nodded. "Probably not, but I'm going to coat it in plaster to take it home. Then when I get there, I'll cut the plaster away from the clay and have a perfect mold of my statue. I'll cast that mold in bronze and have something that will last forever."

"Plaster? You have plaster here?" Sally sat up straighter.

"I brought some because I knew I wanted to attempt this."

"Where is it?"

Logan pointed to a chest near the back of the cabin.

"We can make a cast for my leg with that. My sister did that when a patient had a broken bone. It'll be sturdier than this leather boot, and I can ride a horse more easily. With a plaster cast on my leg, I can get out of here."

She sounded so excited, Logan's heart sank. Of course she wanted out of here. She wanted to be on her way. She wanted to find her family and get on with her life.

He wanted that for her, too. But it made him sad that she sounded so excited. In fact, it made him more than sad. It made him a little angry. He was tempted to refuse her the use of the plaster. She only needed to stay a bit longer. Another week or two and her leg would probably be fully healed.

Besides, he wasn't done painting her yet. He wasn't done kissing her either.

Wise Sister picked that moment to come home.

Logan smiled to think that the old woman had just saved Sally from finding out all the things Logan wasn't done with.

Thirteen

Wise Sister came into sight through Logan's oversized windows and saved Sally from wiping that smug smile off Logan's face with her fist.

Wise Sister moved quietly, smoothly, with no apparent haste, but she was a woman who got things done. She'd left this morning, probably before dawn, and now here she was back with a haunch of venison over her shoulder.

Sally couldn't wait to hear what had happened. She stood, grabbing her crutch.

"Stay put. You'll fall." Logan stepped away from his sculpture toward his stupid painting that looked nothing like her. Well, truly it did look like her, except for that empty-headed expression on her face.

"I'm fine. Go back to your picture." Sally, slowly, experimenting with the pain and the balance, moved to the door. The crutch, tucked under her right arm, worked well to substitute for her broken right ankle. She'd have her hands full getting on and off a horse, but she could manage.

Somehow.

She might need to make a second crutch. Rig a strap to them to hang over the saddle horn. And she'd helped Beth once plaster a broken arm, so she knew how to do that, too. Two crutches and a plaster cast and she was on her way.

She wondered where in the world she was and how to get to Mandy's from here or find Luther from here. The thought of Mandy picked up the pace of Sally's heart. She felt a growing desperation to get to her sister. Or maybe to get away from Logan, she couldn't be sure, but the result gave her both: distance from the painter and her sharpshooting sister at her back.

She thought of Logan's warm kisses and her own odd expression in that painting and did her best to think about every-thing except here. She swung the door open just as Wise Sister came up to the cabin. "Did you see anyone?"

"I found tracks. Two groups. Four men. Much hunting." Her dark eyes gleamed. Sally felt like she knew this woman right down to the bone and she adored her. Smart, strong, quiet. A woman molded by the brutal West and thriving.

"Much hunting for you, Sally girl." Wise Sister didn't come inside. She headed for a stump near the house, stained rust brown from blood. With little noticeable exertion, she heaved the haunch onto the stump with a dull thud.

Sally didn't bother asking why Wise Sister thought they searched for her. She trusted Wise Sister's instincts. "Tell me about the men." She followed Wise Sister the few feet to her butchering block.

"I saw no one." Wise Sister produced a knife from a sheath on her waist.

Sally heard movement behind her and knew Logan had left his precious painting to listen to the talk. She did her best not to sniff at him—the pig who had kissed her and made her feel things then so politely told her he couldn't do her the enormous favor of keeping her as his queen in a fool's kingdom.

"Tell me." Sally watched Wise Sister sharpen her knife with a little round stone that lay beside the stump.

With the scratch of metal on rock, Wise Sister spoke. "One group searches widely, the other wisely. The first, coyotes; the second, wolves." Wise Sister looked up with a smile as sharp as her knife. "I left sign for the wolves."

Sally smiled back.

"What's this talk of coyotes and wolves?" Logan asked, coming up beside her. Too close.

She was tempted to jam her elbow into his stomach. "Luther's close. Wise Sister left a trail for him to follow. It'll lead him here."

"Not a trail." Wise Sister shook her head firmly. "I feared the coyotes would find it. Even coyotes know the woods. But I let them know you lived. To keep searching. That *we* know they're hunting. Your wolves left markers, good, not easy to find. They weren't for me. So they must believe others come."

Nodding, Sally said, "Maybe. The people with me, the colonel and his wife, were important folks. Someone will come hunting. Luther is leaving a trail for those folks to follow." The smile was impossible to contain. Luther was close. She knew it. She fought off a horrifying urge to start leaking salt water. "How long until they're here?"

"Sally, Wise Sister said she didn't leave a trail." He patted her on the arm in sympathy.

The obvious had once again made its way out of Logan's mouth. Luther was going to find the man very annoying.

"Soon." Wise Sister ignored Logan. "They'll find their way."

"And the coyotes?" Sally knew Luther might be pressed to get here before the men who were searching for her.

Wise Sister frowned and told the straight, uncomfortable truth. She tapped her chest with her knife. "I was careful with the sign I left, but coyotes are wily. They may come, too. Even first."

A little shiver of fear ran up Sally's spine. "We'll need a lookout, day and night."

"I've hunted coyotes before." Wise Sister turned to her task and began skinning dinner.

"So have I," Sally said with grim determination. "I've got my Winchester."

"We can't shoot any coyotes or wolves this close to the cabin." Logan gave a firm nod of his head.

Sally pulled her own knife with relish. She raised it just enough to get his attention. Then, after his eyes had widened with alarm, she hobbled over to help Wise Sister.

"Maybe I'll thank that little cowpoke before I shoot him." Fergus stretched his legs out by their fire, enjoying the night and the campfire and the stars overhead.

"Don't know where he got to, but sure enough he hasn't gotten away." Tulsa poured a cup of coal black brew into his tin cup.

Fergus loved the wild land. Having someone to hunt up here was a pure pleasure. "We'll keep our eyes open and prowl around. Maybe I oughta build a cabin up here. Government threw me out of Yellowstone. Maybe they'll keep their paws offa me up here." The scalding coffee burned Fergus's tongue, but nothing could lessen his pleasure. A stick broke in the fire and sparks shot skyward, scenting the air with wood smoke. "I reckon I've been living in the high-up country for forty years now, Tulsa. Reckon I'll die here, rich on stupid travelers and fat elk. It's a good life."

Mountains loomed above them, the white caps dazzling in the summer sun. Quaking aspen shivered and twirled their leaves between the lodgepole pine and heavy underbrush. A man could get mighty lost up in this land. But time to time, Fergus had needed to get lost. So he'd come here, knowing well how to live until it was safe to get himself found.

"I ever tell you I had another brother, Tulsa?" Fergus was in a mood to spin a yarn, and thinking of these rough mountains made him think of Curly, and that led to wandering inside his head until he came to his boyhood.

"Cain't say you have. I've got me a coupl'a sisters and a little brother myself. No idea if they're alive or dead. You know where your brother is?"

"Nope. Haven't seen my baby brother in the whole forty years I been up here. He was a lot younger." Fergus's memories soured as he thought of the drunken old man who'd married his ma the year before he and Curly had left. He'd had a heavy hand with Fergus's ma and wasn't against turning his fists on her boys. Fergus remembered well the day he'd finally gotten old enough and mean enough to make the old man back down.

"The man, Reynold was his name." Fergus shook his head. "He was kin to my real pa. He had the same white stripe in his hair that Curly and I have. Called it the family mark. Different last name though. He tended a saloon and helped himself to the whiskey. Moved around a lot because he'd get fired." Fergus had put himself between the old brute and Curly all the time and taken what beatings he could to protect his little brother. He'd done his best with his ma, too.

"Came a day when Reynold couldn't push me around anymore. He was giving my ma a thrashing and I stepped in, got in a lucky hit that put my ever-loving daddy onto his knees and ended up stomping the old man into the ground."

"Did your ma finally feel safe from him? Did you throw him out?" Tulsa leaned forward and lazily refilled his cup.

"Nope, I got thrown out instead."

Tulsa froze with his coffee half poured, and the flowing liquid overflowed the cup, streaming onto Tulsa's leg. With a shout of pain, he dropped the pot and cup and jumped up to swat at his leg. The pot landed bottom side down. The coffee was spared, so Fergus made no mind of Tulsa's dancing.

Finally the man settled down and looked at Fergus. "Your ma tossed you out?" A cynical frown curved Tulsa's lips down.

Fergus knew Tulsa had a real good idea of how it'd been for

Fergus and Curly. Fergus wondered what had happened to the baby Ma had just borne when Fergus had lit out. He'd always felt bad leaving the little one to his scared ma and brutal pa.

"Yep, Ma gave Curly 'n' me the egg money and told us Reynold would kill us if we were there when he woke up."

"Why didn't she go with you?"

"Scared he'd catch us, maybe." Fergus caught at the streak of white on his temple. "Ma used to talk about my real pa some. She said there was family, and if we could find them they'd take us in. Said there was family pride in sticking up for each other. Don't see how that's true. If my pa and Reynold were kin, then it seems like not beating on your children would be part of sticking with your family."

Shrugging, Fergus added, "Ma made my pa's family sound like good folks. Couldn't tell it by Reynold, though. I use his name as an alias. I like the idea of being an outlaw with that man's name. Hope I leave some dirt on it."

Tulsa grunted and reached for the coffeepot.

"So Reynolds wasn't interested in whether we lived or died. Ma liked a man around and had her some trouble finding one. Ma wasn't a woman to be any better'n she oughta be, so decent men weren't interested."

"My ma neither." Tulsa poured more coffee and settled in again, ignoring the splash of wet on his thigh.

"I was sixteen. Curly was twelve but getting tall, and he could do the work of a man. We took out. I managed to steal a couple of horses and we rode west. We found a wagon train and signed on to work for a coupl'a families. Ended up in Denver and then headed into the mountains with an old trapper. Trapped when the trapping was good, stole a payroll and a horse when times were lean. When I found Yellowstone and saw all the people coming in, not wise in the ways of these mountains, I knew it was my own private gold mine."

That's when he and Curly had teamed up with Tulsa, younger

than Fergus by a dozen years or so. Letting Tulsa join up with him and Curly was like having a little brother. Fergus ran his hand into his gray hair with the white stripe. The years were gone. His life more over than not. He sighed and wondered again about that baby.

"Always hoped that brute, Reynold, was nicer to his own child than he was to Curly and me. I've had an urge to go back, see if the baby needed saving. But it's a long way and that baby is a grown man now, and it's too late to change a thing." For all the sinning Fergus had done in his life, that was the sin that gnawed at his guts. Picturing that baby growing up with those heavy fists flailing at him. He'd protected Curly, but he'd left that baby behind to the wolves.

Fergus's yarn was spun and he felt the worse for having talked about it, so he turned his attention to what was in front of them. "I want that cowpoke dead. This is a good life. The livin' is easy. I don't want trouble on my back trail whether I stay here or go." And that long ago memory of his ma telling him the family stuck together, a family Fergus had never known, helped make him hungry for revenge against that cowpoke that had escaped while Curly had died.

Tulsa nodded and pulled his gun to check that it was fully loaded. "A good life for sure. We gotta make sure that cowpoke and whoever is takin' care of him are dead."

Fergus's family stuck together. Or so he'd been told. So he'd stick with hunting the cowpoke for Curly's sake, and he'd stick with silencing a witness for his own.

When this was over, he'd still rule over this land—his own personal gold mine.

And that cowpoke would be dead.

Fourteen

Sally's alive." Luther straightened from the little pile of stones weighing down the leather. The leather had the McClellen ranch brand marked clear, newly cut. The stack of stones had obviously been deliberately left as a marker. "This is off her boot."

He looked up in time to catch a blurry wash over Buff's eyes, almost as if the man was ready to cry. Luther would have made fun of the old coot if he could speak past the lump in his throat. "This is Shoshone sign." Luther looked into an impassable pile of rocks at the base of a mountain. "Sally, or whoever left this, must know there are bad men searching for her because there's no effort to point us toward a trail."

"So where is she?" Buff asked.

Luther studied Clay McClellen's brand on a piece of leather. Only Sally would have known someone would come looking and understand what that meant. "Shoshone markings." Luther pointed to a few other cuts in the leather. "Makes sense that if someone carried her off, it'd be an Indian, a Shoshone. Them and the Nez Perće are almost the only ones left hereabouts."

"I heard they'd driven the tribes off Yellowstone. They might've come up here." Buff stared at the mountains around them. "I did a fair sight of trapping in Yellowstone in the early days, before we was saddle partners, Luth. Figures there might be some native folks in these hills."

"The rain wiped out the trail the same day we found it. But that first day we saw that someone rode away carryin' a load. Maybe Sally riding double with someone." Luther thought of the men they now followed and itched to face them. Two against two, even odds. He'd have done it, but he wasn't interested in arresting them and hauling them to jail a hundred miles away. And he didn't see any point in a shootout that would risk their lives and not bring them one step closer to Sally. So instead they'd dogged the other men. Luther hoped he'd find a sign of Sally first. And, if he didn't, Luther and Buff would be on hand to protect her.

"The marker was set up by a solid wall of rock with nothing to give us a direction. But it was left by a knowin' hand. Someone afraid the outlaws would see it first. So there's no clue to what direction to ride. We'll have us a time tracking our girl down. But maybe whoever was helping her will come again."

"And in the meantime, we'll hunt." Buff reached out and took the bit of leather from Luther's hand and stared at it a long time.

"See anything there that'll give us a direction to hunt?"

"Wise Sister." Buff closed his fist on the leather.

"What?"

Buff shook his head.

Waiting a minute, Luther decided his friend had no more to say. No surprise there. "Let's see if we can pick up a trail from whoever left it there." Luther looked at the wall of rock looming over that marker. "Could they be up in the highlands?"

"Don't see how." Buff's hand clutched at that leather as if he had to hold on to save his life. "There's no way up. Anyway, you'd be an idiot to climb up onto the top of a mountain."

"What kind of idiot builds his house at the top of a mountain?" Mandy was purely perturbed, and considering her earlier decision to stop restraining herself and let Sidney handle the real her as best he could, she would have asked her husband that to his face if she didn't have two sleeping babies on the ground beside her while she sighted her gun on a mule deer.

It was a long shot, but Mandy had to take it. This was the spot her girls had chosen to nap and she couldn't leave them to slip closer. And their cabin was right on the tree line. The new house would be well above it. So her idiot husband had chosen her hunting grounds for her. She couldn't quite bring herself to be grateful for his love of that mountaintop mansion.

The shot was five hundred yards. Worst part was she'd wake the babies up when she took the shot. No, worst part was she was doing her best to hide behind some rocks waiting for some game to wander close. Normally, she'd have stretched out on her stomach and gotten comfortable while she waited. She knew how to be patient when she stalked game. But these days, her round stomach was in the way.

The wee one inside of her gave her a kick and she smiled, looking forward to meeting the little tyke. A boy, she thought, just because it was time. Her ma was living proof that a woman could have long strings of one then the other, so she didn't put too much stock in any notion of it being time.

The deer moved a bit closer as it grazed. Then it lifted its head, maybe catching a scent of her, but she was downwind, though the wind up this high sometimes swirled around, defying a true direction. More likely there was something else in the woods bothering it. Even a bird taking flight or a raccoon too close at hand would startle a deer. Whatever the reason, the timid critter wasn't going to get any closer.

Mandy drew in a long, slow breath and steadied the gun on her shoulder, feeling her nerves cool. Her vision sharpened, her hands steadied, her blood chilled. Her finger tightened on the trigger. She released the breath halfway, then held it and took the shot.

Catherine and Angela jumped and woke up squalling.

The deer slumped to the ground.

She now had supper. And two crying babies.

With a sigh, she calmed her daughters, hung her rifle in place across her back, and then rigged Catherine on top of the rifle. She took Angela's hand and walked to the horse, tied back a ways.

Tom Linscott.

She caught herself thinking about him every time she got near a horse.

As she led the horse to the deer, she reminded herself that it was not *Tom* she thought of. She did her best not to think about him. It was that sturdy little foal and his massive, handsome stallion.

Tom?

No, nothing about him was proper to think about.

As she hung the deer and bled and gutted it, then slung it over the horse's shoulders, Mandy had plenty of time to wonder how Belle Tanner had fared with the foal she'd gotten out of Tom's stallion. But that wasn't thinking about Tom.

She slung the deer over the horse's shoulders. Next she settled Angela on the saddle, swung up behind the cantle with Catherine on her back, and made her way home. She wondered how Belle's mare had handled the long walk home over the rugged trail to the Harden ranch. Had Tom gone to visit the little foal? Had he approved of the care Mandy had taken of it that winter? It was the foal's health that was her real focus.

That had nothing to do with Tom.

Mandy prepared a huge stew that would feed even all of Sidney's workmen for a couple of days. And imagined the powerful muscles and sleek beauty of that magnificent stallion Tom had ridden.

But she didn't really wonder about *Tom*. Nothing there to wonder about.

With Catherine strapped on her back and Angela clinging to her skirts, Mandy finished preparing supper. When her stew was thick with venison and her garden vegetables, she set it to simmering, and the warm, savory smell of meat and onions began to fill the cabin. Then she went back to work finishing the deer.

It did cross her mind to try and figure when Tom would come. Would it be before or after the baby was delivered—a time fast approaching. Wondering about company wasn't the same as wondering about a man.

Returning to the butcher block outside, she lifted her razor-sharp cleaver just as Cooter, the younger of Sidney's bodyguards, came walking alone down the slope from the mansion site.

A chill ran up Mandy's spine. She took one quick glance then paid rapt attention to the work in front of her. Mandy had felt Cord Cooter's eyes on her many times. But both guards stayed close to Sidney. That was their job. So what was Cooter doing down here when Sidney might need his body guarded up by the big house?

Cooter was about Mandy's age, dark hair with a strange streak of white at one temple. He had reddish skin and lips that were too full. His eyes were a cold blue and they didn't miss much. The man had never spoken to her. He'd never come close to touching her. He'd never done a thing that could give Mandy an excuse to ask Sidney to fire him. But Mandy trusted her instincts, and she didn't like this man. He showed what kind of snake he was without saying a word.

Cooter went to the door of the bunkhouse. Then, as he grasped the handle, he turned and looked square at Mandy. Their eyes met and held. The chill in her spine turned to ice. A mean smile curved Cooter's lips. He caught the brim of his Stetson and tugged it, a greeting. But it felt more like a threat.

God protect me.
God protect me.
God protect me.

Cooter went inside.

Mandy turned back to her butchering and felt the ice flowing through her veins. So cold. And the cold went deep. It threatened to take over and rule her. Could a woman that cold love her children properly?

God protect me.

A squeal at her feet turned her attention. Mandy looked down at little Angela, clinging to her skirt, only a foot or so away from the lethal cleaver.

"Mama!" The little sweetie seemed to think she could help.

"You're a little young for meat cleavers, Angie." Mandy smiled and her heart warmed again. She had so much in her life. Yes, Sidney was a nuisance and a disappointment, but her children were wonderful. She noticed at that moment the wet spot on her neck. Catherine had dozed off. When that happened, she rested her baby-soft cheek on the back of Mandy's neck and often drooled in her sleep.

Carrying Catherine on her back, which she did a lot, had taught Mandy to sling her rifle differently, lower, so the hard length wasn't in Catherine's way. The gun was slower to get into action with it that way, but Mandy hadn't needed to be fast in a while. She still needed to be accurate though.

Angela stood on tiptoes, reached, stretching her little body as much as possible, and screamed. "Mama. Mama hep. Andie hep Mama." Angie's voice rose as she tried to grab the knife, only missing by about two feet.

"Help. . ."

Smiling, Mandy knew she might not get much help from her husband, but before long her girls would be help. With a sigh at the high-pitched screaming, Mandy knew no one's life was perfect.

"Andie help, Mamamama!"

Mandy called her Angie and Angie called herself a slurred version of that. Today it sounded like "Andie."

With some ragged exceptions, her life was wonderful. She thought of how hard it had been hunting this deer, then carrying it home and the work of butchering. Luther usually did this. Mandy wondered where he'd gotten to and where Sally was.

God protect me.

God protect them.

"Mamamamamamama!" Angie bounced and screamed just as a hand landed hard on Mandy's shoulder.

She spun around with an indrawn breath so hard it became an inverted scream. One hand went to her rifle and jerked it forward. She clutched the cleaver in the other, which was a mistake if she needed to aim and fire. Her nerves iced over.

"Don't shoot, Mrs. Gray." Cooter put up both hands with a smile that didn't reach his eyes. He took a quick step back, but it was too small a step and well he knew it. He still stood too close.

Mandy didn't level the gun, but she had it in hand, the muzzle pointed toward the ground, her finger on the trigger. The cleaver she held high enough to keep it from Angie. If it seemed to Cooter like she was threatening him with it, well, that suited her just fine.

"Did you. . ." Mandy's voice shook with the cold, not fear. She cut off the words and drew in a long, slow, steadying breath as she got control of herself. "Did you need something?"

She had only to look in his eyes to know he'd deliberately put his hands on her. Angie had fallen silent as if she'd been frightened by this man. That was something Mandy took very seriously.

He'd touched her knowing she'd hate it. He'd scared her child. She felt a sudden, clawing desire to lift her rifle and pull the trigger. It shocked her so much that her nerves went even colder and she no longer felt anything but calm determination that this man would never come near her again.

"I was going to offer to butcher that deer for you, Mrs. Gray." The offer was a decent thing. But his eyes crawled over her like insects.

494

"I'm fine, Mr. Cooter. A person who lives in a wild land gets in the habit of pointing a gun fast. I will tell you clearly that I don't want your hands on me. I won't warn you again."

"Is that a threat, Mrs. Gray?" He licked his flaccid lips as if he liked the taste of something. His blue eyes had no lashes and seemed rimmed with pink. His brows were dark and heavy. Showing below his hat, she saw that streak of white in his hair that seemed to emphasize a coldness in the man so deep and wide it left frost on the outside. "You'll complain to your husband that I offered to help with some heavy work?"

That is exactly how it would sound to Sidney. Cooter offered to help, and Mandy caused trouble with her unladylike ways.

"I make no threats, Mr. Cooter. I tell you clearly to stay well away from me. How my husband feels about that doesn't come into it because I handle my troubles myself."

Their eyes held. Hers determined and clear and cold. His hungry and cruel.

After too many seconds of silence, Angie caught hold of Mandy's skirt. "Mama, Andie hep." Her daughter made a grab for the cleaver.

"If you'll head on now, Mr. Cooter, I need to get back to work and I'm sure you have work elsewhere, too."

Cooter stared a few seconds longer. Then a scornful smile quirked his lips. He tugged on his hat brim, pulling it low enough to cover the white, then turned to walk back up the hill.

Mandy never took her eyes off of him.

"I'd be glad to help you anytime you want, Mrs. Gray," he called over his shoulder. Then just as he stepped onto a trail that would twist upward and take him out of her sight, he turned back. "Day. . .or night. . ." He paused for too long. "You come to me if you ever need a *real man*." He stressed those words ever so slightly as his eyes crawled over her again, his insulting intent clear. "I'll be. . .watching. . .waiting for you."

The contempt was clear. Contempt for Sidney, as if he wasn't a real man. Contempt for her, as if she'd turn to another man for what his eyes insinuated.

The worst of it was Cooter had never acted like this before. She'd always known he was a dangerous man, but he'd acted loyal to Sidney from the first. He was showing this side of himself because Luther was gone. Was he the one who'd been prowling around the cabin at night, thinking he could find something in their cabin that would give him access to Sidney's gold, stashed in a vault in Denver?

A dishonest man might have many reasons for threatening a woman whose husband was defenseless. Sidney hiring body-guards announced to the world he couldn't take care of himself and his family.

But what Cooter didn't know was that *Mandy* wasn't de-fenseless. She wasn't a woman to cower. Her hand reached down and clutched the muzzle of her trusty rifle.

She'd never shot a man. Never come close. Never drawn a bead on a human being and known she might have to make that choice. A bitter cold place in her heart knew she could do it. She took no pride in knowing it, but she did. She'd never be a helpless maiden in need of rescue by some big, strong man.

And then Mandy thought of Tom Linscott again. This time she didn't even pretend that she wasn't thinking of that strong, kindhearted man. Tom would use his fists on any man who treated a woman like Cooter had just treated her. He'd do worse if needed.

So would Pa.

So would Luther.

And Mandy stood here uncertain if Sidney would even *fire* Cooter. Unless Sidney thought Cooter was a threat to Sidney's gold.

The way to get rid of Cooter was to tell Sidney his money was in danger. That he'd take seriously. Something died inside her to know that—to get Cooter off this property—tonight she'd tell

Sidney exactly that. And that might well force Cooter's hand and turn him from sly and threatening to a blatant danger.

Another interesting question: was he in league with Platte or not? If it came to shooting trouble, would Platte side with the Grays or with Cooter?

Mandy pictured Cord Cooter's dangerous, piggish eyes. Her skin crawled as she thought of his hard hand on her shoulder. She remembered his full lips moving as if they wanted to eat her up.

Not telling Sidney meant keeping a deadly dangerous man in their midst.

Telling Sidney might well tear this mountainside wide open.

Fifteen

We need to cut strips of cloth." Sally tried to remember all Beth had done. "Then dip the cloths into the plaster until they're coated. Then wrap the strips around my leg."

The harsh rip of cloth pulled Sally's eyes around to see Wise Sister at work turning a pile of what looked to be old shirts into strips. Babineau's maybe?

Logan brought a bowl over. "I know how to mix it so it will set up solid. It should be the same as I'd use to mold my clay sculptures, right?"

"Makes sense, I reckon." Sally tried to be calm as she thought about unbinding her leg. It still hurt something fierce, although she could recall the first day she'd been hurt and knew it was much improved.

Logan kept his eyes respectfully on his work, carefully preparing the plaster and not looking at her leg. By the time he was done, Wise Sister had a small mountain of cloth. She gently removed the leather brace and unwound the cloth holding the splint in place.

"Much better." Wise Sister slipped off Sally's sock and ran a hand over a small swollen spot close to her ankle. "The break is right here."

Sally looked up to see Logan studying her leg, bare to the knee.

Wise Sister elbowed him in the stomach.

He jumped and quickly turned back to his plaster.

"I—I—uh—remember Beth wrapped the ankle in something before she put on the plaster, to protect the skin." Sally hadn't done much doctoring for her family. Beth had always stepped forward to do it, and Sally had been glad to avoid the chore. Being gentle wasn't really her way of handling things. She preferred a bullwhip.

Wise Sister got a clean sock and, with tender care, covered Sally's leg. It helped Sally feel less disturbed by Logan's touch. "You, soak the cloth." Wise Sister thrust the stack of fabric at Logan.

Sally was relieved that Logan wouldn't be allowed to touch her. Logan's touch had proved to be extremely unsettling.

When the first strip was soaked with the sticky white goo, Wise Sister took it and pressed it against Sally's stocking-covered leg. The damp cloth soaked through the sock and tickled. Then it downright itched. Reaching for her ankle, Sally's fingernails touched the cloth.

"Don't touch." Wise Sister slapped her hand with a scolding look that made Sally feel like a misbehaving five-year-old. "Don't move."

It was then that Sally remembered thinking disparaging thoughts of Logan when he'd sheepishly admitted he was scared of Wise Sister. Looking up, she caught his eye and he gave her a look that clearly said, "You see what I mean?"

It was all Sally could do not to laugh. But that would almost certainly qualify as moving, and she didn't want to be chastised again so she resisted the temptation. "Tell me more about

Yellowstone, Logan. Or painting, or something before this soggy stuff makes me crazy." Sally looked at him, prepared to beg. But she instantly saw that she'd asked the perfect question.

His hands were busy pulling strips of cloth out of the plaster so he was trapped there just as surely as Sally and Wise Sister. "I first decided to come out here when I saw a painting by Thomas Moran. He came out with a group called the Hayden Expedition in 1871 and he made sketches and watercolors of all the beautiful, mysterious sights in what is now Yellowstone. I saw a lot of them as a boy, and it was just crystal clear instantly that I had to come."

Smiling, Sally said, "Like I wanted to be a cowboy right from the first."

"I suppose it's just like that." Logan handed over a strip without Wise Sister having to ask.

They were working like a team now. Wise Sister winding, Logan holding the strips, Sally being still. She suspected her job was the hardest of the three.

"I could hardly believe the stories I heard about the place, geysers and boiling mud. Ponds that changed colors and were hot right out of the ground."

"I have a little trouble believing in it now," Sally said quietly.

"My paintings of Yellowstone all got shipped back East already. I'd love for you to see them. I have some sketches I'll show you later."

"I'd like that."

"Moran's painting made the place so alive for me, and it made me almost crazy to see it and paint it myself."

"Almost crazy?" Sally made sure to smile when she said it.

Logan took her teasing with good grace. "It was more than just Yellowstone. It was the way Moran gave the whole world a look at something they could probably never hope to see. Until he came back from this expedition, there were reports of the wonders of the place, but a lot of people didn't even believe it, it was so outlandish."

"And you realized you could teach people with your painting. Open the world up for them."

Logan jerked his chin up and looked at her. His eyes blazed. "Yes, exactly. I could go, just me, and bring it back for everyone. It's more than just loving to paint. There are beautiful places back East. It's about sharing something rare and wonderful."

Logan handed over another strip then looked at her, and their eyes locked. The gaze shared something rare and wonderful. It changed Sally inside. Hardened and bound them together as surely as the plaster hardened around her leg. She knew this was wrong, wanting to learn more about Logan, wanting to feel more about Logan. But it couldn't be stopped. It could only be ignored. She had to get to Mandy, help her big sister. She had to and she would. But it wasn't going to be easy.

A grunt from Wise Sister broke the connection, and Logan quickly fumbled for a strip of plaster-soaked cloth and handed it over.

"Tell me more." Sally didn't want it to end, this tie that bound her to this man.

He talked but he didn't look, as if he knew that there was still time, that they weren't firmly encased in whatever wrapped around them. And he would do nothing to further that and maybe trap himself with her.

But Sally knew, at least for her, it was too late. She didn't know if she was in love with Logan, but she knew she loved him. Maybe at this point she could tell herself that she loved him as God called each to love others as themselves. It was more than a dutiful, Christian love though. It was laden with admiration and respect. And longing.

That wasn't romance and marriage and a home. But it was very, very close, and she pulled back from the brink before she tumbled headlong into love with a man who'd already told her he'd make a terrible husband.

The next morning she awakened alone.

Wise Sister planned on scouting the lowlands again today.

The plaster was dried rock solid and Sally felt an almost desperate need to escape. While she could still call her heart her own. She could get out of here now, but Wise Sister scolded and said the leg needed more time.

Sally hadn't been able to force her wishes on anyone while she lay there flat on her back with her leg encased in stone and propped up high on a stack of folded blankets.

She began her second crutch that day and had it done by nightfall, including two handy straps of leather so the crutches would hang from her saddle horn.

The next day she practiced moving around on her crutches, with the heavy cast dangling, and knew she had to get better at this before she struck out on her hunt for Luther. But she found herself able to do the cooking chores, and she even found some vegetables ripe in the garden.

"I said I'd do that." Logan fumed from where he crouched beside her in the potato patch.

"You admitted you didn't know a potato leaf from a weed. I can do this faster if you just leave me alone." Sally knew she was being unfair. She'd chastised Logan for not helping, and now that he wanted to, she was shooing him away because he didn't know how. Sally knew better than that. She'd taught Laurie and her little brothers to tend the garden. She was a hand at teaching. "Fine," she forced herself to say, when she wanted him to go away. "Get down here."

Logan dropped easily to his knees and Sally envied him his two functioning legs.

They worked companionably together for about an hour before Logan looked up at a cloud that cast a shadow over them. "Look at that." He stood, staring upward.

Sally couldn't control following his gaze. Dark clouds boiled overhead off to the west, moving fast. Billowy layers and layers of

502

clouds pushing lighter, thinner clouds ahead of them.

"We'd better hurry."

"You're right." Sally reached for a weed just as Logan caught her around her waist and lifted her to her feet. "Stop. I need to—"

"I'm getting them." Logan handed her the crutches and grabbed the cloth sack of vegetables they'd gathered.

"No, I mean I need to hurry and finish." Sally was talking to Logan's fast retreating back.

"You can get back to the cabin, right?" Logan didn't even look behind her. He was watching those approaching clouds. "You got out here alone. I'll miss it."

Get back? Sally opened her mouth to call after him, "Miss what?"

Logan dashed off and vanished into his cabin.

Sally shook her head to clear it of his strange behavior. Was he afraid of storms? Maybe he'd been scared by a thunderbolt as a child. The storm was coming but not that fast. Still, she might as well head in. She was halfway to the cabin when Logan reappeared with—of course—

Sally did her best not to groan out loud.

His paint.

"God, have mercy," Sally spoke to the building clouds. She'd never spent much time thinking clouds were beautiful, though they were of course, but clouds were God's way of warning people of an approaching storm. They weren't a call to start drawing. They were a call to close the windows and use common sense to come in before it rained.

She moved on to the cabin, practicing with her crutches, planning on starting a meal with those vegetables. She stopped. Her eyes were drawn to Logan as his arm slashed across the canvas—the intensity of his expression, the passion of his movements. The fixation on the boiling, advancing storm was like music.

Drawn closer, she knew he hadn't even noticed her. This is

what he'd been talking about when he said he'd neglect a wife and children.

Dark gray splashed across white canvas. The violence and danger of the storm was there. Sally could feel it moving, threatening, as surely as the clouds did. She wondered if a man had this kind of gift and this powerful calling from God, could a woman maybe, just maybe, rejoice in that? Embrace all that was different about her life? If that man turned all that power and passion on a woman, could she live with the problems that came with a man obsessed with art?

It was like ripping away her skin to pull her gaze from Logan's work, but she did it. Forced herself to do it. Turning to the cabin, she thought of practical things like supper and learning how to walk on crutches.

With one tiny movement, she caressed the beads along the collar of the doeskin dress. Then she ran her hand over the seam where she'd hidden the tiny ribbon. She wouldn't have to hide that ribbon any longer if she stayed here. Logan wouldn't expect her to be boyish in her dress. Logan thought she was beautiful in anything she wore. The intensity of his art was there when he was drawing her, too.

Going soon was essential or she very much feared she'd never be able to go at all.

Wise Sister scolded her into staying home, and another week crawled by.

The only surprising fact was that Sally kept from strangling someone. "Let me ride out with you tomorrow." Sally and Wise Sister had retired to Wise Sister's cabin to sleep. Sally cared for the cabin while Wise Sister did her sneaking around.

Logan painted.

"Can't sneak. Broke leg." Wise Sister prepared for bed quickly and lay down on her pallet.

Sally hated putting Wise Sister out of her bed, but the plain truth was Sally still hurt. It was doubtful she'd have gotten any sleep on the hard floor. "My ribs are fine and my leg hardly hurts anymore since we put on the cast."

It might be more accurate to say Sally had gotten *used* to her leg and ribs hurting, which wasn't the same as *not* hurting, but she saw no reason to bury Wise Sister in details.

"Too many men. I go on foot. You need horse. Can't sneak on horse."

"Have you seen any of the men yet, even a glimpse?"

Wise Sister reached for the lantern she'd left burning until Sally was settled. "No, I see no one. Sleep now."

"Wise Sister, wait!"

To Sally's surprise, the Shoshone woman's hand paused. Usually Wise Sister did as she wished, and Sally had very little success changing the elderly woman's mind about anything.

She'd never get Wise Sister to agree to take her along, but she had a few other things she wanted to say. "The things in this cabin are beautiful."

Wise Sister sat up on her pallet with a small smile. "My home. I make it to please myself."

"Yourself and your husband, Pierre." Sally wondered at the lack of talk of Pierre. Though of course Wise Sister didn't talk much about anything.

"No, *my* home. *My* things."

Looking around at the handwork, the leather, the weaving, the soft animal pelts, the collection of feathers and stones and carved wood, Sally knew that was the truth. "Your husband wasn't here much, then?"

The smile on Wise Sister's face remained but was a sad sort. "Gone a lot. A wandering man, my Babineau. Didn't care after a while."

"You didn't like your husband?" Sally thought of Mandy. From the bits and pieces in her letters, Sally suspected Mandy didn't like her husband one bit.

"At first, yes. Very much. But he couldn't stay. Always itchy to move. At first I moved with him. Then the children came and I stayed in one place. I was a woman for home. He was a restless man drawn to the distant places."

"You have children?" Why hadn't Sally known this?

"Six children. Two girls, four boys. The boys took to the mountains like Pierre. The girls married to my tribe and left for the reservation. No one is near."

"That's sad." Sally knew how they all missed Mandy, hurt to know her babies were growing up as strangers.

"Just life. Not sad."

But Sally heard in Wise Sister's voice that it *was* sad.

"Those"—Wise Sister pointed to a woven mat on the wall, six sides, brightly dyed in six colors—"are my children. I find things of six. One for each child."

Suddenly Sally saw the sprays of feathers, spreading in six directions. The circle of stones, six stones, each a different color. A beaded wall hanging showed a six-sided sunburst. The number was in nearly everything. And in the midst of it hung that painting of Wise Sister and Babineau.

"Does Logan's painting of you and your husband please you, then? Or do you not like your husband's likeness on your wall?"

"Babineau was mine. I was his. We were together even when we were apart. I learned to be content in his absence and his presence. He was strong. He knew the land, and I respected that. I cared for him. A man who stayed with me would be good. But I chose him, not really knowing him, and I lived with my choice."

"I think—I think my sister is married to a man she doesn't like. I think that would be hard."

There was an extended silence as Wise Sister looked at the painting.

Quietly she said, more to the painting than to Sally, "Life is hard. There is right and wrong. We make our choices and live with them. Do what is right especially when it's hard."

There was wisdom in Wise Sister's eyes, and Logan had captured that perfectly in his painting. Patience. Suffering. Contentment. It truly was a beautifully done work. Sally looked closer at Babineau and saw strength and a look in Babineau's eyes of restlessness, wildness. But contentment was there, to match Wise Sister's. They'd found a way to exist together, even though they were very different.

In the end, Sally decided that's the way most marriages worked. Her ma and pa got on well and seemed happy. A painting of them would show little suffering. Beth loved Alex. Some of her sorrow for Mandy's life eased. Mandy would find her way somehow with no-account Sidney.

Sally almost spoke aloud of her confusion about marriage and adult feelings and Logan, but she turned from that, knowing the answer without asking the question. There could be nothing between them. And somehow that made it all the more important that she get out of here fast. "Let me go with you tomorrow, please. If we could ride straight to Luther, he'd protect us from the men who hunt me. We wouldn't have to sneak around."

"Too much hurt. You rest."

The light snuffed out. Sally barely controlled the urge to scream in frustration.

But whether because she was battered and healing took its toll or the high mountain air just agreed with her, Sally fell asleep.

Sally awoke to Wise Sister gone. It was the first night she'd slept through without a single nightmare, and Sally wondered if maybe, finally, she was getting well.

She dressed in her pretty doeskin and hobbled herself over to Logan's cabin. She came upon him standing near a ledge fifty feet in front of his cabin. From that ledge, the ground fell away, swooping to lower mountains, gentle swells, and jagged peaks.

They lived up where the eagle soared. Below the drop, the herd of elk stood in a circle watching a battle. The bull who led the group and the young upstart who challenged him. They'd played at this many times. Sally had seen it. But today seemed more serious. The two huge males snorted and charged, slammed their antlers together, fell back and charged again.

The steep drop reminded Sally of her fall. She hadn't had a nightmare last night. It might well be the first night she'd gotten through without one. But now, looking down, it was like she was plunging again. She had a moment of dizziness. She quickly backed away and sat on the chopping block. She saw his Stetson, pulling it on to block the view, and turned to watch Logan as a way of taking her mind off the memory of her haunting, plunging fall.

He stood, almost attacking his canvas with his knife. His strokes, wild, sweeping, almost violent, left trails of color behind that cried out with strength and vitality. The blue of the sky, the green of the grass, the gray of the rocks, all swirled into a blur around two bulls locked in mortal combat. Their massive antlers clashed, their heads down. Sally could hear the collisions, feel their anger and courage, smell their exertion.

It wasn't a proper painting, where the elk looked like real critters. It was a picture of motion and danger and power. Sally had seen a realistic sketch he'd made when the elk had battled another day. She didn't understand how he took that real world and turned it into feeling and motion and anger.

Sally thought he must be angry. But she watched him look from his canvas to the landscape sweeping away before him and the battling animals far below. Instead of anger she sensed power. Vitality. Strength. Passion.

It didn't sit well to think of him as strong. It wasn't a kind of strength she understood, and respecting something she didn't understand felt...dangerous. It was tied up with her sister Mandy marrying a man no one in the family respected. And Beth marrying a strange man that they all ended up loving, but who looked like a poor bet at first.

Thinking of the two times they'd kissed had awakened a feeling inside her that was as unfamiliar as it was alluring. Sally gritted her teeth. She wanted no part of a man who didn't feel like she did about the land and ranching. She wanted a man like her pa. Her second pa, Clay McClellen. Her ma had married a poor excuse for a man first time out, too.

Sally was determined that, when the day came for her to marry, which she didn't intend to do for a long time yet, she'd pick a sensible man who fit in her life. A man would make a partner for her pa at the McClellen Ranch. Or a ranch very close at hand.

She wanted no part of the nonsense that had afflicted her sisters and ma the first time, when they did their choosing. Sally intended to use her God-given common sense to pick a sensible kind of man, and she'd be happy from the first day.

Logan took one more slash with his paint knife and left a trail of blue on the canvas that exactly matched the blue of the sky in front of him. How did he do that? He had a flat piece of wood in his hand that looked like a dinner plate, streaked with several colors. He'd mix them together with his knife and somehow come up a perfect shade. That in itself was a strange gift.

Sally had helped her ma dye fabric, and she knew how tricky it was to make colors do exactly as she wished. How did he, with sure, racing motions, mix his colors to capture a shade so rare and glorious?

He glanced over. He held another paint knife in his teeth, this one coated with a vivid shade of green. A knife in his teeth, another in his hand, the paint board he'd called a palette in his grip. He had paint on his face and in his hair and on his shirt, and his eyes burned with fire that drew her like a moth.

It was to her shame that he drew her, a man who looked and acted like a complete lunatic.

He set the palette on a chair loaded with small pots of paint and removed the knife from his teeth, so he held one in each hand. He jabbed his blue knife at a second painting sitting beside the first. The one painted with his knives was wild, a confusing clash of color that almost vibrated with Logan's passion for art and the life and death battle of the elk. The other was of the area visible far below them. He'd painted, with complete realism, everything that swept away before them.

He had smeared green paint on his face from clutching the knife in his teeth. He didn't care one bit about being a mess. "I wish you could go down there with me and really be close to the land, hear it, smell it, touch it, taste it. I want all of that to come through in my painting."

"You want someone to be able to taste your painting?" Sally arched a brow.

A lighthearted laugh answered her skepticism. "No, I want someone to see my painting and *imagine* what it smells like and sounds like and tastes like." He wiped his hands on a paint-stained cloth.

"No one can do that. Painting is about seeing." Even as she said it, she glanced at his odd, unrealistic painting and knew she hadn't spoken the pure truth. Sally had witnessed this fight, and Logan had brought it to the canvas in a way that was more than seeing. Logan's work called to all her senses.

"I planned to be out there in nature, ready to catch the sunrise or the racing wind." He stabbed at the landscape and the humor faded from his expression, his eyes snapping with impatience.

Sally saw in them the same passion that showed in his painting. She knew just how frustrated he was. "You're not the only one who's under lock and key, you know. I can't go down there either. Wise Sister scolds. Tells me I'll end up dead."

Logan looked at Sally's crutches.

With two she got around really well. She could do everything, except of course for the one thing she wanted to do most. Escape.

"Too many bad men." Logan frowned down at the view. "Her exact words. I'm going to have to paint this from a distance instead of from down there close. What's the point of being in the Rockies if I'm locked away on this hilltop?"

"I thought you built here because you loved the view." Sally came closer to see the detail of his painting. He hadn't used his knives and a blob of paint with the landscape painting. He'd used the same style she'd seen on her portrait.

"I do love it." Logan wielded his knife at the awe-inspiring panorama. "But Babineau built here for me because his cabin was already here. I wanted to see the whole area, and this was a good central location to all sorts of natural beauty."

"And why did Babineau live up here to begin with?"

"Because it's off the park."

"What?" Sally squinted her eyes to focus on his nonsense.

"Wise Sister's husband has done a fair amount of trapping in Yellowstone over his lifetime, but that's not allowed anymore. And they made it illegal to hunt, too. They'd been in these parts for years so they didn't go far."

Sally couldn't imagine a land where hunting wasn't allowed. What were animals for except to eat and ride?

"The first time Babineau took me up here, the view almost stopped my heart it was so beautiful. After that, I wanted to see more. I'd paint. Babineau hunted. Wise Sister cooked and sewed and tended a garden. I'd go off for a few days and camp. It gets so cold up here that it can snow even in August."

Sally thought of August in Texas and tried to imagine snow. It had snowed during that rainy spell, so she knew it was true. Wise Sister always kept a fire going at night in their fireplace.

"Wise Sister knows this area even better than Babineau, so they were content to stay here. It's close to where she grew up. Babineau built me my own cabin with the huge windows. It wasn't done when I left the first winter, but Babineau had it finished in the spring."

Sally moved closer to Logan's more outlandish elk painting, strangely drawn to it. She thought it was a waste of his life, but she couldn't deny it was skillfully done. She studied it and was only distantly aware that Logan was watching her.

He made a sudden movement of his head that drew her attention. He shook himself as if he wanted to shed water then smiled. "I'll bring a chair out." Logan set his knives aside and hurried into the cabin and back out with a chair.

"Thank you."

"We can sit together and watch the beauty we can't touch." He set the chair down. "How are you feeling?"

"I'm fine." Sally gratefully sank into it, careful to disguise her aches.

"You're still in pain. I can see it in your eyes." Logan leaned close and studied her in the strange way he did that seemed to be looking at the parts of her, to draw them. It made her feel bad, but she wasn't sure why.

Sally glared at him.

His eyes refocused, obviously seeing all of her. "What?"

"You're staring."

Logan flinched. "I do that. Always in my head I'm imagining the picture I want to draw. I've been told by plenty of people that it's a very irritating habit."

"Can't you stop?"

"I don't want to. That's part of why I live out here, mostly alone."

"You live in a wilderness in the West because you have the manners of a pig?"

A smile broke through Logan's discomfort. "No. Well, yes, but not *only* for that reason. I don't want to stop. I want to be who I am. Who God made me to be. I stare. People don't like it. So I stay away from them as much as possible."

Sally was a little tired of Logan blaming everything on God. "It's clear as day that God gave you an ability to draw. Most folks

512

aren't born with such a talent, so it must be a special blessing. But don't tell me it's God's plan for you to be rude."

Logan's brow furrowed. "But it's all part of it. Part of the calling to art."

"No." Sally shook her head. "God sends each baby into the world with strengths—intelligence, a strong will, an easygoing nature, a sturdy back, quickness, or sharp eyes. You should see my sister Mandy shoot. It's a pure gift, no denying it. And Beth, her voice, the way she can whisper to a scared animal or comfort an injured child. I've tried to copy that when I needed to calm a horse. I do all right but it's nothing like what Beth can do. So I know God gives us gifts, but He just gives them to us. The raw material comes along with the baby. What a child grows into is all about his own choices in this world."

Sally thought of Wise Sister and what she'd said the night before about making a choice and living with it. Doing right. Doing one's best.

"Choices?" Logan shook his head.

"Yes, a child can follow the manners taught by her ma, or she can be rude. A little boy can take after his hard-workin' rancher pa, or he can chase after book learning, or he can be a no-account bum. And the choices can come from what their lives are like. How were they treated? Is a child the youngest of ten kids, pampered and babied and fussed over and never disciplined? Is she the oldest with heavy responsibilities resting on her shoulders that make her older than her years?"

Sally thought of Laurie. "My little sister, Laurie, is different from the rest of us. She's had from her earliest years a pa who loved her. Life hasn't been as hard for her as it was for the rest of us. She has no memory of life without a prosperous ranch and nice dresses. Mandy was fighting alongside Ma from the first day she was old enough to fetch and carry. Things got better, but Mandy's character had already been set. But no amount of training could explain my big sister's quickness with a Winchester.

That was a gift she was born with, but Mandy had honed it, too, as we all have."

"My father pushed me hard to be a doctor, and I still became a painter." Logan looked down at the sweeping land. "Look, the elk herd has wandered away. Both bulls will live to fight another day."

"If he'd been really harsh with you, really *forced* you on threat of starvation or a beating, you'd have bent to his will, I reckon. But if he'd done that, he'd have broken you. A parent needs to figure out how to train a child without twisting him. How to understand the nature of the child and respect that." Sally shrugged and looked down at her clothes. "Ma's always pushed me to dress more proper, but she hasn't *forced* me, not out on the range. She thinks I'm an odd one, I suppose, but figures I'm not hurtin' nothin'. Your pa was probably the same. Guiding you, pushing you, but smart enough to let you make your own choices when it really mattered."

"You think what I do matters?" Logan gestured at his paintings.

She looked up at Logan's art and slowly hoisted herself to her feet to really study the elk painting. "I—I don't understand a man passing his days on such a thing. But what you do, whatever is inside of you that comes out onto that canvas—"

She turned from the painting to Logan and their eyes met. "Yes." Somehow it was easy to say that. She held his gaze and felt something warm and beautiful, something already beginning to be born, come fully to life. "Yes, it matters."

"That means a lot to me." Logan's brown eyes flashed with gratitude and pleasure, but he didn't smile, almost as if his feeling went too deep for such a meager expression as a smile. "More than you could know." He reached out and rested one of his paint-stained hands on Sally's shoulder.

"I don't exactly understand what drives you, but I understand you have a gift and that it would be wrong to not use—"

Logan stopped the next word with his lips.

Sixteen

"Sidney, we have a problem." Mandy had waited, choosing her time wisely. Or as wisely as possible when dealing with her notoriously difficult-to-deal-with husband.

Sidney was fussing with his stupid account book. Counting his gold—on paper—like some kind of half-crazed miser. Mandy often saw him swallow as he added and subtracted figures, as if he had to fight drooling over his precious gold. "Not now." Impatiently, he swept one hand at her, dismissing her, his gold ring on his fat fingers flashing in her eyes.

Mandy knew better than to interrupt him at his book, but she also knew he went to bed directly after time spent savoring his wealth. And once on his way to sleep, he was useless. Odd how the man could sleep so well. She'd think he'd be a haunted man.

"Yes, now." She moved from her place at the sink, the evening meal all cleaned up. Facing him, only a few feet away, she plunked her fists on her hips. She'd gone over this a dozen times. How to approach him with this. She'd decided to, well, not lie. A Christian woman didn't tell lies. But to be wily. She couldn't remember a

Bible verse specifically forbidding that.

"Behold, I send you forth as sheep in the midst of wolves: be ye therefore wise as serpents, and harmless as doves."

There were a whole lot of different animals in that verse. Mandy picked her favorite, squared her shoulders, and set out to be a sneaky little snake. "Something happened today that has me worried, Sidney. Your man Cooter, he said something to me that gave me the impression that he might be looking for a way to take your gold away from you."

Sidney jerked forward and rose to his feet, instantly on alert.

"I think he might have been who I heard outside the cabin the other night. I think he's prowling around." To Mandy's way of thinking, none of this was a lie. She just focused on something far less important—the gold—rather than discussing how Cooter had treated her.

"He came down the hill this afternoon." Sidney's eyes narrowed. Her husband didn't have much common sense, but Sidney could always be counted upon to be overly suspicious when it came to his money. "Is that when he spoke to you? What did he say exactly?"

Mandy needed to tread carefully now. If she spoke of Cooter's bold behavior, would Sidney decide that her complaint was about that and not about money?

Cooter clearly thought of being rid of Sidney. He'd never molest her otherwise. And the wretched man must suspect how bad things were between her and Sidney, or he'd have never treated her that way. Which meant Sidney was in danger from a man he paid for protection.

"It wasn't so much what he said. I felt like—well, he ducked out of my sight in a strange way. You know I'm good at hunting. A man doesn't sneak around without my knowing it. But Cooter did. I think, well, he went into the bunkhouse then came up behind me. He'd have had to slip away, down the back side of the bunkhouse, circle the house. I think he was inside."

"Did you lock the door?" Sidney rubbed his chin thoughtfully, his eyes narrowed and blazing, looking through her, considering all the possibilities.

"No, not just to step outside in the yard."

"You should always lock it."

This wasn't an argument she wanted to have. Sidney could always find a way to blame her for everything. "I will from now on. How brazen does a man have to be to sneak into the house when I'm just a few feet away? He must be planning something. Or maybe he's searching for the address of your Denver bank. Could he forge a paper sending for money?"

"Why now? He's been with me a long time."

Mandy knew why now but she'd never dare say it aloud. Luther and Buff were gone. As simple as that. They'd protected her. If only they'd come back.

"What are we going to do?" Mandy ignored Sidney's question and crossed her arms, thinking, knowing it might come down to shooting trouble, hating that danger could come close to her children. She felt a chill calming her as she considered all that could happen.

"I'll have to fire him."

Mandy doubted Cord Cooter would go quietly. "Easy to say. But if he's of a mind to act with violence, that might force his hand."

Sidney continued stroking his chin for long moments.

Mandy didn't offer to back Sidney if it came to shooting trouble. She'd do it when the time came, but it would upset him to speak of it now.

"I'll go to town."

"What?" Mandy felt as if the man spoke a foreign language suddenly. What did going to town have to do with—

"I'll go to town and take Cooter and Platte with me. Once I'm in town, I'll quietly seek out another assistant and hire him. Then, with a new man backing me, I'll fire Cooter. That will leave

Cooter miles from the cabin. If I fired him here he might just ride away, only to circle back."

"He can ride out here from town just as well." And he'd have time to find friends and pick his moment and sneak up on their flank. What was needed was a strong man who could hold what was his, protect his home and family with his will and his fists and his gun if need be. Sidney had none of that, not even the will.

"No, *not* just as well. I'll make it clear that the money is untouchable."

But Mandy wasn't so untouchable. And while she thought Cooter's true aim was the money, he made his unholy interest in her terrifyingly clear. "I'm too close to birthing this baby, Sidney. I don't want to be left here alone. You are always gone most of a week when you go to town."

"I'll make a fast trip. I can do it in five days."

Luther and Buff made it in two all the time, three if things went wrong. It was a brutal ride to make in a day, early mornings, late nights, hunting up the storekeeper to open the store long after closing time so Luther could head out early the next day with loaded pack horses. Sidney liked the carriage and there was no way to make the trip fast with that. Even if he could, Sidney wasn't one to push himself.

"That might not be fast enough. I don't want to be alone here when the baby comes."

"I've never had much to do with birthing the babies, Mandy. I don't even need to be here." Sidney's hands clutched together as if the very thought upset him.

"But I had a midwife out from Helena the last two times. We lived close enough."

"But you didn't need them. It all went fine. No reason to believe it won't go the same this time. And anyway, I'll be back. And"—Sidney's eyes lit up—"while I'm in town I'll see about bringing a midwife back with me. . .or the doctor."

"A doctor can't ride all the way out here. Why are we living so far from town anyway?"

"No, you're right. A doctor probably can't be away from his office that long. But I'll ask around. I'll see if any woman is willing. Maybe someone will need work and be willing to come up here and help you until your sister shows up. You'd like to have a woman about when your time came, wouldn't you?"

Mandy would like that very, very much. And it really was probably still two weeks away or more, but babies had their own timing. It didn't matter anyway. She looked at Sidney's expression and knew he was going. At least he'd be taking Cooter away. "Yes, I'd like that. But I want you to make a fast trip of it, too. I don't like being here alone with the workmen."

Sidney nodded. "No, it's not proper for you to be here, though they seem like decent men mostly. And they'll stay to themselves and keep pressing forward with the house, so you'll hardly see them."

"Is there a man among them who can cook? I may not be able to keep up with feeding them all and caring for the girls." And then, though it pinched, she told him a truth that surprised her. "It's all harder when you're gone."

She wasn't even sure if it was true, because usually when Sidney was gone, Luther and Buff were here, and she'd honestly not noticed her husband's absence much. But now, with her old friends away and Sidney leaving, she felt more alone than she ever had in her life.

"I'll tell them they'll need to make their own meals. It will slow the work down, but it can't be helped."

Silence fell between them, Sidney plotting and planning to be rid of Cooter.

Mandy wanted that badly enough to let her husband go. If she wanted to send him on his way with a kick to his backside, that didn't change that it was worth his leaving to be rid of that dreadful bodyguard.

"You'll be safe here, honey. The men seem decent." Sidney

came and rested his hand on her shoulder.

As if Sidney was any judge. He'd hired Cooter after all. "Yes, I'll be safe. But go right away, tomorrow, so you can get back soon."

He patted her like she was a well-behaved dog.

She was tempted to be less well-behaved and growl, then bite him on the arm.

"How long are we going to skulk around?" Buff tossed the dregs of his coffee on the fire.

"It's gnawing on me, too." Luther looked up from the campfire they'd built to boil up some coffee for their noon meal. The blaze was small so the men they followed wouldn't see it. "If we ride up on 'em, we need to be prepared for shooting trouble, or we'd need to haul them all the way to the nearest town. That's days away, and once we got there, they'd probably be released. We've got no proof they attacked Colonel McGarritt's party."

"It's them." Buff took a long drink of his blazing hot coffee. "As sure as if I'd seen it with my own eyes."

Luther stared at his coffee, tempted, mighty tempted, to find out what those men knew with his fists and his gun. Instead, here they sat drinking coffee while they kept a lookout on those outlaws, searching for any evidence of where Sally had gotten to.

They'd been slipping along in the wake of the men because they were sure these two hunted Sally. They'd fan out searching for markers from whoever was leaving them, hoping to find a trail that would lead to Sally. It was an itch under Luther's skin to worry about his girl and not do something more.

But they hadn't found a bit of evidence telling them where Sally might be hiding.

"I'm thinkin' it's a woman leavin' sign." Luther settled back against a rock wall that faced their fire.

It was a warm day so they didn't need the heat once the coffee had boiled and the beans warmed, but it gave comfort, and in this rocky area, surrounded by towering pines with their needles high overhead to diffuse the smoke, the fire posed no risk. They'd made note of where the two hombres they tailed had set up to cook a meal. Then when it was obvious the two were settling in for a long spell, they'd dropped back and built a fire.

"Yep." Buff poured himself more coffee and leaned back against the trunk of a tall, narrow lodgepole pine. "Woman sure as day. And she knows we're here now, and she knows those other coyotes are here, too. She's protecting Sally, and she's let us know Sally's fine until we can get to her."

"Cautious woman," Luther added. "She knows she could lead trouble to Sally, and she'd rather lead us in circles than endanger our girl. A good woman. Knows the woods, too. Likely Shoshone."

"I knew a fine Shoshone woman once. Real fine." Buff stared into his cup.

Luther waited.

Buff didn't go on.

"Don't rightly know if I like the idea of a woman protecting Sally." Luther tossed his coffee away. "I'd feel a lot better knowing a man was close."

Seventeen

Logan pulled Sally close.

He tilted his head to kiss her better. His arms slid around her waist. He felt half mad with the pleasure of her saying she recognized his gift and knew he needed to use it.

As if he held the most precious thing in all God's creation in his arms, he deepened the kiss, cherishing the feel of her in his arms.

She jerked her head back, but that only made the angle better when he sealed her lips with his own. And she didn't pull back again. Instead her arms wound around his neck and he felt one of her crutches whack him in the shoulder as it fell.

It didn't distract him one whit.

A distant, barely functioning part of his brain whispered that he was better off alone. He was a self-centered man obsessed with his art. He ignored the whisper and pulled Sally closer.

"Trouble comes!" Wise Sister shouted from the woods. "We go!"

Sally jerked out of Logan's arms so fast he almost fell forward and knocked the poor broken-legged woman over. Sally was too quick for him, though. Dodging his clumsiness, she slung the rifle she always kept at hand over her neck, grabbed her crutches, whirled, and headed—Logan couldn't figure out where.

Away from Wise Sister. Was Sally planning to run? She couldn't last in the mountains, which were impassable to the west and north. Wise Sister was coming from the southeast.

While Logan tried to clear his head, Sally was already on the way to—he figured it out. The corral. Wise Sister said, "We go." So Sally was getting the horses.

She might be faster to react, but he could still outrun her, thanks to her broken leg. He caught up and passed her. He had the first horse caught and bridled before she got there. She whipped a saddle onto the horse, with her crutches firmly at hand.

Logan caught a second horse just as Wise Sister appeared from the woods running. He'd never seen her run before.

Sally glanced up, noticed, exchanged a look of alarm with Logan, and finished tightening the cinch then took over bridling the second horse.

Logan grabbed a third. "Just three or do we take all five? Will we need a pack animal?"

Sally shook her head. "I don't think we're gonna do much packing."

"What's going on?" Logan used every bit of skill he'd learned in the West to cut down the time.

"I don't know, but if Wise Sister says we need to ride, I'm going to ride first and ask questions later." The rapid slap of leather as she tightened another saddle underlined the fear Logan knew he'd felt when Wise Sister, so soft spoken, so slow moving, yelled and ran.

Wise Sister ducked into her cabin as Sally and Logan finished with the horses. She emerged with a quiver full of arrows and a gun belt around her plump waist. It was Babineau's, but he'd never seen her with it. She moved so fast she didn't pause for even a moment to close her door.

Logan took one second to realize that while he led the third horse up to where Sally stood with the saddles, which lay hooked over the fence.

To leave a door open and ride away was to turn your home over. Bears would move in and eat what was there within hours. They'd tear the building apart from the inside out within days. Wise Sister was saying they were never coming back. Or there wasn't time to worry about whether they did. "Coyotes come." She rushed toward them carrying a heavily loaded cloth bag in one hand.

Logan grabbed the two prepared horses and led them from the corral. He went back to Sally. "Let me help you." Their eyes met. This young lady, who had more skill on a horse—or so Logan suspected—than most cowboys, didn't like needing help. But she had a broken leg and this moment was beyond pride. He grabbed her around the waist, hating the thought of her bruised ribs, and tossed her up with no ceremony. Then he rushed to the other horses and led one to Wise Sister's side. He went to boost Wise Sister, but she vaulted into the saddle with less trouble than a bird might have. Logan was mounted seconds later.

"That way." Wise Sister pointed to the most forbidding stretch of mountains Logan had ever seen.

A shiver went through his gut as he looked at those soaring, white-capped peaks and the dense woods on ground so broken he couldn't imaging walking through it, let alone riding a horse. He'd never even hiked that direction.

He jerked his head at Sally to go ahead. Rebellion flickered across her face, and he knew she wanted to bring up the rear. He thought of her exposed back with gunfire possibly coming after her. "Go. Now!"

She tugged on her reins and followed Wise Sister. Logan followed, and before they'd left the grounds around the cabin, Wise Sister had them moving into that forbidding wilderness at a full gallop.

They passed into a thicket of trees with a trail Logan couldn't see even as he rode on it, and then Wise Sister pulled her horse to a stop and dismounted. Sally followed, so Logan did the same, not sure what their next move was.

Slipping silently up to the thicket, Wise Sister dropped to her knees. Logan knelt beside her on her right and Sally was on his right.

We're like wild game, hiding in the weeds from hunters.

He heard Sally whisper, "God, have mercy."

Logan leaned forward as two men emerged into the clearing around the cabins, riding hard. Wise Sister made a guttural noise of contempt. Sally shifted on her knees and swung her rifle off her back.

Logan had known her long enough to fight back the impulse to block the gun as she pointed it. Sally was tough, but she wouldn't shoot those men from cover, even if they were, as Logan suspected, the men who had killed her friends.

The men—one skinny with a potbelly and a twitchy manner that reminded Logan of a ferret, and the other a stocky man with massive shoulders and arms, wearing a coonskin cap, carrying a rifle on his saddle, and wearing two pistols and two ammunition belts slung bandolier style across his chest—pulled their horses to a stop in front of his painting.

Only then did Logan realize what an unexpected sight it must be for these two, who looked trail-wise and rugged and dangerous, to come upon two paintings, standing side-by-side on an easel, in the middle of nowhere. Logan had a sudden, world-tilting vision of just how odd he was with the life he led.

The broad-chested man swung to the ground and walked up to the painting Logan had just created this morning—the elk fighting, the swirl of color, his knife and his new love for the strange Impressionist style he'd learned over the winter. The man pulled his pistol and aimed it at the picture.

"No!" Logan lurched up.

They'd finally found what they were looking for and now no one was around.

Fergus itched to hurt someone. His eyes went to the freakish picture standing out here in the middle of nowhere. He was drawn to it just because he couldn't make out nothin' in it but two elk fighting. It was slopped on the paper like a baby had smeared paint on the wall. For some reason, he could feel the killing fury of the elk and it became his own.

Pulling his Colt six-shooter out, he emptied his gun into the stupid picture.

Gunfire brought Luther's head up. He sprang to his feet from where he crouched beside the tracks they'd found this morning. He was running for his horse before the first volley died away.

Buff swung up on horseback with an agility that defied his sixty hard years. They were galloping flat out before the gunfire died away.

"Straight that way." Buff guided his horse toward what looked like a jumble of rocks, spilled down from an endless, broken mountain. Trees grew out from what looked like impassable stone walls.

They'd ridden by this area before, but even with careful studying Luther had never seriously considered there was a way up the mountain here. This morning it was simple because the men they trailed had left sign easy enough to follow. Their horses picked their way and it was a treacherous ride, but the horses moved on, obviously following a clear route. About halfway up the steep, stony cut, Luther smelled smoke. They could go no faster. Panic rode Luther's shoulders as he thought of those bullets cutting into his sweet Sally.

"Luth!" Buff was coming behind Luther.

The hissed shout pulled Luther's attention from his fretting. He looked back at Buff, who pointed. One of those signs they'd been finding. A stack of stones whose main meaning was simply that they'd been stacked in a deliberate way. The Shoshone woman had left it for them, hoping they'd come up and see it but not directing them because she'd known that to direct Luther and Buff up this trail was to direct the men hunting Sally.

But those men had beaten them to the trail, and now Sally might be dead.

A hand slapped over Logan's mouth before the word had a chance to gain volume. Someone landed hard on him, carrying him backward onto the dank forest floor.

Gunfire rolled on up by the cabin. He was so desperate to stop the men from destroying his work, Logan wasn't fully aware of just what was going on for a few seconds.

"Shut up and lay still!" The words hissed at him like a Rocky Mountain rattler he'd sketched last August.

He focused and realized Sally was lying flat on top of him. Her hand was flat on his mouth, all her weight pinning him to the ground. Except her weight was negligible. That's when he realized Wise Sister was sitting on his legs and glaring at him around Sally's shoulder.

He quit fighting. The gunfire ended.

Sally leaned close. "Do I have to tie you up? Because I will."

"What was that?" Fergus turned to the far side of this little level spot, the only flat place for miles in a world that went up, down, and sidewise.

Tulsa looked at the place Fergus was staring at. They hadn't stayed alive in the wild all these years without trusting their eyes and ears and noses.

Nothing moved. No further sound.

"See if you can find anything in the small cabin, money or an idea who these people are." Fergus pointed to a small strip of leather lying on the ground in front of the bigger cabin. "Looks like Shoshone beadwork on that strap."

"Must be who took that cowpoke away from the cliff that first day." Tulsa strode toward the smaller cabin. "Brung him all the way back up in here. Makes no sense."

The whole thing made no sense and it grated on Fergus bad. They'd spent a long time in this country, which seemed bent on killin' anyone who passed through. And all over a witness to murder who should'a died that first day. Gut shot and the cowpoke rode away.

It made Fergus want to unload his gun into something else. "Get whatever's worth gettin' out of that cabin then burn it."

"Sorry." Logan's word was muted.

Sally got the idea, but she still didn't trust him, since he'd just proved himself to be a lunatic. She lifted her hand an inch.

When he remained silent, she caught a handful of hair and yanked it until his neck arched back. "Use your head." She did her best to burn him to death with her eyes. "You need to save yourself, so if they wreck your pictures you can paint more of them."

Logan nodded again.

It went against the grain to stop hurting the lunkhead, but Sally released his hair. Suddenly she became aware of the strength and weight and vitality of him and climbed off quickly, none too careful where she whacked him with the ten pounds of plaster on her leg.

Wise Sister eased to his other side with a glowering look of warning.

"We stay hidden." Sally reached down, grabbed Logan by the

shirt front, and nearly lifted him back to his knees.

"Yes, I'm sorry." He acted contrite, but she still didn't trust him. The man didn't seem to have a lick of common sense.

"If you go running out there, I'm going to have to open fire on those men. I've never killed anyone in my life. I don't want to start now." Though she spoke at a whisper, considering murderers were up the hill a few yards, she saw the impact. Good. It was almost as good as if she'd hit him with her fists.

Logan might cause her to kill and maybe die. For him. Because of him. To save him.

She saw him thinking it through and knew when he was done because shame washed over his face. Nodding, he leaned forward, hesitated, then looked.

The skinny man came out of the cabin with the painting of Sally in his hands. She felt tainted, as if the filthy man was touching her rather than a portrait.

Sally reached over and clamped one hand on Logan's arm. His muscled forearm clenched but he didn't shake her off.

The two men looked at the picture and laughed in a way that made Sally's stomach lurch. Skinny held the portrait, about two-by-two feet in size, in both hands, staring at it. Then he tromped on the elk painting, laying shot to pieces, flat on the ground, and heaved the portrait over the side of the cliff.

Logan's hand rested on top of Sally's but he didn't make a sound.

Skinny came back to the elks, talking as he moved. Sally heard the low rumble of their voices but couldn't make out any words. Skinny laughed, raised a boot, and kicked the bullet-riddled elk painting over the cliff, too.

The bigger man went into Logan's cabin. Sally thought of that huge painting in there, *Blazing Land*. He loved that picture so much Sally's grip on his arm tightened, just in case he lost control. Maybe they'd had their fun and they'd ride on.

She heard the first crackle of fire. A puff of smoke came

out of Logan's cabin.

Wise Sister's hand slapped on Logan's mouth. Sally looked but saw he had control of himself now. He shook his head and gave Wise Sister an impatient look. She arched a brow doubtfully but lifted her hand.

"All I've got to do," Logan whispered, "is picture Sally and you bleeding to death. That's enough to keep me here."

Wise Sister nodded, her stoic expression showing a hint of approval. If Wise Sister was satisfied, that went a long way toward reassuring Sally.

Grimly squaring his shoulders, Logan turned back to face the destruction. All his work, all his paints, all his canvas and pencils and sketchbooks. The summer was over for him. He'd go home empty-handed.

A soft sound drew her attention to Wise Sister, watching the men do their damage. The skinny man walked into Wise Sister's cabin. Unlike Logan, who had a home and family back East and money in the bank, that cabin contained Wise Sister's whole world. She had a lot more to lose than Logan did. Moments later Skinny emerged, carrying a cloth bag loaded down. Smoke began billowing out behind him.

All of Wise Sister's precious things. All her art made with six children in mind.

"Smoke signals," Sally whispered. "It'll bring Luther."

Logan turned to her. "So, I lose a summer's work. Wise Sister loses *everything*, but you get rescued. You're a lucky woman, Sally McClellen."

"I'm sorry. I wasn't thinking about my friends rescuing me. I was thinking of Luther and Buff fighting at our side. They're tough men. They'll help us. If these are the men who killed the colonel, then they're evil. We'll be a lot safer once Luther and Buff are here."

A shout from Skinny drew their attention. He pointed at the

ground and his finger swept along a line that led straight to where they crouched in the undergrowth.

"He's found our trail." Sally grabbed for her rifle.

Eighteen

Luther didn't stop, nor even slow. The climb was steep and relentless. Their horses' hooves rang hollow on small stones that rolled and slipped.

Luther had lived in the mountains for years back when he'd been a trapper and a good friend of Clay McClellen's father. He'd watched Clay grow up and had a hand in teaching him how to live with the land. He'd felt like an uncle, and after Clay's pa had died, Luther had left the mountains to live in Texas near Clay and his family. He'd taken on the role of grandfather to his girls and now a great-grandpa to Mandy's young'uns. Though they were not blood relations, he was family and he'd fight for his family to the end.

The smell of smoke grew stronger as they neared the top of this precipitous climb. When they were within a few steps of the top, gunshots rang out again. It took every ounce of Luther's considerable self-control not to spur his mount. It would only abuse his horse because they were going as fast as they could.

They topped the cliff. Luther saw smoke and flames billowing up from two cabins. Nothing else moved. He slapped his horse hard on the rump and bent low over the saddle, mindful of that gunfire he'd heard. The ground was better here, a plateau that appeared to plunge down another mountain on the far side of the cabin. They were in front of the cabin in minutes. He threw himself off the horse, ground-hitching it as it shied back from the flames. An inferno ate at the log structure. Luther saw Buff rushing toward the smaller of the two cabins.

Could Sally be inside? Could she have been shot and left to burn? Could she, if she was in there, possibly be alive?

Bending low, Luther charged the door, ducking through the completely consumed frame.

Sally centered her rifle on her back then grabbed her crutches. She rushed toward her tethered horse. She felt strong hands on her waist as Logan hoisted her up on the horse before she could scramble up there herself. She'd've managed, but he sped things up some.

She jammed her crutches over the pommel of the saddle as Wise Sister took the lead. Sally kicked her horse into motion. Wise Sister headed down the wash of a dry spring.

Logan swung up on horseback just as a shot cracked the air. Wise Sister spurred her roan gelding and Sally moved fast behind her, glancing back to see Logan kick his horse. Over the thunder of their hoofbeats, Sally heard a bullet slam into the trunk of a tree only a few feet from them. Another bullet followed, then a third.

Sally leaned low on her horse until she almost hugged the back of her black mustang. She glanced back and saw Logan imitate her actions just as a bullet whined over his head. It passed over him and slammed into a tree, in such a perfect line it would have killed him if he'd been sitting upright.

The men must be able to see movement in the trees, though

the forest was heavy. A few heart-pounding seconds followed as bullets rained on them. Sally's mustang moved deeper into the woods, the trail dropping sharply. The gunfire stopped, but galloping hooves sounded from behind.

Wise Sister raised her hand. At first Sally thought Wise Sister was stopping. Did she mean to stand and fight? Sally couldn't imagine pulling the trigger at another human being, killing a man. Then she imagined that bullet hitting Logan and thought maybe she could do it. She put her hand back to check, and of course her rifle was there, firmly in place across her shoulders as always.

Instead of turning to fight, Wise Sister slowed to a fast walk. Still, they continued at a reckless pace. This trail could trip a horse and break a rider's neck.

Sally stayed low, the trail nothing but the path of a dry waterway. Trees stretched their limbs out. Overhead were the branches of older lodgepole pines. Younger trees were thick all through the forest and they slapped at the horses. Sally looked behind her and saw Logan straighten for a second, take a swat from the needled branches, and then bend low again. He was trainable at least.

The horses seemed to understand what those bullets meant and kept rushing. Sally looked alongside her mare's neck to see where Wise Sister was going. She led them with the precision of a forest creature. The slope was downward, long and treacherous, and the dry spring bed was uneven and full of rocks.

They rode on, the silence broken by the harsh breathing of terrified horses and the racket of hooves on the rocky ground. Long minutes passed and they kept slowing. Sally could only follow Wise Sister and match her speed.

As they reached the bottom of the slope, Wise Sister veered off onto a patch of scattered rock. They now rode almost straight north along the side of the slope. They moved on until the rocks underfoot became bigger and impossible to traverse.

Wise Sister turned again, returning to a more westward path.

They reached a solid stone ledge. A sheer cliff rose on their right, solid, impenetrable woodlands on their left. Sally knew this was no piece of luck. Wise Sister was very carefully choosing her way.

Her already huge respect for her Shoshone friend bloomed even bigger. Wise Sister had known exactly where they were going. She'd known this land long before anyone had had a thought of closing Yellowstone to private ownership or opening up Montana for settlement. Either that or she'd been practicing, preparing for trouble. Smart lady.

They approached a massive, sheer stone wall straight ahead, and Sally pulled up when Wise Sister did, waiting for the next move, loving the cunning old woman.

Logan had expected better of Wise Sister. She'd led them to a dead end, with murderers on their trail.

Wise Sister raised her hand again. Sally stopped and Logan followed suit. The Shoshone woman swung down off her horse with such agility, Logan's jaw went slack. She rarely sat a horse, or rather he'd never noticed.

It occurred to Logan that for a man obsessed with the world around him, he wasn't very observant, at least not when it came to people. He knew more about the habits of the bull elk that lived near his cabin than he did about his housekeeper.

Coming up beside Sally, Wise Sister spoke in a quiet voice. Logan had to lean forward in time to hear her say, "That trail." She pointed to what looked like an impassable wall of trees downhill of the rock. "I go." Wise Sister looked in the direction they'd come. "We lose them at the dry spring. Your people will come, Sally girl. They follow the coyotes, and the coyotes will go on downhill. I get your friends."

"If the coyotes don't find us first." Sally looked back the way they'd come, searching the trail as if, by staring hard enough, she could see all the way to those men and fight them.

"I'll go." Logan knew out of three people, one elderly, one wearing a cast, and one able-bodied man, He was least equipped for trouble. But it grated not to protect his women.

Sally and Wise Sister looked away from their back trail to him, as if they'd forgotten he was even along. They wore matching expressions that clearly suppressed smiles. It ripped at his pride.

"You stay, protect Sally girl." Wise Sister jerked a thumb at the wall of trees. She returned to her horse, caught its reins, and walked past both of them so swiftly Logan didn't get a chance to protest again.

Sally headed straight for that wall. Logan opened his mouth to ask how in the world they'd pass through that, when Sally turned her horse to the left and vanished.

Logan quickly nudged his horse forward, hoping the animal could do the same magic trick the other horse did. He glanced back at Wise Sister. She'd vanished, too. For a few seconds, Logan had a wild wash of fear to be so completely alone in these woods and mountains. He'd haunted them for three years now, craved being alone in them. But he'd never faced danger.

He felt such contempt for himself at that moment it nearly choked him, to be protected by two women this way. Then his buckskin, far wiser then he on the trail—and why should his horse be different than everyone else?—turned onto an invisible trail between the rock and the closest tree. Because the tree was a bit closer to Logan than the massive stone, it looked like they butted up against each other, but there were in fact several feet between them and a faint trail that his horse moved along easily.

Logan heard Sally's horse snort ahead, but he couldn't see her in the dense undergrowth. To find Sally, he asked, "How did she find this?"

Sally's voice came from only feet away. "Scouting around you find these things."

Logan's horse turned at a corner that twisted the trail back on itself so sharply he realized he'd been side by side with Sally even though he couldn't see a sign of her.

"She was probably tracking a deer and saw it go down this way."

They were soon on the other side of that massive stone and once again moving along on a solid rock ledge.

"How far do we go?" Logan asked. He had a feeling he should know.

"Until we find a likely place."

"A likely place for what?"

"To hole up." Sally looked over her shoulder for too long.

Logan wanted to paint her smiling, daydreaming, working. He'd wanted to capture every one of the open expressions that passed so freely across her face. He'd actually felt hungry to explore every aspect of her beautiful face. But this expression. . .

"We need a good field of fire."

. . .made his stomach hurt.

"I'll hunt for shelter and—more important—cover."

It made him sick to think of putting this on canvas. He never wanted to see it again. "Cover from those men shooting at us?" He forced himself to say it aloud.

"That's right, Logan." She turned away from him. "We're looking for a likely place to kill." Nudging her horse forward, she added, "Or die."

Luther felt the flames cutting at him, his skin seared as he passed through the licking, consuming blaze. Once in, nearly blinded by the smoke, he took a desperate look around, rushing farther in to make sure no one lay unconscious in the corner, bleeding from bullet wounds.

No one. He headed out and saw a picture of Sally, drawn in pencil, lying on the floor near his feet. He grabbed at the drawings and felt a stack of things under it. He took them all as he staggered out of the choking blaze to drag fresh air into his lungs.

He looked around as he struggled to breathe and saw Buff abandoning the other cabin with something good-sized in his hand.

"No one in there." Buff had a picture, too. This one not a sketch but a painting.

"She was here." Luther lifted his picture as he and Buff moved away from the smothering fire. They saw the corral with two horses fidgeting and snorting because of the commotion.

"They either took her or she ran." Buff began studying the ground. It was the work of minutes to pick up the trail, grab their horses, and set off for the far side of this small flatland.

As they rode, Luther looked down at the picture of his Sally in his hand. She looked so much like Mandy, but she was completely herself. The toughest little wrangler in Texas, to Luther's way of thinking.

Buff held up what he'd brought.

Luther expected to see another picture of Sally. Instead he saw an old woman, dressed in a Shoshone doeskin dress, standing beside— "That's Pierre Babineau." Luther remembered the tough old codger well. He'd been haunting these mountains for years.

"And Wise Sister." Buff lifted the picture for just a second and looked at it. "She's gotten old. Reckon I have, too." He went back to his tracking.

"Never knew her." Luther saw where the trail dipped into the woods. Savvy spot to pick, with a dry spring eating a pathway, rough but passable, into that tangled forest.

"Babineau was a wandering man." Buff looked again at the picture. "Wise Sister stayed to home. I was in these parts before. Years ago. Did some trapping and mining on the Yellowstone River. I knew Wise Sister well, even before she married Babineau. If Babineau and Wise Sister have our Sally, then our girl's in good hands."

Luther's chest expanded with the most hope he'd felt since

they'd found that first sign and knew Sally was alive. "Is she the one who drew these pictures?"

Buff shrugged. "Never heard of her doin' no drawing. S'pose it's possible. Shore cain't be Babineau. That man made a mark instead of signing his name. He drew me a map once to where he'd found good trapping, and I could barely make hide nor hair of it. He had no interest in anything that had him sitting around."

"Look at this trail. Three rode away first, then two came after. The ones we've been trailing. Three. She's with Babineau and Wise Sister."

"Babineau was almighty savvy in the woods. But it was Wise Sister leaving markers for us. That don't make sense. Pierre wasn't a man to stay to home while his woman did the tracking."

"Maybe he's stoved up these days." Luther smoothed his heavy beard and thought about the harsh winters he'd lived through since following after Mandy. It suited him, these mountains did. He felt like he'd come home. But it was a rugged life, took its toll. "Hard, cold mountains might have gotten to his joints by now."

"Whatever's going on with Sally, those outlaws are dogging hard on her heels." Buff exchanged a grim look with Luther.

"We're close. We're almost there." Luther went down the trail as quickly as he dared, only to glance back and see Buff was off his horse. Luther pulled up. "What are you doing?"

Buff tucked the picture carefully into his saddle bag. It stuck out some, but he managed to fit it in. "I can't toss this away. If this is Wise Sister's, she can come fetch later."

Luther arched a brow as Buff took a long, close look at that painting. There was something in Buff's expression that Luther had never seen before. With a shrug, he said, "Stick these under that tree."

Buff saw them and mounted up. They moved on down the trail, mindful of those men who had gone this way only moments ago. Men who had killed before.

That oughta be a lot more interesting to Buff than a painting of an old friend.

539

Nineteen

Sally pulled her horse to a stop so hard the animal fought the bit and reared. It backed away from the ledge while Sally's heart threatened to pound out of her chest. Her horse stumbled into the one behind it.

Then Logan was beside her. Not because he'd ridden up, but because she'd backed into him. Her horse had stumbled into Logan's then kept backing thanks to her iron-hard grip on the reins.

The trail wasn't wide enough for both of them. The mountain rose up steep on her right and rubbed hard against the cast on her leg. Then on the left the whole world slid away into a steep woodland. But somehow she managed to squeeze in beside Logan without shoving him off the trail on the downhill side.

Logan grabbed her horse's bridle as it came even with his hand. He stopped her or she might have backed all the way to Texas. "What is it?"

She realized what she was doing and eased up on her poor horse. Though her grip on the reins lessened, fear didn't lessen its grip on her. Her vision blurred and all she could see were trees rushing toward her as she fell and fell and fell. "We need to go back." She tore a hand from the reins to point back the way they'd come. "We must have. . .have. . .m–missed—"

"You said it was this way. You said Wise Sister gave you clear directions." Logan was watching her so intently she could hang on to that look, and some of the panic left her.

Then she looked at the trail ahead and saw rushing trees as she fell, then jerked her head around to look at Logan again. "We—we can't—the trail isn't—" Sally couldn't finish a sentence.

That searching look in Logan's eyes shifted from her to the trail. The awful trail Wise Sister intended them to take to reach safety. Logan tugged on the reins and pulled them free of her hand, as if he was afraid she'd turn and run if he let go of her horse. He began riding forward, leading her black mustang as if he meant to go straight over that cliff.

"No!" Sally's shout was more like a scream. Humiliating. Girly. Pa would be so ashamed. He might quit loving her. No man would love her if she acted like a weakling.

Logan stopped and twisted in his saddle. "I'm not going down the trail. I just want to see it."

But did he mean it? Or was he lying to make her face this stupid fear? She'd scrambled all over the steep, broken land back in Texas. There were no mountains like these, but it was plenty steep and plenty rugged. She'd never been afraid of a tough trail or a steep descent until—

"Is this because of the fall you took?" Logan turned his horse on the tight mountain path and rode up to her so he was only inches away.

Swallowing, nearly unable to force the words past her throat, she said, "I—I don't know. Maybe. I didn't know. I've never—I— I'm just being—a girl. I'm sorry." Sally tried to force her shoulders to square, but it was as if a thousand-pound weight of fear held them slumped. She swallowed again. "I—I can do it." She looked from the ledge to Logan and back to the ledge.

"Sally." His voice was hard. Commanding. Not at all the easygoing tone he usually took. She had so neatly concluded he was a weak, no-account kind of man. He didn't even mind a female crying. What kind of a man put up with that? But this wasn't the voice of a weak man.

"I'm not weak." Tearing her gaze from that drop, she faced him and knew she was lying.

"Of course you're not. You're the strongest woman I've ever known." Logan held on tight to her reins, belying his words.

"I can handle it." She could *not* go over that ledge. A scream built in her chest and began forcing its way out of her throat. Tears burned her eyes and twisted her stomach with the sickening admission of being a weakling, a female.

As if he knew she was on the ragged edge of control, Logan reached out and plucked her off her horse. He was so strong he lifted even the heavy cast so it easily cleared the saddle. He wasn't weak. Not at all. Not like her. Not about this.

He slid himself back on his horse, behind the cantle, and set Sally sideways on the saddle, still warm from his occupying it. This close, with one arm around her back against her pretty doeskin dress, holding his reins and hers, she felt some of his strength seep into her.

Shameful to need strength from another. She needed her own. Her pa loved her best when she was tough and didn't cry and did a man's work.

The need to scream fought to get free. Compulsively, her eyes went back to that awful, treacherous trail. "On—on a good mountain-raised horse we–we'll be fine." Her throat went bone-dry.

He caught her chin and tugged her face around so their eyes met. "You went through something no human being should ever face, Sally. Falling like that, somehow surviving. You're as strong and courageous as anyone I've ever known."

Sally couldn't pretend it was the truth. "I'm shaming myself. I've always pretended to be strong, but it was always a lie. I cry sometimes. When I'm alone. And I love pretty, girly things—ribbons and lace and curls. I'm a coward." Panic had jarred loose her deepest secrets. Next she'd admit she got tired of riding the range and trying to outshoot the other cowpokes.

"No, you're not."

"I can do it." She couldn't imagine how. She'd faint or fall off her horse. She'd start screaming and crying and not be able to stop.

"We'll go back. We don't even know if those men found our trail. There's a very good chance they didn't. We'll be careful, go the way Wise Sister did, go past my cabin and ride out that way."

"Which might take us right into the teeth of those back-shooting coyotes. If they'd—if they'd face us, I could handle that." Sally realized then her fear went deeper than falling. Deeper than admitting to tears and softness. It turned her pure yellow to think of killing a man. She remembered firing, firing, unloading her gun, reloading, spinning it to cock it as her mother had taught her, as she'd fought with the colonel on that terrible mountain trail. She'd done it without thinking, but now it came rushing back. Had she killed a man?

Dear God, please have mercy if I took a man's life.

"Sally, it will be all right." Logan's eyes carried such strength, such calm. The calm helped. Not much, but some.

"What's wrong with me?" Her voice was barely above a whisper.

"It's normal, even reasonable to have a terrible experience leave behind fears, Sally." Logan's lips brushed hers and gave her something to think about besides sheer terror and wrenching guilt and her pa's love. Her pa had never asked her to be a tomboy. In fact, he'd often tried to shield her from the hardest work, and he'd assured her that he loved her for herself. The things she did. The way she acted didn't make a difference.

Beth had talked with her a few times, quiet talks, about their first pa and how much he'd wanted a son and how hard Sally had tried to be one for him. And how she'd kept that up when Ma had remarried. Beth had tried to encourage Sally to put on a dress and enjoy being a girl. But Sally hadn't trusted Pa to love her unless she helped him and never complained and never cried.

And now here she was, shaming herself in front of Logan. But Logan had never feared her tears. And yes, Pa might actually fear them, but he'd never withheld his love for any reason.

"There's nothing reasonable about what I'm feeling, Logan. Um, let's—let's get on with it." Her heart pounded faster. The trees, the falling, her vision blurred and she was somewhere else. Falling. Fighting it, she whispered, "Put me back on my horse. Give me a minute to steady my nerves, and we'll go."

"Are you sure?"

"Yes, yes, of course." Her voice barely worked.

"We can go back, Sally. There's no shame in not facing that trail. It's a bad one."

"Let's go. Help me back on the horse." She glanced down at her heavy cast, wrapped in Wise Sister's cleverly made moccasin.

Logan didn't obey her one bit about returning her to her saddle. Instead he backed his horse around and faced forward. Still holding her solidly, he made short work of detaching one of her horse's reins, tying it to the other to double its length, then lashed Sally's rein to his saddle horn.

The reins were long enough to leave her horse a couple of paces behind his. She wasn't sure what he intended by that. Did he intend to lead her down? That might be best. "Yes, put me down and I'll—" They neared the point where the trail fell off the edge of the world. Her vision blurred and trees rushed toward her and slapped her and clawed at her as she fell and fell. She wrapped her arms around Logan and buried her face against his chest.

"I'll just keep you right here, I think, pretty Sally."

"No, no, I'll be fine, I just need a little more time." Her voice rose until it was a squeak. Her eyes clamped shut. She felt the horse under her moving, heard its hooves clomping with dull, slow thuds on the rocky trail.

The ground suddenly sloped and Sally's eyes flew open. She looked along Logan's broad chest and past his left shoulder and saw. . .nothing. Air. The ground was gone for a hundred yards below. "Logan, no. I need time—"

"After I kissed you, you said you looked stupid in that picture. I thought you looked wonderful."

"What?" Sally's eyes were riveted on the vast expanse of nothingness as the horse picked its way down, sure-footed, slow and steady. Her heart hammered until she thought it would explode.

Logan caught her chin again, gently but unshakably. "What did you see in that painting that was stupid? I saw a woman who'd enjoyed a kiss. Who wanted another."

"Logan! Pay attention to the trail." Sally's hands clutched the back of his shirt frantically. She was going to scream. She was going to fall. Fall and fall forever, never stop. Never—

He kissed her. Pulled away quickly. "There you go. That's the kiss you wanted, right? That's what was in your eyes after I kissed you." Logan smiled at her.

"No." The man wasn't even watching the trail.

"Liar."

That insult got her attention. Calling a person a liar in the West was shooting trouble. "I *didn't* want another kiss."

"You took the second one I gave you without complaining."

"Watch the trail!" She felt her hands full of broadcloth on his back as if she could sink into him completely.

"A person has to trust his horse on a slope."

"But you should be watching."

"You want another kiss right now." It wasn't a question. He stated it as a fact.

And it wasn't true. What she wanted right now was to go back up to the top of this trail where it was safe. "That's the last thing on my mind, you big dumb—"

His hand slid from her chin and sank into her hair at the nape of her neck and he kissed her again. Deeply, gently. Sally thought of that picture he'd painted as she lost herself in the kiss. A woman whose mind had been emptied.

Of course her mind wasn't *empty* really. It was full, just full of only one thing. One huge thing that left no room for anything else. It was full of the notion that she'd arrived somewhere she'd been heading all her life. The notion that she'd come home to a man and a place. There'd been room for nothing else after that kiss, nor during this one.

Logan had captured that in his painting. Seeing it had terrified her because he was nothing she wanted or respected.

Tilting her head back firmly, Logan slanted his lips hard across hers, which distracted her from thoughts of what she didn't want. In fact, he did a fine job of emptying her head of everything but him just as before. She shuddered to think what he'd paint if he had his brushes handy right now.

As he kissed her Sally knew, no matter what her plans were, they were all gone. All forgotten. She had to plot a new trail that ran alongside Logan's. Her hands let go of his shirt and slid until they wrapped tightly around his neck.

Rocks scattered and the horse shifted and slid a few inches, but all Sally could think of was Logan's strength, his wisdom, his talent for finding truth in his painting. For making a picture that a body could hear and smell and taste and feel. He'd made her beautiful with his art, and now he made her delight in being a woman with his kiss.

Logan raised his lips. "There, we're down."

"What?" Sally's eyes flickered open, her mind truly, once again, empty of all but one thing. "Down where?"

"Down at the bottom of the cliff of course." Logan smiled.

Focusing her blurred eyes, she looked up and up and up behind them. They'd come down a pencil-thin trail, and she'd never even noticed. She realized she'd been nearly reclining against his arm with no mind to whether that might throw off her horse's balance on that death-defying trail.

Empty-headed indeed. Empty except for Logan.

Smiling, he tugged on his reins until he was side by side with her horse. "You ready to take charge of your life again, pretty Sally? Ride your own bronc?"

Her empty head filled again. He'd tricked her. He'd distracted her, this man who'd already broken the news to her that he couldn't do her the honor of marrying her. And because of her foolish fear, she'd let herself fall into a daydream of the future. One he'd already told her could never happen.

He reattached the reins then carefully lifted her with his unexpected strength onto her horse, mindful of her broken leg and her soft doeskin skirt. He had to put the reins in her hands and close her fingers around them.

She was too dazed to do it. Too ashamed.

She'd made a fool of herself for sure, because though he didn't need to know it, she'd just fallen completely in love with Logan McKenzie. And after all he'd said about never marrying.

He'd been dead serious when he'd said it. Which left her without a shred of hope that she could end up with him, even though—if he asked—she'd agree to stay forever and follow him wherever he went, to see whatever he wanted to paint next.

God, have mercy.

Because in the way of a wise Texas woman, Sally knew deep in her heart that he was the only man she'd ever love. And even if Luther came for her today and she rode away from Logan and never saw him again, she'd love him and only him for the rest of her life.

"Let's go." She turned to the trail, a game trail barely visible but not dangerous now. She'd need to take the lead. It was the only place she could put herself and be sure he wouldn't read what she was feeling with those sharp, all-seeing artist eyes.

God, please, please, please have mercy.

"Sally, wait." Logan reached for her. "We need to talk."

She kicked her horse into motion so he couldn't catch hold of her or see her or hear her. "No, let's go," she shouted over her shoulder.

They were the last words she spoke for a long time because the silent sobs choked her throat shut. And it was a good thing the horse was trail savvy because the tears made it so she couldn't see where she was going.

Twenty

Normally Mandy was relieved when Sidney went to town. Having Luther and Buff away had altered Mandy's thinking. She'd never realized quite how much she'd come to depend on her pa's old friends. For everything.

But with Luther and Buff hunting for Sally—

God, protect her. Protect my little sister.

Mandy had spent hours in prayer since Sally had gone missing. There was hardly the tiniest corner of her life that didn't, suddenly, seem to be a disaster.

Catherine cried from her crib in the bedroom, and Mandy felt that little voice center her. That's what her life was about—the children, protecting them, loving them, raising them to marry wisely. . .unlike their mama.

With the men here working on the house, and Cooter's frightening behavior, Mandy was on her own in a way she'd never been. She considered herself to be a tough woman. But maybe it was easy to respect your abilities when you never had to prove anything. She'd wanted to beg Sidney to stay. She'd wanted to shout at him, because he was no protection even if he was here. But if she'd said those words, they could never be taken back so she'd let him ride away.

The first hammer blow rang out on the house, and Mandy glanced out the window to look up, up, up and see that ridiculous house really taking shape. It was stone. Gray stone. Everything in Sidney's world was gray. Mandy looked at her dress. A dull blue only because she'd gotten it before Sidney had become obsessed with his name and turning his whole world gray to match it.

But he'd bought Tom Linscott's blacks. Because no doubt they were so expensive Sidney couldn't resist.

Diverting herself from thoughts of Tom, she looked at her house again. To be surrounded by a mountain covered with logs yet build a house out of stone, at terrible expense, with an over-whelming amount of effort, was embarrassing. Most everything about her husband was an embarrassment.

The day, the third since Sidney had ridden away, caught her and dragged her into it. She'd hoped Sidney would be back by now. She'd told him to hurry. But she kept busy. There were the children to care for, the house to tend, the garden to weed.

Just after noon, with the girls fed and down for naps, she turned her attention to firewood. If she pushed hard she could get wood split before they woke.

She lifted a length of oak to the chopping block. Buff had cut a good supply before he left, but it was going fast thanks to the builders arriving and needing to keep the bunkhouse warm and cook their own meals.

Slamming the razor-sharp ax into the log with a single, smooth stroke, it split perfectly. She took pride in being able to turn her hand to anything, though it was a chore with her stomach so big. She should stick with this until she'd gotten four days' supply, but she already knew she'd be lucky to stay with the chore until she had wood enough for the evening meal and breakfast. And the evenings got cold so she needed more yet to keep a fire in the hearth.

Lifting another log into place, she raised her ax and swung. The impact shook her. She felt the muscles of her arms reach deep into her body, into her stomach, and pull painfully on something.

The sound of hooves spun her around, the ax in one hand, the other going for her rifle, strapped on her back as always.

That's when she admitted she'd been scared all morning, expecting trouble, expecting Cooter. Expecting to hear that Sidney had been shot and Cooter was back to do her harm. But it wasn't Cord Cooter who appeared on that trail.

Tom Linscott rode in leading two magnificent horses, a matching pair, shining black. Mandy barely noticed because her eyes were riveted on Tom.

She dropped the ax and felt his eyes on her, registering everything—that she was pregnant, that she was still doing Sidney's chores. That she was irrationally glad to see him.

The battle to keep herself from rushing toward him was almost more than she could win. And maybe she'd have lost the battle and shamefully thrown herself into Tom's arms.

If she hadn't felt a flood of warm liquid, as her water broke.

★ Twenty-one ★

Wise Sister!" Buff dropped from his horse and rushed toward the underbrush.

Luther heard Buff's words, saw his friend's actions, and pulled his horse to a halt in one short second. They'd found Wise Sister, and that meant they'd found Sally. He felt tears burn his eyes and covered them by blowing his nose and paying strict attention to urging his horse forward to the bushes.

In the seconds it took to reach Buff's side, an elderly woman emerged from the forest. "Here, get off the trail. Bad men come." Wise Sister caught Buff's hand and dragged him to his horse, caught the reins, and led both animal and man down a stony bit of ground eaten by water runoff. They would never have recognized this as a trail.

"Sally?" Luther followed after Buff's horse, aware that he was being completely ignored by both Wise Sister and Buff.

"Sally girl just ahead with Logan, the man whose cabin burned," Wise Sister answered.

"Logan? Is he the one who brought her here? Is he the one

who drew those pictures?"

"Yes. No time now for talk." Wise Sister and Buff kept walking.

Luther couldn't help noticing that she was still leading both the horse and Buff, although from here it looked for all the world like two people holding hands.

Luther rode slowly. Wise Sister led Buff around a bend to her horse. She let go of his hand, they exchanged some words too quiet to hear, and then she swung up on her horse with the lithe agility of a young girl.

Buff mounted and followed her. Luther didn't expect Buff to say much to him, but had the man even asked if Sally was hurt?

It didn't strike Luther as a smart time to start hollering, so he fell in behind Buff and set out.

"They didn't come this far." Tulsa pulled his horse around with a savage jerk on the reins.

Fergus hadn't seen a sign of a trail for a long time, but on this rugged land, that didn't mean much. Right now they'd reached a flat land with some gathered silt that coated the entire narrow trail. No one passed this way without leaving sign.

Tulsa turned and looked back up the trail. "I didn't seen no sign of 'em leaving the trail neither."

Staring at where they'd been, Fergus considered the time since they'd caught that glimpse of the riders, no more than an hour ago. "Then let's go look at places they could have left the trail *without* leaving a sign." He jerked hard on the reins as he wheeled his horse aside to let Tulsa go first. Fergus was good on a trail, but Tulsa was better, and only a stubborn fool didn't use the talents of the men around him.

Fergus wasn't sure about stubborn, but he was sure as certain nobody's fool.

Mandy's knees went limp as she realized what had just happened.

Tom was off his horse and at her side before she could hit the ground. He swept her up in his arms. "What's the matter? Where's the worthless bum?"

Sidney. Mandy hated to admit it. "He's gone to town."

"To Helena? When you're this far along with a baby? When is it due?"

A cramp made her grab for her belly. "Now."

"Now? You're having the baby right now?" Tom's light brown brows arched in pure fear right to his hairline. His hair had bleached to nearly white in the summer sun.

Mandy found her hand caressing the ridiculous length of it, hanging below his Stetson. It reminded her of her pa. "Never time for a haircut."

"What?" Tom turned toward the cabin, carrying her as if she weighed nothing.

At that moment Angela cried out, up from her nap.

"What's that?"

"My baby."

Tom's eyes went to her belly.

"No, my two-year-old."

Another thinner cry sounded with Angela. Catherine was up.

"And my one-year-old."

"I was here just over two years ago."

"Closer to three, actually." Mandy was sure.

"This is your third baby in that time?"

The pain in her stomach grew into a tight spasm, and Mandy didn't want to spend another second talking. "Tom, I'm going to have this baby." She couldn't mention her water breaking. It was too shameful. And there was no woman anywhere. Luther had stayed with her for the last two births while Buff had raced to town and brought back a midwife in plenty of time for there to be no need for a man dealing with something so personal.

"What do you need? What can I do to help?" His voice wasn't entirely steady and his darkly tanned skin turned a sickly shade of gray, but he said the words. A brave man.

The babies cried again and Angela yelled, "Mama!"

Mandy couldn't allow Tom's help. It was too outrageous to even think such a thing. No, this one Mandy was going to have to do on her own, but it would be all she could do to birth the baby, at least toward the end. She didn't have time for her little girls.

Which meant, "Have you ever done any babysitting?"

Logan goaded his horse forward and caught hold of Sally's reins, jerking her mustang to a stop. "You are not going to kiss me like that then ride away as if it meant nothing."

Sally was crying. He saw it the instant his words left his mouth.

"Sally, sweetheart." He leaned down, drawn to her so strongly it was beyond his power to resist the urge.

Sally was made of sterner stuff. She swiped the long sleeve of her dress across her eyes. "I'm not going to sit here talkin' while men hunt us."

Logan straightened. The flame that had drawn him had turned into a fire that threatened to burn him right to the ground. "We need to talk—"

"Wise Sister said to go to the top of this trail and I'd find a hidden cave." Sally stabbed a finger at the trail in front of her. "We can hole up there until she comes. Then we can talk."

The trail climbed again. Everything around here was at some kind of an angle. Up, down, and sideways—God had turned this place on its side rather than laying it flat. Logan was grateful for that because it was magnificent to paint. But it wasn't all that practical.

"No man with a lick of sense would want to jabber away when he's being hunted."

Logan handed her a handkerchief to save her pretty dress.

She took it and blew her nose.

Which gave him too much time to talk. "I'd say I had the sense to get us down that cliff side."

Sally's eyes went to the trail they'd just descended and some of the color leached from her tearstained face, leaving her eyes glowing red and her nose shining. And her lips still swollen from his kissing her all the way down that long, long trail.

Crazy thing to do. He hadn't even watched where his horse was going; though he'd have been little help to his horse so it might be just as well.

He could have kicked himself for reminding her of what she'd called weakness, as if a human being wasn't allowed to have serious doubts about a hairpin trail like that, especially when she'd recently gone sailing off a cliff.

Sally mopped her face off a bit then shoved the soggy kerchief into his hands.

"I wouldn't dishonor you by kissing you if my intentions weren't honorable, Sally." Logan knew his fate was sealed as far as finding a life with Sally now. He'd have to convince her to live in the mountains and spend the winters in New York. Or he'd have to change every plan he'd made. He wondered for a moment if the scenery in Texas was beautiful. It might be worth checking.

"I remember your honorable intentions well enough. You said your painting would always come first, and any woman in your life could plan on being ignored. No thank you, Logan."

"But that was before—"

"You're not going to say that's changed, are you? Because I won't believe you."

"I wouldn't lie." Logan was all stirred up. He was overreacting, but Sally calling him a liar made him furious.

"I don't think you would lie. I think any nice thing you said to me right now would be the absolute truth."

Mollified, Logan nodded. "Well then, good."

"But I think tomorrow you'd see an eagle flying over our heads, and you'd forget every pretty word you said to me." Sally's jaw firmed and the color was mostly back in her cheeks, thanks to her anger.

"I would not."

"And I'd expect you to, Logan. I'd respect you for that."

"What? You'd respect me for ignoring you?"

"No, I'd *hate* that you ignored me. I'd *respect* you for being yourself. For following your God-given dreams and using your God-given talents. And I'd understand that I had a weak moment, and you stepped in and saved me from that weakness, and because you're a hero right along with being an artist, it confused you for a bit about what you're feeling right now."

"You think I'm a hero?"

Sally pulled her Stetson off her head and whacked him with it. He lifted his forearm to protect his face. "Pay attention. Your words and feelings right now aren't the man I've been getting to know for the last few weeks. I've got to believe this is the exception, not the real you."

Logan wanted to argue with her, but he was momentarily distracted by the sight of a young buffalo emerging from a clump of trees far down the mountain. Its mother lumbered out behind it. His fingers itched for his sketchbook and pencil.

The Stetson swatted him again. "You've just made my point, Painter-Man."

Logan had forgotten she was there, but just for a second. Well, a few seconds. No more than a minute.

"Now let's ride to that cave Wise Sister told me about and hole up until she finds Luther and brings him here. Then I can get out of here and go see my sister, and you can go draw another picture of an elk."

All his work was in ashes. All his paints and canvas were destroyed. He had to leave, go home. It was devastating thinking of all he'd lost. That's when Logan realized she was right. He felt so terrible about that loss that he'd gotten his priorities temporarily twisted. But this was only today, while he was saving

her from her fear. Tomorrow he'd be right back to the self-centered
clod he'd always been. And if he persuaded Sally to throw in with
him, stay and marry him—the image he got of that drove every
thought of painting from his head—he'd soon be back to his old
selfish ways. He knew. She knew.

Logan looked at her. Their eyes caught, hers bright blue and
red rimmed. He wanted to paint her when she'd been crying. But
he had no paint. "You're right, Sally. But you're the only woman
I've ever met who made me even want to think less about art. I
doubt I could really be good to you, but I care enough that I'd feel
awful when I wasn't, and that's no kind of life for either of us."

She nodded. With a tug on her reins, she turned her horse to
aim up the trail, searching for a place to hole up.

With a good field of fire. So, if called to fight, he might get
a chance to kill a man.

Sick with dread, Logan fell in behind her and tried to force
himself to think only about the scenery and what he'd do if he had
a pencil and sketchbook and time. But instead he fixated on the
beautiful woman riding away from him.

A woman he could try to capture on canvas for the rest of
his life without ever exploring all the expressions that flitted
across her amazingly lovely face.

A woman he'd just kissed mindless then thrown away with
both hands.

★ Twenty-two ★

"Right there, Fergus." Tulsa raised his rifle in one smooth motion to his shoulder, sighted along the gun barrel, and took aim.

Fergus looked in the direction his saddle partner was looking and saw two riders. Far up the slope.

Tulsa jerked his gun down with a grunt of disgust. "Too far. All a shot would do is warn 'em."

"One of 'em looked like—a woman." Fergus couldn't take his eyes off what he'd seen. "An Indian woman with a gun strapped on her back."

"They're too far away to be sure of that."

"I know it. But I'm sure just the same. And the other one was too big to be the cowpoke you shot."

Fergus and Tulsa exchanged a long look.

"There could be other people out here. Maybe these aren't even the ones we've been hunting. That cabin might belong to someone with no stake in this game." Tulsa jabbed his gun muzzle at the place where the riders crossed just as they vanished into a cluster of trees.

"That gun, the one the woman had strapped on—that's the way the man I shot wore his gun. You don't see that much."

"You think the man you shot was a woman dressed in man's clothes?"

Slowly shaking his head back and forth, Fergus rubbed his hand over the bandolier crossing his chest. The belt of bullets reminded him of how the little Indian gal had worn that rifle. How the cowpoke wore his, too. He tried to sort it out. "He was little enough to be a she, I reckon."

"I regretted shooting that woman off her horse when we waylaid those folks. I haven't seen a woman in too long." Tulsa's smile was pure evil, and Fergus knew the man wasn't talking about *seeing*. "Maybe we can have another chance."

Fergus knew the man was now more determined than ever to catch up with that pair riding far above; and that suited Fergus just fine. "They got off that trail somehow. We'll figure it out." Fergus gathered his reins.

"Not that way." Tulsa kept his eye on the spot they'd last seen the pair.

"How else?" Fergus looked at the land between him and the riders. It was a terrible thing to imagine, jagged, no broken trail, impenetrable forest broken in places by sheer rock.

"We go forward, find a way up from this end instead of going back. We'll cut miles off the trip."

"You think we're going to climb that mountain?" Fergus slung his reins around his pommel then lifted his hat with one hand and ran the other through his hair, agitated. Scared. Like that streak in his hair was a streak of cowardice.

"Yeah. It can be done. Even if we have to go on foot. We'll climb up there and get ahead of 'em, lie in wait, shoot 'em and strip 'em of their money and guns, and climb back down for our horses. Or we'll take theirs and spend all the time we want riding back to ours. Let's go." Tulsa kicked his horse into a trot without waiting for Fergus to say yes, no, or maybe.

Which made Fergus's fingers twitch to put a bullet in the man's back. When Curly had been alive, this'd been Fergus's gang. He made the decisions, and Curly backed him. Tulsa never did anything but go along. Now, without it being two to one, Tulsa was giving orders, and Fergus didn't like it. He took one long moment to think of killing Tulsa, taking all the money in those stuffed saddlebags of his, forgetting that pair riding high above, and lighting a shuck for San Francisco. It would be easy. Tulsa wasn't even watching his back. But they'd been riding the outlaw trail together a long time. Right now, Tulsa Bob Wiley was the only friend Fergus had in the world.

On the other hand, Fergus knew how much money he had, and Tulsa had an even cut. If Tulsa died, Fergus was a much richer man. And he could stay rich if he kept away from poker and whiskey and women. A man got poor having that kind of fun. Though what was the point of being rich if you couldn't have some fun?

Fergus set aside the idea of blowing his cousin out of the saddle. He could always kill his only friend later, should the need arise. He kicked his horse into a fast walk to catch up. It was unwise to turn your back on a back-shooter. Family sticking together wasn't as tempting as cash in hand.

Tom carried Mandy into the house with such quick, determined steps she had the feeling he wasn't saving her so much as running to a place he could put her down so he could escape.

Both babies yowled now from their bedroom.

Tom looked at Mandy, his eyes so wide she could see white all the way around the pupils. His eyes darted from her, to her belly, to the door to the girls' room. Mandy suspected that if he'd been in a room with three sticks of dynamite, their fuses all lit, the man wouldn't have been any more upset.

He bent to set her down on a chair then straightened without letting go. "You should go to bed. No, you should sit out here. No, let me take you in with the babies. Two did you say? Two babies and one on the way? In under three years. Is your husband a complete idiot?"

Mandy could think of no response that should be uttered aloud.

"I left my horses standing there untied." He whirled around with her still in his arms as if he meant to go put up the horses, carrying her the whole time.

Mandy's belly relaxed and she could think again. And take charge. Someone needed to. Her husband wasn't the only idiot man around. "Put me down."

Why, oh why hadn't Sally gotten here in time?

"No!" He shouted the word and looked at her as if she'd asked him to hurl her over a cliff.

"I'm fine. The baby is coming but not this very instant. I'll go check on the girls while you tend to your horses."

"I'm not leaving you alone!" Tom practically roared the words at her. "If your husband was here I'd snap him in two like a twig."

Mandy patted his arm. "Well, if he was here you wouldn't be all upset because he isn't here, now would you? So here or not, you don't end up getting to snap any twigs." She managed to catch his eyes, which were still darting around the room.

It reminded her of a little bluebird that had fallen into the house through the chimney one day. The brightly colored bird had crashed frantically into the walls and ceiling while Mandy rushed to open every door and window, hoping the poor little animal would get out before it hurt itself.

She hoped Tom's blue eyeballs didn't go flying out like that bird had once it'd found an escape hatch.

"Put me down." Small words. Spoken slowly, loudly. Direct orders.

He seemed to be responding. Setting her on her feet, he hovered as if he expected her to keep sinking right to the floor.

When she stood, that went a long way toward calming him.

"Put the horses in the barn."

Shaking his head no frantically, he said, "Okay."

"Now, Tom. Hurry."

Those fluttering, flying eyeballs seemed to understand the word *hurry*. He turned and dashed out of the house so fast Mandy was relieved the door was standing open or, right now, there'd be a Tom Linscott-shaped hole in it.

She focused on the crazy man who'd stopped by, to keep her from thinking of what lay ahead. Turning to the girls' bedroom, she went to it, forcing a serene expression on her face, hoping not to signal to the girls all her many fears.

The door swung inward as soon as she'd turned the knob. Angie, out of her crib, was working to escape.

"I'm sorry Mama was slow, honey." Smiling, Mandy scooped her up and gave her a hug. "I'm sorry I left you and baby Catherine to cry for so long."

"Mama sad?"

Mandy tried to decide if there was something in her expression that prompted Angela's question, or if she thought the word sorry meant sad. Giving the little imp another hug, she said, "No, Mama is very happy. We have company."

Angie's brow furrowed. And why not? How could this little one know what the word company meant? Since no one had ever stopped by to visit before.

Mandy carried Angie to Catherine's crib, did a quick diaper change for Catherine, and helped Angie with her own newly learned potty skills in the little commode they kept inside. Then she scooped both girls into her arms with a hard hug and went back into the main room of the house. She settled them at the table and got two tin cups of milk ready and a slice of bread and jelly.

Thank heavens the cow finally bore her calf and we have milk again.

The girls finished their little snack while she had another contraction, this one so long and hard it scared her, but she didn't think the girls noticed. It passed, and she picked them both up and headed for the rocking chair just as Tom came sprinting through the door she'd still never closed.

"Put them down!" He rushed at her and scared the girls to death. When he reached for Angie, she shrieked and wrapped her arms around Mandy's neck so tightly it threatened to strangle her.

Mandy felt another contraction begin.

Tom started pacing back and forth across the room.

Oh yeah, you're going to be a lot of help.

★ Twenty-three ★

Sally had an itch between her shoulder blades that told her to keep riding hard and fast.

"Stop!" Logan pointed.

Sure enough, there was a cave opening with rocks in the front that gave them nice protection and a good field of fire. Too bad all her instincts told her to keep moving.

"I wonder how far we are from Mandy's." What a dream come true it would be to reach Mandy's house. To have her fast shooting, deadeye sister at her side to face down these bad men. But Luther and Buff should be coming. Surely Wise Sister had found them. Surely they'd be here soon.

Logan shrugged. "You have no idea exactly where she lives?"

"There was a hand-drawn map from Helena to Mandy's house, but I never had it. Pa got it in the mail from Luther and gave it to the colonel, who died with it in the gunfight. One of the men in our party knew this area so we trusted to him when we left the train to take a shortcut. He did his figuring and we were following him. I saw the map from Mandy and I heard the man leading us talk about how he planned to go. But I don't know the area so it didn't make much sense to me. I just knew the general direction. Then after I was unconscious, you took me on a day-long ride in the *wrong* direction."

"Not the *exact* wrong direction." Logan shrugged.

"I can't even figure out if we rode toward Mandy's or away. I know you said we headed mostly west, some north. I think Mandy's cabin is mostly west, some south. We might be closer than we think."

And what if they were close? Sally thought of leading two back-shooters to Mandy and abandoned the idea of even trying to keep moving. "Up until now we've followed Wise Sister's orders; no reason to stop now."

Logan nodded and swung down from his horse in front of the tall cave opening. There was space between the pile of huge rocks in the cave mouth to lead the horses inside. Sally saw nowhere likely to tie them up out here.

Logan stepped in, leading his horse. "No, this isn't possible. It can't be." His voice echoed out of the black opening that swallowed up his mount. He sounded strange, almost scared.

Sally swung down and hobbled after him, not using her crutches. The cast supported her leg without pain. She was still a little edgy, as if even now someone was watching them, drawing a bead.

Entering the cave with her black mustang following placidly along, she stumbled over her feet to a haul at what she saw. Then she forced herself forward to get herself and her horse under cover.

There was a huge room that reached up at least twenty feet, but that wasn't the unbelievable part. Weird columns of stone stood reaching from floor to ceiling like a dozen support pillars. The columns seemed to glow in the dark of the cave. Sally leaned close to the nearest one. It was whiteish gray and wet. She reached her hand out. "Don't touch it."

"Did you see that, Fergus?"

Snapping his head around, Fergus looked where Tulsa pointed. Straight up a sheet of rock that was mighty short on handholds. "See what?"

"A horse. We rounded this clump of trees just in time for me to see the back end of a black mustang going behind those rocks."

"Which pile of rocks? This whole place is nothing but a pile of rocks."

"That mound chest high, in that clear spot." Tulsa pointed as he urged his horse closer to Fergus. "There must be a cave behind that granite. I only saw one horse, but there's not room behind there for two."

Tulsa's eyes shone with a greedy, hungry gleam. "We've got 'em cornered if we can get up there fast enough."

Fergus looked all the way up that slope and gulped. It was a long, risky climb, several hundred yards. The last stretch looked purely impossible, but they'd decide if it was when they got up there. If they hurried, they could get within shooting distance in time to pin down this pair in the cave and take their time closing in on 'em.

Fergus ran a hand down the bandolier of bullets on his chest. They had enough ammunition to start a war. They could pin those riders down for a long, long time. One of 'em could cover the cave mouth while the other climbed and got into position. With two of them, they could take all the time they wanted climbing up there.

"Let's go." Tulsa rode his horse forward as far up the incline as possible. Then he swung down to use a scrub tree for a hitchin' post.

Riding along behind, it burned Fergus bad that Tulsa was giving orders again.

"Move faster," Tulsa said. "We finish this today, then ride for San Francisco for the winter. I've got a hankerin' for some whiskey and a hand or two of poker. I'm tired of living hard and cold."

Hard was the way Fergus wanted to hit Tulsa. Cold, well, that might well be how Fergus left his saddle partner. Cold and dead after they finished with those riders hiding in the cave. Fergus needed Tulsa to make sure there was no one left to tell the tale. They'd finish this then Fergus would double his money with one smashing bullet in Tulsa's back. It'd be the best day's work he'd ever done.

Tulsa yelled a few more orders as they clawed their way up that cliff.

Fergus almost enjoyed how much that irritated him because it would make killing his friend a whole lot easier.

Snatching back her fingers, Sally wondered if the columns held the roof up. "I've never seen anything like this before."

"They're stalactites. Dear Lord God in heaven, thank You." Logan's voice was so reverent Sally knew the man was truly praying.

And well he should be. She was glad these stone columns were here, too. "These are great. If those vermin catch up with us, we'll have a great shield. All we've got to do is get behind these. As far to the back of the cave as we can."

"Wise Sister had to know they were here. How could she not have told me?" Logan reached out and rested a hand on one a few feet ahead of the one he'd forbidden Sally to touch. He had no reaction to her mention of gunfire.

The man was a moron. A moron she was in love with.

And what did that make her?

"This is an artist thing, isn't it?" Sally's jaw clenched. She'd been being a good sport about his painting, hadn't she? But there were limits.

"I've got to get canvas. I've got to find a way to paint this."

He didn't seem to have heard a word she said. Well, his head would clear when lead started flying.

568

Of course maybe they were safe, far from trouble, and the itch she felt was just her being overly cautious. In which case, once she was sure they were safe, she might clear his head by slamming it into one of his *stag-tights*, or whatever he called them.

Ignoring him, she led her horse into the cave to find a place to protect the mustang. The cave was deep, too, as if it sank into the heart of the mountain. Water dripped everywhere, and those weird columns glowed like lanterns, yet cast no light, so she could only see with the bit of light from the cave door. The cave floor was wet enough she paused to take her crutches off the saddle to keep her cast dry. Then she wove carefully between the pillars on the rough floor until she found a small spring near the back corner. Her horse moved past her, its nose reaching for the water, its hooves echoing in the cave.

Though Sally worried about the water being safe to drink, a mountain horse like this little mustang was probably a better judge than she was, so she let the thirsty animal have its head.

Going back, she relieved Logan of his horse while he stared at the column as if he could use it to see into heaven. Logan's horse was soon beside Sally's drinking with soft, rushing contentment. Unable to resist, Sally lay down on her belly to drink. She wondered if she'd have to lead Logan to water, like she had his horse.

When she'd had her fill, Sally stood and wiped her mouth with her handkerchief. Then using one crutch only, she walked back to the front door.

As she passed him, since her broken leg wasn't doing anything anyway, she used it to kick Logan in the shin.

"Ouch!" Scowling, he turned to her. "What did you do that for?"

Resisting the urge to give him one more sound kick, she asked, "Are you going to help me watch the front entrance, or do you want to start drawing pictures?"

"I don't have my sketchbook."

"You really don't have a brain in your head, do you?"

A deep furrow appeared between his brows. "I thought you said we were safe here. Why can't I look at these beautiful stalactites columns for a while?" He turned and pointed to one side of the room to where a column wasn't fully formed. It looked like a set of fangs, one upper and one lower tooth—each about five feet long. "Look at that one. It's dripping down from the top and building up from the bottom, but it hasn't met yet. Isn't it great?"

Sally spared the corner a look. "You shore 'nuff described it perfectly." She deliberately spoke her worst cowboy slang in her deepest Texas accent. Maybe it would remind him of why he shouldn't be kissing her. More importantly, maybe it would remind her of why she shouldn't be in love with him. They were from two different worlds. His was a world where you looked at a rock and wanted to draw it. Hers—where you looked at a rock and saw a place to duck behind when lead started flyin'. When you're dodgin' bullets, I recommend you pick the fattest one."

She smirked at him. "And you know what? Choose one that's solid all the way through. That empty middle part on that one"—she pointed to the giant fangs—"won't stop a bullet worth nothin'. So solid's a real good idea. You can hide behind it while I protect us."

"Those men might shoot at us!" He wasn't asking a question. It was more like he had at last awakened to the danger. It took him long enough.

Well, good. Finally. He needed to be worrying about saving his worthless hide.

"We have to save these beautiful stalactites."

Sally's hands tightened on her Winchester. Oh, she wouldn't shoot him. That wasn't called for. But just one good whack with the butt of her gun. Just one to get rid of some tension and maybe knock some sense into his head. And if there was not a butt stroke hard enough to do that, at least he'd be flat on his back, out of the range of rifle fire. "You're in danger from more than just those coyotes on our trail."

She didn't identify herself as the threat. Instead, she whirled around and hobbled to the cave mouth. "Get a drink. There's water in the back. Just follow the horses. They're not so stupid they don't know to get some water in their bellies when they have a chance."

Sally was just resting the muzzle of her rifle against one of the rocks protecting the cave when Logan grabbed her arm, just below the elbow, and whirled her around.

"Don't treat me like I'm a fool." He leaned down until he nearly touched her nose with his, just like he didn't even see she was furious and heavily armed. "I know there's trouble. That doesn't mean I can't stop for a moment and appreciate something God created with pure beauty in mind. I think you're the one who's *stupid* to be able to see what's in that cave and go right back to water and bullets. You need to open your eyes and see the beauty around you. What's the point of living if you don't?"

Sally jerked against his grip, but he didn't let go so she rose on her tiptoes—well, one tiptoe; her broken foot wasn't of much use—to yell right in his face. "You need to open your eyes and see the ugliness around you. What're the chances of living if you don't?"

They glared at each other, mad enough to light a fire in the air. She yanked at her arm again and managed to drop her crutch and let her rifle swing down so it was out of the way between them. Logan tugged so her forearm pressed against the solid wall of his chest.

"Let me go," Sally spoke through clenched teeth.

"You're not going anywhere." Logan acted as if his height and weight and strong will were enough to force her to do his bidding.

The moment stretched. Sally's temper built. A red flush of fury darkened Logan's neck.

Then something snapped in Sally's anger and turned it upside down, to a different kind of fire. Sally caught the collar of his shirt with her free hand and dragged him down just as he wrapped an arm around her waist and lifted her off her feet—foot.

Logan's kiss wiped out every shred of common sense she possessed. He dragged her back into the cave, then turned and pressed her against the wall, turning his head to deepen the kiss. He raised his lips the least whisper of an inch. "Sally, tell me you'll stay here with me."

His words were nearly lost because Sally wouldn't let the kiss go long enough to let him speak a whole sentence. "I have to. I am so in love with you."

Logan shuddered.

Sally felt that all the way to her heart.

"Yes." His hands slid to her face, and he pulled away so she could see him. See he meant it when he said, "I love you, too. It's madness. You'll end up hating me."

"No, never." It was reasonable that she would get tired of a man who spent his time on nonsense, but she knew it would never stop her from loving him. "I can't hate you ever." She pulled him back to her and lost herself in his embrace.

Logan suddenly wrenched his head to the side, breaking the kiss. He rested his face against the side of hers and she kissed his cheek, his hair, his ear.

"Stop!" With a groan of almost pain, Logan pulled away from her and turned his back, running both hands deep into his hair.

Sally sagged against the stone, pressed a hand to her swollen lips, and tried to think of something, anything except this man and how strange he was. . .and how wonderful. She'd completely lost her mind.

She needed to be doing something else. What? What else? Watch the trail, find something to eat in the bag Wise Sister had brought along, study possible hideouts down the hill where someone could get a shot off at them?

"We're going to be together." Logan turned to her, his eyes

blazing. "I'm not letting you go."

"Good." Now more common sense invaded Sally's muddled brain. Her dearly loved parents, the rest of her family back in Texas. Her big sister in need. Good reasons why she *should* go. She was staying anyway. "Because you're not getting rid of me no matter what you do." She launched herself into his arms again.

He caught her and laughed, his beautiful, searching artist eyes seeking her every thought. Well, let him look. She wasn't hiding anything from him.

Then he dodged her kiss, grinned, and said, "You need to be a bit more practical, woman. This isn't the time and place for this."

Sally smiled, then even laughed. "Name the time and place, Logan."

"How about we live through this, find Wise Sister and your friends, then go hunt up a preacher in the nearest town and get married?"

"Go to town?" Sally widened her eyes in mock surprise. "Tell the truth, is that so we can get married or so you can buy a new sketchbook?"

Logan didn't even flinch. Instead he looked her square in the eye. "It is all about marrying you. If you promise to keep kissing me like that, I'll follow you anywhere."

"I had the same thought myself."

Logan leaned down and kissed her again, hard and quick. "Let's go stand watch to make sure no one sneaks up on us until Wise Sister shows up with your friends." Logan turned her so they were side by side. He slipped his arms around her waist, over her rifle. He helped her hobble along, and somehow they fit together just perfectly.

They reached the cave opening, more focused on each other than on the danger. They stepped out in the narrow space behind the rocks piled by the cave mouth.

A bullet whizzed between them, hit stone behind, ricocheted, and tore a hole through Logan's Stetson.

Sally grabbed at Logan, but he was already grabbing at her, and they dived to the rocky floor.

Gunfire whizzed overhead like murderous bees.

Logan threw himself on top of her to shelter her as the first bullet tore a chunk off one of the stalactites. With a shout of outrage, he said, "They're going to ruin this cave!"

"Those bullets are going to ricochet off the rock and kill us." Sally grabbed the front of his shirt in her fist and tried to decide whether to drag him to safety or strangle him.

★ Twenty-four ★

Luther heard the gunfire and hit the ground before it made impact.

Silent as a ghost, he slipped into the undergrowth on the downhill side of the trail and advanced toward the shooters. He heard Buff and Wise Sister moving, separating whisper-quiet just ahead of him, using every ounce of caution and every shred of cover they could while still moving fast.

More shots rang out, but there was only the volley aiming up the mountain, no return fire. What if they were too late? What if they'd gotten this close to Sally only to have her shot dead minutes before they could protect her?

Luther moved faster, his jaw clenched to keep from roaring in fury. He was falling behind Buff, though Buff was going straight while Luther was on a downhill slant.

The bullets hit stone and caromed with a sharp whine. Two men. Rifles. Probably farther downhill from Luther. He eased on down the slope using the trees to hold him on that steep side of the mountain. It wasn't fit for a man to walk on, but Luther'd never met the mountain that could best him.

He saw a flicker of movement above and saw Buff waving to catch his eye. With a few quick hand gestures, he told Luther to keep moving down while Buff covered the higher end of the trail. It was more dangerous up there, but this was no time for Luther to jaw with Buff about a plan.

Luther faded down even lower, keeping silent, gripping sturdy trees that wouldn't give away his position by shaking their tops when he grabbed ahold.

He got below the shooters without their noticing, based on the fact that they were still unloading their guns on something up the hill. That made Luther feel a bit better. This was wild shooting, meant to get in a lucky hit. They didn't have a real target.

He hoped.

Grim determination twisted Luther's lips as he saw the first man just ahead, methodically unloading his gun up the hill to a cave opening about a hundred feet ahead and above them. Those hundred feet would be tough ones to climb, which probably explained why they were doing their dirty work from down here. This had to be one of the men who had waylaid Sally's party. For a back-shooter, he wasn't watching behind him a bit good.

The man's focus was fixed on that cave, firing, reloading, firing again. Luther knew what bullets could do inside a cave. A body could be riddled by the ricochet. A wild shot, bouncing off stone over and over, had more than its share of chances to kill.

Luther didn't aim his gun. No sense drawing that deadly fire when his first shot could only put down one of these rabid coyotes. Luther had no belly for killing either. He'd do it to save Sally, even to save himself. But he'd never killed a man and, if he could avoid it, he didn't intend to start now.

He moved fast while he studied the situation. Gunfire from a second outlaw told Luther that man was farther away and a bit higher on the trail.

A heap of stones covered most of the cave opening, but there was enough room to get a well-aimed bullet past them. Sally could already be cut to ribbons. Luther rushed recklessly now, hoping the shooting covered any sound he made, using cover for all he was worth but moving whether it was good enough or not.

He'd nearly reached the closest man when the outlaw whirled and fired into the brush, right where Luther figured Buff to be.

A muted cry of pain told Luther the man had hit what he'd aimed at.

Sally crawled on her belly toward the back of the cave with the front of Logan's shirt firmly in her grip.

She didn't have to drag him though. He was cooperating.

Bullets thundered and echoed in the cave. One caromed off the ceiling and struck within inches of her hand. She sped up. In the far back there was one big column, close to the water. There might be room there to hunker down and outwait this barrage of bullets.

Something smacked Logan and knocked him onto his side. Sally glanced at him as she resolutely hauled him back onto his stomach. Blood streaked the side of his face, dripped onto his arm and hers. His eyes were open but dazed. While she moved, Sally tried to see if he'd been shot in the head, but it looked like a graze to her. She hoped.

One of the horses screamed. Whether from fear or pain Sally couldn't say. They crowded the back of the cave, as many of those weird columns in front of them as they could get. Only the sound of the raging gunfire coming from the front of the cave kept them in place. They looked crazy with fear.

Sally was mindful of their stomping hooves as she headed for the corner they'd chosen.

A blow to her leg felt as if a bullet had found her. It was the broken leg. The pain wasn't enough to stop her, so she didn't bother to look back.

A loud crack in the midst of the nightmarish rolling thunder drew Sally's attention. She dropped flat on her face in time to duck a massive white stone hurtling toward her head. One of Logan's stalag-things. She was glad he wasn't thinking right, except that probably meant he'd been shot. But if he was only knocked for a loop, then she was glad. Because he'd have felt terrible about the destruction going on in this unusual and beautiful cave.

She felt terrible herself. But then she was being shot at. Feeling terrible made sense.

She dodged a horse's hoof, caught Logan by the front of his shirt, and lunged behind a thick white column. It was fat at the base, nearly three feet wide, and there was about two feet of space between it and the farthest back corner of this cave. There was nowhere safer for them to be.

She dragged Logan's feet behind the stone and sat him up, without much help from him. His eyes blinked owlishly. Blood coated the side of his face, black and ugly in the dim light. Awful to see.

Noticing her cast was busted up from where she'd been shot, she saw no blood pouring out, and the leg worked so she ignored it. Whipping out her kerchief from the pocket of her dirty, blood-stained doeskin dress, she pressed it to Logan's face.

His hand rose unsteadily to take over holding the kerchief. "Thanks, I'm okay. I think. It hit hard but it didn't go in. Just a scratch."

The gunfire stopped. Her ears still echoed with the deafening roar of it. The cave was thick with dust kicked up by the barrage.

Sally waited, gathering her strength. She needed to go to the cave door, see if she could spot their attackers, get her rifle into action. But just two more deep breaths first, if they didn't choke her.

Logan reached for her rifle. "I'll go."

"You can't go." She knocked his hand aside. No possible chance that she'd give up her gun. Not to anyone, least of all an artist who meant something all wrong when he talked about a fast draw.

The gunman raised his rifle to aim at Buff again. He rose so quickly his hat fell off and revealed a weird streak of white in his hair.

Luther recognized that and it twisted his gut, but he didn't have time to deal with it now.

The outlaw's finger tightened on the trigger, and Luther cracked a single butt stroke, hard enough to put down a bull buffalo, across the varmint's skull. The gun went off but the bullet went wild.

If this man had killed Buff, Luther wasn't sure he'd be able to keep himself from coming back and using the other end of his gun.

One more to go. As he thought that, Luther realized the shooting from the other outlaw had stopped.

That same instant a rod of cold steel jabbed hard against Luther's backbone. "Lower that rifle or I'll cut you in two." The voice was shaky and nervous, but that gun held as cold and steady as a Montana mountain peak.

One wrong move would end this for Luther and then, with Buff down, maybe dead, that left only Wise Sister to protect Sally and get her help if she was hurt.

Luther held his gun with both hands, because of the way he'd used it as a club. Now he lowered it. No chance to take a shot, not with the steady feel of that gun between his shoulders and the nervous edge to that voice.

"Drop it. Toss it away from you."

The voice did something to Luther, hit a chord, sent a chill down his spine that had nothing to do with the gun. He'd heard it before. But when and where?

With no choice to make, he tossed the gun well away from his body. He had a knife in his boot and another in a scabbard under his shirt. Getting to them would require that this hombre get careless. Wherever this man had crossed Luther's path, there was left only a whisper of feeling that he was dangerous. This was not a careless man.

"Get your hands up where I can see 'em." The gun jabbed so hard it would have cut Luther's back if not for his buckskin coat.

"Who are you, mister?" Luther's hands raised about level with his neck. He was closer to the knife in his shirt with his hands up. And Luther'd had plenty of experience getting it out fast. "What are you on the hunt for?"

"Shut up." The gun jabbed hard. "I'm not answerin' any questions. Fergus kilt your saddle partner in the woods. I saw him go down. Now we'll get your friends to come out and say howdy."

Down wasn't dead, and Luther knew it. He prayed this man was wrong about Buff.

"But why?" Luther hesitated, wanting to slow the man down, start him talking, give Buff a chance to wake up, Wise Sister a chance to get in position with that deadly bow, Sally a chance to get away if she was still able. The cave had been as silent as the tomb from the first. "What'd they do to you?"

"One of 'em made the mistake of livin'. I ain't gonna leave no witnesses to talk about what we do out here."

Sally had gone over that cliff. Luther had read that sign. And this man hadn't been satisfied that she was dead. He'd hunted for her body. When he didn't find it, he'd stalked her like she was a rabbit and he a hungry coyote.

Luther's fingers itched to make a grab for his skinning knife. He wanted to take his chance, but that gun didn't waver. He'd die and leave Sally defenseless, though none of the McClellen girls could ever be described as really defenseless.

"You need to run. Forget this killing and get away. You killed a cavalry officer and his wife on that trail. People will come hunting you. I'm the first, but I won't be the last. Killing all of us won't stop what's on your trail now. You should quit this country, lose yourself in a city somewhere. That's your only chance."

"No one can find me in these woods."

"I did."

The gun jabbed again. "You call this you findin' me? I'd say I found you."

"Gettin' the drop on me just means I'm here. I found you. If you take out now, I won't come after you. I'll mislead the posse that's gonna be on your trail, might be on it already. The only thing I want is for you to leave those folks alone in that cave."

"They won't be in there for long." Then the nervous voice rose. "Come out of that cave." The shout carried a long way in the mountains and echoed back, eerie and evil. "I've got your friend out here, and I'll kill him if you don't get out here *now*."

Luther would have shouted for Sally to stay inside if he didn't think this man would put a bullet through him on the first word.

The gun eased off Luther's spine as the man shouted again. "I'll give you the count of five, then your friend here dies!"

Luther swallowed, bracing himself for a bullet, easing his hands one fraction of an inch closer to his knife with each breath.

"One."

A rustle in the trees near that cave entrance drew Luther's attention. The scrub pines up there were mighty thin. Luther saw no way someone could find enough cover to slip out of that cave. And with Luther standing smack in front of this back-shooter, Sally couldn't get a shot off if she *did* get a chance.

"Two."

The voice was a few steps farther back and to Luther's left. Where had he heard that voice before? He eased his hand closer to his knife. There was a definite shake of a small scrub bush near the cave. Someone was alive up there. Sally. It had to be Sally. If only Luther could keep her alive...

"Three."

The man Luther had knocked cold stirred, and Luther knew if that man, Fergus, woke up and bought into this game, they were done. Right now the lone man had to split his attention, which gave Luther a fighting chance. The man couldn't kill all of them, so it stood to reason someone would survive this. Luther vowed it would be Sally before him.

But if Fergus came around and was up to covering his partner's back, both of *them* were a lot safer. And Sally's chances of surviving got a lot slimmer.

"Four."

"I'm coming out." A man's voice sounded steadily.

"No!" Luther shouted.

The outlaw smacked the back of Luther's head so hard stars burst in his vision and he sank to his knees.

Fighting to remain conscious, Luther didn't provoke the man again. Instead, with blurred vision, he watched the cave mouth, listened to the man behind him, waited, and inched his hand closer to his knife.

"Step out where I can see you. Hands up."

A tall, dark-haired man stepped out. This must be Logan, the man who drew the pictures. The man who had found Sally and saved her and hid her until help could come. Luther'd gotten that much and precious little else from Wise Sister. And now here Luther was, and no help at all.

The artist watched the outlaw with more sense than his chosen profession would have indicated he possessed. He carefully stepped away from the boulders protecting the cave, his hands in plain sight.

Seconds ticked by while Luther wished for a back way out of that cave, prayed Sally had found it and was running away right now.

But the man wouldn't have stepped out if there'd been one. And his Sally wasn't much of a one to run.

"There were two of you. A woman was ridin' with you. I want to see her now."

The outlaw's voice! If Luther could remember where he'd

heard it, maybe he could use that to divert the varmint's attention.

Sally eased her head up from behind the biggest boulder. It covered her to the neck, but her head was right there, a perfect target, and this man had spent the last weeks of his life trying to kill her.

"It's you, isn't it?" The man sounded as if he didn't believe it. "You're the cowpoke Fergus gut shot who fell over the cliff. Bested by a woman. But your luck has run pure dry."

Luther heard the crack of the outlaw's hammer drawing back and grabbed for his knife, knowing he'd draw that bullet.

Somehow he'd stay alive long enough to save Sally.

★ Twenty-five ★

Calm down. Let me sit." Mandy made her way to the chair as a new labor pain began tightening what felt like her whole body. She dropped quickly into the chair, trying to remain calm for the girls' sake.

Tom whirled from his pacing and followed her to the chair, his arms still outstretched, the panic on his face almost comical. Almost.

"Now girls, don't cry." Crooning to the girls while her belly tightened was about all she could do. Tom was going to have to wait if he wanted her to talk to him. She did look up, meet his eyes, and say, "Sit down, please. You're scaring the girls."

She did her best not to look at him again. The girls were both clinging. Angela had crawled up Mandy's body until she nearly wrapped around Mandy's head. Little Catherine had her face buried in Mandy's neck.

Tom stumbled backward without looking where he was going and managed to more or less fall into a chair by the kitchen table.

Angela turned her head so her cheek was pressed to Mandy's.

Tears soaked Mandy's neck while she patted her girls and murmured comfort. She hoped it comforted poor Tom, too.

She smiled at him. Almost more than she could do over the slowly receding wailing, the slowly growing tightening of her body, and the slowly building fear about what lay ahead of her, alone—yet not alone—miles and miles from help.

Mandy wanted her own mama so bad she almost started in crying and hollering "Mama" along with her girls.

God, protect me. Protect my girls. Protect this baby coming into the world. Protect Tom Linscott from panic.

That quirked a smile on her lips, which she would have guessed was beyond her at this point.

An afterthought shamed her. Because she hadn't prayed for her husband.

God, protect Sidney.

Cooter's cold eyes and that streak of icy white hair appeared in her mind, and she imagined Sidney telling the man he was fired.

Sidney's going to need protection more than all of us.

She rocked, quieting the girls, breathing slowly to conceal her discomfort until the labor pain ended. It had come hard and too fast. With the girls, her water hadn't broken until long after her pains had started. Things were much different already with this one.

Rising briskly, she said, "Now, Angie and Catherine, I want you to meet this nice man." Her tone carefully light, she eased Angela to the floor. Angela gave her only token resistance, which boded well if Tom could keep from yelling. Holding the toddler's hand and carrying the baby, she walked over to Tom, who seemed to have calmed a bit. "Tom, why don't you sit down on the floor so the girls can get to know you?"

"Why?" Tom blinked those clueless blue eyes at her. The man still hadn't figured out he was in for an afternoon, evening, and possibly night of child care. He might not have much time to get it in his head.

"Do it!" she snapped. She hadn't meant to yell, but that's the way it ended up.

Slipping quickly to the floor, Tom found himself at eye level with Mandy's two-year-old.

"Angie, this is Tom Linscott." For propriety's sake she should introduce him as Mr. Linscott, but Angie probably couldn't say Linscott anyway. Of course, maybe she couldn't say Tom either. But the odds were a little better.

"Hi." Angie grabbed the skirt of her little blue calico dress and bounced on her tiptoes, smiling shyly.

Mandy wondered how much longer it would be before the children were all dressed in gray.

Mandy was so proud of Angela. She loved her little girls, and she loved this baby on the way. They were the brightest part of her life.

"Hi, Angie."

With a sigh of relief she saw Tom playing along.

Thank You, dear Lord God in Heaven.

"Mr. Linscott is a friend of Pa's who is going to help us this afternoon. He brought us some new horses. Your papa bought them, and Mr. Linscott delivered them today."

"Sit down in front of Mr. Linscott, Angie. He'll tell you all about his horses." Mandy eased Catherine down, too, and the little tyke seemed almost jealous of her sister because she plopped down a bit closer to Tom than Angie.

Mandy walked around the little circle and pulled close the chair Tom had used. She very much doubted she'd be able to get up if she sat on the floor.

Catherine smiled at Tom then shoved a handful of her little dress into her mouth, flashing her diaper while she wiggled her bare toes.

Tom smiled at the two little girls. Then very slowly, using surprising wisdom for a man who didn't have children, Tom reached out his hands to Catherine, and when she didn't pull back, he lifted her onto his lap. "Hi, Catherine."

The baby giggled through her mouthful of calico.

It surprised Mandy. Then she had a thought that wasn't a bit comfortable. "Do you have children, Tom—uh—Mr. Linscott?" Why had it never occurred to Mandy that Tom was a married man? He was of an age to be such.

"No, I'm a bachelor, but my sister Abby has a baby between Catherine's and Angela's ages. A little boy, and he is almost as cute as these two." He spoke the words to the girls, not her.

Angela scrambled onto her hands and knees and crawled quickly to join her little sister on Tom's lap. Both girls seemed content there, which was good because Mandy felt another contraction coming on.

"So the horses?" she prompted, hoping Tom and the girls would sit and talk while she dealt with a labor pain far too strong to be happening so early. This baby was going to come fast. But it could never be fast enough that Tom wasn't going to have his hands *very* full with some *very* upset little girls.

Tom looked up and their eyes met. A furrow on his brow said he knew she was hurting.

So much compassion, so much worry, so much admiration that she was quietly suffering, so much gentle understanding that she was trying to keep things calm for the girls.

Mandy got more true respect and kindness from one little wrinkle on Tom Linscott's forehead than she'd gotten from her husband during their entire marriage.

A devastating thing to admit while she was in the process of having her third child.

"Get back in there!" Logan spoke under his breath when he wanted to scream.

"No. I'm not letting you draw a bullet."

"So you'll get shot instead of me? No man would ever agree to that. And I won't live with knowing you died in my place."

"Not in your place, Logan."

Logan watched the man at the bottom of this nasty cliff. The skinny outlaw never took his eyes off of Sally. She was going to die.

Logan knew it. She had to know it, too.

With that watchful villain aiming straight at her head, there was no way to get her gun into action in time. Of course, Logan didn't have one. Like the idiot he was.

Sally inched her rifle higher behind the stone. Logan could see it but Skinny couldn't. If the gunman would look away for one split second. . . If anything, however small, would draw his attention. . .

Logan knew that had to be either Luther or Buff kneeling, bleeding from the back of his head. Unable to provide a distraction. From this vantage point, Logan could see the other one of Sally's two friends lying sprawled on his back in the underbrush, out of everyone's sight, but in no position to help. Where was Wise Sister?

Searching the area, he couldn't see her anywhere, and he knew she was in this to the end.

Logan stood there, useless.

That rifle of Sally's inched higher. She was doing her best to look calm, not visibly move her shoulders, which the man could see. Logan had seen her handle that thing. One second of distraction and she'd have it leveled and fired. That skinny, twitchy man kept his eyes riveted on her like she was bread at the end of a forty-day fast.

So she was willing to die for him, was she?

Logan couldn't allow it. Couldn't live if it happened and he'd done nothing to save her.

When there was a crisis, Sally knew she reacted faster than

almost anyone on earth.

Every movement was lightning-quick, but to her it felt like molasses. Her vision became almost painfully acute. Every sound was information she used without conscious thought.

She and Beth and Mandy had talked about this a lot. This calm in the middle of trouble. Mandy got cold, but Sally and Beth never did, and they'd decided long ago that it was the icy edge to Mandy's nerves that made the difference. So Mandy could outshoot Sally, but precious few other people on earth could.

But this wasn't a quick draw. That outlaw had his gun aimed and cocked. No one could get a gun into action fast enough to beat the quick pull of a trigger. She needed one second, one split second of distraction. But the outlaw wasn't budging an inch.

Logan dove straight forward. Straight off the cliff. He flew off the ledge straight toward the nervous-looking man with his gun aimed straight between Sally's eyes.

He was a perfect target. His move meant sure death. If the fall didn't kill him, the gunman would.

And she knew why he did it, too. He'd known she needed the man to look away.

Logan was dying to save her. No greater love.

The outlaw's gun dropped away from Sally and aimed at Logan.

Her rifle came up, cool, smooth, unerring, despite wanting to scream and cry and give Logan a thrashing for what he was doing.

In one instant that didn't stop her aim or slow her speed, she saw the colonel's wife dying in a pool of blood. The colonel, shooting, fighting, honorable and good and courageous, battling this coward.

She felt herself falling, falling, falling. Trees slapping at her as she tried to grab hold. She saw Luther bleeding and beaten to his knees. Buff was off to the side, visible from here. Down, maybe dead. Logan soared downward.

From out of nowhere, Luther had a knife in his hand and was spinning.

Sally's Winchester leveled and aimed straight at the outlaw's black heart. Her finger tightened on the trigger.

The gunman fired.

An arrow whistled through the air—and slashed deep into the outlaw's chest, slamming him backward.

Logan slammed onto the ground and skidded along flat on his belly.

Sally never fired a shot. She shoved her rifle behind her, mostly ignored her broken leg, and darted out from behind the rock.

Logan didn't move.

She saw blood. Too much blood.

The gunman was flat on his back, choking and thrashing and bleeding with an arrow surely pinning him to an afterlife of eternal torment and fire.

Wise Sister rushed out of the woods, tucking her bow over her head and one shoulder as she ran. Buff staggered to his feet and came limping behind her, bleeding through his right pant leg, his gun drawn. Luther stayed on his knees and reached for Logan, who lay still as death.

Sally looked frantically around for a way to get to Logan. It wasn't going to be easy, but she'd do it. She dropped to sit on the ground, swung her feet over the lip of that trail, rolled over onto her belly, and slid over the edge.

Going over a cliff for the second time in her life. But this time by choice.

Sally clawed her way down that cliff, pain radiating out from her heart in waves a thousand times worse than when she'd gone over that cliff before.

★ Twenty-six ★

Mandy fought against the scream.

This one, just control this one. Please, please, please.

"*Please!*" That last please slipped out long and loud. She couldn't control the cry for help. Her belly felt as if a grizzly had its teeth sunk into her, shaking, tearing her apart.

She clamped her jaw shut, listening for a cry. The girls had to be asleep by now. Poor Tom had a fight on his hands because Mandy had said good night and come to her room to have this baby in private and heard the racket. They'd made it through supper, though Mandy hadn't cooked it or eaten it. But she'd been there, doing her best to care for the girls as the contractions came closer and closer, harder and harder.

The sun had set, the evening had turned to night, and finally she'd managed to get the girls into their night clothes and into bed. But she hadn't been able to sit there and sing and read stories. It was simply beyond her physical capabilities. So she'd put them in bed and left the girls to Tom. She'd come to her room and let their crying tear her apart along with her labor pains.

Now here she lay, close to an hour later, the pains coming one on top of the other. Nowhere to go for help, no one to turn to, not even for comfort.

"Mandy, I'm here."

Realizing she'd had her eyes slammed tight shut, she forced them open. Tom could not be in here.

"I'm right outside the window."

Frantic to find where this man was during this extremely personal time, she saw that her bedroom window was open but the curtains hung over them. Outside she saw a lantern, deliberately held so that Mandy would know someone was out there.

She could see his silhouette through the gingham curtains, his square jaw and straight nose, his Stetson pulled low on his forehead. She could see nothing more and, to her relief, he could see nothing at all of her in the darkened bedroom.

"You should step away. It's not right—"

"I'm not going anywhere unless—unless the girls need me." He sounded unsure and nervous, but so kind. "I understand why I can't come in, but I can be out here. I can't see a thing from here. But I'm close enough you don't have to go through this alone."

Mandy's contraction eased, but she knew another one would be coming soon. With the last she'd felt that terrible bearing down of her body that meant it was pushing the baby out. She was only too glad that had finally come, even though the contractions were agonizing.

"It will be soon, Tom. The baby's close to coming." Mandy would have blushed at the improper topic if she hadn't been exhausted and scared beyond embarrassment. She was in the mood to hurt any man she got her hands on, too.

"If you need me in there, I'll come."

"No, absolutely not. Never."

"We may have to forget what people say is right and wrong. I *will* come in there if I decide I need to. But for now, I just thought you ought to know the girls are fast asleep for the night, and I'm here. You may be in that room by yourself, but I am one second away. You're not alone."

Mandy only realized at that exact instant how terribly isolated she'd been feeling. Having Tom say those words was like someone had thrown her a rope as she dangled off the edge of a cliff. "I'm glad you're here." Treacherously glad. Sinfully glad.

"Talk to me, Mandy. When your pains aren't bad, in between them, just talk. Anything you want. Just to know you're not alone."

"I—my life isn't a good one to talk about."

There was an extended silence, followed by a sigh. "You've got a lot of money. Two healthy daughters. A fine home. You just bought two of the prettiest horses west of the Mississippi." Even now she heard Tom's pride in his fancy horses. He added, "You don't have such a bad life."

Mandy laughed, or tried to. "You're right. I'm dwelling on the bad, and there's so much that's good."

"The bad." There was a long silence. "Like your husband."

And Mandy knew how improper it was to speak to another man about Sidney. But her mouth wouldn't obey her mind. "Sidney had a. . .a chance to be a good husband, I think. At the beginning."

Mandy didn't mention the part of the beginning where she'd found out Sidney was already married to someone else. True, that someone else had died before their wedding, but Sidney hadn't known that. No, he'd stood beside her, in front of her parents and family, and taken vows before God to be hers and only hers for life. All while he thought he was married. A vile, sinful falsehood.

Forgiving him for that hadn't come easy. With a slashing moment of honesty, Mandy realized she never had. She'd tried. She'd swallowed the shame and rage and betrayal and done her best, seeing as how the marriage was legal, to keep her vows to love, honor, and obey. But in her heart, in her soul, the soul that God had cleaned and forgiven, Mandy had not been able to do the same. It was a sin, and if she had been able to move, she'd have gotten to her knees and asked God to remove that sin from her heart.

She spoke of none of that to Tom. Instead she thought of Sidney after they'd had it out about his first marriage, after she'd pretended—even to herself—to forgive him.

And before the gold.

"The first winter together, Sidney seemed to respect the skills I brought to our marriage. He wanted to learn. He tried hard." Some days he'd tried hard. Others he'd been his usual pouty, sullen self. "He made some real progress taking on the chores of a pioneer. He tried."

"One winter?"

"We had part of the fall, then the whole long winter, and a short time in the spring where Sidney listened to me. . .and Luther."

"I've met Luther and Buff. Good men."

Where were Luther and Buff? Where was Sally? What had happened to them all? She didn't expect Sidney back, but she'd thought for sure Luther would move mountains to be here for her when her time came.

"Yes, Sidney let them teach him, and he treated me well." Once in a while. Even then he'd looked down on her. Mandy knew that now. "He showed promise."

"And then he discovered gold." Tom sounded so sure.

Mandy wondered what people said about her husband outside of his hearing. She suspected he was regarded to be a fool.

"Being rich hasn't been a good thing for Sidney. When there was no money, for a time he seemed to be trying to fill that hollow part of himself with working the land, caring for the cabin, learning to be a good husband. Then he found gold. Now, it's like he's hollow inside and desperate to fill that emptiness with the things money can buy. Worthless things for the most part."

"Hollow?" Tom just being out there, speaking, listening made this bearable.

"He was very poor growing up." Mandy couldn't relate the scandalous things Sidney had survived with a disreputable mother and no father. But poverty was enough of an explanation, though a poor one. Most poor people were honorable. "It's like he's trying to make up for a deprived childhood. He wants a bigger house, higher on the mountain, as if that makes him important, powerful. He wants a nicer buggy. A flashy ring, silk shirts, all of it just to brag. I hope you charged him a fortune for those two horses."

"I charged him a fair price." Tom sounded insulted.

Mandy's belly started tightening again, and she fought down a whimper, focused on Tom's arrogance. "Well, you should have doubled whatever you thought was a fair price because spending a lot on something seems to suit Sidney. And heaven knows he can afford it."

"He paid plenty." There was something smug in Tom's voice, and Mandy knew that Sidney hadn't bartered at all. Tom had made himself a pot of money on Mandy's foolish husband.

He'd more than earned every penny of the extra by being here today.

A cry of anguish slipped from Mandy's lips. Not loud—she fought that.

The baby pressed, ready to get out, more than ready. Mandy was ready, too.

"Are you all right?" Tom's worried voice drew her attention and she could see he was closer to the window, one hand on the sill. His silhouette looked poised as if he intended to leap through.

"Shut up," she shouted without meaning to and tried to sound more calm. "Just shut up for a second." Not so calm. "I mean, I mean, let me get—*ge–e–et*—" The pain turned the last word of what she'd hoped would be a rational little speech into a scream.

She was beyond listening for Tom, beyond telling him to stay out.

"Logan!" Sally fell most of the way down that cliff, but she got down fast and in one piece and it didn't matter if she had some bumps and bruises. She jumped up and stumbled to her knees because of her stupid cast, then crawled to reach her man's side.

He lay sprawled on his stomach.

Gently she leaned down and pressed her lips to his head. Then she reared back onto her knees, tears burning her eyes. "He's dead." He'd been shot! She turned to the man who had sent that bullet flying toward the man she loved. The only reason she didn't kill him was because he was already dead.

Luther knelt across from her, his skinning knife still in hand. Their eyes met. Sally felt the strength and relief in Luther's eyes that she was alive and well, and also the question. He'd witnessed her tenderness toward Logan. But this was no time for a talk.

Logan lay between them, flat on his belly, still as death. Luther's shirt was soaked with blood from his head wound.

Wise Sister joined them and dropped to Logan's side, nearer his head on the same side as Sally. "Scoot. Let me see to him."

Pure tyrannical orders. Sally wouldn't have dreamed of disobeying them. She remembered Logan saying he was kind of afraid of Wise Sister. Sally knew exactly what Logan meant. She moved closer to Logan's feet.

Wise Sister looked up at Luther, fury in those black eyes. "See to Buff."

Luther might have been a little bit afraid, too, because he flinched and looked past Wise Sister to his decades-long friend. He jumped to his feet, staggered as if his head reeled, then steadied himself just as Buff limped up to them. "Where'd he hit you?" Luther spared one loathing glance at the still-unconscious outlaw, lying face down beside his arrow-shot friend.

"Leg. Not bad." Buff sank to the ground. "Just a burn. Slowed me down some."

Wise Sister pulled a good-sized leather pouch out of her belt and tossed it to Luther. "Bandages. Moss. Pack Buff's wound. See to your head. Hurry. Need it for Logan."

Sally got to her feet and rounded to Logan's other side. "Where was he shot? That man couldn't have possibly missed at such a close range."

"Tulsa Bob Wiley. That's the guy's name." Luther pulled his knife again. "Sit down and let me clean out that wound."

"No bullet hole I can see." Wise Sister ran expert hands down Logan's arms and legs. She ordered Sally, "Turn him over."

"Get away from me with that knife." Buff staggered to his feet and backed away as if Luther was aiming for Buff's heart.

"I'm just gonna cut open your pants leg. Bandage the wound." Luther advanced on Buff.

"No!" Buff's voice was a loud whisper, as if he only wanted Luther to hear, but every word was clear to Sally. "You're not cuttin' my pants offa me in front of Wise Sister."

Sally was distracted from her worry about Logan by Buff's strange behavior. She'd never seen him act nervous. Was he hurt more seriously than she'd thought?

His pants were slick with blood low on his left thigh, just above the knee. But it wasn't bleeding that fast, and why mention Wise Sister but not Sally? Buff wasn't a man to talk much, and Sally had never seen him worry for one moment about what anyone else thought.

"Help move Logan." Wise Sister glanced over her shoulder at Buff and sniffed. "We won't look. Just hurry."

Luther advanced toward Buff. Buff backed away quickly enough Sally had no chance to worry, because they reached a clump of aspen trees and vanished from sight.

Noticing the lengthening shadows, Sally looked up to see the sun low in the sky, ready to set and leave them on this mountain in the dark.

From low muttered words, Sally could tell Buff was letting Luther tend his wound.

Sally and Wise Sister eased Logan onto his back. There was no blood, except for a single rivulet coming from his temple.

A blood-stained stone under his head explained how that had happened.

"I can't believe he missed. I can't believe it." Sally dragged a kerchief out of her sleeve, folded it, and pressed it to the cut on Logan's forehead. Through her fear, she noticed Logan breathing steadily. His face was ashen under the blood, but if his only injury was being knocked senseless, it would take time and nothing else to fix him up.

Wise Sister gave one furious look over her shoulder at Luther, who had walked off with her bandages, then pulled the corner of Logan's shirt up, produced a lethal-looking knife, and slit the fabric. "Move your hands. Bigger bandage."

Leaving her kerchief in place, Sally let Wise Sister add her pad of cloth. Wise Sister pressed down hard to staunch the bleeding.

"Ouch! That hurts!" Logan's eyes flickered open.

Her husband-to-be was waking up. And wouldn't she just know the first words he said would be unmanly?

Sally was so relieved she felt another bite of tears just as Logan's eyes flickered open and locked on hers. With an unsteady hand, he reached for her and pressed his hand to her cheek, which jarred loose some of that blasted salt water.

"Logan." She leaned down and kissed him full on the lips. At least it hid her tears from Luther, who, if he could see through those trees, would be horrified and ashamed that she acted so girly. The kiss might horrify him almost as much. It didn't matter. Luther was ignoring her in favor of stopping Buff's bleeding.

When Sally pulled back, Logan was alert and—for a bleeding man who'd just jumped off a cliff into gunfire—he seemed pretty happy. She leaned down to kiss him again, and Wise Sister shoved at Sally's shoulder and shook her head. Probably not the time or place for kissing.

A sharp crack of a bullet being jacked into a gun barrel pulled Sally's eyes up straight into the muzzle of a rifle.

"Everyone just stay calm." A stocky man with a streak of white hair leveled his fire iron at them as he leaned against a sturdy tree.

Sally had seen him lying unconscious then forgotten all about him. One of the two coyotes Wise Sister said were hunting her.

The man's eyes darted toward his dead friend, but Sally didn't see a lot of grief. Then he scanned the area and must have known Luther and Buff were close by. He aimed his rifle straight at Sally's head.

"You men get out here or I'll kill her."

"Just back away, mister." Sally felt that odd, almost crazed calm that came over her in times of trouble.

"We stay right here." Luther's voice sounded as sure and solid as a mountain from where he was behind that tree. "We'll let you ride out like you rode in. But if your finger even twitches on that trigger, you'll die. You can't kill us all. Your only chance of survival is to walk away."

The outlaw's eyes stayed beaded on Sally for a long, long moment, and she felt as if she was staring straight into her own grave.

God, have mercy.

"Don't be stupid, mister." Buff added his voice. "There's only one way for you to live through this day."

Sally saw Luther move in the forest. He was making himself a target, she knew, trying to draw this man's deadly gun to himself. Sally's fingers twitched to reach for her own rifle. She saw Logan's hand slide to the sheath on his belt that held his knife, and she remembered that he'd tried to die for her once already today.

God, have mercy on us all.

"That streak of white hair," Luther said. "I've seen that before."

"Me, too," Buff added; and from the location of his voice, Sally knew Luther and Buff had spread out to make themselves even harder to hit.

Sally watched the outlaw and saw the instant he hesitated and shifted his eye. They had him. He'd figured out he had to run.

"You get out here." The man's voice rose with nerves. "I mean it. I'll kill the girl, and even if I die, you'll have lost your friend."

Sally heard the soft whisper of Logan's knife inching out.

No, please, stop this. Have mercy on us, God.

"You can't win this fight," Sally said. She had to save Logan. She couldn't let him die. She couldn't live without him. "You can kill one of us, and we don't want that, but then you'll die. One man alone can't take all of us."

"That thatch of white hair," Luther said, moving back and to the right as a snapping twig told Sally Buff continued to move forward and to the left. "It's just like—"

"How about two men?" A new voice entered their conversation.

Sally looked up high overhead, to the mouth of that cave, and saw another man.

"Two could do a lot of damage." A younger version of the man down here held two pistols aimed in the general direction of Luther and Buff. Sally wasn't sure what the man could see from up there.

"Cooter." Luther's voice sounded like he was spitting. "He has hair just like Cooter's."

"Your name is Cooter?" The man down on their level asked.

"Yep, that's my name. Least it was a long time ago. And my pa and my brother had that same streak of white."

The two men exchanged a long glance, but their guns aimed true.

"I think that makes you my big brother."

"Cordell, is that really you?"

"Yep, sure enough. I came west huntin' you. I heard tell of a man with this mark. I've kept my eyes open, but never run you to ground."

Cooter and Fergus held their whole conversation without shifting their eyes or lowering their guns.

"Cooter works for Sidney," Luther said.

Wishing Luther would shut up, Sally knew he was trying to draw the men's attention. Give her a fighting chance. She straightened slowly, gradually, to shift her gun so the muzzle wasn't pressed against the ground. Then Sally thought about what Luther had said. "He works for Sidney? Mandy's Sidney?" Which reminded Sally of her big sister and the fact that she was somewhere, very soon to have a baby—if she hadn't already. Sally needed to get to her.

"We're not gonna shoot it out with you folks." Cooter spoke like he was chitchatting over coffee and huckleberry pie. "I've got my eye on the mother lode, Fergus, if you want in."

"Why not? I'm shy a saddle partner." The older man jerked his head toward the dead outlaw.

"I think they're right that we won't be able to get out of here without taking some lead. But they'll take their share. Not a winning hand. We'll back off."

Sally straightened a bit more. No time for relief yet.

"I'll keep 'em covered while you get to your horse, Fergus."

Fergus shuffled back. A mighty careful man. "Head south and I'll catch up with you."

"Their only horses close to hand are up here in this cave so they'll be a long while climbing up here to get 'em. I'd steal 'em, but if I got in that cave, these folk'll scatter and I won't be able to get out. Their horses'd slow us down too much anyway, and the plan I've got, we can buy all the horses we want. I've already got a spare, and you'll have your partner's. With the climb ahead of these folks, we can be well away by the time they're on horseback."

Sally wasn't sure where Luther had left his horse, but it couldn't be anywhere close by. Luther, Buff, and Wise Sister had climbed down here on foot if they'd been on the trail she and Logan had taken. Cooter had it figured out about right.

No one moved as Fergus vanished from sight. The man above them kept his eyes and aim steady.

At long last, just as the sun slipped below the mountain, casting them into twilight, a whistle from far below caught their attention. The man above touched two fingers to his forehead and backed into the brush alongside the trail. He never once slipped up with his aim until he ducked out of sight.

Luther charged forward, still pale, his shirt soaked with blood from his head wound. "The mother lode is Sidney. We've got to get to Mandy's house fast."

"You stay with Logan and Buff," Sally ordered Wise Sister as she limped for the trail above and the cave where their horses were sheltered, hoping neither of the animals had been wounded.

"No!" Logan surged to his feet. "We're all going. You're not facing those two men alone with a broken leg."

Buff stumbled forward, too, pants blood-soaked but well in place, limping but moving. Wise Sister was the only one of them that was at full strength. Sally was second, but a poor second.

"We won't be alone. We'll have Mandy." Sally didn't think Logan understood, but she'd rather have Mandy fighting at her side than an army.

Sally kept moving toward the cliff and scrambled up, using the meager handholds and sparing her battered cast as much as possible. It wasn't an easy climb, but she managed it, even in her doeskin skirt.

As she rolled over the lip of the cliff onto the trail, she looked back and saw Wise Sister right behind her. Logan, Buff, and Luther had vanished.

"They go for the other horses and come hard behind us. We tied the horses not far back that way. But there's no cliff. Logan and Buff get dizzy climbing this cliff, maybe Luther, too."

"Who decided that?" Sally would have preferred Luther at her side. She stood, testing her leg. Still no pain. She hoped that meant it was fully healed because the cast was a wreck. Her gaze went down to the dead man with Wise Sister's arrow in his throat. Sally centered her rifle across her back and decided having Wise Sister to back her was for the best.

"I lead." Wise Sister was issuing commands now. "I watch for coyotes. I know the woods."

"But do you know the way to Mandy's?" Sally hobbled into the cave, dingier now than ever with the sun gone. She snagged her crutch off the ground and hustled to the horses, which were back drinking at the pool. They looked no worse for being in a shooting gallery, though Sally saw a bullet lodged in her mustang's saddle.

"Buff and I talked as we came after you. He told me where your sister's cabin is. I know enough to set out. He'll be with us before the trail branches out."

"Are you sure Logan and Buff are up to a long ride?" Sally caught her mustang's reins and led him out of the cave.

Wise Sister was right behind her. "Better they keep moving."

It ate at Sally, the worry over Logan, the strange, almost pulsating pressure she felt to get to Mandy. Almost as if God Himself was telling her to hurry. She got her horse outside, limped to the saddle, and, using her broken leg for support, got her good foot into the stirrup and climbed clumsily aboard.

"If those men head straight for Mandy's house, they may beat us there. And it's close to Mandy's time to have a baby."

"Then we hurry." Wise Sister pointed up the trail, the same direction Cooter had gone, and without asking, kicked her horse forward and passed Sally, taking the lead. Which also meant Wise Sister would draw the first bullet.

Swallowing hard, Sally let Wise Sister go. She knew the way, she knew the mountains, but Sally hated it.

As they rode fast up the ever-climbing, twisting mountain path in the ever-deepening darkness, another thought occurred to Sally. "You ever deliver a baby?"

Wise Sister shook her head. Then Sally heard a sound she'd never thought Wise Sister would make. Laughter. "All six of my own."

"Alone? You had all six of your own alone?"

"Oldest girl helped later. But the first four? Yes, alone. And I've helped with a few hundred others."

"Let's ride faster."

★ Twenty-seven ★

Anyone else feel like a weakling?" Logan looked at Luther and his blood-soaked shirt, Buff and his bleeding leg, then touched the rough bandage tied around his own head. "You know Sally's got a broken leg."

It seemed necessary to point out that the women weren't completely unscratched. Wise Sister was, but that woman defied all attempts to stop her from anything she set out to do.

"Still carryin' that painting?" Luther rode alongside Logan. They set a fast pace, despite the pain they were all in.

"Painting?" Logan knew only one painter around here. He looked at Luther, who was looking back at Buff bringing up the rear.

Buff's saddlebag was tied shut funny, as if whatever was in there didn't fit, and the flap that closed over it was stretched.

"What painting?"

"One you did of Wise Sister. Babineau got mostly burned off, but Wise Sister is still there. Buff knew her back a long time ago."

"You knew Wise Sister when she was younger?" A branch

slapped Logan in the face and he turned, bent lower, and kept moving. They weren't closing the distance with the women at all. Sally and Wise Sister were moving fast and had a good head start. Which meant if they got where they were going, they might run right into gunfire.

"Yep. And Pierre." Buff didn't add to that, and Logan got the impression Buff was a man of few words.

"How far to Sally's sister's house?"

"Not far. If we ride hard." Luther leaned down over his horse's neck to duck under a branch.

"Not far" was about the most useless bit of information Logan had ever heard. The trail could barely be called such. Tracks were clearly going this way.

"You're sure we're following Sally and Wise Sister, not those two outlaws?" Logan shouldn't have asked, but it goaded him that, yes, he could see two sets of hoof prints. *But what if the outlaws had met up? What if*—A particularly unfriendly aspen slapped Logan in the face and cut off his worries.

"Don't matter. This is the way to Mandy's and we need to get there. Sally and Wise Sister know that. Quit yapping and ride." Luther pulled ahead of Logan as the poor excuse for a trail got even more worthless. The three of them strung out in a fast-moving line.

Logan wanted to ask a lot more questions. But it stung to be accused of yapping so he fell silent and rode.

They reached a particularly treacherous stretch of the trail. The horses scrambled to find footholds. Faint tracks showed in the occasional bit of dirt blown onto what was mostly stone. They were on the right trail.

They crested the rise and found a trail clinging to the side of the mountain they were scaling. Luther kept climbing. Logan urged his horse forward. No small task because this easier trail let them move faster, and Luther was pushing his horse hard.

"Do they live clear on the top of this mountain?" Logan

wondered if they had a pretty view and opened his mouth to ask.

"Yep. Mandy's husband is an idiot."

Logan closed his mouth. They reached a civilized stretch of the trail and the horses broke into a canter.

"So, what are your intentions toward my girl?"

Logan looked up to see Luther glaring over his shoulder. Cold eyes burned into Logan's hide.

"Your girl?" Logan considered dropping back. Luther hadn't shown much interest in talking, but this question he clearly thought was worth the effort.

"I have treated Sally with nothing but respect since she's come to stay with me." Logan thought if he got that out quick he might dodge Luther's fist.

Luther grunted and fell back by Logan's side. "Not what I asked."

Buff suddenly pulled up so Logan was between them. Logan felt trapped, with one mountain man on each side. He seriously suspected that was exactly what Buff and Luther wanted him to feel.

"I asked Sally to marry me. She's said yes. She has to get to Mandy first and make sure her sister is all right, but after that, we're riding to find a preacher."

"And live up here and paint pictures the rest of your life." Luther sounded like he was spitting when he said "paint pictures."

"Sally respects my work. Knowing she does is an honor. She said she'd be willing to stay with me, work beside me."

"You mean she's willing to break her back keeping your house and feeding you while you sit around and look at the scenery?"

"No, that's not what I mean," Logan retorted, embarrassed into anger because that sounded like what he expected Wise Sister to do.

"I'm used to people not understanding my work. I expect nothing else from most. But Sally understands." Logan hoped.

And he hoped that the feelings Sally had for him right now, when their life and death struggle heightened everything, survived during the mundane years ahead when he neglected her to chase the elk or the spewing geyser or the crimson sunset.

He loved her and knew he always would. Right now, at this moment, she loved him. But how could that love survive disillusionment and hardship?

Giving her up would be the honorable thing to do. Send her away. Leave her while she still cared rather than binding her to him and watching her grow to hate him.

Logan looked at Luther. "I hate justifying myself to people. I live with contempt from almost everyone. But I can see you love Sally, and she loves you. It would mean a lot to me if you'd approve of us." But how could Luther approve when Logan didn't really approve?

"I might approve," Luther said, "if you followed her back to Texas, got to know her family, gave her parents a chance to know you."

And how could Logan go to Texas when he needed these soaring mountains to live? And all his time away from them was saved to see his own beloved family. And he needed New York City as a market for his paintings. The people who would open a museum or buy a sculpture were few and far between in the West.

"You'll drag Sally away from her family and ranch life, then hope she still loves you as the years pass." Luther urged his horse around a curve in the mountainside.

Logan saw that they had another hard climb in front of them. He silently thanked God that this conversation would have to end.

Just as Luther pulled ahead to the trail that narrowed until they couldn't ride abreast, he glanced over. "That's what Mandy did when she married Sidney. When you meet Sidney, you'll see why it's a bad idea to marry for love."

"Nothin' wrong with love," Buff interrupted.

Startled, Logan turned to the taciturn man. Could Buff possibly be on Logan's side in this?

"There is if your lives don't match." Luther scowled at Buff.

"Love's enough. Real love." Buff eased his horse back so he fell in behind Logan.

Looking back at his friend, Luther had an expression on his face Logan couldn't quite define. Annoyance, amusement, a bit of worry. Mainly surprise.

"Maybe love's enough." Luther glared at Logan. "Real love. But who's to say what's real?" Then Luther turned back to the trail and took the lead as they passed into a wooded stretch clinging to a steep mountainside.

From that point on they concentrated on not falling off the mountain.

Mandy lost track of everything but the waves of pain and the man just outside, who seemed like an anchor holding her to this world while her body tried to hurl her into the next.

This contraction seemed endless and the next and the next. No break in between to relax and prepare to face another assault.

Then as if it was too much for the mind to deal with, Mandy felt an almost detached clarity. She realized in that moment something amazing about having a baby. God made her body to work. He created birth and women and babies out of His great love and endless wisdom. And He knew what He was doing.

This baby was going to come on out and join the world no matter if she had a doctor, a husband, a passing horse salesman, or two crying little girls. There was freedom in feeling that, even utterly alone, her baby would be fine. God created a beautiful world, and His world worked.

Her child, forcing its way into her life. There was no stopping it. No point in much planning ahead really, despite all her worrying. Her child would come in a way as natural as all newborn creatures. It would emerge to join the family on a wave of mother's tears. Mandy was only distantly conscious of crying out and giving an occasional shout she didn't plan and couldn't control.

As her time came closer, an almost audible snap in her mind erased her fear, leaving her with an almost insane serenity. A sense of power had her think fleetingly of Sidney's mountain and his mansion. That sense of independence and arrogance and victory and power. The power of it. Of surviving alone.

She'd decided to never twist herself around in Sidney's presence again to suit some notion he had of proper womanhood. She'd stood up to him a couple of times, but there hadn't been many chances. Now that confidence, pride maybe, though she knew that for a sin, exploded on a crest of pain.

She would never, never again back down from anyone. She had the strength to make her own life. And if Sidney or anyone got in her way, she'd trample him to the ground beneath a stampeding herd of longhorns.

Tom's voice intruded distantly on her heady fury. His words didn't make sense in the midst of her travail. She didn't need him. Didn't need anyone. And as soon as she was done having this baby, she'd prove that to the whole world.

Suddenly there was a massive surge of her body and another and another. It went on and on until Mandy knew she could survive it no longer.

Time stood still. It could have been moments or hours or days because to Mandy that moment was the stuff of eternity.

"This is taking an eternity!" Sally wondered why the menfolk didn't catch up. It wasn't like they were waiting for them, but still, they should have been here by now. Never a man around when you needed one.

Of course, Sally probably didn't need one, but it still would have been nice.

"God, have mercy, what is this?" Sally rode up closer to Wise Sister, who led the way. A trail blasted out of the heart of the mountain. Still narrow, so deep, but passable. Better than what they'd been following.

"We're close now. This is as Buff described. Sidney used blasting powder to widen the trail to his home." Wise Sister slowed her horse but continued forward on the steep uphill slope.

"Widen? This is widened? A wagon can barely pass." Sally entered the odd stretch of trail. The walls of the mountain rose over her head fifty feet. Someone above her on that trail could rain deadly fire down on anyone who passed. If Mandy's husband controlled the high ground, then his home was an impregnable fortress. But if someone else somehow gained that, no one could pass through this trail and expect to survive.

"Move faster." Sally thought of the two outlaws who had ridden off with their talk of the mother lode, Luther's certainty that they were talking about Mandy.

The really strange part was that no one seemed to be up there keeping a watch on this trail. That meant Sidney felt safe enough to neglect this single outpost. Sidney hired that vermin, proving he had poor judgment indeed.

Wise Sister didn't respond but she picked up the pace.

They rode on in silence until they'd passed through the gap.

Sally drew in a shaky breath as they found a mountain valley, still rugged but thick with grass and water. A small cabin stood at the far side of the clearing.

Mandy's house. They'd made it! In her excitement, her eyes followed the rising mountain and— "Good grief, look at that!"

A mansion. A huge structure was visible, half built, on up the mountain to the right near the peak.

Wise Sister grunted but didn't respond. She kicked her horse into a ground-eating gallop, and they drew near the house in time to hear a heart-tearing scream of agony.

Sally raced for the house and leapt off her horse as a stranger, a tall blond man, rounded the side of the cabin. They both froze for a second. Sally blinked. Who was this?

"Mandy's giving birth. She needs help." The man reached for the door, then froze and stepped back. "Uh. . .you go."

Sally didn't have time to consider who he was or how he knew something so personal about her sister. The only thing she was sure of was, though she hadn't seen Mandy's husband for years, this wasn't him.

Another scream spurred her into the house, Wise Sister on her heels. They ran inside in time to hear the high-pitched cry of a baby.

★ Twenty-eight ★

New life. An eternal soul entering the world.

Mandy tried to force her body to respond. To reach for her wailing child, but she couldn't, not yet. But she'd manage it soon. Now she knew God had created her to be capable of doing what was needed, completely alone.

The door slammed open and Mandy clawed at the blankets she'd thrown off to shield her body.

"Mandy!"

"Sally?"

An elderly woman pushed past Sally, swinging the door closed. Mandy caught the smallest glimpse of Tom, just his form. He'd been coming in.

Thank You, God, that he didn't. It would have been a terrible sin to let him see her.

The Indian woman reached Mandy's side and smiled with a wisdom as solid as the mountain. She took a quick look to make sure the door was closed, then brushed the blanket aside and lifted the baby into her arms.

Sally came to Mandy's side and they looked at each other and both burst into tears. "Pa would have our hides for crying." Sally leaned down and pulled Mandy into her arms.

"It's a boy." The elderly woman looked down and a smile creased her wrinkled face.

"This is Wise Sister." Sally pulled away from Mandy, though Mandy didn't want to ever let go.

Mandy looked at the older woman holding her squalling, wriggling child. "A son." Mandy smiled through her tears.

Then new voices were added to the racket her little boy made. Two crying youngsters. No doubt disturbed by all the commotion.

Tom's heavy boots thudded as he went in to the girls. His deep voice began soothing them.

Mandy looked from Sally to her baby, too exhausted and confused to know what she should do next.

Wise Sister took the child and began bathing him in the water Mandy had prepared.

"Where have you been?" Mandy asked, suddenly furious.

Sally laughed and pulled Mandy into her arms again. There was considerable talking as Sally told of her adventure.

"You ran in here on a broken leg?"

"I'm a McClellen. Of course I did."

Wise Sister rested the baby in Mandy's arms. "Time for him to eat. I'll see to helping you clean up."

Mandy took the little boy.

Wise Sister tidied the room, changed the sheets with only a little help and a minor break in the talking, and made sure all was well.

"I'm no help at all." Sally sank down on the bed, her eyes fixed on the tiny baby. "I wonder what I expected to do if I'd gotten here alone?"

Mandy looked away from the baby and started to cry again. "I'm so glad you came."

"Too late to do any good."

"No, you're doing me a world of good right now, just by being here."

The door to the cabin opened again and they heard someone speak.

"Is that Luther?"

"Yep, he and Buff and Logan must have finally caught up."

"You've talked a lot about Logan?" Mandy made it a question.

"I'll explain later. Where's Sidney?"

Mandy's tears dried up, and she looked down at her son. With one trembling hand she reached out to touch the little hand that flailed near the baby's cheek. With a few gentle brushes, Mandy got the baby to open his hand and cling to her finger. "Sidney is in town."

"You're sure? We met a man named Cooter on the trail, and Luther was afraid he meant you and Sidney ill."

"Cooter?" Mandy looked up. "Sidney was planning to fire him."

"He held a gun on us. He and the man chasing me lit out, and Luther thought they were heading here." Sally told Mandy briefly what had transpired.

"I wonder if he hurt Sidney." Mandy was exhausted and overwrought. That was surely the only reason that speaking of Sidney possibly being dead didn't give her a single twinge of sadness. She remembered her vow, as her child was born, to need no one, to stand on her own. Maybe that's why she wasn't overly worried about her absent husband.

Sally leaned close and whispered, "Who is that man out there?"

"What man?" Mandy knew exactly what man.

"A tall blond man who looked to be coming in at the same time I was."

"Tom Linscott. He brought a team by right when the baby started coming. He stayed around."

He did all her chores and took care of the girls when she couldn't. He saved her sanity. "I wouldn't let him in here, of course, but I reckon I did some hollering there toward the time the little one came. I must have scared him into ignoring my orders that he stay out."

Sally's brows arched nearly to her hairline. "He was coming in?"

Considering all she'd been through, Mandy was surprised to find out she had the strength to blush. "Must've been."

Wise Sister interrupted. "I take the baby. Show him to the menfolk. They will wish to know how you and the little one fare." She gently lifted the baby from Mandy's arms, adjusted the tiny blankets a bit, and said, "You need to sleep." Then she took the baby and left.

Mandy looked at her son as he disappeared. "Who did you say that is?"

Sally gave Mandy a huge hug. Mandy clung to her sister as if Sally was a floating log in a rushing river. A life saver.

"That's Wise Sister. She'll take good care of the baby, Mandy. When I was hurt and broke my leg, she took care of me. She's almost as good a doctor as Beth."

"How'd you say you broke your leg again?" Mandy's eyelids seemed to weigh about ten pounds each.

Sally lifted her battered cast and Mandy perked up, but soon her eyes grew heavy again. "I'm going to let you rest for a while." Sally squeezed Mandy's hands then rose from the bedside.

Mandy held on tight when Sally tried to let go. "You won't leave, will you?"

Sally hesitated for just a second. "Of course I won't leave."

For some reason Mandy was sure Sally was lying. "Please don't leave."

Tears burned her eyes again and she remembered how she'd decided to never need anyone again. But maybe she did need her sister. For just a little while.

"I'll be here when you wake up, Mandy. I'm here for a little while. Don't worry about a thing. You've got lots of help."

I don't need any help. Mandy thought it but couldn't quite manage to say it out loud for fear Sally would believe her and leave.

Sally's brow furrowed as she watched Mandy.

Mandy almost begged Sally to stay in the room with her. And that reminded Mandy again that she'd taken a vow to never depend on anyone again. She let loose of Sally's hands.

"You get some sleep now. I'll take care of your little ones."

Well, she'd start being independent just as soon as she woke up from her nap. "Thank you, Sally. I'm so glad you're here."

Mandy's eyes fell shut as she heard the door close, leaving her completely alone. Her last thought as she felt herself sinking into sleep was she'd have cried her head off if she hadn't been so tired.

Sally emerged from the room to find quite a party going on.

Luther held Catherine on his lap. The little girl was grinning and tugging on his beard. The tall, blond stranger held two-year-old Angela as if they were old friends. Wise Sister held the baby and stood next to Buff, who admired the little tyke, as proud as a grandpa rooster.

Sally limped over to Logan's side. Her foot didn't even hurt anymore. The cast was hanging by shreds of fabric. As soon as things settled down, she'd cut it the rest of the way off. As she stood by his side and looked at the people here, she could almost see him sketching the scene in his head.

Everyone was talking quietly, if they were talking at all, except Angela, who was jabbering away to the stranger. Sally caught the word "horsie."

"Yes, I have a big horsie." The stranger smiled at Angela, bounced her on his knee, and listened to her as if every word was etched in gold.

Who was he?

Logan smiled down at Sally. "Your sister's okay, then?"

"Yes, she is. She's fine. She was glad to see us, but she managed the whole thing herself. She's a tough woman." Sally looked at the three little ones. All three little more than babies. Her sister was tough indeed. "I've never even met my nieces before." Afraid her voice would break, Sally swallowed hard before she went on. "And a nephew. They shouldn't be so far away from family."

"Sidney is her family now."

Snorting, Sally looked sideways at Logan. Was she going to do this? End up somewhere so far from loved ones that her children never knew their aunts and uncles and grandparents? Was that a reasonable life? To give up everyone else for a man? It might be a good deal if it was the right man, but how could anyone know? Mandy had adored Sidney. Sally remembered Pa's unhappiness with Mandy's choice, but Mandy would not be turned aside from having him.

Luther turned Catherine so she straddled his knee and introduced the little girl to her new brother. Once Catherine's attention was caught there, Luther looked up. "We need to get ready for trouble."

"What trouble?" Tom Linscott responded immediately. Sally noticed he wore a revolver on his hip, and his weathered skin and sharp blue eyes spoke of living a hard life and conquering a hard land.

Luther explained about Cooter's threats, speaking calmly to keep from upsetting the children. "We need to put someone on lookout through that gap. If we own the high ground, no one can get in. Anyone who lives in here ought to have sense enough to post a guard."

"Where's Sidney?" Sally hadn't even though of him until Luther spoke of someone needing more sense.

"He went to town." Tom faced Angela outward and began bouncing her on his knee. Good thing, because the little girl might have been frightened by the fierce anger on Tom's face. He let none of it sound in his voice, and he kept jiggling Angela as if he didn't have a care.

Everyone in the room fell silent. The baby chose that moment to howl.

"See da baby." Angela reached up and slapped Tom in the face, then looked up and laughed. Tom smiled back—but there was no smile in his eyes.

"We need to post a guard." Sally looked at the wounded warriors around her—Luther still covered in blood, Buff needing his leg tended. Wise Sister needed to do the tending. Logan probably ought to be at least sitting down. Tom was healthy but this wasn't his problem.

That left her. "I'll go." Her cast was so battered she didn't think it was doing any good anymore. But her leg seemed to be holding up.

"I'll go." Logan stepped forward. He looked reasonably steady. But had the man ever even aimed a gun?

Sally couldn't help but *not* feel reassured.

Luther jabbed a finger at Sally. "You need to help with the young'uns. I'll go."

But Sally thought Luther looked unsteady under his gruff exterior.

"I'll go," Tom said. "I don't mind staying up all night. I just came way too close to helping deliver a baby. I probably won't sleep for a month. And I'll probably have nightmares for the rest of my life." Tom stood with Angela in the crook of his arm. "But if that no-account Gray comes riding through that gap, I can't promise not to fill his backside with buckshot."

All things considered, Sally wasn't sure she could make that promise herself.

"Then tomorrow I'm going to ride in to Helena." Tom handed Angela to Buff. "Find Sidney." Tom drew his Colt as soon as his hands were free. "Kick that worthless excuse for a man in the backside for going to *town* when his wife was ready to have a baby." He cracked open the revolver. "And send what's left of him home." Tom checked the load with quick, practiced motions then snapped the gun shut.

"Then I'll contact the U.S. marshal." Tom returned his gun to his holster with a soft *whoosh* of iron on leather. "And give him a description of the two varmints who drew their guns on you folks." Tom settled his Stetson more firmly on his head. "I've seen Cooter." With one tug, Tom drew his hat down nearly to his eyes. "If his big brother looks as much like Cooter as you say—"

"He does," Luther interjected.

"Good, then I can describe 'em both well enough that the authorities will know just who to look for." Striding to the door, Tom reached for the knob. "Then I'll make sure the sheriff rides out to find the body you left behind." He turned the knob hard as if crushing the doorknob was a substitute for crushing an outlaw—or Sidney. "And then I'll send a wire." Tom looked back, sliding his eyes over each of them.

Sally knew they were a battered-looking group. She suspected he was assessing their fitness to stay here and take care of Mandy. What was Mandy to him?

"And get ahold of someone who knew Colonel McGarritt." They must have measured up because Tom turned back to the door and jerked it open. "So they can get a bead on the men who killed the group you were riding with and wipe 'em out and put an end to the danger Mandy is in." Tom stormed out, slamming the door behind him.

Which set the baby to crying again.

"A man of action." Sally looked after him, impressed. That's the kind of man she should be marrying. She smiled up at Logan. Too bad for common sense, she was in love with the paint slinger instead of the gunslinger.

Wise Sister took control. "Sally, you get a bedroll and sleep on the floor in Mandy's room." She bounced the fussing infant. "I'll take the youngsters into the other bedroom and get them settled. Their eyes are heavy. They'll sleep soon."

Wise Sister turned to Buff. "Then I'll see to your leg. It needs tending. All of you men find a spot on the floor and get some sleep. We'll need you at full strength in the morning."

A woman of action. Sally was glad someone was taking charge.

Or course, Sally would have liked a bit of time alone with Logan to try and reassure herself that loving him was enough to overcome their differences. But who could stand up to Wise Sister?

They all obeyed like a herd of mindless sheep. Mindless, wounded sheep

★ Twenty-nine ★

Mandy woke to find an Indian in her bedroom.

She'd have screamed if she thought it was real. Probably a dream. Her eyes fell shut.

"No, come back. It's morning." The lady gently rocked Mandy's shoulder.

Mandy realized her shoulder being rocked was what woke her to begin with. She felt sleep ease away. It was the kindest wake-up she'd ever had. Mandy moaned and stretched, aching oddly, still mostly asleep.

"The baby needs to eat, little mama."

"Baby?" Mandy's eyes flew open and focused. She'd had the baby. "Where's Tom?"

Mandy clamped her mouth shut. That wasn't the first question she should have asked.

The baby let out a thin yowl, like a hungry kitten, and Mandy sat up, groaning at the battering her body had taken yesterday.

"Let me help, Mandy." Sally slid an arm under Mandy's shoulder.

"Sally!" Everything came back to Mandy in a rush. Mandy's eyes met her sister's, and they launched themselves into a hug.

While her little sister, who was taller than Mandy these days, held her in arms made tough by long hours doing a man's work, Mandy felt that stupid, weak urge to weep again.

That thin cry sounded again.

Sally eased Mandy back then smiled. "Hi. Yeah, I'm here." She propped a rolled-up blanket behind Mandy's shoulders.

Wise Sister carefully helped Mandy settle the baby in to a meal.

"What time is it?" That was a dumb question. What difference did it make what time it was? It was feeding time. That would be her only clock for a long time. Except it felt like she'd slept a long time. And she'd expected to be awake all night caring for a baby.

"The sun rises already in the east." Wise Sister, that was the Indian lady's name. Shoshone.

With a clear head and no baby being born, Mandy could recognize the dress and the beadwork as Shoshone. She looked at Sally and saw that Sally was wearing a doeskin dress similar to Wise Sister's. How had anyone gotten Sally into a dress?

"I can't believe I slept all night." Mandy's head cleared more with every word. That full night of sleep had been incredibly healing.

"We tended the little one," Wise Sister crooned, smoothing back Mandy's hair. "You needed rest."

Mandy took a few deep breaths and enjoyed the presence of women. So wonderful to have a woman around. Then her shoulders squared. She was the big sister, the pioneer wife, the tough Texas ranch girl, and the fastest gun and deadliest shot in the West. . . and she'd believe that until someone proved her wrong.

"Where have you been, Sally? What happened to you? Are you all right? Tell me everything even if you already went over it last night. Did you say you've got a broken leg?"

Sally lifted her leg up. It looked fine. "Wise Sister cut the rest of the cast off last night. I feel almost whole again after I got shot off a cliff."

"What?" Mandy felt her brows slam down over her eyes. "Start talking. I want to know everything that's happened."

Sally jerked her chin, sat down on the bed, and started at the beginning.

The baby was almost finished with his meal by the time Sally got to yesterday.

"Cooter! He held you at gunpoint?" Mandy's fingers itched to get her rifle. The nursing baby slowed her down.

"I think he'd have just shot us where we stood except Luther and Buff were a few steps behind some undergrowth. Buff was shot in the leg and Luther had to stop the bleeding. Wise Sister and I were tending Logan, who was knocked insensible after he dived off that cliff to save me." Sally kept taking fascinated peeks at the baby. "Even with two guns held on us it was too risky for the outlaws to start shooting. Cooter struck me as a cautious man and a thinking man. Which makes him mighty dangerous."

"The yellow-haired man stands lookout on the gap into your home," Wise Sister said.

"Tom." He was still here, still taking care of her. Mandy swallowed and turned her thoughts away from how much she admired him. Which made her think of her husband and how much she did *not* admire him. "What about Sidney? Did he come home? Do you think Cooter killed him?"

Sally's eyes widened.

Mandy realized how she'd sounded. Her voice had been too brisk, too indifferent.

"We don't know. Cooter talked about finding the mother lode then held the gun on us until his brother, Fergus, could get away. He didn't say anything about where Sidney was. Luther's sure Cooter was talking about you and Sidney and all your gold. The two of them rode off, and we headed here fast, afraid they were coming straight for you."

"No, there's no gold here." Mandy turned all the possibilities over in her mind. "I'm sure Cooter knows that. But I'm sure he's has been working out a plan to get his hands on it. Somehow. He wasn't referring to a direct attack. Or at least I doubt it. Sidney put the gold in a bank in Denver and made sure people far and wide knew it so there'd be no point in attempting to steal it from here or there. He picked one that's got a safe that has never been robbed. Cooter must have some idea about the money, but I have no notion what it might be. I don't see how he'd think coming here would help him."

Sally nodded. "Good, then there's no immediate threat." Sally then told Mandy what Tom planned to do with his day.

Mandy relaxed. "That'll put the U.S. marshals on the trail of the right men. It'll make this area dangerous for them, and if they're not caught, it'll be because they quit the country, at least for now. But I very much suspect they'll be back."

"We'll be ready for 'em," Sally said with a mean look in her eyes that Mandy had missed very much.

"Yes, we will. Now, who's Logan?" Mandy watched fascinated as her mean, dangerous little sister turned all pink and shy.

A woman stepped out of the bedroom, dressed and a bit shaky, but not that much considering she'd had a baby all by herself last night.

Logan was stunned by how much she looked like Sally. They weren't identical. Sally was two full inches taller, her hair a shade darker. And while Mandy was a pretty woman, she didn't hold a candle to her beautiful little sister. But the resemblance was uncanny. "How many girls are there in the family?"

"Four." Sally walked out right behind Mandy, close, as if her big sister might collapse and Sally wanted to be handy to save the day. Sally held the baby in her arms, so Logan walked over, thinking he could do the big sister catching it if was called for.

"All as pretty as you two?" Logan was already dreaming about a painting. All four of them. Mandy the pretty little mother. Sally the rugged ranch hand. "You said one of your sisters is a doctor, right?" He could already see the doctor's bag and the no-nonsense intelligence. It would make a fantastic portrait, catching their similarities and their differences.

"Yes, and the fourth is almost a woman these days."

"She still as prissy as ever?" Mandy asked.

"Yep, and as pretty. Taller'n me these days. And she's got men coming around all the time courting. She has a parasol to keep her skin from getting burned. Can you imagine?"

Grimacing, Mandy said, "Pa must be as nervous as a long-tailed cat in a room full of rocking chairs."

Mandy and Sally shook their heads in mutual disgust. Logan wasn't sure if it was over their sister or their pa or both.

Luther came into the cabin carrying baby Catherine, with Angela dogging his heels and jabbering away. Luther had a free hand to lift his Stetson and scratch his head as if confused. "Strange doin's." Luther handed the one-year-old to Logan.

The tyke came to him easily. But the day was wearing on, and he'd spent considerable time with the little ones this morning. He'd never painted children before, but these were so pretty. He'd love to try, see if he could catch their innocence and softness, the love and trust in their eyes.

Logan wondered for the tenth time this morning where their pa was. Gone to town, leaving his pregnant wife alone with two toddlers. Then he thought of his own inclination for neglecting people when the sunrise called to him. Would he be any better of a father and husband than Sidney?

Catherine took that moment to grin at him.

He smiled back. A furious wolf awakened in him, and it was a struggle to keep that off his face. The thought of someone doing these babies wrong. He'd fight and die for his own child. By golly, he'd fight and die for *these* children. *Yes*, he would be a good father. A good husband, too.

He turned to look at Sally, standing there cradling a baby. Logan waited until she looked up, then he smiled. Her eyes slid to the precious child in her arms, and her brow furrowed. She came to his side, but too slowly to suit Logan.

What was going on in her female head? Logan leaned down to get a closer look at the little boy, and the baby's waving hands punched him in the face.

Catherine giggled.

Logan almost stole a kiss from pretty Sally, right there in front of everyone.

"Strange doin's about what?" Mandy moved to a rocking chair by the stove and sat down with a faint groan.

"About Buff." Luther went to her, frowning, with Angela clinging to the fringe on his buckskin coat. "Somethin' wrong with him."

"His leg?" Sally asked.

"Nope, that seems to be fine, sore but the wound is already closed. It's just that he was talking with Wise Sister for a while last night when she tended his gunshot. Quiet-like and I couldn't hear. But they were goin' on about something for a long time."

Logan realized that Wise Sister wasn't in the cabin. He'd seen her going in and out of the bedroom all morning. She'd fed them all breakfast with Sally's help. Her quiet efficiency was missing right now from the crowded house.

"Then Buff spelled Tom at lookout early this morning. Tom set straight out for town without even eating anything. I went to spell Buff and he said—he said—" Luther shook his head.

"Said what?" Mandy frowned.

Logan didn't think it was wise to worry a new mother overly.

"He said"—Luther swallowed with a gulp so hard it hurt Logan's throat to watch—"him and Wise Sister are getting. . . getting. . .m–married."

"Married?" Sally's voice rose. The baby jumped in her arms and started crying.

"Today." Luther looked dizzy. "He said he was sorry I couldn't go, stand up with him."

"Buff?" Mandy asked.

"W–We decided I'd better stay here and help out. He promised to be back in two days."

"Wise Sister is getting married?" Logan felt a sufficient flash of shame to stop himself from shouting that he needed her.

Bouncing the baby, Sally's brow lowered then it cleared. She exchanged a look with Mandy, and they both smiled. "That's wonderful."

"It is?" Logan was losing his biggest helper and a true friend who actually respected his work. Except now Sally was a mighty good friend. Still—

"I guess they knew each other way back. He trapped alongside Babineau in the early days. Babineau was always going off and leaving her for months on end. Sometimes he'd get snowed away from her for the whole winter. Buff got so he'd stop by her cabin, almost more often than Babineau, when she had little ones hanging onto her skirt. He'd stay awhile, do some hunting. Help with the chores for a time. He says he loved her even back then but never spoke of it, seeing as how she was married. She cared for him, too, I guess, because she said yes."

"Well. . ." Logan cleared his throat. He'd be happy for her if it killed him. "Buff's a lucky man." An impulsive need to stake his claim to Sally, before he lost another friend, made Logan turn to her. "We should have ridden along to town. Made it a double wedding."

Mandy gasped out loud. "I asked you about Logan. You never said anything about a wedding."

Sally gave Logan a surly look, and he considered that she might have wanted to make the announcement herself. Well, too late for that. "This is no time to discuss something like that."

Logan's stomach sank at the look in her eyes. She was measuring him. He knew it. She compared him to Sidney and thought she saw a bleak future.

"I'm not leaving Mandy alone to run off with you." Sally made it sound definite and permanent.

"How 'bout if we get married, then come back here and stay with Mandy." Logan was willing to agree to almost anything Sally wanted, as long as they managed to include a wedding in there.

"I said we'd discuss it later." Sally's face was stiff with annoyance. Logan wondered if by pushing her, he'd pushed her away.

Luther cleared his throat loudly. "I think you ought to wait awhile, Sally girl. You haven't known Logan all that long and—"

"Hey." Logan cut him off. "Don't try and talk her out of it. She already thinks I'm strange enough." He looked down at Sally uncertainly.

She softened a bit. "I'm a little strange myself."

"I'll let you wear cowboy clothes all you want." Logan leaned close and whispered, "And I'll let you wear ribbons and lace, too."

Her eyes warmed. Logan thought he saw agreement in her expression.

The door burst open, and Sidney barreled in. He had a black eye. "Mandy, do you know what Tom Linscott did to me? I've got half a mind—" Sidney fell silent at the sight of so many people.

No one spoke.

Logan wondered how long it would take the idiot to notice that his family had grown in his absence. He was tempted to blacken his other eye, but holding a toddler in his arms dissuaded him.

"So, Sid," Mandy's voice sounded distant, cold, hard, "I see Cooter didn't kill you." She didn't sound one bit relieved.

"Of course not." Sidney sniffed like an overconfident bull right before butchering time. "I fired him and that was that."

Logan looked from Mandy's chilly frown to the soft light in Sally's eyes. Could that coldness one day be aimed at him if he was a bad husband? He couldn't imagine the day he wouldn't notice, and Sidney didn't seem to.

Shaking her head, Sally said to her brother-in-law, "Hi, Sidney. I got here just a few minutes after Mandy had the baby all alone."

"Baby?" His eyes roamed the room and landed on the squirming infant in Sally's arms. His eyes widened in surprise. "Tom said something about me being gone from home when I was needed. I suppose he was referring to the baby. Is it a boy this time?" Sidney sounded petulant.

Logan clenched a fist.

"It *is* a son, Sidney," Mandy said from where she rocked. Logan noticed that a rifle had somehow ended up on the floor right beside her rocker.

Sidney came over to look down at the little mite. Unwise, considering Logan's uncertain control of his fists.

The child had a dusting of dark hair. Logan was afraid the little guy was going to be the image of his father. Hopefully only on the outside.

"I have a son." Sidney smiled and touched the baby's hand. The infant clutched Sidney's finger.

Catherine, in Logan's arms, said, "Papa!" and nearly threw herself out of Logan's grip.

Logan held on, and it was a good thing because Sidney only had eyes for his baby boy. He didn't even look at his reaching, smiling, yelling daughter.

He picked the baby up out of Sally's cradling arms. Logan saw Sally's scowl, but she didn't stage a tug-of-war, which showed some self-control.

The little boy's eyes opened. His arms jerked and he opened his mouth and wailed by way of saying hello.

"We'll call him Sidney Gray, Jr." Sidney didn't ask Mandy about it; he just pronounced it. Sidney took the child and went to the table to sit down and continue staring. Angela ran to his side and pulled on his pants leg. Sidney didn't seem to notice.

"Sidney *Jarrod* Gray," Mandy said. "My grandpa who lived in these mountains was named Jarrod."

"Fine." Sidney didn't even give his wife a single look. It would have forced him to quit staring at his son.

Sally gave Mandy a worried frown. "Are you all right, Mandy? How are you feeling this morning?" Logan knew Sally was hoping to jar black-eyed Sidney out of his fixation on the baby and remind him there were others in this family who needed attention.

"No, I have everything I need." Mandy's voice lowered, and it sounded as strong and unshakable as the mountains. "I've got my own strength, a charitable God, and my children are safe. I don't need a thing."

Logan thought he saw an almost irrational fervor strike Mandy. She really didn't need anything. She brought that baby into the world without a doctor or another woman or her ma or her husband. She didn't need anyone.

That expression held an almost crazed sense of power.

The baby thrashed its little fists, and Mandy looked at him as Angela gave up on her papa and ran to climb onto Mandy's lap. "Sidney Jarrod Gray for his father who couldn't be bothered to be home when his first son came into the world." She settled Angela on her lap.

"Huh?" Sidney looked up for a second then went right back to adoring his son.

Mandy didn't repeat herself. But when the baby started crying, Logan noticed that Mandy, the independent, powerful warrior, hugged her daughter close and cried, too.

Sidney didn't notice.

Sally did, and when she looked between her big sister and her brother-in-law, her eyes went hard.

Logan felt her slipping away.

631

Thirty

Logan handed Catherine to Buff, then turned and grabbed Sally's hand.

"Hey, what are you doing?" Sally didn't have time to react before they were outside.

Logan strode along, dragging her and her only recently un-plastered foot.

She thought of using it as an excuse, but it didn't really hurt. "What are you doing?" Could this be one of his artistic quirks?

"I don't like what I saw in your eyes."

She must have been moving too slowly to suit him, because he turned and swept her into his arms, then continued walking.

"What you saw?" Sally's temper rose. She was going to *insist* that Logan quit reading her mind. She slid her arms around his neck, just for balance, not because she wanted to cuddle up to the big dope.

Logan stopped walking and turned to face her, but he held on tight. "Yeah. I saw you comparing me to that worthless Sidney. Like you think I'd neglect you."

"You already told me you'd neglect me."

"Well, I take it back."

"You can't take something like that back."

Logan ignored her and kept talking. "I would *never* leave you when you were set to have a baby. I would *never* favor one of my children over the other. You know me better than that."

Sally let go of his neck and shoved against his chest. "Put me down."

"I'm not letting you go until we have this out."

She quit fighting and glared. Their eyes locked. Then her anger wavered. "How do I know?"

"What?"

"Mandy was completely in love with Sidney when they got married. He ended up being the wrong man for her in every way, but she didn't know that until after she'd married him and followed him halfway across the country. He lied about being married. He lied about being a lawyer. He lied about having a job waiting. Now here you are, wrong for me in every way. And asking me to follow you."

"But you just said it yourself."

"Said what?"

"Sidney lied. I haven't lied. You know exactly who I am."

"Yes, I do. I know you're all wrong."

"But you fell in love with me knowing who I am and what I do. Would Mandy have fallen in love with Sidney if she'd known the truth?" Logan's eyes widened, and he let her slide down to stand on her own two feet as if his arms couldn't hold her anymore. "He was already married?"

"Yes. Sidney's first wife died before the wedding, but Sidney didn't know that."

"Well then, would Mandy have fallen in love with a married man?"

Her jaw tightened, and for a second Sally thought she might slug him. "My sister is an honorable woman. Of course she wouldn't have fallen in love with him. He courted her, wooed her, flattered her, charmed her, showered her with presents and attention. She'd have *never* let any of that happen if she'd known. Plus Pa would have shot him right out of the saddle, so it wouldn't have mattered what Mandy thought."

"You're making my point, Sally. Sidney lied. I haven't. You may think we're not right for each other, but you love me." He leaned down and took a quick kiss.

Sally let him and knew she'd miss him terribly if she used her God-given common sense and sent him away.

"And I love you. Knowing exactly how different we are, I still fell in love. And you fell in love with me." Logan slid one strong, artistic hand along the side of her face and tilted her chin up. "Didn't you?"

He looked so vulnerable. So in love. And he was right. She knew almost too much about Logan—the good and the bad—because he'd warned her long and hard about what he wanted in life and how much he cared about his strange bend toward painting pictures.

She couldn't lie to him, which meant she couldn't lie to herself. "Yes, I did. I fell completely in love." She closed the inches between them and felt Logan's shoulders slump with relief, even as he slid both arms around her waist and lifted her to her tiptoes and kissed her. She clung to his shoulders then to his neck. His warm, thick hair was like silk beneath her fingers.

"No more doubts, Sally. We get married with our eyes wide open. Knowing how different we are, respecting those differences, and working hard to get along despite them. Whatever happens, we make this work because I never want to be without you."

"I never want to be without you either." Tears flooded Sally's eyes.

He leaned down and kissed them away.

"Do you mind much a woman crying?"

Logan pulled away to meet her gaze. "I love every emotion

in you. I love that you're capable of love and rage, tears and tenderness. I love how you looked staring down at that new baby. I want every bit of how you feel to always show in your face. It's the most beautiful, expressive face I've ever seen. I don't even need Yellowstone or soaring eagles or snowcapped mountains. If you marry me, I'll have all the beauty I can bear, right in my arms."

His eyes studied her in that deep, detailed way, and she realized she'd gotten used to being stared at. She'd even learned to love it. "You mean you don't mind if I cry?"

"I never want to miss one second of what you're feeling."

It didn't sound true. No man *liked* a crying woman.

"I hate the idea of you being hurt by me or anyone, so if I caused any tears I wouldn't like that, and I promise to do my best to never make you cry." He snuck in a kiss.

Sally noticed she wasn't fighting him off, which must mean she liked the whole idea of being with Logan, no matter how outlandish it was.

"Besides, my mom raised four boys, and she cried at the drop of a hat. She cried when she was happy, when she was sad, when she was scared or tired or mad or. . .hungry. I swear that woman was always crying. I got real used to it and learned not to panic." Logan smiled then kissed her again.

It made a certain amount of sense. Her pa hadn't been around women as a child, out here in the Rockies. He might have grown up with no experience. Sally decided then and there to tell Mandy it might be fine to cry if she was of a mind. It might even be good and honest. And, unless Pa came to visit, there'd be no harm done.

Before today, Sally had never seen her big sister in tears, and she suspected Mandy had never seen Sally cry. Sidney didn't appear to notice. So maybe Mandy should save the salt water for someone who cared.

Then Logan broke off kissing her, and Sally realized she'd missed part of it for all her fretting about tears. She decided not to fret anymore. If she felt like crying, she'd cry and that was that.

Logan let her stand on her own two feet again. "We're getting married." It wasn't a question. It was an order.

Sally found she liked the idea of a man ordering her to marry him. As long as it was Logan. "But I need to stay here with Mandy for a while. I don't know how long."

"Then we'll stay. I'd like to ride to town and get married, then come back past my cabin and see if any of my paintings survived. Remember that one of you that outlaw threw over the cliff? We might be able to find it."

"But then we can come back here?" Sally hoped some bald eagle didn't distract Logan on the ride. Then she remembered he had no pencil or sketchbook and thought they'd probably be safe.

"Yes, for as long as you want. All summer. . .all winter, too." Logan looked up the mountain and grimaced at the mansion. "If they ever get that done, they ought to have plenty of room for us."

"Or maybe they could live up there and we could stay in this cabin." Sally looked at the really nice-sized cabin Mandy now lived in and wondered why anyone needed more.

"Unless Wise Sister and Buff want it."

Sally nodded. "We'll figure out something, because, yes, Logan. Yes, I will marry you." Her arms went around his neck again just as the cabin door slammed open and Sidney came flying out of the house to land belly down on the ground.

Sally saw Luther standing in the doorway and Mandy peeking out from behind Luther, holding the baby.

"You'll come back in when you can watch your mouth!" Luther raged.

Then he turned to Sally and Logan and said, "Get in here!"

Sally remembered thinking Wise Sister could give orders. She couldn't hold a candle to Luther in a rage. Maybe they'd just go on in. She reached down and took Logan's hand and they exchanged a look.

"Let's go tell 'em we're getting married," Logan said, not acting all that afraid of saying something as stupid as Sidney must have and incurring Luther's wrath.

Clinging to Logan's hand, Sally feared she'd have to drag him, but he came along willingly, walking past Sidney groveling in the dirt. They headed right into the teeth of Luther's rage.

Sally knew she'd finally found a man strong enough to let her be a cowboy, kind enough to let her have a few bits of lace and ribbon, and wise enough to keep his mouth shut about both. "Logan?"

"What, honey?"

"Luther's had a bad day with losing Buff and dealing with Sidney. Maybe you'd better let me do the talking."

"There's one more thing you'll find out as you get to know me better, Sally."

"What's that?" She smiled at Luther, who bared his teeth and glared at the hand she had entwined with Logan's.

"I'm not a foolish man." Logan shifted so Sally was standing directly between him and Luther. "I've taken so much abuse for my painting over the years that it's really hard to wound my manly pride."

"Which means?" Sally sort of felt like she was in a kill zone between the two men. Though in all fairness, no one would probably get killed. Exactly.

"I'd be glad to let you do the talking."

"Good, I'll start by inviting everyone to the wedding." Sally looked over her shoulder at Sidney, crawling to his hands and knees and spitting out dirt. "Except him."

★ Thirty-one ★

Buff and Wise Sister brought a preacher back.

Sally saw the man wearing the black suit and thought Buff had hired a new bodyguard for Sidney.

He might yet need one to protect him from Luther, and even more so from Mandy. Nils Platte was still hanging around, but whatever arrangement he'd had with Sidney for protection apparently didn't stretch to include protection from a wife.

When Buff dismounted, he had the most peaceful smile on his face Sally had ever seen on the taciturn old man. "We had our wedding." Buff nodded toward Logan, who was holding Wise Sister's horse. "Now it's time for yours."

A smile bloomed on Sally's face. "Luther isn't too wild about the idea of me marrying a painter. Looks like you're okay with it."

Buff jerked one shoulder. "Wise Sister likes him. Says he's a good man. I trust her."

Platte came out of the barn and took both horses. He didn't seem to be staying all that close to Sidney these days.

"How'd you manage to not get shot when Sidney ran Cord

Cooter off?" Sally had been dying to know.

"Mr. Gray told me what he was planning. I convinced him to make a hard day's ride of it to Helena. He wouldn't do it for his wife, but he decided his own life was at risk so he was willing to get the firing done fast then run for home and set up a lookout over that gap. I've suggested guarding that gap before, but this time Mr. Gray seemed to believe he was in danger. I expected Cord to follow after us, thinking to get some lead into me and take Mr. Gray, maybe force the information about his gold out of him."

Wincing to think of how cruelly Cooter would accomplish that, Sally moved closer to Logan. They'd been under Cooter's gun. Either of them could have died so easily. Logan rested his arm across Sally's shoulders, and she couldn't believe the comfort of that single touch. She really did know him. It was all honest. Yes, they were different, but she knew that and she loved him anyway.

Wise Sister asked Platte, "Why didn't you get home earlier?"

Platte's jaw clenched. "Mr. Gray wasn't done with his town business. He insisted we leave the trail and let Cooter go past, then ride back into town."

"And leave his pregnant wife here unprotected, with Cord on the way?" Logan snarled.

Sally was happy to see Logan firmly on the side of those who despised Sidney. If he wanted to fit in the family, he really needed to do that.

"Mr. Gray didn't see it that way. He figured Cooter wanted him, not his wife. He didn't think she'd be in any danger."

"That man is mighty unconcerned about his wife and children." Logan pulled Sally closer.

"Seems right fond of his son." Platte spit on the ground with contempt. "Maybe he'll take better care of all of them now, with a boy in the mix."

Sally realized that if Cooter hadn't come after her, he'd have been back right during Mandy's birthing. Even her tough big sister would have had a time of it defending herself. "Why'd he go after us?"

"I talked with Luther some about the trail you took. You were close enough he probably heard the gunfire. Might've even thought it was Mr. Gray, gone off the trail."

"We were close to Mandy all this time, and I didn't even know it." Sally shook her head.

"There were a few things barring the way, Sally." Logan's grip loosened enough that she could breathe, but she didn't mind his holding on tight. "A cliff or two stood in the way. Miles of treacherous trail, a broken leg."

Nodding, Sally said, "It all slowed me down some."

"So why do you reckon Cord never came back? After he met up with his brother, I figured they were headed this way."

"Looked that way to me, too. Never cared for the way he looked at Mrs. Gray. I didn't agree with the boss that his wife wasn't in danger. But Cord's not in here, and I've posted a watch up there so he can't get in." Platte looked back in the direction of the gap then scratched at his bristly jaw. "Sometimes Cord would get to talking and he was crazy on the subject of his family. He asked everyone we ever saw if they'd seen a man with a streak of white in his hair. Said it was a family trait and he wanted to find two brothers he hadn't ever met. Or leastways not since he was too young to remember. He had a few folks say they'd seen such a mark, sometimes on one man, some would say on two. There were definite sightings around these parts, but no one could give him any solid information about just where the man lived."

"Fergus and the man Wise Sister shot had that white streak in their hair. Those must be his brothers."

"Cord talked about how his family always backed each other. Cooters stick together. He must've said it a hundred times. Figured it for big talk since I never saw a sign of any family. They sure weren't sticking by Cord."

"The dead man we saw where the outlaws shot Sally and killed the colonel and the others had that streak." Buff frowned. "He must be family, too."

"Then I say we need to be ready for trouble." Platte looked so serious it sent a chill down Sally's back. "Cord will be bent on hunting down anyone who harmed his family. Like I said, Cooters stick together. That's how he'll see it. He'll want revenge."

Sally watched Platte, Buff, and Wise Sister exchange a grim look. She felt pretty grim herself.

"So, is there gonna be a wedding or not?" Buff shook his head as if to throw off the tension.

Logan looked at Sally then turned to Wise Sister. "Where will you go? Will I ever see you again?"

Wise Sister moved to Buff's side so the two of them faced Sally and Logan. "Buff and I plan to build a cabin where mine was before. We'll build another one for you and Sally there, too, if you wish."

A smile bloomed on Logan's face.

Sally couldn't enjoy the moment, though she loved the thought of having Buff close by. "What about Mandy? She needs us here. She needs someone."

"I'm staying." Luther came up beside them, with Angela sitting atop his shoulders. The little girl's hands were holding onto the long gray hair surrounding Luther's bald crown.

"And we'll be a day's ride away." Logan lifted her hand up and kissed it. "We can come several times during the summer to see your family. And as soon as things are settled down, I'd like to go spend about half the winter in Texas and get to know your family."

The thought of spending months with her family thrilled her.

"And then spend the second half of it in New York so you can get to know mine."

Sally's eyes went wide. The thrill was gone. "New York City?"

Logan lifted one shoulder sheepishly. "Only if you want to. We'll decide all of that together. After we're married."

"I'm kinda scared of New York City." Which made her a little mad because Sally didn't like being afraid of anything. "Maybe we'd better decide that before the wedding."

Shaking his head, Logan smiled. "Nope. We'll work out everything else, but there's nothing left to decide about a wedding. We're getting married. Today. Let's get your sister and get this wedding started."

Deciding that suited her right down to the ground, Sally said, "Don't move," ran to the house, and called Mandy's name.

Her big sister came out carrying a baby, with a toddler hanging from her skirts.

Sally plucked Catherine up so they could all move faster toward saying the vows.

They had their wedding guests gathered in two minutes— little more than the time it took the preacher to walk the kinks out after his long horse ride.

Sidney even waddled over and watched, though he'd been inspecting the house and no one had invited him. He just happened to be coming down to the house to gloat over his son at that moment. Both of his eyes were black now.

Sally stood Catherine on her own two feet, thinking it was a more proper way to conduct a wedding, but the little tyke hung from her doeskin skirt and babbled.

"Dearly beloved. . ."

Turning to Logan, Sally decided those words described him perfectly.

"We are gathered here. . ."

An absolute truth. They'd simply gathered everyone here and started in.

The ceremony, such as it was, lasted about five minutes, but Sally took those vows, to marry a man who painted pictures instead of herding cattle. Logan said his promises right back, and he'd seen her wearing chaps with his own two eyes.

When the parson finished, Logan leaned close and took

both her hands in his. "There is truth between us, Sally. I know who you are, the tough wrangler, the pretty woman, the tears on occasion, the ribbon you always wear. I love you and know you and promise to respect you without trying to change you."

Sally heard some faint grunt from Sidney that sounded like he didn't agree with such a statement. A quick glance at Mandy told Sally her sister had heard that noise, too. The man was purely lucky he didn't have any eyes left to blacken.

But this was no time for her sister's problems or her brother-in-law's whipping. This was a sacred moment.

"We do know each other, Logan." She gripped his hands tighter. "We don't think alike about a lot of things, but about the big things, I think we're in wonderful agreement."

She looked deep in his eyes, those eyes that had a way of studying her, reading her every expression until he was almost reading her mind. Things that she'd come to depend on. "You can paint all you want and I'll still love you. In fact, I'll love you because you paint all you want."

"And you can wear anything you want and I'll still always love my little wrangler in petticoats." Logan leaned down and kissed her.

With that kiss, Sally sealed her vows, knowing as they began their future as two people, very different and very happy, they would always be true to themselves and to each other.

Discussion Questions

1. It is historically accurate, even in the West, to always put women in dresses and let them ride side-saddles. Few western novels do this though, preferring riding skirts and riding astride. Why do you think such an impractical way to ride and dress was asked of women?

2. Sally is tough and Logan is a wimp—or that's what Sally thinks. But Logan is strong in things she doesn't respect or understand. Talk about the differences between their value systems. . .seeing the land as providing a living versus seeing it for its beauty.

3. Both Sally and Logan learned to appreciate each others viewpoint. How have you changed due to being near someone you respect and love who thinks very differently from you?

4. Mandy's marriage has changed since it began, mostly for the worse. How has the West changed Sidney? Or explain how it is just revealing his true character.

5. Has Sophie done wrong to let her daughter Sally be such a tomboy? Explain how you feel Sophie's choices were right or wrong.

6. When an elk walks near the house, Sally reaches for her rifle, and Logan reaches for his sketch pad. Talk about how that creates conflict between them.

7. Why do you think Sidney wants to build his house at the top of a mountain?

8. How normal is it for a woman to conform herself to keep peace in her home, like Mandy does?

9. The West had a way of swallowing people up. They'd head west and never be seen again. Why do you think people went to such a dangerous place? What was drawing them there?

10. Did you like Tom Linscott? He's got a cameo in all three books in the Montana Marriage series, but now he's got his own story. Do you remember him? Did you want to know more about him?

11. Do you like the books being woven together with Lassoed in Texas and Montana Marriages? Explain what you like and don't like about series in general.

12. Today, with Internet and cell phones and air travel we can stay more connected, but distance can still make a difference. Have you ever had someone in your family move away and you've lost touch with them, or nearly? Explain how that affected your relationship.

Sharpshooter *in* Petticoats

One

Montana Territory, August 1884

Tom Linscott slid backward five feet before he caught a slender rock ledge and clawed at it to stop himself from plunging a hundred feet more.

The rock was nearly sheer. He felt blood flowing from his fingertips. His grip was shaky already, and now it was slippery. He clung to that ledge like a scared house cat, afraid to move, fighting to slow his slamming heart and steady his breathing. He'd been climbing a long time, and he had a long way to fall if his grip didn't hold.

Then he did what any thinking man did when something scared him. He got mad.

So, he clung to the side of that stupid mountain, gathered his strength to go the last twenty-five or so feet, and fumed. He was a rancher not a mountain goat. He should *not* have had to climb up here.

No woman should be this hard to get.

His handhold felt solid; his footholds were all of three inches wide. He needed a minute of rest before he went on to a more precarious spot. And while he hung there, dangling over a dead drop that ended in jagged granite, he looked up and saw her.

The woman he'd come for. Lady Gray.

She lived in a fortress, cut off from all the people she considered beneath her. The rumors about her were legion and harrowing. Ruthlessly dangerous, some said. A witch, others had called her. She'd put a curse on the land she ruled over.

Tom hadn't told anyone of his plans until just before he left home. But he'd listened for any whisper of her name, any passing reference to the legendary Lady Gray.

She was the most dangerous woman in the West. As fast and deadly with her rifle as any woman alive.

That last part Tom suspected was true. The first, well, he hoped she wasn't dangerous to him, but he was minutes away from testing the theory.

He'd had to admit he was coming right before he left because there were arrangements to make. That's when one of his cowhands told Tom with dead seriousness that he'd lived in this area and it was widely repeated and believed that to approach Lady Gray meant certain death.

But Tom knew something none of the rest of them did. He knew what had brought her to this place. He understood the roots of her reputation. He knew who she was before the legend had been born. And he knew she was no witch.

That didn't mean she might not blow a hole in him with that blasted Winchester if he wasn't real careful.

Right now she stood motionless, looking up, clearly visible in the starlit night. He watched her and stoked his temper while he hugged this stupid cliff that he should *not* have had to climb. The fool woman should have invited him to come right up to the front door of her fortress.

As he watched, a mountain breeze billowed her dress and

cloak and scarf in the night, and in the moonlight it was as if living power swirled around her. Everything she touched was more alive, more vital, more beautiful. A half moon glowed in the cloudless eastern sky, while she faced the west.

As her dark cloak and light hair danced around her, Tom knew exactly why her reputation had reached the level of the mystical. Back when Tom had last seen her, she'd been beautiful and wounded and sweet.

No one put those words to Lady Gray now. Untouchable was more often repeated. Untamable certainly, as if anyone would consider trying to tame a witch. She was called cold, but Tom had seen the warmth. Life might have forced her to hide that away, but Tom would never believe the warm, intelligent, vulnerable woman he knew wasn't there somewhere. Merciless. That might be true. Tom was sneaking in after all. He didn't want to risk finding out she had no mercy. Unbeatable, too. A warrior with nerves as steady and strong as the stones of her castle.

But all of that reputation wouldn't keep friends nor enemies away. She had a large supply of both.

A rifle, now, that made people fight shy. But even the rifle wouldn't keep Mandy Gray's family back. They were a salty lot. But the danger of knowing her was so intense that she'd begged those she loved to stay away, and they'd let her alone.

Tom had heard the grumbling, had done some of it himself. Her pa had come and tried to pull her out of her mountain fortress, one of her sisters, too, and some faithful old friends. She'd run them off to save their lives. And Tom knew, even if no one else did, that her coldblooded rejection was rooted in love. Or maybe he just believed that because he'd been run off, too.

Her cloak stormed and twisted around her. Her hair, loose in the wind, danced white, like living smoke curling around her head. It went with the gray of her clothes. It was said she always wore gray to match her name and her castle and her mood. But in the night, who could say what she wore? Everything about her looked gray, even her eyes, which Tom knew were a flashing sky blue.

It gave Tom grim pleasure to know he was dressed in pitch black. That suited his mood.

A desire to yell at her, tell her he was coming, coming to rescue her from this self-imposed exile, clogged in his throat as he saw the butt of that deadly accurate long gun poking up at an angle by her left shoulder. She always wore it that way. The rifle and her lightning-fast reflexes were as much a part of the legend as her beauty and isolation.

She'd be real glad to see him. He was sure of it. But she had a reputation for shooting first and asking questions later, so he didn't want to startle her.

Mandy Gray and that rifle. Tom bit back a growl that she'd made it so hard for him. He fully intended to own Mandy, and he'd use that rifle on her backside if she didn't come along quietly.

But he'd tell her all that a bit later, after he had her disarmed. The element of surprise increased his chance of survival.

Since she was right where he wanted to be and there was no way to gain that high ground as long as she was there, Tom settled in to his precarious perch to watch her and pick his moment to stake his claim. Considering she was the most beautiful woman Tom had ever seen, watching was no hardship.

As he waited, a long tube appeared over her head as if she were taking aim at the sky. A thrill of fear raced up his back as the irrational thought flickered through his head that Lady Gray was having a showdown with God. She'd declared war on the whole world, why not God, too?

Tom followed the line of the tube and saw a falling star streak across the sky, then another. As if maybe God was shooting back.

Shaking that madness away, he knew she hadn't made a move toward her rifle. Tom was watching too closely to miss even Mandy Gray's wicked speed.

She pointed upward and held the tube to her eye, riveted

somehow, completely unaware of her surroundings. Tom tried to figure out what had caught her attention until he realized that her utter focus on the sky gave him his chance to move.

Wiping his bleeding fingertips on his black shirt, to make them less slippery, he resumed his stealthy climb, glancing every few seconds at Mandy and that tube and her frozen fascination with...something.

He'd never seen anything like it before.

The sky is falling.

Mandy's heart trembled and she enjoyed it—the fear.

For so long she'd feared nothing. Felt nothing. Not joy, not fear, nothing. She loved her children, so she felt that to some extent, but her love translated into protecting them, and to do that she needed to remain in control.

Beyond the love of an angry mama grizzly, her heart was as dead as her husband.

She didn't fool herself with romantic notions that her heart was dead *because* her husband had died. No, she'd been finished with feelings long before Sidney had assumed room temperature. The men who'd shot Sidney had hardened what few feelings she had left.

So now the sky was falling.

Maybe the end of the world. Maybe Jesus coming again.

That suited her.

White lights shot across the sky. She lost count. She stood and watched through Sidney's telescope and *felt*. For the first time in a year she wasn't ice cold all the way to her soul. It was as close to free as she could be in the stronghold of her home, Gray Tower.

Logic told her that the world probably *wasn't* coming to an end. That would be too easy. She hadn't had an easy day in her life. West Texas wasn't what anyone would call easy, and certainly there'd been no ease since she'd come to Montana.

She pulled the telescope away from her eye and watched white slices of heavenly light. Content with the goose bumps of fear, her spirits rose. Assuming the world wasn't ending, she'd come to a good place out here. Her children were safe. She was safe—bitterly lonely but safe.

And at night she looked at the stars and dreamed of being far away. And dreamed of making sense of that map Sidney had left, a map that would take her to a gold mine and give her a way out of her troubles.

But the map with its odd star markings as a starting place made no sense. And the gold and the freedom it could buy might as well be as far away as those slivers of slashing light. But the stars changed. She'd learned that since she'd begun studying them. And every night the stars were out, she looked and hoped Sidney's map made sense.

Tonight, here she stood again and watched the sky and stayed safely in her tower. The Shoshone people who lived around her had made this land impenetrable. And she hadn't had a report of someone trying to gain access for months.

A few reported deaths weighed on her. And there was one nightmarish night when they'd gotten through the watching Shoshone and come upon her. She'd survived that life-and-death fight on a moonlit night, but with a scar on her soul—the knowledge that she had killed another human being.

What choice did she have? Running her thumb over the little callus on her trigger finger, she knew she could fight or she could die, and her children with her. When evil men preyed on a woman, they had no right to hope for mercy, and neither the Shoshone nor she showed them any.

Another star shot a streak of white light, and she shivered in that lovely fear, the first real feeling she'd had since the cold had sleeted through her veins on the night she took a man's life. The fear gave her hope.

Maybe, finally, even without Sidney's gold, she could believe she was safe. She could dare to believe the men who hunted her had finally given up.

A hard hand clamped over her mouth. She went for her rifle to find it locked between her body and whoever held her.

"Hold still," a voice hissed in her ear. "I won't—ouch!"

Mandy struck hard with her telescope, going for the kill. She slammed her attacker in the nose. Even as she landed the blow, she knew it wasn't hard enough. His arms never relented. His grip on her trapped rifle never wavered. Then somehow her telescope was gone, thrown aside. She heard glass shatter as it landed against the rocks. Then it bounced and clattered over the cliff. The telescope she needed to study the stars and save herself.

With a sickening twist of her stomach, she knew she'd failed her precious babies. That thought made her desperate, and she twisted, fighting the iron grip. Her hard boots stomped but missed the man's foot. With a sinking stomach, she knew this man was tough.

Her elbow rammed his stomach. He grunted and his grip tightened, pinning her arms. She could get no force behind the blow. He lifted her off her feet. She kicked with her heavy boots. Grunting in pain, he wrapped one leg around both of hers and they fell backward.

The grip knocked the wind out of her even though she landed on top.

"Stop! Mandy, quit." The man still whispered.

Mandy instantly knew he was aware of her Shoshone friends and was careful not to alert them. Where were they? They were so diligent.

"Will you please—"

Writhing against him, panic drowned out his words. She didn't need to hear to know the man would spew threats and gloat with pleasure at her sure death.

Her children! What would become of them? What plans did

this evil man have, all because of Sidney's filthy gold. She sank her teeth into the hand over her mouth and clawed at the muscled wrist.

"Mandy! Will you stop that?" The voice was deep. "Ouch!" Raspy. "Get your teeth out of me." Familiar.

She froze. She knew that voice.

"Are you done trying to beat the stuffing out of me yet?"

Tom Linscott.

Mandy's taut muscles relaxed. She opened her clenched, attacking jaw and sagged back against the hard length of him. She wasn't going to die today.

Looking toward the heavens, she saw yet another streak of light. The sky wasn't going to fall after all. Her world wasn't going to end.

Tom's hand lifted from her mouth. "I knew I had to quiet you down before I tried to talk to you." He rolled sideways, tipping her off of him.

She kept moving and gained her feet, ignoring an almost instinctive need to go for her rifle.

Standing, dusting his backside, Tom gave her, and her rifle, his full attention.

"Get out of here. You need to go. I'll signal the Shoshone people so they'll know you're coming out the gap." Mandy frowned and looked over the ledge. "Did you climb up that cliff?"

Taking his hat off and slapping it on his leg, Tom said, "Yep."

"How'd you do that? Wise Sister's family would have seen you. They know this is the only other way in."

"Not exactly a 'way in,' Mandy. It took me two hours of hard climbing in the pitch dark. My fingers are bleeding." Tom scowled at his hands, black tipped with blood.

Mandy noticed some teeth marks, too. "Well, you're in." Mandy took an uncertain step forward when she said those words.

He was definitely.

In.

Then she, who thought everything over and had complete control of her actions and complete death in her emotions, launched herself into his arms.

He caught her and lifted her onto her tiptoes and kissed the living daylights out of her. A moment stretched to a minute, then two. Her arms tightened on his neck.

He pulled back. "Mandy, I've been—"

"Shut up." She tilted her head to deepen the kiss and put an end to his ridiculous talking for long minutes more. He cooperated fully, and Mandy realized she could feel so much more than just fear.

When she regained her senses, she found her toes dangling about three inches off the ground, not quite sure when he'd lifted her. He pulled away and, even with his face shaded by his Stetson in the dark, she saw him smile.

"Hi." His white teeth flashed as pure as shooting stars.

She dove for his lips again but he ducked. "We're going to talk now. I've come to get you out of here."

In one second, with one poorly chosen sentence, Tom cleared Mandy's head of nonsense.

"I can't leave." She pushed against his shoulders. "I'll be killed."

"I'll protect you." He ignored her pushing.

"You can't." Her shoving hands turned into fists. "You'll be killed."

He lowered his head and kissed one of the fists that was curled upon his chest. "I'll hire enough people to guard us."

"No!" Her struggling paused as she watched his soft mouth touch her taut fingers. She shook her head to clear it. "They'll be killed."

"I've got tough men. We'll protect you and your young'uns."

"I can't take the children out." Shaking her head frantically, Mandy knew they'd come to the real reason she stayed trapped in here. "They'll be killed."

"Will you stop saying that!"

"No, because—"

"Will you shut up, or do I need to gag that mouth again?"

Mandy frowned but didn't speak the obvious. He'd clearly heard her already.

"There is no reason on earth you have to stay up here."

"Yes, there is. I'll be kill—"

An extremely rude snorting noise cut her off. "There have been other rich people, Mandy. Many of them have lived to an old age."

"They didn't make enemies of the Cooter clan. There doesn't seem to be any end of them. And they all have a grudge, aimed straight at me."

"The Cooter feud against you is famous, no denyin' it. But the solution isn't to hide up here for the rest of your life."

"Yes it is." It was a stupid solution; even Mandy knew that. But it seemed to work, and the alternative was death. "If I go out in public, they'll come for me."

"Then they'll be stopped, arrested, and hung."

"You can't arrest them all. They're like cockroaches. They keep coming. I've already been shot at twice. Hit once." Mandy rubbed her arm, long healed but not forgotten. "Sidney is dead."

"No great loss."

"Buff was shot."

"That was before the feud."

"Luther was shot."

"I know. A bunch of Cooters have been arrested. Several are dead."

"But there are always more of them. There's no end to it."

"Buff and Luther weren't hurt badly."

Sidney sure had been, but Mandy didn't mention that. "In the last few months there've been no attacks." That she did mention. A tenuous peace, but the best she could hope for. "They seem satisfied as long as I stay up here, like they've got me in prison, I suppose. But every time I try to leave or someone tries to get in, they come and keep coming. The Cooters and their kin will hurt anyone who gets in their way."

"Then they'll have to go through me."

"That's exactly right, Tom." The night wind tossed Mandy's gray cloak around, whipping it, lifting it until it floated around her like smoke, drifting and tossing her hair. "They'll come through you. I'm not risking anyone else. I'm here. I'm safe. I hope the really spiteful members of the Cooter clan will die out by the time my children need to leave. Until then I stay."

"Then I'll stay with you."

Shaking her head, Mandy said, "You've got family, a sister and nephew, a ranch."

"Two nephews, now. My sister had another son."

"My family is all in Texas. The Cooters haven't gone that far to bother them, mainly because they've gotten the notion I've cut my family off."

"Wonder where they got that idea?"

From Mandy herself. She'd started the rumors about her family begging for money. All nonsense and a blow to the McClellen family pride. Ma and Pa would never have accepted the lie she put about. But then Luther was shot trying to get in to see her. He was lucky to survive. After that Mandy's family had respected her wishes and left her alone.

Tom wasn't leaving.

"I'm not staying." Tom crossed his arms and planted his feet as solidly as if they were rooted to the ground. "I've got a ranch to run. Let's get packed. We can be well away from here by morning. The way through the gap is clear tonight."

"We can't be sure of that."

"I'm sure of it." Tom reached out and grabbed her so hard his fingers bit into her arm. She'd have bruises tomorrow. Fair enough, she'd punched him in the face. He'd have a few bruises, too.

"I'm not going." Mandy yanked against his grip.

Tom jerked her forward so suddenly she stumbled into his chest. His arms went around her waist, and he lifted her up to eye level. Mandy didn't think of herself as a short woman. But then she was mainly surrounded by toddlers, so compared to them she was quite tall. Tom was a big man, though, and he made her feel tiny and very feminine. Just look how he'd grabbed her and kept her from getting to her rifle. It was galling.

Now he lifted her straight off her feet. His muscles were the iron hard bands a man earned fighting nature to run a ranch. He dangled her there with no apparent exertion and stared straight into her eyes. "How about we do it this way, Mrs. Gray?" Tom swooped down and kissed her until she didn't have much left in her head, surely no sense.

He pulled back, only inches, his intense eyes and stubborn jaw filling her whole world. Made her want. Made her feel. "I'm taking your children out of this fortress tonight. You can come with me or stay behind."

Made her crazy. "I won't let you."

"You can't stop me." He fell silent and waited. A big, tall stack of pure stubborn.

Going for her rifle wasn't really an option since she'd just admitted keeping him alive was her first reason for not going. Still, her fingers itched to grab for the barrel.

When she didn't respond, Tom set her on her feet, turned, and stalked toward the house, as if he planned to pack the three children up and take them without her permission or company.

She reached for her rifle and grabbed. . .air. Looking down by her right hand where the muzzle was always waiting, she realized it was gone. Looking up, she saw Tom carrying it.

"Looking for this?" He raised his arm high so the gun was silhouetted against the starlit sky.

The growling noise in Mandy's throat surprised her. Yes, she was definitely feeling again. Rage, terror.

God forgive me, I feel attraction, caring, desire. Worst of all, hope.

Shaking her head to dislodge that ridiculous notion, she couldn't wipe away the hope. And really hope was the worst because she *knew* better. Tom letting her believe there was a way out was the cruelest thing he could do.

Running her thumb over her trigger finger, she liked it better when her emotions were dead. Going back to that thrilling fear that the sky might be falling would be wonderful.

He reached the house, that stupid gray monstrosity Sidney had named Gray Tower after himself. Sidney Gray. He'd named his son after himself. He'd have named the whole wide world after himself given half a chance. It was a wonder he hadn't tried to pay the state of Montana to change its name to Gray.

She glared at her home. It looked like a castle out of a fairy tale. All they needed was a moat and a fairy godmother.

Tom grabbed the knob and went in, slamming the door behind him. He'd never find the children in there. Too many rooms.

She dashed after him. . .not to help him find the children. . . to get her long gun back.

T w o

W e're not setting up camp for the night. Not this time." Cord
Cooter jerked his reins so hard the horse reared up and fought
the bit.

"Eight of us dead." Cord stayed in the saddle but not without
some difficulty. "The Grays have killed eight of our kin. I'm ready
to settle accounts."

He wheeled his temperamental horse around and looked at
the six men with him. They were barely visible in the dim light of
the heavily wooded trail.

One of his cousins, rattlesnake-mean J.D., rode up beside
Cord. "I ain't gonna ride into that gap. She's got it staked out by
ghosts. I swear we've lost men without hearin' 'em die nor findin'
their bodies. There's somethin' ain't right about the mountains
around her. They're cursed. The woman's a witch. And that place
is surrounded by haints."

"She ain't no witch. I've talked to her. I've had my hands on
her." Cord had touched her one time. One time only. And he
could still feel her slender shoulder. . .and her fear. It made him

hungry to feel both again. . .and more. "She's human enough."

One hand, for one second, two years ago. He didn't tell his family that. Cord's fingers clenched into a fist, and only the memory of a broken nose and two black eyes—barely healed from the last fight with one of his cousins—kept him from swinging a fist at his cowardly, superstitious cousin, J.D. He was an old man more interested in sitting on a rocking chair than avenging their family.

"I'm content to stake out the trail to Helena in shifts and wait to pick her off if she rides to town." J.D. looked around and nodded.

Cord heard a lot of agreement in the grumbling.

"You're gonna let that woman kill all those Cooters and not pay? Grandpa'd skin you yellow bellies alive if he could hear you now." They were about five miles from the gap that led to Lady Gray. Mandy Gray—Cooter didn't like thinking of the reputation she'd earned up in these parts. They could be there in an hour, and Cord was tired of waiting. They should strike tonight and be done with it. He'd given up on having Mandy and the gold and had a plan that would let him be done with the rugged life he'd been living for the last two years.

"Grandpa set it down that we'd back each other." J.D. snarled like a hungry wolf. "Cooters stick together. We done that, Cord. But corralling Lady Gray in that gap is good enough. She can't enjoy all her gold. She can't get out. No one can get in. I don't have a belly for killin' a woman anyhow, and what happens to her children if we kill her? I think blasting that gap closed is worse than killing her without getting blood on our hands. You've seen her standing on that cliff, late at night, aiming her gun at the stars like she's aiming to shoot God right out of heaven. She's in league with the devil. We've got her trapped, and I say as long as she stays trapped, we're getting our due for our cousins. Getting more of us killed ain't gonna make nuthin' better."

Cord looked at the men. The faces were different, but no

one would look twice and not know they were family. The white shock of hair was mostly covered by their hats and concealed by darkness, but their stocky build was the same. They all had a few weeks' worth of grubby dark whiskers on their chins. And the set of their jaws and the cold eyes were of a kind. He was mighty proud of his family, but he was by far the youngest. The rest of 'em were getting soft.

"More Cooters should be drifting in to Helena soon." Fergus turned his horse so he stood side by side with Cord. They were brothers. Two of a kind. And even Fergus had no belly for that gap and that witch woman. "Cord's right that we've gotta make her pay for what she's done." Then Fergus turned to Cord. "But not till there's more of us, brother. Let's keep the trail covered and wait for the train. There's something ain't right about that gap and the land around it. We've lost too many men."

"It's Old Nick, I'm telling you," J.D. shouted. "She sold her soul, and now she's under the protection of the devil hisself. We've lost men right while we could see her. We know it ain't her what killed 'em because we could see her standing all the way up there, her rifle aimed at heaven, with her out of range so she couldn't'a shot any one of us anyway. And if she did, there was no crack of a rifle. And never a body found."

A chill went down Cord's back. J.D. had the right of it. His cousins had vanished as if the ground had opened and they'd been sucked right down into the brimstone. But Cord didn't believe in God, so that meant there was no devil neither. Couldn't have one without the other to his way of thinking. His cousin was just a superstitious fool. Chances are those no-account cousins had picked their moment, slipped away, and run off. Their horses were gone, too, weren't they?

"We know she's not shooting anybody." Fergus urged his horse a step closer to Cord. "But we're down to five of us. If this is a blood feud, then we're losing too much blood. Instead of a head-on attack, let's wait for more help and go at her hard."

Cord appreciated his brother standing by him physically even if he didn't support Cord's plan.

Fergus went on, now looking at Cord. "Until then, she's stuck in that fool's house. Judging by the way she stands up there, every night, and aims her rifle at God, I'd say she's lost her mind. And we're the cause. I like your idea of trapping her behind a pile of rock where she lives. Make it her tomb. We'll as good as kill her without drawing the blood of a woman. But we need to wait for more Cooters."

"But this is different than when we've tried to get through that gap and take her. We don't have to go far in. We just dynamite it shut. We wouldn't have to stay around to put a bullet in her." Cord almost agreed that the gap was haunted. He'd felt a hot brush on his neck a time or two like the breath of the devil, as if someone was out there, watching, ready. Rushing at his back. But he'd whirled around and there'd been nothing.

Fergus's eyes flared. "Dynamite would do the trick."

Cord and Fergus had ridden into Helena for it a few days ago, but now no one had the belly to plant it.

"If we slipped in quiet and set it off," Cord said, trying to sway his stubborn family, "we'd be done with this."

"Last time we rode in we lost two men, and that was long before we got to the gap. Why're you so sure we can even set the dynamite?" J.D. groused.

"We'll do it because we're Cooters, and when we stick together we can't be stopped." Cord nodded.

His cousins did, too, grudging but tempted to do this and be on their way. They'd been stalking this woman for too long. Cord and Fergus had been at it for two years, though they'd waited awhile for their family to come at first. None of the men here tonight, except for Fergus, had been in on the start. Those men were all gone. Somewhere.

Lady Gray was proving to be mighty hard to kill.

"This time we all stay together. Before, when we've lost men, it happened when we got separated." He looked at his cousins and saw the stubbornness, but they wanted this done. They wanted to go to town and forget the woman holed up on that mountaintop.

Shifting his horse around, Fergus clapped J.D., the oldest of the Cooter cousins, on the back. "We'll set the charges. Then we'll blow that gap and leave that woman in there." Fergus looked at the cousins one by one and added, "Buried alive."

They all nodded.

With grim satisfaction that they were doing something instead of standing watch on a trail, J.D. said, "This is gonna be over before the rest of our clan even show up."

"We'll do for that woman what she done to us." Cord jerked his chin, satisfied. "And people'll learn the price they pay for hurting a Cooter. The family's pride will be upheld." He wasn't all that eager to ride into the teeth of that witch woman's gunfire. The dynamite suited him fine.

Cord reined his horse in a circle and led the way for the old codgers. This group was so motley he was almost ashamed to be a Cooter. But this would restore their name and show that Cooters were men to be reckoned with. Strange to be ashamed of his family at the same minute he was ready to kill for their pride.

With Fergus galloping at his side, Cord knew that, finally, tonight was the end of this. There'd be no gold for him, and he'd never get his hands on her again, and that chafed. But it was almost enough to picture Lady Gray buried alive.

The vicious pleasure told him they were doing the right thing.

"Tom, you get out of my house." Mandy rushed up behind him and caught his arm as he grabbed for the doorknob on the second room down her entry hall.

Tom purely liked her hanging from him, so he didn't protest. He just dragged her along. "Quiet, woman." Tom had decided before he'd started this he wasn't going to discuss any of it with her. He was *telling* her, and that was that. "I'm hunting for your children so I can save them. I'm getting them out of here and taking them to my ranch, with or without your cooperation."

She held on as he kept walking, and he heard the heels of her boots skidding along on the stone floor.

"This is the dumbest house I have ever seen." Tom reached the next door and swung it open.

"Try living in it." Mandy threw herself in front of Tom as he pulled his head out of the store room he'd just checked. "Try heating it."

"You can't stop me." Tom glared at the stubborn female. "I'm taking your children and, just like a wild mama longhorn, I'm betting you'll traipse along behind them. If you're real good, I won't make you stay in the barn when we get to my ranch."

"You did *not* just compare me to a cow."

"If you're *real* good, I'll let you live in my ranch house and be my wife."

"Wife?" Mandy's throat moved as if she were swallowing hard.

"It's about time, don't you think?" Years past time, Tom thought.

"It is never going to happen." One pretty little hand, rough with calluses, caught his arm as he tried to go around her.

"It's already happened." Tom peered down into her eyes in the shadowed hallway. "We've been meant for each other from the beginning."

"We have not!"

Remembering the day he'd come to her home to visit the foal born out of his stallion and Belle Harden's mare, Tom could still feel the connection that had sprung up between them. He refused to believe a word of her denial. "Why do you think I've stayed single?"

"Because no woman would have you?"

Tom shook his head. "Nope."

"Because there are no women in Montana?" She might have

actually growled when she said that.

"No women wouldn't have stopped me. I'd have gone and hunted one up if I'd've wanted someone else. Nothing much stops me once I've got my mind set on something."

"To—o—om!"

A single lantern burning in the long stony hallway barely dispelled the gloom enough so he could see her face. He saw a lot of defiance, but he also caught a glimmer of hope. This was no time to be a pessimist, so Tom refused to believe he imagined it.

But, being a man of action, just in case the defiance outweighed the hope, he picked her up and kissed her again. That seemed to have a persuasive effect on her before, at least in the sense that she quit trying to punch him.

By the time he was done being a man of action, he was tempted to just grab ahold and tote her off to a preacher-man. From the way she kissed him back, he was hopeful she'd cooperate. . . eventually.

But first he had to find those children. Setting her on her feet like a bucket of fresh milk, he said, "Tell me where they are. With or without your help, I'm finding them and taking them. So you might as well help. Getting out of here in the dark is a lot safer than waiting till daylight. You want your children to be safe, don't you, Miz Gray?"

Taunting. He knew it. He was so disgusted with her for marrying that worthless Sidney Gray he could hardly keep from turning her over his knee. Knowing she'd probably find a way to shoot him if he did helped keep him from acting on that impulse.

"But they won't be safe if you take—"

Tom walked around the little road block.

"Come back here."

He went on down the hallway. "I'm gonna start yelling pretty soon, Mandy girl. That'll wake 'em up, and I'll just follow their cryin'." He stopped and looked back.

She was dogging his heels, still yapping like an ill-tempered hound. Convincing her wasn't part of his plan. Who had time for that?

"Are these rooms all full of furniture?"

"Of course. Who has a house without furniture?"

"It's coated with dust and looks like you've never been in the room." Tom kept moving.

Open the door. "Kitchen." Slam.

Open. "Pantry. Not much food." Slam.

Open. "Closet." Slam.

"I'm getting a sense that the kids are upstairs." Tom wheeled and headed back toward the front door, where he'd seen a flight of stairs. He almost ran over Mandy while he walked.

She jammed a shoulder into his belly.

"That does it." He hoisted her and tossed her over his shoulder.

"Tom Linscott, you can*not* come in here and just take over my life!" Her yelling near to raised the rafters.

And Tom heard a thin cry of "Mama" from overhead.

"Shame on you for waking your babies, Miz Gray." He almost swatted her on the backside, it being within convenient swatting distance. But the thought of how much he'd enjoy that convinced him it was sinful. "By the way, we're changing all the children's names to Linscott."

"Put me down." She pummeled him in the center of his back.

She had a good wallop, but nothing he couldn't handle. He held her legs real tight though. She could do some damage with those feet.

He was glad he'd tucked her rifle into the first room he'd searched and she'd been too busy scolding and fussing to notice and go hunt it up. If he'd have slung it over his shoulder as he'd originally planned, she'd no doubt be unloading it into his backside about now.

Dealing with Mandy Soon-to-Be-Linscott, the sharpest shooter and fastest draw anyone in the West had ever heard tell of—male or female—was a powerful sight easier if she was disarmed.

669

He trotted up the steps, shaking her a bit more than was absolutely necessary. When they reached the top, he needed his hands to carry the young'uns, so he swung her back in front of him and caught one of her flying fists with the hard slap of flesh on flesh. She took another swing and he caught that hand, too, just as she'd have slugged him in the nose.

Again.

"Mama!" A new voice, tearful but a bit more mature than the squalling baby, was added to the racket. A little girl. Probably Angela—she'd be four years old by now. Tom was partial to her because she'd learned his name the last time he was here. Nearly two years ago. He fancied the notion that she might remember him, though he knew it was unlikely.

Didn't matter anyway. She was going to have to start calling him pa.

"You can't take three little children out of here, Tom. You don't have enough hands."

"I've got it planned." He smirked. She was so cute in the dim light of another long hallway. "The oldest can ride piggyback, and I'll carry the two younger ones in my arms. I also intend to steal a horse."

"Now you're a horse thief?"

"That's right, Miz Gray. I'm planning to steal the two horses I sold to that fool you were married to. They deserve better than to live stuck away up here. So it's more like I'm rescuing them. Get the sheriff if you object. Except, whoops, you'd have to leave your fortress to do that, now wouldn't you? Well, since you're runnin' to the law, maybe you'll carry one of the youngsters for me. I can get by without any help, but I wouldn't refuse it."

"How did you get in here anyway? How could you have slithered past all the guards?"

"I had Wise Sister talk to her Shoshone family and convince them to look the other way whilst I climbed that mountain." Tom relished telling her that. Her trusted guardians had betrayed her.

By letting him in, they'd as much as said they were picking him for her.

"She did not!" Mandy sounded horrified and also loud.

A new voice added to the mix. "Mama!" An outburst of tears followed the word.

That must be the three-year-old, Catherine. "You know a decent mother wouldn't stand here yelling, scaring her babies. What is the matter with you anyway?" Tom frowned and gave her one more chance. "You want to carry one? Or do I have to handle them all while I turn horse thief?"

"That is kidnapping. A worse crime that horse thievin', Tom Linscott!"

"That's right, practice your new name."

"That's not my new name you big, dumb—mmphf."

Tom yanked her hard against his chest and kissed her until she forgot about yelling. He slid one hand into her wild white hair and tilted her head back so he could pour all his loneliness and eagerness to have her into one single kiss.

With no ability to yap at him, she turned into a full partner in that kiss. Her arms wound around his neck, and he knew, whatever words came out of her mouth, this was truth. She wanted him. She was meant for him. This was the destiny God had laid out for the two of them.

She calmed and went along so enthusiastically Tom tried to figure out a way to speed up their wedding vows to tonight.

Since they were about two days' ride from the nearest preacher, nothing came to mind, so, when he quit, he wheeled toward the first door. All the crying was coming from there. "A house this big and the children don't even get their own rooms."

Mandy's hand landed hard on top of his as he gripped the knob. "They don't *want* their own rooms. Guess what. I sleep in there with them. I don't want *my* own room. This place is spooky. Worse yet, it's cold. If we stay together, then we only have to heat up one room to survive the winter."

Tom looked down and smiled. "You're coming, aren't you, Mandy girl?"

All the defiance and temper melted from her expression, replaced by fear. "It's not safe for you, for any of us." She had her mind stuck clear in a deep old rut.

"I know. But I can't help it. I need a wife and you're the only woman I can imagine being such." He considered kissing her again if she kept arguing. He decided that when she went to nagging it was almost like she was begging him to kiss her.

"I will *never* be your wife. I'd just as well sign a warrant for your death."

She was worrying about him; that seemed like a good sign. "I gave you a year since that worthless husband of yours died, but you never came nor mailed me a letter asking me to come."

"That's not my place."

"Figured you might see it that way, seein' as how we've only met twice before. But I knew how it was meant to be between us right from the start. And I'm sure you did, too." Tom flipped his hand over, off the knob, to grab hers. "Didn't you?"

There was a long moment of silence. Well, silence not counting three crying babies.

Finally, with a frown so fierce it hurt Tom's heart, she said, "I was a married woman."

"That was a big old avalanche blocking the trail between us, I'll grant you that." Tom smiled at her confusion.

"And now trouble comes riding with me." Mandy shook her head, and in the dim light of the hallway, he saw her eyes, so light blue they looked gray, fill with tears. "Terrible trouble. I won't bring that to your door."

"Finally figured that one out, too." He interlaced his fingers with hers and held on, hoping she got the message soon that he was planning on holding on forever. "That's why I quit waiting for you and came to fetch you home."

One more kiss, then he opened the door and went in to meet

his children for the second time. He approached the oldest girl, Angela, such a pretty little thing with long, wispy blond hair half escaped from a braid.

Behind his back he heard his stubborn almost-wife snarl, "I *am* home."

Tom sighed but kept a smile on his face for the little girl's sake. Someone around here had to think of the children's best interests.

"And I will *never* marry you."

Smiling, he lifted Angela into his arms and said, "Hey, little girl. Call me Pa."

"Pa?" Angela tilted her head and the tears slowed.

"Yep. I'm your new pa. We'll practice it until you learn it well."

"Tom, don't you dare tell my daughter to—"

"We've got plenty of time, because with your ma bent on talking me to death, this is shaping up to be a long night."

Sidney Gray had tried to level a mountain. Pure stupid.

Cord had figured him for a halfwit from the first, but a halfwit in possession of a fortune. Cord was able to take orders from the man who was paying his salary. The money had been good, and he'd seen no way to separate Gray from that fat pot of gold he had tucked away in a Denver bank. So Cord had handled dynamite for one long summer, learned how to run a long fuse and get clear and how to pick a spot that would do the most damage quickly. Even back then Cord had seen how easy it would be to bring that whole gap right down on a man's head.

The way it worked out, Sidney had paid Cord by the month to learn exactly what he needed to know to trap Mandy in this place forever.

There were cracks all over the walls of that gap, torn there by the blasting. Toward the end of the summer, they'd quit drilling holes for the dynamite sticks and just used the cracks that were already there. Some of the crew of skilled blasters had pointed to specific spots and warned Sidney that the wall was weak. They'd warned Gray that his gap would someday come tumbling down. Not could. . .would. They'd been sure the stone lining this gap was undermined and had warned the high and mighty Lord Gray that he was courting trouble.

Gray had just scoffed and said if the gap collapsed he'd blast it open again.

Cord had listened and watched, and in the dozens of times he'd passed through that gap, he'd located the exact spots where he could plant explosives. He'd have that gap closed in minutes.

Fergus rode up alongside him. "I've told the men to stay tight together. You may not want to believe in haints, Cord, but there's for sure somethin' in these woods. Wolves'd howl. A grizzly bear would kick up a ruckus if it attacked. Both of them critters would leave plenty of blood behind. We've seen no sign of Indians or outlaws. And that witch woman is usually up there where we can see her, pointing her gun at the sky like a madwoman. She's not down here picking the men off."

A cold chill crawled up Cord's spine. It was the honest truth that men had disappeared. "Gotta be Indians."

"There ain't no Indians around here, Cord. The army moved 'em off years ago."

Cord saw the gap in the distance, the rocks black and threatening. The other Cooter kin rode so close behind that Cord was ashamed of their cowardice. He was also glad to have them near to hand. They approached the gap. Cord saw the tall, narrow opening yawing in front of him and felt like it was a huge, gaping mouth, waiting to swallow them whole. Where had all Cord's kin gone?

"Pull up." Cord refused to admit it was because he was losing his nerve and needed a few seconds to build his backbone up. "I want to get the blast rigged and ready so we just ride in there, plant it, and pull out fast, running the fuse until we're clear. The second we're out, we detonate the sticks of dynamite and then we hightail it. We'll be in and out in a few minutes. So fast no ghosts nor curses are going to have time to stop us."

He reined his horse off the trail and felt the woods surround him. Cord swung to the ground and pulled the dynamite from his saddlebags and began cutting the fuse.

"Use plenty," J.D. said. "I want to do this once and be done for good."

Cord curled his lip in contempt, without telling his cousin that he'd already pulled out about double what they'd need. Cord wanted out of here, too.

"Did anyone see that woman up there tonight?" Cord paid attention to the dynamite but not so raptly that he failed to notice that no one rode away to check. They all studied the top of that gap from where they sat on horseback. There was no witch woman silhouetted as she took aim at heaven with her long gun.

The men were well and truly spooked.

"Nope, no sign of her. Bright night, too." Fergus had stayed on his horse.

Only Cord had dismounted. It made the woods close in, and he felt that odd warm breath on his neck. The devil breathing on him.

Working faster, Cord stuck a fuse on plenty of dynamite. And he gave each stick plenty of fuse so they could be well away before they lit it.

Cord was a coward, too. That thought sneaked into his head before he could stop it. He shook it off the best he could, but it stuck to him like a burr.

He felt eyes watching him right where he stood. The eyes of a crazy woman. A crazy woman he'd touched and wanted. A woman who was no witch. She was warm and beautiful, with eyes that looked straight into his soul and found him wanting.

He hungered to crush the contempt he'd seen in her eyes. Drag her down until she was thankful for a man like Cord Cooter.

But tonight he gave all that up. It was lost to him and it chafed, but there was no other way. They couldn't get in, so tonight they were going to bury her alive.

Three

Mandy was going to be buried alive. They rode toward that gap, and her throat closed, and her breath battled to squeeze through her clenched jaw.

The gap stood between her and death. Inside it she could survive. Outside, death roved and snarled and snapped like a pack of rabid wolves.

And not just her death, but the deaths of any she'd be called upon to kill. A shiver rushed up her arms and shook her spine. Cold. She needed the cold to face what lurked outside the gap.

More than the cold, she just plain needed to stay inside. She rubbed on that callus she'd grown by keeping her rifle always to hand. Hating the bit of hardened skin, she knew her heart was just as hard and just as terrified of what was waiting for her outside that gap.

But Tom was leaving, and he was taking her children with him. So now here she rode straight for death with no way to get control of the situation. And that made her crazy.

Being crazy probably described her pretty well as she headed for that gap like she wasn't afraid to die or nuthin'.

"I can't believe that idiot husband of yours didn't manage to do harm to my horses." Tom was riding one of the horses Sidney had bought from him two years ago.

They were beautiful animals. Mandy had cared for them with utter devotion, hoping Sidney never noticed how tenderly she watched over them because she knew they were a little piece of Tom.

Now they rode away from Gray Tower on the matched team of blacks Sidney had bought from Tom, leaving the huge house and all its lavish furniture behind without a second thought to its value. She'd also abandoned closets full of stupid gray clothes. The furniture had just been more to dust for Mandy. The clothes, she and her children wore because she had no others.

Tom had Angela in his lap and nearly two-year-old Jarrod in the pack strapped on his back. The little tyke was chunky and given to running wild. He was dark while his sisters were fair, and Sidney had proclaimed the boy his spitting image. Mandy thought Jarrod took after her pa.

Mandy had taken the bare necessities with her. Diapers and Sidney's map. She ran her hand over the map she'd slipped inside the bodice of her dress and fretted to think of her shattered telescope. That telescope and this map were what she'd always hoped would lead her to freedom.

Right now Jarrod was settled in that pack and acting contented, waving cheerfully at Mandy, almost as if he wanted to taunt a smile out of her when she was feeling so grim.

Tom carried the chunky little boy in that pack without a sign of effort, though he loaded Mandy's arms or back down heavily these days. Mandy stared at her wriggling, grinning son, who yelled, "Bye-bye, Mama."

Bye-bye Mama indeed. God protect me. Protect us all.

She slid her hand to where her rifle should be on her back and wanted to go pound on Tom because she felt so helpless without it. If she had possession of it, they had a chance. Besides, she needed to touch the muzzle to bring the chill rushing through her veins, the cold that helped her pull the trigger.

Tom and two of her children were riding straight into the teeth of the Cooter family's gunfire. Mandy followed along, knowing she should somehow run Tom off with her Winchester. But the man was canny enough to have possession of her children. Even as sure a shot as Mandy was, she couldn't be sure of not hitting one of them. And even if she could be sure, none of that was possible because she didn't have her gun.

In near despair, she admitted to something even worse than that. Her heart wasn't in killing him. Confound it.

"Hurry up. I hear something." J.D.'s whisper sounded loud as a rifle shot. Cord heard the man draw his six-shooter and cock it.

"Shut up." Cord would have said more, but he was rushing through the job. This was the last stick of dynamite to place. The fuses where ready to be doled out and attached to the plunger. Cord fastened the last blasting cap to the stick of dynamite and began backing out of the gap.

He thought he heard something, too, but he ignored it. His imagination was running wild in this pitch black pass with his brother and cousins as jumpy as spit on a red hot skillet. The gap pressed on Cord until he could hardly breathe.

Fergus held a lantern, but it barely cast enough light to work. It did nothing to push back the weight of these high walls, looming, threatening to collapse and bury them all.

"Bring my horse." Cord eased the fuses out hand-over-hand, careful not to pull on them and maybe loosen the connection so they wouldn't detonate.

They neared the mouth of that gap, and Cord hurried toward it, eager to breathe deeply again. He fed out the fuse.

His family was slower, and they'd strung out behind him as he stepped out of the black pit those gap walls created.

"Move faster. I'm going to blow that thing. Can't you keep up?"

He rounded a pile of rocks well out of range and dropped to his knees. Immediately he fastened the fuses to the plunger, so hungry to bury that woman alive he was drooling.

"Can you keep up?" Tom snapped at her like she was a private in the army and he was the almighty general.

"Let me have my rifle back." Resuming the argument she'd already gone through ten times, she reached the inside edge of the only way out of this place—unless she turned mountain goat like Tom—and nearly turned and galloped back to the house.

To keep from doing just that, she kicked her horse into a trot, forcing the beautiful thoroughbred to enter that narrow gap. The stupid place Sidney had blasted out with dynamite— barely wide enough for a small wagon to squeeze through. All because he wanted to live atop a mountain. The gap snowed shut all winter. Though it melted open in the short Rocky Mountain summer, it didn't matter because there were Cooters outside that gap trying to kill her.

The gap was easy to guard against the whole, back-shooting world. . .but it hadn't stopped one pest of a rancher who wasn't afraid to scale a cliff. It was all wrong that she found that appealing.

"I'll give it to you when you catch me." He had the nerve to look back, and even in the black belly of that gap, she knew he was gloating.

The gap was too narrow for them to comfortably ride two abreast. The steep sides cast them in deep shadows as they rode farther in, until it cut off even the starlight—which reminded Mandy again that she'd lost her scope.

She needed it to study the night sky. She'd been doing it ever since she'd found Sidney's map and the stars he'd used to lay out a direction to his treasure. She'd never made sense of the map, but staring at the heavens night after night reminded her of her place, her low humble place in God's creation.

Sidney had been fascinated by the stars once his fortress was finished. Mandy didn't think he was in awe of how small he was. Instead, she suspected he resented the heavens for daring to be above him. And maybe the moron was looking for a way to build way up there.

Sidney had hauled home books about the stars. Mandy had listened when he talked of constellations and the North Star and the phases of the moon. And after he'd died, she'd found peace in the night and the stars.

Now she'd lost her telescope. She'd have to remember she was lowly without any help.

Except Tom would probably remind her.

And she'd lost that one tool that might help her find Sidney's gold. Gold that would help her buy freedom.

The sides of the gap rose to a dizzying height. Mandy could see her rifle in the boot of Tom's saddle. He'd also scrounged through her house and taken four pistols, a shotgun, and a Bowie knife.

It had been left to Mandy to remember to bring diapers for Jarrod.

Men!

Instead, mainly because Catherine was on her lap and Jarrod was watching her from the pack on Tom's back, Mandy said, "I'd like it now, please, Mr. Linscott."

A far more earthy phrase full of dire threats and insults was pressing to escape through her lips. But the children were close at hand.

"Call me Tom." Then Tom tilted his head and in the dark seemed to look down at Angela. "And you can call me Pa, little girl."

"Pa!" Angela kicked her feet, which stuck out almost straight on both sides of the broad-backed black Tom rode. Mandy could just barely see her little moccasins.

"Do *not* call him Pa." Mandy could not sit idly by while that travesty occurred.

"Pa!" Catherine, on Mandy's lap, twisted around and grinned up as if the order were a joke.

Jarrod's legs were encased on that papoose-like pack on Tom's back, but the little boy's arms were free, and he waved them wildly and yelled, "Papa!"

"That's right. I'm your pa. You might as well call me that right from the start."

"My other pa is dead." Angela's high-pitched voice carried back to Mandy.

Tom bent down and responded, but Mandy couldn't hear what the coyote was saying to her daughter.

Shaking her head, Mandy couldn't believe the actions of this night. If things continued to progress as they were, maybe her order was a joke. Maybe she was destined to marry Tom. And maybe Tom and Mandy's children were all destined to die under the blazing guns of the Cooter clan.

Tom had announced they probably would never come back, and he'd picked the horses he'd sold Sidney and let the others loose. He handled the long-legged black spitfire mare so easily, Mandy wondered if the horse remembered him. He hadn't offered to bring a pack horse or let Mandy bring any extra clothes, and she hadn't asked. There was nothing in that stupid fortress she wanted.

The gap wasn't all that long, and she could see gray against the pitch black past Tom's broad shoulders. She swallowed audibly.

"You all right?" The varmint sounded kind, like he was reading her mind. Or maybe he'd noticed that Mandy hadn't corrected Catherine when she'd said, "Pa," and from that he judged she was either ready to stop arguing or in a complete mindless panic.

She was neither. She was just resting up to start all over again nagging until the man saw sense.

"I—I just haven't been outside this gap in—in. . ." She was whispering, and so was Tom, as if they were in church. At a funeral. She hoped it wasn't their own.

"In over a year. I know. I've talked to Luther and Buff and to a few of Wise Sister's guard dogs."

"They're not guard dogs!" Mandy hissed this time. Now she was turning rattlesnake. Well, it was bound to happen as upset as this had made her. She had an Arkansas toothpick in a sheath in her skirt, and it would stand in nicely for a set of fangs.

"They are the finest, bravest, most generous people in the world."

"You don't have to tell me." Tom laughed softly. "I meant guard dog as the highest compliment. It's a fine thing to be able to protect someone from harm."

The laughter seemed unnatural. It wasn't his usual state of mind. He seemed more comfortable being a bad-tempered grouch. "They let me past, didn't they? I love those folks. How'd you get a tribe of Shoshones to protect you?"

"I own the land all around here. Sidney bought it for miles in all directions."

"Your husband bought a mountain's worth of wasteland? He was an idiot."

Mandy didn't argue. "So now I own it, but it's really their hunting ground, always has been and, to their way of thinking, it always will be. So they don't respect the fact that I own it one bit."

"Neither do I, but for a completely different reason." Tom's horse neared the exit to the gap.

"Wait." Mandy's soft cry of fear made Catherine jump and Tom pull his horse to a quick halt.

"Did you hear something?" Fumbling with the fuses, Cord froze.

Fergus had stayed at his side. The others had eased back

behind a bigger pile of rocks. Cord intended to follow them the minute he hit the plunger.

"Haints, called up here by that devil woman." Fergus knelt at Cord's side.

"There's no such thing as ghosts, nor the devil neither." Cord didn't believe in that because he didn't believe anything survived after a man was dead. And it made no sense to believe in the devil if one didn't believe in God, and Cord didn't. But still, he felt the blood thundering in his ears. Which was probably what he'd heard.

He turned back to his fuses, just a few more seconds. He'd set three blasts. He'd blow the gap closest to the house first, so the fuses closer to him didn't get torn loose by falling rock. But they'd all go almost at once. He intended to detonate all three of them as fast as he could.

"Fergus, here's the first one." He handed the plunger to his brother.

Fergus lifted it and grabbed the handle to shove it down.

"Not yet!" Cord worked frantically now, wanting this done. "Wait until we can blow them almost all at once. I go first. You hit yours after the second explosion I set off."

"Hurry it up then. I'm eager to turn that woman into the walking dead, leave her alive inside her own tomb." Fergus laughed with ill-concealed greed. "She's killed her last Cooter."

"What?" Tom jerked his horse to a stop so hard it reared up, but he brought it instantly under control and kept the children safe. He turned to Mandy with his Colt six-shooter in hand, aimed upward, as he scanned the gap.

"Don't you feel it?"

He felt nothing but irritation. "Feel what?"

"There's someone out there." Mandy rode close enough that her horse's head drew even with Tom.

"No, there's not. What is the matter with you?"

"I'm afraid for you to go out the mouth of that gap." The gap was so narrow Tom could block her from passing him simply by turning his horse sideways.

"Don't go out there. Please. We can turn around." She tried to push past.

Tom would have to move for her to get ahead of him, and he wasn't budging.

Leaning forward, she caught Tom's gun arm. "Let me go back. Then you climb back down that cliff. Don't go out that entrance. Just leave us."

"I'm not going back, and I'm not leaving these children. You can come if you want." Tom jerked against her grip.

"We can't." Her nails bit into his forearm through the fabric of his shirt and he flinched. Her voice dropped even lower. "Tom, they're out there. I can almost hear them breathing, waiting. You'll die. We'll all die."

"No, they're not out there. Wise Sister's friends made sure there's no one near abouts. They went all over the area to make sure. Now they've dropped back to let us pass. We're safe, Mandy." He wished she'd believe him, but it didn't matter. They were going out.

"We're *not* safe. If they're cleared out tonight, then they'll be back tomorrow. If I'm gone from here, then they'll find out and come to where I am."

"How'd this start anyway?" Tom asked.

"Sidney's bodyguards shot two Cooters. You remember Cord. He was Sidney's bodyguard when Sidney bought these horses from you."

"Yep, I met him. Never cared for the man."

"No one did but Sidney—and that only lasted until I convinced him Cord was after his gold."

"Convinced him? What do you mean? *Wasn't* Cord after the gold?"

Mandy shuddered, and Tom was glad she was holding his arm or he might have missed the telling reaction in the dark.

"What is it? What did Cord do to you?" Tom figured out enough from that one little shiver.

"I had to convince Sidney Cord was after gold, but Cord didn't really *do* anything. He was a man with bad things on his mind. The reason I didn't like him was the way he spoke to me. I knew he was dangerous."

"Which means"—Tom's disgust for Sidney deepened, which Tom hadn't believed was possible—"if Cord bothered you, that wouldn't have been enough to make Sidney fire him?"

"He did nothing except frighten me. And even that was mostly what I sensed. I knew it wasn't enough to make Sidney fire him. So I lied. I made up a threat to Sidney's precious gold, which wasn't a lie. Cord wanted the gold right enough. Sidney sent the man packing almost instantly. He made a trip to town then fired Cord in Helena so the man was well away from our cabin. Sidney hired a new bodyguard and ran for home, hoping to beat Cord here. I warned Sidney it might come to shooting trouble."

"That's where Sidney was when Jarrod was born. I remember. And Luther and Buff and Wise Sister and Sally ran afoul of Cord, along with that painter greenhorn."

"That greenhorn is my brother-in-law now. Be nice."

Tom snorted. "I remember them talking about Cord teaming up with a brother of his. When Luther and the rest of 'em got to your house they were pushing hard, sure the Cooters were on their way straight to you. But they never came."

Mandy nodded.

"Your worthless husband was in town. He'd left you alone to have his child and came straggling back in after you'd had him all alone."

"Not alone, Tom." Her claws relaxed, and Tom felt her gratitude. "You were there."

It had been the finest experience of Tom's life. He could barely speak past the feelings that recalled themselves when he thought of how he'd been there when Jarrod had come into the world. This boy was Tom's regardless of who had fathered him. No one would ever convince him otherwise. And since the boy was Tom's, it figured his sisters were, too. He was the father of three. And he was coming to the job a lot later than suited him.

"I remember your husband getting all excited about his longed-for son and ignoring the girls who were begging him for attention." Tom had thought Mandy could've used some attention, too, but he didn't see any reason to point that out. "I wanted to stomp the man into the dirt right then."

"Luther did it for both of us," Mandy said. "But firing Cord wasn't what caused the worst of the trouble. That started when a Cooter died."

"Before that, Cord and Fergus teamed up to get the gold."

"Yes, and brought in some cousins. They attacked us, but we had a lookout at the gap by that time, and a couple of those cousins died. Turns out they've got a passel of cousins and a taste for vengeance against anyone who does their family wrong. I heard someone say that Cooters really stick together."

"Then they're fools. They think they can attack honest folks and if those folks fight back they've got good reason to start a feud over that?"

"So it would seem," Mandy replied. "And Sidney hired more guards. I didn't like them either, but they fought for the brand while they were here. They ended up in shooting trouble with the Cooters, and a couple more Cooter cousins died. There have been several clashes, and Sidney was killed in one of them. That was before Wise Sister's Shoshone family moved into the woods around our house. Killing my husband wasn't enough for 'em. I'm alive, and to their way of thinking, I still need to pay."

Tom had heard the rumors. A blood feud. "What kind of polecats turn their blood feud on womenfolk?"

"The Cooters have made it clear all of Sidney's family would die."

"Even the women and children?"

"Everyone. That's what I heard, and hard as it is to believe, I got a bullet lodged in my shoulder one time, and another shot missed. The hate in those people makes me sick. It's obsessive, murderous." She let go of Tom, and he had to stop himself from checking to see if her nails had drawn blood. The woman had herself a grip.

"If I could give them all my gold to buy peace, I'd do it, though it galls me to pay the Cooters for their brutality." Mandy ran her hand over the front of her dress in a way that drew Tom's attention. "But their hate is a deadly thing."

That got Tom's eyes back where they belonged.

"Cooters died at the hands of Sidney Gray's guards. It's a blood feud that they've sworn will last until the last Gray or the last Cooter is dead. There seems to be no end of the Cooters, but there are very few of us Grays."

Tom was quiet, watchful in the dark. Mandy wanted to scare him off, but he knew better. He knew deep down she was terrified he'd leave her. She did want to be saved. But she was so unselfish, so honorable, so brave, so sweet, that she'd chosen a life of pure loneliness rather than endanger someone else.

He cupped her chin, leaned in, and kissed her.

Half expecting her to fight him, knock him back, his heart burned with pleasure when she kissed him back.

When the kiss ended, she whispered, "They're out there." She sounded just this side of crazy. But Tom suspected anyone who had survived what she had would be right on the ragged edge of losing her mind. But she'd held on. And now he was here to take over all her worrying.

"No, they're not." Tom flicked the tip of her nose.

"Yes, they are. I can feel them."

"You can't feel nuthin'."

"They're out there."

"No one's out there."

"They're waiting."

"You're making up something to worry about." Tom went straight back to kidnapping her children, knowing she'd follow along.

"You sound loco, Mandy girl. I'm purely worried about you."

She made a sound that made him glad he hadn't given her the rifle back. She was a crack shot, he'd heard. Chances are she could pick him off and not harm either of her youngsters.

"I'm telling you to get back here."

Tom turned his horse and headed out of the gap. "Quit yapping and let's move out."

"You're going to die, Tom. I know they're out there and ready."

Four

Are you ready?" Cord set both his plungers on the ground and took a grip on both handles. In the dark, Cord could just make out Fergus's nod and his own hand on a third plunger.

"Ready."

"On the count of three, I go. One." Cord leaned his weight forward. "Two." He braced himself for the blast.

"Cord! Fergus! We got trouble."

Cord jerked his hand away from the detonator like he'd been struck by lightning. Fergus pulled back, too. Both were kneeling. Cord didn't stand. He whirled around and looked through the underbrush.

J.D. was scrambling forward with Dugger on his heels.

"What?" Cord tried to penetrate the darkness but could see no danger.

"Two of the men're gone." J.D. tripped and fell on his belly, breathing hard like he was scared to death

"What?" Fergus's voice dropped to a deadly whisper.

"You heard me." Thrashing forward, J.D. got to his knees,

facing Cord and Fergus. Dugger stood back, leaning over them like the halfwit he was. The three of 'em on their knees might well be attending a prayer meeting.

"I thought you were going to stay together." Cord realized as he'd said it that the men with them hadn't stayed together at all. They'd left Fergus and Cord to wire the dynamite and faded back into the woods. Cord had forgotten all about what his cousins were doing.

"We were together, all four of us. Keeping low, waiting for the blast. My brothers were right behind me." J.D.'s eyes were as wide and round as a spooked horse, and Cord didn't blame him. They could look for the brothers, but Cord knew it was a waste of time. They'd never find a trace of them. "And now they're gone, without a sound, no trace of them anywhere. Just like the others. I tell you these woods are haunted."

Cord did not believe in ghosts. But there was something out there. There had to be.

"Let's blast that hole and get out of here." Fergus reached toward his plunger.

Tom rode on with two of her children.

The big, dumb kidnapper.

She watched and waited for one of those awful, vicious Cooters to shoot Tom right out of the saddle. Her eyes burned, and she fought it, but there was no stopping the tears. She could not believe she would pick a moment like this to waste her time with such nonsense. "Tom, don't ride out there yet." No gunfire split the night. "You've got to give me that rifle back. I want to be able to fight." She'd have said more, but her voice wasn't working.

"Come on up and get it." Tom rode straight on out.

There was no shot. Only silence, broken by quiet hoof beats and the sounds of the forest at night.

Mandy stopped the tears by getting mad. "You're an idiot."

"I'm marrying a crazy hermit with three children. I reckon that makes me an idiot all right." He just kept on riding. And he was still alive. "But Sidney was an idiot, and you married him. You've shown a bent for that. So why not do it again?"

"Maybe I learned my lesson."

"Doubt it." Tom turned to the south.

"And you have no survival instincts."

He was out of the gap, still riding.

Mandy goaded her horse and caught up to Tom in seconds.

Without looking at her, he pulled her rifle out of the boot of his saddle and held the gun out straight at his side.

She snagged it. She felt more in control when, with economical motions, she slung it across her back, butt side up by her left shoulder, muzzle down within grabbing distance of her right hand. She could breathe again.

"I've got my stallion picketed off this way. We've got to stop for him."

"Let's move fast. If you want to get away from here, let's not dawdle." She kicked her horse and didn't even threaten to shoot Tom but rather listened and smelled and opened herself up to the land around her, watching for trouble.

"So, the Shoshone like you, huh?" Tom asked, catching up to her and matching her blistering pace.

"Yep, there was some trouble between them and Sidney."

Tom snorted. "No surprise. There was trouble between Sidney and everyone."

"But they've forgotten him, I guess," Mandy would probably have hit Tom if she hadn't been busy looking for two-legged predators. "Because they work well with me. They live on that land. My title to it keeps others away—except those vermin Cooters—so the Shoshone can have the land to themselves, and I get some credit for that in their minds. They know the Cooters mean me harm, so they watch out for me. It's as simple as that."

"They're mighty fierce protectors."

Mandy knew that to be the honest truth. It was a blessing pure and simple, and she owed it almost entirely to Wise Sister, Buff's wife of two years. "They haven't set up a regular village because the government might send troops and move them if they realized they were here. They live quietly in the woods, and I stay on my side of the gap. We have peace between us."

Mandy and Tom rode side-by-side, though he was picking their trail. She remembered Belle Harden had lived quite a ways from Helena. She'd mentioned the town of Divide, and Mandy had learned vaguely where that was. Belle's mare had unexpectedly given birth to a foal bred to Tom's stallion. Which must mean Tom lived near Belle. Mandy felt her throat close with the thrill of getting to see Belle again.

They found Tom's stallion exactly where it was supposed to be. The horse did his best to fight Tom every second while Tom saddled and bridled the big animal. Then Tom swung on its back. Their three horses were a matched set—black and strong with beautiful lines. Mandy's pair so obviously offspring of Tom's stallion.

Tom led the second horse as they headed out. With every step, Mandy remembered death rode with her. She would be bringing it straight to Tom. It wasn't a possibility; it was a certainty. She had to get away, get back to her fortress. But for now, with her baby strapped on Tom's back, she had to follow.

The silence was eating at her, giving her too much time to worry. "Where do you live anyway?"

"Southeast of Divide." Tom picked up the pace, as if he meant to run away from her questions.

Well, let him try. "How close to Belle Harden?"

"She lives a long way to the northwest, but I run across her once in a while."

Something moved in the woods.

Mandy's hand was on her rifle before she was aware of the motion.

"Careful, it's one of the—"

"I know." Mandy cut Tom off, furiously. "Part of being good with a rifle is knowing what I'm shooting at. Did you think I'd just start unloading bullets into the underbrush?"

Mandy's heart pounded because she'd come perilously close to doing just that before she recognized the slender Shoshone brave, riding his horse, shadowing them in the woods. The horse's unshod hooves barely sounded on the soft forest floor. The man emerged, long and lean, dressed in buckskin pants and no shirt, carrying a spear and riding a pinto pony bareback.

The trail widened, and they were riding down a smooth meadow, sloping away in the moonlight. Mandy knew this land well and knew they could make good time for the next hour in this direction.

"Let's put some space between us and that gap." Tom's voice was hard, commanding. And he didn't wait to be obeyed. He kicked his horse and began a steady, ground-eating gallop.

Another Shoshone appeared silently as a ghost from the woods. The hoof beats became a steady drum like the rolling of distant thunder as more and more of her friends rode out of the night. They drew nearer until they were riding, surrounding her, flowing with her over hills and down swales, around rocky outcroppings between wooded areas.

"What's that?" A deep rumbling from behind them caused Tom to pull his horse up and wheel back toward the direction they'd come.

"Thunder?" Mandy looked over her shoulder into the night sky. Starlit, no sign of an approaching storm.

"That's all this night needs is rain." Tom turned and rode on.

"An avalanche, maybe." Mandy's skin crawled for no reason she could understand, and she rode quickly after Tom. Whatever that was, it was far behind them and made no difference to this journey. The only difference it might make was if that gap had collapsed, something Mandy used to worry about when she passed through it.

Now, she turned her attention to the far more likely possibility of being cut down by gunfire.

Cord stood from behind the sheltering rock. The air was still full of dirt, but all the rock had settled down. In the darkness, he could see that they'd turned the gap to rubble.

"Now let's hunt for my brothers." J.D. was a tough man, but he couldn't keep the tremor out of his voice.

Cord wanted to go out and holler up to that overlook where the witch woman lived, make sure she knew who'd locked her in. Whether it was the explosion or his own pleasure at finally taking action against the woman, Cord felt none of that spookiness that had plagued him almost from the beginning.

The woods felt safe, empty. Even the night critters were scared back into their holes by that explosion.

"Start hunting."

J.D. knew better than to hunt.

"We've never found a single man, J.D." Cord would have hunted, though, if it'd been his brother.

"This time I'm not stopping until I do." J.D. whirled, like he was going to storm off on his own. But he didn't. No one wanted to be alone.

"This'd be a good time to remember Cooters stick together. Let's not go off alone." Cord wouldn't have gone along except for the faded sense of spookiness.

Maybe they'd driven off the evil spirits with the dynamite. "First light will be coming soon. Then we'll keep looking until we piece together what's happened."

J.D. jerked his chin, satisfied with the decision. They went as a pack to study the place where J.D.'s brothers were last seen.

There were four or five Shoshone riders in front of Mandy and as many behind her. It was the whole family, children, women, young men and old.

No one talked as they galloped along. She'd certainly spoken to her friends and protectors in the last year. But they were a quiet people, and she wasn't even sure of their names, though she recognized faces.

They weren't even really her guards. And they were good-hearted, peaceful people. But they did walk the woods all around her home. And they could defend that land if forced to. Their very presence kept the Cooters back. She rarely spoke to them or even saw them, but a few times one of them would come to the house for some reason. She'd heard stories in their broken English of Cooters being stopped, but she didn't ask how. She did know the villains had chosen to leave her alone as long as she stayed in her mountaintop home, and she gave these people credit.

They reached a narrow spot in the trail that wound sharply downward. Tom, who kept the lead, slowed his horse to a fast walk along the treacherous path. The trail dipped lower and widened.

Mandy rode up beside Tom to check on the children. Both were fast asleep. Catherine was dozing on her lap.

The trail wound back and forth across the face of the mountain. Jagged peaks rose high over their heads as they descended.

"Let's stay to a walk for a while. The horses are blowing hard." Tom glanced at her, his face weathered, his expression determined, as if he expected her to start fussing at him again.

Like a nagging woman rather than one of the straightest shooters in the West.

"Why did your husband build up there anyway? Stupid place for a house."

Mandy sniffed. "Isn't it obvious?"

"Reckon I'm not quite dumb enough to figure out what Lord Gray was thinking."

"Lord Gray, that's about right."

"And you're Lady Gray. That's why you dress as you do, right?"

"I dress in gray because it was one of Sidney's quirks. It seemed like he came up with a new one with every sunrise. Gray clothes, gray like his name."

"And he dressed you?"

"No, he went to town. I didn't."

"Never?"

"I had three small children, and Helena is a brutally hard day's ride. Why would I go to town?"

"So you wear gray because. . .?"

Mandy saw clearly he didn't get it.

"Because if any clothing or fabric was purchased, Sidney bought it, and he bought gray. I could make my clothing and the children's clothing in gray, or we could go without. I'm lucky the man didn't make the children wear gray flannel diapers. I suspect it's hard to find, or he'd have done even that."

"I've mentioned this before." Tom arched one eyebrow. "But your husband—"

"Was an idiot." Mandy cut him off. "I know."

"And is that why he built his home all of gray stone?"

Mandy almost laughed. It ended up being more of a snort. A cranky snort. "Well, Tom, stone is gray almost all the time, in case you haven't noticed."

"So the color of Gray Tower is just a coincidence?"

"Actually it is mostly. Although he could have just built a log cabin. But Sidney loved building himself a castle, and castles are made of stone. It probably is what set him on his gray clothing obsession. Gray for his name, Gray Tower for his house, gray suits. And he built up there because it suited him to be above everyone. He could play at being a king."

"It's a wonder he bought my black horses."

"He wouldn't have later on, after he became obsessed with all things gray."

"All on top of a gray mountain. And why'd he build it up there, so far from everything?"

697

Mandy sighed. "For the simple reason that Sidney had a thirst for looking down on people."

"But he was an idiot; everyone thought so. There's not a man in these mountains that doesn't consider him a fool and look down on *him*. They laughed when he died and asked how the no-account managed to survive as long as he did. How could he look down on anyone?"

"I doubt you said to his face you thought poorly of him."

"Well, no, of course I didn't."

"The answer is simple then. He didn't know. He thought highly of himself because of his money and assumed everyone else felt the same." Mandy shrugged. "I'm not sure Sidney was completely rational toward the end. He couldn't have noticed anyone who disagreed with his delusion. It made no sense to imagine being high up in some far-off place made you important. Someone had to see you showing off to be impressed. And someone has to speak to you, to tell you how powerful and important you are. I think in his calmer moments he knew that. He never even stayed in that house much. He'd go to Helena at least once a month, often twice. And he'd stay away a week or more. The shortest trips he made were six days. He took longer trips occasionally."

"You said Helena was a hard day's ride."

"Yes, and Luther always made it in two days. Once in a while it would take three. But Sidney didn't care much for roughing it. He preferred leisurely two-day rides in. Then, once he was in town, he stayed and conducted business. Lived in the best hotel, ate good food."

Spent time with dance hall girls. Mandy didn't say that aloud.

"Leaving you up here alone with the children?"

"Like I was when Jarrod was born."

Tom had come to deliver horses and ended up next thing to delivering her baby. She'd known back then how things were between Tom and her. A bond had formed that day. It was the kind of shared experience that made a man climb a mountain to get to a woman. And made Mandy ignore common sense and ride out into the dangerous world with him.

"Sidney's trips to town usually lasted a week or two. Sometimes he stayed away more than a month. He told me he rode to Denver on those occasions to have a visit with his gold." That hadn't been true, as Mandy found out much later.

She'd given Sidney the bad news, after Jarrod was born, that she'd never share a bed with him again. There would be no more babies born between them. He'd kicked up a fuss, but Mandy hadn't been able to stand the thought of his touching her. She'd blamed it on Sidney's behavior, but now she wondered if it wasn't at least partly because of how she felt about Tom.

"After Jarrod's birth, Sidney stayed away even more. I. . .I strongly suspect. . ." Mandy hadn't meant to start this. She did a lot more than suspect. Sidney had flaunted it.

"That there was another woman?"

Mandy nodded. "I wasn't going to risk being alone with another baby to birth, and I told him so. He got difficult. He seemed to no longer care what anyone thought of him, as if everyone was beneath him, and that most definitely included me. I suppose that means he did care for me, at least a little, if I could hurt him that way. But I was too angry to be swayed, and he had his son. That was enough for him.

"He'd gotten self-indulgent and sullen. He gained an amount of weight that should have been impossible in the West, with it taking so much work to provide food. But Sidney lived high when he was away from home. Or so I assume. Lavish meals, not a minute's worth of hard labor. His appetite for food was as large as his appetite for grandeur. He completely quit paying attention to me or the children, even Jarrod. When he was home, he sequestered himself in a huge room in his stupid fortress, with a masterful view of all that was beneath him." Mandy hesitated. "And he began watching the stars."

"The stars?" Tom's brow furrowed.

Mandy realized she could see him quite clearly. The night was waning, and the sun was pushing its way toward the horizon. Another day began. How many did they have before the Cooters came?

"Yes. When he spoke at all, he spoke of constellations and comets and planets. I think he begrudged anything that was above him."

"Even the stars?" Tom laughed, but there wasn't much humor in it.

"Yes. I was watching the stars when you jumped me."

"A scope? Was that what you held? I thought at first it was your rifle."

"No, it was Sidney's telescope. I've taken a liking to stargazing. The scope went flying over the cliff when you tackled me. It's the one thing I'll miss from that fortress."

"Because now *you* begrudge anything that is above *you*?"

"No." She controlled the urge to punch him as they moved along side-by-side in the dampness of dawn. "Just the opposite. To remind me of how small I am. How alone. How completely I have to depend on God who could create the heavens."

"Nothing like the Montana Rockies to remind a person of God." Tom looked around and saw that they had a clear stretch ahead. "My horse isn't breathing hard anymore. Let's try and make some time."

He kicked his horse into a gallop, and Mandy fell in behind him again, glad that the talk had ended. Glad to think of something other than her wretched marriage.

"Cord, over here. I found two sets of tracks." J.D.'s voice brought everyone running.

"Your brothers didn't come riding out of that gap." Cord studied the ground, and those tracks were clear. And enough debris had settled on them that it was undeniable that someone had ridden out of that gap shortly before the dynamite had gone off.

"She got away!" Fergus howled like a wolf with his tail in a crack.

"But she broke from cover." Cord suddenly had a chance at what he'd thought he'd lost. Like a bird that'd been flushed from the scrub brush, Lady Gray had run. That meant she was away from this awful haunted ground. Maybe there was still a chance he could have everything he wanted. The lady and the gold. He faced the direction the tracks led and almost smelled the running prey. "We can get her now."

His cousins and Fergus all got it the first second he spoke out loud. Lady Gray had left her fortress, and she'd left this spooky, cursed woodland.

"Let's ride." Cord swung into the saddle and kicked his horse into the fastest gallop the trail would allow.

F i v e

The ride went on, slow in spots, faster when the terrain allowed. Occasional breaks when one of the little ones had to be seen to in some way or other.

Mandy noticed several of the Shoshone braves pick up speed and ride ahead as if Tom had ordered it. But Mandy'd been watching, and Tom had given no order. How long had he been planning this?

Catherine slept in Mandy's lap, and she saw no sign of the children being active on Tom's horse.

The sun began to show itself. Mandy knew she should be exhausted, but she was exhilarated. She was free.

And the Cooters were now free to come for her.

God, forgive me. I'll bring trouble with me to Tom and anyone else who tries to protect me. But it feels so good to be free. Thank You. Protect me. Protect my children. Protect Tom and these wonderful people who have guarded my home and all the new people that I will brush up against.

Mandy knew she needed to get away from everyone who

mattered to her. But how? How could she protect her children away from the fortress?

The land grew more civilized, at least compared to where Mandy had been living. There were open valleys, pastures full of cattle. They startled a herd of elk and, as they forded a stream, scared a mama grizzly bear and her two cubs.

Enough of the land was rugged that the horses walked and had a rest from time to time. The Shoshone people stayed at her side like a human barrier from attack, and it tightened Mandy's throat to see their loyalty. Though she'd tried to be a good neighbor to them, mainly their loyalty came from the love of these people for Wise Sister. That love and loyalty might well get them killed.

The burden of that had kept Mandy sequestered for this last year. And now, to be out, to be free. . . The guilt and the longing were so powerful she was reduced to following Tom's orders. Like a brainless sheep.

Standing idly by while a man came courting Emma was killing Belle Harden, and when something went to killing Belle, her very first instinct was to kill it right back.

It was in that spirit that she kept an eagle eye on Emma's beau.

It was the longest night of Belle's life. And she'd had four wedding nights, given birth to six children, and married off a daughter against her will. Belle's will, not Lindsay's. Lindsay had been all for that wedding.

But none of it had been this bad.

Marrying off Lindsay had been bad, but it had been quick. This could drag on for a long time. It'd better.

But that meant it was awful to watch.

Silas had rounded up the young man, and Belle hadn't been quick enough on her feet to prevent the meeting.

"She's not old enough for a beau, Silas," Belle hissed in his ear, feeling for all the world like a rattlesnake. She had fangs, too, and she wasn't afraid to use them.

"She's a woman grown, Belle. What was I supposed to do when Linscott asked if the young man could meet my daughter?" Silas stood beside her on the tidy porch of the house he'd built for them right after their marriage. He'd added on a bedroom since then. Good thing with the family growing.

"You could have shot Linscott. That man has been a thorn in my flesh for years." Belle thought of the beautiful black stallion that had been born to one of her older mares from Linscott's runaway stud and almost forgave the varmint.

The varmint being Linscott. She forgave his stallion easily enough.

Linscott had shown up and tried to make Belle pay the outlandish stud fees. They'd both known he was wasting his time, but it had given Belle a chance to gloat, so she'd let him stay and complain for a while. The gloating, combined with that beautiful foal, now one of her top horses and earning her stud fees of her own, had been enough fun that she'd almost forgiven Linscott.

But not quite. And now she could draw on that old grudge to stir up her temper into a wicked storm complete with lightning bolts coming out of her eyes and stabbing right into Mark Reeves.

Belle's eyes slipped to where Emma and that whippersnapper walked, a good three feet of space between them, along the corral, talking horses, Belle hoped. They neared the corner of the barn, and to keep the young couple squarely in sight, Belle leaned sideways and conked her head on the post that held up the roof of their porch.

Silas rubbed her head and grinned.

Which made Belle mad. "Mark Reeves, what kind of name is that?"

"What kind of name is Belle Tanner-Svensen-O'Rourke-Santoni-Harden?" Silas caught her arm and turned her to face him. Then he slid one strong arm around her waist and pulled her close.

"That's not my name." For a change she didn't have a big belly to hold them apart. The baby was almost two months old, her second son. She didn't bother trying to shake off Silas's grip. She liked his hands on her. She hadn't felt them on her in quite this way since before the baby was born. In fact she did the exact opposite of trying to shake Silas off. She surprised both of them by shivering and taking a quick peek at Silas's lips.

"It sure enough isn't your name. It's Mrs. Belle *Harden* and nuthin' else." Silas smiled and rubbed his hand up and down her spine. "So, feeling rested up from childbirth yet, Mrs. Harden?"

She was suddenly feeling rested up to beat all. But she forced herself to frown. "I'm staying right here on the porch to watch that young man court my daughter, and you know it."

Without his smile slipping an inch, Silas said, "I'm not going anywhere either, ma'am. For now." He glanced over at the young couple. "But there is always later."

Silas's sideways glance reminded Belle she'd quit keeping her eye on Mark and Emma.

The couple had vanished behind the barn.

She gasped and turned.

Silas turned her right back and kissed every thought right straight out of her head.

Every thought but one. And that one had her wrapping her arms tight around Silas's neck.

He eased away from her, his brown eyes—more like her hazel ones than any husband she'd ever had—glittered in the setting sun. "And later, Mrs. Harden, I might be interested in going somewhere. With you."

"We. . .uh. . .we need to—"

Silas's arms went around her waist. He yanked her forward and shut her up. Then, much, much later, he pulled away. "Shame on you, Belle. You're supposed to be checking on our daughter.

He released her and helped her let go of him. He'd kissed enough starch out of her knees that they failed her. She sank down hard and sat on top of the porch railing. Good thing Silas had built it sturdy.

"Stay put." He jabbed a finger right toward her nose.

Sighing, she obeyed him. She obeyed far too often lately, confound it. But still she stayed put and smiled up at her cantankerous husband.

"I'm going to go see if young Mark needs any help checking out the backside of our barn." Silas tugged his Stetson low over his eyes and turned to walk at a very fast pace toward where Emma and Mark had disappeared.

If Belle hadn't been so bemused from that kiss, she'd have been shocked at the complete confidence she had in Silas being fully capable of pinning back Mark's ears. And it wasn't that she didn't trust Silas. It's just that when it came to abusing suitors for her girls, Belle enjoyed seeing to that chore personally.

"Thanks for agreeing to coming out for a walk with me, Emma." Mark was having trouble pulling in a deep breath. Here he was standing next to the prettiest girl he'd ever seen, and she didn't seem opposed to the idea of his being here.

"You really asked Tom Linscott to talk to my pa to get permission to call?" Emma sounded flattered.

Mark should have let that stand, but he was having trouble thinking of things to say—which wasn't like him. So he could hardly ignore the only thought in his head, now could he?

"I didn't really do it to be proper and respectful, Emma."

"You didn't?"

Maybe Mark hadn't put that right. "What I mean is I saw you in Divide, and you were so pretty. I asked the boss about it, and he told me to stay as far away from you as I could because your folks were the orneriest parents he'd ever known. He said your pa would beat me into the ground then run a herd of stampeding cattle over me, and your ma would shoot what was left of me and bury me under a tree on your ranch that even now was surrounded by the graves of worthless men who'd come calling."

"Linscott said that?" Emma surprised Mark by smiling.

Shrugging, Mark smiled right back. "Actually I'm prettying it up quite a bit."

Emma laughed.

Every minute he spent near her was pulling him down deeper. "But I did get the message loud and clear that I'd be unwise to just come riding out to your place and bang on your front door and expect you to come out and ride off with me."

"So you saw me walking down the street, and that was all it took." Emma's smile faded. "I happen to know there aren't all that many women in Montana. I suppose you'd have come chasing after any female you clapped eyes on."

Shaking his head, Mark said, "Nope. It wasn't seeing you that did it. Although once I saw such a pretty woman, I was definitely watching you close, or I probably wouldn't have seen what it was that caused me to hunt up Linscott and ask questions."

"What was it?"

Was Mark supposed to talk about another woman to Emma? Mark liked women. Liked talking to them, liked looking at them. But he was a restless man, and he had a lot of building to do before his thoughts turned much to women. But when he'd seen Emma— "You went up to your horse, a fidgety roan mare who was pulling at her reins against the hitching post and looking hard at Tom Linscott's stallion."

Emma's eyes widened. "She was a lot more interested in that stallion than she was in letting me load my saddlebags. But what of that? Why'd that make you ask about me?"

"She was fighting the reins, and you waded right in there next to her stomping feet and jerking head and ran your hands down her neck." Mark stopped and swallowed hard. The way she'd touched that horse, her hands so strong and gentle. It'd hit Mark hard, and he'd been transfixed. "And you talked to her."

So much like one of the McClellen girls. Beth, especially with her gentle touch, though Beth was older than Mark. Sally was Mark's age, and she'd been a better cowhand than most men, certainly better than Mark, and Mark thought he was pretty good. He'd seen Emma Harden and almost felt her hands touching him, almost heard her voice talking to him, gentling him. He'd stared until his eyeballs had near to gone bone dry.

Then he'd headed straight to one of Tom's hired hands and been laughed at.

Threatened with Belle Harden and, almost as an afterthought, Silas.

It hadn't deterred him. He'd gone to Tom and been warned. Belle Harden again.

When Mark'd persisted, Tom had gone to Silas. And Tom had ridden off to do some chore with someone named Lady Gray. There hadn't been much talk of what exactly. And Mark had been given a day of freedom and directions to the Harden Ranch.

Seeing Emma handle that horse with such skill had made Mark homesick so bad it'd taken all his will to not just ask Tom for his pay so he could ride home to Texas. Instead, he'd filed on a homestead and come calling.

"I talk to horses. Don't you?" Emma gave him a narrow-eyed look as if she expected him to make fun of her.

"I do. But I—I just—there was a family of girls back near my home. Blond girls who were good with horses and cattle." Mark reached out and caught Emma's hands just in case she didn't like him talking about other girls and tried to make a break for it.

"So I remind you of someone?" That didn't sound like it suited her much.

"You remind me of a kind of woman I respect." He turned Emma to face him. "The kind who's tough enough to work alongside a man and strong enough to tame a hard land without ever being anything less than beautiful and gentle."

Emma's eyes widened, her lips softened.

Mark shouldn't be looking at her lips, but he'd accidentally taken a peek—or two.

A very gentle tug brought her closer to him than he'd ever been to a woman. Which wasn't saying he was so honorable, really, though he liked to think he was. He'd certainly done his best to charm a few women, but they just hadn't been much interested.

Another quick glance at her lips—which weren't frowning at him one bit—made him hope that maybe, just maybe, Emma *was* interested. He pulled her toward him and, hallelujah, she came.

"So, you finding what you're hunting for back here?" Silas Harden's voice made Mark drop Emma's hands like he'd gripped the business end of a red-hot branding iron.

He had his back to Silas, and Emma was blocked from her pa by Mark's body. They exchanged one long, lingering look before Mark turned to face Silas, not touching his daughter in any way.

Tom kicked dirt over the fire and rose. "We'll be in Divide by mid-afternoon today."

Mandy had thought the journey would never end. But now it would. And she'd stop. . .and the Cooters would find her.

She turned to the Shoshone people who had stayed by her side for the last year, women, men, old, young. "Thank you so much for your protection."

Swallowing, she said what was very likely the truth. "I'll never come back to that house on the mountaintop." Most likely she'd be dead, and she had no wish to be buried there.

An older woman who looked much like Wise Sister, stout and silent and strong, bounced Jarrod on her ample hip and listened, as did all her people. Mandy held Catherine. Angela ran in circles, singing quietly, on the far side of the smoking campfire.

"That house is yours if you want it." Of course they wouldn't want it. "And anything in it, though it's full of such foolish things I doubt much of it will interest you. There's some food and blankets. Take anything you want."

"Thank you." Tom spoke to Mandy's guardians. He acted as if they'd done something for him. Or as if they'd done something for his woman. "We'll let you return to your home now." He lifted Jarrod out of the Shoshone woman's arms and settled him into the pack on his back.

The Shoshone people immediately mounted up and rode off in their quiet way.

Fighting the urge to cry out with fear at being alone here in this dangerous world, with only Tom and her children to pay the price for the Cooters' vendetta, Mandy remained silent. There was no reason to believe the Cooters would be here. They'd come soon, but not right now today.

Tom caught Angela when she ran too near the fire. He growled like a grizzly bear while he hoisted her high then nearly dropped her.

Angela screamed then laughed and yelled, "Again."

"Say, 'Again, Papa.'" Tom hoisted her up.

"Again, Papa."

"That's my good girl." Tom hugged her tight and scratched his whiskery face on Angela's neck.

"Tickles, Papa." She giggled and squirmed and hugged onto Tom's head, right under his Stetson.

Mandy wanted to pound her head against something hard.

The drum of hoof beats drew Mandy's head around, and she reached for her rifle.

"Don't shoot, Lady Gray." Tom stepped in front of her as a group of cowboys rounded a bend in the trail. "These are my men." Tom set Angela on his hip, raised his hand, and waved.

The cowpoke in the lead waved back.

So, they weren't to be on their own. Tom had arranged protection for the whole journey.

A dozen trail-hardened cowboys rode up with a thundering of shod hooves. And in with them Mandy saw a woman, her hair flying free, long and blond and snarled.

Mandy knew with one glance that the woman rode like one of the Shoshone. She had no saddle on her horse. Her back was ramrod straight but leaned forward until her body was almost a perfect line with the horse's regal neck. She moved with a stallion—that had to be another offspring of Tom's black—as if she and the animal were one. It was a nearly perfect match for Tom's horse.

"We've been watching the trail. No sign of trouble." The first cowboy spoke to Tom, but he smirked at his boss holding a toddler in his arms and carrying another on his back.

"Let's go." Tom didn't seem to notice he was being laughed at. Or if he did notice, he didn't care. He hugged Angela tight, then, with her in his muscular arms, he mounted up with no extra effort due to the two extra people he carried.

Mandy was on her horse a second later, with Catherine in her arms. She kicked her horse forward, riding into the midst of the Linscott hands.

Her eyes focused on something that could not be. A young cowpoke wheeling his horse to head for Tom's ranch was undeniably familiar. Mandy guided her horse toward the blond man. "Are you one of the Reeves boys?"

He turned when he heard the name.

"You are." Mandy pulled up beside him.

The man's face widened into a huge smile.

"Mandy McClellen." He moved his horse until he rode side-by-side with Mandy.

Ahead, Tom noticed and turned to glare, as if he was ready to give his cowhand an order.

"Which one are you?" She could barely say the words through the lump in her throat. Someone from home. Someone left from the childhood that seemed so long ago it had never existed.

"Mark." He smiled and that rascally Reeves charm was clear to see. "I work for Tom Linscott, and so does my cousin Charlie."

Mark jerked a thumb at his saddle partner.

"Mark, it's so nice to see a familiar face." Mandy remembered all the trouble this scamp and his brothers had gotten into back home.

"He said he was going for Lady Gray and someone would ride in for us when it was time to meet him." Mark shook his head as if he still expected it to clear and she'd vanish or maybe turn into a stranger. "He never said your first name, and I wouldn't have known Mandy Gray anyhow."

Without really even knowing she planned to do it, Mandy reached across the small gap between her. She wanted to launch her whole self into Mark's arms. He was a man now, strong enough to catch her. But she had Catherine on her lap, and all she could spare was one arm.

"I've missed you," she whispered into his neck. She didn't miss Mark Reeves. Honestly, she'd never been able to stand Mark Reeves. But she missed home, her parents, her old life where she was safe and respected and loved. And suddenly she felt as if she had missed Mark Reeves desperately.

It was all too much. Mandy broke down and cried.

"Mama cwy?" Catherine slapped her cheek gently. Then Catherine was gone.

Mandy grabbed for her, afraid the little girl was falling. She looked and saw the woman on the black stallion settling Catherine on her lap. The baby was safe, at least until the Cooters found them.

Knowing it was shameful, Mandy wept harder, and both her arms went around Mark, who held her in arms so strong they couldn't belong to the skinny, half-grown boy Mandy had seen years ago.

Then, just like she'd lost her grip on Catherine, she lost her grip on Mark when she was lifted, gently but firmly, away from her old nemesis.

Mark had made school a nightmare at every opportunity with

his antics. He'd tortured teachers, tormented girls, gotten into trouble, a ringleader with the other boys—his brothers especially— but he had a knack for talking other boys into nonsense, too.

Mandy had spent a good portion of her growing up years wanting to strangle Mark Reeves. She'd never been so happy to see anyone in her life.

Clawing to hang on, Mark pried her arms loose. She looked at him, wondering why he was betraying her.

He had his hand on his gun as if ready to fight for her. Then the fierce expression cleared, and he shook his head as if to joggle his senses back around to sanity.

That's when Mandy realized Tom had her. Tom had pried her arms loose, not Mark. Tom had Jarrod on his back, but Angela was sitting in front of a dark-haired man with green eyes who rode alongside the blond woman.

"Lead her horse, Reeves," Tom snapped and rode forward holding Mandy on his lap. "Make yourself useful."

"Yes sir, Boss." Mark's deep voice shocked Mandy. Even more, the obedience in it. No boy could change that much. Mark had never obeyed an order respectfully in his life.

Mandy needed someone to hold on to so she looked up at Tom, who was watching her with kind blue eyes that did not go with such a cranky man and his brusque orders.

"I'm sorry I'm crying." She thought of her pa and how much the man hated tears then threw her arms around the big jerk who'd just stolen her from Mark Reeves, the terror of Mosqueros, Texas.

"Me, too." Tom sounded resigned.

At least he didn't cringe and run like Pa would have. Of course she was hanging on really tight. And to be fair, her pa wouldn't run. But Mandy would know he wanted to.

The tears were nowhere near spent, so they broke free again and Mandy, barely aware they'd started riding again, soaked the front of Tom's shirt while she cried out a year's worth of tension and fear. . .knowing she couldn't really cry it out. It'd still be right there waiting for her when the foolish tears were over. As surely as the Cooters would be waiting.

And that made her cry all the harder.

"Get off the trail, fast!" Cord had ridden ahead to scout. Now he raced toward the three men. There were only four Cooters left, until the next pack of 'em showed up.

All three men scattered. Fergus to the uphill side of the trail, J.D. and Dugger, J.D.'s last living brother, to the downhill side.

Cord went with Fergus.

"What's going on?" Fergus had dropped back a long way and now he waited for Cord to explain himself.

"Shoshone coming. A war party. Let's ride forward so we're away from where you left the trail." Cord looked out and saw it had been a rocky stretch. Add in that they'd been following a big group—probably including these Shoshone—so the trail was torn up enough to conceal new tracks.

Cord hissed loud enough that J.D. let himself be seen across the trail. Cord waved his arm forward to let J.D. know to keep moving. They'd been riding for about five minutes when the Shoshone came through. The group, women and men and a few youngsters, were moving fast. Cord stopped and held his breath as the party rode straight past the stretch of trail where J.D. and Fergus had ducked out of sight.

As soon as the Shoshone wound around a curve, Cord and his kin returned to the trail and set a fast pace to put distance between them and that band.

"Those Indians will eventually see we rode along behind them." J.D. was such a complainer that Cord was wishing whatever happened to his brothers had also happened to J.D.

"They might not," Fergus growled.

"That's who's been haunting the woods around that gap." Cord knew he was right.

"But we looked for Indians. We saw no sign."

"Usually they'd have a village, and we'd find signs of teepees and fire. But they were laying low. Careful. Probably watching us the whole time." Cord felt a shiver of fear race up his back. "We're lucky that witch woman left that fortress of hers. She don't have no protection out here."

"Good, because we owe her." J.D. scowled.

"Are we gonna have to get even with all them Indians, too, J.D.?" Dugger was none too smart, but he took orders well and talked very little. "They must've killed our brothers when we were blasting that gap. Does Granddaddy's rule about sticking together mean we've gotta take on a whole village of Shoshone?"

Cord wished like crazy Dugger'd stop talking.

There was something wrong with Dugger. He'd stayed childlike in his head while his body had grown into a man. Mostly he was quiet, and when he did talk Cord always had a powerful wish that the fool would stay silent.

"I think Granddaddy will understand that we can't start a war with the Shoshone. That's just too big a fight." J.D. looked at Cord nervously.

Truth be told he was none too fond of his cousins, and honestly he'd never even met his big brother, Fergus, until a year ago. Or he'd been a baby when Fergus had taken off, so it was as if they'd never met. What kind of stupid rule was it that they all had to fight to defend family?

"Then let's make tracks." Cord pushed hard, glad of an excuse to stay ahead of J.D. and Dugger. No sense admitting out loud that Cord didn't want to start a war with the Shoshone neither.

Six

This is wrong, Tom. All wrong." Mandy grabbed a handful of Tom's soggy shirt front and got a hunk of skin while she was at it.

"Ouch!" The leaky woman had finally quit crying and commenced to scolding. Sighing with relief, Tom'd gladly admit to the whole world he preferred scolding to salt water.

"I've got to get into that gap and back to my house where it's safe."

Scolding got old, too, though. Why couldn't the woman just ride quiet? He started looking back fondly on the last half hour or so. Sure it had been filled with sobbing and his shirt was soaked through, but at least it had been quiet sobbing.

"We're almost to the Double L. Another hour or so until we get home. We'll get married. Then tomorrow we'll ride into town and get you and your young'uns some new clothes. Gray is an ugly color." Tom waited for her to thank him for rescuing her.

She frowned so deep Tom braced himself to get walloped. But he didn't let her go. He liked holding her close in his arms. Idly as he cantered toward home, looking at his future wife's cranky expression, he wondered if he'd ever get to hold her when she wasn't shedding tears or being kidnapped.

Well, he'd kissed her a time or two with her full cooperation. Right at the beginning. Of course that might have been before he'd announced his kidnapping plan. Or at least before she'd believed him. "If you didn't want to marry me, you shouldn't have come home with me."

"You kidnapped my children, you big dumb—mmmph."

Tom kissed her to shut her up. The woman'd marry him, whether she knew it or not. In fact, she was so stubborn that they'd probably be married and have three young'uns, in addition to the three she already had, before she quit squawking about it.

He had no doubts about his ability to get her to say "I do," though. He hadn't faced up to much in his life that he hadn't gotten squared away to suit himself. Why should marrying an unwilling woman be any different? He was sure, despite her definite statements to the contrary, she was planning to marry him. The fact that she was letting him kiss her right now was a really good sign.

Which made him think of Mandy launching herself into Mark Reeves's arms. Tom held Mandy closer just in case Reeves hadn't gotten the message that Tom'd staked his claim on the woman. Mark was to keep his hands to himself.

He pulled back from the kiss, his stallion carrying both their weights without breaking a sweat. He loved this animal.

"I'm not going to marry you, Tom." Her lips were swollen, and she was staring right at his mouth. He decided that outweighed her words. "It would be a death sentence for you. I might as well just pull the trigger myself."

"I appreciate you worryin', but I'll be fine." Tom sped the horse up, and his men fell in until the pounding hooves and fast pace made talking impossible. He contemplated exactly what he'd say to get her to come around to his way of thinking.

Poetry, flattery, bribery?

Nope, none of that would work.

He needed to kidnap one of her children again. He mulled over just how to arrange that. How did a man hold a child on the far side of a wedding vow and force the child's mother to come on across the line?

Tom glanced down and saw a little spitfire in his arms, shooting daggers with her eyes, arms crossed, completely trusting him to keep her on his saddle. He wondered if she realized what that trust meant. No sense pointing it out.

With an effort he kept the grin off his face. He contemplated getting all that fire into his life, into his cabin, into his heart. He was determined to do it before the sun went down. Just because she said no was no reason to change his plans.

Mandy McClellen wasn't going to spend one more day. . .or night. . .not being his wife.

Mark Reeves controlled himself when he reached for his gun. But he was shocked by that sudden reflex to protect his Mosqueros nemesis, Mandy McClellen. He'd never felt such a thing before. For anyone.

He was raring to protect Mandy, and her children to boot. He noted, even though he could only see Linscott's back, that the man was kissing the livin' daylights out of Mandy.

Mark'd have his hands real full stepping in there and taking Mandy back. Then he saw Mandy's arms go around the boss's neck and suspected Mandy wasn't going to cooperate if Mark went to saving her right at this time.

"It don't look like she's being hurt at all, Mark." Charlie Cooper smirked.

Mark would have never made this trip out west without company. He'd had a herd of boys around him all his life. When none of his brothers would come, he'd ridden to see his cousins and talked Charlie into heading for the frontier. His aunt Hannah had almost skinned him for making off with one of her children.

Mark had done a good job of getting around Aunt Hannah and persuading Charlie. They'd signed on with Tom Linscott early in the spring.

"I see that look in your eye, Mark. If you mess with Linscott and get yourself fired and run out of the country, can I have Emma?"

Mark whirled to face Charlie and saw him fighting not to laugh.

It calmed Mark down some. "You stay away from Emma Harden."

"But we're a team. You as good as dragged me away from Sour Springs, right when Ma and Pa were fixing to have another baby. Now you're gonna up and get married and leave me alone." Charlie sounded like he was teasing, but Mark wondered if there wasn't a spark of truth about it. Charlie was crazy for family, having lived the first ten years of his life without one.

Which reminded Mark of a very simple solution to Charlie's worries. "You know Emma's got a sister, right?"

"Really?" Charlie lost the teasing gleam in his eyes. "I wasn't in town the day you saw Emma. You never mentioned a sister."

"Guess I've been mostly talking about Emma, huh?"

Charlie's blue eyes flashed mischief. "That's a fair statement."

"Well, she's got one. A woman grown, too, though young. Her sister wasn't in town. I found out about her when I went calling. I barely saw her when I was at Emma's house. But Sarah Harden is about the most beautiful thing in the whole world next to Emma. Red hair that looks like it'd be hot to touch. Green eyes that I noticed even though I only saw her for a few minutes and was only thinking of Emma. You could marry up with her and stake a claim, and we could settle here and build our ranches side by side."

Charlie smiled. "You always were one for making a plan, Mark. I need to be careful or you'll talk me into marrying some woman I've never even clapped eyes on. I'd never even heard of Belle Harden until you started talking about Emma. Not too many women out here."

Mark slapped Charlie on the back. "Better get a look at her before you make any wedding plans. But you're going to be real interested."

Mark's eyes slid back to Mandy, and all his pleasure in teasing Charlie faded. "I've got to find out what's going on."

Charlie nodded and Mark kicked his horse to ride over to Abby Sawyer, carrying the bigger of the little blond girls in her lap. The tyke reminded him of one of the McClellen girls from back in the day.

Looking down, Mark saw the front of his shirt was still wet from tears. Mandy was powerful upset. What if she didn't welcome Tom's advances? What if she was so vulnerable she couldn't stand up for herself and she grabbed onto whoever was closest?

"That's Lady Gray?" Mark asked Abby, Tom's sister.

Mark had been working for Tom Linscott since the spring branding. He'd learned that Tom's sister was almighty tough. She'd come over for a visit and found out Tom wanted a group of his hands to ride out to meet him on this trail and escort him back to the ranch, riding shotgun to protect Lady Gray.

Abby had decided to come along. When Linscott's foreman told her no, she'd taken to sharpening her knife until the foreman said yes. The woman didn't take orders worth spit. She reminded him a lot of Belle Harden. And Emma for that matter.

Riding her horse with a grace and ease Mark had rarely seen before, Abby kept an arm wrapped around the little girl with dandelion wisps of white hair. "I understood my brother was going to fetch Lady Gray," Abby said. "So that must be her. The woman has a reputation as wide as these mountains, but I've never seen her before."

"No one's ever seen her." Mark had heard talk, too. "She lives in seclusion on that mountain in a fortress. The bits I've heard made it sound like she was loco. Crazy."

And it was Mandy.

Mark felt sick wondering what had brought one of the toughest, smartest young women he'd ever known to such a place. The McClellen girls were impossible to tease or torment. A boy learned soon enough that doing it only brought pain. Mark knew that from personal experience.

His big brother, Ike, had been sweet on Mandy for a few years, but Clay McClellen was a scary man, and Ike hadn't been enough in love to risk his neck.

"I've heard she's deadly with her rifle. I admire that." Abby patted the little girl and smiled down at the upturned face. "I've never been so good with a firearm."

Mark wanted to know more, but he hesitated to even speak to Abby Sawyer. He hated calling her Abby. It felt improper. But she took to sharpening her knife when anyone called her Mrs. Sawyer, so Mark didn't dare do that.

"Not loco," Abby went on, "not according to my brother. He spoke of her only in passing. A few words in a few years' time, but enough that I thought he knew more than most."

Riding up beside Abby came Wade Sawyer. Wade Sawyer was the largest rancher in the area since his pa's death. Silas and Belle Harden were second. Tom's Double L was a close third.

Mark had filed on his modest little homestead in a valley he'd scouted out in the mountains, not all that far from Belle Harden's spread. He needed to have a cabin built on it before snow fell so he could set to proving up on it. Between now and then he was earning his living with Linscott, who had promised to pay him in cattle instead of cash money.

Mark knew Abby Sawyer lived in a teepee in the woods near Wade's huge ranch. Rumor had it that sometimes when it was really cold she deigned to move into the house. But mostly Wade lived in the teepee with her, or so Mark had heard. It was some cock-eyed deal Wade had made with her when they'd moved to Wade's ranch.

Wade had a slightly older girl in his lap. Mark swallowed hard at the sight of the two girls. They were the image of those little girls he'd known from school and church. They were Mandy McClellen's children through and through.

He opened his mouth to tell Wade and Abby what he knew then closed it. Maybe Mandy didn't want everyone to know where she'd come from. Why did she live up there like that? How had she become Lady Gray? Mark knew he had to talk to her alone before he ran off at the mouth.

"I heard someone call her a witch." Wade spoke quietly, their words not for Mandy's and Tom's ears.

All three of them stared as Tom pulled farther ahead. Mandy's arms were still tight around his neck.

"They said she put a curse on the hills around her mansion. A curse that would swallow up anyone who came to bother her."

"It looks like my brother got through." Abby sounded smug.

He did indeed appear to be through whatever defenses Mandy had built around herself.

Tom twisted in his seat and yelled, "Let's get home. Pick up the pace."

The dark-haired baby boy on Tom's back jumped and hollered. The little girls started squirming and fussing, too. The girl on Wade's lap looked up and behind her. She took one long look at Wade and squalled.

"Better go let her see that her ma hasn't run off." Wade patted the baby with the big hand he rested on the girl's tummy. Wade grinned at his wife, who also had a fussing little girl.

Mandy was looking around Tom's shoulders, a furrow on her brow.

Wade kicked his horse gently and picked up speed. Abby fell in and left Mark behind. Full of questions. Twisted up inside with worry for his old friend.

Tom Linscott was a tough boss. The man was quick with a fist, and he'd sent a few no-accounts down the road since Mark had signed on. But the ones he fired deserved it. Tom rewarded hard work with decent pay and good food. They had a clean bunkhouse, Sundays off if there wasn't trouble, and Tom treated them with respect, something Mark was grateful for beyond everything else.

With a grim clench of his jaw, Mark knew he wasn't going to just let Tom sweep Mandy off her feet and plunk her into his house, not if it wasn't Mandy's wish. If it meant losing his job, Mark was going to make sure Mandy was safe and happy. He'd even take her back to Texas to her folks if that suited her.

Except what about Emma? How was he supposed to get to know Emma better, get himself a cabin built, and earn enough money to get a start on a ranch, if he was traveling half the country to get Mandy and three children home?

And yet right now, he knew that taking care of Mandy was something he could not shirk. Shaking his head, Mark picked up the pace just as he was told.

They came into a valley that was part of Linscott's vast range, and Mark saw the herd of prized Angus at the far end of this pasture. They were beautiful. Mark had never seen a black cow such as these before. A few Herefords and plenty of longhorns in all colors, including black, but these cattle of Linscott's were famous in this corner of Montana. And his name was rapidly spreading. Mark had come to this ranch particularly because of Tom's reputation.

As they rode past them, Mark spotted the old bull that had started all of this. He stood proud and watchful on land a bit higher than the herd. A mean old beast Mark had been warned to steer well clear of. Mark had heard the same warning about the boss's old black stallion.

Tom's Angus cattle, his thoroughbred stallion. The boss was a strong man, but he had brains, too, and no one could deny it.

Mark studied the massive shoulders on those Angus, the deep bellies, the wide backs and hindquarters. Linscott had found himself a goldmine without lifting a pickax. Mark had heard enough about Linscott's ideas and the financial risks the man took. . .and the amazing wealth he'd amassed in a few years because of the sleek black cattle and the stunning thoroughbred foals ranchers were willing to pay a premium for. There'd been plenty of talk about Linscott's success as Mark roved around the West, working cattle drives, hunting for a place to put down roots.

Finding the Linscott ranch felt like going to college, which three of his brothers had chosen rather than do the respectable work of ranching. Mark could have been a doctor like Ike or aimed for lawyering like John or studied business like Luke. Mark knew he was uncommonly smart, and his ma, a teacher, was all fired up about education.

But Mark wanted the land.

When Abe decided to stay on and ranch with Pa, there just wasn't anywhere for Mark. The Reeves ranch would support two families, but not three. Mark struck out on his own, looking for a likely place and saving money for the day he found it.

He'd lived for a while near his aunt Hannah and uncle Grant and their passel of kids. Mark had been sweet on their daughter Libby, but Libby'd had other ideas, and Mark had moved on.

He thought he'd found his place here in Divide, Montana. He'd scouted out a likely valley and homesteaded. And he'd met Emma Harden. He could picture his life laid out tidy before him.

Except here was Mandy McClellen. Mark could no more deny his need to protect her than he could stop breathing.

He could figure out a way to do everything he wanted. If he just had a plan.

"I seen 'em, Cord." J.D. came riding in, back from scouting the trail. "There's a passel of 'em, though. The four of us can't take 'em all on."

"How many?" Since the Indians had left off guarding Lady

Gray, Cord had been sending out the men to find an overlook, a likely spot to finish this. They knew a crowd rode with her, but they'd been pushing to catch up and hadn't taken the time to sort out all the tracks.

"Twenty and they're all armed. A salty-lookin' bunch."

No overlook was good enough for the four of them to kill twenty hardened men.

"Now what?" Dugger asked.

They rode along while Cord pondered. Wait for more cousins? It didn't suit Cord to attack directly even if he had Lady Gray's men outnumbered. But he sure as shootin' wasn't coming straight at her where the Cooter clan was so short on men. Attacking head-on wasn't Cord's way anyhow. He preferred to have the odds in his favor. The cousins seemed to come in two or three at a time. They'd be awhile collecting twenty men.

And that's when a sight greeted Cord's eyes.

"Look at them cows." Fergus spoke first.

"They're beauties." Cord stared at the heavily muscled animals. "That bull is the biggest I've ever seen."

A huge, shining black bull stood to one side of the herd, back a ways as if standing guard. His head lifted, and he looked straight at Cord with the arrogance of the biggest, meanest critter on the land. A beast who had never met an animal to best him. The sun shone down on that bull, and his coat gleamed like a black jewel set down in the middle of the mountains.

"I've heard there's a rancher in these parts, Tom Linscott who breeds black cattle and horses like the one leading the group with Lady Gray," Fergus said. "Reckon that's Linscott?"

"Seems likely." Sweet satisfaction lightened Cord's dark thoughts. "What if there was a stampede? Any rancher would take his cowhands after the runaway cattle, 'specially if he thought they were being rustled. That'd leave Lady Gray to us."

Of course they'd have to split up. He'd send J.D. and Dugger to run off those cattle with as much noise as they could muster while he and Fergus finished things for the Cooters with that witch woman.

Cord would have preferred to scout out the land, learn who he was dealing with, figure out all the back trails in the area, and pick the best route to run off the cattle. But there wasn't time for any of that.

"Don't figure on getting away with the herd." He caught J.D.'s eye and knew the fool wanted those cattle. Well, let him try for 'em, but Cord doubted they could sell those black beauties anywhere without Linscott finding out about it. "Just get 'em moving. Make sure those cowhands are after you, and then cut and run, get back on the trail Lady Gray is following, and try to catch up with Fergus and me and back us in the fight."

"I wouldn't mind me a few beeves to sell, Cord." Dugger was always the first one to complain. "There ain't much money in chasing after that woman." And he had a rare knack for saying the absolute truth, right when it irritated Cord the most.

"If this lot is as salty as you say it is, you decide if you want to try and get away with that herd with them on your trail."

Dugger's stubborn chin weakened fast.

"Tom Linscott looks to me like a knowing man. We don't want him or his cowhands on our back trail, Dugger." J.D. gave his halfwit brother a slap on the back. "We'll just stampede the herd and circle around."

J.D. was the only one of them who had gotten a good look at Linscott and his cowhands. Whatever he'd seen must have really scared him.

If Cord could have gotten his hands on Granddaddy, he'd have shaken the old man until he changed his mind about Cooters sticking together. But for now, Cord didn't see as he had much choice. "Give Fergus and me some time to get in position; then start the stampede."

Seven

Tom should give his horse a breather.

Not that the black stallion seemed to get tired, but he was carrying double. Triple if he counted Jarrod in the backpack. . .and Tom *didn't* count the little guy. And the trail was a hard one. Still, Tom felt so pushed to get home it was almost like an itch in his shoulder blades. The kind of itch that made a man look around for men aiming their guns.

Tom's eyes slid over his prized herd of Angus. Before long there'd not be a cow left on Tom's place that wasn't shining black. He kept this herd close to his cabin mostly just to be able to enjoy looking at them every day. His eyes paused on the massive black bull that was the kingpin of his herd. He'd added bulls, bought 'em, and raised a bunch.

Not one single one of those black cows had a rifle aimed at him or Mandy, though, and his shoulder blades still itched. Most likely, thanks to his soon-to-be wife, he'd be having that feeling pretty much all the time—maybe for the rest of his life.

"Wade," Tom barked at his brother-in-law and realized that

he'd started to get used to Wade. The man let Abby push him around, and that galled Tom. But then Abby was a feisty little woman. She pushed Tom around most of the time, too. Tom just put up more of a fight. Wade seemed to *like* taking orders from his wife.

Wade galloped up, and Tom asked, "Did you send word to Red that we'd be in town?"

"Yep, and it's Saturday, so I expect he'll be close to hand." Wade carried Angela in his arms. The four-year-old was fussing, and when she got this close to Mandy, she started hollering in earnest.

"Good, go in and get him. Bring him out to my ranch." Tom caught Mandy's arms as she reached for her child. "I need to ask you something before we take Angie back."

Wade hesitated, giving Mandy a chance to decide whether to go along with Tom's orders.

"Give her to Mark." Mandy looked around for that blasted Mark Reeves, which stuck in Tom's craw. "He's got a lot of little brothers. He can keep her happy for a few minutes."

Wade tugged on his hat brim and turned his horse back toward his wife, probably to get her permission before he rode off.

Tom was too slow and didn't get a chance to sneer at Wade. He looked back with regret to see Wade hand the little girl off to Reeves. What was that kid doing riding alongside Abby as if he was a friend of the family? And now he got to take one of the young'uns?

"I can't believe how nice it is to see Mark." Mandy stretched her neck to see around Tom and stare at that young whelp.

"How do you know him?" Tom had meant to ask right away, but he'd let Mandy finish her crying first and then gone to kissing her witless, and he'd forgotten about snatching her out of his cowpoke's arms.

"We grew up together in Texas. He was my mortal enemy in school. Always in trouble. I had to practically run that school single-handed for years while every teacher tried to make Mark and his brothers behave."

"So you hated him then?"

"Couldn't stand him, nor any of his brothers."

"Then why were you sitting in his lap?"

With a wobbling smile that Tom was terribly afraid would bring on a new bout of tears, Mandy said, "It made me homesick is all. Reminded me of Ma and Pa. I wish I could see my mother." Her lip quivered as she stared at Mark, now holding her daughter and teasing a smile out her.

Tom had to fight down the urge to stop the tears with a kiss. It would be no hardship. Although at the rate his woman shed tears, if Tom didn't think of some other way to put a stop to all the crying, he might end up kissing her almost constantly for the rest of his life. Tom shifted restlessly in his saddle as he enjoyed the thought of being saddled for life with that sweet chore.

Wade took off galloping toward Divide, and with a suppressed grin, Tom figured out exactly how to distract Mandy from a new bout of tears. "Wade is going for the preacher so we can get hitched before nightfall."

"What?" Mandy's head snapped around so she was only looking at Tom. There was plenty more yelling to come, and that was why Tom hadn't wanted Angela in Mandy's lap.

"That's more like it." He had her undivided attention now.

"I am not going to marry you."

That troublemaking Reeves kid came riding up just as Mandy made that announcement. Tom had seen the kid's eyes, and he'd seen the young man make a quickly aborted move for his gun. Mark wanted to protect Mandy. Tom respected that. At the same time it made Tom want to plant a fist in the youngster's face.

The kid was a good cowhand, but he was given to dumb stunts and reckless behavior that had brought Tom right to the brink of sending him down the trail a few times. Tom had held off, though. The kid knew cattle, and he was a worker. The nonsense always came during his spare time.

Tom had been a stubborn kid, too, refusing to come west with his family, staying behind in the East, hoping to win the favors of a foolish young girl. Tom's selfish decision back then had left his family to die and Abby to be raised by the Flathead Indians. Regret over that still saddled Tom with guilt, so he had a little bit of patience with young men and their nonsense.

He'd given Mark Reeves a chance. Most young men grew up. But now Reeves saw a lady in need of rescue. Saving Mandy would appeal to him.

Tom sullenly admitted it appealed to him, too.

"You don't have to do anything you don't want to do, Mandy." Mark had Angela in his arms.

"Mama, pick me up!" Angela fussed and reached across the space between the horses.

"Reeves, drop back. We're talking and we don't want the young'un to hear." Tom didn't want Mark to hear either, but yelling at the whippersnapper wasn't a smart thing to do when Tom was trying to lure Mandy into a wedding. Well, trick her into it was more like it. Threaten her into it. Bully her into it. Yeah, he wanted Reeves to drop back bad.

Punching Reeves in the mouth wasn't a great idea. But Tom didn't rule it out completely.

"No, I'm not dropping back." Reeves squared his shoulders and looked Tom right in the eye. Tom had to give the kid credit. He knew Reeves was as good as begging to be fired.

"Mandy. . ." Tom looked down at the bundle of cranky woman in his arms. Her eyes were only for her fussing daughter.

"What?"

"Tell Reeves it's all right."

"I think I should see to Angela. She might—"

"Not yet," Tom cut her off. "Tell him we need to talk."

Mandy arched one blond brow at him in a way so threatening Tom felt a little curl of fear. Surprisingly, the fear was a pleasant, tingly feeling. He was fully prepared to be scared to death by his wife for as long as they both shall live.

And Tom intended for that to be a very long time.

"And tell him you aren't one to be pushed into doing anything you don't want to do." That part was true enough, which was why Tom was going to have to push real hard.

Tom took a second to wonder why he couldn't have chosen a more easygoing woman. Then he thought of Abby and that wicked knife. Belle Tanner Harden and her long line of dead husbands. The West didn't breed too many easygoing women, and that was as it should be. The strong survived out here.

"So, if I don't shoo him off then I'm a coward?" She sounded so sweet. "Is that what you're saying?"

Tom almost smiled at the gently asked question. He already knew Mandy well enough to suspect he was about one wrong word away from being assaulted. Looking at Mark, he said, "Drop back."

"No." A stubborn look on Mark's face impressed Tom at the same time it made him want to punch the young pup. "Mandy needs to know she's got a choice. I don't know what's going on, but Mandy is one of the toughest women I've ever known. She was already that in grade school."

Looking down at his sweet almost-wife, Tom said, "Really?"

Mandy nodded with a dangerous kind of smirk.

"And if something has upset her to the point she'll hug up against me—who she's never been able to stand—and cry—which I've never once in my life seen her do—then it's not fair to push her into any decision right now."

That struck Tom as being wise, sensible, and fair. But this was no time for nonsense of that sort. He needed to crush Mark Reeves like a bug. Tom decided to appeal to Mark, man-to-man. "If I don't next thing to force her to marry me when she's overwhelmed with all that's going on—"

"What is going on?" Mark interrupted.

Ignoring him, Tom went on, trying to make the little pup see reason. "Mandy wants to marry me something fierce."

"I do not."

Tom resisted the urge to gag his woman. "But she's got a lot of trouble on her back trail. She's got a band of outlaws looking for revenge for something her idiot of a dead husband did, and they've been after her for a long time."

"I never said I wanted to marry you something fierce, you big dumb ox." Mandy jabbed Tom right in the chest with a finger that was almost as sharp as Abby's knife.

"And anyone who gets close to Mandy comes under the guns of the pack of coyotes who are hunting her." He glared down at her. "Don't they?"

"That is the absolute truth. That's why I can't marry you."

"And that's the *only* reason you won't marry me, right?" Tom forgot Mark and focused completely on Mandy.

"That's right." Mandy slapped her hand over her mouth. From behind her fingers she said, "No, that's *not* right. I don't want to marry you for a whole lot of reasons."

Tom looked at Mark and arched a brow.

Mark's belligerent expression had eased and his focus had shifted from confronting Tom to understanding why Mandy was saying no—and being on Tom's side. Mark saw clearly that Mandy wasn't trusting Tom to protect. An insult to all men.

"I helped deliver Jarrod." Tom jabbed a thumb over his shoulder at the little boy he carried on his back.

Mandy lifted her hand off her own mouth to slap it over Tom's. "Don't tell him that."

"Are you calling me a liar? Did I help or not?" Tom noticed Mark Reeves's eyes grow wide. To deliver a baby, a man that was neither Mandy's husband nor her doctor, was shocking. There were few people in the world who could imagine something that intimate passing between an unmarried man and woman.

Mark looked at the baby. "You've got to marry him then,

Mandy. If your pa gets wind of this, he'll come up here and kill Tom before those outlaws get within a hundred miles."

"He's welcome to try," Tom snarled. "But I'll bet your pa will side with me and help me drag you in front of a preacher."

"It's not like that." Mandy's eyes narrowed and threatened certain death.

"It's exactly like that." Tom looked at Angela, glad he'd carried her and coached her most of yesterday. "You remember me, don't you, sweetheart?"

"Papa!" Angela's little fingers quit reaching for her ma and stretched toward Tom.

"Are you—I mean—no, you're not really—you can't be the older children's—pa—too?"

From close behind them, Catherine squealed from where she sat on Abby's lap. "Papa!"

The little angel was copying her big sister. Tom hadn't gotten a turn with Catherine. He intended to have plenty of time with all three of his children.

Jarrod said, "Papa," and bounced against Tom's back, waving his arms. "Papa, Papa." The little boy yelled it every time he bounced. Tom had noticed Jarrod calling the horse papa and his supper and his toes, but no sense pointing that out to Mark right now.

"All three of them? And you're not married?"

"Tom Linscott!" Mandy made a fist. It was cute. As long as he watched her Winchester, he thought he could take her. "You stinking—"

"I'm your pa, aren't I, Angie?" Tom thought this was going nicely. He reached over and tickled the little girl under her plump chin.

"I love you, Pa." Angie giggled.

A few more seconds of this, and Mark would pull out a shotgun and force the marriage. And that was good because Tom figured it might take both of them.

"We need to get your pa married to your ma right quick, don't you think?" Tom asked Angie, while shifting his grip subtly on Mandy to keep her from getting to her shooting iron, always handily strapped on her back. And it was blasted uncomfortable carrying her with that thing.

"Papa," Jarrod hollered, getting into the spirit of the thing.

Abby rode up beside them, scowling. "These are your children, and you've never seen fit to bring the woman home?"

Lucky for Tom no one knew much about Mandy's life. She'd managed to get those who knew her to leave her alone. And to everyone else, she was a legend. Some even doubted she existed up on that mountain. He held a legend right in his lap.

"Mandy McClellen, is this true?" Mark had changed sides fast.

Tom smiled down at Mandy.

Who swung a fist straight at Tom's nose.

Tom grabbed her fist in his bare hand and pretty much had her pinned down. "For you to say no shames you and labels me for a coward who would leave you up there alone because I didn't want to face your enemies."

Turning to Mark, Tom gave him a man-to-man look.

Mark jerked his chin.

Angela screamed, "Papa!" and reached for Tom again.

"You have no honor, Thomas Linscott." Mandy tugged at her captured fist.

Tom had a firm hold, though.

"What enemies?" Mark asked.

Tom ignored the youngster. "Say you'll marry me. Restore my honor." Tom didn't smile. This was too serious. If he couldn't marry her with her cooperation, he'd use underhanded means and cheer her up later. "Whatever you say doesn't make one speck of difference. You're marrying me. That's that. You know we're meant for each other. Say yes, Mandy honey. Say you'll marry me."

She lay there, fuming, her arms pinned, her gun out of reach, her fist enclosed in his big hand.

Angie yelled, "I want Papa."

And the toughest woman Tom had ever known crumbled right before his eyes. Tears brimmed in those confounded, always-leaking eyes. She whispered, "Yes."

Before she could say more and muck it all up, Tom kissed her quiet. He raised his head and realized they were getting close to the Double L.

He looked at Mark Reeves, who didn't seem pleased. Like maybe he was torn between drawing on Tom to rescue his old friend Mandy. . .and drawing on Mandy and taking part in a shotgun wedding to restore the honor of his boss.

Deciding not to give the kid time to think, Tom hollered, "Let's get home." He spooked his stallion—that wasn't hard, the feisty animal was always ready to bolt—and the horse took off running.

Which suited Tom just fine.

Mandy was dizzy from the changes of the last days. That's the only excuse she could possibly give for what she was about to do.

Condemn Tom Linscott to death.

Herself, too, certainly. But she'd known that ever since she'd stepped foot through that gap.

If it was just her, she'd take her chances, rely on her speed and toughness and live as she pleased away from that fortress. But her *children*, Tom, Luther, all the people who'd side with her would be at risk. And yes they were tough. They wouldn't die as easily as Sidney. But a bullet could cut someone down from cover, and that was the Cooters' way. That's how they'd wounded Luther.

The Cooters were a pack of treacherous, back-shooting coyotes. Would they really kill children? The first Cooter was killed shortly after they'd started posting a guard over the gap to their home. The Cooters had tried to rush the gap, apparently believing they'd find gold or the information they needed to go on a treasure hunt. There'd been a gunfight. Sidney's guard had held the Cooters off and managed to kill one of them. Shortly after, they'd gotten word that the death of a Cooter began a blood feud and the Gray family had to die.

But children? Toddlers? What kind of animals were these people? Deep in her heart of hearts, Mandy could not believe these villains really intended to kill children. In fact, she thought they weren't all that bound and determined to kill a woman. That explained why they'd left her alone, as long as she stayed in her fortress.

But now she was out. And she was on the verge of getting married. Whatever scruples the Cooters had, they wouldn't hesitate to kill Tom. And yes, Tom was tough, and he had a salty bunch of cowhands. But the Cooters just kept coming and coming. There was no end.

The dread of what she was bringing about by marrying Tom twisted in her gut. The honest, soul-deep desire to be married to him lured her, enticed her. . .caused her to be willing to risk his very life. The longing for him and the terror for him combined to leave her frozen with indecision.

Not so Tom. He was the king of decision making.

He rode into what must be his ranch yard, swung down from the saddle with her still in his arms, and tossed his reins to Mark. "I want half of you men to ride out and check the herds and be on the lookout for trouble." Tom strode straight toward Wade Sawyer.

She'd never heard of the man before, nor seen him, but she'd learned his name when Tom had sent him for the preacher. Wade was another man who would most likely be at risk if he worked here for Tom. Mark, too, might die, and his cousin Charlie. Maybe the blond woman.

Mandy reached to push Tom's arms away so he'd set her down. Before she could get loose, she noticed a redheaded man holding a Bible in one hand and a baby in the other standing next to Wade.

Tom's cowhands rode out in small groups of two or three, in different directions, while Tom carried her around like a parcel.

Beside the redheaded man stood a pretty, dark-haired young woman, not much older than Mandy, with children of a similar age. There was an older girl with braided hair that hung over her shoulder and dropped nearly to her waist. A little boy with out-of-control red curls clung to the young mother's skirts and looked like the image of the Bible-toting man, who held a carrot-topped infant.

Without setting Mandy down, Tom paced straight toward Wade and the others. He stopped a few feet ahead of them. "We're getting married, Red. Let's get on with it."

"Let me go." Mandy felt herself blush, and she was tempted to take a swipe at Tom, but the parson was watching.

"Are you going to put that rifle down for our wedding?" He ignored her order to release her.

"No." Narrowing her eyes, Mandy dared him to disarm her.

"How about for our wedding night? Will you take it off then?" Tom's eyes held heat that had nothing to do with temper.

Mandy found herself totally disarmed. Literally.

Because while she was bemused by Tom's statement, her gun—and her gumption to resist him—both vanished.

He extended her rifle to the blond woman who'd been holding Catherine for so long. The woman—Abby—Tom's sister—Mandy was losing track of everything—swung down off her horse with Catherine tucked comfortably on her hip. Abby grabbed the Winchester and tucked it into the boot of her saddle, then came to stand beside Tom.

Like she was the best man?

For some reason that made Mandy fall a little in love with her possibly unless-she-could-get-control-of-her-life-right-this-minute sister-in-law. Mandy had missed her sisters something fierce.

Wade stepped close and lifted Jarrod off Tom's back and stood beside his wife. Another witness for the groom.

As always, Mandy had no one. She glanced at Mark, who came up beside her holding Angela. Which made Mark Reeves her. . .bridesmaid?

With a jolt, Mandy realized she had no children in her arms. In fact, someone else had cared for her children for hours. Something that hadn't happened in a year. She'd been all her babies had, day and night, for everything. Food, clothes, safety, teaching—*everything* they had came from her hand or it didn't come.

The Shoshone had helped. They'd brought in food on occasion from a good hunt. But they left it quietly, often without Mandy seeing them, sometimes with a few words in broken English about rumors that had reached their ears about the Cooters.

Mandy was fairly certain her children didn't even know there'd been any other adults in the world.

"I'm Red Dawson." The preacher touched the brim of his Stetson. "I'm the preacher in Divide."

Mandy wanted to gather her children into her arms and run. She held off for just a few seconds thinking God might not approve of her being blatantly rude to a parson. "I'm Mandy Gray."

"Not for long." Tom took her arm and faced Red. "Let's get on with the ceremony."

"You'll be killed." Mandy tugged on her arm, but Tom had her well and truly caught.

"He'll be killed if he marries you?" Red narrowed his eyes.

"I'll be fine." Tom nodded at Red. "Let's go."

"Tom, there's no rush." Red sounded reasonable. Like a really nice man of God. Like a strong, wise friend. Mandy liked the looks of his wife, too. "If Mandy doesn't want to get married, I'm not going to perform the ceremony. We need to be certain of God's will in something this important."

"God wants us married. Mandy's got her doubts, but God doesn't."

"Listen, you big—"

Tom bent down and kissed her.

From Abby Sawyer's arms, Catherine yelled, "Papa."

Giggling, Angela reached from Mark's arms for Tom. "Papa kissing Mama."

Jarrod, bouncing in Wade Sawyer's arms, waved his hands, giggled, and yelled, "Papa, Papa, Papa, Papa!"

The kiss ended, and Mandy had forgotten what they were talking about. And where she was. And she wasn't all that sure of her name and if it was winter or summer. And for a second even she wasn't all that sure Tom Linscott *wasn't* her children's papa.

Vaguely, she did notice that Red's brows had arched almost to his hairline. "What is going on here, Tom?"

"I'm trying to marry the mother of my children."

The parson's face darkened into an expression that seemed to promise fire and brimstone. "Now see here, Linscott. I want to know—"

Mandy was so distracted by Tom's kiss that she didn't even find the grace to blush. In fact, she didn't even find the wherewithal to listen to the parson.

"And she's being stubborn about it." Tom leaned close until his cheek rested on hers, and she forgot all about her children and Red and her Winchester.

"I'll not have a member of my flock carrying on without—"

The voice of the local holy man was like a faint buzz she couldn't quite understand because of Tom's sliding one strong arm around her waist.

"You will—" He caressed every bump in her backbone while he whispered into her ear.

"Mandy, you don't have to get married today if you don't want to. I'll—" Mark patted her on the shoulder while Angela yelled, "Papa." But that barely penetrated her ears after Tom's kiss.

Each whispered word Tom spoke sent a little tingle straight into her brain, which made thinking sensibly impossible. "Marry me."

That was no proper proposal.

"Tom," Mandy heard Wade throw his voice into this mess, "you need to let Mandy have time. A day or two to decide."

A day or two? Mandy couldn't imagine things getting better in a day or two.

"Mandy girl, say yes." There was that voice, that touch, that strength drowning out everything even though he whispered.

"I want some answers. Who are these children, and why are they calling you—" The parson yammered on, but Mandy didn't quite have the gumption to go into a long explanation. Not when her bones were melting as she listened to a man order her around.

In the normal course of things, Mandy never followed orders unless she got ordered to do something she fully intended to do anyway. But now disobedience wasn't so easy with shivers running down her neck, spreading far and wide.

"You've been coming to my church for a long time now, and you've never said a word—" Red waved the Bible at both of them as if he was prepared to beat the sin right out of their lives.

"My brother will do as he wishes and—" Abby was talking now.

Mandy took a moment to truly and deeply appreciate that the dark-haired woman standing next to the cranky preacher remained quiet.

This was the strangest wedding ceremony Mandy had ever seen. Her first one had been tidy and proper, though, and what a dumb move that had been.

"Now, Red," Wade broke into the preacher's rant. "Tom wouldn't do a thing—"

But really, who could pay attention to all the talking when Tom was so close and her bones were liquid? All the voices just a steady roar, like the wind blowing, easy to ignore.

"Say yes, sweetheart." Tom brushed his lips across her ear and nodded his head, slowly, gently.

Mandy found her own head nodding right along.

"It's time." Tom eased back, still nodding. "Finally, it's time for us."

Mandy nodded right along.

And what reason could she possibly have for not marrying Tom anyway? She'd wanted him for years. Shamefully, sinfully, she'd known he was a much better man than Sidney. She'd kept all of that to herself when it was such a dreadful betrayal of her wedding vows. She'd denied it so completely she'd not even admitted it to herself.

Well, maybe she'd admitted it a few times—for a second or two each time—but there was no reason to deny it now. Sidney was gone. Tom was here. Her chance for a life with a man she respected was within her grasp.

Why not? Why not reach out and grab this chance at marriage to a good, strong man?

Because Tom was going to die.

"Now, Tom." Wade broke into her thoughts. He sounded reasonable and sane. But since when did sanity have any place in her life? "I think Mandy needs time to—"

"I love you, Pa." Angela just would not stop.

"Where did three children come from that call you pa?" Red interrupted. "You will answer me now, Tom Linscott. There are three innocent, impressionable children involved, and I—"

"Let's talk"—with a glint of annoyance, Tom quit tempting her and turned to Red—"about *your* wedding for a few minutes, shall we, Preacher-man?"

Mandy looked between Red and his wife and saw them both blush just a bit. Red went so far as to quit scolding. The wife, with her china white skin and pure complexion, got very busy wiping her perfectly tidy baby's chin while the palest hint of peach darkened her cheeks. Red, with his Irish coloring, red hair, and freckles, turned a far more vibrant shade of red and he clutched his Bible a little tighter. What had happened to these two?

"How Cassie and I got married has nothing to do with this." Suddenly Red sounded a lot less like he was holding a revival meeting demanding sinners repent and a lot more like a young awkward rancher.

"Sure it does."

"No, it doesn't."

"You married a woman you didn't know."

"I knew her a little." Red moved closer to his wife's side.

"You said your vows while you were both standing on the freshly dug grave of her husband."

"We didn't *pick* that spot." Red frowned.

"And you"—Tom turned to Wade—"traipsed your horse over the grave and kissed Cassie in front of a throng of men and tried to take her for yourself."

Abby scowled at her husband.

Wade smiled at her, which struck Mandy as very brave. "Things were different back then, Tom."

"And you"—Tom glared at Abby—"spent more time pulling a knife on Wade—"

"And me," Red spoke up, looking a bit relieved that Tom wasn't talking about him anymore.

"And me," Tom added.

"Your sister tried to stab you?" Mandy was liking Abby better all the time.

Through all of this, Tom's strong hand remained on her back, holding her close. Her children took turns yelling "Pa."

The chaos and Tom's gentle touch almost distracted Mandy from the fact that she was bringing certain death to the man she wanted to marry. And wasn't that what it all came down to?

Mandy made her decision. "It doesn't matter."

God, protect me.

She turned to Tom. "You're a fool to do this."

God, protect Tom.

"I'm probably evil, certainly a weakling, to marry you."

God, protect us.

"We're putting my children at an even greater risk outside that fortress, and I hate that."

God, protect them.

"But you're determined and I—I—" She reached her hand out to run her fingers gently down a face that she adored. "I want to be your wife more than you want to be my husband."

God, protect this marriage.

"That's not possible, Mandy girl."

"Yes. May God protect us, *yes.*"

Tom's expression altered from determination to satisfaction.

"I'll marry you."

Red looked worried.

"It's about time." Tom's satisfaction turned to pleasure.

Wade looked resigned.

"And God forgive me for it."

Abby looked like she'd gladly pull her knife right now if need be.

"God's going to bless you for it." He kissed her quickly, lightly, but with a kiss that promised a lifetime of more. "No forgiveness required, darlin'."

Angela yelled that Pa was kissing Ma.

"You're sure, Mandy?" Mark's hand rested on her back. "I'll see you get home to Texas if you want me to. I'll take you."

Angela waved at Tom from Mark's arms and said, "I love you, Pa."

Before the whole storm could fire up again, Mandy said, "I'm sure, Mark."

Sighing, she looked at Tom. Shaking her head at the foolish, foolish man, she let her hand slide from his face, down his arm, until she held his hand. And he gripped hers as if he'd never let it go.

"I hope and pray you're right about God blessing us, Tom Linscott, because we're going to need Him to survive."

Eight

Dearly beloved..."

Tom almost choked when he heard the words. Crazy as it seemed, he really hadn't given much thought to the fact that he was actually getting married. He'd been too focused on bringing Mandy around to saying yes. And heaven knew that was a big enough job.

He hadn't pondered actually *being* married. Much.

He'd been a bachelor for a long time.

"We are gathered here today to join this man and this woman..."

Of course he'd planned this day up to this point down to the last detail. That included plotting with the Shoshone, picking a day Red would be handy, arranging for the Shoshone to protect their escape, and making sure his cowhands met him and took over their protection. And that didn't mention kidnapping his woman and dragging her to his ranch and using every trick, threat, and bribe he could think of to force her to stand up here and say, "I do."

Sure, he'd done all that to bring about getting married, but that wasn't exactly the same thing as *being* married. He had a little trouble paying attention to Red and listening to his wedding vows, and that was no doubt a Rocky Mountain–sized sin.

His feet turned to pure ice. He had an itch between his shoulder blades that told him the Cooters would be coming plenty soon. And he had a soon-to-be wife who could outshoot him, out-yell him, and had knocked him in the head with her telescope not all that long ago. He probably had a black eye to show for this twisted courtship.

"Do you, Tom Linscott, take this woman—"

Abby jabbed Tom in the ribs.

He looked at her.

"Say, 'I do,' white man." Abby hadn't drawn her knife, though, and Tom took that to mean he hadn't acted in any way that was truly offensive.

But the day was young.

"I do."

Mandy couldn't believe he'd said it. Even more, she couldn't believe she was about to say it right back.

Red turned his attention to Mandy. "And do you, Mandy Gray, take this man to be your lawfully wedded husband, to have and to hold from this day forward, for as long as you both shall live?"

"I"—gunfire exploded in the distance—"do"—Mandy whirled around to face the trouble, reaching for her rifle. . .which wasn't there—"need my gun."

"You do need your gun?" Red shook his head, took one lightning quick glance at his Bible as if trying to remember where that part of the wedding vows came from, then turned toward the gunfire and produced a Colt six-shooter.

A different kind of preacher, no denying it.

The shooting came from the direction they'd just ridden.

Right where Mandy had seen that herd of all black cattle.

"Rustlers!" A cowhand came riding into sight, leaning low on his horse's neck. Even from a distance, Mandy could see bright red blood on a scalp wound. "They're running off the herd. They've shot Tex and Lefty."

All thoughts of getting married obviously fled Tom's mind as he sprinted for his stallion.

Mark shoved Angela into Mandy's hands and ran.

The cowhands all followed.

Tom vaulted into the saddle and turned to look straight at— Abby.

That bothered Mandy some. The man should have looked at her.

"Get everyone in the house and make sure Mandy has her Winchester."

Mandy decided Tom was showing some sense at last.

"Wade, Red, you protect the woman and children. And Red!"

The preacher-man turned to look at Tom's thundering shout. "What?"

"You finish this wedding." Tom jabbed a finger straight at Red. "I don't need to be here to hear the pronouncing." Tom wheeled his horse and raced toward the rolling gunfire.

Mandy had known she'd married a man of action, but honestly, even she was a little overwhelmed. And a wedding certainly didn't count if her not-quite-husband wasn't around to hear it.

"Let's get inside." The preacher caught her by the arm.

Abby slapped the rifle into Mandy's hands.

Mandy slung it over her shoulder, almost conking the preacher in the head, and felt safer than she had ever since she'd been disarmed.

Red ushered Mandy and his wife and all the children to Tom's house.

Mandy saw that it was almost a stockade. Solid log walls with opening slits just wide enough to use for gun sights. Those inside could shoot out, but it would be mighty hard for those outside to get a bullet in.

Before they'd gone ten steps, Mandy felt a bitter-cold chill rush up her spine that she'd felt only a few times before, and every time it had meant—

"Cooters." Mandy broke from Red's grip. "This is staged. Everyone, in the house now."

Mandy remembered who she was in that moment. She wasn't the weak-spined critter that had agreed to marry Tom Linscott for the stupid reason that he made her pulse race and she respected and maybe even loved him. And she wasn't that mysterious witch woman, Lady Gray, with the cursed forest. And she certainly wasn't the woman who had tried to win Sidney's respect by twisting herself around to suit him during their marriage.

She was Mandy McClellen, the fastest, surest gun in Mosqueros, Texas. And maybe in the whole West. And if she wasn't the fastest, she was still almighty fast.

She had six children to protect, two women, a rancher, and a preacher-man. Maybe the rancher, Wade Sawyer, would be some help. Except she saw that Jarrod was in Wade's arms, and Abby had Catherine. Which left Wade out of the shooting.

Red had his infant in one arm. His wife had the redheaded toddler and was running with her hand holding the little dark-haired girl.

"Let's go." Mandy waved a hand at the preacher. "Faster. They'll be coming from a different direction than the gunfire. That's a diversion." A bullet whizzed past Mandy's head seconds after she spoke.

Angela howled in fear and set the other children off.

Mandy caught Red and shoved Angela into the hand that held his Bible. "Inside! Now!" She rushed the house, whirling to move backward as fast as she could and still bring up the rear.

Her blood took on the feel of the Rockies in January. She aimed and fired, aimed and fired. There was no thought involved.

She didn't look down her gun sight. There was no time. She didn't need to anyway. She could feel where those bullets were raining from. Two gunmen, both with rifles, high on the hill south of the cabin. She used her own body to shield the preacher and her son and the other little one the preacher had.

Prodding the rest of them ahead of her with her voice, her eyes picked out the puff of smoke curling from the guns firing at her. With deadly accuracy, she unloaded her Winchester, whirled it in the air one-handed to cock it, fired again, cocking and firing faster than the eye could see.

In the way of every fight she'd ever been in, the world slowed. Mandy had time to aim and fire. Time to reload. Time to look side to side and behind her back and over her head. Time to plan her next shot and figure where she might need to aim next.

Glancing back, she saw Abby, with Mandy's daughter in her arms, look at Mandy's rifle and understand the skill, the speed, the deadly aim. Mandy read all of that without missing a shot.

Abby turned away and ducked inside as a bullet cut a chunk out of the door inches from her blond head.

Wade had a drawn Colt revolver, but it was useless at this distance. Besides, he was carrying Jarrod. He had to get to shelter, and he did, disappearing inside.

Two of her babies were safe. Mandy snapped shells out of her ammunition belt and reloaded almost as fast as she could fire.

"Go! Get inside!" Mandy saw Red turn back to her, worrying about her, his eyes wide as he noted her speed and accuracy and frigid control. "I'm right behind you. Move!" She had complete awareness of everyone behind her, the outlaws firing on them, where the door was, where her rifle would hit.

She heard a shout of pain from up on the hill, and one of the shooters' guns fell silent. The dry-gulchers moved, ducking sideways. She followed them with flying lead. They crouched behind a pile of rocks. Both gunmen were firing again. She knew exactly where they were by the sound of their thundering guns and the sheer cold calculation she was capable of.

Gunfire caromed off the ground behind Mandy's running feet. Red picked up speed, thank the Good Lord. Her rifle exploded steadily. Angela cried only a few steps behind Mandy, but even that didn't penetrate the cold in her veins.

Red's wife was in. Then Red, Jarrod, and Red's own child in his arms were swallowed up by the door and those heavy log walls.

Mandy had five steps to go. Three. A bullet buzzed so close to her ear Mandy felt the heat. And she was inside. The door slammed behind her, and bullets peppered the sturdy slit logs of the door.

The gunfire continued from outside, steady, lethal.

Red set a massive brace across the door.

Abby had a knife in her hand and was watching through one of the rifle sights.

Wade pulled guns down from a rack in the large room, one side half-covered by a stone fireplace. He loaded guns as fast as his hands could move.

"There's a crawlspace under that rug." Abby pointed at a bearskin rug in the center of the living room. "Cassie, get the children down there."

Red's wife stood her toddler on his feet and scooped both children out of Red's arms.

Mandy watched all of this while she reloaded her Winchester with hard, quick movements.

With a jerk of a strong arm that didn't really seem to go with being a preacher, Red opened the trap door, lifting rug and all, and waved Cassie inside, with all six children.

It reminded Mandy sharply of the crawlspace under her home in Texas. She'd been forced to go in there for cover once. It was a good position. Red dropped the door shut, and the rug settled over it so no one would even know it was there.

Mandy could turn her attention to the fight knowing her children were safe. "What's in the back of the house? Can they come in that way?" Mandy, rifle in hand, moved to peer out the gun portal on the south side of the room. She could tell from the direction of the gunfire that their attackers had moved.

"The shots all came from the front," Abby shouted over the sound of blasting lead.

"They're a pack of back-shooters. They'll come at us from behind if they can."

The gunfire stopped as suddenly as it had started. The Cooters were cold-blooded and smart. They'd probably hoped to finish this in a single hail of bullets. When that failed, they knew to save ammunition.

"I'll go keep an eye on the back of the house." Red strode that direction, shouting orders. "Wade, get upstairs and see if you can get an angle on where they're shooting from."

"They're on the south," Mandy yelled. "But they're on the move, too."

"Tom will hear the shots and come running." Red rushed out.

Wade jerked open a door and vanished up a stairway.

A second later, Red popped his head back in the living room and his steady gaze nearly pinned Mandy to the log wall. "By the way, I now pronounce you man and wife." He turned those blue eyes on Abby. "You're the witness."

Abby nodded.

"That does *not* count," Mandy called after him.

The only response was Red slamming the door on his way out.

"It doesn't!" Mandy glared at Abby.

Who shrugged. "Talk to the preacher, not me."

Mandy scanned back and forth, high and low. She saw no sign of movement, no outlaw to draw a bead on. Once she decided there was no one to shoot at, she had a chance to think.

That running cowhand had shouted that they'd shot Tex and Lefty. "Death." It had already begun.

"What?" Abby leaned a rifle against the log wall but kept her knife in hand as if that was her weapon of choice.

"I brought death to your brother."

The blond woman's brow furrowed.

Mandy wouldn't blame Abby if she threw that knife straight at Mandy's heart. In fact, that might be best for everyone. Surely they'd leave the children alone once she was dead. Surely they'd leave Tom alone if she never married him. Then he wouldn't risk his life every time he stepped into the open.

For a second Mandy's stomach roiled and the muscles in her knees wavered until she thought she might drop right to the floor from the thought of Tom, even now, running straight into the teeth of evil guns.

"What do you mean by that?" Abby peered through the narrow slit in the front wall of the cabin then moved to the far side of the room to look out. She was restless, watchful, careful. . .furious.

Mandy couldn't help liking her. "The reason I've stayed up in those mountains alone. . .well, alone with my children. . .is because a family named Cooter has declared a blood feud against my family. My husband's bodyguards killed a couple of Cooters when they attacked us, and the whole Cooter family came running to take up arms against us."

"Feud?" Abby shook her head. "Against a woman and children? What sort of cowards are these?"

"The sort that come and come and come." The sort that could talk family and feuding but would probably leave her alone if there weren't a fortune in gold. "There seems to be no end. A group of Shoshone lived in the woods around my home and kept them back. The Cooters seemed content to leave me alive as long as I was trapped in my cabin. When Tom came, I told him the Cooters would come with guns blazing. I know that's what's going on now. They ran off Tom's herd as a diversion so they could attack the house and try to kill me. They've probably already killed some of Tom's men. They won't stop."

"So why did you come to him, then? Why didn't you send him

away when he asked you to marry him?" Abby looked at her knife. Sunlight, through the slit in the wall, glinted on the blade.

"He didn't *ask*." Mandy deserved to have Tom's sister hate her. Mandy would hate anyone who brought danger to her family. "He *told* me we were getting married. When I refused, he kidnapped two of my children. Then he spent the whole ride here teaching them to call him pa."

Abby stared at Mandy for a long moment. Then a smile quirked her lips. "That sounds like something my stubborn, know-it-all brother would do." She turned back to keeping watch.

"But I need to go back. I need to leave here and take the trouble with me."

Abby kept her eyes straight forward, alert, listening but not distracted from her lookout post. "Here's what I think."

For some reason, Mandy felt as if this was important, epic even. Abby was a tough woman, and she obviously cared about her brother.

"To stay in hiding to protect your children is a wise thing, if that is your only hope to save them."

Exactly as Mandy had thought. Her stomach sank. The wise thing to do was to go home. Back through that gap. Back to seclusion. Her throat seemed to swell as if the idea of going back to that bitterly lonely life would choke her to death.

"But that *isn't* your only hope." Abby's blue eyes blazed like the heart of a flame.

Even from across the room Mandy felt the woman's strength, and Mandy, who considered herself as strong as any woman alive, wanted to lean on Abby Sawyer.

"My brother is a strong man. My husband is strong, too, in his own way. Strong in kindness and decency. A stronger man in many ways than my brother. My husband is wise, and he recognizes that true strength is inside, in a man's soul, in a man's faith in God."

"Tom isn't a believer?"

"He is. But even God doesn't seem to be able to control

Tom's red-hot temper."

Mandy had seen that temper a time or two. It didn't bother her. Mandy could handle a cranky man.

"You shame my brother by living away from him, not giving him the respect he deserves to protect his family."

"We are not his family." Mandy left her gun sight and moved to the far end of the living room. She saw no movement outside. Not the least whisper of activity that would give her a target.

"You are." Abby roved between the two sides of the room. "You spoke your vows before God. I'm the witness. But even without the vows, my brother has claimed you in his heart. That isn't a gift he gives easily. To turn your back on that gift marks you as a weakling and a coward. You give these Cooters the power to decide where you live and with who."

"A weakling? A coward?" Mandy's spine stiffened. She was reminded forcefully she had a temper of her own.

"What would you call it?" Abby turned from her vigilant watch to look Mandy in the eye.

From the length of the wide living room, it occurred to Mandy that they looked alike in general ways. Long blond hair, blue eyes. Abby was taller, leaner, burned brown from the heat of the Montana summer. But Mandy bet, even with that gleaming knife, Abby *wasn't* tougher. "I'd call it keeping my children alive."

"I say you're the rabbit and the coyotes have driven you into a hole. The speed that you had when you leveled that rifle tells me you're *not* frightened, defenseless, and cowering. You're *not* a rabbit. So why do you let them rule you? Get back out into the world. Face these coyotes. Give my brother the respect of letting him protect his woman and children. If he can't do it, then you do it yourself."

"I've already—" Mandy's voice broke. She didn't know if she could say what she wanted to. The words had never passed her lips. Her heart picked up speed, and her throat tightened, telling her to keep quiet. And yet Abby's steady eyes and challenging words dragged the words out. "I killed a man, Abby."

Mandy was sick to admit it. She'd never spoken the words aloud to anyone. But in the early days, shortly before Luther was wounded, she'd been standing watch and a man with that white thatch of hair had jumped her, gun drawn, and Mandy had killed him. He'd been no match for her speed and accuracy. He'd been no match for the cold-blooded way she fought.

"It's a scar on my soul." Mandy looked into Abby's eyes, begging the woman to understand. "No matter how much evil a man does. No matter how much he may deserve to die. No matter the danger to me and my children if I *don't* fight back. No matter that I had no choice but to pull that trigger—" Mandy realized in a flash that her true cowardice and weakness was buried behind these words. "It's a terrible thing to take a human life."

She never wanted to do such a thing again. Did the fact that she'd killed put her beyond heaven?

"Thou shalt not kill."

It was stated as clearly as anything in the Bible.

When she thought it all the way through, Mandy knew God could forgive anything. But it shouldn't happen.

The worst of it was knowing she'd cut off a man's chance for eternal life if he died, unrepentant, by her hand. Because the man coming after her was evil, she had very likely, with one twitch of her trigger finger, sent a man to eternal fire.

It made her sick to think it might happen again at any time. Today.

"I was safe from this." Mandy lifted her Winchester. The weapon fit her hand as comfortably as her fingers. "I was safe from having to kill again."

"I saw the way you shoot. I've never seen more accuracy, more speed."

"I'm too fast." Mandy looked at her rifle. "I've always been greased lightning, fast and cool and deadly. When there's trouble, I get cold inside, calm, cruel. I'd kill again to protect my children.

And I can't let them kill me and leave my children with no one. I *can't*."

Abby looked down at her knife. "And you don't want to kill again?"

"No, never again. As long as I was up there, hiding like a scared rabbit"—that's exactly what it had been like, quivering and frozen in her dark hole of a mansion—"I didn't have to kill. Now, out here, I'll have to. And it's not just me. Because of me, your brother will have to kill, or his men will have to. Some of your brother's men may be dead already. I brought death to Tom's door, even if he always wins against the endless stream of Cooters."

"I see." Abby nodded. "Yes, maybe you're not a coward then, nor a weakling. It takes strength not to kill with all the force at hand when danger comes." Abby's gaze lifted from her blade and smiled. "No wonder my brother wants you."

To her surprise, Mandy felt a smile curl her lips. She really did like the idea of having a new sister.

"You said your vows."

"But Tom left in the middle of it. We aren't married."

"Red says you are. He's a man of God. He's probably right about it."

"I can't do it to Tom."

"You think he'll come riding back in and say, 'Forget the whole thing. You're more trouble than you're worth?'"

Mandy had no such hope. "I'd decided to say yes, just because—selfish as it is—I *want* him." Mandy's eyes rose again to Abby's. "I want him so badly. We met years ago, when I was married. Even then, sinful as it was, I wanted him, wished for him. I fought dreaming of him but failed too often. We never spoke of it, but I knew it was the same for him. That's true weakness."

"Stay with your decision to say yes to my brother, Lady Gray. And let the Cooters come. We'll all protect you. Besides, you're already married to him."

"I am not!" Mandy thought of Tom out there chasing those

back-shooting Cooters. She thought of the preacher, then of the preacher's pretty wife cowering below the house with all the children. "So many people called upon to risk their lives, to fight and maybe die, all for me."

And all for gold, which was at the root of this. If Sidney hadn't found gold, none of this would have happened. Mandy needed to get her hands on that gold. She'd use it to put such a high price on the head of every Cooter they'd have to leave her alone.

Mandy turned back to her gun sight. She saw nothing, but she didn't expect to. These were Cooters. They wouldn't come straight at her. They'd play coyote. They'd shoot her from cover. And Tom and Abby. Anyone who got in their way.

And if Tom won today, it would mean he'd killed a few Cooters. And the blood feud would expand to include him, married to her or not. He'd put a target on his own back.

Mandy couldn't let this happen. In one blinding instant, as if she'd broken from all her worries and guilt, she knew what she had to do. She'd declare her own feud. Her blood chilled as she thought of it.

Dare she risk hunting for brutal men? To protect her children and the man she loved, could she choose a path that would separate her forever from God?

Tears cut at her eyes. These she didn't even worry about. If a woman deliberately chose a path of murder—deliberately turned from the most fundamental of all commandments—surely that was a decision that warranted a few tears.

She'd always prayed, *God, protect me.* She wasn't even sure when she'd picked up that habit. About the same time she'd realized just how deadly she could be with her rifle. And Mandy knew that the deepest desire of her heart, God's protection, was for this moment. Protection from the decision that would set her on a path that led straight away from God. But it was the only way she could think of to protect her children and all these people she loved.

God, protect those I love.

But she didn't say that prayer for herself. If she set out on this course she would no longer deserve such protection. Truth be told, she would no longer need it. With her rifle in hand, it was the rest of the world that needed protection from her.

She raised the Winchester in front of her eyes, and it felt as if it were welded to her hand, burned into her soul. Her course would leave her forever marked as a killer.

She already was one, but that killing had been forced on her. Now she would choose to kill.

God would not protect such a woman, but it didn't matter.

"I'll protect myself."

Nine

Tom leaned low over his horse as he saw his purebred Angus bull disappear over a far rise, leading the rest of his herd.

The animals flowed like black water. Two men pushed them.

Tom knew even as his horse thundered up the trail after the beeves that this was a diversion. There were more Cooters, and even now they were closing in on his ranch house, coming for Mandy.

He knew how strong the walls of his cabin were, how well laid out the Double L. No one could breach the walls. There was no good place for an outlaw to lie in wait.

He'd only built it a couple of years ago. By then he'd lived out here long enough to have learned how to make his home safe. And he'd already pictured Mandy in his house, though he'd held out little hope that she'd ever really be there, what with her being a married woman and all.

So, she was safe back there, and he'd picked right to leave her with Red, Wade, and Abby. But still, it ate at him. He wanted to be at her side. But the real way to make her safe was to round up these stinking, yellow-bellied Cooters and lock every one of them away. No matter if there were two of them or fifty.

He urged every ounce of speed out of his stallion. The horse had put in days of hard work with precious little rest, and now Tom was asking more of the magnificent animal. The horse didn't disappoint him, but the Black had to be worn down.

The stampeding herd raced up a crest and were visible again. Tom saw the outlaws drive the cattle up a trail Tom knew all too well.

Mark Reeves came alongside Tom on one of the Black's offspring.

Tom snapped at him, "The trail they took is the long way around. We can cut them off if we take that trail between the aspens."

Mark leaned low over his galloping horse's neck, intent on keeping up with Tom. He yelled to be heard over the hoof beats. "I know the one."

The outlaws had just made a mistake that gave Tom the advantage. Except—

"But a lot of my cattle will go off the cliff overhanging the river if they're moving too fast. We've got to cut the herd off before they reach the narrows at the peak of that trail. Plenty of the cattle won't survive that fall."

Rage went all the way to the bone as Tom pictured his beautiful Angus cattle plunging to their deaths. Tom would be starting his own feud if that happened. "We've got to stop them." Tom turned and yelled at his twenty or so cowhands, all riding close behind him, fighting for his brand. "Half of you follow me."

He felt pride in the men who'd thrown in with the Linscott ranch. He liked a lot of them almost as much as he liked his black stallion. "We can cut through that low valley and come around. Mark, take half the men and go up after them. If we stop them in time, those yellowbellied Cooters will turn and try to run. That'll bring them right at you. They're cowards so they might surrender without a fight, but be ready in case they try and shoot their way through your line."

Tom hadn't meant to put Mark in charge, but the kid was closest. It made sense to give him the order to pass on. Tom veered his stallion toward the lower but less visible trail tucked between the trees. He urged every drop of speed out of his powerful thoroughbred in a race against time to save his cattle, put a stop to the Cooters, and get back to his wedding.

The aspens slapped Tom in the face as he dashed through the woods. The trail went straight toward the end of that high, climbing trail. The Cooters were going to be taken out of this fight before it ever started.

Tom reached the point where the curving high trail met up with the low trail and turned to race upward. He finally heard the thundering hooves of his cattle. "We've got to stop them," he yelled over his shoulder. "Turn them back."

Tom's stallion blew from the fast ride and the steep climb. They had to get to the cattle and turn them back before the narrowest part of the trail, and it would be close. It made Tom sick to think of it, but he might have to kill a few of them in the lead to stop the rest.

The men came up beside him on the trail, still wide enough to ride four abreast, and two more rows of nearly that many men rode behind Tom. The hill reached its peak ahead. On the right, a mountain soared overhead. On the left, it dropped off for a hundred yards to a fast-moving river. A man might survive such a fall, but it would be a chancy thing. If Tom's herd plunged over that drop, many would die.

They closed in on that crest. The sound of those pounding, runaway cattle, laced with an occasional wild bawl of fear, drew nearer.

Tom glanced to the left and right and saw some of his best men. They might well die today, thanks to Tom's determination to have Mandy Gray. He was well and truly married to her now, so there was no going back. This was the bronco he'd saddled, and his drovers rode for the brand. Any one of them was free to turn around and ride away right now. It did his heart good to see their loyalty.

They reached the crest. The cliff was only yards away. Dust kicked up by a hundred head of runaway cattle was visible ahead.

Tom charged forward, and at last his herd came into view. He drew his gun, mindful that he'd sent men up behind the herd, and fired into the air, shouting, his cowhands firing and waving, creating as much racket as they could to halt the terrified Angus.

Tom and his men raced ahead. The Angus came on. A few at the front twisted and skidded along, pushed by those behind. Reining back on his stallion, Tom watched the herd shove toward him, to trample him and his cowpokes. Tom reared his stallion up, hoping to make himself and his horse as big a barrier as possible. His men did the same, shouting, firing into the air. His big bull stumbled and went down. Cattle from behind him shoved on ahead, bawling.

Looking at the crowd of slowing cattle, Tom saw his own men down the trail. Mark Reeves had gotten into the middle of the herd somehow and was turning the farthest cattle back around. A few were already trotting downhill. The pressing mill of animals slowed. The gap between Tom and the beeves narrowed.

His bull reared up, still alive, but Tom knew he had to be injured. Then the old guy was lost in the dust.

No sign of the rustlers who had started this. Tom holstered his revolver and pulled his hat off, waving it, hollering.

Reeves got between more of the tightly packed animals and turned them aside. The bunch that would hit Tom and his men was smaller now, a few dozen head. But they were propelled forward, the front cattle unable to stop. Tom braced himself for the impact.

In an instant he was swallowed up by the herd. The roiling dust blinded him. He felt a steer collide with his stallion, and the horse staggered but stayed on his feet.

He could lose his most valuable animals today—his stallion and his bull. What a wedding present.

Tom slapped his hat in the faces of the black, bawling critters who surrounded him and pushed him and his horse toward that cliff. Battling for each foot, Tom resisted being pushed back, wondering what was happening to the men behind him.

Then, as suddenly as he'd been surrounded, all was still. Tom could barely make out where they were, and that death drop might be one wrong step only inches to the side. He held his horse in place.

The cattle shoved, and he saw the big heads turning, mooing, packed too tightly against each other to move.

Mark Reeves emerged from the haze. With a coiled lasso, he slapped at a single steer, turning him and heading the big brute down the hill. Tom's Angus bull came into view in the middle of the herd, and Mark went for the big guy next. With soft, soothing noises meant to move the animals without startling them into another run, Mark hazed the bull until he turned and headed back the way he'd come.

Tom breathed a sigh of relief knowing his bull had survived this mess. The bull moving broke the logjam of cattle, and they followed the bull. Tom saw the cattle walking placidly away. The big lugs looked exhausted from the stampede.

The dust cleared enough that Tom could dare to move. His horse was so close to the edge, a chill of fear raced up Tom's back. He quickly put space between himself and that ledge. A few cattle had gotten past Tom, but his drovers had turned them and sent them ambling after the rest of the herd.

"What about the shooters?" Tom turned to Reeves. "Did you get 'em?"

Mark shook his head. "We saw the trail they took. Once they got the herd running fast, they turned off and left them to stampede on their own. I watched close, we all did, but there was no likely spot for them to dry-gulch us."

"I reckon that's the only reason they didn't. This had to be set up to draw us away from the cabin. But once they all got inside, they'll be safe. No one can breach my cabin."

"As long as they managed to get inside." Mark's eyes were sharp for such a young man.

Tom nodded and said, "Let's make tracks for home."

"They're gone." Red emerged from the back room, and Wade came downstairs. "I caught a glimpse of them riding away. Two men are all I saw."

"Two shooters." Mandy checked the load on her rifle then felt in her pocket for bullets. "Where were they headed?"

She strode toward Tom's rifles, mounted on the wall beside the fireplace, and helped herself to a bandolier, dropping it over her head to cross her chest. She added a second and tucked two boxes of shells in the pockets of her gray dress.

"I saw them running over the rise to the southwest. There's some mighty wild country up there."

"Show me the trail they took."

"Let me get the young'uns out of the cellar first, Mrs. Linscott." Red walked for the bearskin rug.

Mandy caught his arm so hard he flinched. "The trail first, while it's fresh in your mind." Mandy directed her attention away from Red for a second. "Abby, you take care of the children."

Abby arched a brow as if no one gave her orders and lived.

Mandy ignored her. "And I'm not Mrs. Linscott. My almost-husband ran off before you made the pronouncement. It doesn't count."

"It counts," Red said easily.

"You're sure we're married?" Mandy thought of that for a long second and realized that now, if she died, someone else would be responsible for her children. If she could stop the Cooters—

even if she died trying or even if she didn't die but ended up in prison. She felt the heat of shame and wished for the comfort of her usual icy nerves. "Shouldn't we have a marriage certificate of some kind?"

Red produced a sheet of paper from his pocket. "I made it up before you and Tom rode into the yard. I'm signing it now in front of both of you." He looked around the room and spotted an ink pot on a desk, with a pen beside it. He strode to the desk, dipped the pen, signed it, and then gave the certificate to Abby. "You sign just below."

Abby swiftly signed it, giving Mandy a defiant glance. "There. You're my sister."

"You're sure this is legal?" The man was a parson. Why would he lie about such a thing?

"It's legal." Red showed not one speck of doubt. "He said, 'I do.' You said, 'I do.'"

Mandy had actually said, "I do need my rifle," but this wasn't the time to quibble.

"That's what matters." Red thrust the paper and pen toward Mandy. "Sign."

"I'll swear to that." Abby reached down for the bearskin.

Making her decision, Mandy grabbed the pen, dipped it again, and signed boldly. Then she dragged Red into the kitchen. "Which trail?"

Red pointed.

"Okay." She stared hard, memorizing the way, checking landmarks so she could find whatever trail must be up there.

"I'm going to go make sure my wife is all right. You might want to come and comfort your children." The preacher-man sounded like he was chastising her.

Mandy controlled the urge to give him a butt stroke across the back of his head. That said more about her current state of mind than whether he was an annoying man. Instead of slugging him, she handed him back her marriage license.

Red seemed to sense her violent attitude. He gave a little shake of his head, rolled his eyes heavenward, and then left the room.

Which suited Mandy just fine. She sure hoped Abby got her meaning when she told the woman to take care of the children. She was now legally their aunt.

Mandy jerked the door open and within minutes was on horseback, riding one of the beautiful offspring of Tom's stallion, rushing after those mangy varmint Cooters. She'd end this by killing every mother's son of them or dying in the attempt.

Either way it would be over.

If Red said she was married, and Abby said she was married, and Mandy had signed the paper swearing she'd made her vows, then that was that. Tom was her children's father. Tom was free to raise her children, should she not survive this madness.

Her Winchester hung heavily on her back. The weight of the bullets threatened to drag her to the ground. In the end she was afraid today's choices and this load of deadly ammunition would drag her right down into Hades. But it was the price she'd decided to pay to protect the people she loved.

God, protect me.

That old prayer came to her, but Mandy shook her head and spoke aloud to the sky. "I don't mean it, God. I don't deserve Your protection on this path of killing I'm on. But protect my children, Lord. And my husband. Reckon I took my vows before You and meant every word. But when he finds out what I've done, he may just tell Red to rip up that paper and forget the whole thing."

At a ground-eating gallop, she aimed her horse for that trail Red had pointed out. While she rode, she wondered if a woman could be hanged for stealing a horse from her own husband.

T e n

Che stole my horse?" Tom's voice rose to such a high pitch it hurt his ears.

"I don't think a woman can rightly steal a horse from her own husband." Red shrugged.

"And now you can't find her?" Tom clenched his fists and stormed straight toward Red and the worthless man Abby had married.

"I think she took out after the men who were shooting at us." Wade stepped in front of Red. It was his brother-in-law's way to draw a fist to his own face to protect someone else. He might even have thoughts of Tom's soul, not wanting Tom to slug a parson.

"She can't have gone far." Red came up to Wade's side. Calm, strong, wise, a hard man to thrash for a lot of reasons, confound it. "We just realized she was gone a few minutes ago."

"She took enough bullets with her to start a war," Abby added.

The whole lot of them had realized Mandy was gone and gathered outside by the time Tom came riding into the ranch yard.

"She left her children behind?" Tom couldn't believe a woman would do such a thing.

"I reckon they're your children now, too, Tom." Red lifted his shoulders as he stated the obvious. "Just like your horse is hers."

"So we're married for sure?" Later, Tom intended to beat the tar out of both Red and Wade for losing Mandy. But right now he had a missing wife to track down.

"You oughtta sign it, too." Red handed Tom a piece of paper with a neatly written record of the marriage, signed by Red, Abby, and Mandy, all three. "But even if you don't, you're still married."

Red said that as if he expected Tom to argue, but being married to Mandy, the little horse thief, suited him right down to the ground. Tom grabbed the paper. Red produced a pen and a bottle of ink. Tom scrawled his name and thrust pen and paper toward Red.

"It's yours." Red refused to take it.

Tom folded it roughly and jammed it into one pocket.

"Abby, tell me what went on around here. Sawyer, pack me some grub."

Abby talked while Tom led his stallion to the barn.

When his sister paused to take a breath, Tom jerked his chin at the stallion. "Will you take care of him? Everyone else on this ranch is scared to get near him."

Abby agreed and kept talking, letting him know all that had unfolded. She made a point of talking about the way Mandy handled her rifle. Tom had heard a similar story years ago from Belle Harden, who had met Mandy when she was a new bride.

He'd asked too much of the black. He strode toward the corral where Tom's second favorite horse was held. The most perfect colt to ever come out of his stallion, and that was saying something because his stallion bred true.

Tom stumbled to a halt when he reached the corral. A dozen horses grazed in the pen, none of them the one he wanted. "She stole my *best* horse?" Though it was no time for such a thing,

Tom laughed. He had married himself one beauty of a woman.

"Borrowed, Tom. Not stole." Red had tagged along to the corral.

Tom remembered well his plan to beat Red within an inch of his life. Right now time was too tight. "Which way did she go?"

Red pointed to a trail in the distance Tom could only see because he knew his land so well. "She asked me where I saw the men riding, the ones who shot up your house."

"And you told her?" Tom wheeled to face Red head on. Maybe he'd take the time for that beating after all. "Why would you do a stupid thing like that?"

Red shoved his face right up into Tom's, which reminded Tom that Red wasn't just a sky pilot—he was also a rancher who'd come out here and tamed a mighty mean stretch of land. "I *told* her because it never occurred to me that a woman would abandon three children and a man she'd just married to go hunting a pack of killers. What kind of woman did you marry anyway? She's acting crazy."

Tom shrugged. He couldn't really argue Red's point, though arguing came real easy. "I married me the sharpest shooting woman in the West, I reckon."

"That you did, Tom. I saw her in action." Abby bridled Tom's second choice for a horse while he saddled.

"I saw her, too." Red shook his head in wonder. "I've never seen anyone shoot like that. Why do you want a woman who appears to have a taste for killing? What are you thinking to pick a woman like that?"

Tom looked past Red and saw Red's wife, sweet little Cassie Dawson, quietly tending all six children, both the Dawsons' and Mandy's—

Tom caught that thought. They were his children now, too. He liked the sound of that.

Tom's temper would have crushed Cassie like a bug the first week of their marriage. Shrugging, Tom felt a little sheepish, but this was a man of God. It'd be wrong to lie. "Honest, Red, that's what I like *most* about her."

Tom got a notion that would make things safer for *his* children and threw a few orders at Abby.

"Good idea. I'll do it." Abby would obey him because it was a good idea, and for no other reason. The woman didn't submit to a man worth spit.

He grabbed the bag of grub from that jelly-spined Wade Sawyer—the perfect man for Tom's sister—then he set his horse to galloping before he left the ranch yard. He was in a hurry to drag his gun-slinging wife back home and get started on his honeymoon.

Mandy caught up to them at sunset. She could read sign like the written word. She'd seen where the two men shooting at Tom's ranch house had met up with two others. Now she was almost within shooting range of four Cooters, and she intended to leave them all dead in the dirt before she slept tonight.

The sin of what she planned rattled at her like a longhorn bull dodging a branding iron.

She ignored her conscience. Ignored a lifetime of teaching. Ignored the hurt she'd cause her parents and sisters and children. She couldn't tackle four armed men head-on. So she'd unload her gun into their mangy hides as they sat around their campfire. She'd dry-gulch them and keep firing until they were all dead or she was.

Then she'd sit back and wait for the next Cooters to come, and the next. She'd left honor and her children and any claim to decency behind when she'd set out on this path. And she knew it.

She edged her way up the dirt, on the ground above where they were settling in for the night. An inch at a time. She wanted no motion to draw the Cooters' attentions, no sound to stir their suspicions.

She heard the crackle of a campfire and knew the lazy coyotes were settling in for the night. They hadn't run as far as she'd expected when she'd seen the far trail they were on. Of course they hadn't. Because, though today's attack had failed, they'd now begin their planning for the next one, and the next.

It was why they had to die.

She had only another inch to go and they'd be visible. Then with equal slowness, she'd aim her trusty rifle. Four shots. A hot hunger in her gut had her hoping she could kill them in four shots. It was evil, the greed to kill.

It was the path she'd chosen, but still, the pleasure that came with her willingness to kill surprised her. Good and evil weren't far apart in a woman's soul.

She smelled their fire, clean and crisp from dry wood and leaves. Not like the sulfuric fires where she'd spend eternity.

Her mouth watered as her hand tightened on the trigger. The one thing she hadn't been able to summon was the cold. For some reason it eluded her. And killing the Cooters flooded her with heat straight from the heart of the devil.

"I'm done waiting, Sophie." Clay felt his spine crawling for some reason he couldn't imagine. But he'd felt it a few times before and he trusted it.

His wife looked at him, and their gazes locked. She knew exactly what he meant. "Why now?"

Shaking his head, Clay couldn't explain it, but then Sophie was pretty good at figuring his thoughts, so he usually didn't need to. "It's riding me, and I'm not going to sit quiet anymore."

"She's a grown-up woman, Clay. She made her wishes known, and we should respect them."

Clay didn't think even his stubborn wife sounded quite as sure as usual. They'd had this fight a dozen times. He wanted to get to Montana and fetch his daughter home, and he was going to do it.

If he had to fight off some mob of men to get to her, so be it. If he had to fight Mandy, so be it.

The boys were sitting quietly at their studies. Smart sons, good ones. Clay took a hard minute to realize he was riding into danger and might well not come back. But to sit here safe while his daughter was in trouble went against every bit of his grain.

"I'll go along, Pa." The most talkative of the twins, Cliff, spoke up. He'd be of some help. His boys were tough and savvy, no denying it. But he wasn't going to put them in danger.

Although from Mandy's letters, the very few there had been, Clay knew getting involved in this stupid feud could draw those Cooters down on his whole family.

"Nope, your ma needs you here." His eyes went to Laura. She was grown up enough that she'd be the next daughter he had that would come dragging some idiot husband home. A half crazy doctor for Beth, a painter of all things for his rough and tough Sally, and for Mandy, that worthless Sidney Gray.

Alex Buchanan had gathered his wits and ended up being a solid husband for Beth. Sally's husband, Logan McKenzie, was not what Clay would have picked. Clay's eyes went to a huge painting on the living room wall of a spectacular mountain scene that reminded Clay of his childhood in the Rockies. Truth was Logan adored Sally, and the nomadic life they lived seemed to suit them. They came through the area and stayed for a month about twice a year. There was a baby on the way now, and Logan had promised to settle somewhere once there was a family to think of. Clay believed him.

Sidney Gray. There was no explaining that. Although to be fair, he'd seemed like the most solid and sensible of the three men when Mandy had picked him. Of course Clay had loathed him, but that was the normal state when a man came bothering one of his girls. A lawyer, solid, educated, prosperous. It had all been lies. At least the lunatic doctor and rootless painter had been honest.

Clay vowed there and then to just shoot any man who got

near Laura and be done with it.

"You need someone to ride with you, Clay." Sophie had that look in her eyes, the one that said she was about to take the bit in her teeth.

"I'll send a wire to Luther and tell him to meet me. I'll need someone to guide me to that mountaintop where Mandy lives anyway. Maybe Buff will come, too. I'll ride careful, check with the law when I'm in the area." Clay held Sophie's gaze.

After far too long, she jerked her chin. "Fine. I have the feeling it's time for us to go, too."

"No, not us. Me. First light. I need to go talk to the men."

"I'm going, Clay." He heard her muttering, "Help me, Lord. Help me, help me, help me," as she turned to begin packing a sack of food.

When his Sophie started praying that prayer, there was no stopping her. So Clay didn't try.

"Boys, come on along so you'll know what's going on." Clay plucked his Stetson off a peg by the door and went out, his sons, sturdy boots clomping on the porch, falling in behind him.

He wondered how he'd go about running off the women when they came hunting his sons. How did that even work?

Sally threw off the covers of her bedroll with a quiet growl of frustration and reached for her broadcloth pants.

In the dim light of morning, she saw Logan's eyes flicker open as she dressed.

When he focused on her, his brows rose nearly to his hairline. "You haven't worn those in a while." He sounded scared.

She would have grinned if worry wasn't eating at her. "I've got to go see Mandy." One moment of indecision had her running her hand over her slightly rounded stomach. She had a baby to think of now. Her hand drifted upward to the bit of ribbon on her chemise, then she turned to drag her favorite cowpoke shirt over her head.

God, have mercy. On my sister, on my child, on me.

"It's dangerous." Logan got up and began dressing. He knew her very well. Protest all day long, but he knew how this had been riding her, and he knew she'd just snapped. "You know I want Mandy to be safe, but we can't just go diving into the middle of a feud with—" Logan gestured at her belly.

"I want this baby to be safe more than I care about my own life." Sally slung her rifle across her back even before she put her boots on and felt a fraction safer. She still wore it all the time, but honestly, life was pretty safe with Logan. Painters just didn't draw trouble, thank the good Lord.

"I've hung back and stayed away as long as I can." She continued to dress. "But I can't do that anymore."

She'd enjoyed the summers in Yellowstone after splitting the winters between New York City and Mosqueros, Texas. Logan had produced some of his most beautiful work. As summer drifted past and Sally's belly got round, Logan kept finding new wonders. Sally could be content with this life forever. Their children would have to learn to live a rugged life and travel back and forth across the country, but with Logan, Sally had found that to be fun.

"Your ma said we should respect Mandy's wishes." Logan was dressing as quickly as Sally. "She's an adult woman, and she asked us to let her be. Told us she was handling her own problems and had no wish to bring them raining down on the rest of us."

Sally cooked and hunted and saw to a shelter, and lately she'd done it all wearing a dress, or a split skirt if she was riding. She'd found she preferred it to pants. Discovering just how much being feminine appealed to her was embarrassing, but with Logan she felt safe admitting she liked pretty things. In fact, she felt wonderful admitting it.

She'd found Logan had a talent for hunting and was better at Western life than she'd first thought, so he helped with the running of the house, especially since they'd found there was a baby on the way. But mostly, he painted. Sally looked at his work stacked against the flimsy walls of their tent. She respected it as much as she respected her pa riding herd.

As she finished dressing, she knew a riding skirt had no place in what lay ahead of her. "I'm going to talk to Wise Sister and Buff. See if they'll ride along." Sally jammed her foot into her boot and stomped it on the ground to get her heel inside.

The boots thudded as she took two long strides before Logan caught her arm.

She turned to him, glaring. It was hard because she loved him with all her heart.

"*We're* going."

"No, you stay here. You've only got a few more weeks before the snows close up Yellowstone. This is your only chance to catch the leaves turning color and the elks with full racks of antlers. And I heard you talking about that big geyser almost due to blow. If you ride with me, you'll miss it."

"And if I don't come along, I'll miss you."

"Logan, no."

He rested his beautiful, graceful, brilliant hands on her slightly rounded stomach.

Sally had fully planned to stay in Yellowstone as long as possible. Then they'd ride the train to Texas, Beth would deliver her baby around Christmas time, and then they'd head toward New York to see Logan's parents and brothers and introduce the McKenzies to their newest grandchild before heading back west for another summer of painting.

Sally adored her in-laws, especially when she saw that, though they were just as baffled by Logan's strange inclination to paint as she was, they accepted it and respected his talent. Though they were city people, at heart they were more like her than they were like Logan. A fact that bonded her tight to them.

"Sally, yes. I'm going." He raised one of those talented hands to rest it on her chest and caress her concealed pink ribbon, the feminine bit of fussiness that he understood better than anyone. "I'm not letting my increasing wife ride into a gunfight while I stay safely behind painting pictures. Either I go or you stay."

"I've got to go."

"Then it's settled."

Scowling, Sally said, "I'll go saddle the horses."

"I'll ask the man running the park to ship my paintings home. We'll ride out of here, but then we're taking the train. It's a long, rugged ride to your sister's home. We're going to be careful. I won't let you exhaust yourself or harm our baby."

"My ma rode horseback right up to the day her babies were born. A long hard horse ride won't hurt me."

"Please. . ." Logan's arm snaked around her waist.

The usual weak-willed agreeableness that flared up whenever she found herself in conflict with her husband took over. "I think there's a shorter way if we ride horseback. Remember how we had to go way north of Mandy's on the train the last time we went there, then ride a long way south to see her? I think if we skip the train we can cut a couple of days off the trip. But I promise I won't ride recklessly."

Logan kissed her soundly. "You are such a good, obedient little wife."

The confounded man knew she hated it when he talked to her like that. He grinned as if daring her to blow up.

Since she was getting her way about the trip, she didn't get too mad at him. But the mad was there, simmering.

He kissed her again as if to dare her to let her temper go, as if he liked it.

Her annoyance turned into something else, something warm and passionate. Throwing her arms around his neck, she kissed him until she almost forgot what she was about. When she let go, she was satisfied to see the friendly look in his eyes. "Finish getting dressed while I saddle our horses."

"Yes sir, ma'am." He sounded like an obedient soldier. Then she heard him laugh as she shoved back the tent flap and stormed away.

Mandy was good in the woods. Not as good as Beth, her little sister, but almighty good. She could sneak up on anyone, and no one would ever take her by surprise.

The next inch would give her the first view of the Cooters. Her hands tightened on her rifle. She could do this. She had to.

Something stopped her, something inside. She fought it. To let these men go was stupid. This was her chance.

Don't do it.

Was that her conscience speaking to her? Or her cowardice?

She had to do this, or they'd be right back. Her children could have died today. She felt those bullets so close to her, so close to everyone, all running because of her. Some of Tom's cowhands already had died.

Do it.

Her heart was beating, her blood running hot through her veins. The cold she felt when she was going into action needed to come. She paused, rubbed that callus on her trigger finger as if it were a genie in a magic lamp and she could get the icy calm to come out if she just rubbed enough.

She wondered if she could shoot without it. Even hunting for game, she'd always felt that chill. But she'd never had time to think before, just react. Leastways not think about shooting a man. She'd never consciously tried to bring that cold.

Don't do it.

I have to. I have no choice.

Do it.

Was that wisdom and courage emerging? Or was the devil on her shoulder luring her into sin? It didn't matter. She knew this was sin. And she had to do it anyway and live with the consequences. She gathered her muscles to rise up, come out of hiding, and fire. She'd do it.

A hard hand slapped over her mouth. Weight like a collapsing mountain crushed her into the ground. She knew in that second that she'd failed. She'd given up everything she believed was right in the hopes of ending this feud. All she'd really done was put herself at risk, abandoned her children, and all for nothing. She hadn't even thinned out the pack of coyotes who wanted her dead.

"You are the most contrary wife a man ever had."

Tom. He knew exactly what was going on.

Her gun was wrenched out of her hand, which was annoying, but it didn't stop the surge of relief and even joy she felt to have Tom with her and to have this deadly choice taken from her.

She turned her head, and he let loose of her mouth and only eased his weight for a second as he flipped her over onto her back.

She smiled.

He kissed her witless.

When she could think again, she pointed toward where the men, still blocked by the woods, were camping. "Cooters." She barely breathed the word.

Tom eased down the hill on his hands and knees, dragging her along, as if she might not follow. The man had her rifle for heaven's sake. What was she going to do up there without it?

He had a hold of one arm and pivoted her so her head was turned downhill. Then he dragged her along on her back, like she was a deer he'd brought down.

It took her a second to get over the pleasure of seeing him. Then she scrambled to her feet and fell into step with him. He had her wrist in one hard hand and her rifle in the other, and he strode with ground-eating steps toward where she'd left her horse.

They reached the horses, now grazing side-by-side; then Tom said, "Mount up. We can't talk this close to them."

He let go of her, possibly because he trusted her but more

likely because he knew she needed her Winchester and figured she'd come along until she could retrieve it. Swinging up on his horse, he glared at her. She experienced a little thrill of fear at his fierce expression.

Feeling unusually obedient, she mounted up and had to move fast to keep up with him as he headed down the trail. They were too far to get back to the Double L tonight, so she expected him to stop riding at some point and yell at her.

Mandy had to admit that at least part of the light spirit she felt was because she'd been stopped from unleashing lead at those Cooters.

They'd put several miles behind them when they reached a trail that turned off. Tom followed it to a rock wall that curved into a perfect shelter.

"Tom, are we—"

"*Do not talk to me*, woman." His shouted words practically took a bite out of her hide. "I'm about one wrong word from turning you over my knee."

No one talked to her like that.

Tom had his horse unsaddled before Mandy could get her mouth shut. She wanted to dare him to manhandle her but was just the least bit afraid he might be serious, so she went to work stripping the leather off her own horse. Tom had a small fire crackling by the time she'd finished with her horse and put it on a lead rope to graze.

And now finally it was time to talk.

"I've made my choice." She stalked over to Tom. "I'm not going to sit like a frightened rabbit and wait for those Cooters to come for me and my children and you."

Tom looked up from the fire, where he was feeding in sticks, with eyes so blazing hot Mandy felt burned.

"So you headed out to kill them, is that right?" He threw in a bigger stick. "You were crawling up that rise to murder those men in cold blood—"

"They deserve to die!"

"Because you don't trust me to protect you, *is that right*?" Tom shouted the last three words.

"I did it to save your life. I know you'd protect me. I know you'd *die* for me. I understand all of that. But I can't let you."

"The one thing you don't seem to know, woman"—Tom surged to his feet—"is that you can't *stop* me."

His arm whipped out quick as a striking rattler, and he yanked her hard against his body. "You're mine." He grabbed a hank of her hair. "You're mine, and I'm through waiting for you." He sank his heavy hand deeper into her hair and tilted her head back. "We're married. I *will* protect you. I *will* die for you."

He kissed her until her knees went weak and her arms wrapped around his neck to keep from falling. Long moments later he raised his head, his blue eyes burning into hers.

"Better than that. I will *live* for you. That's all you need to understand." He swooped his head down, and Mandy had one flash of a moment to think she was still prey, this time to a diving hawk.

She understood. At last she finally and completely understood that she was Tom's, and he was hers.

As he lifted her up in his arms, she accepted it. Tom had just saved her from doing something beyond the pale. He'd stopped her from breaking her covenant with God. God had surely seen to it that Tom arrived in time. God had protected her.

His lips never left hers as he lowered her to a blanket and came down with her to hold her hard against him. She clung to him. His iron muscles, his iron will.

The Cooters would come and come and never stop. But if she'd destroyed them, she'd have destroyed herself.

Then she forgot all about the Cooters. Tom drove them out of her very thoughts, and all she knew was she'd done it right this time.

She'd married herself a strong, smart, decent man.

He was married to a lunatic. Soft skin, beautiful eyes, passionate nature, crazy as a rabid swamp rat.

Tom pulled the loco little vermin closer. She murmured but didn't wake up.

It made him sick to think how close it had been. Mandy had clearly planned to unload her Winchester on those men. Maybe she wouldn't have gone through with it. He hoped and prayed she couldn't have. But she'd considered it. Left his cabin contemplating it. Come close to doing it.

To become a back-shooter, a cold-blooded murder, was the kind of choice people couldn't recover from. It broke their minds, scarred their souls. Tom had never killed a man, and he hoped he never had to. He reckoned he'd do it to protect his life, his herd, and definitely his wife and children. But killing when a man was pressed into it was different than planning ahead to kill, no matter how evil the men.

That was the woman he'd married. There was no way to explain it other than she'd gone completely loco. Hiding up in that mountain fortress for the last year might well have pushed her clean over the edge. He wondered if he'd have married her if he'd known she needed to be strapped into a straitjacket and locked in a cell.

Mandy shifted her weight and rested one of her work-roughened hands on his chest.

Sure he would have. She was a mixture of strength and softness that made Tom a little dizzy when he thought that she was now his. He had the signed papers to prove it.

"Tom." In the still-flickering firelight, he could see her face, see her lips move to form his name, though she barely breathed the word. But she sighed, and her breath was warm on his skin. He moved his arm slowly, to tuck her even closer without waking her, and she flowed against him like warm rain.

Aw shucks. Even now, knowing what kinks she had in her head, he'd marry her again. He'd have to get a net. Keep his eyes peeled. Chase her down and drag her home when she went berserk.

But so what?

He kissed her forehead, and she feathered a kiss across his jaw. He looked down and saw her eyes flicker open, heavy lidded with sleep and contentment.

Though he hadn't meant to wake her, he couldn't really get too upset that he had. Especially when she stretched up to meet his lips with her own. He didn't make her stretch far. As he kissed her, he decided to hire a few more cowhands. That'd give him more spare time to cope with the madwoman he'd married.

And that was the last rational decision he made for a long, long time.

Much later, Mandy lay in her husband's arms, staring at the stars, and saw a comet zip across the sky. She'd been watching these same heavens...how many days ago?

Could a woman's life change so much in such a short span of time.

Another streak of light reminded her that the night Tom had come for her, she'd wondered if the sky was falling. "Tom, have you noticed all the falling stars lately?"

"Hmm?" He was almost asleep.

She lay with her head on his shoulder, one hand resting on his broad chest.

What would Tom have to face to survive being married to Mandy McClellen, Lady Gray?

"I watch the stars. I told you that. Look up there. Maybe you'll see a falling star. They're raining down. It's...almost...scary."

Tom pressed a kiss to her forehead. Then Mandy felt him shift, and a glance at him told her he was staring up. "It's a beautiful night to be camping out."

A star streaked across the sky. They were in an open area

surrounded by woods, so they didn't have a wide view of the sky, but straight overhead they could see. "So strange that there are so many. I wish I'd brought my books with me from Sidney's house."

"Books about what?"

"The stars and planets and meteors. They were fascinating. I read about how sailors found their way all around the world using the stars. Can you imagine?"

"Sure, I can find the stars and get my bearings, know north, south, east, west."

Mandy nodded.

Tom's arm tightened around her. "So you're scared when you look at the stars? How do you have time to be scared of falling stars when you've got Cooters to worry about?"

"The book—one that Sidney got just recently—names all these meteors and comets and says they come again and again. The unusual rain of falling stars is caused by a meteor shower called the Perseids."

"Perseids?" Tom pulled her so close she had a hard time remembering they were stargazing.

It was actually a romantic thing to do, Mandy decided. Lie in her husband's arms and stare at the sky, with no moon tonight but blazing with stars and the occasional streak of light. She'd talked about the stars with Sidney. Or more correctly, she'd listened when he talked. And out of sheer boredom she'd read the books and papers he'd amassed, using his wealth to gather them from far and wide. But she and Sidney had never gone out together. And *nothing* between her and Sidney had qualified as romantic.

"Yes, a meteor that passes close to Earth once a year, during the first weeks of August. The comet has a long stream, a tail following it. With rocks I guess. And some of the rocks in that tail get close enough to Earth and come plunging down, and they leave a slash of light when they do."

"But not the main comet? It doesn't come down?"

Mandy shrugged. "I don't understand how it works. I just

know from Sidney's papers that it does. And I can look at the sky and see the truth of it." Another comet left a burn of light.

"I think, woman, that once I've got you back to my ranch, you're going to be too busy at night to do much stargazing."

Tom moved and blocked out the sky. His face, shadowed by the night, filled her vision, and his lips indeed distracted Mandy from the stars. Mandy was certain Tom didn't give the stars a single thought for quite a while. She was certainly thinking of other things.

Later, as she was lying, relaxed, in his arms, she saw yet another comet leave a stripe of white in the sky. Mandy's stomach growled, and she wondered how long it'd been since she'd eaten. Tom, too, for that matter, but she was too content to move. Too happy to be in Tom's arms. He'd regret soon enough that he'd chosen her to love.

Mandy paused. Love?

Tom's words had all been about possession. He'd said she was his. They were meant for each other. They belonged together. And tonight he'd claimed her as clearly as a man could claim a woman. But he'd never spoken of love.

Did she even want his love? Did she want to love him? Loving a man was such a stupid thing to do. Because if she loved Tom, then she'd want to depend on him.

True, her pa had been dependable. But her real pa, the man who'd been married to her ma when Mandy had been born, had proved unreliable, and Mandy had adored him. And Sidney certainly hadn't been a man to depend on, and Mandy had been madly in love with him at first. Thinking of love seemed dangerous, risky.

She thought of her actions today, how she'd tried to call that cold-bloodedness to herself and hadn't been able to and had planned to kill those men anyway. . .maybe.

It made her sick that she might have done it. It made her just as sick that she'd left those men alive.

Could a woman who wanted to kill love? What man would want that kind of woman in his life?

Terribly glad she hadn't committed murder today, she still wanted the Cooters dead. Her mind chased itself around until she thought she'd go crazy. . .crazier.

Tom pulled her close, and that broke off the circle of worry. Foolishly she felt safe. And she decided to let exhaustion win for now. As she dozed off in the strong arms of her husband, her last waking thought was that she felt a little sorry for the man.

He'd spoken marriage vows with a lunatic.

Eleven

Wake up, you crazy woman."

Mandy jerked awake and saw Tom crouched a few steps away, across an open fire, holding a coffeepot that boiled almost as hot as his expression. In the firelight, he looked grim and dangerous and worried. It was still dark, though Mandy thought she saw a bit of lightness to the east.

As always she looked up and studied the stars. Always the stars. Then she looked back at her ferocious husband. His tone and the grim scowl on his face was not in keeping with the man she'd spent the night loving, but it was a pretty good match for the man who had dragged her bodily away from where she was drawing a bead on the Cooter clan.

"Want some coffee before we talk about what in the name of heaven you think you were doing yesterday?"

Mandy sat up in bed, and when the blankets fell away, she quickly caught them and pulled them to her chin.

Tom didn't seem to notice. It was a shame really because she'd very much like to *not* have this conversation with him.

He poured her a tin cup of coffee and brought it to her. She had to fumble to grab the cup and the blanket both. He went back to the fire and threw some bacon into a red-hot skillet. He went to work on the bacon with his back to her. Deliberately, she was sure, so she'd have a moment to make herself decent.

She came up to the fire, putting the finishing touches on braiding her hair just as he was scooping the bacon out. It irritated her that he'd packed so well for the trip. He'd been just in the nick of time to stop her after all. He handed her a tin plate with bacon and a corn cake on it. This is what they'd eaten on their way from her home to his. Maybe it had all been in his saddlebags already.

"So, you were planning to back-shoot those men, is that right?" Tom settled onto the ground, his back resting on a fallen log. He held a plate in one hand, a cup of coffee in the other, obviously ready to have a calm visit about the fact that he was married to an almost-murderer.

"I was planning to." Except maybe she wouldn't have gone through with it. "I wanted them dead. I don't know. I was tempted."

Tom's eyes slid to her rifle, close beside him on the far side of the fire. Making herself decent included going armed. All that was left was strapping on her Winchester. They were married now, so he might as well know she went armed all day, every day and slept with her long gun on the floor within easy reach. She saw it lying beside Tom and decided, just for now, to leave it there.

"We're going home today. Maybe you remember what you left back home. Your *children*, who need their *mother*." He left off staring at her rifle to glare at her. Fury like she'd never known flashed out of his eyes. The flickering fire made them even more savage.

Husbands didn't really turn their wives over their knee, did they?

786

"You know they've had no one but you for the last year. Think they might be a bit *upset* that you took off yesterday and left them with *strangers*?"

Mandy stood, her breakfast half eaten. "I've got to get back to them."

"Good idea, except they're gone."

"Gone? You said we had to get back to them." Mandy thought of the Cooters. Had they taken them?

"No, I asked you if you remembered them. They're small. You went through childbirth. Probably changed a lot of diapers. There are three, two girls and a—"

"I remember my children," Mandy snapped.

"Okay, good to know. So when you went haring off it was with them firmly in mind, then. You planned to ruin your life and probably hang and never be near them again. That was all planned out. A deliberate choice. Good to know."

"Just tell me where they are so I can go get them. The Cooters didn't—"

"Abby and Wade, along with a few of my cowhands, took them to Belle Harden's house."

"What?" Belle Harden, the toughest woman Mandy had ever known. Mandy wanted to go to Belle's house, too.

"They're safe. Belle lives in a mountain valley with two ways in. I sent enough drovers they can post a guard day and night. It's a lot like where you live, only her husband, being of sound mind, built her a cabin not a castle. And they've got thousands of acres of rich pasture land around them to feed their cattle instead of a few yards of solid rock like you had."

Mandy couldn't leave her children there for long. She took the last bite of her last corn dodger and set her plate aside to scrub her face with one hand. "I snapped yesterday."

Tom made possibly the rudest sound of disgust Mandy had ever heard. "If you'd've killed those men, you'd have deserved to hang. Then who was going to raise your children?"

"You." Mandy looked up from her hand. "You're their father now."

Tom rolled his eyes. "Yeah, they won't even notice you're gone. Is that what you think?"

Mandy had done a lot of thinking yesterday. Frantic thinking, laced with fear and panic and hate. "How many of your men were killed or hurt yesterday? I know they wounded that cowhand that came running in, bleeding. He said more were down."

"Didn't you notice he turned around and rode back out with us? He was barely scratched. It wasn't even a bullet. The bullet hit a tree, and a chunk of bark ricocheted and hit him."

"He yelled two names. The Cooters shot two more of your men."

"Both dove off their horses when the Cooters opened up. One of 'em knocked himself insensible on a rock. The other took a bullet in the leg. Just grazed him. They're going to live. They were already up and on horseback when we got out there."

"I brought death to you."

"The Cooters, not you."

"Well, I brought the Cooters. They'll never stop coming. I just snapped. I wanted to stop them, hurt them, wipe them off the face of the earth."

"And you remembered just how good you are with that stupid rifle. Abby told me she saw you in action."

"I can barely remember it." Mandy looked up and locked her gaze on Tom's. "I've got a reputation with that rifle, Tom, but you don't know—"

"Don't know what?"

Mandy remembered how she'd fought to make herself cold. But her hate had all been red hot. "I don't even like people to know just how good I am. I probably shouldn't tell you now, except Abby saw."

"She was mighty admiring of your skill. She's more comfortable with a blade." Tom said it like he was admiring of a woman who preferred a blade. Well, too bad for him he had a sharpshooter for a wife, and he was stuck with her.

Because of last night, there was no going back. They were well and truly married. There could even now be a baby on the way. Another fragile life in desperate need of provision and protection.

In the clear light of day, Mandy was amazed that she'd so recklessly and eagerly seen to her wifely duties.

"If I don't know the half of it, why don't you tell me?"

"Abby will tell you I'm faster'n greased lighting, but what she can't see is what's going on inside me." Mandy lifted her coffee, clutched the tin cup with both hands as she thought of the cold, and tried to put it into words. "I'm fast and accurate, but there's more."

Glancing at the shining stars overhead, something called to her. She longed for her scope, but more likely she just didn't want to go on talking. "It's as if—as if time slows down. I don't feel like I'm moving fast. I get—calm, deadly calm. So calm it frightens me when I think of it later. I'm firing and aiming, cocking my gun and reloading."

"That's not so unusual. I've talked to men who've been in the Civil War. They say it's like that."

"But I'm thinking, too. I'm figuring angles, moving to get a better shot if I need to move. All of that and so much more is going on, and the gun keeps firing, keeps hitting what I aim at. I—" Mandy broke off her telling and stared at her boots, not wanting to see what Tom thought of his wife.

"You're what?"

"I'm cold." She shoved her toe in the dirt. "Ice cold."

"Keeping a cool head in an emergency is a good thing. Abby said you did that."

"It's more than a cool head. I don't feel—sane—" She took a quick glance at Tom then looked down again. "I'm so detached, ruthless. I do whatever I need to do. I feel no guilt, no remorse. And since this last year, hiding from the Cooters—"

"Abby told me you killed one of them," Tom said quietly.

Mandy glared as she raised her coffee cup in a salute. "For a man who was in a hurry to catch me, you sure had time to do a lot of talking and a lot of packing."

"Abby talked while I saddled my horse. Wade loaded a saddlebag with provisions while I worked. I ordered her to go to Belle's, and she obeyed me because it suited her. Red shoved that marriage paper in my hand and assured me we were legally married. I did all of that and still managed to be on the trail five minutes after I heard you'd lit out."

Mandy shuddered to think what would have happened if he'd taken ten minutes.

"So now we go get the children?" Mandy missed them desperately. When she'd set out yesterday, she'd felt as if she were giving them away. If she'd killed those Cooters, she'd've hanged most likely, but her children would be safe. And her death would end the feud. The Cooters would quit coming if she was dead, Mandy was sure of it. Now that it looked like she'd dodged the noose, she could hardly bear the fear and love she carried for those little ones who were her whole life.

"No, now we go home, and we face the Cooters without having the children to worry about. They'll be safe. Abby's good. She'll make sure they aren't followed. And Belle and Silas will make sure their valley isn't breached."

"While we wait for the next attack?" Mandy felt it again, that sick need to destroy, to fight, to kill.

God, protect me from this ugliness inside.

It was the first time she'd prayed since she'd made her decision to hunt down the Cooters. She hadn't felt that she deserved the help of the Lord, not even the ear of the Lord. Praying now flooded her soul with the life she'd nearly wiped out of it yesterday.

"God, protect us," Mandy prayed aloud.

Tom nodded. "We want God on our side for this, Mandy. How could you be so dumb as to choose a path without any hope of His blessing? It's an act of insanity."

Those blue eyes leveled at her. Asking her a question that she was afraid to answer.

"You brushed aside what I said about the way I feel when I'm shooting, Tom. But insanity might cover it. I had little sisters growing up."

"I met Sally, your sister who dressed like a wrangler."

"We were all good shots. None of them was as good as me, though Sally was mighty close. Beth always thought she was second best, but I'd say she was third—though no one was as good at sneaking around in the woods as Beth." Mandy missed her sisters with the stabbing pain of a bullet wound.

"We talked about it a lot, worked on our strengths and weaknesses. What we figured out was that none of them reacted like me. None of them knew quite what to make of that crazy coldness that came over me." Mandy tossed the dregs of her coffee onto the dying fire and watched it sizzle in the flames.

Then she looked up at her husband and confessed the depths of her ugliness. "I've always believed that I have it in me to be a murderer. I think what happens to me when I shoot is what happens to a hired gun, a professional killer. I'm terrified of that part of myself, and that man I killed. . ." Her eyes fell shut.

"What about it, darlin'?"

"I was too good at it. It haunted me later. But when it was happening. . ."

"You liked it."

Unable to speak, she looked at him, and he looked back until she got control of her tightened throat and clenched jaw. "I felt proud. Proud that I'd beaten him, proud that I'd brought him down hard and fast. It's a feeling, that pride, that is a terrible sin. God speaks of the sin of pride, and I know it to be true."

Tom shrugged. "I'm proud of my Angus herd, proud of my stallion. Proud of my pretty wife and the three beautiful children I have. I'm proud I built a house strong enough to keep you safe from the Cooters. Is that all a sin, too?"

With a shrug, Mandy said, "I guess it's a sin if God convicts you of it. And He certainly convicts me. I felt it again yesterday when I was creeping up that rise to get those men in my sights. I don't know if I'd have done it, but I might have. Worse yet—" She fell silent.

"Worse yet," Tom went on for her, "you might have enjoyed it."

"I might have, at least right at that moment." Forcing herself to turn to her brand-new husband and face him with the truth, she said, "I have this callus on my trigger finger."

She took Tom's hand and rubbed her finger against his. His were so strong and work-hardened she wasn't sure he could even feel it, but he ran his finger gently, carefully over her index finger. In the dark, she knew when he found the right spot. He paused and rubbed the rough skin slowly.

"What of it?"

"It's a reminder to me of what I am."

"You're a beautiful woman, a loving mother, an obedient wife."

Mandy thought Tom didn't sound all that sure of the last part and smiled despite the deadly serious topic. "I'm a sharpshooter. As good as anyone anywhere, I reckon."

"Your hands have calluses other places. Why worry about that one?"

"It's like living proof that I'm dangerous, to myself, my children, my parents and sisters, you. I never want to forget that, because it's who I am."

"It's part of who you are, but not the biggest part." Then Tom said, "You're part of me now, too. Anytime you want to run your hands over me to remind you of that fact, I'll be glad to allow it."

Mandy laughed, but it didn't last. It couldn't last, not while the cold inside her existed. Except this time, she hadn't been able to bring the cold, and that made her wonder what it would have done to her to pull the trigger in the heat. Maybe instead of enjoying it, she would have hated it. Loathed it. In fact, been unable to do it.

Tom shook his head and drew her attention. He looked mighty sad for a man who'd just spent the night in the arms of a woman he claimed to have wanted for five years. "Mandy, honey, I think it's best for the two of us, just privately here, to admit that you are as loco as a rabid swamp rat."

Mandy agreed with him, but she wasn't all that crazy about hearing him say it out loud. "Tom Linscott—"

"What, Mandy Linscott?"

"Good grief, I have a different name. I hadn't even thought of that yet."

"What were you going to say?"

"You should make a point, if you're gonna call me a rabid swamp rat, of always having a firm grip on my Winchester."

"Already thought of that." Tom raised it above his head with one hand while he tossed dirt on the campfire with the other.

Mandy let him keep the rifle while they broke camp. She glanced upward again and tried to figure out what was drawing her eye skyward.

They were half a mile down the trail when they reached a clearing in the woods where the sky opened wider. The soft gray of dawn was winking out the stars.

The wide heavens above drew her eye, just as they had earlier. She slowed her horse then slowed it more as she stared and wondered and suddenly knew. The stars!

Could it possibly be? Could she have, at last, found the key to turn this maddening lock?

Tom was stretching out his lead, but because they'd been riding single file, not talking, he didn't notice he was leaving her behind.

Her eyes darting between the stars and her husband's receding back, she carefully eased Sidney's map out of her pocket and unfolded it with terrible care so the paper wouldn't give a single crackle that might draw Tom's attention.

The map was as familiar to her as her own face. Hours upon hours of studying it, wondering about it, looking through Sidney's books to decipher this stupid map, told her the truth before she looked. With a rush of pleasure so powerful it felt sinful, she compared what she held in her hand to what she saw in the sky. And they matched.

Which meant that at last she'd found a way to escape the brutal violence of the Cooter clan, without using her Winchester.

The clearing ended, and the trees swallowed Tom whole. He couldn't know, not yet. Not when he was still so stubbornly insisting on protecting her. She folded the map as silently as she'd unfolded it then tucked it away without saying a word.

This plan, well, she'd include him. It wasn't likely he'd fail to notice when she disappeared. But he didn't need to know everything, not until it was too late for him to protest.

She ran her thumb over that little callus on her trigger finger and hoped that this madness could end without a blaze of gunfire and the death of her soul.

And she wouldn't even have to tell a single lie. Which wasn't the same at all as telling the absolute total and complete truth.

"Beth, I'm going to get Mandy."

Beth looked up as her pa slammed her door open. Her eyes snapped with satisfaction. "It's about time." She rose from the table where she was eating breakfast with her husband and two children. "Is Ma going?"

"I tried to leave her, but yes, she's going. She's buying supplies right now and sending a telegraph to Luther."

Beth went straight for the rifle she kept hung over her front door.

"Put that gun back. I'm just asking you to watch out for the young'uns."

"I won't be able to, because I'm going with you. Get Adam and Tillie to mind them while you're gone." She looked over her shoulder at Alex. "They'll help you out, too."

"You're not going, Beth." Pa yanked his hat off his head and slapped his leg.

"Fine." With a snort of disgust, Beth wheeled away from her pa and headed for her satchel and the supplies she'd need to pack. "You and Ma go by yourselves to get her, and I'll go by myself."

"I declare I have the most stubborn bunch of womenfolk." Pa rammed his hat back on his head with fierce disregard for the beating the Stetson was taking.

Beth headed for her bedroom, but Alex erupted from the table and grabbed her arm before she could get out of the room. "You're not going without me, Beth."

Turning, she saw that he was concerned for her, not afraid of being left. There was a time that the idea of staying here, doctoring the folks in Mosqueros without her, would have sent him into a panic. Resting her hand on his wrist, she felt the slow, steady beat of his pulse. His heart was tied to hers. But she had to help her sister. She couldn't bear to think of Mandy locked away from them. She'd been chafing to go to Mandy for a long time. Now the waiting was over.

"Somebody's got to watch the children." She looked at her sweet little blond-haired daughter and her sturdy little son who looked so much like Alex.

"Now, honey—"

The door snapped shut, and Beth saw that her pa had left. He wasn't getting away with that. She shut Alex up by kissing him senseless.

When she had his full attention, she unwrapped her arms from around his neck and said, "I've got to go, Alex. I don't want Pa and Ma facing down an army of feuding gunmen alone, not even with Mandy at their sides. There's no way to get hold of Sally, wherever she is."

"I don't want you walking into a gunfight, Beth."

"There's not going to be a gunfight." Beth felt the weight of her rifle on her back and had the good grace to be embarrassed. "I promise to be careful."

Alex's brow lowered. "Fine, if it's going to be so safe, then there's no reason for me not to come along."

Her stomach pitched when she thought of Alex getting mixed up in shooting trouble. It might be too much for him, considering the scars, both physical and emotional, he still carried from war. Beth shook her head. "You're not going."

"Why if it's not dangerous?"

"Because I said so." Beth jammed her fists on her hips.

Alex proved right then and there that he'd come a long way from the deeply traumatized man she'd married, the one who avoided any sort of trouble. He proved it by smiling right into her gritted teeth. "Not good enough."

"You need to stay and watch the children." There, that was a solid reason.

"I'm bringing them along." Alex had the nerve to smirk.

"You're not taking my children to a—" Beth stopped herself before she said—

"Gunfight?" Alex scowled. "Is that what you were going to say?"

"No." Maybe. "Of course not." Probably not. They could probably just grab Mandy and haul her home, and those awful Cooters would get tired of looking for her.

"Well, if the children come with us, then we'll be sure to avoid a gunfight at all costs. Right?"

Beth couldn't really come up with a good enough reason for him to stay. Not without lying, and she respected him too much to lie. She might possibly not respect him too much to keep from slugging him, but she'd never lie. "You're not going."

"Fine. You go see Mandy and the children, and I will go see Mandy and the children. If we happen to take the same train, you don't even have to sit with us."

She decided that when he'd been so upset, when they'd first met, and not pushy at all, those had been good days. "Come then. If you can keep up." Beth headed into the bedroom while Alex wiped the mouths of Beth's precious children.

Good grief, she was taking her children to a gunfight. Well, maybe she could convince Alex to stay to the side and just doctor the wounded.

Alex came in before she had her satchel packed and began shoving diapers into a gunnysack.

It was worse than before. She was taking a *baby* in *diapers* to a gunfight.

"I'd sure like my little sister watching my back. She is pure lobo wolf mean with that rifle of hers. Almost as fast and accurate as I am. Though neither of us can hold a candle to Mandy, of course."

God, give me strength to do what I have to do. Give me strength.

As they swiftly and silently packed, she took a moment to lay her hand on his shoulder, and when he turned to face her, braced for the next round of the fight, she kissed him. When she was done, he held her gaze, and she saw the peace and courage and strength of the man she'd married and couldn't resist kissing him again.

"I'm glad you're coming, Alex."

"Me, too. It'll remind you of why you need to be very, very careful."

Give us both enough strength to take care of Mandy. Give me strength.

Twelve

Belle Harden saw a woman top the rise that led through the low gap into her valley. More riders came behind her.

As soon as the first person became recognizable, Belle smiled. A visit from Abby Sawyer was always welcome. It was a good chance for Belle to get her knife sharpened. No one had quite the knack Abby did.

Then her eyes slid to the others in the group. Two little children. Then one of the riders with a child in his arms twisted in his saddle, and Belle saw a baby slung on that rider's back. Three children.

Wade was along of course. He tagged after Abby everywhere. Strange man. Abby seemed to adore him, and despite a few years of worthlessness in his youth, he'd turned into a decent man.

Belle had a hard time hating him, but she did her best.

There were six men riding with the Sawyers and those children. The Sawyers had only had two children, didn't they?

Then her eyes landed on Mark Reeves. Her smile turned hard and fast downward. What was that polecat doing here?

Belle turned and strode toward the house to have a little talk with Emma.

Silas met her before she'd gotten anywhere near.

"I already spotted the Reeves kid and said my piece, Belle. Emma knows how we feel."

"That she's too young, and Reeves is a no-account pup who needs a whip taken to his hide?"

"Yep, of course Emma knows you'd never take a whip to a pup's hide. But I think she's very sure you'd do it to Mark."

"Good, then you've saved me some time." Belle turned back to the approaching group.

They were setting a good pace and were in the yard before long.

Belle noticed Emma come outside. Betsy came next. Then Tanner tagged after Sarie, jumping and yelling like always. The child had more energy than ten regular people. It was naptime, or there'd be an even larger group to greet the Sawyers and that polecat Reeves.

"What's going on?" Silas asked Wade as the man swung down from his horse.

Abby alit next carrying a three-year-old.

And Mark, the polecat, had the pack carrying one child and held a four-year-old who jerked awake with a little cry when he dismounted. The little girl threw her arms around Reeves's neck and sobbed for her mama. Mark rested a hand on the little one's back and bent his head to talk with her. Except for one annoyingly welcoming smile in Emma's direction, Mark was focused completely on the child, talking sweet nonsense, holding the little one gently.

Emma went to the child as if she'd been lassoed and dragged. Belle frowned, but she could fault neither Mark nor Emma for the unhappy child. And as much as she wanted to hate Mark Reeves, the youngster was doing his best to comfort the little girl.

"These are Mandy Gray's children." Wade helped Mark swing

the pack off his back. "Tom sent us here because there's trouble, and he wanted to get the children out of the line of fire."

The little boy in the pack had his lip stuck out, quivering, as he watched his big sister cry.

"Shooting trouble?" Belle lifted the little boy out of Wade's pack while Wade held on to the leather contraption. "With children involved?" Then another thought struck her. "Shooting trouble Mandy Gray can't handle?"

Belle turned to Emma. "You remember Mandy Gray, don't you?"

Emma reached for the crying girl, and the child shrieked and buried her face in Mark's neck.

Mark gave Emma an apologetic look, then rested one of his big hands on the flyaway white hair and crooned to her.

"Sure. I felt like I'd met a woman after my own heart." Emma looked worriedly at the crying child, inched just a bit closer, which put her that much closer to Reeves. Emma and Reeves exchanged one more of those blasted understanding looks. "Mandy could swing a rifle into action like nothing I've ever seen before."

Sarah came and stood behind Mark's back and started talking to the little one over Mark's shoulder.

Another one of the cowpokes came up slightly behind Mark—right next to Sarah in fact—and nudged him. "Need any help there?"

Mark turned to Emma and said, "This here's my cousin, Charlie Cooper. Charlie, this is Emma Harden and"—Mark looked over his shoulder—"her sister Sarah."

Belle couldn't have been watching her daughters much closer, so she noticed clear as day the way Charlie reacted when he looked at Sarah.

And if Belle wasn't mistaking it, Sarah looked right back.

"Howdy, Emma." Charlie touched the brim of his hat then reached out a hand to Sarah. "Pleased to meet you Sarah."

Sarah took his hand and smiled in a way that made Belle want to reach for her shooting iron.

Angela let out a squall that drew Sarah's attention and probably saved Charlie's life.

"I've got about a dozen little brothers and sisters," Charlie said.

"A dozen?" Sarah actually looked away from the child, and that was unusual. Sarah had always had a special heart for the little ones. "A dozen or so?" A smile bloomed on Sarah's face.

Belle had to admit that comment caught her own interest.

Charlie laughed. A great laugh. So great it made Belle a little sick to her stomach.

"My ma and pa adopted me when I was about ten, off an Orphan Train."

"What?" Sarah's brow furrowed. "I've never heard of such a thing."

Nodding, Charlie went on. "I've never rightly counted, but Pa said I was about the twentieth child he'd adopted. And he kept on doing it all his life."

"Your pa adopted children? Not your ma?"

"Yep. He started before he and my ma got married. Then they kept doing it afterward, and they had a few children of their own."

"How many were adopted, and how many were their real children?" Sarah seemed overly fascinated.

"We're all real." With a brief frown, Charlie said, "I don't rightly remember which are their own and which are adopted. But I reckon we're all real enough. I've got two little brothers with sort of strange speckled greenish brown eyes, though. They look a lot like my pa. I'm pretty sure they were born to my parents."

Then Charlie reached a hand out, and for a second Belle thought he was going to touch Sarah, but instead he tapped Angela on the chin. Looking at Angela, but talking definitely to Sarah, he added, "My parents are wonderful people with a heart for children without homes. I'd be glad to tell you all about them."

Which would give him time with Sarah. Which wasn't going to happen.

Charlie touching Angela turned Sarah back to the unhappy little girl. With skill far beyond her years, Sarah cajoled Angela out of the crying, but the little one didn't quit clinging to Mark until Tanner ran into Mark Reeves's leg and sent him stumbling forward into Emma. Emma caught him, and the two shared a smile.

Belle decided then and there she needed a horse whip. And no horse was in a bit of danger.

"Thanks, Em." Mark stayed far too close to Belle's daughter.

The collision distracted Angela from her tears, but it had almost the exact opposite effect on Belle. She thought Mark took way too long apologizing and asking if Emma was hurt, as if the girl was made of spun sugar or something. And Charlie reached out a hand to rest it on Sarah's arm as if she'd almost fallen in a heap.

"Anyone want a molasses cookie?" Sarah had the knack, and no one could deny it. Though offering cookies to little children was no stroke of genius.

Angela rubbed at her eyes. Emma went to relieve Abby of the child she carried.

The little girl, younger than Angela, screamed, "No! I want Mark."

Abby rolled her eyes, but Mark came over, and Abby passed the child to him.

Shaking her head and smiling, Emma said, "Maybe this one will let me hold him." She took the stout little toddler from Belle.

Even the baby boy stared at Mark but allowed Emma to carry him. They headed for the house with Tanner running between them hollering. Betsy tagged along. It usually fell to her to ride herd on Tanner. Belle had a moment to praise the Lord that Betsy had been able to keep her roughhousing little brother alive all these years.

Charlie didn't go with them—which kept Belle from dropping him with a butt stroke—but he was looking way too long after the little group, and his eyes didn't seem to be stuck on his cousin.

Though her arms remained tight around Mark's neck, Angela now looked between her sister, in Mark's other arm, and Tanner. The racket Belle's son made seemed to drive all thoughts of crying out of Angela's head.

Belle needed to keep an eye on Emma and Mark, but first she needed some answers. "What's going on?"

Abby did the talking as usual.

"Of course they can stay." Silas gave the house a concerned look.

Belle wondered if he was considering building on. "And we appreciate the cowpokes to help guard the gaps. We don't keep drovers, so we'd have our hands full posting a guard around the clock on both of them. And it sounds like we'll need to do it."

"We need to get on home," Wade said. "We've been gone from our own young'uns for too long. But with the six men from the Linscott place, you should have plenty of help."

"Five men," Belle said. "Only five are staying."

"Why only five?"

"Because that no-account Mark Reeves has to go."

"Mark's my cousin. He's a top hand," Charlie assured Belle.

"Four, I want you out of here, too."

"What did I do? I know how to keep watch."

"Don't matter if either of you can lasso the moon and break it to ride. Mark's sparkin' Emma. He can't stay here. If I had my way, I'd post a guard at the gap to keep *him* out. And I saw the way you just looked at my Sarie. You're leaving, too."

The drovers laughed.

"I'm not joking." Belle had long ago perfected a glare that shut most people up. It didn't fail her now.

Except with Abby. "My brother insisted that Mark ride along, and you can see why. The children took to him more than anyone else. Tom's their pa now, and he said Mark had to stay with the little ones. They're a sight upset by all this commotion around their ma when they're used to just living in that house with her alone. Tom would never have sent them here if he didn't think the danger was serious. And you'll need six men to stand shifts on two gaps. You can't do it right with less."

"Mark's had one or more of 'em on his lap the whole time," Wade added.

Belle thought of her own girls and how completely she'd raised them alone. They'd have been devastated if she'd died and left them with strangers. And the older girl especially had clung to Mark. All of them had looked to him. No denying it.

"I suppose it'll upset the children if I have to beat Mark over the head, too." Belle glared at the house. Then she looked back at Charlie. "But I doubt they"ll mind over much if I carve a notch out of you."

She thought Charlie got the message, judging by his wide eyes and respectful silence.

Silas went to the drovers and discussed where to put up their horses while Belle said good-bye to the Sawyers without even getting an edge put on her knife.

Then she turned to her house, bulging at the seams with children, and one polecat.

She strode to the house. She didn't think all those little ones and Sarie combined were quite good enough as chaperones.

Besides, getting those children to trust her and her girls was now top priority. The second job on her list, as soon as she'd earned that trust, was booting Mark Reeves out of her valley.

Thirteen

Emma, if you come stand right beside me and talk to Catherine and Angela, with Jarrod in your arms, I think they'll calm down. See, Catherine is already watching her brother." Mark tilted his head so he could look little Catherine in the eye. "Aren't you, honey?"

Mark looked up and smiled at Emma, who'd come right on over. Mark had a passel of little brothers, and he'd learned a long time ago that a man carrying a baby was a lure to a woman. He'd used it many times in his earlier years. Before Emma he'd never been serious about women, but he'd always liked their attention. Now he used these little ones as tasty bait.

"I only had brothers growing up." He looked at the girls in his arms. Sure he was baiting an Emma-trap, but he sincerely cared about Mandy's little tykes. "My folks only had boys."

Emma kept her eyes on Catherine, her voice gentle and sweet, her hands stroking Jarrod. "Hi, Catherine. I only had sisters until Tanner was born. There were four of us girls."

"Four?" Mark looked around the room, blond Emma,

redheaded Sarah, black-eyed Betsy. "Who'm I missing?"

"I've got an older sister who's married."

Mark smiled and Emma seemed caught in the smile. Jarrod in her arms, Catherine and Angela in his. He could see them as a family. Children of their own. Blue-eyed and blond-haired, Mark reckoned, though obviously Emma came from a family that could churn out children of all descriptions.

"So, you've got a lot of little brothers?" Emma was a tough Montana cowgirl. Mark knew that and it suited him. A woman needed to be strong to settle the West. Mark figured if he touched her hand he'd find calluses as tough as boot leather. And he almost reached out to check but thought better of it. Having two children in his arms slowed him down, too.

She was close to him now, and she'd stay here if he didn't make any false moves. She was as pretty as a spring rose, and her voice washed over him like warm rain.

The thought of having children with her was almost more pleasure than Mark could take. "Yep, five when I left home. But my folks have one every onest in a while, so who knows? Ma's getting older now. She has to be almost forty I reckon."

"My ma's almost forty, and she just had a new baby." Emma tipped her head toward a crib where a little one slept. "Your ma must've been young when you were born."

"She's not my real ma. My ma died having me and my two brothers."

Emma's brow knit with a frown. "Three babies at once?"

"Yep, triplets. We're the only ones I've ever heard tell of."

"I didn't even know babies could be born three at a time. And it killed your mother to have you?"

"Yes." Mark had been having fun until now, luring Emma closer, flirting a bit, acting like a hero because the children took to him. But it hurt to think that his birth had done his ma in. "Pa raised us for the first five years alone. Then he remarried."

Thinking of his pa's second wife helped him shake off that

strange guilt. "She was real young. Seventeen when they got married. I have twin brothers who were ten when Pa married her, so she's closer to their age than his."

"Twins, too?" Emma shuddered. "Did the rest of your little brothers come in batches like that?"

Mark shook his head. "Nope, and I'm glad, because Ma is a good'un. I'd have hated to lose her."

Angela picked that moment to rest her head on Mark's shoulders and fall asleep as if someone had switched off a light. Mark smiled down at her. He'd seen his little brothers do this.

Emma reached up and ran one work-scarred finger across Angela's cheek.

Catherine snuggled closer to Mark and looked to be the next one to nod off.

"You're good with them," Emma whispered.

"I've had my share of practice. And I like little ones." Mark looked down at the little girls.

Angela's eyes, closed in sleep, were still rimmed with tears where her lashes lay white and spiked from all the salt water. Catherine sighed and leaned her head on Mark's shoulder as if the weight of it was more than her neck could bear.

Forgetting his flirting for a second, Mark said, "They're powerful lonely for. . ." He looked at Emma and arched one brow. "Ma."

"It must have been bad for. . .her. . .to leave them. A. . .person. . . doesn't leave little ones easily. I remember when we first met her. She was just in the country from Texas. A young thing to be married. Though a sight older than Lindsay, my big sister."

"You met Mandy when she first came here?" Mark felt the stirring of excitement. If they knew her, it must be all right to tell them he knew Mandy from way back.

"We helped her and her first worthless husband build a cabin. A great little cabin not that far from Helena. There was no need to move up there where they went and build what I've heard called a castle. Ma wrote a letter to her folks back in Texas letting them know Mandy was safe and settled for the winter."

"So you know she was a McClellen, too?" Mark's tone finally pulled Emma's attention away from the children.

Emma leaned closer and spoke in a sharp whisper. "Too? How do you know her? Do you know these children from before?"

Mark might well be imagining it, but he thought he caught just a hint of something from Emma that could count as jealousy.

"I've never seen her children before, but I know Mandy." Mark kept whispering so Emma would have to stay close to hear. Besides, Catherine needed quiet to sleep, now didn't she? "I grew up with her in Texas. We went to school together."

"Did you come up here to see her?" Again that little bite of annoyance.

Mark had to fight to suppress a smile of satisfaction. "Nope, I had no idea who Tom was bringing home. I mean, I heard Lady Gray. I heard the rumors about her being a hermit."

"A witch. Which was ridiculous. She was a nice woman. Ma and all my family took a powerful liking to her from the first."

Mark nodded. "Then when we rode out to meet Tom, I couldn't believe my eyes when he had Mandy. And she recognized me, too. I think the children took to me partly because I felt the connection to them 'cuz I knew their—" Mark stopped himself from saying "ma" and looked down at Catherine, whose eyelids were nearly closed. "I knew Lady Gray."

"Connection?" Emma still sounded a bit tart.

"She's married, Em." A smile just would not be held back.

"Widowed you mean."

"No, I mean married to Tom Linscott. They saw to it before all the trouble started. Mandy was my mortal enemy when we were kids. I was always up to some nonsense in school, and she was the bossiest, most scoldingest girl I've ever met. But I haven't seen anyone from home in a while. And then knowing what I knew about Lady Gray, then seeing Mandy. . .well, I know her and her family, and they're good folks. I can't stand by and see Mandy come to harm."

Emma's fair skin, even burned brown by the summer sun, showed a tinge of blush.

"Why, Em? Would it bother you if I had a connection to some other woman?"

Emma scowled, but she stayed close. . .very close.

"Because the only woman I want a connection to is you, Emma Harden."

"You do?" Emma whispered. Her scowl faded, replaced by the sweetest smile Mark had ever seen.

Which made Mark very aware he was looking at Emma's lips. "Oh, yes, I want that real bad."

He'd thought it through and logically decided that Emma was the woman he wanted to marry. She was everything he wanted, strong and pretty and smart and a God-fearing woman. But until right now his plans had all been made in his head. He'd marry her and be happy with her and build a ranch with her. It made perfect sense.

But as her sweet smile grew wider and her eyes filled with interest in a way that made Mark feel like a king, Mark figured out the difference between logic and love. Because right at that instant he fell headlong in love with this pretty woman with the baby in her arms. Mark had never felt anything so right in his life.

And Emma needed to know that he was more than just mildly interested. He'd come close to stealing a kiss out back of the Hardens' barn when he was here before. But Emma's pa had interrupted before he could work up the nerve.

He was full of nerve now.

"Emma?" He glanced at her lips again and decided to take the little girls out for a walk behind that same barn. Lure Emma along.

"Yes?" Almost as if she'd read his mind and was agreeing. And once she started agreeing, who knew what she might say yes to.

"It's crowded in here and hot."

"It sure is." Emma patted Jarrod on the back but kept her eyes locked right on Mark.

"Maybe we could take the children for a little walk."

"But they're sound asleep. Should we put them to bed?"

"A little fresh air won't hurt them, will it?" He leaned closer as if fresh air was a big secret that only he knew, and ignored the fact that the children had been out in the fresh air through the whole long ride to the Harden ranch.

"No, I don't suppose so." She sounded grateful that he'd shared the idea.

"So, let's you and me—"

"I'll be glad to take those children off your hands now, Reeves." Belle Harden's voice had the effect of the tip of a blacksnake whip cutting a slit in his skin.

Mark straightened away from Emma fast, only now aware of just how close he'd been to her right here in the middle of Belle Harden's kitchen. In about five more seconds, he'd have had that kiss, even with all these people around.

He turned to face a very cranky, heavily armed woman. A woman he hoped would one day very soon be his mother-in-law.

If she didn't shoot him first.

"We're gonna make that woman sorry she left her house." Fergus mounted up beside Cord.

Cord led the way as he always did. He was hopeful that some more cousins would show up soon. They were running purely short.

"Why'd Grandpappy make this rule about Cooters sticking together?" Dugger asked in his childlike way.

"Family pride, that's why," Cord snarled. "You oughta get some."

"The most of our family I know ride the outlaw trail," J.D.

grumbled. "Where's the pride in that?"

"We're hard men and we fight for the brand. That's the Cooter way," Cord said. "Nothing wrong with letting the world know that they're steppin' into a buzz saw when they hurt a Cooter."

Cord felt his chest swell with pride. He'd been raised by his pappy, a mean old codger, but with pride in family and a powerful sense of loyalty. The old man had loved feuding.

Even more so, Grandpappy did. Cord was one of the few of the cousins who ever knew the old man because Grandpappy spent his whole life working long hours. Cord had come along later, when Grandpappy had finally slowed down, against his will.

"You never knew Grandpappy, and I did. You remember the family rules, but I know *why* he made those rules." Cord looked back at Dugger. The man was pure dumb, but this was simple; maybe Dugger could learn it better than all of them.

"Our real name is Couturiaux. You all know that, right?"

Dugger looked lost.

J.D. shrugged.

"Sure. We all were raised hearing that. Stupid long name. I like Cooter better," Fergus said.

Cord preferred it himself. A man would be all day writing his name if it was Couturiaux. "I was raised by Grandpappy Cooter, and he loved to tell stories of the old country. I heard all about how he came to America and got his name chopped up by the only man who'd give Grandpappy a job."

"I always thought the long name sounded stupid." Fergus shrugged.

"Well, Couturiaux was a respected name in France. To be forced to shorten it by a pompous rich man, the only man hiring when Grandpappy got off the boat from Europe, nearly choked him."

"Yeah, well, try getting someone to spell that name. I don't blame the guy for wanting it shorter," J.D. said from where he rode behind Cord and Fergus. "And try getting a poor man to give you a job."

Cord decided then and there his cousins were pathetic. "Look, Grandpappy had his family pride ripped right off his back when his name was changed. And he had to accept the name change in order to feed his family. By the time he got ahead and could start his farm, his sons were grown and started families of their own. All of 'em were used to calling themselves Cooter. Grandpappy knew it was too late to get anyone to change the name back, but it burned him, and he made it a point of family pride to demand we all support each other. He couldn't have the name he wanted, but he could mold the family tight together in other ways."

"Makes sense to me," Fergus said. "When I rode off from our place, I didn't like leaving you behind, Cord. I reckon a lot of that is the family pride you're talkin' about. I know my pa was a harsh man, and I knew you'd have a hard life. It ate at me that I should have taken you along, but you were just a baby and me a young man alone." Fergus frowned.

Cord looked at his older brother, feeling some dismay to think he'd most likely end up looking like Fergus, because Fergus was stout and wrinkled and ugly. Cord might feel family loyalty, but that didn't mean he didn't know a homely man when he saw one. Right then, Cord decided he'd finish this mess with Lady Gray, then leave his family behind and hope to never see a one of them again. He didn't want to end up alone on the outlaw trail. He wanted a soft bed, a soft wife, and maybe a few babies with streaks of white in their hair. But he did appreciate that his big brother had wanted to take care of him. "Thanks, Ferg. I'm glad I caught up with you out here. I'd been looking for a while."

The foursome crested a distant hilltop and looked back. They'd come a long way.

Cord had felt cold for a while last night, like someone was taking a bead at his backbone. He'd decided to put some distance between his family and Lady Gray for a few days.

"Well, will you look at that." Dugger said it, but all of them immediately realized what had happened. They'd found the perfect lookout.

"The Double L brand belongs to Tom Linscott for sure." Fergus had been in this country longer than the rest of them. And that house of his is built like a fort.

"What do you think that cowpoke is doing with Lady Gray anyhow?" Cord saw how impenetrable the house was. He'd learned that well when their first attack had failed. Now, looking down from this far distance, the whole ranch looked well fortified. It was laid out so the few overlooks could be defended well.

"Linscott's a known man. A big rancher with a reputation for raising a top herd of cattle, like those big blacks we ran off." Fergus pulled a chaw of tobacco out of his pocket.

Cord had heard of Linscott, but he'd never ridden these trails nor met the man. He suspected that a man savvy enough to lay out this ranch and build a big spread knew enough to post a lookout. They'd never get as close to Mandy Gray as they had that first day. Not while she was living in Linscott's house. It chafed him that they'd missed that chance. He glanced at Fergus and the red scratches on his neck where rock had exploded under Mandy's gunfire.

Taking one second, Cord let himself remember the way that woman had moved with her gun. It shrank something in Cord's stomach, and that fear made him mad and made him determined to give her a taste of that fear.

"Why did he drag her out of her fortress and take her to his ranch?" Dugger scratched at his neck.

As he considered the Double L, a memory came back to Cord. "Years ago, I was with Gray in Helena, and Linscott was in town with a herd. I remember now Gray bought a matched pair of horses from Linscott, and Linscott agreed to deliver them. Maybe Linscott met Lady Gray back then. Maybe something more was going on between him and Lady Gray, and he came to get her and take her for his own."

Cord had touched Lady Gray exactly once, and his fingers still felt the heat of it. He'd wanted her. He'd wanted that arrogant fool, Sidney, dead, and Cord planned to step in and claim Mandy Gray for his own. He'd have the woman and the mountain of gold Sidney was always bragging about. With heated satisfaction, Cord thought of the dark, streaky-haired children Mandy would give him. A passel of them in fact. Boys. A new generation. Cord had decided long ago his children would bear the name Couturiaux.

Now Tom Linscott had her, and her gold. Any children Mandy would have would be light-haired instead of dark with a white streak. The hungry jealousy almost sent Cord into a rage. It also gave him bitter satisfaction to decide that Linscott had bought into this feud. The Cooters now had someone else to settle with.

"It's miles away, but we can see them coming and going from that ranch." Cord looked at the forest around them and saw ground covered deep in soft pine needles and the nearby trickle of spring water. It was a likely place to camp with a perfect overlook of the ranch, though far out of rifle range. "We can bide our time here, just like we done by Lady Gray's gap. We'll wait and watch and pick our moment to strike."

Cord swung down from horseback and tied his horse to a scrub pine. "Let's set up camp. Then let's start scouting to see if we can find a lookout that's within rifle range. I don't want to wait too long to let Linscott know he's made a big mistake."

Mandy rode into the Double L at a fast clip.

Tom kept up. If he hadn't, she'd have taken a stick to his backside to hurry him along.

Every few yards, without slowing her pace, Mandy turned around to study the trees and hills around them, looking for likely places for dry-gulchers to hide out.

She noticed full well that Tom did the same. At least he was taking the threat seriously. All Sidney had done was hire bodyguards and leave his protection to them.

They cantered into the ranch yard, and Mandy's skilled eye saw that Tom had posted a lookout on every high peak near his cabin.

And what a cabin it was. Sidney had built a castle. Tom had come very close to building a fort. Most people didn't live in such intense security. Since she was the only thing Sidney and Tom had in common, Mandy took a second to wonder if she somehow made men feel endangered.

"What are we going to do about the children?" It was burning a hole in Mandy's belly to think of them, so far away, so cut off from her.

"The first thing we're going to do is talk to the law. I want a U.S. Marshal to know what's going on."

"The law can't stop them, Tom." Her horse sidestepped, and she realized she had a death grip on the reins. Relaxing her hold, she said, "They keep coming and coming and—"

"I know." He cut her off. "You've told me that about fifty times. But I'm going to give the law a chance." Tom nodded toward his oversized log cabin at a tall, lean man wearing a star, leaning on the hitching post right in front of Tom's door. "And there's just the man I want to see. He's the toughest man in the territory."

Tom hollered at a nearby cowhand.

"All I see is a man with a target painted on his back. You. If that man throws into our fight, then there'll be a target painted on him, too. I think I should go to the children, Tom. Belle would see sense and let me go back to the mountain."

Tom turned to Mandy, "You can't go to the children. Sending them away keeps them safe. I don't think any man is a low enough varmint to kill a little child, so I'm hoping they won't even chase after the young'uns. But they might come after you, and if the lead starts flying, I want the children tucked far out of the way."

Tom swung down and handed the reins of his horse to the bowlegged old man who seemed to mosey along but covered the ground fast enough.

Tom took Mandy's reins as she dismounted, and the drover led the horses away.

"Thanks for coming, Zeb. Mandy, this is Zeb Coltrain." Tom shook the man's hand. "He's been chasing bad guys since before you were born. Zeb, this is my wife, Mandy Linscott."

She wondered if the children were Linscotts now.

"Howdy, ma'am." Marshal Coltrain wore a Stetson, but what hair Mandy saw was dark, and his face, half covered by a huge, drooping mustache, had the weathered look of a man used to living much of his life outdoors fighting the elements. However, he was by no means old enough to have been chasing bad guys all that long.

"I been hearing rumors about you, Tom. What kind'a trouble have you stirred up now?" The lawman tucked his thumbs in his gun belt as if he didn't have a thing to do but jaw with Tom, but Mandy saw the sharp awareness in the man's eyes. He had two six-guns, tied down, a knife in his belt, and the coldest black eyes Mandy had ever seen.

She had a terrible mix of hope and dread. Hope he could somehow protect her.

Dread that she'd get him killed.

Pretty much the same things she felt toward Tom. Except she felt a few more things toward Tom. Wifely things. She thought of those things and glanced at him. He caught the look and winked at her in a way so intimate she couldn't help remembering how well she'd liked being in his strong arms. Tom went back to talking to Zeb Coltrain.

Mandy saw a smile quirk Marshal Coltrain's lips, and knew the marshal hadn't missed that little exchange. Surely a lawman learned to watch everything. He stayed alive by picking up subtle clues.

Mandy felt her cheeks flush and decided she very much hoped the lawman couldn't read her expression with perfect accuracy. "Can we go inside and talk about this? I feel like someone is lining up a rifle right at my back."

Tom rested a hand on the small of her back, reminding her that he'd stand between her and any gunfire.

She hated knowing that.

They went inside, and Mandy noticed the bullet holes in Tom's front door. She walked through Tom's main front room, where Mandy had already drawn gunfire, and went through a wide doorway into Tom's tidy kitchen. She filled a coffeepot from a bucket of water near the dry sink.

Tom and Zeb followed her, already talking.

"These Cooters"—Zeb sat at the table in Tom's kitchen—"the rumors about them and their feud have done some spreading. I've heard bits and pieces. But except for your husband, it seems to me the only ones that've been dying are Cooters. That's a stupid way to conduct a war."

Mandy didn't want to tell them about the one she'd personally blown a hole in.

"My little wife here killed one personally that came at her while she stood watch one night."

She glared at her overly talkative husband, but he didn't even notice.

He was too busy throwing wood into a potbellied stove and lighting a match to some kindling. He brushed his hands together.

She crossed her arms so Marshal Coltrain wouldn't see her hands tremble. "I did what I had to do. It was self-defense. I didn't go out hunting—"

"Any man coyote enough to attack a woman deserves whatever happens to him." For a lawman, Zeb here seemed uninterested in hearing about a killing.

Tom sat down across from Zeb. "I had one of my hands ride

in and send word for the marshal. I didn't expect you here so fast, Zeb."

"I was in the area. I had yesterday to send a couple of wires, and I already got one back. These Cooters are like lice the way they've spread."

"Well, they sure as certain make me itchy." Tom leaned back in his chair as if he didn't have a care in the world.

"Mrs. Linscott, ma'am, you're right about there being a passel of cousins. We're trying to get to the bottom of why they're really coming after you. It don't make no sense. One man in town said he'd heard that the Cooters were just crazy for feuding and the granddaddy of the clan kept them all whipped up about sticking tight together."

"But against a woman and children?" Tom shook his head. "Never heard the like. And who started this whole notion of the Cooters sticking together no matter what? Where is this granddaddy? Is he still alive? I'd like to plant my fist in his face for being behind this."

"I've asked a few questions, and like I said, I'm expecting to hear more. But the good part is that there are some Wanted posters on this crowd. I heard tell of a few Cooters back East, in Tennessee and Kentucky, who are honorable, prosperous men. I've got a telegraph to them to ask if they're connected to this mess. I can call in a few more lawmen because there's some reward money on the head of a Cooter or two."

"But which Cooters?" Mandy asked. "How do we find them? They all have that streak of white in their hair." Mandy could still see the man she'd shot. His hat had fallen off, and there he'd been, dead in the night, that stripe showing like a skunk.

Mandy started opening the few cupboard doors in Tom's utilitarian kitchen. Her kitchen now. But she needed to learn it.

Tom rose from the table. "Let me help you." He went straight to a small door and opened it. "Coffee's in here and most food stores."

He looked over his shoulder and smiled at her. "A wife oughta learn her way around her husband's house, now shouldn't she?"

Mandy was sorely afraid she was blushing again, which was ridiculous for a woman with three children. But being with Tom as his wife was an all new experience, and the dreadful blushes kept surprising her. For the moment, she diligently kept her back to the marshal.

"I think we need to hear how this all started, Mrs. Linscott. Between the Cooters and this strange feud business and all the mystery that surrounded the witch woman, Lady Gray, about half of what I've heard is probably exaggerated or outright lies."

The coffeepot made a sharp clink of metal on metal as Mandy set it on Tom's squared wood-burning stove in his kitchen, which had the same strange slits in it rather than windows. Mandy should have found it smothering, but those thick log walls felt like the strong arms of God to her. Safety. "I've kept to myself for a long time, marshal. I'm out of the habit of trusting folks or leaning on anyone."

Tom's strong hand settled on her lower back. His fingers slid up her back slowly, touching each bump in her spine. Beth called them vertebrae, and somehow, when Tom did that, it was like he was sharing his strength with her, offering her his protection, lending his strong hands to help her find her backbone. "Time for new habits, then. Come on." He urged her toward the table.

Though she felt panicky at the thought of talking through the troubles, she wanted Tom's hand to support her enough to go along.

Dragging out a wooden chair, Tom waited for her to sit straight across from the marshal. Then he sat at the head of the table.

Mandy thought of the majestic wooden table in the formal dining room in her mountaintop home and much preferred this rustic rectangular one, clearly made by hand from split logs.

"It didn't start out as a feud. The Cooters wanted Sidney's

gold. Cord Cooter worked as his bodyguard, and I always thought he had a sly, cruel look. But then so did the other bodyguard, and he was loyal to Sidney."

"I met 'em both, Zeb," Tom interjected. "One time in Helena when I sold Sidney a team of horses. Both tough men. Didn't care for 'em myself." Tom leaned back in his chair, watching Mandy in a way that told her he'd protect her from hard questions as surely as he'd protect her from gunfire.

"Sidney fired Cord, and there was a run-in between Cord and my sister, who was coming to visit. Which led him to find a brother. They teamed up with it in mind to get their hands on our money. I heard—" Mandy's throat seemed to quit working, and her eyes shut.

A warm touch brought her eyes back open. Tom had leaned forward and clasped her hand.

It settled her enough to go on. "Cord intended to kill Sidney and force me to marry him. I know his main goal was to get his hands on Sidney's gold. Sidney heard something like that when the Cooters ambushed him and his bodyguards shortly after my sister's visit had ended. Sidney lived, thanks to his guards, a Cooter died, and shortly after that we found that guard dead, shot in the back. A note was pinned on his shirt telling us we'd started a blood feud by killing a Cooter and that every Cooter in the country would come boiling up out of their Tennessee hills to wipe the Grays off the face of the earth. We had incidents that came hard and fast after that. Luther was shot."

"Who's Luther?" the marshal asked.

Mandy explained about the mountain man who had helped raise her pa and been like a grandfather to her all her life.

"But he survived the attack?" Tom slid his hand from hers and went to fetch the coffee.

Distantly, Mandy realized that should have been her job. "Yes. Then there was an attack on the men who were building our house. It was as good as done, which was for the best because the whole work crew quit. We were safe in our gap because there was only one entrance and Sidney kept a lookout posted. But when people would go through it, to town or for any reason, they were at risk."

"You said you shot a man?"

Tom poured her a cup of steaming liquid, and the curling steam helped keep Mandy's shivers away. Even so she rubbed her hands up and down her arms. "Yes, another Cooter. He had the look of them, but I'd never seen him before, so I knew they were telling the truth about the feud." Her fingertips touched the ugly scar on her shoulder. "I was shot myself, but it wasn't serious."

She'd cared for her three children with her arm in agony, because by then Sidney had almost completely cut himself off from her. He sat in his regal office by day and watched the stars by night, and he took every excuse he could think of to ride into town and stay away as long as he could. A risky business considering the Cooters, but Sidney couldn't stay home. In the end his restlessness killed him.

"Sidney was shot down in the streets of Helena. A man was arrested, also a Cooter. Sidney's guards rode out to tell me. I guess I went a little crazy at this new attack. I convinced Luther to leave. He didn't want to, but he knew I was about at the breaking point, and his leg was healing so slow he just made one more person for me to guard. I sent a letter with him to tell the rest of my family to stay away."

"And the Shoshone people who helped you?" The marshal took a long drink of his coffee, which still had to be boiling hot.

Thinking of Buff's new wife made Mandy smile, though her heart was heavy. "Wise Sister is the wife of another good friend of my family, Buff. The Shoshone are Wise Sister's family and friends. She figured out a way to keep me safe. The Shoshone consider the land around my house their ancestral hunting grounds, but the government had moved them off. They came back, but very quietly. They made themselves known to me and occasionally brought in food and a few reports of Cooters who had tried to invade. And they didn't set up a regular village, mainly to keep the government from knowing they were there but also because the Cooters were just as evil to them as they were to me. Since it was my land, private property, no one much cared who lived there. And all my problems stopped. The Shoshone kept the Cooters back, though there were run-ins with them."

Mandy frowned over the trouble she'd caused those fine Shoshone folks. Well, their trouble ought to be over. . .since it seemed to be following Mandy. "With Sidney dead and the gap and land near it guarded, as long as I stayed close to home, I was safe."

Tom and the marshal nodded in nearly identical motions. They were quiet, thoughtful as they drank their coffee.

Mandy joined them, thinking of what it meant now that she had left her fortress. The Cooters had already attacked once. But even while she dreaded what was to come, she looked at these two men.

Tom, much better looking but cut from the same cloth. Western men, forged by harsh elements. So like Mandy's pa. The kind of man she loved, respected, and wanted in her life.

What in the world had she been thinking to marry Sidney?

It was a wonder God didn't strike her dead with a lightning bolt for her stupidity.

Fourteen

It's a wonder God didn't whack you with a lightning bolt for being so dumb as to marry that sidewinder, Mandy honey." Tom meant it kindly. He'd added honey at the end, hadn't he? How much sweet talk did a woman need?

Mandy's eyes flashed a lightning bolt or two of their own. Tom decided maybe calling her dumb hadn't been the right thing to do. But for heaven's sake, she was as smart as any woman he'd ever met. And she'd done a mighty dumb thing. Pointing it out shouldn't get him in any trouble.

"But he's dead, and now you're married to me. I won't be wandering off to town for weeks at a time. You just leave all this Cooter business to me and the law and don't worry your pretty head about it." Tom expected a smile and a thank you.

"This is my problem, not yours."

He was doomed to disappointment. Women were a mystery. Looking at Mandy's beautiful, flashing eyes reminded him that they were a wonderful mystery.

Tom ignored her foolishness. "So, Zeb, what do we do next?"

"I'm going out to where you saw those Cooters camping. I want to read their sign and get an idea what kind of men I'm dealing with."

"They'll shoot you down from cover." Mandy got up and fetched the coffeepot.

The tinkling of the coffee into the tin cups as she gave them a refill warmed Tom's heart. He'd gotten himself a good little wife, except for her stubbornness. . .and her preference for shooting people. And the pack of killers on her trail. And—

"I'll ride careful, ma'am." Zeb interrupted Tom's dark thoughts, which was just as well. Zeb tested the coffee then took a careful sip.

"I hear you're mighty good with that shooting iron, Mrs. Linscott." Zeb gestured at Mandy's rifle with his coffee cup.

That's when Tom noticed she was wearing it across her back, in the kitchen. Partly it amused him to realize he'd gotten so used to her and that always-handy rifle that he barely noticed. Partly it irritated him that she didn't feel safe and trust him to protect her, not even inside his home.

"Why don't you hang that rifle up?" Tom was tempted to disarm her. He'd done it before.

"I never do. Even at night, rocking the babies to sleep, I keep it on the floor close to hand. It's a good habit to have it close."

Tom reckoned she was right, but it pinched to think of how self-sufficient she was. He wanted his woman to trust him to protect her.

Zeb finished his coffee and set the cup down, then swiped his hand across his moustache and rose. "I'm going to do some tracking. If I think those four Cooters are ones from a Wanted poster, I'll bring 'em in."

"Be careful." Mandy's brow furrowed.

Was she just nervous after years of being hunted? Or

did the coyotes really deserve this level of caution from Tom's sharpshooting wife?

"Appreciate the concern, ma'am. And maybe by the time I get back to Divide I'll have some answers to those wires I sent about the Cooters." Zeb headed for the door.

Mandy met Tom's eyes. He could see she was holding back more words of caution.

"He's good, honey." Tom stood and followed Zeb out, Mandy trailing along. Since it wasn't her nature to follow, Tom decided she was hanging back to keep her mouth shut.

Zeb rode off, and Tom came back inside.

"We'll give him a few days and see if he can iron this all out." Tom slid his arm around Mandy's waist. She moved before he could get ahold and remind her how much fun it was to be married.

Snatching her Stetson off the nail where she'd hung it, Mandy slapped it on her head.

"Where are you goin'?" Tom blocked the door or she'd have stormed right out.

Jamming her hands on her hips, Mandy said, "I've got two choices."

"You've got one choice." Tom grabbed her hat. "You stay inside where it's safe and let the law do its job."

"Two choices and neither of them include staying inside."

Sighing, Tom regretted even asking but knew he might as well get it over with. "What are your choices?"

"I can go to my children. They'll be so worried. They've never been away from me."

"And maybe bring gunfire down on them."

"Except you seem to think the Cooters have ridden off so no one's around to follow me."

"What's the other choice?" Tom knew he wasn't going to like this one either.

"I know in my gut that the real reason the Cooters won't quit coming is that gold. They may not even have a notion of getting their hands on it, but they sure enough let it push them into the crazy way they've been acting."

"You don't know that for a fact." Though it sounded pretty reasonable to Tom, unfortunately.

"So, my other choice is to ride to. . .Denver and get that gold out of my life."

Why had she hesitated when she'd said Denver? "What are you going to do? Throw it into the streets?"

"I might. I just might."

"We'll be days riding to Denver."

"Not we, me. You stay here and defend your ranch. I'll go deal with that gold."

"You're not going anywhere without me, and I can't be away that long. It'd take two weeks going there and back. Are you going to leave your children for that long?"

Mandy flinched, and Tom figured he'd just stopped her in her tracks.

"So, you're saying I can go to the children, then?" The expression on her face almost tore Tom's heart out. She could go there, and her location might remain secret, at least for a while, maybe for long enough to let Zeb straighten this whole mess out. But if the Cooters got wind of it, they could come at the Harden clan, and turning a pack of back-shooters loose on the Hardens wasn't Tom's idea of being neighborly.

"You're staying here, woman." Tom stalked up and leaned over her. He was nearly a foot taller and outweighed her by close to a hundred pounds, he figured. That put him in charge. "You heard those wedding vows. Love, honor, and *obey*!" He jabbed his finger right at her nose. "You're obeying me, and that's the end of it. I gave you *one* choice, and you're taking it. Stay inside."

"I'm not going to sit around inside a log fort while men hunt and kill you and anyone else they think has a connection to me."

"Instead you'll go traipsing off and hope when they dry-gulch you that rifle will be able to settle things your way?"

"Which gives me an idea for a third choice." Mandy stepped closer to Tom. Not backing down and agreeing sweetly like a woman had oughta.

"What's that?" He shouldn't ask. He knew it before he opened his mouth.

"Instead of going to Denver or my children, I can take this rifle and head for those Cooters and finish what you interrupted yesterday. I can hunt them down like rabid skunks."

Well, he'd known what he was getting into when he set his sights on marrying the fastest riflewoman in the West. He didn't expect her to be all that easygoing. Still, in this instance, she was going to mind her husband. She'd do things his way or he'd know the reason why.

"You're staying here." Tom put his hands on her waist and lifted her right off her feet until she was eye-to-eye with him. What was she going to do about that? Whatever else her skills were, she couldn't beat him in a wrestling match, and he wasn't about to change his mind.

Mandy's arms went wide, and Tom braced himself for an attack. Then those arms wound around his neck, and her lips near to swallowed him up.

Mandy tried to stay mad at Tom as he brought up the rear on the trail to Divide. She managed it mainly because the man would not stop complaining.

"This is the most ridiculous plan I have ever heard." Tom pulled his stallion up beside Mandy and glared. "We need to stay at my ranch."

Mandy wasn't so much leading the way as making a run for it. True, Tom had agreed to this madness, but only after three straight days of nagging. And she was deliberately riding so fast he had his hands full keeping up. It gave him less time to think.

It also made them harder for a hidden gunman to hit.

She'd heard Tom send men out to scout ahead. The main trail to Divide was the one Tom had chosen. He'd said there was only one spot on that trail that made him nervous. One narrow stretch, lined with trees so thick they would have their hands full turning around if needed. There was a rocky overhang on that trail that would be a perfect position for a shooter. But the Cooters weren't from around here, and Tom assured her they'd need to do a lot of scouting to figure out just how Tom rode to Divide. There were several routes, and if they picked the best way then they'd have to scout for a solid lookout spot. There was one. But though it was well-known to Tom, he also said only a knowing man would be able to get to it. It was encouraging, but still, Mandy didn't ride easy.

She'd spent three straight nights doing her best to persuade her cranky husband to see things her way.

Not even her best persuasions had worked until this morning when Tom had come storming in from riding herd to announce one of the herds had been run off, some of them injured, many missing, all exhausted and turbulent and threatening to stampede again.

"Those varmints are just going to keep coming." Mandy threw him a furious look. "And we didn't see a thing until it was too late to do anything but clean up the mess. That's just the way they operate. We have to do something. We can't just sit here like big fat targets waiting for them to hurt us."

Tom glared at her, the fire in his eyes mostly for the Cooters and the damage they'd done, but Tom's grip on his temper was always shaky. "We can handle this, Mandy. I'll hire more hands. We'll bring the herds in closer."

"How much will that cost you, Tom?" Mandy snapped her fingers in front of Tom's face and made sure he heard the sarcasm when she said, "I've got an idea. Why don't we go to Denver and get the gold I have in the bank? We can use it to put a bounty on the Cooters' heads that will run them off for good."

Grabbing her wrist, Tom shook his head. "This means they're back. They're watching the ranch. I've got men combing the hills, and they'll eventually find this bunch and bring them in. We're not leaving. You're safe here."

"You're not safe." Mandy tugged on her captured wrist.

"I'm fine." Tom held on tight.

"Your cattle aren't so fine, are they?" Mandy wrestled against his grip. It was hopeless to try and get him to let loose, but she was in the mood to fight with him, so she went on with it.

"Stand still." Tom jerked her forward.

"Let me go." She crashed into his rock-hard chest and nearly knocked the breath out of herself. "Not just my arm. Let me go to Denver."

His arm came around her waist, and they stopped arguing. Stopped wrestling.

"Tom, please." Mandy's fist opened and pressed against his shoulder. "I can't stand to think of all I'm costing you. I can't bear to think cowhands and lawmen might die trying to settle my troubles."

"No one's died."

"Yet. And now you've lost some animals." Mandy went on her tiptoes. She couldn't be this close to him and not want to be closer. "You might die. I survived it when Sidney died because I'd quit caring about him and I blamed him for so many of our troubles. I don't mean I wanted him dead. I just. . .what I felt wasn't the grief a wife should have for her husband. All of that had died over the years."

"Thank God it wasn't you." Tom bent down and kissed her.

"And what if—it was you—Tom?" She broke her words up between kisses.

"Would you grieve for me then, wife?" Tom's eyes flashed humor now, rather than the rage when he'd come in to tell her about the stampede.

"Terribly." She slid her free arm around his neck. "Forever."

Tom let go of her wrist and slid his arms around her waist. He lifted her clean off her feet in a way that always made her feel delicate and feminine. Truth be told, she didn't feel like either of those things very often.

"Please, I don't want to sit here and let the Cooters run our lives. I've done that for too long. I want to fight back."

"And you think you can do that with your gold?"

Nodding, Mandy said, "I've seen what people will do for gold, Tom. I think I can make life so hard for those feuding outlaws they'll quit the country and leave us in peace."

"I can make my own ranch secure, Mandy. You should trust me." Tom met her eyes with a solid, studying look.

"But your land is sprawled out enough that you can't hire enough men to cover it all."

"We can't just sit there at the ranch and wait for them to cause trouble, that's for sure." He had the temperament of a grizzly bear most of the time.

Mandy found that suited her. She really was fond of her cranky new husband. More than fond, honestly. "You won't let me go to the children, and as it happens, I agree with you. No sense leading these coyotes to them. But we have to do something, and that gold is like an itch I've been needing to scratch for a long time."

"But what are you planning to do with it? You can't put a bounty on a man's head unless he's wanted for something."

"I'll use it to get rid of them even if I've got to give it away. If I didn't have any gold, they'd never have been harassing me. I don't care what they say about Cooters sticking together."

"You're not seriously going to just haul it out of that bank in Denver and set it on the street and holler, 'Come and get it,' are you?"

"I've given it a lot of thought, and I need to give it just a little more. If nothing else, we'll use it to hire more hands."

"Bodyguards like Sidney hired?"

"No, tough men. Picked by you. Then we really could secure your range." Except no matter how tough those men were, the Cooters would do damage. Men would be hurt or killed because of this feud.

She just couldn't quite decide, but it had become like a burr under a saddle to think of that gold, and the facts she knew of it that no one else did. Somehow that gold meant safety to her.

Finally, with a single jerk of assent, he said, "All right. We'll go. I'm ready to do something to drive those varmints off my land."

Before another hour passed, they were in the saddle heading for Divide, to see the sheriff. "We need to be seen leaving Divide." Mandy urged her horse a little faster.

"So the Cooters will quit the country and come after us?"

"It'll get 'em away from your ranch and my children."

"*Our* ranch and *our* children."

Mandy looked at him and smiled.

"Just ride." Tom's growling went on, but Mandy decided it wasn't even really growling. Not when it came to her husband. This was just normal. When he really started growling, there'd be big trouble. "Wanting them to come after you is even more loco than wanting to ride to Denver and give away all your gold. You're as crazy as everyone said you were when you lived up there in that fortress."

Mandy came to a wider spot in the trail and pulled up for just a second so Tom's stallion could ride side-by-side. They each led a second horse. If they pushed hard, switched saddles, and rode long hours at a fast pace, it wasn't impossible for a rider to make a hundred miles a day. But that was on a good trail. There was nothing good about the route they were taking.

Her heart ached to think of how long she'd be away from her children. To think that maybe she'd never see them again.

And they weren't going to Denver either. Another of Sidney's lies. This one Mandy had maintained. She'd break that news to Tom a little later, just before she led him northwest of town instead of east. He was a bit too knowing of a man to fail to miss that little detail.

When they reached Divide, Mandy went to the general store. There were a few things to buy for the trip, but mostly she knew the Cooters seemed to have a knack for finding her. So, if she let it slip that she was riding out, that word would draw the Cooters toward her. That would protect the ranch and send the Cooters off in the wrong direction, toward Denver. Meantime she and Tom would be riding hard for Sidney's gold.

Mandy gathered the supplies while Tom left to talk with Marshal Coltrain. When he was out of sight, she ducked out the back door of the Bates' General Store and ran for the telegraph office. She needed to warn a few people, because if this went bad on her and she died, she needed someone to raise her children. Tom would probably do it. Belle Harden, too, but it wasn't their duty. Besides, she hadn't sent word to her family in so long it was heartbreaking.

Her days of protecting everyone by keeping them away from her were over. Not by her choice. Tom had dragged her out of her mountain hideout, and now she was forced to stand and fight, and Mandy was in the mood.

She'd find that gold and use it to buy harassment against the Cooters. Or an army of tough cowhands for Tom's ranch. Or, if that didn't work, she'd use the gold to lure those Cooters into a gunfight and have it out with them once and for all. She didn't care how many of them there were. She had lead enough and was savvy enough to win this fight even if it took her the rest of her life.

She was glad now that Tom had stopped her the other night. She knew that had been madness, that desire to slaughter those men. But to face them, to force them to come to her, to track them down and put an end to their stupid feud, that was something she could do and not give up her honor and pride. Killing wasn't anything she wanted to do, but she was done cowering, done hiding and letting them tell her how she had to live.

Done.

Now she'd fight back. They had no idea who they'd picked a fight with. She suspected that if they did know, they'd run like yellowbellied polecats.

No offense to polecats, which were pretty fearless critters.

Tom would be at her side, and that added to her courage. At the same time, she felt the terrible guilt of putting him in danger.

What a dreadful, life-wrecking burden of a wife the poor man had found for himself!

Fifteen

Tom had rounded himself up a sweet little wife, and now he was riding out from his ranch for the first time in years.

Why, it was almost like going on vacation.

Tom had heard of such things, traveling here and there for pleasure, but he'd never taken a vacation before. Never really knew anyone who had.

True, his vacation might include a life-and-death battle with gun-wielding, back-shooting vermin, but a man couldn't ask for everything, now could he?

Smiling, Tom crossed Divide's dirt street from the general store to the sheriff's office. Zeb Coltrain's horse was tied to the hitching post out front. He opened the door and saw the sheriff, Merl Dean, and Zeb poring over Wanted posters.

Zeb glanced at Tom and picked up a poster that lay by itself on the desk. "We've found one. And I've sent out a bunch of wires. I got one back from Tennessee, someone who knows the family and is going to ask some questions to try and figure out what kind of people these Cooters are. Maybe they're a lawless bunch from way back. Maybe if they're wanted in other places, I can get lawmen interested in coming here and forming a posse and doing a roundup. If they've treated other people like they've done your wife and her children, chances are they're wanted. But I've only found one with a poster on him."

Tom took the poster. "This isn't Cord. This one's too old, and he's been around for too long." He read the name aloud. "Fergus Cooter, goes by the alias Reynolds. Wanted for murdering an Army Colonel and his wife. So he's a man that'll kill a woman. Probably came west running from the law. He looks like Cord, though, the dark hair and that white blaze. Gotta be kin."

"Never heard of him, neither as a Reynolds or a Cooter. I bet he's run afoul of the law since, but if he has, he's done it quiet. He's not a known man." Merl sighed and looked mournfully at the sizable stack of Wanted posters still to go through. "If we keep hunting, maybe we'll find more on him or some other of his family."

Merl got up and went for the coffeepot. "Want a cup?"

"Better not. I don't want to leave Mandy alone for long."

"These coyotes wouldn't come into town." Zeb accepted a cup of the black, steaming sludge that looked thick enough to float a horseshoe and hot enough to burn the skin off a man's gullet. "They're back-shooters. They'll waylay you on the trail instead."

Nodding, Tom said, "I reckon she's safe enough with Seth and Muriel in the general store, but no sense letting her wander around loose. That woman is always looking for an excuse to get that Winchester into action."

"What brings you to Divide?" Zeb sipped his coffee, grimaced, glared down at the offending cup, and then took another sip. "I thought you were gonna tighten the lookouts around your ranch and hole up. Give me a chance to catch these varmints."

Scowling, Tom considered denying the whole thing. Lying to a lawman. Better than admitting his wife had the bit in her teeth. "Mandy says she's tired of being a rabbit and she's turning wolf.

She wants to strike out on the trail for Denver, find what's left of her husband's gold and do—I'm not sure what with it. She's a little vague on that, but she's sure blaming all her trouble on Sidney striking it rich."

"Is there a lot of gold she's aiming to get shut of?" Merl looked like he was willing to volunteer to take some of it.

"I saw that castle her loco husband built up high enough to scrape the sky. I wonder if there's *any* of that gold left. It had to cost a fortune. And I heard he had people come from back East, real knowing men, who built that. Took the better part of two years to finish it. No man has enough gold to throw it away like that. I'm not sure if I hope we'll ride into her Denver bank and find the money's gone or not. Will she be relieved or disappointed?"

"If the gold is gone, you're gonna have a tough time convincing the Cooters of that."

"Gray was a secretive man," Merl said. "I heard he dug until he'd found every bit of that gold he struck, then bought a string of horses and loaded them, right down to the last bit of dust, and slipped away alone. No men riding guard duty back then because he wasn't admitting yet that he struck it rich. He found himself the sturdiest vault in Denver. Then he locked his gold up without telling anyone exactly where, paid for a lot of big things in Denver, then came home with a pair of bodyguards and a lot of fancy plans, but he didn't have to ride back with so much as a speck of gold dust to be stolen. Had him some cash but no gold."

"Then he built that monument to himself." Tom shook his head. "You should see that castle. Gray stone like something you'd read in a book. It even has a tower."

"Rich folks get notional about their money," Zeb said. "And I reckon it's theirs to do with as they want."

But Sidney hadn't cared much what Mandy wanted. To Tom's way of thinking, that gold was as much hers as his. She should have had a say. "That house was dark inside. A couple of kerosene lanterns to light the whole thing. I don't think Mandy could get to town to buy more or chop the wood to keep fire going in the fireplaces. She and the three children all slept in one bedroom together. She said it was mostly because none of them wanted to sleep alone in that spooky, cold place."

"I'm surprised she didn't make you pack a string of horses to bring all her folderol down with her." Merl began cleaning his fingernails with his knife.

"Mandy didn't even bring a change of clothes. She brought diapers and her Winchester and the two horses Sidney bought from me back a few years. That's it. She wanted no part of it." Tom turned to Zeb. "So you've heard nothing from your telegrams back East about the Cooters?"

"I've gotten one wire saying they're tracking down some answers. They think this grandfather who started that whole family code of loyalty is still alive. They're going to ask him some questions. They'll let me know more when they do."

"Will talking to the old man make it worse?" Tom had decided to marry Mandy, and nothing would have stopped him. But she'd sure been right when she said trouble came riding with her. "Will he send more Cooters out here to buy into the fight?"

"Near as I can tell, things can't get any worse. The marshals I contacted have heard of this feud. The word is out for Cooters to come a-runnin' and fight for their family, and they've been doing it already for more than a year. A lot of them Cooters are missing. There's a reason they think Lady Gray is a witch. Men get swallowed up when they go after her."

"So how many Cooters are there?" Tom felt tired thinking of how long this fight could last. Would they have to wipe out the whole family before they could have peace?

"I'm just not sure. The answers aren't in yet. I've been out every day scouting the land around your cabin, and I've got a glimpse of a track here and there. I haven't caught up with the Cooters, though. Four of 'em from what I can see. I've got marshals riding in so we can cover more land. We'll get 'em, Tom. Just let me do my job."

"Well, we're trying to take the trouble with us when we ride, but hoping to leave it far enough behind that we draw the Cooters off without getting under their gun sights. Keep your eyes open, and if you see any sign of these coyotes on our trail, toss a loop on them for me." Tom adjusted his Stetson as he strode toward the door. "Now I'd better go keep watch on my wife."

Luther read the telegraph with grim satisfaction. Mandy was finally doing the right thing. And she'd paid for enough words to tell him she'd send a wire to her folks, too. Good.

It was too many miles into Yellowstone to get Buff, though he'd love to have his old friend at his side. He'd love even more to have Buff's tough, trail-savvy wife. And if he could get to Buff, he could get to Sally, and then they'd really be able to bring a fight to those back-shooting Cooters.

But Luther wasn't taking any side trips. He'd been hunting and trapping around Helena ever since Mandy had forbidden him to come and stay with her. Having a broken leg that was stubborn healing had helped keep him away.

But no more. He was in good shape again, and he was done listening to the wishes of a little girl, no matter how fast she was with a rifle.

He wasn't waiting for Clay either. He knew Clay would come, but not in time. And Luther didn't mean to let Mandy stand alone, not even with Tom Linscott at her side. Luther knew Tom Linscott just a bit. The man's reputation was solid.

If Mandy'd had the sense to marry a rancher to begin with instead of a greenhorn sidewinder, none of this mess would have happened. He intended to tell her that, too, but he'd soften it so she wouldn't cry or nothing.

The wire she'd sent included instructions for him to

head for Divide, Montana.

Saddling his horse and packing supplies took ten minutes. He was moving down on the trail to Divide at a gallop in eleven. Too bad he couldn't talk to Buff.

Mandy dashed up the back steps of Bates' General Store and rushed inside, through what looked like a storeroom. She ran down a hallway to the front of the store, slammed into a cracker barrel, caught it before it tipped over, and earned herself a raised eyebrow from the whipcord-lean lady minding the place. "So"— she had to gasp for breath before she could go on—"is my order ready?"

"Yep. I'm Muriel Bates. So, you married Tom Linscott?"

Between breaths, Mandy said, "Yes."

"The man has a hot temper. I'd make it clear right from the start I wasn't gonna put up with it."

"I appreciate the advice, Muriel. I have a temper myself, so I have no room to complain. You know I'm Lady Gray. I've heard that's what I'm called." Leaving a trail was part of Mandy's plan. And this oughta do it.

Gray brows arched over a deeply lined forehead. "I've most certainly heard of you. That there was a—a—"

Mandy could only imagine what this plain-spoken woman was thinking. It seemed likely that she'd say most things that came to mind. "A witch? I live in a castle? My land is haunted?"

"That about sums it up."

"I did live in a castle, I suppose. My first husband found gold and seemed to think if he lived in a castle on a mountaintop that'd make him a king."

Muriel snorted.

Mandy couldn't help liking her. She looked out the front window and saw Tom striding across the street from the sheriff's office. She almost had her breathing under control now. A quick swipe mopped sweat off her brow, but it was a hot day. Sweat could be caused by something other than running.

"So you don't want your husband to know you went down to the telegraph office?"

Swallowing hard, Mandy looked into the woman's eyes. "Uh. . .no, I'd just as soon he didn't, but I'm not sneaking to put something past him. I sent away for help. Figured his pride might get in the way if I asked permission, so I did it behind his back. I'm planning on telling him when we're a few miles down the trail to. . .Denver."

"Denver's where you're headed?" Muriel's skeptical tone told Mandy she'd caught the hesitation.

"Yep." Mandy reached for the loaded saddlebags Muriel had stuffed with goods.

"I've known Tom Linscott a lot longer than I've known you. Why would I lie for a witch?"

Mandy looked straight into Muriel's eyes for far too long. Then a grin snuck onto Mandy's face. "Because us women have to stick together?" Sort of like the Cooters, only way better.

Tom shoved open the door.

Muriel grinned back. "Good a reason as any, I reckon."

"Reason for what?" Tom walked over and lifted the saddlebags out of Mandy's hands.

"We were talking about female things, Tom. You really want to know?" Muriel crossed her arms.

Mandy hoped sneaking wasn't a female thing. She'd like to think men did their share.

"No, good grief, no. I don't want to hear it." Tom shook his head almost desperately and turned to Mandy. "Let's go. We're burning daylight."

Running her hand over her dress pocket to make sure the directions Sidney had left her were still there, Mandy nodded to Muriel. "I'll be a good wife to him, Muriel. If I don't get him killed, that is."

Muriel closed her eyes as if she were exhausted. "Enjoy the ride to. . .Denver."

"I found an idler in town willing to make some money. He nosed around real quiet-like to see if anyone knows much about Linscott." Fergus eased himself down by the fire.

Cord was sick to death of standing watch on that ranch. They didn't dare get closer, within rifle range. Linscott's hands were too savvy. They'd run off a herd of beeves to see if that would clear the lookouts and draw off the men who stayed around the ranch house, but Linscott seemed to have enough hands to always keep a solid guard posted and track down stampeding cattle.

"Do you have to ride in again tomorrow to talk to him?" Cord decided he'd be the one who'd ride in. He needed to do something or go crazy.

"Nope." Fergus took a long pull on a bottle of whiskey, then corked it and tossed it across the fire to J.D., who was practically licking his lips at the sight of liquor.

"Take one long drink, and then we're hitting the trail." Fergus had a smug smile on his face that made Cord's heart beat faster.

"You found something?"

"Tom Linscott and Lady Gray hit the trail today. . .for Denver."

Surging to his feet, Cord said, "Then why are we sitting here? Let's ride."

"We're sitting here, little brother, because I trailed 'em. The man in town pointed to the trail they took, and I could make out the hooves of those big black thoroughbreds easy as if someone were holding up an arrow. And I saw their trail head northwest."

"Northwest?"

"Yep. They should be coming up the trail straight toward us. I rode hard to beat them here. We've got plenty of time to get set up. Then we finish this."

Kill a woman.

Cord didn't like it much. But Grandpappy wanted them to stick together, and that woman had killed a Cooter.

"The man also said she'd married Tom Linscott."

Cord froze. "So Linscott has to die, too?" Tom Linscott was a salty man with a lot of friends. One thing to hunt a lone man who lived like a hermit on the mountaintop. Another thing to finish his wife who had killed one of their own and who kept to herself. Cord didn't like it, but it was a blood oath, and he couldn't turn away.

But Linscott was an established rancher. Attacking Linscott could bring a whole load of trouble right down on their heads. But so what? The feud was well known, and Linscott had bought in knowing he'd joined the wrong side.

"Chances are we'd have had to kill Linscott anyway if he was riding with her," Dugger said, taking his turn with the whiskey bottle and drinking half a pint in a few gulps.

"But what if we don't get him?" J.D. asked. "He'll come after any man who kills his wife. Once Linscott's in this, we'll be fighting tough men who'll keep coming."

"We'd better be sure to get him when we get her, that's all." Cord thought he sounded confident, but it wasn't coming from his belly. This whole feud was making him sick. He'd been earning an honest living riding for Lord Gray. He'd had ambitions. He'd wanted to get his hands on Gray's gold somehow. But until he'd made that move on Lady Gray, he'd been earning the best honest wage of his life.

It had eaten at him that he rode for a man he considered a fool. Lazy, leaving his security to others, ignoring that beautiful woman and those young'uns to go to Helena and Denver and Ogden to flash money around and spend time with dance hall girls. Building himself a mansion somewhere no one could see it, of all stupid things. Then leaving the house he'd spent a fortune on to stay in a hotel room in a frontier town for weeks at a time.

Sidney'd had everything, and Cord wanted it. All of it, right down to the three children. And somehow Cord had thought he'd find a way to end up with what Lord Gray had. If watching Gray act like a king had given Cord a little taste for acting the same, the only way Cord could satisfy that taste was to take it.

He'd goaded these others and fed them with family pride and Grandpappy's rules. Fergus had never even heard of the family rules, and he'd said, since he heard, that Curly had been killed in a shooting. Cord knew if he pushed it, Fergus would agree to go chasing off after whoever had killed their other brother. But Cord had enough to do. And chasing after Lady Gray made sense, when there was a fortune in gold at the end of the chase.

Cord had always planned to get Lady Gray under his gun sometime and, rather than kill her, make her an offer of marriage she couldn't refuse on pain of death. She was a strong woman, and Cord doubted she'd take him over death if it was only her. But for her children, she'd marry him. She'd put herself at his mercy to save them.

Yes, he'd planned it all. Even down to how he'd enjoy crushing that arrogance in her. Sidney had it, too, but it was phony, built on a foundation of gold and foolishness. But Lady Gray carried herself like true royalty. And Cord had seen how easy she was with that rifle. He'd never seen her fire it until that day at Linscott's cabin. She was pure greased lightning with that thing. But he'd always seen she was comfortable with that fire iron across her back.

The first thing he'd do was separate her from that Winchester. Then he'd teach her to say, "Yes, Cord. Right away, Cord." He'd teach her with his belt if he had to. Many's the time he'd had brutal imaginings about humbling that woman.

But all these daydreams faded with Linscott in the game. They'd have to kill them both because both would fight to the death without the children to use as leverage. And with Mandy and Linscott fighting side-by-side, the two of them went a long way toward evening the odds a bit.

Linscott had to die fast under a hail of bullets. And once he was dead, there'd be trouble because he wasn't a man whose death would be ignored, even snickered at like Lord Gray's had been.

For the first time, as Cord sat there feeling all his plotting and planning unravel, he really felt that thirst Grandpappy had bred in him—thirst for family pride, thirst for his name Couturiaux from the Old Country. The castle, Gray Towers, had been sealed off forever. The gold was locked away somewhere, and only Lady Gray could get it.

Lady Gray—Mandy, Cord knew her name well enough—was going to die on this trail, right here tonight under the Cooters' guns. They'd have to kill her hard and fast to have any hope of defeating her. And when that happened, she'd take the secret of that gold to her grave.

Years spent in scheming and Cord had nothing left but pride. He looked at Fergus and J.D. and Dugger, a sad lot, but Cooters to the bone. Couturiauxs right to that flash of white hair.

Fine, if this was all he had, then he'd fight for the family, fight for the brand. He pulled his six-gun from his holster and checked the load, and then he turned to Fergus. "What trail will they be using?"

Fergus rose from the fire with a flare of evil in his eyes. "I'll show you, and we can scout out a place to lie in wait and finish this."

Like back-shooting coyotes. Could a man take pride in that?

"Then we can head for town and get more whiskey," J.D. added eagerly as he drained the bottle.

It was all Cordell Couturiaux had.

Sixteen

W hat do you mean we're not going to Denver?" Tom followed his wife off the trail trying to catch her. He'd yelled that she'd taken a wrong turn.

She'd laughed. The little spitfire had laughed at him. Then she'd taken off to the north, through a dense stand of woods that might well stretch all the way to the Idaho border and beyond.

"Catch me, and I'll tell you all about it." Mandy looked back with a smile on her face that made Tom lean low on his horse's neck and urge it forward on the uneven ground, bent on catching himself a wife—for the second time this week.

He caught her all right and persuaded her to bed down for the night before the sun had even set. There was no talk of maps nor gold nor Denver. There was only Tom with the woman he'd wanted in his arms for five years.

Now he had her. He'd stormed through all her objections and taken her for his own, figuring himself as the sensible one of them. Smiling, he lowered her to their bedroll and let every minute of that frustrated waiting show in his kiss and his touch.

One of the very best things he liked about his wife was she seemed to have a few years of frustration of her own to relieve.

Much later, they sat by the crackling campfire in the lowering sun, Mandy in his arms, sitting between his legs, resting her back against his chest while he held her tight. "We're gonna have us a good life, Mandy girl."

And a few more children if Tom had anything to say about it.

She looked up over her shoulder with a beautiful, private smile that made Tom think of those long, lonely five years again.

Her endless white blond hair was loose and messy, raining over Tom's arms and her shoulders. It drooped over one eye, but he could see enough. She was relaxed and at peace for the moment. That look of fear and regret that always, always shadowed her face was missing right now, and Tom wished he could figure out a way to make it stay gone forever. She'd lived with fear and regret for long enough.

He wrapped one arm tight around her middle to pull her even closer, then smoothed her hair back and unwound it from his arms and her shoulders. He brushed it off her forehead. His hands were coarse and awkward, too rough for someone so beautiful, but he couldn't quit touching her. Watching the shining strands of her hair slide through his hands, he couldn't remember much in his life that was more perfect than this moment.

"I haven't had much family in a lot of years, Mandy. Having you and the young'uns is going to make my house a home."

"What about Abby, your sister?"

Tom hated to think of all his sister had been through. "I've only really known her for a few years."

Mandy twisted around to look at him. "How can you not know your sister?"

Tom wanted an excuse to keep holding her, so he decided to talk. "Abby came west with my family years ago. She was still really young."

"You didn't come?"

Shaking his head, Tom went back to caressing Mandy's hair. He needed to learn to braid so he had a chance to touch her more. "Nope. I was a full-grown man of sixteen years. When my folks decided to go west on a wagon train, I stayed behind. I had a job and a girl and my future all laid out in front of me."

Mandy sat up straight and frowned over her shoulder. "You've been married before?"

Mandy obviously didn't like to think he'd had a wife. All things considered, this little woman had a lot of nerve to object to the nonsense in Tom's past.

"Never married her. But I was determined to when my family moved away, so I told them good-bye. I was headstrong and so sure I was all grown up."

"I suppose most sixteen-year-olds are sure." She subsided back into his arms, watching the crackling fire.

My folks had been gone about a year, and I missed them so bad, but I had my girl and my pride. I was getting by."

"What happened to her?" Mandy's hands rested on his thighs, her fingers flexed as if she were comforting him.

"I lost everything. The girl I gave my family up for found herself a rich man, leastways rich compared to me. And since I was working in her father's store, I got fired when she got herself engaged to another man."

"I'm sorry. I know how it hurts to have your dreams die, even if those dreams aren't very sensible. I was madly in love with Sidney when I married him. It took me a while learning that I didn't even really know the man."

"Yep, it hurt." Shaking his head, he added, "I was so young. I really don't blame her for picking someone else. I had no hope of caring for a wife and supporting children on the salary I was earning. I suppose I had it in my head that her pa would let me be a partner in the store, but she'd have been crazy to marry me."

He could still remember the feeling of his heart breaking in two. He'd covered it with anger and told himself he didn't really want her, but she'd torn down everything he saw for his future with a few careless words.

"She'd have been lucky to marry you, Tom. Store clerk or rancher, whatever you turned your hand to, you'd do well. You'd take good care of a wife and children."

Tom kissed her neck, just for the kindness in her voice. He could have used that kindness back then. He'd been devastated.

His arms tightened on her waist so she was pulled snug against him. Mandy lay her head back on his chest and hugged his hands wrapped around her belly. He opened one hand to lay on her stomach and wondered if maybe he'd managed to get a child of his own started with his wife. The idea was so appealing he couldn't talk for a moment.

What if she wasn't expecting yet? Tom decided he needed to do more to make sure she was. He was ready to turn her to him when she started talking again.

"So after things ended with your girl and your job, what did you do?"

He was no longer in the mood to talk about his childhood, but he found himself in the mood to be very obliging to his wife right now. "I got another job for a while, but finally pride became a lonely companion. I found a wagon train headed west and set out to throw in with ranching with my family."

"But you said you haven't had much family in years."

"When I got out here, they were dead." Tom found himself in need of swallowing before he could go on.

Mandy made a sound of such pure sympathy that for a minute, Tom had a struggle to hold back tears. And that would be so embarrassing that the horror of it settled him down. "A fever had gone through and killed a lot of people, my family included. I hadn't been told. They lived a long way out from town and didn't really know anyone, so no one ever visited to see they'd died. I got here, and there were records of their claim, so I found where they'd homesteaded. I rode up there thinking they'd be so excited to see me, and I was crazy lonely for them."

The silence stretched as Tom remembered that ramshackle cabin. In bad shape because no one had done a thing to it in over a year. "I found an empty cabin. Then I found graves." Tom had thought that girl had broken his heart, but Tom knew as he stood there over those windswept graves what true sadness was. "It's the same place I live."

"Tom, I'm so sorry. But Abby was alive."

"Abby was gone. I—" His voice quit working. This went beyond grief to guilt and regret that was almost unbearable. He never let himself think about it. "I thought she'd died, too. I just assumed she had."

Mandy sat up and turned fully to face him, drawing her legs beneath her until she was next thing to kneeling between his legs. "You assumed? But where was she then?"

"A band of Flathead Indians had found her alone in the cabin, the rest of the family dead. They took her in. I didn't hear from her until just a few years ago."

"She lived with the Indians all those years?"

Nodding, Tom said, "They were good to her. She's very loyal to them. Don't act like you feel sorry for her when you see her next time because she'll pull that wicked knife and start sharpening it right in front of your eyes."

Mandy laughed. "Sorry, I'm sure it's not funny to you."

"It's just something else I did wrong. I should have been there to help."

"And died of the fever yourself?" Mandy met his eyes.

"I might have lived. Abby did."

Gently his pretty wife rose to her knees and wrapped her arms around his neck. "I'm glad you're here."

All Tom could think of for the next hour was that he was very glad he was here, too.

Finally, long after the flickering flames of their fire had turned to glowing red coals, it was time to go back to what he'd been going to ask before they'd started talking about Abby. "Why didn't you trust me with Sidney's map from the first?" He shouldn't ask when they were so content and relaxed, in harmony for once, but it had to be spoken of sometime, and tomorrow would be a long hard-riding day.

"I've always trusted you, Tom. Too much when it was the wrong thing to do. When I was a married woman."

He gathered her wildly tousled hair in one fisted hand and eased it over her shoulder. "That's not real trust. Not the kind where we talk about whatever's on our minds."

"I begged you to stay with me when Jarrod was being born. That's trust."

"You were alone with two toddlers and terrified. You'd have begged a grizzly bear if that was all the help that was to be had."

"Probably right." Mandy flashed her white teeth at him.

He was glad he hadn't gotten her stirred up and mad yet. "And yes, for anything to have happened between us back then would have been wrong. I'm not asking you why you didn't share all your secrets with me back then. But I dragged you out of that stupid castle days ago. You didn't tell me about the map until you turned off the trail a couple of hours ago. Why?"

Mandy reached her long, graceful neck up and kissed him on the side of his jaw. He was so much taller than she was, so much bigger all over. He should have worried about the delicate little lady. But she was strong. Tom caught himself hustling to keep up with her and rarely had a spare second to think of her as fragile.

He turned his head and met that kiss with his own and almost let her distract him from their little problem about trust. Almost.

He eased back and lifted one of her hands to his lips. He noticed the callus on her index finger and kissed it with special attention. It was part of what made her the most interesting woman he'd ever known.

Pulling her to a sitting position, he moved them around so the bit of glowing light made her more visible. With the starlight and his excellent night vision, he could see her well enough. "Braid your hair for me. Let me watch."

Her brow furrowed. "What?"

"You heard me." He picked up her hair, hanging nearly to her waist down along her left arm. "I want to watch, learn how to do it."

Their eyes held. More passed between them than seemed possible without words. Finally she nodded and picked up her hair. "Separate it into three parts. Like this." She demonstrated.

He helped, making it much harder but getting a feel for it before long. He'd done some braiding, he realized. Turning strips of bark into sturdy whips. Turning hemp into rope. He hadn't done it for a while, but it came back.

They worked, their hands tangled up together. Mandy watching as her braid shaped up.

"It wasn't because I didn't trust you, Tom. I just wasn't alone enough with you. I didn't want to take a chance on anyone else hearing what I had planned. I've gotten in the habit of"— she took a quick peek at him—"feeling watched, pursued. In that castle I felt like the walls had eyes and ears. It was spooky. And the Shoshone people who lived near, well, they never eavesdropped, but they were so quiet. They came and left a haunch of elk or a buffalo hide or something like that quite often. I loved them, but it added to the eerie feeling."

"So you really felt like someone was hanging around while we were alone in the house?" Tom didn't quite believe that. His house was really open. There was nowhere to hide.

"Maybe, just because it's an old habit to always feel that way. And besides, I didn't really know I was going to get my gold until yesterday. Until then I was trying only to figure out how to make it safe for the children. That day I went after the Cooter clan I could only think that I was tired of being hunted. I was ready to be the hunter. When you stopped me from that, I didn't know how else to hunt. Then I thought of the gold. I'm going to use that money for something worthwhile. Finally. I'm going to use every cent of it to buy peace."

"The real reason you didn't tell me was because you didn't think I'd go. You had your hands real full convincing me to ride to Denver. You were afraid I'd never agree to follow Sidney's map with you."

Mandy shrugged. "My hands have been real full with you."

Tom almost laughed, which would have let his stubborn little wife off the hook. "We should have given the law more time. Let the marshal work."

"I need to get to my children, Tom. They won't understand any of this. I know Belle Harden well enough that I trust her to take care of them and comfort them. But letting them stay in her care is cruel. I hate it. I—"

"You're not cruel." Tom twisted the heavy rope of her hair around his fist twice and drew her face close using the silken length. "You're smart and tough and too kindhearted for your own good. We're leaving them there because that's what's best for *my* children."

"But I need to be there. They won't understand where I've gone. They'll think I—"

He shut her up the only way that had proved to work a bit well.

And later, because they'd made such a mess of it, she had to teach him how to braid her hair all over again.

"Wise Sister!" Sally shouted as she strode toward the tent Buff and Wise Sister lived in when they were following Sally and Logan around.

Wise Sister pushed back the flap almost immediately. Her serene eyes took in everything. The loaded horses. Sally's cowboy clothes. Logan's harassed expression.

"We'll come."

"I've got to see to Mandy." Sally looked past Wise Sister to see Buff reach for his saddlebags and begin shoving provisions in.

"Ten minutes." Wise Sister dropped the flap. It hadn't been a request.

Sally turned to Logan, fuming. "They can catch us. Let's go."

Buff came out before Sally had finished speaking, carrying two saddles. He headed for the makeshift corral behind their tent. He looked over his shoulder. "Help me." Another order.

But it kept Sally busy for the few minutes it took Wise Sister and Buff to get ready to go on a trail ride that could take weeks. It was possible they wouldn't get back to Yellowstone this season, and if that happened they'd lose everything they'd left behind. It was even possible they might die in a feud that had nothing to do with them.

Neither of them hesitated a second.

As they swung up on horseback, Buff said, "Luther know you're going?"

"Nope, no way to tell him. I heard he was trapping up closer to Mandy. No way to even send him a wire."

"He'll know." Wise Sister set a brisk pace as if she and Buff had been fighting the need to make this trip for a while. She only knew Mandy a bit, but it was Wise Sister's village that had protected Mandy all this time. The Shoshone woman never went anywhere and never seemed to have company, but somehow, if anyone had news about Mandy, it was her. If Wise Sister said Luther would know, Sally believed her.

Sally fell in behind Wise Sister, determined to push hard all the way to Mandy's fortress. She'd lead this group if they didn't move fast enough to suit her. But she could never quite catch up, which made Sally wonder if Wise Sister had reason to hurry beyond Sally's sudden fear.

Sally's hand crept to her belly.

God, have mercy on us all. God, have mercy on my baby. God, have mercy.

Seventeen

It got chilly in the Rocky Mountains at night, even in August. Mandy was only mildly surprised to wake up and find a dusting of snow covering the bedroll she shared with Tom.

It was warm as toast under the wool blankets, but an itch between Mandy's shoulder blades told her she needed to be moving. They should have ridden longer last night. Gritting her teeth against the cold, she shoved back the covers in the gray light of pre-dawn.

"Hey!" Tom woke up with a jerk as a layer of snow drifted down onto his bare chest. Mandy grinned at him as she dressed with quick, efficient movements. By the time she had a coffeepot in place, Tom had the bedroll bundled and was saddling the first horse.

"Why did I ever think marrying a city boy was a good idea?" Mandy watched Tom do all the things a man needed to do to get on the trail.

He turned to her and quirked a smile. "I reckon you needed to get up here to these mountains somehow."

"Tough way to travel, with Sidney in tow."

"Warm up some of that jerky, too. Something hot will taste good this morning, and you can do that right quick."

"Okay, but I want to be on the trail within a half hour. The sun will be up past the horizon by then."

The dusk was already light enough that they could be traveling. Mandy knew they were lingering, which made no sense. Urgency had been riding her hard ever since they'd set out from Divide.

Turning back, she crouched beside the fire, grateful for her leather riding skirt and long sleeves. Even her ugly gray cloak. She needed to buy something in a different color, and if she lived through these next few days, she'd do it.

She'd be hot later in the day and wish for lighter clothes. She could shed the cloak, but the leather skirt and long sleeves were all she had. A woman couldn't have everything.

The goad to hurry reared up as she pulled a cast-iron skillet out of Tom's pack and tossed a few pieces of the tough jerky on to heat. It would only take a minute or two to warm it up. Then they'd chew on it while they moved down the trail.

"I smell smoke, Cord." Dugger pulled his horse so abruptly to a halt Cord almost collided with him.

Cord smelled it, too, now that Dugger mentioned it. Dugger might be childlike in his head, but he had better sense in the woods than any of them.

The four of them left the trail, Fergus and Cord uphill, J.D. and Dugger downhill.

Cord and Fergus eased along. The smell of smoke became stronger. Then Cord heard the crackling of flames.

Cord came to a rock wall so rugged it was tempting to just forget getting over it. But if Cord's nose told him right, that fire was set up right in front of these rocks. If Cord could get above whoever had that campfire, he could pick them off like ducks frozen on a pond. He gestured to Fergus that he was leaving his horse to climb up.

"Got it." Fergus's whisper was softer than a breath of wind. He pointed at a path that took him around the rocks, then caught Cord's horse's reins and faded back into the woods.

Cord inched his way up a pile of rounded stones that looked like a giant had been stacking massive marbles. Trees grew here and there, seemingly out of solid rock. He raised himself, silent as a ghost, to the top of the rocks, swept his Stetson off, and eased forward, an inch at a time, to see who was below him. Even if it wasn't their quarry, if the travelers had good horses and guns, it would be worth the taking.

"Let's saddle up."

The female voice froze Cord in his tracks. Whoever it was stood directly below him. But what other woman could it be than Lady Gray? A trickle of cold sweat ran down Cord's backbone as he thought of that witch woman loosing her Winchester on him.

Tightening his hands on his own gun, he knew his first shot had to take her down and the second had to finish Linscott. Even as he crouched behind the cover of rocks in the dim morning light, Cord felt like things weren't quite stacked enough in his favor.

He saw a space where two rocks were heaped together so there was an eyehole about three inches across at most, big enough for a rifle and for him to draw a bead. The opening was at the bottom of a rock. That was as safe as a man could be.

He slid his gun onto the lip of that little hole and rose up from his crouch to get a dead shot at his target. The gun was still angled upward, but as he rose the muzzle lowered and lowered, and there she was.

He remembered that witch woman all right. He'd had his hands on her once, just once. And she'd backed him off, insulted him. Now she crouched by a pack, shoving two tin cups into it. He wanted to own her. But that wasn't going to be possible, so he'd do what he had to do. His gun came lower, and he slid it forward just enough to clear the rock.

Cord smiled.

Mrs. Gray rose from her crouch to make the middle of her back an even more perfect target.

Cord smiled and leveled his weapon just slightly.

A pebble rolled from where the gun was braced.

He pulled the trigger.

Mandy dove sideways at the sound of that rolling stone. A gun exploded into the last of their dying campfire and sprayed cinder and ash into the air. It would have slammed into the back of her head if she hadn't moved.

Her gun was in action before she'd hit the ground, and she twisted to land on her back. Her blood turned cold and flowed like molasses in January.

Mandy spotted the exact direction where the shooting came from. She fired. A cry from that circle told her she'd hit her mark.

Firing again, she levered bullets into the chamber with a hard, whipping turn of her hand, twirling the rifle, firing, twirling, firing. Moving, she put trees and stone between her and the attacker, shooting, always shooting.

The rifle protruding fired again, but wildly. Overhead leaves shredded, hit by the erratic bullets. Then the gun muzzle was gone and silent.

In a fraction of a second that seemed like hours, she saw Tom bring his gun up and aim away from where the bullets had originated. Her eyes followed the direction he looked, and she saw two gunmen, running and dodging forward. Mandy fired at the nearest one. She had plenty of time to pick, to see which one had the best aim at Tom, the best chance of making a hit. Her bullet slammed into his gut. The gunman cried out and went down under her withering fire. His hat toppled off, and Mandy saw the white slash of hair at his temple.

Cooters.

But she'd known that already. She turned to the other man, leveled, and fired.

Tom was shooting and weaving to put trees between him and the second shooter.

A bullet from another direction spit up rock and dirt near Mandy's feet. She wheeled and fired. That gunman staggered back, and his shot went wide.

Mandy saw it all, as if the bullet inched along. This fourth man's wild shot lodged into his own kin. A Cooter killing another Cooter. She hoped they declared a feud against each other.

She fired again, and the fourth man was gone, running. She'd winged him, but it wasn't a fatal hit. Unless the bullet got septic and killed him later.

With a quick glance she saw the two gunmen down. Dead most likely. One killed by her. All she felt was icy calm.

Two had run off. She raced after them. Something hit her hard in the back. Bringing her gun around, suddenly it was swept out of her hands.

"Mandy, it's me."

Mandy made a grab for her rifle.

Tom flipped her onto her back and held her to the ground with his full weight stretched out on top of her. "Stop. They're gone."

"I can get them." Her voice sounded unnatural, guttural and savage and distant, like it came from miles away. The woods were vivid. She was aware of each leaf that fluttered in the wind. She heard the receding footsteps of two men. Both wounded, she was sure. Her blood moved like sleet in her veins as she took in every sight, sound, scent, touch, and taste. She felt all of that, but no remorse, no regret, no weight of the sin of killing.

Mandy knew she had it in her to be a monster. "We need to end this, Tom."

His weight made struggling a waste of time.

She finally gave up and let herself go limp beneath him, but inside she was still coiled like a rattler. Her heart pounded until she felt like her whole body vibrated with it. She smelled the sulfur from the gunfire, the ashes from the camp. The blood. Tom's shirt pressed on her, and in her heightened state of awareness the coarse fabric was like sandpaper under her fingers.

"You're not going after them." He sounded wrong—strange mix of fury and tenderness—when what he ought to sound like was loathing. He knew what he'd married now. "You're not running blind into those woods."

"Blind?" Mandy laughed a ragged, vicious sound she didn't understand. "I can see everything. I swear I could see through stone. What I can't see I can hear and smell."

As he held her, her eyes finally focused, not on the whole world and every detail in it, but on Tom. He was staring at her, willing her to calm down and come back to him from wherever she went when the cold-blooded murderer took over.

"Are you all right now?"

Mandy managed to nod her head. She noticed that Tom didn't let her up. The man was starting to know her.

Suddenly, Tom's head came up. "One of them's riding away but not both." He leapt to his feet, shoved her rifle at her, and raced into the woods.

Amazed he'd given back the Winchester, Mandy was on her feet running, studying the woods. Tom was fast enough that he was kneeling by a fallen man when she caught up.

The man struggled, but one arm wasn't working, and blood poured, sapping his strength. Galloping hooves faded in the distance.

Tom tossed a rifle one way and a six-gun the other.

Mandy was on her knees across from Tom just as her husband relieved the man of a skinning knife. Another Cooter, the white thatch of hair, the same glowering face, though pale. The man's arm was bleeding fast.

Tom jerked the Cooter's kerchief off his neck and tied it tight around his arm, with no regard to gentleness. "I know a U.S. Marshal who'd like to ask you some questions."

"This isn't over." The man gasped with pain as Tom knotted the kerchief. His face went gray; sweat flowed off his brow. His eyes flickered shut, but he kept talking. "Cooters will keep coming until you're all dead. We stick together."

"Real family loyalty." Tom gave the kerchief one last tug, and the bleeding slowed to a trickle. "Your kin didn't even stay to boost you on your horse. He just rode off and left you. Whoever that was is a coward, just like the rest of you."

Tom stood and jerked the man to his feet. Mandy saw the horse tied nearby and went to lead it over. Her fingers itched to do something evil to the man, but she didn't. Her sanity had returned, and she was close to normal again. As close as she got.

But she had to goad the man somehow. "Did you notice that you killed one of your own? Maybe the Cooter clan will leave me alone and start hunting you." She positioned the horse to stand beside the Cooter.

Mandy thought of the other men dead. One of them was her doing. No one could deny that. The cold in her blood receded, and guilt washed through her heart straight to her soul.

God, what is wrong with me? Protect me from what lives inside me, Lord. Protect me. Protect me. Please.

Tom was strong enough he tossed the outlaw onto his saddle. Then he bound the man's hands to the pommel and began leading the horse back to the clearing.

"Hunt to the downhill side of our camp for the other horses, Mandy."

Mandy wasn't sure if she was honored by the respectful way Tom gave her a job and expected her to do it or annoyed because he was giving her the job that kept her away from their prisoner, as if he wasn't sure whether she'd go berserk and kill this man, too.

She was pretty sure she wouldn't, but just in case, she headed for the horses.

"I'll get the other two ready to move and finish packing our gear. We'll head back to Divide, leave these men for the sheriff and marshal, and get on with our trip to. . ." Tom glanced at the sullen man clinging to his horseback and spoke carefully. "To wherever you say we need to go."

Cord felt that witch woman taking aim at the dead center of his back. He felt her tightening her finger on the trigger. Felt a bullet seconds away from slamming into his spine.

He drove his horse with a vicious continual goad of his spurs. He'd seen Fergus go down and knew J.D. and Dugger were down and dead. All three of them killed by that woman and her wild, whirling gun.

Reaching up with a shaking hand, he found the slits on his face and blood pouring down. His eye was already swelling shut.

Kicking his horse brutally, he rode and rode until his horse stumbled on a talus slide and went down hard. Cord flew over the horse's head and landed flat on his belly. He slid, twisting his body, clawing at his six-gun to aim at. . .nothing.

Seconds passed. No one came.

Waiting, waiting, knowing she was coming. His hands shook. The muzzle of the gun wavered.

He'd *never* seen anyone handle a rifle like that. He trembled, smashed into the dirt and rock, and waited for her to come roaring out of the woods, that witch woman with her whirling guns and deadly accurate bullets. The noise and the sulfuric smoke made him think of the afterlife and how Hades would be. The memory of how she looked grew until she was magic, pure deadly black magic.

She'd seen through rock. Aimed and hit an opening twenty yards away that was a three-inch circle. His rifle had saved his life because she'd hit it, jammed it back into his shoulder. The gun had been destroyed, and Cord had staggered back, slashed by fragments of metal and shards of shattered rock. He'd still been able to see her through that hole, stunned into frozen awe. She knew he was no longer a threat and whirled from him and unloaded that gun at J.D. and Dugger, coming from the opposite direction. He saw the bullet hit J.D. and kill him. A gun she'd had one split second to aim. Then she'd turned as Fergus had opened up from yet another direction. She was just as deadly.

Cord had been only slightly aware of Tom Linscott also firing. What Cord saw in that woman stunned him beyond noticing much else. Her Winchester seemed like a living thing with its own mind, flaring in all directions, almost at the same time. Her gray cloak flew as she turned and fired until she was a dark cloud, thunder and lightning with a Winchester.

He lay shuddering on the ground now and stared at the trail and heard her coming. His chest heaved. His hand trembled. His eyes, burning from oozing blood, riveted on the place he expected her to appear.

But she didn't.

The seconds stretched to minutes, and slowly the panic receded, and Cord realized she wasn't coming. When his blood quit thundering in his ears, he knew the pursuing hoof beats coming at him like the hounds of Hades were in his own head.

His breathing slowed. His heart rate slackened to as near to normal as he was ever going to be again.

She'd killed three more of his family. Three more Cooters dead at the hand of that witch woman.

And now he lay here on the rocky trail, crushed into the ground like discarded trash. She'd made a fool of him. Terrorized him. And his fear shamed him. So he changed the fear to hate.

Hate wasn't shameful. It was strong because it made a man do what he needed to do.

Gathering his scattered courage, he slowly rose. He fumbled

for his kerchief, tearing it off his neck and sopping up the blood. His face was clawed up, but he wasn't blinded. The wounds were little more than deep scratches, and the bleeding had stopped.

The horse that had stumbled and thrown him stood just a few yards down the trail, trembling with exhaustion, its sides heaving, its head down.

Cord wanted to get on that horse and ride away, defeated, beaten into rubbish. But he couldn't quit. And he couldn't go back and face her alone. The cousins he'd sent for might be in Helena by now, awaiting him. There might well be dozens, and even Lady Gray couldn't defeat that many men.

With grim determination, Cord stalked to his horse and was astride. He didn't spur the horse this time, contented to walk. Cord was as exhausted as his mount.

He'd get to Helena soon enough. Give himself a few days to heal so the cousins wouldn't think he'd been bested. Then he'd gather his family and come back with overwhelming strength to avenge his name.

Dugger, J.D., and Fergus, all dead. That was enough to keep the feud alive. He'd use that to inspire his cousins.

But Cord's real thirst for blood came from knowing there was a woman who could defeat him, humble him, and make him fear.

That woman had to die.

Eighteen

Mandy, this one's alive." Tom's heart picked up speed. He'd seen Mandy hit this guy hard. It had looked deadly. Tom didn't want this scar on her soul, and when he saw the man's chest rise and fall, he rushed to him, hoping he could be saved. Tom knew what it had cost her to kill once before.

Mandy appeared from the woods leading two horses. Her eyes sharpened. She walked quickly toward where Tom rose from the man's side.

"I know I hit him in the heart, Tom." Mandy sounded grim.

"It's dead center on his heart." Tom swallowed hard to think of his wife's aim, in the middle of a gunfight. "But there's something in his shirt pocket. The bullet's nearly stopped by a little book."

"Nearly?"

"He's bleeding." Tom unbuttoned the man's blood-soaked shirt. "It went through. It's lodged in his chest, and I guess it knocked him cold, but it wasn't a killing shot."

Mandy knelt beside Tom. "Yes, it was." Mandy looked up from the wound.

Tom met her eyes and saw the guilt and pain and danger of his wife. "Yes, it was. And I'm glad you're as fast as you are, or we'd both be dead. In case you didn't notice, I never hit a thing."

"You kept their heads down. You messed up their aim."

"While you finished them. And now we've got three of them in custody, and you haven't had to commit murder."

"Then why do I feel like I have?"

Tom looked at the still man on the ground. He lifted his head to study the man slouched over his pommel, apparently unconscious. "I don't think you do feel like you have."

"Yes, I do."

"No, I don't think you know what you'd feel like if you committed murder. As awful as you feel now, that would be worse, and a different kind of pain. Uglier."

Mandy's eyes went to the freely bleeding wound in the man's chest. "This is pretty ugly."

"Then be glad it isn't worse, woman. Be very glad." Tom made quick work of digging the bullet out of the man's chest and wrapping a rough bandage over the wound. The man never woke up, and Tom noticed that he had a knot on his head the size of a chicken's egg. That was the reason he was unconscious.

Tom boosted this man as well as the dead one on the horses Mandy brought. "Let's haul them to town. That's the end of this bunch, except for the one who rode away, and he's wounded. And one man alone, especially a coward like these Cooters, isn't much danger. Alone, he won't even come at us from cover."

They made a quick trip back to Divide and left the men with the doctor, who thought both could survive. Then they made a report to the sheriff.

Tom finished being questioned then went outside to find his sharpshooter of a wife.

Mandy sat on a bench outside the sheriff's office, staring into space.

Sitting beside her, Tom said, "You want to tell me about it?"

Pulling herself with visible effort out of whatever daze she'd been in, Mandy turned to look at Tom. "About what?"

"I saw you in action. That's the first time, though I've heard tell. It's somethin' to see." Tom smiled. He was careful not to touch her because she looked like she might just explode.

Pulling in a breath so deep her whole body shuddered, Mandy said, "I'll understand if you want to get me out of your life. Any man would want to—" Her voice broke. She lifted her chin and stared straight out into the middle of the street.

Tom saw the fight for control. "If a woman can't shed a tear when she's been attacked and nearly killed and forced to fight for her life, then when can she?"

Tom saw tears brimming in her eyes as she turned to face him. Her shoulders, so square, so strong, shuddered, and she threw herself into Tom's arms. "I hate what happens to me. I'm evil. I'm—"

Tom kissed her quiet right in the middle of the day in Divide, Montana. Once he thought he'd taken her mind of that "evil" nonsense, he pulled back. "The sheriff said we can leave town. One of the outlaws, the one who shot his kin, is a wanted man. The others were riding with him, and that's enough. We can go"—Tom leaned so close no one could overhear—"on a treasure hunt."

Mandy set a blistering pace.

They were three days on the trail and getting close to their destination, when Tom pulled up abruptly. "Tracks!" He pointed at hoof prints of an unshod pony obviously carrying a load.

Indians.

"We walk from here." Tom snapped out the order, even though he was whispering. He dismounted.

Mandy didn't even consider disobeying. She'd found it didn't suit her much to take orders from anyone, especially a man, but why bother squabbling about such a thing when the man in question was right?

"How close are we?" Tom eased off a barely visible trail into the thick woods that surrounded them.

Mandy pulled the map out in the waning light. "Close." She looked up. "I'd say it's right up at the top of that rise. Then there's a mountain valley and directions where the gold is hidden."

Tom looked at the peak. It was still miles away and only visible through the heavy forest because it was so high. He turned to Mandy. "Let's pull back, set up camp for the night, and figure out how we do this tomorrow."

Shaking her head, Mandy said, "I've already been gone from the children too long, Tom. I just can't wait any longer. Worrying about them is eating me up inside."

With a long look, her cranky, bossy, short-tempered husband seemed to take her word for it that she was telling the truth. She really was about ready to snap.

Nodding, he said, "Let's see that map."

They found a spot and sat side-by-side on a boulder.

"The trail that rider was taking looks to lead to that low spot on the mountaintop." She studied the map and the mountain. "But Sidney says the treasure is far to the northeast side of a huge mountain valley, just beyond that rim."

"Maybe we can go north and slip into that valley without the Indians knowing." Tom sounded doubtful.

"That's not what the map says to do." Mandy tapped her lips as she considered that. "In fact, the map seems to follow the exact trail of those unshod hooves."

"Your husband isn't the kind of snake who would leave a treasure map behind for his wife that would force her to risk her life to find the gold, is he?"

Mandy set that thought aside as she remembered how well the Shoshone folks who lived around her knew what went on around them, even in the dark of night. "It's possible those are

Shoshone tracks. If they are, the people may know of me, even protect me. We might just be able to ride in there and tell them what we want."

"There are other tribes in the area, though. I think this used to be Flathead land. In fact, I think these might be the people my sister lived with for a few years after my parents died."

"Your sister? Abby? She lived here?"

"Yes, and they were good to her. She doesn't talk about them much but I know it ended badly. Her village was massacred by a gang of outlaws. She was left alive because she was white. Because of that, there was bad blood between her and the few native folks that survived."

"Can you speak their language?"

"A few words. My sister tends to lapse into Flathead when she's mad. And she spends a good part of her time mad, so I've had a chance to learn what some of it means."

They shared a look that stretched long. "Do we dare just ride into the middle of a Flathead village and hope they'll be friendly?" Mandy's heart sped up with fear.

"Do we dare try and sneak past a bunch of trail-savvy Flatheads and hope they won't notice?"

Mandy finally shrugged her shoulders. "How about we do both? Sneak and, if we get caught, try and talk to them."

"How about we ride back to Divide, abandon the gold, and forget this ever happened?"

Shaking her head, Mandy stared at the mountain for a long time, thinking. What was bothering her about this? "It's so far from where our cabin was when Sidney was gold mining. How did he ever find this place?"

After an extended silence, Tom said, "Is it really that far?"

"We've ridden for days, and this map starts from Divide. It's shown us every step from there."

"But how about from your castle? We rode for days south from your place to Divide. Now we've ridden west and north from Divide to here."

Mandy's brow furrowed. "We might be closer to my house than I think, but I can't be sure from this side of the mountain."

"Maybe your husband deliberately laid out a hard path, thinking no one would ever understand where he was sending them, a way to make it even harder to find his gold. A way that would lead into the heart of a hostile Indian village."

"But he left this map where I'd find it. It wasn't easy to find, but it wasn't impossible either. That would mean Sidney wanted me to never find the gold, and if I did, he'd put me in danger." Unfortunately that did sound like her husband, the sneak.

"It's possible that if we went up over that rim and across that high valley and over the other side..." Tom fell silent studying the mountain. "That stupid Gray Tower might be an easy ride from where the treasure is hidden."

Mandy's temper flared. "And that explains how my husband could get on a train, ride all the way to Denver, come home with his gold, and never let anyone see where he'd gotten it. Because he probably went up to get the gold before he even left for Denver. Sidney always was too suspicious and sly for an honest man."

"So do we walk in and try to deal honorably and directly with the Flatheads? Or do we turn weasel and try to sneak past them?" Tom turned to her, and in the fading light their eyes met and held as they weighed the possibilities.

"I think we'd better sneak."

With a smile, Tom said, "Me, too."

"And the best sneaking goes on at night."

"And there's no sense waiting for the next night when we've got a perfectly good one right here." Tom nodded. "Let's get on with it."

"This train is crawling!" Clay wanted to jump out of the

slow-moving train with his horse and storm the Rockies.

"You know we're making better time this way." Sophie rubbed his shoulders.

Beth sat across from him. Alex was down one seat with one baby on his lap and the other stretched out on the seat.

Clay couldn't believe they were taking two little children to a gunfight.

Both women were in a fury from Mandy's telegraph, but they were holding it inside. Clay struggled to be as strong.

"She's married?" Clay couldn't believe it. Finally he'd gotten up the gumption to go fetch his daughter home, and before he could get there, the girl got herself hitched to someone else who lived half a country away from him.

"Tom Linscott." Beth said what they all knew. "So she's in a little town called Divide. We can travel on the train all the way to town."

"Slow, slow way to travel."

The train labored up a grade. Clay could have gone faster on foot. "A horse can run faster than a train." He knew he was just on edge. This was the fastest way to get there. But sitting in comfort while Mandy was in danger made him crazy. If he'd been on a galloping horse, at least he'd have felt like he was doing something.

"But it can't run for as long." Sophie's hand rubbed harder on his shoulders. "If we'd had a string of horses and kept changing saddles, we might have been able to beat the train, but probably not if we ran into rain or outlaws or one of the horses came up lame or threw a shoe. It all slows things down. The train goes slow but steady."

The rubbing changed until she was almost beating on him. He looked sideways and saw that his wife was on the brink of snapping, just like him.

The train went around a curve ahead, and for a while he could see all ten cars. There hadn't been a car to sleep in, so he and the family had been sitting up for days.

Clay knew he wasn't making anything easier with his ranting. "I'm going to check on the horses again. Make sure they're holding up."

"You're just back from checking them, Pa." Beth gave him a level look that almost settled him down. The kind of look a young woman might give to her misbehaving children.

He couldn't stand it. "Then I'll go for a walk. I need to move, or I'm going to get my horse and jump off the train and ride." He erupted to his feet and stormed toward the front of the train. He hadn't been up there, preferring to stay close to his horses. As he neared the door that would let him outside, between the cars, it slammed open, and he stepped back, thinking to let some other impatient person go through.

An old man with lines cut deep in his face stepped in. He looked cranky and irritated and about ready to jump off the train right along with Clay. The only thing noticeable about the scowling old coot was the slash of pure white in a head of hair that was turning gray.

The old man looked up, and his eyes locked on Clay's, and they stayed there, direct and defiant, like he was looking for trouble.

Mandy set a blistering pace on the treasure hunt.

She glanced behind her in the shrouded night woods and saw with satisfaction that Tom was keeping up. It might have been shadows cast from a full moon, but she thought he had a look on his face just as determined as hers.

He didn't want the gold. He wasn't a man to search for treasure. He expected to work for his keep. But Tom knew this was important to her. He might even agree with her that a staggering price on the head of every member of this family of feud-loving coyotes could end this almost instantly.

She looked back at the nearly invisible trail she'd found heading for the far north end of the valley. Her map told her the gold was at the end of this trail.

Trees surrounded them, and she often was forced to slow to a walk as the trail grew steep until they were going up as much as forward. The moon was full, and that helped, but mostly she trusted to her horse to pick his way along the rocky landscape.

What critter had created this trail anyway? Mandy suspected it was a herd of mountain goats. But Tom's horses were game and strong and surefooted.

They scrambled along on the climb until suddenly the forest thinned. The trees were shorter and farther apart. Mandy saw the increasingly gnarled limbs as they moved onward, upward. They must be nearing the tree line. Seconds after she realized it, the sky opened up above her. The moon was so bright she couldn't see many stars, but there were a few, enough to tell her she was on the right trail.

She pulled her horse to a slow walk and continued forward. When she finally saw a clearing ahead, she pulled to a stop. The land became impossibly rugged. It was more rock than grass and sloped steeply upward within a few feet of the trees ending. The mountain goats might have been able to scale it, but no thoroughbred was going to.

Tom came up beside her. "We walk from here?"

Nodding, Mandy dismounted. "There's grass. The horses won't mind standing for a few hours."

"Let's see that map one more time before we go. Sidney's got it marked that he's hidden his stash on this end of the valley, right?"

Mandy secured her horse while Tom did the same. Then they mulled over their next step.

"We'll be exposed for a while once we walk out of these trees." Mandy looked at Tom and considered, not for the first time, that getting mixed up with her might be the death of him.

"Yep. I don't see any sign of Flatheads around here, and most

Indians don't hunt at night. I think. Besides, why hunt in this steep woods when there are better places to the south?"

Pointing to the land above the tree line, Mandy said, "We're going to have our hands full getting up there and over the rim. Sidney's map says it's possible."

"Your husband drew this map long after he'd found that gold. You know that, right, Mandy honey?"

"I know. He must have found the gold coming into that valley from the north. Then he scouted a trail to the south to create the map, just to keep anyone who found the map confused. Then he used the night sky as his guide. None of that made sense to me from our house. But once I studied the night sky from where we slept out the night of our wedding, it was easy to follow."

"So, you weren't really fascinated by the stars in the night like you said at first. You were trying to understand the stars well enough to find the gold." Tom studied the land, as Mandy did, making sure the coast was clear before they stepped out of the scrub pines. He looked around until their eyes met. "You wanted that gold almost as badly as Sidney did."

She hated to admit to anything that compared her to her deceased husband. "Not for the same reason, though. I always saw that gold as a way to buy freedom and safety for my children."

"Hired killers? Bodyguards?"

"Bounties, Tom. I'm going to put bounties on the white-thatched head of every Cooter I can find who's related to this bunch."

"You said that before you'd give a reward for their capture. But you've got to prove they're wanted. It's not enough for you to say a few of them pestered you and you want them all in jail."

"I know. But I think I could make things hot enough for them that they'd back off. I can definitely get the sheriff and Marshal Coltrain to name Cord as a wanted man. And they found that one Wanted poster."

"But that was for Fergus, and he's already locked up."

873

"We might find a few others that qualify. I can pay some people to look into it more carefully than the sheriff can. And I can raise those rewards then put out the word that anyone who bothers me can expect the same treatment, even after my death if need be. I can set a reward so high the whole Cooter clan will go away and stay away."

"It's not a bad plan." Tom looked around again. "I've got some money these days. We could probably make your plan work with the cash I have on hand."

Which was just Tom saying one more time she should trust him to protect her. "You'd break the ranch doing it, Tom. After all your years of hard work, marrying me might ruin everything you've built."

"We could make it work, Mandy. We don't need to sneak into a valley full of very smart, possibly hostile Flathead Indians in hopes of finding a treasure."

"It's got to be huge, Tom. If it isn't, it'll just make the Cooters mad and drive them to come at me even harder." Mandy took a deep breath and stared at her husband.

"Last chance, Mandy girl. Let's go home. Let's fight this out, use the law, do it right."

She knew he was right, but she wasn't turning back. "I'm going. If you don't want to, I'll understand. I won't think less of you if you—"

"Just go then. Don't insult me by telling me to leave."

Nodding, Mandy turned.

Protect me, Lord. Protect Tom.

She stepped into the clearing and almost immediately found herself scaling instead of walking. Her husband grumbled behind her, but she noticed he kept coming after her. That seemed like a real nice quality in a husband.

Tom had a new respect for mountain goats by the time he'd

gotten to the rim of this canyon. And he'd respected 'em quite a bit before.

The sun was casting the first bit of color across the sky to the east but it was still dark enough. He grabbed Mandy's ankle, which was just an arm's reach over his head. "If that map is right, the gold ought to be just a few hundred yards ahead. We can get in there, grab the gold, and get out before the sun has risen fully."

She jerked against his hold, but when he didn't turn loose, she glared down at him. "I heard you. I agree. Now let go."

His throat went dry. "I should have talked to Abby first, asked her what to expect. She might have been willing to try and talk to the Flathead. She speaks their language and knows how they think."

'Too late now." Mandy, his stubborn-to-the-bone wife, went over that rim like she was a goat herself.

Scowling, Tom followed the she-goat into the valley of the Flatheads. When he wriggled over the rim, he found the going easier. Steep but not straight up and down like the outside of the bowl-shaped valley.

Tom couldn't see much—the rising sun wasn't up high enough to penetrate this highlands. Good, less chance of being seen. He heard water running nearby and caught a glimpse of a spate, silver in the darkness, gushing out of a rock.

"The map said there'd be a spring." Mandy kept moving.

His wife was slithering down the slope, so Tom tried to catch up and keep a sharp eye out for trouble at the same time. Though she was moving with reckless speed, he had no doubt his wife was being careful. There was just no denying that Mandy was a wily one. He'd learned she could be fast and cautious at the same time with no trouble at all.

Tom saw no sign of life. He couldn't make out too much, but there didn't seem to be a tree line inside this valley. The moonlight helped, but mostly the terrain was shrouded in darkness. He scampered down and down, afraid he'd lose his wife. She had the map after all. So, he stuck with her.

The land leveled a bit. Not real level of course—there seemed to be nothing purely level in the whole state of Montana—but better.

Tom was able to walk upright, hurrying to find that stupid treasure and get out of here before the light revealed them to a tribe of bloodthirsty Indians.

Honesty forced Tom to admit that his sister, on the rare occasion she spoke of her years with them, had always talked of the Flatheads as a gentle people. But then she'd known them as an orphaned child. Tom really didn't want to count on them being all that friendly to him.

Mandy stopped so suddenly that Tom ran straight into her. He had to get the woman some clothes that weren't gray. It was like trying to keep track of a wild cat in the dark. He wondered if her eyes would glow if he carried a lantern.

Tom caught her so he didn't knock her flat on the ground, and she hissed—another cat-like attribute. "This is the spot." She waved the map in his face and pointed at a triangular rock jutting out just to one side of that spring. "That's got to be the stone from this map."

Tom realized his wife, the sharpshooter, had eyes like an owl by night and an eagle by day. If he managed to survive marriage to her, she was going to be handy to have around.

Dropping to her knees, Mandy began pulling at a small pile of stones stacked at the base of that triangular rock. Tom hadn't paid that much attention to the map, not the details. He'd never figured to get this close. But now he pitched in, pulling at stones sized from about even with his fist to bigger than his head. They weren't stacked in here in a natural way. It was clear that they'd been moved in to bury something. He felt a little hum in his veins thinking about finding a fortune in gold.

Gold fever, was it possible he might be catching it? He almost hoped so. Then he could blame madness on being here treasure hunting. Better to be crazy than to think rationally that this was a good idea.

They dug industriously for long minutes, the silence broken only by the tumble of stones. They cleared the rocks and found sand. Scooping with bare hands, they dug faster. Dirt kicked up. Sand flew. Tom's hands were coated with dust and gravel.

He took a quick look at his wife and saw that she must have touched her nose because her face was streaked with dirt. He reckoned his was, too. He went back to digging.

Mandy froze. "I found something."

She turned to Tom, and he realized he could see her clearly. The sun wasn't over the canyon rim, but it was pushing back the dark. Indians weren't famous for sleeping the daylight hours away. They had to get out of here.

She tugged and Tom's hand brushed against heavy leather coated with dirt and sand. She pulled hard, and for a long moment everything was frozen—the bag, Mandy leaning backward, even the dirt seemed to stop to catch its breath. Then it gave all at once with a *whoosh* of exploding sand and dirt.

Mandy flew backward. Tom snagged her in midair, or she'd have fallen into the stream that rushed away from that spring.

She sat down hard and began swiping at the dirt on what looked like ancient saddlebags. She uncovered a symbol of some kind. Her fingers ran along an indentation, looked for the edge of the battered leather. What looked like a crest appeared, with a helmet of some kind engraved above the crest.

Tom would have liked to see it better, but in the dim light there wasn't much detail visible, even without dirt.

Tom saw her hands slide under a flap on the edge of the bag. When she went to lift it, a knotted strip of leather held it in place. She fumbled with the leather thong that tied it shut.

Tom rested one big hand on hers. "Leave that until later. We need to get away from here."

Mandy smiled at him. "You're right."

He planted a kiss on her dirty face. "Are you sure there isn't anything left in that hole?"

They both dug, but the ground turned to solid rock just inches below where they'd unearthed the bag.

"There's nothing else." Mandy swiped at her forehead.

Tom saw her leave a damp trail of dirt and knew she was sweating. But though they'd been working hard, it was a cool mountain morning. The sweat came from tension more than labor.

"Sidney buried it here, probably moved it here from wherever he found it."

Nodding, Tom said, "Let's get out of here."

Mandy lifted the heavy saddlebags.

Tom heard a dull sound from the inside like something hard rattling. Gold. His heart sped up as his wife lifted the treasure.

"The solution to all my problems is in this saddlebag."

"Gold don't usually fix what's wrong with our lives, Mandy honey."

"This gold will. I just know it." Rising to her feet, she smiled. "Now I've got enough money to buy some safety, some peace, some happiness.

The sharp crack of a gun being cocked stopped them in their tracks.

Nineteen

Luther rode hard for Divide, trusting that the Cooters were busy tracking Mandy and weren't looking for him these days. It was a hard ride through about the worst that this rugged land had to throw at a man, but Luther was used to it. His horse was game, and his cause was life and death.

He pulled into the streets of the dusty little frontier town just as the sun lowered behind the towering mountains to the west. Following the instructions in Mandy's wire, he rode straight to the sheriff's office.

A stout man with knowing eyes looked up when Luther shoved open the door.

Those eyes went straight to Luther's six-gun. "You huntin' trouble, mister?"

"Nope. Not with you anyway. I'm hunting a man named Tom Linscott, and more important his wife."

The sheriff rose slowly from where he sat behind a scarred wooden desk. "Your name Cooter by any chance?"

Luther relaxed. The sheriff was clearly well informed. "Nope.

But Mandy sent me a telegraph saying she'd moved here and was ready to accept some help from an old friend. So, I came a runnin'. My name's Luther."

Sinking back into his chair, the sheriff nodded at coffee steaming on a potbellied stove that was casting off unneeded heat in the summer evening. "I'm Merl Dean. Pour yourself a cup. Tom and his new wife have told me their story, and I've been doing what I can to see the Cooters brought to justice. Pull up a chair, and let's talk about what's to be done."

The door slammed open just as Luther reached for a tin cup. Luther had his hand on his Colt as he whirled to face whoever had crashed in. Then he laughed out loud. "Sally!"

He charged for one of his favorite people in the world and hoisted Sally. . .McKenzie up in the air. It was hard to get used to her new name.

"Luther, you're here. Where's Mandy?" Sally's arms wrapped around his neck. He remembered when she was just a little thing, no bigger'n a sprite, tormenting him with her chattering and tagging along, determined to out-cowboy all the cowboys.

"I'm just in the door, looking to find her. She told me to come to the sheriff's office and he'd fill me in." Luther set her down and grinned, then looked past her, and his smile faded at the sight of her husband.

Logan McKenzie. Strange man. Strange business painting for a living. Not a man's way to earn his living, to Luther's way of thinking.

Logan did make a living, though. And the wandering seemed to suit Sally. Not like the way everything Sidney Gray did annoyed Mandy.

"We'll ride out to her place together." Sally smiled then jabbed her thumb behind her. "Buff and Wise Sister are with us. They're stabling the horses for the night."

"How far have you travelled?" Luther thought his girl looked tired, and Sally was a hearty little lady.

"We're riding in from Yellowstone." Sally quit grinning. "I got such an itch to see Mandy and drag her off that mountaintop she lives in that I couldn't stand it. It hit me one morning so hard I couldn't stay still. I'm going to ride in there and drag her and her youngsters out of there."

"Mandy left that fool house Sid built, and she's married." Luther pulled the wire out of his shirt pocket.

"Married?" Sally gasped. Her eyes narrowed. "God have mercy."

Luther didn't blame the girl a bit. Mandy would have done better to let someone else pick her next husband. She'd shown no talent for it.

"Yep, and living here in Divide." Luther handed over Mandy's brief message then turned back to the lawman. "'Is'zat right, Sheriff?"

"Come on in and I'll tell you everything I know." The sheriff waved a weary hand. "We've got two men under arrest and one dead after a run-in with your sister and Tom Linscott."

"What?" Sally looked at the empty jail cell.

"They're over at the doc's, but they're expected to pull through . . .eventually."

"That sounds like my big sister." Sally wouldn't have minded a crack at those outlaws herself. She might just go ask them a few questions later. "Tell us what's going on."

Buff came in before they could get settled, with Wise Sister at his side.

Luther was happy for his old friend to have found a wife, but he missed him something fierce. It had been okay when Luther'd been around Mandy and had someone in his life. But since he'd gotten shot and Mandy had told him to stay away, Luther had hurt with the loneliness.

The two exchanged a hearty handshake and very few words; then they turned to have it out with the sheriff. "So where's Linscott live?"

"His ranch isn't too far out of town, but he and his new wife are gone."

"Gone?" Luther had to fight to keep from growling like a rabid wolf. "Gone where?"

"Just this morning they hit the trail east for Denver. They'll be—"

"We came on the main trail from the east," Sally interrupted. "We'd have met them if they were heading for Denver on horseback."

Luther looked from the surprised sheriff to Sally to Buff. "Did you see anyone on that trail who looked like one of the Cooters?"

"No, the trail was plumb empty." Sally pulled off her gloves, and Luther noticed in passing that his girl was dressed like a cowboy. She'd given a lot of that up after she'd married, but it appeared she hadn't given it up completely.

He'd have smiled if he hadn't been so worried. "Well, if there weren't any Cooters, then they can't be in too bad of trouble."

Mandy had her rifle aimed and pointed, her finger on the hair-trigger, before she'd seen who it was. A dozen grim, black-eyed Flathead warriors, half armed with steadily aimed guns, the rest with tomahawks and knives. All primed for trouble.

Ice cold all the way to her soul, she eased her hand slowly, carefully away from the Winchester.

God, protect me. Protect Tom.

Mandy risked a glance at Tom. He was raising his hands in a slow, steady way so as to not startle anyone.

The warrior in the center spoke something Mandy couldn't begin to understand.

Tom said some guttural words that were similar in tone to the words she'd learned trying to communicate with the Shoshone who lived around her home. None of those tones shaped themselves to being a word Mandy could recognize.

The warrior pointed his rifle at the saddlebags that had fallen at Mandy's feet.

Tom moved so slow he'd've lost a race with molasses in a blizzard, crouching, an inch at a time, to fetch the saddlebags.

"No!" Mandy couldn't lose that gold.

Every brave raised a weapon. They aimed evenly between her and Tom as if they'd planned well beforehand, given out the responsibility of who to take aim at.

Had they been watching them ever since they'd ridden into the valley? Or ever since they'd entered their hunting grounds outside this mountain canyon? After a year living surrounded by those sharp-eyed Shoshone, Mandy was ashamed of herself for underestimating any native folks.

"No help for it, Mandy girl. I've got to let them have it."

A thousand words crowded to get out of Mandy's mouth; any one of them could get Tom killed. And that was just why she'd resisted marrying him.

"If we make them real happy, they might let us out of here with our hair."

Her throat had gone bone dry, which helped her keep quiet.

Tom eased forward, the saddlebags dangling from his fingertips.

Giving it all away. All her hopes. In that second of crushing despair, Mandy knew she was a fool to put her hopes on gold, just as Sidney had been.

When had that started? She'd gotten Sidney's map and recognized the markings as from the sky. But the sky didn't make sense.

She'd watched the sky and dreamed of finding her way to that gold. But she'd also learned a lot about how beautiful the sky was, how powerful God was to create it all. She'd learned humility as she thought of the One who'd set it in motion and made such a beautiful world work.

She'd learned from her watching and from what she'd read

in Sidney's books that the stars changed through the night and through the year. She'd hoped that the day would come when her map made sense and she might find her way to the gold and safety. But that hope had been vague as long as the sky didn't fit the map and there was no way out of her prison.

The Flathead brave nearest to Tom moved forward just as slowly as Tom until he reached the saddlebag and lifted it away. The brave fell back quickly, focusing on the bag. The rest of the tribe kept their attention strictly on Tom and Mandy.

Mandy was frigid inside, her senses registering every sound and smell and movement. She rubbed the little callus on her finger and knew, with cold, hard logic, that she couldn't win with all these guns. She was glad she had no possible chance of going for her rifle. She and Tom were the intruders here. To open fire on these men, who were just guarding their home, would be an awful thing to live with. Even knowing that, Mandy felt that cold, that sleet where her blood should be flowing in her veins.

She wondered, in the detached way of her chilled heart, if she saw an opening, a chance, would she grab her rifle and open fire? She hated knowing it might be beyond her control.

The warrior holding the saddlebag backed until he was at the brink of the stream cut by the gushing spring. He took his knife, so sharp it gleamed in the early morning light, and slashed through the leather thong that held it closed. He flipped open the saddlebag and pulled the mouth of it wide. Leaning down the man grunted, a sound of confusion.

Mandy had expected a gasp of pleasure at the sight of all that gold. But maybe Indians were too sensible to care about a golden rock.

A few harsh-sounding words drew two more warriors away from Mandy and Tom. Mandy glanced at Tom to see if he was considering that now, at about nine to two, this was a fight he'd buy into. A hard single shake of his head told her not to go for her rifle. Her fingers itched. Her blood ran cold, but she knew he was right, and she held off.

Suddenly the three men studying the contents of the saddle-bag laughed, and the one who was the leader lifted the bag high in the air.

The gold, they'd realized what it was. They'd realized how their lives could be changed with this wealth. Mandy felt sick to think of how close she'd come to possessing it. And what a fool she'd been to think money could solve her problems.

A quick, guttural statement by the Flathead leader brought a smile to the face of nearly every man there. Then the man stretched his lifted hand to the side and stretched his arm wide until he held the bag over the fast-moving stream. And he poured.

"No!" Mandy jumped.

Tom grabbed her around the waist as she saw. . .dirt.

Dirt and stone and nothing else poured out and splashed and was swept away.

"Where's the gold?" She couldn't tear her eyes away, willing it to turn gold.

The drab gray and brown poured, dropping into the water.

Mandy held her breath, waiting, waiting, waiting for that moment when the stones and dirt would sparkle, when whatever was on top of the gold finished falling out and the gold coins followed, lost forever in that deep, rushing water.

The gold never came. The dirt and rocks quit pouring. The bag was empty.

"Nothing." Tom was behind her, his arm clamped around her waist. It wasn't lost on Mandy that the way he held her pinned her rifle to her back. She couldn't get it into action. She knew Tom well. His grip was no accident.

The leader finally tossed the now flat leather bag aside and turned to Mandy and Tom. Somehow Tom moved so he tucked Mandy behind him. She noticed he'd left her the rifle.

Harsh, cutting words came from Tom. They were returned at about double the speed by the warrior. Back and forth the two men talked. Tension built. The other Flathead men kept their black, angry eyes on Tom. Their tomahawks and knives and guns at the ready.

The cold grew and spread in Mandy's body, swallowing up her limbs, her heart, the breath in her lungs. She wondered if the cold was of the devil and would soon swallow up her soul.

Suddenly the warriors lowered their weapons. A few more harsh words were traded between Tom and their leader. Then Tom reached his hand back, as if to corral Mandy, and began easing up the hill, the way they'd come.

"Tom, what—"

"Quiet," he cut her off. "Move."

Mandy shut her mouth and moved.

One step at a time. The Flatheads no longer had their weapons aimed, but neither did they take their eyes off their white visitors.

"Go ahead of me." Tom's voice was low, barely audible to Mandy. "Climb. Hurry."

Mandy had to quit staring at the men to watch where she was going. She began climbing in earnest. Faster, running away from danger. Leaving behind her dream of safety bought with gold.

She crested the steep edge of the mountain valley, and as she topped it and began descending she took one long second look back and saw what remained.

Nothing. The warriors had vanished as if they'd never been. All that was left was the spent, flattened saddlebag with the odd, ancient crest. "Sidney's gold. Where is it?"

"It's gone, Mandy girl."

"Gone where? We have to find it!"

"No, not gone, like it's been moved. Gone, like spent."

"Spent by who?"

"By your husband. I did my best to talk with those men, and they say no one's been in here since they took over this valley. They're sure of it. They know their land well. That means Sidney hasn't been in here for the gold in years. He may have come the

886

first few years to get a bit more when he needed it, but building that house must have taken it all."

Mandy thought of her mansion. She could imagine that it had drained a Spanish treasure chest to construct it.

They hurried, dropping lower and lower in the full morning light now that they were on the east side of the canyon. Their feet skidded on the stony ground, kicking up dust that permeated the cool morning air.

"Then why leave the map?" Mandy glanced behind her, able to stand mostly upright as they reached slightly more level ground.

"Maybe he never intended you to find it. Maybe he made that map strictly for himself." They had only a few dozen yards to go to reach the tree line and their horses, and then ride like the wind to put space between themselves and those Flatheads.

"But we decided he deliberately marked the map to confuse me." Mandy wanted to get her hands on Sidney and shake him until he wasn't worthless.

"It made sense if he left that map for you." The land became smoother. They rushed for the trees. Tom's hand rested on the small of her back. "But I think he must've drawn it earlier. He'd have wanted to be very careful not to lose track of it."

"But why draw it so it led out of the valley to the east when he came in from the west?" Mandy could almost feel those Flatheads back there, changing their minds, getting worked up and deciding they should never have let people intrude on their land without paying a price.

"Just being sneaky I reckon." They reached the tree line, the first scrubby pines that barely reached waist high.

"He drew the map so he could understand it and no one else." Mandy brushed hard against one stumpy tree as she rushed past. It scratched her hand and filled the air with the scent of pine.

"Makes sense. Anyone might find a streak of weasel in his soul if he'd found a treasure trove. You wouldn't want anyone finding it."

"Including me?" Mandy asked bitterly. The trees grew taller, head high. Mandy could almost breathe again.

"I doubt he created that map intending to cause trouble for you. I doubt he intended to die." Tom steered Mandy with his pressuring hand and guided them straight to where they'd tied their horses, hours ago in the pitch dark.

Mandy thought with cold satisfaction that if Sidney had tied those horses there, he'd have never found them again, the big dope. The big gold-wasting dope.

Mandy unlashed her horse from the scrub pine where it had been quietly grazing. She looked over the back of the magnificent black, into the eyes of her magnificent husband. He caught the pommel to swing himself up, but his eyes met hers, and he stopped. Between them something stretched, as if he'd lassoed her and now stood, a tough cowpony that had her completely bound to him.

A smile crept across her face as she thought of it.

"What? Something funny happen in that valley? You lost your gold. You lost your chance of buying your way out of Cooter trouble. You almost lost your scalp."

"It's not funny, but it does occur to me that I found something in there, too." Mandy wanted to be away from here, but she didn't know where to go. Back to Tom's? To Belle Harden's to get her children and bring them into the path of danger? Where in the world could she find safety?

"Nope, all you did was lose."

Shaking her head, Mandy quietly said, "I found you, Tom."

"I wasn't lost."

"I found a man who stood between me and danger."

"I've done that before a couple of times."

"A man who's going to stick even though there's no gold."

"Gettin' that gold was always a hare-brained idea."

Mandy's smile stretched. "I found a man I can respect. A man to ride the river with."

Tom's disgruntled eyes softened, warmed, heated.

"A man to love."

"You're just figuring out now that you love me?" Tom shook his head in disgust. "I knew that five years ago."

"So did I, but it wasn't something I could admit, or even let myself think."

"Nothin' stopping you now."

"Not a single thing."

If Tom would have moved, Mandy would have gone to him and let him wrap her in his arms. But a big part of why she loved him was that he had too much sense to take time for kissing and hugging when they were within spitting distance of a tribe of irritated Flatheads.

Tom swung up on his horse instead of rounding it to drag her into his arms. That made her love him even more. "Let's go home, wife."

"Home or to get the children?"

Tom picked up his reins, then frowned and turned to her as Mandy mounted up. The gaze between them held. Mandy knew he was thinking, just as she was, weighing the danger.

Finally, reluctantly, he said, "I think we need to get them and bring them home."

"The Cooters will keep coming." But Mandy was in agreement. They needed to start as they meant to go on. She was sick of hiding.

"And you need to trust me to protect you."

"You've seen me shoot, Tom. You know I'm not used to relying on anyone to protect me."

"My delicate lady wife don't need much help, and that's a fact." A smile bloomed on Tom's face. "But I'll see if I can make myself of some use."

"I 'spect you'll be right handy to have around." Mandy smiled back.

"For now, I reckon we've thinned 'em out and backed 'em

up a few steps. Maybe we can have a few good days before they show up."

Nodding, Mandy said, "Then let's get the children and go home."

Twenty

I'll take a watch, Miz Harden." Mark was sorely tempted to call her ma just to see if he could do it and walk away with his head still on his shoulders. He always had liked taking a risk.

She had to know he was sweet on Emma, and yet he was still allowed to live. It was probably because of the babies.

Belle turned, scowling, to face him. Her arms crossed, her jaw a hard line.

He sat on the ground, behind her cabin, with the boy on his lap, eyelids heavy in the afternoon sun.

Angela was busy strangling Mark from behind. Catherine talked his ear off and tugged on his hair.

Mark was kicking himself for not getting it cut recently.

Even Tanner had taken to hanging on him and was trying to yank off one of Mark's boots. Betsy, with her black eyes and riotous black curls, sat in the dirt beside him making faces at Angela as if she were encouraging the girl to torment Mark.

Why wouldn't Tanner and Betsy hang around? Mark had possession of all the Harden children's best playmates.

It didn't really make sense that Mandy's young'uns had taken such a liking to Mark, except that he'd felt such a powerful need to protect Mandy and that stretched to include her children. They must be able to tell his concern for them was real and deep.

Emma had just gone inside carrying her baby brother. They had a good chance of getting Jarrod to sleep, too. Then Emma said the rest of them would have cookies. Before that she'd been out here with him while they cared for the six best chaperones God had ever put on this earth.

"You plannin' to take all the children with you to the lookout?" Belle asked with cold contempt.

Seven best chaperones.

Now was the time to point out that he really was indispensible because of how attached the children had gotten to him. Except he feared that *indispensible* wasn't a word Belle Harden used when it came to menfolk. . .at least not when they were sparking her daughter.

"I reckon they'd be fine here with you and Sarah and. . . Emma." He had a hard time saying Emma's name right into the cranky face of his future mother-in-law. As if five children weren't enough, Belle had been a better chaperone than an army of Catholic nuns. He hadn't gotten a chance to steal a single kiss. A shame because he had a strong sense that Emma would go along nicely with the plan. She hadn't forked a horse to check the herd since Mark had arrived. He understood that to be out of the usual way of things.

"Just stay put. We're handling the lookout just fine without you."

"Miz Harden." Mark swallowed hard, hopeful Belle would hesitate to kill him in the presence of small children.

"What?" Her voice was so hard it landed on Mark like a rock.

"I want you to know I—I—" Mark fell silent. There really was nothing he could say that would ever make Belle like him. "As you know, I have asked to call on Emma."

"I believe I have some vague memory of that." That hard voice was turning into an avalanche rather than one lone rock.

"I have only the most honorable intentions for your daughter, ma'am. She's as fine a woman as—"

"She's too young."

"How old would you say is old enough?" Mark heard that tone he sometimes got that riled up schoolteachers and made men narrow their eyes at him. It was left over from the antics of his childhood. He was a sober, thoughtful man now.

"You want to stay on this ranch, you watch your mouth." Belle didn't like one bit of sass unless it came from herself. Mark made a note of that for the future.

"I'll wait until whatever age you say is old enough, ma'am." Mark had no intention of waiting. In fact, he fully planned to be living in a house with Emma as his wife before the snow fell. And it was getting on toward the end of August already. It didn't make him a genius to refrain from being fully honest about *that* part of his honorable intentions.

He hoped he and Emma didn't have to run off and get married. Would Emma protect him against her own ma?

Emma came out of the house without the baby. Mark had yet to see the day all of these tykes decided it was nap time at the same minute.

And Belle never slept.

Emma came over and crouched beside him and reached for Jarrod, dozing despite the rambunctious children surrounding him. "Let me get him settled."

Mark looked up into those blue eyes and was lost in the notion of Emma coming to lift a child out of his arms. Soon it would be their child.

Then his eyes went past Emma's pretty face and reaching arms to see Belle, her jaw so tight it was a wonder her teeth hadn't been worn down to nubs.

A spark of defiance flared to a flame Mark couldn't quite

control. "Emma, when do you think you'll be old enough to consider taking a husband?"

Emma froze. Her eyes wide. Her reaching hands not coming a bit closer. He saw her throat work as if she were gulping down something she hadn't meant to. "I—I reckon I'm a woman grown now, Mark." Those frozen eyes thawed.

From behind Emma, Mark heard a noise similar to one he'd once heard from a mountain lion that he'd startled. Part snarl, part scream, all terrifying.

A hard hand landed on Emma's shoulder and pulled her to her feet. Belle stepped between Mark and Emma.

Mark struggled to get to his feet, without stomping on Tanner or knocking any child to the ground.

"I told you she's too young, Mark Reeves. You do your talking to me, not Emma."

Emma came around Belle and hoisted Tanner into her arms. She thrust the boy at Belle. Then Emma tore Angela off Mark's back. That left Catherine yammering around Mark's knees and Jarrod asleep in his arms and Betsy jumping at his side.

Very deliberately, Emma stepped closer to Mark and faced her mother. "You've always told us we're not to let anyone force us into marriage, Ma."

"I'm not going to force you—"

Emma grabbed Mark's forearm and sank her fingernails in so hard Mark shut up to keep from yelling in pain.

"But I don't think I'd let anyone force me into *not* getting married either. You raised me to be strong enough to take care of myself, and that includes making decisions for myself."

"Not about this. Not when this polecat is acting as if he's such a good caretaker of children. He's doing it to charm you, Emma."

"I am not. I—ow!" Mark closed his mouth before he ended up with scars on his arm.

"He's taking care of these children because Mandy is an old friend of his family, from back in Texas."

Belle's dark eyes slid from Emma to Mark. "First I've heard of that."

Mark glanced at Emma to see if she was going to let him talk. Her nails retreated from his skin a bit, so he took that as a good sign.

"I didn't speak of it at first. Tom Linscott and everyone with him saw that we knew each other. I didn't hide that. But I didn't tell about where we'd met. I wasn't sure how Mandy had ended up there on that mountaintop, with the name of Lady Gray. When I saw her—" Mark looked at Emma. He'd already told her that Mandy was important to him, but not in the way Emma was. He hoped Emma knew that.

He hoped Belle did, too.

"I just—I hadn't seen anyone from home—" Mark thought of how hard it had hit him, to see all the trouble that had landed on his old rival. How it made him feel when she launched herself into his arms and started crying.

"Mandy and Tom had to send the children to safety. I couldn't help Mandy. Tom was doing that." Mark's throat ached at how badly he'd wished he could do more for Mandy.

"But the children needed someone. I think they can tell I care about—" Mark's voice broke. Horrified, he quit talking and crouched down and got real busy gathering Catherine into his arms, keeping his head down, and taking far too long to shift Jarrod to one side. His pa would be shocked. His brothers would torment him forever. A man didn't *cry*.

Emma's hand on his arm slid away as he crouched. He got the burning of his eyes under control, and the embarrassment of it all eased the thickness of his throat, but now his cheeks burned as if he'd turned ten shades of red.

This was *not* how he'd planned to court Emma, by arguing with her ma and showing himself to be a weakling in her presence. He squared his shoulder, braced for the sneer he'd see on Belle's face and the disdain on Emma's.

He looked at Belle first because he couldn't help himself and saw. . .kindness.

He almost dropped Catherine.

"Let me take Jarrod." Belle relieved Mark of one of his burdens. She now held two children in her arms without looking overly burdened. He shifted so Catherine was on his right hip.

Then he dared to look at Emma. Her eyes shined right into his, and there was only softness and sympathy.

Could crying possibly be useful in attracting women? Mark had never considered such a thing before. He wondered if he'd be able to learn to do it on command.

Emma moved Angela to her left side and rested her arm on Mark's back, not even looking at her mother and not a fingernail to be found anywhere. "I think it's wonderful that you've been so good to Mandy's children. Wonderful."

Mark wished like crazy that Belle Harden would just take these children and go away. In fact, he wished it so bad, he turned to her. "I want a private word with Emma, Miz Harden. We won't go far, and we won't go for long, but if Emma's agreeable—"

"I am."

He snuck a quick look at Emma when she said that. And liked what he saw.

Turning back to Belle, he was having a little trouble even being scared of her, which was just pure down-to-the-bone stupid. "Please."

Belle's kindness faded, but she replaced it with worry and just a hint of sadness, which made Mark feel like a worm. The woman was just trying to protect her daughter. Here Mark stood with all these children, children he'd die to protect. He could feel exactly what Belle did, only her feelings had been going on all Emma's life. His had started when he'd met these children a few days ago.

"Betsy, help me get the children inside." Jerking her head toward the cabin, she added, "Let's go get some cookies."

Angela raced for the house with Betsy on her heels. Catherine started wiggling, and Mark let her down to run for the promise of sweets.

Tanner started squirming and tugging on Belle's hand to get loose. He yelled, "I want a cookie!"

Belle let him go, which left her with a sleeping baby and a scowl. "Don't be gone long." Belle turned and stomped toward her cabin.

Mark could barely breathe as he reached out to Emma and she caught hold. There were lookouts everywhere. Mark couldn't think of anywhere he could possibly be alone with her.

Emma dragged him straight for the barn. She pulled him inside, swung the door shut, and turned.

He tried to work up the nerve to say what was in his heart.

Emma launched herself at him and wrapped her arms around his neck.

He laughed, caught her around the waist, and lifted her right off her feet. The words wanted to all get out at once, and for a moment Mark wasn't sure he'd be able to say anything. "I've homesteaded some land only a couple hours' ride from here. I'm planning on having a cabin built before the snow falls. Will you—"

"Yes!" Her smile was blinding bright.

"Marry me." Mark said the words, but he didn't need to hear more. He laughed, spun his woman around in a tight circle, then set her on her feet, lowered his head, and kissed her.

It was his first kiss. He'd have taken one a few times before, but he could never convince the girls to go along. He suspected, considering Belle's extreme watchfulness, it might be Emma's, too.

They were both fast learners.

Mark pulled away reluctantly. "I can get the cabin built fast, but it won't be much at first." He ran one hand over Emma's beautiful hair, pulled back in a no-nonsense braid that reached down to her waist. He wanted to see her hair loose. He wanted to have the right to ask her to leave it swaying around her shoulders, just for him.

"I don't want to wait until spring." He kissed her again. He desperately didn't want to wait until spring. "But what I'll have up by the time snow flies will be a humble home. We'll be able to stay warm." He had no doubt of that. "But—"

"Can we ask my pa to help build it?"

"Your pa?" That got Mark's attention. He frowned. "I don't want him to think I can't provide for you, Emma. I wouldn't ask you to marry me if I couldn't. We'll be okay."

"He helped build Lindsay's first house when she got married." Emma was a tough Montana pioneer woman, and Mark knew that. But she was acting purely female now, with a coaxing smile and her hands brushing across his neck.

He was sorely afraid he'd agree to anything. "I'd love the help, but—"

"It don't matter. I'm not sure you can stop him."

"Truth be told, I'm mainly worried about your ma." Mark could almost feel Belle Harden burning a hole in the barn with her eyes.

"She let us come in here. That means she's going to be okay. She might not ever admit it. And she might threaten to kill you from time to time, but that's just tough talk."

"Tough talk?"

"If she really gets mad, you'll never see her comin'."

Nodding, Mark slung his arm around his brand-new promised-to-be wife. "Well, let's go give her the good news. Right now. Before Mandy's young'uns figure out they don't need me and your ma can run me off her range."

Emma laughed and slid her arm around his waist. "You'd better let me do the talking."

"Don't you think your ma will judge me a coward for that?"

"Nope, I think she'll be impressed with your good sense."

Mark walked out of the barn holding on to Emma, trying to figure out just what kind of family he'd be joining. And not caring one whit, because he'd be getting Emma. As for making her ma like him, well, he'd figure that out later.

When he stepped outside, he saw Belle and Silas. Silas looked grim. Belle had her six-gun tied down.

The first thing Cord saw when he rode into town was a man with a streak of white in his hair. And he wasn't alone. He found a new passel of Cooter cousins waiting for him in Helena.

Striding up to the first man he saw with the odd hair tuft, he thrust out his hand. "You're a Cooter, aren't'cha?" He saw a small army of men standing behind this one. Not all with the family hair. Maybe time in America was breeding that out of the Cooters. Cord hoped so. He hated that hank of white.

"Yep, we're from all over the country. We've been gathering for weeks waiting to hear from someone."

Another man from the group said, "We heard a Cooter'd been gunned down, and we're here to see the killer pay."

Cord didn't want to explain the whole truth. When it had been only a single woman against the Cooter family it had been a little bit embarrassing. But now they had someone to war against. "Tom Linscott has a ranch about three or four days' ride south of here. He's just killed three more of us." Cord was pretty sure Lady Gray had killed them all. It stung bad that a woman could be so salty.

"He even got my brother Fergus, and they almost got me." Cord knew the scratches still showed on his face. He was glad they did because it helped stir up his family.

Another of the nearly two dozen men standing in the crowd pushed himself forward. "I rode with Fergus a few years back. Anyone who killed Fergus is going to pay."

Cord wasn't absolutely sure Fergus was dead. After that terrible racing panic had eased, Cord remembered that Fergus had been running away just a step behind. What had happened to his brother? Cord wasn't about to admit he'd run and left a wounded brother behind, not when he'd been the biggest talker when it came to sticking with family.

It didn't really matter, except Cord didn't want his kinfolk to find out he'd left Fergus behind. For a man crazy to stick with his kin, Cord was surprised how little he cared about his brother. They'd only met a couple of years ago. It wasn't like they'd grown up together.

Cord took in the look of the group. A shady crowd. He knew there were poor Cooters, rich ones, honest ones, and outlaws. This group looked like a poor band of outlaws for the most part. Worn clothing, battered saddles. Weary-looking horses and boots that were down-at-the-heels. Probably no-accounts. He suspected they hadn't all ridden here on a train, because the tickets were too expensive.

"We need to end this now," Cord said. He heard the grumbling of agreement. Good. "And we've got enough men that we can attack hard and fast and finish Linscott and his men all at once."

And his wife.

Again Cord kept that to himself. Cord would see to Mandy Gray personally. Even that wicked shooting iron couldn't stand up to this many men. "Let's saddle up and ride."

They headed straight for their horses, mounted up, and were galloping before they'd reached the edge of town. As his kin thundered along beside and behind him, Cord's throat swelled with pride. His family was here. Enough men to start a war. Now, with all of them thrown in with him, and that cursed land around Gray Towers not haunting them, the Cooters finally had a real chance to show the world they were a family to be reckoned with.

Cord counted down the hours until they could finally make this right. With luck, if they pushed hard, they could rain down like fire on the Linscott ranch in three days.

★ Twenty-one ★

We'll be three days getting to the Hardens if we stop for the night. We are *not* stopping."

Tom reined his horse to a stop. "Yes, we are."

"You said it's only about four more hours. We can keep going that long. And we'll be at Belle's house when the children wake up."

Tom was careful to roll his eyes before he turned to face his nagging wife. Once he was looking at her, he did his best to be real respectful of the battle-ax he'd married.

"I am not riding up this trail in the dark." He caught her reins and thought he might catch a fist in the face.

But despite her protests, her endless protests, her endless cranky protests, he was pretty certain Mandy was ready to stop for the night. It just seemed weak to her, so she was fighting it. And him. "I've ridden a lot of hard trails in my life."

For an observant woman, Mandy didn't seem to notice that he was tying her horse up, alongside his, and stripping off his saddle. He might have to strip hers off with her still sitting on top of it.

"Come on down. That trail is a killer in the full light of day. I'm not riding up it with exhausted horses and exhausted riders. We'll set out the minute the sky lightens in the morning."

Tom knotted her horse's reins tight enough she'd have to dismount to untie it. Once her feet hit the ground, he'd steal her saddle, and then he'd have her. Watching for his chance, he started building a campfire.

The growling behind him continued, but finally she got down. Ready to lunge, he was pleased to see her working the cinch loose. He went back to setting up camp, glancing up occasionally to make sure she hadn't stolen the horse and run for the upland trail. He relaxed when she took to rubbing down the black mare she was riding. He had a fire crackling before she was done.

She grabbed a small pot and filled it with spring water for coffee.

"There are talus slides on that trail." Tom wasn't opposed to talking sense to his wife. Being reasonable, explaining his actions. It just proved to be a waste of time up till now. "It winds around like the great-granddaddy of all timber rattlers. I haven't been on it in years. There are spots that cave off and drop away for a hundred feet."

"If it's so bad, we might not even be able to get through that trail into the Harden spread." Mandy set the coffee on to boil and pulled fixings for supper from her saddlebag.

"We'll get through. We might have to pick our way, lead our horses, and clear the trail in spots. We can't do all that in the dark."

She grunted but quit her nagging. Tom thought the quiet sounded like a slice of heaven. They worked quietly side-by-side setting up camp and getting supper.

"What are we going to do to keep the children safe? We should have—"

Closing his eyes in near physical pain, he knew she thought of something new to complain about. But she was upset. Tom didn't blame her.

While she fretted, they finished their quick meal. The coffee was black and hot. Tom poured them both a cup in the cool mountain night then edged back from the fire to rest his back against a nearby log. Even in August it got mighty cold at night in the mountains.

With a sigh of contentment, he took a sip of the wicked brew and sighed again when his brand-spanking-new wife sat down beside him. "I'm sorry we couldn't get there tonight, Mandy girl. You know I'm right."

Mandy grunted. Which was an improvement over the nagging. Tom thought he could handle the racket, though. He wanted a wife with her own mind.

"And I know how much you want to get to your young'uns."

Mandy took a long sip of the slowly cooling liquid then sighed deeply. "They'd be asleep when we got there anyway." She looked sideways at him.

In the flickering firelight, he was reminded of the first night he'd seen her. Well, the first night since he'd gone to drag her out of that tower she lived in. Her hair loose and white, her clothes as gray as the stones that surrounded her. The blue in her eyes washed gray by the firelight. Her eyes glittering—spooky. Beautiful.

"I'm just so crazy to get to them. I should never have—"

His lips stopped the beating she'd been giving herself all day. He pulled her coffee cup out of her hand and took that stupid rifle off her back and eased her sideways until they lay on the ground, between the log and the fire.

"Stop, Mandy. Please." He ran one hand deep into her hair. "You thought long and hard before you left them."

"No, I—"

Silence again reigned. Tom was almost starting to like her criticism of herself. Better than him. Besides, it gave him a great excuse to distract her.

When he eased away from her pretty lips, they were stretched out on the ground. "Enough. You're too smart to waste this much energy fretting about something you can't undo."

With his body blocking the fire, he couldn't see her eyes anymore. Her hair flowed like milk over her arms and chest, and he realized he'd pulled the leather thong away and let her braid loose. He caressed the silken weight and wished it were full daylight so he could read her expression better. As if she was making any secret of how she felt.

"I know. And you're right. It's been an exhausting day. If that trail's half as treacherous as you say, we'd be lucky not to kill ourselves or our horses. We have to stop. I'm sorry I've been fussing at you, Tom." She smoothed his forehead with her fingers. It was the sweetest touch he'd ever known.

He wasn't much in the mood for sweet right now.

She closed her eyes and rolled so her back was to his. "We need to get some rest and get an early start tomorrow. Good night then."

He caught her shoulder before she could get comfortable and rolled her flat on her back. "Not quite yet."

"What?"

"You've been worrying about your children, and I know they're mighty important."

"Important? Well of course they are. They're the most important things in my life."

"I suppose that's fair, but a husband ranks right up there, doesn't he?" Lowering his head, he said, "I think you need to worry about me for a little while."

He kissed her and didn't stop until she was thinking only wifely thoughts, and plenty of them.

"This doesn't worry me one bit." She slid her arms around his neck and smiled.

Laughing softly, Tom said, "Well, maybe I'm not doing it right then."

Mandy came awake slowly, feeling as if she were wrapped in comfort. Feeling safe. Strange, unfamiliar feeling. She looked skyward and remembered how the stars had almost seemed to speak aloud to her the first night she and Tom had spent in each other's arms. She'd been lying just like this.

At peace, even in the midst of the madness of her life, and the stars had hinted that there was a way to read them so Sidney's map made sense.

They weren't talking now, but then Mandy had learned what that map and those lights in the sky had to say already.

Instead she wondered how long she'd slept. Her head was fuzzy, but it wasn't heavy with exhaustion. The stars told her dawn wasn't far away. Tom was warm and solid beside her, letting her use his shoulder for a pillow.

They should get up. By the time they'd built up the fire and warmed up what was left of last night's coffee and eaten a biscuit or two, the sun would light their way.

She felt Tom stir beside her. Though she hadn't moved, she'd obviously disturbed his sleep. Or something else had disturbed them both.

Mandy listened, but nothing alerted her, and she trusted her wood-smarts.

"Let's get moving." His voice was scratchy and gruff. It stroked something deep inside her, almost an ache but not really. Too pleasant for that.

Mandy rolled up on her elbow so she looked down on her new husband. The moonlight lit his eyes. "I'm sorry I've brought trouble to you, Tom."

"Now, Mandy girl, don't start that again."

"But trouble or not, I wish now I'd come storming out of that stupid castle the minute Sidney was dead. That sounds awful and so unloving, but I wish I'd packed up the children and come running straight to you. I knew I could. I knew you'd take me in. But all I could think of was the trouble I'd bring." She knew the sun was coming close to rising because she could see the surprise and satisfaction on his face.

"I wish I'd been married to you for a year already." She leaned down and kissed him.

His arms were hard, as strong as oaks. Strong enough to protect her. Maybe her constant prayers for protection had garnered her the lightning speed with the Winchester, and now God had added a tough-as-nails husband.

"We'll get the children today." Tom stroked the hair back off her forehead. "We'll take them home and start living our life tomorrow. We'll be on guard, and the sheriff and the marshal will do their jobs. Worrying day and night about survival isn't going to be your life from now on, Mandy. We'll find a way to live in safety and as much peace as a body gets in the Rocky Mountains."

Smiling, Mandy nodded. "We will."

They were in the saddle soon after and riding out in the gray light of pre-dawn.

Before they'd ridden a hundred yards up the trail, they were stopped by a slide.

"This is awful." Mandy led her horse around the worst of it. Tom was in the lead, so he pushed rocks off a steep cliff on their left when necessary. They'd mount up and ride, then have to stop and lead their horses again. By the time they reached the top of the trail, the sun was fully up. But Mandy's nerves were strung tight from the mean, twisting trail.

"Glad we waited until we were rested?" Tom looked over his shoulder and gave her his usual "I told you so" smirk. She was almost starting to like it.

Mandy rode up beside him when the path widened enough to allow it. "I'm learning something about marriage from you, Tom."

He aimed his horse down the much more civilized slope that must lead them to the Harden ranch. The bottom of the trail was visible, and it seemed to end in a lush, grassy valley. There was no sign of a ranch house. Mandy had never been here before, but Tom seemed to know where he was going.

"What's that?"

"When you're married to a man you respect, it's a lot easier to let him lead. I know a man's supposed to be the head of the home, but with Sidney I never trusted him enough to even consider letting him take charge of much."

"You mean you built that castle?" Tom's lips quirked, so Mandy knew he was only teasing.

"Nope, that was all Sidney. But I didn't let him take care of the children. I never trusted him to find food or chop wood. Maybe he'd have done it if I'd let him get cold and hungry, but my children and I would have had to get cold and hungry, too, and I wasn't willing to trust him enough to leave it to him."

"But you might let me do important stuff?" Tom's smiled bloomed fully.

"I very definitely might."

Laughing, Tom said, "I am fully honored, Mrs. Linscott, that you might let me run my own household."

"Well, you oughta be."

Tom reached a smooth stretch of the trail with no rocks to roll beneath the horses' feet and kicked his horse into a ground-eating trot. Mandy kept up, eager to see her children. As they rode, she remembered the last time she'd felt this excited about life. It had been the day she'd married Sidney and had gotten on the stagecoach to leave Mosqueros, Texas, and start her new life with him.

And look how badly that had turned out.

"Look who's here." Mark lifted Angela off his lap and stood, turning to face Mandy and Tom. "Your ma's back."

He looked from Angie to Catherine in Emma's arms. Emma

was watching the oncoming horses. Jarrod was taking a mid-morning nap. Mandy was still a ways off, but Angela howled and reached for her mother and started crying her head off. Catherine joined in at once, though Mark didn't think the little girl knew exactly why she was crying.

"I guess I should've waited to mention it." He looked at Emma.

"I reckon." Emma had to shout to be heard over the wailing children. She rolled her eyes at him.

He smiled to think of a lifetime of Emma and her sass. "Let's walk out to meet them. Maybe if we act like we're hurrying it'll stop their crying."

"I'll tell Ma they're coming first." Emma hurried to the ranch door and was back in a trice.

The oncoming riders had goaded their horses into a gallop and were closing in so fast Mark didn't bother walking toward them. Instead he fussed over Angela, teasing her out of her tears with nonsense.

Emma reached his side with her own fretful child just as Mandy and Tom rode up.

Mandy was off the horse and running the few feet to her children before her horse had come to a full stop. Mark looked over Mandy's head to see Tom dealing with the horses. Belle came out of the house carrying a sleepy Jarrod with several more children on her heels. Mark and Emma both set their wriggling girls free to run to their mama.

Her arms full of crying children, Mandy hugged and kissed and comforted her girls. Mark heard her apologizing repeatedly.

Tom came up and said, "Got a howdy for your pa?"

Angela looked up, quit crying, and stretched out her arms. "Hi, Papa."

Tom scooped her up and tossed her into the air. The tears were forgotten as Angela giggled and Catherine yammered for a turn.

Mark whispered to Emma, "You don't think he's really their pa, do you?"

"Of course not." Emma shook her head. "Mandy's a proper, decent woman."

There wasn't a real strong sense of assurance in Emma's voice, even though Mark thought she was right. Probably.

Mandy reached for Jarrod when Belle got close enough. His legs were pumping as if he were running toward his ma, even though Belle still had him in her arms. Smiling, she handed the boy over. Then Belle gave Mandy a hug, even though the children were in their arms.

When the riot calmed down, Belle said, "Come in and sit a spell."

"We need to get back to the ranch," Mandy said.

There were tears in her eyes. Mark couldn't get past how fragile Mandy McClellen had become. It stirred him until he wanted to fight someone just to take the pressure off his gut.

He went to Mandy when Belle turned loose of her and pulled her into his arms, children and all. "Are you all right?" He pulled back so their eyes met. So much passed between them.

"You have never been nice to me a day in your life, Mark Reeves." Mandy's eyes were watering, but he saw her spunk. She was in better shape than when Tom had first brought her to his ranch.

"You didn't deserve nice. You were bossier than my parents and the teacher combined, you pointed out more of my sins than the parson ever did, and you never quit nagging me for a minute." Mark grinned.

"And you tortured perfectly nice teachers and disrupted the school, and you earned every sharp word I ever spoke."

Mark caught himself before he dropped his head and kicked at the dirt in the sullen little boy way he'd had whenever his pranks had caught up with him. Instead he stepped back and said, "I believe you said on a number of occasions that I was born to hang."

"And yet here you are walking around." Mandy's tears eased and she smiled fully. "A testimony to years of desperate prayers your mother sent heavenward."

Mark glanced behind him and saw Emma watching him with narrow eyes. He made a quick move and snaked his arm around her waist—right in front of Belle Harden—and pulled her to his side. "And now I've got another good woman with her work cut out for her."

Mandy looked from Mark to Emma. Mark noticed a faint blush on Emma's tanned skin.

"Well, since she didn't slam the butt of her six-gun into your skull, it must be true." Mandy looked at Emma, who nodded. "Emma, we've got to find a time to talk privately. I know all the best ways of punishing Mark when he's up to no good."

Emma smiled. "Have you got things straightened up? I thought you were on your way to Denver. We didn't expect you back for days and days."

Tom came up to Mandy's side and hoisted Catherine out of her arms. "We let everyone think we were heading for Denver, but that wasn't our goal. We've done what we set out to do."

Mark had no idea what that meant exactly. Tom definitely wasn't telling all he knew.

"Now we're going to go home, make sure the ranch is secure, and let the law handle the Cooter clan." Tom looked down at Mandy.

Mark thought he saw just a hint of warning in Tom's eyes, a bit like what he'd seen in Emma's. Maybe Mark had oughta quit hugging married women.

Then Tom glared at Mark. "Are you coming with me, or are you staying here with the Hardens?"

"He's going with you." Belle stepped up close. "Let's get you something hot in your stomachs. Trail food gets old after a while."

They turned to the house. Mandy and Tom walked ahead with all three children, still clinging.

"Have you talked with your family, Mandy?" Mark might be wise not to hug her, but he couldn't help wanting to protect her. "Do they know what's going on? I didn't send a letter or a wire. I wasn't sure if I should."

Mandy looked back, frowning. "Are you coming back to Tom's place?"

"*Our* place, Mandy girl," Tom said.

"Our place." Mandy smiled at Tom a private kind of smile that made Mark restless to have his very own wife.

He reached out to pull Emma close, and Belle was there. She knocked his hand aside. "Let's get inside."

"You know I'm really starting to like you, Ma." Mark braced himself to take a fist to the jaw.

Instead Belle smiled. She wiped the smile away quick but not quick enough.

"I saw that."

She scowled, and Mark didn't push his luck. He headed after Mandy and Tom. He needed to ask his boss about the cattle he had coming for pay. He needed to get on with building a house and arranging a wedding.

If he had his way, he'd get it all in order by the end of the week.

Mark saw Charlie riding in from his stint standing watch. Charlie had done his best to sneak a word or two with Sarah, but it'd been a challenge.

Silas rode alongside him, and the two were talking. Silas looked plumb depressed.

It occurred to Mark suddenly that Charlie was talking to the man of the family. Why hadn't Mark thought of that? It was the proper way, and it had the advantage of going around Belle instead of through her.

Silas swung down off his horse and handed the reins to Charlie, who started leading the animals toward the barn.

Sarah stepped to the door of the cabin. "I've got some stew heated up."

Her pretty voice drew Charlie's head around, and he stopped in his tracks.

"Let's get inside now," Belle ordered.

Silas came up to Belle and said something in a voice too low for anyone to hear.

Belle shook her head and looked horrified.

Tom and Mandy went inside along with the children.

"Sarah, come out here." Silas's voice was hard and cranky. Belle's jaw was so tight he doubted she was capable of speech.

Sarah had backed into the house as the crowd moved in, but she came back out so quickly Mark knew she'd been paying close attention to what went on outside. She headed for her parents, but her eyes went to Charlie as if they were beyond her control.

Charlie turned back from the barn, and Mark said to Emma, "I'm going to see to the horses. I'll be right back."

Emma looked past him and saw Charlie walking toward her ma and pa and Sarah, and her eyes went round with surprise.

"We can live next door to 'em if you want. There's another nice stretch of land close to mine that will suit my cousin." Mark paused as Emma sorted all of that out. Then he added, "And your sister."

Emma whispered, "See to the horses. I'm going to say a prayer for Charlie."

Mark nodded and made quick work of taking the horses to the barn, leaving his cousin to his fate.

★ Twenty-two ★

I can't seem to get my breath." Mandy looked behind her at the receding gap they'd just ridden through. "That place seemed safe. Now we're out here, exposed. We need to ride hard for your ranch, Tom."

Angela was asleep sitting in front of Mandy. Catherine was asleep in Tom's arms. Mark had Jarrod on his back. Six cowhands rode strung out behind them. Including Mark Reeves, though Mandy had wondered for a while if he'd agree to go.

"You're looking at it wrong, Mandy girl."

"How so?" She kicked her horse to up her speed from a ground-eating canter to a flat-out gallop.

"You're still thinking like a rabbit. Running from hole to hole. Your stupid Gray Tower was safe, Belle's was safe, my ranch is safe."

"Well, they are." Mandy felt her heart pound hard at the wide open spaces. She looked at the cragged hills and thick forests. Well, not wide open exactly.

"We're not going to live like that. We'll be cautious, but we are not going to run into my house and pull that heavy door shut behind us and hide."

"Yes, we are."

"We're going to live." Tom reached over and caught Mandy's reins and slowed her horse. "We can't keep up this pace all the way home. The horses can't handle it. Settle down."

Mandy wanted to knock Tom's hands away from her horse and spur the animal faster. Of course she had no spurs, but she'd manage to wring speed out of the poor critter. And she wanted it so badly, so desperately that she suddenly knew Tom was right.

She was thinking like a rabbit. Half rabbit, half rabid swamp rat.

With a sigh, she quit fighting over control of her horse, and when she quit, Tom let go. They settled into a fast, steady walk that the horses could keep up all day.

"I can feel them out there, Tom. I can feel them drawing a bead on my back."

"I've got good men with me, and I know these hills. There's nowhere to lay in wait along here. The trail is too rugged. There aren't good overhangs. Farther down the trail toward the Double L, I'll have the men split off and make sure no one's around, but for now we're fine."

"We're not *fine*, Tom. We'll never be fine as long as one Cooter is still living."

Mandy settled in to rail at her husband for the rest of the long ride home when a wider spot in the trail allowed Mark Reeves to ride up beside them. Mandy clamped her lips shut and glared at Mark. He grinned back. Mandy suspected she looked a lot more like his old enemy when she was glaring.

"Can I talk to you, Boss?"

Mandy waited for Tom to tell Mark to beat it so they could discuss important, life and death things.

"Sure, what do you want?" Tom didn't even look at Mandy.

She wondered if maybe she'd done a bit too much nagging.

914

It didn't seem to be having much good affect.

"I've asked Emma Harden to marry me."

Mandy gasped and looked sharply at Mark.

"Any reason that's a bad thing, wife?" Tom's voice sounded a bit too harsh.

"Yes, of course there's a reason. I've got to warn Emma to run for her life."

Tom's harsh tone was lost in a quick laugh.

Mark scowled at her, but there was a twinkle in his eyes. "Too late."

"Maybe I'll talk to Belle, then."

"She's already given her blessing, or as close as she's ever apt to get when a man comes courting her daughter."

"How close?"

"She hasn't threatened to shoot me for nearly two days."

Tom laughed again, and Mark joined in. Mandy closed her eyes then was helpless not to laugh, too. "Well, if Belle's given you her. . .sort of. . .blessing, then who am I to oppose poor Emma signing on her future with you."

"Silas is Belle's fourth husband. The rest were a worthless lot. I think Emma will be okay with me because she's had some terrible men to compare me with." Mark grinned.

Mandy was tempted to swat him. He wasn't quite close enough, though. And that might not be accidental.

"So are you telling me you want to draw your time?" Tom reminded Mandy that Mark had started this for a reason.

"You said you'd pay me in cattle. I've homesteaded on a holding up in these hills." Mark pointed straight at a bunch of trees no one could begin to see through. "There's a nice mountain valley I scouted out a few miles to the north of Belle and Silas's. It turns out Emma's sister lives to the north. Belle knows the place I picked and seems to be pleased with it. I'll need the cattle. I'll work as long as I can, but I want to get a cabin up before first snow, and I—"

"I'll send some men with you to put up the house." Tom looked at Mandy. "In fact—"

"You don't have to do that," Mark interrupted before Tom could go on. He had a tinge of pink on his cheeks as if his temper was up. "I can take care of my own wife and build my own cabin."

Tom glared at Mark. "Neighbors help each other out here. You think I built my house single-handedly? And maybe Mandy and I could come, camp out with the young'uns. Get away from the ranch for a while. Let the Cooters hunt around for us."

"It wouldn't be hiding, and yet they'd have a hard time figuring out where we went." Mandy liked the idea real well.

"But I thought I'd work another month or two. I figure I've earned five or six head of cattle. I'd like to add a couple more, get a better start for Emma and me."

"I'll make it ten—nine cows bred Angus and one young bull."

Mark jerked a little and looked surprised and delighted.

"We'll have to camp on the trail tonight. But we'll get home midday and leave as soon as we can, maybe tomorrow if I don't run into anything at the ranch that slows me down. I have to get in to Divide to talk to the law, but we can swing through there on our way to the building site. We'll take all the men the ranch can spare and get the cabin up and finished while the sheriff and marshal do their jobs." Tom looked satisfied.

Mandy liked it, too. It wouldn't be hiding. She wasn't a rabbit if she was helping a friend build a cabin.

"Well, I suppose—"

"It's an order. And go back right now and tell Silas about it. He'll need to come along with Emma, and he's a good carpenter." Tom shrugged. "No, forget that. Just tell Emma you want her to have say in how we build the cabin. Don't even bother telling Silas. He won't let his girl ride away from his place with you. He'll come whether you ask or not."

With an expression that made Mandy wonder if he was dizzy from his life being planned for him, Mark said, "I'll go back and talk to her, then catch up with you wherever you camp." He wheeled his horse.

"Wait a minute," Tom ordered.

Mark turned back instantly.

"Leave Jarrod with me." Tom shook his head as if Mark didn't have possession of a lick of brains.

Grinning, Mark said, "I've gotten used to him." He slung the pack off his back, and Tom donned it. Then Mark headed back in the direction they'd just come.

Tom gave a firm, satisfied jerk of his chin then headed for home carrying two of Mandy's babies. He was protecting them. And Mandy. She'd brought terrible danger into his life, but he was strong enough to handle it all and build a house for one of his cowhands in his spare time. "The horses are rested. Let's put some miles behind us." Tom sped up, and Mandy fell into a gallop, keeping up with Tom's fast pace toward home.

He was carrying more than just her children. He also had her heart.

Cord crested a high ridge in the trail and pulled up. "Look down there." He pointed at a spot to the west of the Linscott ranch.

There was room for several of his cousins to come up beside him. "What're ya lookin' at, Cord?"

"It's Linscott. I recognize his black stallion. I'd know that big beast anywhere." It was getting on toward noon. They'd ridden late last night. Then one of his cousins had produced a bottle or two of rotgut, and they'd stayed up late playing poker and talking.

Cord knew they needed to push hard, but he'd enjoyed the whiskey himself and had needed the sleep this morning.

"You said his ranch was to the east of here." One of the cousins was a whiner.

Cord could taste the victory, and it would cost far less than he'd planned. A direct assault would have brought a lot of Cooters down. Cord had been ready to do it, but now he saw a way out. "He's heading for Divide. He's got a few men riding with him, but he's not barricaded like he'd be at the ranch."

And he had Lady Gray with him. With cold pleasure, Cord focused on her white braid. He saw a toddler strapped on Linscott's back. Cord suspected the other two children were on someone's horse, but he couldn't see them from this distance.

Thinking of that, the children, twisted his gut. This was a blood feud, and those young'uns had bought in just by being born. But he hadn't really thought of bringing those little ones under his gun. Unless he was killing mad, he didn't think he could do it. And he was sure the rest of his kin hadn't given it much thought.

But how could he spare the children if he was raining fire down from an overlook? If he tried to be careful of them, he'd miss his chance to finish Lady Gray and Linscott. He settled it by nursing his grudge and letting the need to avenge his family turn his mind from an act even he couldn't stand to think about.

He glanced at his kinfolk. "We can take the high trail right here, instead of going down. We'll get ahead of Linscott and cut him down where he stands." He studied the landscape then pointed to a high outcropping of rock. "That looks like it looms right over the trail. A perfect place for an ambush."

A lot of heads nodded, and more than a few seemed relieved. They hadn't complained, but Cord sensed they weren't eager to launch a frontal attack on a well-defended ranch. He wondered what flowed in the blood of the Cooter family that made them inclined toward back-shooting. He preferred it himself.

He turned his horse, not half the animal Linscott's stallion was, and headed straight north on the highlands. He didn't know the country around here, but he knew the woods, and there was a faint but clear game trail. These were mountain-bred horses—at least his was. If a deer or a mountain goat could leave a trail, his mustang could follow it.

"This is gonna be over in a couple of hours." With renewed

energy, his family followed him to the final showdown.

Tom set a blistering pace. He wanted to talk to the marshal and Sheriff Dean then do his best to get into the highlands before nightfall. They'd find the place where Reeves's cabin would be built and have themselves a few days of hard labor, in complete safety.

He loved his ranch, but the whole time he'd been there this morning it'd itched at him that the Cooters would be coming. They were pure weasel, but they were dependable.

Without slowing up, he hollered back, "Reeves!"

Mark came up beside him. "Here, Boss."

"There's a narrow spot in the trail ahead. It's the only place where someone could get a good shot at us from cover. We can't scout the trail without it taking half a day, there's just no way up to those rocks." Tom pointed at an overhang in the distance. Then he glanced back at Mandy and met her eyes.

She nodded, taking in every word.

He made no attempt to keep anything from her. After what he'd seen of her in action, there was nobody he'd rather have fighting at his side. She might be worried about becoming a killer, but Tom wasn't overly. He suspected he could keep her from hiring out to settle range wars if he watched her close.

She was trailing him, but only because it was too narrow to ride three abreast, especially at a gallop.

"What do you want me to do?" Mark asked.

Tom tried his best, but he was having a hard time getting really mad at this little punk who'd known Mandy for so long and had such a deep connection to Tom's children. "Drop back and tell the men we're going through hard. I'll signal you when I'm ready to pick up speed." Tom shifted his grip on the reins so he held them in his left hand, which was busy holding Catherine on the saddle. He raised his right hand in a fist. "That'll be the sign. I don't want to yell and wake up the children. Tell the men to ride low to their horses until I signal you to stop. We'll make it. The Cooters wouldn't have any way of knowing where we are. My men have been scouting around the ranch, and there's no sign we're being watched. But even so, we ride hard, keep low, and be ready for trouble. Tell 'em."

A firm jerk of Mark's chin was the only response before Mark let Tom ride on ahead.

That tight stretch in the trail was still a ways ahead. Tom had ridden this trail a hundred times and knew it right down to the trees and game trails. Within the hour they'd pass through what felt to him like a death trap all of a sudden. Rugged rocks rose high on the right side and dropped away on the left. Swallowing, he realized he'd never given it much thought before. Despite the hard life, most of the danger out here came from rattlesnakes and grizzlies and blizzards, not gunmen. Even the outlaws tended to run off a few head of cattle and avoid coming under anyone's gun.

Being married was going to be tricky, what with Mandy always halfway ready to run away, thinking to protect him. He looked down at Catherine, deep asleep in his arms. He'd have to guard the children to keep their stubborn mother in line. She wouldn't run off without them. Then he realized she already had once.

Hugging Catherine close, he felt the weight of Jarrod on his back and thought of what would happen if dry-gulchers opened fire on him or Mandy. The children would be right in the line of fire.

Tom's fury tightened his whole body, and Catherine shifted in her sweet sleep. Forcing himself to relax, lest he squeeze her until she woke up, Tom set his jaw and looked ahead. One more hour and they'd be through that narrow stretch of trail and likely be safe.

His big hand nearly covered Catherine's tummy, and he wished his hand were iron, a solid barrier for the little girl.

One more hour.

"We'll be down there in less than an hour." Cord pointed to the outcropping of rock that loomed over the trail the Linscott party was traveling. "We'll have time to set up and be waiting for them."

A grumble of satisfaction from behind pulled a smile onto Cord's face. This was all going to be over. He thought maybe he'd move to California once this was done. He was tired of the Rockies in winter. He had no taste for homesteading or ranching. Maybe he could work for someone like he'd done for Sidney Gray. That had been the best job he'd ever held. Easiest, too. With a smirk he thought of how that fool Gray had ended up dead at his hand.

It flickered through his head that if he hadn't mistreated Lady Gray and gotten himself fired, he might have instead continued to protect Sidney. Sidney might still be alive, especially since Cord had killed Gray personally.

For one second his whole world tilted as he considered that he had set all of this in motion. He had lost the best job he'd ever had through his own behavior. Now he daydreamed about getting a job just like that again.

Shaking his head to avoid the unsettling notion, he remembered when he'd gone up behind Lady Gray and put his hand on her shoulder. Offering her protection and. . .male companionship. She should have been honored. Cord knew the way Sidney treated her. She should have jumped at the chance to be friendlier with Cord. Instead she'd been offended and had him fired. Gray had acted like it was about the gold, but Cord knew the truth. Mandy had spoken to her husband, and Cord got booted out of his job. The sting to his pride was still there.

He looked down the tree-covered slope to the trail where he'd seen Linscott. It was hidden from sight, but Cord knew it was there. He knew Lady Gray was there. He'd teach that woman a lesson.

Then he touched his face where she'd nearly killed him. She'd hit, near as Cord could tell, his rifle right in the muzzle. As good as sent her bullet straight up the barrel of his gun. If she'd really been aiming for the muzzle, then she'd hit a target less than an inch in diameter. And she'd done it while she was moving, ducking, diving. Shaking his head, Cord knew no one was that accurate. Lucky shot. But Cord couldn't deny she was greased lighting with that Winchester. Well, he'd see how she did against two dozen hardened men.

He also decided he'd take his pick of spots. Even with him high above in a surprise attack, she'd get her rifle into action. He suspected she'd keep firing even if she were dying. It'd take a well-placed bullet to bring her down, and if they didn't place the bullets well, it'd take a hail of them.

The first bullet out of Cord's gun was already marked just for Lady Gray. He saw the game trail he was following narrow, which was next to impossible because it was already so narrow it was little more than a rabbit track. It curved downward sharply, and Cord had to slow his horse. Tree branches reached out and would have knocked a man off a running horse. Keeping low, Cord wondered if they'd have to end this on foot. Could his horse even get down to that overhang?

He wished he could see the Linscott crowd, but they were out of sight. That lone stretch of rock topped by the outcropping would be the only place they'd have a clear shot. They'd gained ground. Cord suspected they'd pulled well ahead of the Linscotts. Now they just had to get into place and bide their time, patient as hungry cougars.

Cord liked that image. He was coiled and ready to spring. All he needed was a rabbit to pounce on.

★ Twenty-three ★

For the first time in years, Mandy didn't feel like a rabbit being stalked by a pack of coyotes. She followed Tom's broad shoulders, feeling like he could block the whole world for her. Hating that she'd put him in danger, but still glad not to be on her own anymore.

And they were nearing Divide. Somehow getting to town seemed like the end of all the danger. They'd consult with the marshal, find out hopefully that they had the situation with the Cooters under control, and then make tracks for Mark's homestead.

If they needed to build Mark an eight-bedroom mansion, they'd do it and stay at that homestead until the Cooters were arrested and no longer a risk to anyone. If her husband would just agree.

Tom looked back over those broad shoulders. "We're almost to that narrow stretch."

He spoke softly, so as not to wake the children. Trying to smile, she barely managed a brief upturn of her lips and a terse nod.

Tom wasn't fooled. He knew her very well considering how short was their acquaintance.

Looking ahead to the tapering trail, Mandy swallowed hard and held Angela closer. The trail twisted and climbed. They could only see a few yards ahead. It led to a woodless rocky stretch. The whole trail was narrow and heavily forested, except this one stretch. For a few yards, it would be so tight it almost grabbed Mandy by the throat. They just needed to get through it, and the mountain on the right dropped away. There was nowhere to ambush riders on the trail after that one spot. After that was a fairly safe route to Divide.

They'd be passing through it in minutes. Mandy was scared right down to the ground, but at least, finally, she was no one's rabbit.

Cord didn't speak a word. They were too close. Chances were the heavy forest would drown out any sound, but he wasn't taking a chance. The trail was so sheer now his horse took a single step at a time. They were cutting it close, but they'd get there. A trail had to go somewhere after all. And though Cord wasn't familiar with this area, he was dead certain that this trail led straight to that rocky knoll.

He caught a glimpse of a rider far below, still well behind the Cooters. All he had to do was reach that stack of boulders, and that was only a few hundred yards ahead.

Salivating, Cord could taste the victory. He'd like to get his hands on those beautiful black horses of Linscott's. He'd like to get his hands on Lady Gray's gold. He'd like to get his hands on Lady Gray. He doubted he'd manage any of that because he was going to come down on that party like iron fire raining from heaven. Lady Gray was too fast and too accurate to risk leaving her alive or aiming carefully to spare those horses. The horses were too well-known anyway. Someone would identify them as

Linscott's, and that would tie the Cooters to their deaths. He was content with just finishing this business and riding away with the slate wiped clean, the feud settled.

He reached a sudden drop-off in the middle of the trail that forced him to stop. He could clearly see tracks. Deer and mountain goat, heading down, straight for that overlook. But his horse had finally reached the limits. It balked and wouldn't go another step. What's more, Cord knew the horse *couldn't* go another step. It couldn't handle this sheer descent. But a man could.

Grimacing with anger, he looked back at his kin. "There's no trail from here on, not one a horse can handle. We've got to go on foot."

His family grumbled, but they all knew there was no time to hash out a new plan.

Swinging down, they tied their horses to the nearest limb, and there was an abundance of them. Cord looked again at that drop-off. Easy enough on foot. He'd just have to jump. It might have been twenty feet of sheer rock, but Cord could swing down, hanging on with his fingertips, then drop the last bit. He checked that his six-gun was firm in his holster and took his rifle. He'd need the long gun to make that shot. Even from where he wanted to lie in wait, it was a long shot to make a hit. But he had no doubt he and his cousins could do it.

From up here they were out of rifle range. There was no chance to even draw a bead on the Linscotts because the trees blocked their line of sight. Which was fine. That let the Cooters get close without being detected.

Cord slid his belly over the drop-off and, with his rifle in one hand, hung for a second from the other, then dropped. Simple.

He looked up into the eyes of one of his cousins above, nodded, and turned. They still had plenty of time to set up at that overhang, take aim, and fire.

"Reeves!" The trail was too narrow to ride two abreast, but for a few seconds, if they were careful, they could manage it.

Mark eased up beside him.

"Take Catherine." Tom slid the boneless, sleeping girl into Mark's arms. "I don't want Jarrod on my back when we ride through there." Tom swung Jarrod around front and held the sleeping toddler, sheltering him as well as possible.

Mark jerked his chin and dropped back. A glance told Tom he fell behind Mandy, too. Guarding her from the rear along with six more men behind Mark. Good men, men to count on in a fight. None of that would protect them if lead started raining down on them from overhead.

They'd be in that tight neck and out before those Cooters could take aim. And, considering that the Cooters weren't even there, it'd be fine.

Still, Tom saw no reason to hope for the best. His eyes rose to that overhang of rock. Perfect cover for an ambush.

Tom asked everything of his horse, himself, and his God as the trail narrowed.

Sliding more than walking, Cord didn't try and stop his descent. He needed to get down there in time to take aim, and all his cousins with him.

From behind he heard all the men coming. Dust and small rocks dislodged under his boot heels, and a few clattered down on his head kicked from above. The dust rose up until a small cloud formed. Was it visible to riders below?

Cord clung to his rifle and kept heading down.

Tom pulled Jarrod close to shield him, then raised his fist and spurred his horse.

Teeth gritted together with rage, he hated to think those coyote Cooters were so bent on their feud they might kill one of

Tom's children—and they *were* Tom's children. Whatever their father's name, they were *his*, and they were Linscotts to the bone because Tom decided they were.

He pushed ahead fast without checking those behind him. The men were solid. Mandy was as dependable as the sunrise. They were right where they needed to be.

The trail continued to rise, and it was more narrow by the stride. His horse was game, though, and it didn't falter as it raced for a stretch of trail that could become a death trap.

With a tight hold on his rifle, Cord hit a slightly less treacherous stretch of the trail. It still slanted sharply downward, but he was on his feet now instead of his backside. He ran flat out. Closing the distance, listening, hoping he didn't hear the sound of oncoming hooves.

Not yet. He threaded his way through a clump of aspens, hitting one with his shoulder and setting it to quaking. The shiver of the tree startled a deer out of the brush slightly down the trail. Running, the deer vanished into the trees, but his direction went right along this trail.

"We're on the right track." The deer was leading them, proving this was an established trail. He chanced a quick look back at his family, all racing along after him. His heart pounded hard, as much from excitement as from exertion. All these Cooters working together. He was proud of his family. Proud of their loyalty to each other. Lady Gray was about to finally realize just how foolish she'd been to aim her rifle at a Cooter.

With his eyes squarely on the path ahead, Cord risked a smile.

All they had to do was get there in time.

Trees on both sides slapped at Mandy's shoulders. Galloping as they were, she ducked a branch and still took a swipe in the face from whipcord-thin branches of aspen.

The aspens grew more up than out, which told Mandy just how narrow the trail was. If they'd wanted to turn around, they'd be hard pressed to manage it. The horse could rear and wheel around probably, but it would be difficult and slow, especially with so many riders packed tightly and traveling fast. They were as good as forced to go forward.

Tom rode this trail every time he went to Divide. He should have widened it. Cut trees for his cabin from this spot. She'd spend awhile nagging him to do just that as soon as he'd worked out all the other trouble that came along with marrying her.

Pine trees occasionally replaced the aspen and clawed her. She focused on speed and protecting her little girl. With one hand busy blocking blows to Angela's precious face and the other guiding her horse, she wasn't able to spare herself.

A ponderosa pine nearly unseated her. She crouched lower, using her shoulders and her stinging face to protect Angela the best she could.

She'd ridden this trail once with Tom, the day they'd gone to town. They had come from another direction when they'd ridden in from Gray Tower and from yet another way when they'd come back from the Flatheads' valley and the Harden place. This tight passage had been hard to endure on the earlier trip when she *didn't* feel like she had a gang of outlaws on her trail.

Now, knowing the Cooters might have regrouped and come back, it was a hundredfold worse. Every breath she drew was a struggle as her throat tightened with fear. She felt the cold creep into her blood, her muscles, her nerves.

Surely Cord, the only one of those last four men unaccounted for, hadn't found more cousins already. But Mandy and Tom had taken three men into the sheriff, one dead and draped over his horse. They'd ridden to the Flathead village and back.

A good chance he couldn't gather any help in that time, but Cord could be up there alone. And he could do terrible damage from that overlook.

Mandy desperately looked forward to getting through this gauntlet.

Cord saw the deer ahead of him. Then he saw it leap gracefully over. . .nothing. Straight ahead he saw the end of the world.

He threw himself flat on his back.

"Stop! A cliff!" A strangled yell of warning was all he had time for. His shirt tore on a projecting scrub pine and he felt his back being cut and scoured by the rock and grit of the mountain. He slid to a stop just inches from the ledge.

A cousin came sliding fast. Cord grabbed at him. His cousin stopped with his legs hanging out over. . .Cord wasn't sure what.

The next few seconds were a fur ball of tumbling and grabbing and muffled shouts. But when the dust settled, no one went over the ledge. When they all lay, scattered like battered branches after a wind storm, Cord finally had the time and gumption to lean forward and see the pit he'd almost gone flying into. There was nothing but a huge crack in the mountain.

Straight across the crack stood the deer that had led them this direction. It had jumped, probably without giving it a thought. The deer arched its neck, and a rack of proud antlers rose as the animal seemed to sneer at Cord. Then it whirled and ran straight to that outcropping of rock and posed there as if it was the king of this whole mountain. Then it vanished into the woodlands beyond. Of course this trail worked for a deer.

Cord looked down. This crack dropped into a pit so deep Cord couldn't see to the bottom.

Heart pounding, gasping for breath, Cord's stomach clenched so hard at the near miss he thought he'd toss his breakfast right into the depths. He fought that off and then had time to really look, up the mountain and down. If they could get across, that outcropping of rock that overlooked the trail was only a few dozen feet on the other side of this split in the earth.

It might as well have been on the moon. The crack stretched as far as the eye could see up, and on the downhill side looked to go all the way to the trail Linscott was on.

He could just faintly see where Lady Gray and her guards were riding through the trees far below. And he wouldn't have known he could see it at all if he hadn't watched riders, visible for fleeting seconds, passing.

"We missed them." Cord's terror twisted into fury. But they wouldn't miss them for long. "Let's get down there and finish this." Cord turned, ignoring his kin, and charged back up the slope, twice as hard and half as fast as he'd come down.

He heard his family grousing, but he didn't wait. The Cooters would come. He knew the kind of men they were. They'd belly-ache maybe, but they were loyal. They were men who understood what was important.

In the end, Cooters stuck together.

"Did you hear something?" As they cleared the narrow stretch of trail without incident, Mandy rode up beside Tom.

"Nope." He lifted his head and listened with keen con-centration for a few seconds, then looked up and behind him as his horse moved along at a gallop. "Smells like dust or something." Tom shook his head and pulled his horse to a fast walk. "Probably kicked up by the horses. Who knows."

Looking over her shoulder, Mandy saw a magnificent mule deer with a huge set of antlers step up on the rocky overhang as if he were their lookout. As if he ruled the world.

"That must be what I saw."

Tom looked back just as the deer turned and darted away. "Well, no one up there, or a deer wouldn't be hanging around."

Mandy felt the chill recede as she accepted the movement and slight sounds of the deer as the reason why she'd felt so itchy. For a second she'd been ready to reach for her rifle, and she already knew exactly where she'd have aimed and fired. And Mandy was one to trust her instincts.

"We made it through that gap. There's no real good place to stake out the trail from here on in." Tom's horse emerged from the heavily wooded stretch into a flatter land, grass and some scrub brush but no highlands edging the trail. And no trees big enough to hide behind.

"Those back-shooting Cooters won't face us head-on, so with that bad stretch behind us, we'll be fine now." Tom smiled then looked down at sleeping Jarrod. "Can you imagine feeling this safe?"

Mandy reached across and brushed the flyaway brown hair off of Jarrod's forehead. "I think I already knew how to load Ma's rifle at this age. Definitely by Angela's." She tightened her grip gently on the child in her own arms. "And Sally could already rope a moving calf from the back of a good cowpony when she was just a bit older."

"We can get started training the girls to rope and shoot as soon as we get done building Reeves's cabin. Get 'em their own rifles."

"Tom, I don't think—" Mandy looked up and saw the sparkle in her husband's eye.

"Maybe we wait a little longer, huh?" He chuckled.

"Maybe just another year or two." Shaking her head, Mandy smiled. "Let's get to Divide. I'm going to be mighty glad to be done with this trail."

They walked awhile, the heat of the summer, the scent of the pines at their backs, the jagged white peaks all around them, the soft clop of the hooves.

Mandy dropped back when Angela woke up and started chattering. Her horse was inclined to move along following Tom, and it required almost no effort from Mandy. Jarrod riding on Tom's lap was chattering, but the boy wasn't a big talker yet.

Mandy heard Tom's deep voice—probably going over and over that the boy was to call him Pa. The thought made Mandy smile, and it eased her tension. She looked back and could see Catherine sitting with relaxed contentment on Mark's lap.

Mark smiled at Mandy and gave her a reassuring nod. A world where Mark Reeves was mature and helpful just made no sense to Mandy at all.

When the horses were rested, Tom picked up the pace, and it wasn't long until they rode into the sleepy little town of Divide.

Mandy had told herself she was safe before, but now the weight that lifted off her shoulders told her she hadn't really believed it.

"I want to see Sheriff Dean first thing," Tom said to Mandy. Then he turned to his cowhands. "See to that list of supplies. Mark, do you mind keeping Catherine? We can take her."

"I'm fine." Mark smiled down at Catherine as if to ask her if she was happy. Catherine giggled.

Mandy was a bit surprised at the way Mark accepted the children's attention. He'd never shown much patience as a child. Though his little brothers had begun popping up in school before Mandy had grown up. And he'd always included them in his nonsense. Mandy had considered him more a bad influence than a caretaker.

Tom rode straight up Divide's single dirt street for the jailhouse, and Mandy followed.

She'd only been in town briefly, but she was struck by how quiet it was. No tinny music coming out of the Golden Butte. No wagons or horses on the street. Not a single soul anywhere.

Tom swung down, carrying Jarrod as if he didn't weigh an ounce. As Mandy's feet hit the ground, the sheriff's door burst open, and she saw—

"Sally!" Mandy ran and threw herself into her sister's arms.

Angela was between them, but Mandy didn't let that stop her from hugging Sally tight and long and deep.

★ Twenty-four ★

Luther came next. Tom remembered him and Buff and Wise Sister. They all poured out of the sheriff's office, talking a mile a minute.

Well, at least Mandy and Sally were. Sally snatched Jarrod out of Tom's arms. Tom didn't even try to keep up with the chatter. She might have asked nicely for the little boy.

"Mark Reeves?" Sally shouted the name, sounding stunned.

Tom saw Reeves, carrying Catherine, turn, flash a smile, and come back at a near run.

It burned a little. Tom had told the men to lay up supplies. But there were more than enough men for that. He just hadn't wanted the whole bunch of them crowding into the sheriff's office.

Mark swept Sally up in his arms just as Logan McKenzie came out of the sheriff's office. . .and started scowling.

Tom hadn't seen any of these folks since Jarrod was born, and then he'd met them once and not for very long. But he felt an instant brotherhood with any man who didn't like Mark Reeves hugging his wife.

Tom reached out a hand to Logan and drew his attention. "We're brothers now, I think."

"Why, because you don't like that guy touching my wife either?" Logan didn't take his eyes off Sally.

"No, because I married Mandy. We really are brothers."

Logan's brow smoothed, and he smiled. "You finally got Mandy to marry you, huh?"

For some reason it gave Tom fierce satisfaction that someone else had known how he felt about Mandy. And how much sense it made that they'd be married now.

"That kid with his hands all over your wife is one of my cowhands. He knew Mandy—Sally, too, it looks like—back in Texas."

"Hmm—" Logan's smile faded.

"All those years I told everyone you were born to hang, Mark Reeves." Sally grinned and slapped Mark's shoulder. "Guess I owe Beth five dollars. I bet her you'd never live to be an adult."

"It's not ladylike nor Christian to wager, Sally." Mandy looked stern, but Tom saw the twinkle in her eye.

"You're right. But with Mark I never figured it for any kind of a gamble."

Mark laughed and slid an arm around Sally's waist, and she let that arm stay right where it was.

"That's how Mandy talks to him, too." Tom drew Logan's eagle eyes away from the little group. "In fact, she called him her childhood enemy. I've decided he's no threat."

Then Mark put his other arm around Mandy, and Tom wasn't feeling quite so charitable.

"Still don't like it," Logan muttered.

"I'm planning to fire him." Tom nodded.

Luther bulled his way into the reunion and had Mandy in a bear hug.

Tom waited until the fuss had calmed down, not that hard considering Luther, Buff, and Wise Sister barely spoke, and Logan was busy glaring. It boiled down to Mandy, Sally, and Mark, who were talking like magpies, and Mark was touching them again.

Finally Tom reached for the sheriff's door. "Let's go see what Merl found."

"He's not there." Logan shook his head.

"He left the door unlocked?"

"Yep, he rode out this morning to check on some cattle rustling in the area. He said he wouldn't be gone long."

Looking around, Tom realized there wasn't a single horse tied at a hitching post. Not a single man walking down the street. No music coming from the Golden Butte.

"What's going on? Divide's a little town, but this is too quiet." Tom frowned. He'd thought that a town full of rough Western men meant safety.

"A cattle drive came through the other day hiring and paying top wages. Took every able-bodied man in town. Even Seth and Muriel at the general store hired on as camp cooks. Thought it'd be fun to get away for a couple of weeks. They left one of the few women in town to run things."

"How long have you been in town?" Tom asked Logan.

"Just a few days. Sally decided she wasn't going to put up with Mandy living on that mountaintop anymore. We came through Divide on our way north and met Luther here, just coming from Mandy's castle. The sheriff told us you weren't at the ranch, that you'd headed off for Denver. But we knew you hadn't gone to Denver because we came up that trail. He told us to wait here for you."

Belle Harden chose that moment to ride into town with Emma. She came from the west, crossing the train tracks that bordered the town on that side.

"Reeves!" Tom had to yell to get Mark to quit with the girl talk. Maybe if the halfwit didn't have the sense to keep his hands off his boss's woman, he'd figure out he shouldn't be hugging his boss's woman in front of his fiancé. When Mark looked up, Tom jabbed a finger toward Emma.

Mark wheeled around and smiled a greeting.

"What are they doing here?" Tom asked Logan that question, but it was clear with one glance at Logan's expression that the man had no idea who these newcomers even were.

And as the Hardens dismounted and Mark rushed to her side and slipped his arm around Emma, one more crowd rode in. Red Dawson with his wife and three young'uns, along with Silas Harden.

From yet another direction, Tom saw his sister coming in with Wade. And they'd brought their two children with them.

"I sent a rider out to tell them we were going to build a house," Tom told Mandy. "Abby wants to help. She thinks white people build unwisely at times."

"Unwisely?" Abby had ridden close enough to overhear the remark. "I think my exact words were that white people are fools who would try to close the whole world inside." She swung off her bareback horse in a fluid leap that always drew Tom's admiration.

"White people?" With one brow arched, Sally looked from Tom to his blond sister.

"I'll explain later," Mandy whispered.

Mark and Emma were talking fast, and a grin spread so wide on Mark's face, Tom thought the boy's head would split in half.

Then Mark gave a yell that'd make a wild Indian back down. He lifted Emma in his arms and whirled her around. "We're getting married," Mark announced at the top of his lungs.

Belle must have given her the go-ahead and sent Silas for the preacher.

"Well, we were going to build them a house," Belle muttered, glaring at Mark. "Emma decided she wanted to get married and live in it."

They all gathered in a circle to discuss the details. The loud click of a gun being cocked whirled them around to face two dozen heavily armed men.

Most of them bearing white streaks in their hair.

Tom had his gun drawn, but he froze at the sight of all that firepower, aimed right at them. His first thought was that his children were in the middle of this. Red Dawson's children, Abby's children. And too many women. The Cooters didn't open fire. But it was clear from the fanatic hate gleaming in Cord Cooter's eyes they'd come to finish their feud.

Today they weren't back-shooters. Today they planned to face this feud as men. Men who'd put children and women under their guns.

Tom's opinion of the family didn't improve. "Let the woman and children step away from us," Tom ordered. As if these coyotes obeyed any civilized law.

"All but Lady Gray." Cord's eyes went straight to Mandy. "She's part of this, and she's not going anywhere."

Sickened, Tom looked at Mandy, knowing she'd never back down anyway. She had her rifle in her hands. With one look, Tom could see the cold in Mandy. She was detached, ready to fight and keep fighting. Fire that Winchester until she won or died.

He hated that for her. He knew how that scared her, that part of herself. He'd hoped to give her a safe enough life that she never had to let that cold flow in her veins again.

It's a wonder she hadn't just started mowing down Cooters the second she saw that white streak. Only about half of them had it, Tom noticed. Maybe, if they could breed that streak out of a man, they could breed the evil out of him, too.

"Let 'em go, Cord." There was grumbling from behind Cord. "I'm not shooting women and children."

Cord nodded.

"The little ones and all the women but Lady Gray can go," Cord agreed quickly.

Tom realized that even a snake like Cord Cooter didn't have a belly for shooting children.

"I'm not going." Belle Harden had her six-gun drawn.

In the distance, a sharp, high whistle blew. The train, which came through once a week on a good week, would be in town in a matter of minutes.

"I'm staying." Sally had her own rifle. She'd pulled it from a sling around her back just like Mandy had.

"Cass honey, you take the little ones."

"No, Red." Taking his eyes off the Cooters for only a second, Tom saw the tension on Cassie Dawson's face. She wanted to stay just like the other women, but her eyes went to the children, and Tom knew she'd do as she was told to save them.

"Please, Cass honey, take 'em and go. Get 'em out of here."

"This is madness." Tears brimmed in Cassie's eyes, and Tom knew she had the right of it.

"I know, Cass. Please. Stay in the church until this is over and get down. Flying bullets don't respect even a house of God."

"Yes, Red." Reluctantly, Cassie started shooing children. Cassie Dawson was inclined toward obedience.

"Go with her, Emma." Mark Reeves sounded real bossy for a man who didn't have a prayer of getting his way.

"I'm staying." Emma wasn't so much inclined.

Tom knew better than to even waste his breath ordering any of the rest of these women around. Mark'd learn that soon enough. But a wild country wasn't settled by weaklings. It figured a lot of Western women would buy into a fight someone brought to their doors. Not that Cassie was a weakling. She was just a sweetheart, and she couldn't seem to stop herself from minding her husband. And someone had to get these children out of here.

Tom felt a moment of pure envy before he stepped closer to his wife. Then he focused on those drawn Cooter guns and felt sick. They needed to stop this or a lot of people were going to die. When had the Cooters stopped being dry-gulchers? Why'd they pick today of all days to grow backbones?

"I'm a man of God." Red Dawson stepped forward as Cassie herded the children out of harm's way. "I'm telling all of you men to stand down. There's no reason for this. What is your purpose for coming at us with guns drawn? What is calling you to such a terrible sin as shooting at honest folks, including women?"

The train steamed closer. Tom saw a blast of black smoke belch out of its chimney and heard the first squeal of the brakes.

"It's a feud, Preacher-man. It was started by Lady Gray." Cord gestured at Mandy with his pistol. "Today it'll be finished by Cooters. The minute she shot one of our family, she drew this onto herself. Cooters stick together, and that's why we're here. When we're done, no one in the West will dare to pick a fight with one of us. We'll have a name to be proud of. A name to fear."

"There's no pride in this." Red's voice was kind. Tom didn't know how he managed it when talking to scum like this. "And now with the train here there are witnesses."

"We *want* witnesses," Cord sneered. "We want everyone to know, and be afraid."

"It's murder. A waste of lives. And the folks on that train will know, and those of you who live through this will be brought to justice."

"Those of us who live will remember every one of you who stood by Lady Gray. Our feud will be against all of you, and all your kin."

There was a shifty look in the eyes of several of the two dozen men who faced them. Tom suspected that given half a chance they'd back down.

Tom stepped up beside Red. "We're wasting time. These men don't know a thing about right and wrong. They only know revenge and hate."

Tom saw Cassie get the last of the children inside the church. She gave one last long look back. Even from here, Tom could see tears in her eyes.

"I reckon you're right, Tom. But I had to try."

"You step out, too, Red. It's not fitting that a parson be involved in this."

The train pulled up, and the engine passed them, slowing, the brakes squealing.

"I'll stay. I won't let it be said I backed down and let the evil happen without fighting back."

"Enough of this." Cord raised his gun. "We end this today."

Feeling sick, Tom exchanged a long look with Mandy. She was standing in the front, far too many of those guns aimed right at her. She wasn't going to live through this no matter how fast she was. Tom braced himself to jump in front of her.

An elderly man jumped off the still-moving train with surprising agility and strode straight for the standoff. "Hold your fire!" He was an elderly man with a wide white streak in his hair.

"Grandpappy?" Cord lowered his gun.

Mandy looked past the old man and saw her pa getting off the train. Even better, her ma. Mandy had to fight every reflex in her body to keep her rifle aimed and not run to throw herself in her mother's arms.

Pa was walking just a pace behind the old man. Grandpappy Cooter, who'd laid down the rule that Cooters stick together. If there'd been a chance the Cooters would back down, that was over. The man behind all their feuding was here to lend them his backbone.

The train bumped to a haut, and a crew of men jumped off the train, ignoring the goings-on in town, striding down to what looked like a cattle car that was dead even with the Cooter clan.

Grandpappy walked smack into the middle of space that would be filled with flying lead in just a few seconds and stalked right up to Cord.

As if time suddenly slowed to a crawl, Mandy braced herself.

"Protect me, Lord. Protect all of us." Mandy didn't see how even God could protect them all.

"God, have mercy." Mandy heard her little sister behind her, praying, maybe dying today because of Mandy.

"Lord, help me." That was Ma, striding right into the middle of this madness.

Her throat swelled when she saw Beth step off the train. Beth took in the nightmare in a single glance, walked straight toward the worst of the trouble praying, "Give me strength."

Sally stepped up beside Mandy on the left, Beth on the right. The gentle-voiced doctor in petticoats, who'd been back East to medical school and dedicated her life to healing, had her rifle leveled. Ma was there, ready to fight for her daughters, as she always had been.

Belle Harden shoved between Sophie and Tom. Tom's eyes were narrowed and ready.

If her blood hadn't been so cold, Mandy would have wept to think she was bringing death to the people she loved so well. But the tears were frozen solid behind her eyes.

Silas was between Belle and Tom, back a step just because Belle wouldn't have it otherwise, but he was ready.

Pa was there, too. Farthest away, with Luther and Buff at her side, Wise Sister stood with her bow drawn. Abby had a knife in her hands that gleamed in the sunlight. Red Dawson, a man of God who didn't want this but wouldn't stand by while evil men killed the innocent. Mark Reeves with Emma at his side. There were cowhands from Tom's ranch, too.

But even with all of these, there were more Cooters. They were outgunned, but they'd make a fight of it.

Mandy's cold blood chilled to frigid, solid ice as she waited for the old man who had started all this with his rules and twisted sense of pride to turn and fire.

He reached up a gnarled hand and. . . "What are you buncha no-accounts doing?"

He knocked Cord's gun hand aside.

"Uh, that woman over there shot a Cooter." Cord suddenly looked about ten years old as he fumbled with an explanation.

"Why?"

Two men started opening the wide side doors of the baggage car. The scrape of those doors was the only sound in the whole town.

Mandy, with her sleeted nerves, seeing everything, hearing everything, noticed other people getting off the train, a man carrying two little children.

"Why what?"

Mandy wondered, too. Why had they waited so long to kill someone who'd harmed a Cooter?

"Well, 'cuz her husband's guards shot Amos and a bunch of others."

"And what was Amos doing when they shot him?"

Cord got a mutinous look on his face. "It don't matter what he was doing. You're the one who said Cooters stick together, Grandpappy."

"Yep, I said that all right. They stick together to uphold the family honor. There's no honor in this."

Pa reached Mandy's side. "Lower your gun so I can give you a proper hug."

"Not now, Pa. Not until this is over." The ice in her veins began to thaw when Pa touched her arm, but she was still cold, unnaturally calm, and ruthless and ready. Maybe that old man could stop this, but she wasn't trusting him. Not yet.

"I rode on the train with that man. He's the head of the Cooter family. He said the law came to him back East and asked about this feud. As soon as he found what his kinfolk were up to, he set out. We've been riding the train together since Denver. He's going to put a stop to this right now."

Mandy heard that wavering, elderly voice ranting and raving at the Cooters. She started to believe it might really end without gunfire. But she remembered the hate in Cord Cooter's eyes and kept her rifle leveled.

More passengers got off the train. Mandy saw Sheriff Dean

ride into town from the north. The baggage handlers shouted as they rigged a ramp from the side of the train and, using wooden poles, carefully controlled a huge wooden keg rolling out of the car's belly.

Cord had a burn of red on his cheeks. His head was bowed like a chastised child. Grandpappy was yelling. All of the Cooter guns were lowered.

The keg reached the ground and was pushed to the side to unload a second one. Mandy saw the word MOLASSES stamped on the side of the keg. Supplies for the general store.

"I'm ashamed of all of you, do you hear?" Grandpappy waved his arms wildly.

Cord's eyes rose. Mandy didn't like what she saw. Cord wasn't a boy any longer, and being scolded clearly didn't sit well.

"All my life I've fought hard to make the Cooter name stand for something, and now you run around like a pack of yellow dogs chasing one woman. She's made you look like fools. She's shamed you, and you've shamed the Cooter name."

Suddenly, at the word "shame," Cord snapped. Mandy saw the second it happened. The sleet in her veins lanced through every part of her as Cord raised his gun, his eyes straight on hers.

"Look out!"

A shout from the train didn't pull Mandy's eyes away from Cord and his gun. She was busy raising and aiming her rifle.

Then just as Cord's eyes told Mandy he'd fire in the next instant, the runaway keg slammed into the whole crowd of Cooters. They began to tumble like tenpins, knocking one into the other until they went down in a heap, Cord at the bottom of the pile. The stack of Cooters groaned and shouted and shoved.

Grandpappy Cooter missed being bowled down by inches. The keg split open, and molasses poured out over all of them.

The sheriff jumped off his horse and waded into the mess, plucking guns out of molasses-coated hands. The men were too busy howling in disgust to resist.

Grandpappy helped disarm them.

Wondering what molasses did to a fire iron, Mandy's gun lowered. She clearly saw that the danger was past, but she was still as cold as death inside.

Until Tom had his say. "I guess what Cord said is right."

She turned to him. Just seeing him brought her back from that arctic place. As their eyes met, the heat in his look made her feel alive and warm and hopeful. "Cord was right about what?"

"Those Cooters really do stick together."

★ Twenty-five ★

Just because Mandy no longer wanted to hide didn't mean Mark and Emma didn't need a house.

Mandy introduced her family to Tom while the sheriff locked up so many Cooters it was likely the whole western half of the nation had been stripped clean of them.

Grandpappy told names and, angry at this blight on the family name, pointed out any he specifically knew were wanted men. "There are lots of honest men who bear the name of Cooter. I'll not have the family shamed by defending vermin just because they've got streaks of white in their hair and share my name."

The sheriff groused about the molasses ruining his jail cell, but in the end, all the right folks were on the business side of a door with iron bars.

"So, Tom"—Pa had that old look in his eye, the one that had run off so many men over the years—"you got the means to take good care of my girl?"

Tom smiled. He winked at Mandy then said, "Come and look at my stallion."

Jerking his thumb at the black thoroughbred, Pa's interrogation was diverted, and he went with Tom to study the horse more closely.

"And I'm running a herd of Angus beeves."

"Black cattle?" Pa ran his hands along the stallion's front shoulder, clearly admiring all that muscle. "Not longhorns? How do they handle the cold weather?"

Mandy would have stayed in her ma's arms all day except she had to keep taking turns hugging her sisters. And there was Alex to meet and all the children to fuss over.

Ma shocked all her girls by crying over Mandy's three little ones. Mandy, Beth, and Sally created a little circle around Ma as she crouched to hold Angela in her arms, hoping to block the sight of tears from Pa.

Alex and Logan did their best to act interested when Tom and Pa talked ranching. Mandy knew neither of them had much to do with it. But they must have figured out something to talk about.... Maybe McClellen women in general, because they seemed to be having a good time.

The talking went on for a solid hour until Belle Harden snapped, "Red, you gonna perform this wedding ceremony any time soon?" Belle Harden couldn't exactly sound excited about the wedding, but she sounded impatient with life in general, so scolding Red seemed to suit her.

"We get on with this, or I'm taking Emma back home." She'd seemed okay talking to Abby and Cassie, but apparently she'd been faking her agreeableness.

Mark flinched. Silas broke off talking with Red and Wade. Emma grinned and went to stand by Mark.

They had the wedding in the little Divide church then headed out for a house raising.

With all these knowing hands, Mark and Emma had a nice roof

within a few days.

Better'n he deserved, Mandy thought, though she was having trouble hating the kid like she'd once done. And she'd fallen in love with Emma...the poor thing.

Mandy spent so much time crying she thought maybe, just maybe, her pa actually got kind of comfortable with tears.

Tom seemed to have the time of his life with Pa, Ma, and Belle Harden talked together for hours.

As they worked on Mark's house, Mandy learned everything that had gone on with her sisters and her ma for the last few years.

The cabin was a good-sized one, thanks to an abundance of hardworking men. But not *too* big thanks to Abby.

Belle had stocked the larder for a long winter, along with providing cattle and horses and so many wedding presents Mark had taken on a permanent irritated scowl.

Except when Emma stood beside him and whispered in his ear. Then he got purely cheerful. Mandy decided Mark Reeves had found the perfect woman to tame him.

The last day of building came. One family at a time—the Sawyers, the Dawsons, and the Hardens—packed up and headed home. The McClellens were leaving soon to spend a few days at the Linscott ranch.

The women were hanging curtains in the house while the men finished some work on the front porch railings. Emma and Mark were taking their turn watching over Mandy's and Beth's children so the work could be finished in peace.

Tom came in with a cupboard and carried it to a spot where it would hang on the kitchen wall. "Mandy, can you lend a hand here?"

Mandy went eagerly. She'd barely spoken to Tom in days. And certainly she'd had no time alone with him.

The only ones allowed time alone were Emma and Mark, which rankled Mandy a bit since she and Tom were almost as much newlyweds as those two. She wouldn't have minded getting Tom off by himself.

He adjusted the cupboard carefully. "I want to fasten it on tight. I've got the weight on the pegs I hung earlier, but I want to level it." He moved it one way and then another until he was satisfied. "That's good. Hold it steady."

He glanced at her, standing very close, her hands on the shelf, her eyes on him, her mind not on her work at all.

Tom read her mind and closed the distance even more. "How long are we gonna have to build this stupid house? I want to take you home."

She shivered under his heated words, and it wasn't the kind of cold that worried her one bit. She hadn't felt so much as a twinge of the coldness that she often feared would come one day and never go.

She was so distracted by his words and the intent in his eyes that she forgot what she was doing with the cupboard and let go to wrap her arms around his neck.

The cupboard dropped, and Mandy jumped back to catch it. A rough edge jammed a splinter right into her index finger. "Ouch!" Mandy saw blood welling up and an ugly shard of wood protruding.

Tom steadied the cupboard. Not level, but it would stay up. He turned to her finger and bent his head low over it. "Let me get it out for you."

With his head bent so low, Mandy was almost nose to nose with the man. Lip to lip. He smiled then turned to his doctoring. Mandy never for an instant considered calling for help from her doctor sister.

With his strong white teeth, Tom bit into the nasty piece of wood and pulled it out of her finger.

Red blood oozed from the wound, and Tom murmured sympathy. With the splinter gone, Tom pressed her fingertip into his mouth to soothe the pain.

It worked because instead of pain she felt a tingle that started where his mouth touched her and spread up her arm until it reached all the way to her heart. "I love you, Tom." Mandy tried to remember what it was like living on that mountaintop with no one to care for her. No one to share any burdens with her.

When he raised his head next, her finger looked raw. The bleeding had stopped, but that warm tingle had gotten far worse. Somehow it pushed out the cold so completely that Mandy couldn't even worry about it returning. She knew now that if it did, it would never be who she truly was, never take over and not recede. Not with all the warmth of love Tom brought into her life.

"I love you, too, Mandy girl." He smiled then studied her finger again. "Hey, look."

Mandy followed the direction he was looking, to her wound.

"The callus." Shocked, she looked closer. "It's gone."

Nodding, Tom kissed her finger again. "I live a pretty quiet life at the Double L. I reckon we'll never have enough trouble for you to grow in a new one."

"Maybe, or maybe now that little sore on my finger will scar over, and I'll be stuck with a tough spot on my trigger finger for life."

"Don't matter none." Tom kissed her palm then her wrist. "I want you to be just who you are. That means you're fast with a rifle. I'm proud of that. I'm proud of you."

"I doubt you'd have married me if you'd known how fast I was. I'm told it's a pretty scary sight."

"Well, I've seen it, and I love you as much as ever. As much as a man can love a woman. I think I've rounded up the best little ranch wife a man ever had."

"You might as well think it because you're stuck with me." Mandy couldn't stop the silly tears she'd found such a talent for since she'd married Tom. As the first one trickled down her cheek, she felt Tom flinch, but he stayed close.

A strong arm slid around her waist. He drew her into his arms and lifted her clean off her toes, then raised his head and froze.

Mandy twisted her head to see her sisters standing nearby, watching her, crying.

She looked past Sally and Beth to see her ma turning from the curtains and her pa coming in the cabin door, with Alex and Logan just behind him.

"What's going on here?" Pa sounded panicky.

"Sorry." Mandy sniffled. "I'm just so happy."

"That is a pure waste of salt and water, Mandy. You know better'n to cry." Pa looked behind him as if to check to see if the coast was clear. He didn't run, but Mandy suspected it was a near thing. "Sally, not you, too?"

Sally sniffled, and Logan went to her side.

"You've raised yourself up a nice brood of daughters, Sophie and Clay." Tom turned so Mandy could see her sobbing family better. "But I think I got the best of the lot."

Alex and Logan shook their heads, but they didn't stop smiling.

"I don't care how fast you shoot, Mandy," Pa fussed. "Or how well you doctor, Beth. Or Sally, how good a hand you are with cattle. You girls have gone soft since you've grown up."

The waterworks had turned loose, and there was no stopping them. When Ma started crying, Pa sighed and went to pull her into his arms.

There was a long, sweet, quiet time while the women in the McClellen family ignored Clay's Rule Number One for about the ten-thousandth time.

Discussion Questions

1. Did you read the books in the Lassoed in Texas series? Do you think Mandy is true to the child she was in *Petticoat Ranch*? How so?

2. Did you know Tom Linscott would be the hero? Why?

3. Did you wish Sidney would have died in the story? Would you have liked to see him come to a bad end in explicit detail? Explain your feelings about his life and death.

4. Have you ever known a family with a distinctive mark like the Cooter clan's white dash of hair? What set them apart?

5. Were you happy to see Mark Reeves, or did you assume he'd come to a bad end based on what a pill he was as a child? Describe him as a child from *Calico Canyon*.

6. Did you feel sorry for Emma? Were you rooting for her or Mark, and why?

7. Talk about the returning characters in this book. Could you keep them straight? Could you remember them from *Calico Canyon* and *Gingham Mountain*?

8. Do you think Mandy had a cold-blooded nature? Why?

9. Did you struggle to empathize with a woman who was so deadly with a rifle? What was admirable about her?

10. Have you ever had someone on your mind so intensely that you phoned them or went to see them, only to find out they needed a friend and prayer? Do you think God talks to us in this quiet way? How so?

11. Have you ever ignored a feeling like that only to really regret it later? How could you have made a better decision and be more prepared the next time the feeling comes?

ABOUT THE AUTHOR

MARY CONNEALY is a Carol Award winner and a Christy Award finalist. She is the author of the Lassoed in Texas Trilogy, which includes *Petticoat Ranch, Calico Canyon,* and *Gingham Mountain.* Her Montana Marriages series includes *Montana Rose, The Husband Tree,* and *Wildflower Bride.* She has also written a romantic cozy mystery trilogy, *Nosy in Nebraska*; and her novel *Golden Days* is part of the *Alaska Brides* anthology. You can find out more about Mary's upcoming books at www.maryconnealy. com and www.mconnealy.blogspot.com.

Mary lives on a Nebraska ranch with her husband, Ivan, and has four grown daughters: Joslyn (married to Matt), Wendy, Shelly (married to Aaron), and Katy. And she is the grandmother of one beautiful granddaughter, Elle.

Mary loves to hear from her readers. You may visit her at these sites: www.mconnealy.blogspot.com, www.seekerville.blogspot. com, and www.petticoatsandpistols.com. Write to her at mary@ maryconnealy.com.

Other books by Mary Connealy:

LASSOED IN TEXAS
TRILOGY

MONTANA MARRIAGES
TRILOGY

JOIN US ONLINE!

Christian Fiction for Women

Christian Fiction for Women is your online home for the latest in Christian fiction.

Check us out online for:

- Giveaways
- Recipes
- Info about Upcoming Releases
- Book Trailers
- News and More!

Find Christian Fiction for Women at Your Favorite Social Media Site:

 Search "Christian Fiction for Women"

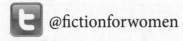 @fictionforwomen